AF528828

The yellowbacks... classics of popular fiction

The yellowjackets or yellowbacks were a great series of bestselling adventure and crime thrillers that had its origins in the mid to late 19th century following on from the 'penny dreadfuls'. They virtually began the mass market revolution of the early 20th century with a clear standard format and imprint/series livery (what would today be called branding). Hodder & Stoughton published the yellowjackets in two main series with series run dates of: 1923-1939 and later 1949-1957.

As the tagline ('where thrillers really began') on the back cover implies, the imprint and series focused on thrillers that were the bestsellers of their time. This current reissue or retro revival if you will, brings back many of these masterpieces, now classics in their own way and extends it further by including key titles from that period that were either great crime or thriller or even general commercial fiction (including sub-genres of noir, horror, gothic, romance, westerns, etc.) influences of their time. There are some perennial favourites and many rarities either lost or not easily available being revived in the current series. Writers and characters ranged from adventure heroes like Bulldog Drummond, Allan Quatermain, Richard Hannay or the Saint through thriller grandmasters Edgar Wallace and E. Phillips Oppenheim, crime and mystery maestros like Patricia Wentworth, GK Chesterton, Agatha Christie and the Detection club, to western and swashbucklers like Zane Grey, Max Brand, Captain Blood and even romance or general fiction classics like Hermina Black, Denise Robins, Marie Corelli or Stella Morton. These were books that had storytelling at their heart and always entertained.

The yellowbacks had both hardback (with varying design elements) and paperback (which built the series look) versions with the latter still carrying the imprint 'yellowjacket'. The current reissues pay tribute to both and use an amalgam of elements from both editions while retaining the complete yellow (or 'mustard-plaster') livery with the author's name in blue beveled type with a 'simulated emboss' effect and a white outer 'outline', and the book title in black. These reissues retain the distinctive size of the original mass market paperback and follow the three main category variations—the thrillers (crime, westerns, mystery, adventure) had blue lettering for the author's name, while Romance and softer general fiction had red; and other categories like humour had green.

For more detail and a full list of titles visit https://www.hachetteindia.com/home/yellowbacks

THE COMPLETE CHARLIE CHAN

VOLUME II

THE COMPLETE CHARLIE CHAN

Earl Derr Biggers was born in Warren, Ohio on August 24, 1884. Years later, while attending Harvard University, Biggers showed little passion for the classics, preferring instead writers such as Rudyard Kipling and Richard Harding Davis. Following his graduation from Harvard in 1907, he worked briefly for the Cleveland Plain Dealer and at Bobbs-Merrill publishers. By 1908, Biggers was hired at the Boston Traveler to write a daily humor column. Soon, however, he became that paper's drama critic. It was at this time that he met Elanor Ladd, who would later become his wife and who would have a marked influence in his writing. He is best know as the creator of Charlie Chan

THE COMPLETE CHARLIE CHAN

Earl Derr Biggers

VOLUME II

The Black Camel

Charlie Chan Carries On

Keeper of the Keys

hachette

The Complete Charlie Chan
The Black Camel first published in 1929; *Charlie Chan Carries On* in 1930; and *Keeper of the Keys* in 1932 – all by Bobbs-Merrill

1

The texts in these editions in most cases have been reprinted as is, with minimal editorial changes and by and large no bowdlerizing for political correctness; though in some editions, a few words and phrases considered archaic, or those considered offensive now, along with archaic punctuation may have been modified in places to make the text more accessible to today's readers. The narratives, language, beliefs, social mores and/or cultural depictions, in these volumes are a reflection of their times and must be viewed as such. They may also contain certain cultural, racial and gender prejudices and stereotypes that may be outdated or clearly wrong then and wrong today; but their removal would be tantamount to claiming these prejudices never existed. The Publisher does not endorse or support those depictions or stereotypes; and these books have been made available for a discerning audience that will read it for entertainment value and a chronicle/record of popular fiction of past times.

Cover design by Priya Singh adapted from the original classic yellowjacket by Hodder & Stoughton.

Cover illustration by Ishan Trivedi.

Series note: Some of the books in the series (unless otherwise credited) may have cover or inside illustrations from the original yellowbacks or early editions, and while full restoration has been attempted, some images may be grainy or faded due to the condition of the original material. The end notes or bonus material or blurb details may have been sourced from the public domain or free use publications such as Wikipedia and attribution is hereby made also allowing similar free use reproduction from here. Sources requiring further specific attribution may write in and further detailing and/or corrections shall be made in subsequent printings/editions.

Reprint specifications may be subject to change including but not limited to finishes, paper, colour sections.

ISBN: 978-93-5731-151-9

Hachette Book Publishing India Pvt. Ltd.
4th & 5th Floors, Corporate Centre,
Plot No. 94, Sector 44, Gurugram - 122 003, India

Typeset in Electra LT STD 10/12.5 pt by Manipal Technologies Limited, Manipal

Printed and bound in India by Manipal Technologies Limited, Manipal

CONTENTS

The Black Camel

CONTENTS

I

MORNING AT THE CROSSROADS

The Pacific is the loneliest of oceans, and travelers across that rolling desert begin to feel that their ship is lost in an eternity of sky and water. But if they are journeying from the atolls of the South Seas to the California coast, they come quite suddenly upon a half-way house. So those aboard the *Oceanic* had come upon it shortly after dawn this silent July morning. Brown misty peaks rose from the ocean floor, incredible, unreal. But they grew more probable with each moment of approach, until finally the watchers at the rail were thrilled to distinguish the bright green island of Oahu, streaked with darker folds where lurk the valley rains.

The *Oceanic* swung about to the channel entrance. There stood Diamond Head, like a great lion—if you want the time-worn simile—crouched to spring. A crouching lion, yes; the figure is plausible up to that point; but as for springing—well, there has never been the slightest chance of that. Diamond Head is a *kamaaina* of the islands, and has long ago sensed the futility of acting on impulse—of acting, as a matter of fact, at all.

A woman traveler stood by the starboard rail on the boat deck, gazing at the curved beach of Waikiki and, up ahead, the white walls of Honolulu half hidden in the foliage behind the Aloha Tower. A handsome woman in her early thirties, she had been a source of unending interest to her fellow passengers throughout that hot monotonous voyage from Tahiti. No matter in what remote corner of the world you have been hiding, you would have recognized her at once, for she was Shelah Fane of the pictures, and hers was a fame equal to that of any president or king.

"A great piece of property" film salesmen had called her for eight years or more, but now they had begun to shake their heads. "Not so good. She's slipping." Golden lads and lasses must, like chimney-sweepers, come to dust, which is something the film stars think about when they cannot sleep of nights. Shelah had not been sleeping well of late, and her eyes, as they rested on peaceful Tantalus with its halo of fleecy cloud, were sad and a little wistful.

She heard a familiar step on the deck behind her and turned. A broad, powerful, keen-looking man was smiling down at her.

"Oh—Alan," she said. "How are you this morning?"

"A bit anxious," he replied. He joined her at the rail. His was a face that had never known Klieg lights and make-up; it was deeply lined and bronzed by tropic suns. "Journey's end, Shelah—for you at least," he added, laying his hand over hers. "Are you sorry?"

She hesitated a moment. "Rather sorry—yes. I shouldn't have cared if we had just sailed on and on."

"Nor I." He stared at Honolulu with the bright look of interest that comes naturally to British eyes at sight of a new port, a new anchorage. The ship had come to a stop at the channel entrance, and a launch bearing the customs men and the doctor was speeding toward it.

"You haven't forgotten?" The Britisher turned back to Shelah Fane. "This isn't journey's end for me. You know I'm leaving you behind here tonight. Sailing out at midnight on this same ship—and I must have your answer before I go."

She nodded. "You shall have it before you go. I promise."

For a brief moment he studied her face. A marked change had crept over her at the sight of land. She had come back from the little world of the ship to the great world whose adoration she expected and thrived on. No longer calm, languorous, at peace, her eyes were alight with a restless flame, her small foot tapped nervously on the deck. A sudden fear overwhelmed him, a fear that the woman he had known and worshiped these past few weeks was slipping from him for ever.

"Why must you wait?" he cried. "Give me your answer now."

"No, no," she protested. "Not now. Later today." She glanced over her shoulder. "Were there reporters on the launch, I wonder?"

A tall, handsome, hatless youth with a mop of blond hair waving in the breeze rushed up to her. His energy was a challenge to the climate.

"Hello, Miss Fane. Remember me? Met you when you went through here on your way south. Jim Bradshaw, of the Tourist Bureau, press-agent of beauty, contact man for Paradise. Our best aloha—and here's a lei to prove it." He hung a fragrant garland about her neck, while the man she had called Alan moved quietly away.

"You're awfully kind," Shelah Fane told him. "Of course I remember you. You seemed so glad to see me. You do now."

He grinned. "I am—and besides, that's my job. I'm the doormat on the threshold of Hawaii, with 'welcome' written all over me. Island hospitality—I have to make sure that my advertisements all come true. But in your case, I—well, believe me, it isn't any strain." He saw that she looked expectantly beyond him. "Say, I'm sorry, but all the newspaper men seem to be lingering in the arms of Morpheus. However, you can't blame them. Lulled as they are by the whisper of the soft invigorating trade winds in the coco-palms—I'll finish that later. Just tell me what's doing, and I'll see that it gets into the papers. Did you complete the big South Sea picture down in Tahiti?"

"Not quite," she answered. "We left a few sequences to be shot in Honolulu. We can live here so much more comfortably, and the backgrounds, you know, are every bit as beautiful—"

"Do I know it?" the boy cried. "Ask me. Exotic flowers, blossoming trees, verdant green hills, blue sunny skies with billowy white clouds—the whole a dream of the unchanging tropics with the feel of spring. How's that? I wrote it yesterday."

"Sounds pretty good to me," Shelah laughed.

"You'll be some time in Honolulu, Miss Fane?"

She nodded. "I've sent for my servants," she told him. "They've taken a house for me on the beach. I stifle in hotels—and then, too, people are always staring at me. I hope it's a large house—"

"It is," Bradshaw cut in. "I was out there yesterday. They're all set and waiting for you. I saw your butler—and your secretary, Julie O'Neill. Speaking of that, some day I'd like to ask you where you find secretaries like her."

Shelah smiled. "Oh, Julie's much more than a secretary. Sort of a daughter—almost. Though of course that's absurd to say, for we're nearly the same age."

"Is that so?" said the boy—to himself.

"Julie's mother was a dear friend of mine, and when she died four years ago, I took the child in. One must do a good deed occasionally," she added, modestly looking down at the deck.

"Sure," agreed Bradshaw. "If we don't we'll never be tapped for the Boy Scouts. Julie was telling me how kind you've been—"

"I've been amply repaid," the star assured him. "Julie is a darling."

"Isn't she?" replied the boy heartily. "If I had my rhyming dictionary along, I'd give you a good description of the girl right here and now."

Shelah Fane looked at him suddenly. "But Julie got in only two days ago—"

"Yes—and so did I. Made a flying trip to Los Angeles, and came back on the same boat with her. The best crossing I ever had. You know—moonlight, silver seas, a pretty girl—"

"I must look into this," said Shelah Fane.

Two of the passengers joined them: a weary, disillusioned-looking man whose costume suggested Hollywood Boulevard, and a dashing girl of twenty. Shelah yielded to the inevitable. "Mr Bradshaw, of the Tourist Bureau," she explained. "This is Miss Diana Dixon, who is in my new picture, and Huntley Van Horn, my leading man."

Miss Dixon lost no time. She sparkled instantly. "Honolulu is an adorable place. I'm always so thrilled to come here—such beauty—"

"Never mind," cut in the star. "Mr Bradshaw knows all that. None better."

"Always happy to have my ideas confirmed," bowed the boy. "Especially from such a charming source." He turned to the man. "Mr Van Horn—I've seen you in the films."

Van Horn smiled cynically. "So, I believe, have the natives of Borneo. Has Shelah told you anything about our latest epic?"

"Very little," Bradshaw replied. "Got a good part?"

"It always has been a good part," Van Horn said. "I trust my rendering of the rôle will not impair its future usefulness. If it does, many of our leading studios will have to close. I'm a beach-comber, you see, and I've sunk lower and lower—"

"You would," nodded the star.

"I'm wallowing in the depths, and quite comfortable, thank you," went on Van Horn, "when—if you can believe it—I'm saved. Absolutely rehabilitated, you know, through the love of this primitive, brown-skinned child."

"Which child?" asked Bradshaw blankly. "Oh, you mean Miss Fane. Well, it sounds like a great plot—but don't tell me, don't tell me." He turned to the star. "I'm glad you're going to take a few shots in Honolulu. That sort of thing makes us very happy at the Tourist Bureau. I must run along—one or two other celebrities on the ship. Fellow named Alan Jaynes—very wealthy—"

"I was talking with him when you came up," Shelah said.

"Thanks. I'll go after him. Diamond mines—South Africa—he sounds good. We're strong for the arts in Hawaii, you know, but as for money—well, when that appears in the harbor, then we really get out the flags. See you all later."

He disappeared down the deck, and the three picture people moved over to the rail.

"Here comes Val," said Huntley Van Horn, "looking like the man who wrote the tropics."

He referred to Val Martino, director of Shelah's latest picture, who was rapidly approaching along the deck. He was a short, stocky, gray-haired man, dressed in a suit of immaculate white silk. Above a flaming red tie loomed his broad heavy face. It was almost the same shade as the tie, suggesting that Mr Martino had never concerned himself with such trivial matters as blood pressure and diet.

"Hello," he said. "Well, here we are. Thank heaven, Tahiti has been attended to. From this on, I'll take my tropics after they've been ruined by American plumbing. Was that a newspaper man you were talking with, Shelah?"

"Not precisely. A boy from the Tourist Bureau."

"I hope you laid it on thick about the new picture," he continued. "You know, we'll need all the publicity we can get."

"Oh, let's forget the picture," returned the star a bit wearily.

The *Oceanic* was drawing slowly up to the pier, on which a surprisingly meager crowd was waiting. Shelah Fane gazed at the group with interest and some disappointment. She had rather hoped for a vast throng of schoolgirls in white, bearing triumphal leis. But this had happened when she went through before; she could not expect history to repeat itself—and it was, too, only seven in the morning.

"There's Julie," she cried suddenly. "There—near the end of the pier. See—she's waving." She returned Julie's signal.

"Who's that beside her?" Van Horn inquired. "Good lord—it looks like Tarneverro."

"It is Tarneverro," Miss Dixon said.

"What's he doing here?" the leading man wondered.

"Perhaps he's here because I sent for him," said Shelah Fane.

A quiet black-garbed maid stood at her side. "What is it, Anna?"

"The customs men, madam. They're going through everything. You'd better come. They want talking to, it seems."

"I'll talk to them," said the star firmly, and followed the maid into her suite.

"Well, what do you know about that?" Van Horn remarked. "She's sent for that phony fortune-teller to come all the way from Hollywood—"

"What do you mean, phony?" cut in Miss Dixon "Tarneverro is simply wonderful. He's told me the most amazing things about my past—and about my future, too. I never take a step without consulting him—and neither does Shelah."

Martino shook his great head impatiently. "It's a rotten scandal," he cried, "the way most of you Hollywood women have gone mad over voodoo men. Telling them all your secrets—some day one of them will publish his memoirs, and then where will you be? A few of us try to lift the industry to a dignified plane—but, oh, lord—what's the use?"

"No use, my dear fellow," said Van Horn. He looked across the intervening stretch of water at the tall lean figure of the fortune-teller. "Poor Shelah—there's something rather touching in such faith as this. I presume she wants to ask Tarneverro whether or not she shall marry Alan Jaynes."

"Of course she does," Miss Dixon nodded. "She wants to know if she'll be happy with him. She cabled Tarneverro the day after Jaynes proposed. Why not? Marriage is a serious step."

Martino shrugged. "If she'd only ask me, I'd read her future quick enough. She's nearly through in pictures, and she ought to know it. Her contract expires in six months, and I happen to know—in strict confidence, you understand—it won't be renewed. I can see her taking a long journey by water then—going abroad to make a picture—the beginning of the end. She'd better grab this diamond king quick before he changes his mind. But no—she's fooling round with a back-parlor crystal-gazer. However, that's like you people. You won't grow up." He walked away.

The formalities of the port were quickly ended, and the *Oceanic* docked. Shelah Fane was the first down the plank, to be received by the eager arms of her secretary. Julie was young, impetuous, unspoiled; her joy was genuine.

"The house is all ready, Shelah. It's a knockout. Jessop is there, and we've found a Chinese cook who's a magician. The car's waiting."

"Really, dear?"

The star looked up into the dark deep-set eyes of the man at Julie's side. "Tarneverro—what a relief to see you here. But I knew I could depend on you."

"Always," said the fortune-teller gravely.

What the crowd lacked in numbers, it made up in noise and confusion. Anna, the maid, was overwhelmed with boxes and bags, and seeing this, Tarneverro went to help her. There was no condescension in his manner; he treated her with the same courtly grace he would have shown the star.

Alan Jaynes and Bradshaw appeared on the scene. The latter went over to greet Julie with as much warmth as though he had just arrived after a long hard voyage from some distant port. Jaynes stepped quickly to Shelah's side.

"I shall be damnably anxious," he said. "This afternoon—may I come then?"

"Of course," she nodded. "Oh—this is Julie—you've heard about her. Julie, please tell him the number of our house. We're just beyond the Grand Hotel, on Kalakaua Avenue."

Julie told him, and he turned back to Shelah. "I shan't keep you—" he began.

"Just a moment," said the star. "I want to introduce an old friend from Hollywood. Tarneverro—will you come here, please?"

The fortune-teller handed a couple of bags to Shelah's chauffeur, and came at once. Jaynes looked at him with some surprise.

"Tarneverro—I want you to meet Alan Jaynes," the star said.

They shook hands. "Glad to know you," remarked the Britisher. As he gazed into the other man's face, he experienced a sudden sensation of deep dislike. Here was power; not the power of muscle, which he had himself and could understand; but something more subtle, something uncanny, inexplicable and oddly disturbing. "Sorry, but I must dash along now," he added.

He disappeared into the crowd, and Julie led them to the waiting car. Tarneverro, it appeared, was stopping at the Grand, and Shelah offered to drop him there.

Presently they were bowling along through Honolulu's streets, under a flaming blue sky. The town was waking to another leisurely day. Men of many races languidly bestirred themselves; at the corner of King Street a boy offered the morning paper, and a fat brown-skinned policeman lazily turned a stop-go sign to let them pass. Shelah Fane, like all passengers newly descended from a ship at this port, felt rather dazzled by the brightness and the color.

"Oh, I shall enjoy this," she cried. "I've never stayed here longer than one day before. What a relief to be out of the South Seas."

"But they're romantic, aren't they?" Julie asked.

"The illusions of youth," the star shrugged. "I shan't destroy them. Only don't mention Tahiti to me again as long as I live."

"Not quite like the books," Tarneverro nodded. He sat, mysterious even in that bright world, at Shelah's side. "I discovered that for myself, long ago. You're staying here for some time, I take it?"

"A month, I hope," the star answered. "A couple of weeks still to go on the picture, and then, I trust, a fortnight's rest. I want it badly, Tarneverro. I'm tired—tired."

"You need not tell me that," he said. "I have eyes."

He had, indeed, eyes; eyes that were cold and piercing and rather disquieting. The car sped on past the old royal palace and the judiciary building, and turned off into Kalakaua Avenue.

"It was so good of you to come over here," Shelah told him.

"Not at all," he replied evenly. "I started the day after I got your cable. I was due for a vacation—my work, you know, is not precisely restful. Then, too, you said you needed me. That was enough. That will always be—enough."

Julie began to chatter about the islands: she mentioned the warm caressing waters of Waikiki, the thrill of haunting native music in the purple night, the foreign pageant of the streets.

"All of which," smiled Shelah, "sounds very much to me like James Bradshaw in one of his more lyric moods."

Julie laughed. "Yes, I guess I was quoting Jimmy. Did you meet him, Shelah?"

"I met him," the star nodded.

"He's really very nice," Julie assured her. "Especially when he isn't talking shop."

The pink walls of the Grand Hotel appeared at that moment through a network of majestic palms, and Shelah directed the chauffeur to turn in at the gates.

"I must talk with you very soon," she said to Tarneverro. "I have so much to ask you. You see—"

He raised a slim white hand. "Don't tell me, please," he smiled. "Let me tell you."

She glanced at him, a little startled. "Oh—of course. I need your advice, Tarneverro. You must help me again, as you have helped me so often in the past."

He nodded gravely. "I shall try. With what success—who knows? Come to my apartment at eleven o'clock—it is number nineteen, on the first floor. There is a short flight of stairs leading to my corridor just at the left of the hotel desk as you enter. I shall expect you."

"Yes, yes." Her voice was trembling. "I must settle this thing today. I'll be there."

Tarneverro bowed from the hotel steps, and as the car drove off Shelah was conscious of Julie's frank young eyes fixed on her with a disapproval that was almost contempt.

The head bell-man touched Tarneverro's sleeve. "Excuse. There is a man who waits to see you. This one."

The fortune-teller turned to perceive a bulky Chinese who approached him with an amazingly light step. The ivory face was wearing a somewhat stupid expression; the black eyes were veiled and sleepy-looking. Not a very intelligent Chinese, Tarneverro thought, wondering vaguely what this visit presaged.

The Oriental placed one hand on his broad chest, and achieved a grand bow despite his waistline.

"A thousand pardons," he remarked. "Have I the undisputable honor to address Tarneverro the Great?"

"I am Tarneverro," answered the other bruskly. "What can I do for you?"

"Permit that I introduce myself," continued the Chinese, "unworthy of your notice though I am. The name is Harry Wing, and I am humble business man of this island. Do I extend my remarks too far when I say I wish to see you alone?"

Tarneverro shrugged. "What for?"

"The matter is of pressing urgency. If I might suggest—your room—"

The fortune-teller gazed for a moment into that placid mask of a face, behind which life seemed nonexistent. He capitulated. "Come along," he said. Obtaining his key at the desk, he led the way.

Once inside the door of number nineteen, he turned to confront his odd visitor, who had followed on noiseless feet. The curtains of the sitting-room were drawn back as far as they would go, and the place was flooded with light. With his customary forethought, Tarneverro had selected an apartment on the mountain side of the hotel, and a restless cool wind from the Koolau Range swept in at the window and stirred the papers lying on a desk.

The countenance of the Chinese was still without expression, even under the piercing scrutiny the fortune-teller now gave it.

"Well?" said Tarneverro.

"You are the famous Tarneverro," began Harry Wing in a respectful singsong. "Among Hollywood people you have vast reputation as one who lifts dark veils and peers into uncertain future. Black as lacquer that future may be to ordinary eyes, but to yours, they say, it is clear as glass. Permit me to add this reputation pursues you even to Hawaii, dogging like shadow at your heels. The rumor of your mystic skill floods the street."

"Yes?" put in Tarneverro shortly. "What of it?"

"I am, as I say, business man of small importance to everybody but myself. Now I begin to speak to you frankly that opportunity arouses itself in my path. I can amalgamate my business up together with that of my cousin from a north province. Future looks bright, but qualms assail me. Will the merge have success? Is my cousin honorable as cousin of mine should naturally be? Can I trust him? In fewer words, I desire dark veil lifted, and you are man to do the business. I stand ready to make generous payment for this lifting."

Tarneverro's eyes narrowed, and for a long time he stood staring at this unexpected customer for his wares. The Chinese waited motionless as a Buddha, with his hands in his trousers pockets, his coat thrown back. The fortune-teller's glance rested for a moment at a point just below the fountain-pen pocket on his visitor's waistcoat.

"Impossible," he said, with sudden decision. "I am here on a vacation, not to practise my profession."

"But rumor remarks," objected the other, "that you have already done work with crystal—"

"For one or two of the hotel managers—as a friendly gesture," Tarneverro cut in. "I received no fee of any sort. I will not do this kind of thing for the general public."

Harry Wing shrugged. "The matter then becomes sad disappointment for me," he answered.

A grim smile spread over the seer's dark face. "Sit down," he said. "I have spent some time in China, and I understand how great is the interest of your people in fortune-tellers. So for a moment, while you were telling me why you came, I thought you were speaking the truth."

The visitor frowned. "I am now rapidly failing to understand you."

Still smiling, Tarneverro dropped into a chair facing the Oriental. "Yes, Mr—ah—er—Wing, I believe you said—momentarily I was deceived. And then a certain little gift of mine came to my aid. You have been kind enough to speak of my success. I have succeeded—why? Because I happen to be psychic, Mr Wing—"

"Chinese people are psychic, too."

"Just a moment. As I stood there listening to you, a psychic wave swept over me. I had a feeling—a feeling of—what? Of stern men who sit in police stations and are sworn to enforce the laws. Of detectives pursuing evil-doers, landing them at last—and then, a court of justice, so-called, a learned judge.

That, my friend, is the feeling I had. Rather amazing, don't you think?"

His visitor's expression had lost suddenly all its stupidity. The little black eyes snapped with admiration.

"Amazing smart act on your part, yes. But as for me, I do not think it was psychic feeling. A moment ago I beheld your eyes resting with fierce understanding on locality of my own waistcoat from which detective badge was recently removed. The pin has left indelible marks. You are number one detective yourself, and I congratulate you."

Tarneverro threw back his head and laughed. "*Touché!*" he cried. "So you are a detective, Mr—er—"

"The name is Chan," said the bulky Chinese, grinning broadly. "Inspector Chan, of the Honolulu police—former times Sergeant, but there has been upheaval in local police department, and I am rewarded far beyond my humble merits. Trap which has just failed so flatly, I add in justice to me personally, was not my idea. I informed Chief it would not work unless you happened to be extreme dull-wit. Since you turn out clever beyond expectation, it did not. No bitter feelings. I pause only to call attention to local ordinance which says men like you must not practise dark arts in this town without obtaining permission. A word being spoken to the wise, I rise to accomplish my exit."

Tarneverro also stood up. "I am not going to practise among your townspeople," he announced. He had dropped the tense air of mystery which he evoked for the benefit of film stars, and seemed quite human and not unlikable. "It has been a pleasure to meet you, Inspector. As for my own detective prowess, I may say in confidence that it is rather useful in my work."

"Must be so," returned Chan. "But such skill as yours should be at service of public. Frequently in Los Angeles murder mystery leaps into print and never gets solved. I study them all with fiery interest. The Taylor case—what an amazing happening was there—*haie*, it is still mystery. And case of Denny Mayo, famous actor of handsome countenance, dead in his home at night. How many years—three and more—and Denny Mayo is still unavenged by Los Angeles police."

"And never will be," added the fortune-teller. "No, Inspector, that is not in my line. I find it safer to dwell on the future and soft-pedal Hollywood's past."

"In such course, wisdom may abide," agreed Chan. "None the less, how happily I would welcome your aid if some such worrisome puzzle stared into my face. I will say goodbye, Mr Tarneverro. Memory of your cleverness will linger in my poor mind for long time to come."

He slipped quietly out, and Tarneverro glanced at his watch. With a leisurely air, he placed a small table in the middle of the room, and taking from a bureau drawer a gleaming crystal, stood it thereon. Then he stepped to the window and drew the curtains part way across, shutting out a goodly portion of the bright light outside. Glancing about the darkened room, he shrugged his shoulders. Not such an impressive stage-setting as his studio in Los Angeles, but it would have to serve. Sitting down by the window, he took out of his pocket a bulky letter and, slitting the flap of the envelope, began to read. The curtains, caught in the fierce grip of the tradewind, swirled about his head.

At eleven o'clock Shelah Fane knocked on the door, and he ushered her into his sitting-room. She was gowned in white and appeared younger than she had at the dock, but her eyes were clouded with worry. Tarneverro's manner was professional now; he was cold, remote, unsympathetic. He seated her at the table behind the crystal; then, drawing the curtains all the way, plunged the room into almost complete darkness.

"Tarneverro—you must tell me what to do," she began. He sat down opposite her.

"Wait," he commanded. He looked fixedly into the crystal. "I see you standing at the rail on the boat deck of a steamer, under a brilliant moon. You are wearing a dinner gown—it is gold and matches your hair. There is a scarf of the same color about your shoulders. A man is standing at your side; he points, and offers you a pair of glasses. You raise them to your eyes—you catch the last faint glimmer of the lights along the front at Papeete, the port from which you sailed a few brief hours ago."

"Yes, yes," murmured Shelah Fane. "Oh, Tarneverro—how do you know—"

"The man turns. I can see him only dimly, but I recognize him. Today, on the pier—Alan Jaynes—was that his name? He has asked you a question—marriage, perhaps—but you shake your head. Reluctantly. You want to say yes—yet you don't. You put him off. Why? I feel you love this man."

"I do," the star cried. "Oh, Tarneverro—I really do. I knew him first at Papeete—only a week—but in a place like that—The first night out—it was just as you say—he proposed to me. I haven't given him my answer yet. I want to say yes—to have a little happiness now—I've earned it, I think. But I—I'm afraid—"

He lifted his piercing eyes from the crystal. "You're afraid. Something in your past—you fear it will return to haunt you—"

"No, no," the woman cried.

"Something that happened long ago."

"No, no—it isn't true."

"You cannot deceive me. How long ago? I cannot quite determine, and it is necessary that I know."

The tradewind mumbled at the curtains. Shelah Fane's eyes wandered helplessly about the darkened room, then came back to Tarneverro's.

"How long ago?" the man demanded again.

She sighed. "Three years ago last month," she said in a voice so low he had to strain to hear.

He was silent for a moment, his mind racing like an engine. June—three years ago. He gazed fixedly into the crystal; his lips moved. "Denny Mayo," he said softly. "Something about Denny Mayo. Ah, yes—I see it now."

The wind tore the curtains apart, and a wide strip of dazzling light fell across Shelah Fane's face. Her eyes were staring, frightened.

"I shouldn't have come," she moaned.

"What about Denny Mayo?" Tarneverro went on relentlessly. "Shall I tell you—or will you tell me?"

She pointed to the window. "A balcony. There's a balcony out there."

As one who humors a child, he rose and looked outside. He came back to the table. "Yes, there's a balcony—but no one is on it."

He sat down again, and his bold commanding eyes sought hers. She was trapped, and helpless.

"Now!" said Tarneverro the Great.

II

THE HOUSE ON THE BEACH

After a brief twilight, the dark sweeps over Waikiki Beach like Old Man Mystery himself. In the hours before the moon, like a climbing torch, ascends the purple sky, the sense of hearing comes into its own. Blackness covers the coco-palms, yet they may be heard rustling at the tradewind's touch; the white line of the breakers is blotted out, yet they continue to crash on that unseen shore with what seems an added vigor. This is night in the real sense of the word, intriguing, awe-inspiring, but all too short, for the moon is waiting an early cue.

A solitary floor lamp was burning in the huge living-room of the house Shelah Fane had rented at Waikiki. The paneled walls, the furniture and the floor, all fashioned of rare native woods, gleamed faintly in the half-light; the green of exotic plants was everywhere. The French windows that faced the street were closed, but those on the ocean side, leading on to a great screened lanai, stood wide, and through them at regular intervals came the roar of the surf, which was running high.

Shelah Fane came into the room. She walked with a quick nervous step, and in her eyes was a look of apprehension—almost of terror. It was a look that had been there ever since her return from that interview with Tarneverro in his apartment at the Grand Hotel. What had she done? She asked this of herself over and over. What had she done? What was the secret of this dark man's power that he had so easily dragged from the inner recesses of her mind a story she had thought safely buried for ever? Once away from the strange influence of his presence she had been appalled at her own indiscretion. But it was too late then for anything save regret.

With her unerring instinct for the spotlight, she sat down under the single lamp. Many cameras had clicked in Hollywood since that distant time when, like a rocket, she had flashed into the picture sky, and nowadays the spotlight was none too kind to her. Kind to her hair, yes, which seemed to spring into flame, but not so considerate of the lines of worry about her eyes, about her small tense mouth. Did she know? Longer than most rockets she had hung blazing in the sky; now she must endure the swift lonely drop in the dark.

Her butler, Jessop, came in, a spare elderly Englishman who had also found in Hollywood the promised land. He carried a florist's box. Shelah looked up.

"Oh, Jessop," she said. "Did Miss Julie tell you? The dinner hour is eight-thirty."

"I understand, madam," he answered gravely.

"A few of the young people are going for a dip before we dine. Mr Bradshaw for one. You might show him to the blue bedroom to dress. The bath-houses are dark and need cleaning. Miss Julie and Miss Diana will dress in their rooms."

Jessop nodded, as Julie came in. The girl wore an afternoon gown, and her face was innocent of make-up. She was enthusiastic, happy, young—a touch of envy darkened the star's fine eyes.

"Don't you worry, Shelah," Julie said. "Jessop and I have planned everything. It will be like all your parties—a knockout. What's that, Jessop? Flowers?"

"For Miss Fane," explained the butler, and handing the box to the girl, left the room.

Shelah Fane was looking about her, a frown on her face. "I've been wondering, Julie. How in the world can I arrange a good entrance on the party, in a place like this? If only there were a balcony, or at least a broad flight of stairs."

Julie laughed. "You might come suddenly through the lanai, strumming a ukulele and singing a Hawaiian song."

The star took her seriously. "No good, my dear. I'd be entering on the same level with the guests, and that is never effective. To make the proper impression, one must appear suddenly from above—always remember that, darling. Now, in Hollywood—"

The girl shrugged. "Oh, just come in naturally for once, Shelah. There's a lot in novelty, you know." She had torn the cord from the box of flowers, and now she lifted the lid. "Lovely," she cried. "Orchids, Shelah."

The star turned, without interest. Orchids were nothing new in her life. "Nice of Alan," she said languidly.

But Julie shook her head. "No," she announced, "they're not from Mr Jaynes, evidently." She read the card aloud. "'With love from one you have forgotten.' Who could that be, Shelah?"

"Who couldn't it be?" smiled the star a bit wistfully. She rose with sudden interest. "I wonder—let me see the card." She glanced at it. "'With love from one—'" Her eyes lighted with quick understanding. "Why, it's Bob's writing. Dear old Bob! Just fancy—with love—after all these years."

"Bob?" inquired the girl.

Shelah nodded. "Bob Fyfe—my first and only husband, dear. You never knew him—it was long ago. I was just a kid, in the chorus of a musical show in New York, and Bob was an actor, a legitimate actor—such a good one, too. I adored him then, but along came Hollywood, and our divorce. And now—with love—I wonder? Can it be true?"

"What's he doing in Honolulu?" Julie asked.

"Playing in stock," Shelah replied. "Leading man at some theater here. Rita Ballou told me all about him, this morning when I called her up." She took the orchids. "I shall wear these tonight," she announced. "I never dreamed he would even speak to me. I—I'm touched. I'd like to see Bob again." A thoughtful look crossed her face. "I'd like to see him at once. He was always so kind, so clever. What time is it—oh, yes—" She glanced at a watch on her wrist. "Seven-twenty. What was the name of that theater? Rita told me. The Royal, I think she said—"

The doorbell rang briskly, there ensued a snappy bit of dialogue in the hall and Jimmy Bradshaw burst through the curtains. He was, it seemed, in a light-hearted mood.

"Here we all are," he cried. "Everybody who really matters. Well, Miss Fane, how does it feel to be foot-loose and carefree on a palm-fringed shore—way down in the warm southern seas?"

"It's really very restful," Shelah smiled. She nodded at Julie. "I'll be back in a moment. I want a pin for these flowers."

She disappeared into the hall, and Bradshaw turned quickly to the girl.

"You're looking great," he cried. "It's the climate. Not that you didn't look fairly good at the start—"

"Tell me," she cut in. "What do you think of Shelah?"

"Shelah?" He paused. "Oh, she's all right. Nice and friendly but—a bit artificial—a good actress, on and off. In the past two years I've met enough screen stars to start a Hollywood of my own, and what I always say is—doffing my hat to southern California—you can have 'em."

"You don't really know Shelah," protested the girl.

"No, I guess not. She's been kind to you, and that makes her aces up with me. But my own preference in women—and I've looked very carefully over the field—"

"Oh, you have, have you?"

"My ideal—since you've asked me, and I'm glad you have—is a rather different sort. Lovely, of course, young, innocent, ingenuous—and pretty crazy about yours truly. That—and you may quote me freely—is the girl for me."

Diana came suddenly through the curtains. She, too, still wore an afternoon gown.

"Hello, big boy," she said. "You ready for that swim with me?"

"Sure," replied Bradshaw. "With you—and anybody else who wants to come along." He looked at Julie. "Let's go. Before the moon rises is my idea. It's the best time. Anyone else going—or is it just—the three of us?"

Julie shook her head. "No one else, I guess. The others are afraid of spoiling their make-up."

"Which is one advantage of youth over doddering age," the boy returned. "Well, come along—"

Shelah appeared, wearing the orchids on her shoulder.

"Just about to dip into the world-famed waters of Waikiki," Jimmy informed her. "Won't you join us?"

"Some other evening," she told him. "You know, I'm hostess tonight."

"You are missing," said Bradshaw impressively, "one of the thrills of a lifetime. The silken surf beating on coral sand, the dark, star-strewn sky above, perhaps the pastel loveliness of a lunar rainbow—boats run from Los Angeles and San Francisco once a week, and the fare is within the reach of all—"

The doorbell rang again. Accompanied by Shelah, the young people went out into the hall.

"Get your suit," Julie said to the boy. "I'll show you where to change. Let's make it a race. The first one into the water gets a prize."

"I'll win it," answered Bradshaw. "I'll name it too." They clattered up the polished stairs.

Again the bell sounded. Shelah was just beside the door, but she did not open it; she considered such an act beneath the dignity of a star. Instead she returned to the living-room and waited for Jessop to do his duty. After a brief delay, he did it, and two new guests appeared in the living-room. Shelah advanced to meet them—a dark, rather faded woman of thirty, followed by a big blond man who had an air of nonchalant authority.

"Rita Ballou," the star cried. "Why—it's ages! And Wilkie—I'm so glad."

"Hello, darling," said the woman she called Rita.

The man came forward. "Look here, Shelah. What time did you say dinner was to be?"

"Eight-thirty—but it doesn't matter—"

Ballou turned to his wife. "Good lord—can't you ever get anything straight?"

"What's the difference?" the woman replied. "We can have a chat with Shelah before the others come." She turned to the star. "So sorry we missed you when you went through before. We were on the mainland."

"Haven't missed you this time, thank heaven," added Wilkie Ballou. "By gad, you're as blooming as ever."

"How *do* you do it?" inquired Rita sweetly. Her cold eyes flashed green with envy as she looked at Shelah.

"She's found the fountain of youth," suggested Wilkie admiringly.

"I've always heard that was in Hawaii," smiled the star. She looked hard at Rita. "But it isn't," the look added.

Rita understood. "Not at all," she said grimly. "It's in the beauty shops of Hollywood, and you know it. Over here, women fade quickly—"

"Nonsense," protested Shelah.

"Yes, they do. Oh—I've learned my lesson—too late. I should have stayed in Hollywood and gone on with my career."

"But, my dear,—surely you're happy with Wilkie?"

"Of course. The way I would be with the tooth-ache."

Wilkie shrugged. "Overlook it, Shelah," he said. "We've been rowing all the way out here. Rita's nerves, you know."

"Is that so?" remarked his wife. "I guess anyone would have nerves with a husband like you. Honestly, Shelah, he's got a better imagination than what's his name—Shakespeare. If he'd only drop sugar planting and go in for writing scenarios—but never mind us. Tell me all about Hollywood. I'd love to be back."

"I'm making a long stop here—we'll have lots of time to chat later," Shelah explained. "Some of the crowd are going for a swim before dinner. Care to go along?"

Rita put one hand to her perfect coiffure, and shrugged. "Not for me," she cried. "I'm so sick of swimming I gag at the sight of my tub. You've no idea, my dear—three years married and living in Honolulu—these people over here are like fish. They suffocate when you bring 'em ashore."

They heard the noise of a new arrival in the hall, and Alan Jaynes came into the room, handsome and upstanding in his dinner clothes. Shelah's heart sank suddenly at sight of him. While she was introducing him to the Ballous, Julie and Jimmy Bradshaw rushed in, wearing gay beach robes over their bathing-suits. They paused, with obvious reluctance, for further introductions.

"Where's Miss Dixon?" Bradshaw inquired. "She hasn't gone out, has she?"

"Nonsense," cried Julie. "Diana will take ages. She always does."

"Then the race is between us two," said the boy, and dashed through the open window on to the lanai, with Julie at his heels.

"What a good-looking boy," Rita remarked. "Who is he?"

Shelah explained Mr Bradshaw's place in the world's work. Rita stood up.

"Let's all go down to the beach," she said.

"The beach—in high-heeled slippers?" protested Wilkie.

"I can take them off, can't I?" Rita demanded. She was moving toward the window.

"Go along," the star said. "We'll follow later."

Rita went out.

Without enthusiasm, Wilkie lifted his great bulk from the chair. "That means I go, too," he explained, and did so.

Shelah turned to Alan Jaynes with a nervous little laugh. "Poor Wilkie—he's so jealous. And with reason, I'm afraid—at least, he had reason in the old days."

Jaynes came quickly to her side. "So sorry I couldn't see you this afternoon. Your headache—it's better, I trust?"

She nodded. "Much better."

"I've brought you a bit of an offering. It's hardly worthy of you, of course." He handed her a corsage bouquet wrapped in tissue-paper.

She unwrapped it. "Lovely," she said.

"But too late," remarked Jaynes. "I see you're wearing someone's orchids."

Shelah laid his gift on a table. "Yes, Alan."

"I hope that doesn't mean—" he began, frowning. "Shelah—it can't mean that. I—I couldn't go on without you."

She faced him. "You'll have to, Alan. I'm so sorry. But I—I can't marry you."

His expression clouded. "It's true, then," he said.

"What's true?"

"The thing Van Horn told me this afternoon. I refused to believe it of you—it's too childish—too ignorant. You sent for that damned fortune-telling charlatan, and he decided it for you. He advised you not to take me." She turned away, without speaking. The man's face flushed with anger. "If you had any sane reason," he continued, controlling himself with an effort, "I'd take my medicine quietly. But this—this is too much. To let a fakir—a crystal-gazer—a cheap fraud, come between us—by the lord, I won't stand for it. I thought on the boat you loved me—"

"Maybe I did," she answered sadly.

"Then nothing in this world shall stop me—"

"Wait, Alan, wait, please," she cried. "It's for you—I'm doing this for you. You must believe that. There could be no happiness for us—"

"So that's what he told you, eh?"

"That's what he told me, but he was only repeating what was in my heart. The past, Alan—the past won't die—"

"I've told you I don't give a hang about what's past."

"Oh, but you don't know, Alan—and I can't tell you. I'm trying to do the decent thing—you're so fine and straight—I couldn't bear it if I ended by dragging you through the dust. Please, Alan, please—"

"I don't want to understand," Jaynes cried. "I only want you—to love and take care of—see here, my time is brief, so pitifully brief. I must leave at midnight—you know that. Forget this fool of a fortune-teller. I can't understand your faith in him, I can't approve it, but I'm willing to overlook it. You aren't to blame, I fancy. Your temperament, your way of life. Forget him, my dear, and give me your word before I go—"

She shook her head. "I can't," she said brokenly. "I can't."

For a long moment Jaynes looked at her. Then, with great dignity, he turned on his heel.

"Where are you going?" Shelah cried.

"I don't know," he answered. "I must think this thing out."

"But you're dining here—"

"I don't know," the man repeated. "I couldn't talk to your friends just now. I want to be alone for a few minutes. I may return later." He seemed dazed, uncertain of himself.

Shelah was at his side, her hand on his sleeve. "Alan, I'm so sorry—so unhappy."

He turned, and took her in his arms. "By heaven—you loved me on the ship. I won't give you up. I can't." His glance fell on the orchids, fastened to the shoulder-strap of her gown by a small diamond pin. "No one shall take you from me," he cried and, releasing her, went quickly out.

Shelah Fane walked slowly to a chair, and dropped into it. Pain and a desperate unhappiness were in her face, and she was not acting now. For a few moments she sat there, then gradually came back to her surroundings. She glanced at her watch—a quarter of eight. Quickly she rose and went to the French windows at the rear.

The moon was still in hiding, and the broad lawn that lay between the house and the pounding surf was shrouded in darkness. She heard, far away, the exultant cry of Julie battling with a breaker, and then the answering call of Jimmy Bradshaw. There was an odd air of expectancy about her as she stepped out on the lanai. She crossed it to the screen door that opened on to the lawn and stood there, peering out. Under a nearby hau tree she thought she saw, in the blackness, an even blacker shadow. Suddenly it moved. With a little cry of recognition, she flung open the door and ran swiftly across the grass.

Meanwhile, Alan Jaynes was striding grimly along Kalakaua Avenue in the direction of the Grand Hotel. Five minutes brought him to the cool lofty lobby of that famous hostelry. He passed the head bell-man, whose smile of welcome froze suddenly on his face as he caught the look in the Britisher's eyes.

Jaynes turned to the left, moving past shop windows filled with jade and Oriental silks, then past the flower booth where, earlier in the evening, he had purchased the bouquet which now lay unappreciated on Shelah Fane's table. In another moment he reached the entrance to the big lounge of the hotel, and stood there at the top of a short flight of steps.

It was a beautiful room, with those three great arches opposite the entrance like triple paintings of the tropic sky. But Jaynes had no eye for beauty tonight.

Most of the guests were at dinner, and the lounge had a deserted air. Seated not far away, however, talking pleasantly with an elderly couple who had the look of tourists, the Britisher saw the man he wanted.

He descended the steps, and crossed to this man's chair. "Stand up," he ordered in a husky voice.

Tarneverro the Great looked at him with an expressionless face. "I should have expected a bit more courtesy," he said evenly. "But then—I scarcely know you."

"Stand up," Jaynes repeated, "and come with me. I want a talk with you."

For a moment the fortune-teller sat, quietly measuring the man who towered above him. Then he rose, and making his apologies to the two old people, he walked at Jaynes' side down the long room.

"What is all this—" he began.

They stopped at an archway near the far end. Outside a series of brilliant lights bathed the hotel lawn in white, making an ideal stage-setting for some drama of the tropics. But the stage was empty; the drama was all inside the lounge.

"I want an explanation," said Jaynes roughly.

"An explanation of what?"

"I have done myself the honor of asking Miss Shelah Fane to marry me. I had every reason to believe she intended to do so—but today she consulted you about the matter—a matter that concerns you not at all. You advised her against a marriage with me."

Tarneverro shrugged. "I do not discuss with outsiders what goes on at my readings."

"You're going to discuss it with me. Make up your mind to that!"

"Suppose I did—what could I say? I tell my clients only what I see in the crystal—"

"Rot!" cried Jaynes. "You tell them whatever happens to suit your fancy. What was your reason for this advice to Shelah?"

He came closer and stared into the seer's face. "Are you, by any chance, in love with her yourself?"

The fortune-teller smiled. "Miss Fane is most charming—"

"We don't need your evidence on that point—"

"Most charming, but I do not permit myself the unwise luxury of a sentimental attachment for my clients. I advised her as I did because I saw no happiness possible in this proposed marriage." His tone grew serious. "Incidentally, whether you appreciate it or not, I did you a favor today."

"Really?" said Jaynes. "But I'm not asking favors of a mountebank like you."

A dark flush spread over Tarneverro's face. "There can be no point in prolonging this interview," he remarked, and turned away.

Jaynes seized him quickly by the arm. "We'll prolong it this far. You are going to Miss Fane at once and tell her you're a fraud, a fake, and that you wish to retract all you said to her today."

Tarneverro shook off the other's grasp. "And if I refuse?" he said.

"If you refuse," Jaynes answered, "I propose to give you a thrashing you won't forget for many a day."

"I do refuse," said Tarneverro quietly.

Jaynes' arm shot back, only to find itself in a surprisingly firm grip. He turned. Val Martino, the director, was at his side; his was the grip on the Britisher's arm. Beyond Martino, Huntley Van Horn, resplendent in Hollywood evening garb, looked on with an air of amused interest.

"Now, now," bellowed Martino, his face even redder than usual. "Cut this out, please. Too much of it in the pictures already. We can't have it, Jaynes, we can't have it."

For a moment the four stood motionless. A new figure strolled upon the scene, a broad bulky Chinese in a dinner coat. Tarneverro hailed him. "Ah, Inspector Chan. Just a moment, please."

Charlie came closer. "It is Mr Tarneverro," he remarked. "The lifter of the veil."

"Inspector," the fortune-teller said, "may I present Mr Van Horn, and Mr Martino? And this is Mr Alan Jaynes. Inspector Chan, of the Honolulu police."

Chan bowed gracefully. "The honor is immense. Distinguished company, as a blind man could see."

Jaynes glared at Tarneverro. "Very good," he sneered. "Hide behind the skirts of the police. It's what I would expect of you."

"Now, now," Martino interposed. "A slight misunderstanding, Inspector. There will be no trouble—I am sure the good name of the industry is too precious to all of us. It is certainly very precious to me."

Van Horn looked at his watch. "Eight o'clock," he announced. "I believe I'll roll along down to Shelah's. Anybody coming?"

The director shook his head. "Not yet. I'll be down presently." The actor walked slowly away. Martino, his grip still firm on the Britisher's arm, sought to lead him off. "Come out on the terrace," he pleaded. "We'll talk this matter over."

Jaynes turned to the fortune-teller. "I'm not sailing until twelve," he said. "In the meantime, we may meet again." He permitted Martino to lead him down the room.

"I trust that last prediction falls short of truth," Chan said to Tarneverro. "I do not have much liking for light I observe in gentleman's eye."

Tarneverro laughed. "Oh, he'll come around. I have offended him, quite unintentionally." He looked thoughtfully at Charlie. "By the way, Inspector, this is a happy meeting. I was thinking of calling you up. Just how do you plan to spend the evening?"

"I attend Rotary Club banquet in this hotel," Chan explained.

"Good. You'll be here some time?"

Chan nodded. "I fear so. It happens very few after-dinner speeches are equipped with self-stopper."

"Until eleven, perhaps?"

"It seems terribly possible."

"I am dining at a friend's house down the beach," Tarneverro said. "At the house of Miss Shelah Fane, in fact. Some time between now and eleven o'clock I may have a very important message for you, Inspector."

Chan's eyes opened slowly. "A message? Of what nature?"

Tarneverro hesitated. "This morning you happened to speak of certain murder cases in Los Angeles that remain unsolved. I told you then that I preferred to keep out of that sort of thing. We are not always able to follow our preferences, Inspector." He moved away.

"One moment," said Chan. "You have sought to quench the fire of my curiosity by tossing upon it a handful of straw. May I repeat my question—what sort of message?"

The fortune-teller gave him a long look. "A message calling upon you to arrest the murderer of—but there, I mustn't say too much. There's many a slip, as you have no doubt learned from your own experience. I shall be happy to have you so near—until eleven, at least. After that I presume I can reach you at your home?"

"With ease," Charlie told him.

"Let us hope for success," smiled Tarneverro cryptically, and went to rejoin his elderly acquaintances in the center of the lounge. For a second Chan looked after him. Then, shrugging his broad shoulders, he turned to find the banquet room.

III

FLOWERS FOR SHELAH FANE

Huntley van Horn strolled down Kalakaua Avenue in the direction of Shelah Fane's house. On this tiny island in the midst of the rolling Pacific, few outward signs of a romantic past survived. He might have been on Hollywood Boulevard: the parade of automobiles along that stretch of American asphalt was constant, a trolley clattered by, he walked on a concrete sidewalk under the soft yellow glow of modern street-lamps. Yet, beyond the range of those lamps, he was conscious of the black velvet of a tropic night. He caught the odor of ginger blossoms and plumeria, a croton hedge gave way to one of hibiscus, topped with pale pink flowers that were doomed to die at midnight.

He came to the number Shelah had impressed on his memory and turned in through the gates on to a broad drive that curved before a wide front door. Passing beneath a prolific banyan tree, two centuries older than the motion pictures, he rang the bell. Jessop admitted him.

"Oh, Mr Van Horn," the butler said. "I'm happy to see you again."

"How have you been?" the actor inquired.

"In splendid health, sir. I trust you enjoyed your little jaunt to Tahiti?"

Van Horn tossed down the straw hat he had substituted for the silk topper in which he had won the approval of several million women. "A primitive country, Tahiti," he smiled. "It would have reminded you of Hollywood, Jessop."

The butler permitted himself a discreet smile. Van Horn pushed on into the living-room, and Jessop followed.

"No one here?" the actor cried. "Lord—am I as early as all that?"

"Oh, no, Mr Van Horn. Some of the guests are enjoying the bathing, which I understand is rather famous in certain quarters. A few, I believe, are on the beach. Would you care to join the—er—the other young people in the water, sir?"

Van Horn grinned. "The diplomatic service lost a good man in you. No—much as I am tempted to classify myself with youth, the matter involves too damn' much dressing and undressing. I shall remain, high and dry, on the shore."

"Just as well, sir," nodded Jessop. "It is already eight-fifteen, and the dinner hour is rapidly approaching. I shall be forced to summon them in shortly."

Van Horn stared about the room. "What—no cocktails?"

"There has been a slight delay, sir. The gentleman who was to supply us with the raw material—the very raw material, between you and me, sir—has only just come. I was busy with the shaker when you rang." He went over and stood by the French window opening on to the lanai. "You will find the ocean just out here, sir," he explained.

Van Horn laughed, and stepped on to the lanai. The butler followed him to the screen door, and held it open.

"Ah, yes," said the actor. "I hear the roar of surf. No doubt I shall find the sea in that same general neighborhood." He paused in the doorway, and indicated a light gleaming through the trees some distance to the right. "What's over there?"

"It's a sort of summer-house, or pavilion, sir," Jessop explained. "At least, it would be a summerhouse in England, where we have summers. It may be a few of the guests are in there."

Van Horn went out on the lawn, and started across it in the direction of the light. Suddenly he heard, above the pounding of the breakers, voices on the beach. He stood for a moment, undecided which way to go.

Jessop, meanwhile, returned to the living-room. An old bent Chinese came shuffling in.

"My dear Wu Kno-ching," the butler protested, "in a well-run house, the cook's place is in the kitchen."

The old man blandly ignored the rebuke. "What time dinnah?" he asked.

"As I have told you, the dinner is set for eight-thirty," replied Jessop. "It may, however, be somewhat delayed."

Wu Kno-ching shrugged. "Wha' kin' house this is? Dinnah mebbe sometime plitty soon aftah while. I get dinnah leady boss say wait dinnah goes to hell." He departed, murmuring further reproof.

The screen door slammed behind Wilkie Ballou; he crossed the lanai aimlessly and entered the living-room.

"I fear this idea of a swim is going to delay dinner, sir," Jessop said to him.

"What? Oh, yes—I suppose so. Have you any cigarettes here? My case is empty."

Jessop proffered a box containing cigarettes, and taking one, Ballou dropped into a chair. The butler officiated with a match, then retired to the kitchen.

Returning fifteen minutes later, he found the Honolulu man sitting just as he had left him.

"Things are getting rather serious, sir," Jessop remarked. He carried a large dinner gong. "I had always supposed, from my reading, that the Chinese are a notably patient race."

"They have that reputation, yes," nodded Ballou.

"Their representative in our kitchen, sir, is doing nothing to sustain it," Jessop sighed. "He informs me with great passion that dinner is waiting. I'll just go down to the shore and see what this will do." He nodded toward the gong and disappeared. Presently he could be heard in the distance, beating a not unmusical tattoo.

Ballou lighted a fresh cigarette. Jessop returned, and at his heels came Rita Ballou and Van Horn.

"You should have stayed, Wilkie," Rita said. "I've just been getting all the latest Hollywood gossip."

"I'm not interested," Ballou growled.

"Poor Wilkie," his wife smiled. "It's close to his bedtime, and he hasn't even had his dinner. Cheer up. It won't be long now."

Diana Dixon arrived, quite out of breath. "I suppose we're late," she cried. "You should have been in with us. It was glorious—but not half long enough. I could have stayed for hours. Cocktails—that's an idea."

She took one from the tray which Jessop held before her. The other guests likewise needed no urging. Huntley Van Horn lifted his glass.

"To our hostess, if any," he remarked.

"That's right—what's become of Shelah?" Rita Ballou said. "We saw her for a moment when we came—"

"Shelah," said Van Horn, with a cynical smile, "is no doubt lurking in the background waiting to make a grand and impressive entrance. She will ride in on a white charger, or descend on us from a balloon. You know, she goes in for that sort of thing—"

Julie and Jimmy Bradshaw rushed in, glowing and in high spirits. "Hello, Mr Van Horn," the girl cried. "Are you all that's come?"

"To think," he groaned, "that you could be so rude to me."

"Oh, you know what I mean," she laughed. "Where are all our other guests? Val Martino, Mr Jaynes, Tarneverro—"

"Tarneverro coming?" Van Horn lifted his eyebrows. "In that case, I will have a second cocktail. Thanks so much."

Quite unexpectedly there was the sound of steel guitars at the front door, and of many fresh young voices singing a Hawaiian song. Julie cried out with delight.

"A serenade from Shelah's admirers," she said. "Isn't that sweet? She will be pleased." Her beach robe streaming behind her, she ran to the door and threw it open. She stood gazing out at a vast throng of high-school girls, laden with flowers. They stopped their song, and a young Japanese girl stepped forward. "We would like to see Shelah Fane, please."

"Of course," said Julie. "Just wait, and I'll get her. While you're waiting, if you don't mind—will you sing *The Song of the Islands*? It's Miss Fane's favorite, you know."

She left the door open and returned to the living-room. "Come on, Jimmy—we'll find Shelah. I think she's in the pavilion."

"Sure," said Jimmy. They went out on the lawn.

"Couldn't be better," Julie cried. "For Shelah's entrance on the party, I mean. That crowd outside serenading her as she comes in—she'll love it."

"Good lord," said Bradshaw, disapproval in his voice.

"Oh, I know," the girl answered. "It's silly, but poor Shelah's what she is. Her life has made her so, and she can't change." They went on across the soft lawn under the hau trees and the algarobas. The sweet haunting strains of *The Song of the Islands* came to them on the evening breeze. "Hurry," Julie said, "Shelah must get in there before that song ends."

She ran up the steps of the pavilion, with Bradshaw close behind. He pushed open the door of the single room. For a second he stood there, then he turned swiftly and caught the girl in his arms.

"No, no," he cried. "Don't go any farther."

His tone frightened her. "What do you mean?"

"Turn around and go back," he pleaded, but she tore away from him and ran inside.

"You'll be sorry," he warned.

And she was sorry, it seemed, for above the voices of the serenaders and the distant whine of steel guitars, her own voice rose in a sharp cry of fright and terror.

Shelah Fane lay on the floor beside a small straight-backed chair. She had been stabbed through the heart; her priceless ivory gown was stained with crimson. Outside, that little group of her admirers continued to sing fervently their serenade.

Julie knelt by the star's side, and Bradshaw looked away. In a moment he went over and lifted the girl to her feet. "We'd better go," he said gently. "There's nothing we can do."

He led her to the door. She looked up at him through her tears. "But who—who—" she murmured.

"Ah, yes—" he answered. "That, I'm afraid, is the big question now."

He found, on the inside of the pavilion door, an unexpected key. They went outside, and the boy locked the door, putting the key in his pocket. Slowly they walked back to the house. Huntley Van Horn greeted them.

"Did you tell Shelah?" he said. "The stage is all set. Her guests are gathered in the living-room, her great public is singing lustily at the door—it's a grand entrance—" He stopped at sight of Julie's face.

"What's happened?" cried Rita Ballou shrilly.

Bradshaw stood looking about the little group. Jessop came in and, picking up the silver tray on which he had served the cocktails, prepared to collect the empty glasses. Outside the door, *The Song of the Islands* trailed off into silence.

"Shelah Fane has been murdered in the pavilion," said the boy in a low voice.

There was a sudden crash. Jessop had been guilty of his first error in forty years of service. He had dropped the silver tray.

"I beg pardon," he said to no one in particular.

Outside, Shelah Fane's admirers began another song. Bradshaw dashed through the curtains to the front door.

"Please," he cried. "Please—no more tonight. You must go away now. Miss Fane can't see you. She is—she is ill."

"We are so sorry," said the girl who seemed to be the leader. "Will you give her the flowers, please?"

They began to load him down with fragrant blossoms. Presently he staggered back into the hallway, his arms filled with a riot of color. Julie was standing there, her eyes wide, her face deathly pale.

"Flowers," said Bradshaw. "Flowers for Shelah Fane."

With a choking cry, Julie fell in a heap at his feet.

IV

THE CAMEL AT THE GATE

Down at the Grand Hotel, Charlie Chan was well started on what he perceived was going to be an excellent dinner. The hour of Rotarian oratory was not near enough to worry him, the food was good and he felt at peace with the world. He did not know the name of the small fish that lay on the plate before him, but one taste had led him to approve most heartily of its quality. He was leaning forward to apply himself with increased diligence to the task at hand, when a bell-boy touched him on the shoulder.

"You are wanted on telephone very quick," said the boy.

A sense of vague unrest troubled him as he walked down the long lobby to the telephone booth. He would have preferred a life of quiet meditation, but a ruthless fate was always breaking in upon him with some new problem that must be solved. What now, he wondered, as he entered the booth and pulled the door to behind him.

He was greeted by an excited young voice. "Say, Charlie,—this is Jim Bradshaw of the Tourist Bureau. Huntley Van Horn told me I could find you at the hotel."

"Yes—and now you have found me. What is it that has brought you to this state of high disturbance?"

In jumbled phrases Bradshaw poured out his story. Charlie listened calmly.

"Shelah Fane," the boy was saying. "You know what that means, Charlie. This news of mine will be cabled all over the world tonight. You're going to be in the limelight as you never were before. Better get down here as fast as you can."

"I will arrive at once," Charlie answered. Was that a sigh, Bradshaw wondered, that came over the wire? "Let nothing be touched until I touch it," the detective added.

He hung up, then called the police station and gave certain directions. At last he came from the booth, mopping his perspiring brow with his handkerchief. For a moment he stood motionless, as though gathering his strength for the task that lay before him. Another case, another murder, and he knew that what the boy had said was true: this time he would work in a bright spotlight indeed. Shelah Fane! Not for nothing did he have numerous children who, as he often said, were movie crazed. He knew only too well the interest that had always centered about the woman who now lay dead a short distance down the beach.

"A thousand-mile journey begins with one step," he sighed, and took it—in the direction of his hat.

When he returned to the door of the hotel, he encountered Tarneverro. The fortune-teller also carried a hat, and seemed on the point of going out. "Hello, Inspector," he said. "You haven't finished your dinner already?"

"I have not," Charlie answered. "I am rudely wrenched away by important business. The most important I have encountered for some time."

"Yes?" returned Tarneverro lightly.

Charlie's small eyes were fixed upon the other's face with a fierce intensity. Not too soon to collect impressions, to weigh, to measure, to study.

"Miss Shelah Fane," he said slowly, "is just now found murdered at her home."

For hours afterward he was to speculate upon the look that crossed that dark mysterious face.

"Shelah!" Tarneverro cried. "Good God!"

"You were on your way there, perhaps?" Charlie continued.

"I—I—yes—of course—"

"Do me the honor to ride with me. I desire to ask questions."

Val Martino hurried up. "I say, Tarneverro—are you going down the beach?"

Tarneverro told him the news. The director heard it with surprising calmness.

"Too bad," he said evenly. He was thoughtful. "Well, there goes six months' hard work. That picture's ruined. I'll never find anybody to double for her—I've tried it—"

"Good lord, man!" cried Tarneverro angrily. "Shelah is dead, and you babble about your picture."

"Sorry," said Martino. "Sorry for poor Shelah. But even in the movies, the show must go on."

"What became of that fellow Jaynes?" Tarneverro asked suddenly.

"Right after we left you, he shook me off and strolled down the beach. He was in a state of mind—well, you saw that. Wasn't coming to the dinner—but I fancy I'd better find him and bring him down, eh?"

"Yes, yes," Chan said hurriedly. "I must see him. Come, Mr Tarneverro. Speed is necessary." He led the fortune-teller out to the drive, where his battered flivver was waiting. "The vehicle is none too grand," he apologized, "but it moves. Will you kindly leap inside?"

Silently Tarneverro climbed into the little two-seater. Charlie started the car.

"This is a terrible thing," the fortune-teller said. "Poor Shelah—I can scarcely realize it."

Charlie shrugged. "Time to be philosophical," he suggested. "You have perhaps heard old Eastern saying. 'Death is the black camel that kneels unbid at every gate.' Sooner or later—does it matter which?"

"I know, I know," Tarneverro continued. "But, in a way, I'm afraid I'm responsible for this. Oh, lord, the more I think about it, the clearer it becomes. Poor Shelah's blood is on my head."

"Your remarks have interesting sound," Charlie remarked, as the car moved through the hotel gates on to the avenue. "Explain, if you will be so kind."

"This evening," the fortune-teller went on, "I told you I might call on you to make an arrest in a very important murder case. I fully expected to do so. I'll tell you what I meant by that, as briefly as possible.

"Shelah Fane had cabled me from the ship, asking me to meet her here. It seems that this fellow Jaynes had proposed to her, and she wanted my advice. For some time past she had been in the habit of coming to me with all her problems. She loved Jaynes, she wanted to marry him—but she was afraid of what the future might hold in store. She feared that at any moment the world might discover that for three years or more she had gone about burdened with a terrible secret."

"What secret?" Charlie inquired.

"This morning," Tarneverro continued, "you spoke of Denny Mayo, who was found dead in his home in Los Angeles some three years ago. The police have been at sea on the case from the start. But Shelah Fane—she knew who murdered Denny Mayo. She was in Mayo's house, paying a harmless call, on the night of the murder. The doorbell rang, and she foolishly hid in another room. She saw the thing done. All this she confessed to me this morning. What is more, she told me that Denny Mayo's murderer is at this moment in Honolulu."

Charlie's eyes gleamed in the dark. "She told you the name?"

Tarneverro shook his head. "I'm sorry. She didn't want to, and I made no effort to press her. Her reason, of course, for not revealing her connection with this affair at the time, was that to do so would ruin her career. She has kept silent all these years, but she hesitated to marry a man of whom she was really fond and perhaps drag him through some very unpleasant publicity later on."

"A natural hesitation," Chan approved. "You encouraged it?" He had stopped the car in the drive of Shelah's house, but he made no move to alight.

"I did, of course," Tarneverro said. "More than that, I strongly advised her to lift this burden from her mind and find peace at last. I assured her that if she revealed the name of the guilty person of her own accord, no police in the world would be inclined to punish her for her long silence. I trust I was right in that?"

"Speaking for myself only, yes," nodded Charlie.

"I suggested she refuse Jaynes for the present, and go through with this unpleasant duty which I felt she owed to society. I said I thought it would be extremely foolish for her to marry any man with such a threat hanging over her happiness. If he really cared for her, I pointed out, Jaynes would marry her in the end. If he didn't care that much, then it was better to discover it now."

They alighted and stood under the banyan tree. Charlie peered into the fortune-teller's face. "And if Jaynes did not marry her—" he suggested.

Tarneverro shrugged. "You are on the wrong track there," he said. "I had no sentimental interest in Shelah Fane. But I didn't fancy my rôle—the secret she confided in me was a bit more than I'd bargained for. I felt, too, that for the sake of her own happiness she ought to get rid of this burden at last. So I pleaded with her to make public the name of the guilty person in the Mayo case."

"And she agreed?" Charlie asked.

"Not precisely. The idea rather frightened her. She said she would think it over, and give me her decision tonight. 'Write me a brief statement, with that name included,' I told her, 'give it to me at dinner this evening, and I will make everything as easy for you as possible.' I was confident of gaining my point, or I would never have spoken to you about it. Yes, I would have gained it—but now—now—"

"Now," Chan said, "the killer of Denny Mayo has silenced this woman for ever."

"Precisely."

"But in what manner did this person discover she was hovering on a point of revealment?"

"I can't tell you," Tarneverro replied. "There is a balcony outside my room. That's a possibility, but not a likely one, I fear. Or it may be that Shelah consulted the killer, told him—or her—that she could no longer remain silent. It would have been like her. She was indiscreet, impulsive." They moved toward the steps. "I hope that what I have told you will prove helpful, Inspector. It gives you the motive, at least, and it narrows your search. Believe me, I shall be at your side through this investigation. You are going to have all the help I can possibly give you. I want, even more than you, the name of Shelah's murderer."

"Your help will be valuable indeed," Chan told him. "What did I say to you this morning—you are number one detective yourself. I did not dream that so soon we would be working side by side."

Jessop admitted them, and they went into the living-room where the two Ballous and Van Horn sat in gloomy silence. Charlie stood gazing at this small group with thoughtful deliberation. Jimmy Bradshaw entered behind him, his bathing-suit abandoned for dinner clothes.

"Hello, Charlie," he said in a low voice. "You're needed here, all right. In the pavilion—clear over to the right on the lawn. I locked the door as soon as we found what had happened. Here's the key."

"You are bright boy," said Charlie, pleased. "That fact has long been apparent as the morning sun." He turned to the others. "It will naturally be understood that no one leaves this house until I grant permission. Mr Tarneverro, will you kindly accompany me?"

He walked with the fortune-teller in silence across the lawn, white now under the rising moon. Chan went up the steps first, and unlocked the door. With marked reluctance, Tarneverro followed.

Charlie went over and dropped down on one knee beside Shelah Fane. Slowly he looked from her to the fortune-teller. "Long time I have been in present business," he said softly, "but rough blunt feelings do not come natural to me yet. I am sorry for this lady. Never before this moment have I seen her—yet I am so very sorry." He stood up. "The black camel has knelt at plenty famous gate tonight," he added.

Tarneverro remained some distance from the body. He seemed to control himself with an effort. "Poor Shelah!" he muttered. "Life was very sweet to her."

"It is sweet to all of us," Charlie nodded. "Even the beggar hesitates to cross a rotting bridge."

"I can never forgive myself," the other continued. "What you see here began this morning in my apartment."

"What is to be, will be," Chan comforted. "We will not move unfortunate one until arrival of coroner. I have already telephoned the station. But we will look about, Mr Tarneverro. Do not forget—you are to help." He knelt again, and lifted Shelah Fane's left arm. "Here is already some evidence. There has been a struggle, and wrist-watch was smashed in process. Crystal is broken, and"—he placed the watch to his ear—"the working of the timepiece immediately ceased to function. The hands remain stationary at two minutes past eight. So soon, without an effort, we know exact moment of tragedy. That is indeed something."

"Two minutes after eight," Tarneverro said. "At that moment, Jaynes, Martino, Van Horn, you and I were in the lounge of the hotel. Remember—Van Horn looked at his watch, remarked it was eight o'clock, and said he was starting down here."

"Of course," Chan nodded. "The alibis arrive in one huge flock." He pointed to the orchids, crushed on the floor. "Further evidence of the struggle. Bouquet was torn off, trampled under foot."

"All of which looks a bit like jealousy," responded Tarneverro, frowning. "Can we be wrong about the motive, after all? No—it might be anger, too."

Charlie was crawling about the rug. "Peculiar thing," he remarked. "Flowers were fastened by pin—you may note the shoulder-strap is torn—but no pin is here now." He examined the orchids, and made a thorough search of the floor, while Tarneverro watched him. "It is true," he added, standing up, "the pin which fastened flowers is strangely missing."

He stepped to an old mahogany dressing-table, a handsome piece in its day, but now banished to the beach house. The table had a glass top, and leaning over, he studied this with a microscope he had taken from his pocket. "One more point," he said. "This corner here has lately received fierce nick. What can that mean?"

Tarneverro had picked up an expensive gold mesh bag that was lying on the table, and was studying the contents. "No use," he said. "The usual compact, and a few dollars. For a moment I had a crazy thought that perhaps Shelah had already written down for me that name we want. It would have been a very happy chance. The case would have been over before it started."

"Cases do not permit themselves the luxury of such easy solution," sighed Chan. "If letter such as you warmly desire had been in this room, murderer would have it now. No—fate is never so kind. We must take long way round. Come—we have finished here for the present. Much more to be done later."

They went out, and Charlie locked the door. As they moved across the lawn, he enumerated the clues. "A watch stopped at two minutes past eight in fierce struggle. A bouquet of orchids crushed in same, the pin that held them in place oddly lost. A fresh nick on glass corner of dressing-table. Enough for the moment, maybe."

As they entered the living-room, Jessop was ushering in Martino and Alan Jaynes. The latter's face was pale beneath its bronze, and he was obviously much upset.

"We will all acquire chairs," Chan suggested. "Many questions must now be asked."

Jessop came forward and faced Tarneverro. "I'm sorry, sir," he said. "With all the excitement, I quite forgot it."

"Forgot what?" asked Tarneverro, surprised.

"This letter, sir." He took a large elaborate envelope from his pocket. "Miss Fane requested me to give it to you the moment you arrived."

Tarneverro stretched forth his hand, but Charlie stepped quickly between them. He took the envelope. "So sorry. But the police are in charge here now."

"Naturally, sir," Jessop bowed, and backed away.

Chan stood there, a rather helpless-looking figure, holding the letter in his hand. Could it be true? Was the answer to this puzzle so soon within his grasp? A long understanding look passed between him and Tarneverro. The room seemed filled with people, milling about, seeking chairs. Charlie lifted his right hand to slit the envelope.

The floor lamp furnished the only illumination in the room. Chan took a step nearer it; he had the envelope open now, and was about to remove the contents. Suddenly the lamp went out, and the room was plunged into darkness. There followed the sound of a blow, then another, a cry and the fall of a rather solid body.

The place was in an uproar. Out of the blackness came an insistent demand for lights. The lamps in the wall brackets flashed on, revealing Jessop at the switch.

Charlie was slowly rising from the floor. He rubbed his right check, which was bleeding slightly.

"Overwhelmed with regret," he said, glancing at Tarneverro. "Famous god Jove, I hear, nodded on occasion. For myself, I fear I have just taken most unfortunate nap." He held out his left hand, in which was a tiny fragment of envelope. "Vital portion of letter," he added, "seems to have traveled elsewhere."

V

THE MAN IN THE OVERCOAT

For a long moment Chan stood with that fragment of letter in his hand. His expression was calm and unruffled, a very inaccurate indication of what was going on in his heart. Before a room filled with people some person had tricked and therefore disgraced the famous detective of the Honolulu police.

Charlie Chan had lost face in the presence of seven witnesses. Though he had lived many years in Hawaii, he was still Oriental enough to feel a hot bitter anger that startled even himself.

He sought to conquer that feeling immediately. Anger, he had been taught, is a poison that destroys the mind, and he would have need of all his faculties in the ordeal that impended. In this affair he was face to face with an adversary who was not only in a desperate mood, but who was also clever and quick to act. Well, so much the better, Charlie told himself; he would find all the more satisfaction in defeating such an opponent in the end. For he would win out; on that he was fiercely determined. The unknown person who had killed, first Denny Mayo, and then, to protect that secret, Shelah Fane, would be brought to justice at last, or Inspector Chan could never find peace again.

Tarneverro was glaring at him with ill-concealed indignation. "So sorry," he remarked coldly, "but the police are in charge here now."

Chan nodded. "You are eminently correct in that sneer. Never before in my life has such a happening aroused itself in my path. But I give you my word"—he looked slowly round the little group—"the person who struck that blow will pay. I am in no mood that turns the other cheek tonight."

He took out his handkerchief and applied it to the cheek that had, unfortunately, been already turned. It did not need the trace of red on the white linen to tell him that the hand that had hit him wore a ring. His right cheek—then the blow had probably come from someone's left hand. On the left hand of Van Horn, he noted a large seal ring; he turned to Wilkie Ballou, and on that gentleman's left hand he caught the glint of a diamond. Covertly he pursued his study; Bradshaw, Martino, Tarneverro and Jaynes were all innocent of jewelry.

Tarneverro held his arms aloft. "You may start with me," he said. "You are, of course, going to search everyone in this room."

Charlie smiled. "I am not quite such fool as that. Person who favored me with vigorous blow is not likely to hold incriminating letter in guilty possession. Besides," he added casually, as he walked away, "the matter is of small importance anyhow."

Tarneverro lowered his arms. It was quite evident from his expression that he heartily disapproved Charlie's omission of what he considered an essential move. But Chan ignored him. The detective was making a swift examination of the cord which stretched from the lamp to an electrical socket a few inches above the floor. The plug, wrenched from its place, lay before him, its two protruding prongs mute evidence that its removal had been a simple matter. It had only been necessary to step on the cord anywhere along its length, move the foot a short distance away from the wall, and the thing was done. Simple, yes, but a bit of quick thinking on someone's part. Charlie restored the plug, and the lamp flashed on again.

He came back to the center of the room. "We waste no time in fruitless search for letter now," he remarked. "I propose instead to fix in my mind our little group of characters, and perhaps learn from their lips just what they were engaged in doing at two minutes past eight tonight." He stood gazing at them thoughtfully. "I have some hesitation where to begin. Mr Ballou, yours is familiar face, so I will start in your vicinity. Will you kindly state position in this house of yourself and Mrs Ballou?"

The millionaire looked at him with all the arrogance of the white man who has lived for a long time among what he considers inferior races. "Why should I do that?" he inquired carelessly.

"Murder has been committed," replied Charlie sternly. "I recognize your high position on this island, but you are not above question. Will you deign to reply, please?"

"We came here as dinner guests," Ballou said. "We are—we were—old friends of Miss Fane."

"You knew her in Hollywood?"

"Yes."

"Mrs Ballou was, before her marriage to you, herself actress on famous silver screen?"

"What if she was?" flared Ballou.

"Why not be polite, Wilkie?" rebuked his wife. "Yes, Inspector, I was in the pictures, under the name of Rita Montaine. And if I do say it, I was rather well known."

Chan bowed. "Could one of your charm be otherwise? May I inquire, please, how long you have been married?"

"Three years this month," she told him amiably.

"You resided, perhaps, in Hollywood up to moment of your marriage?"

"Oh, yes."

"Do you recall—was Mr Ballou in Hollywood for some time previous to that marriage?"

"Yes—he hung around for several months, pleading with me to give up my career and take him." Her husband snorted. "You may not recall it now, Wilkie, but you did."

"What the devil," cried Ballou irritably, "has all that got to do with the murder of Shelah Fane? I believe, Inspector, that you are exceeding your authority. You'd better be careful—I'm not without influence—"

"So sorry," said Chan soothingly. "I will come at once to the present. You arrived here tonight at what hour?"

"At seven-thirty," he answered. "The dinner was not until eight-thirty, but Mrs Ballou got the invitation over the telephone, and as usual"—he glared at his wife—"she balled things up."

"At seven-thirty," put in Chan hastily, cutting off Rita's reply. "Describe actions down to present moment, please."

"What are you getting at?" objected Ballou roughly. "You don't think I killed Shelah Fane, do you? By gad, I'll speak to someone down at the station about this. Do you know who I am—"

"Oh, who are you, anyhow, Wilkie?" his wife put in wearily. "Why not tell the Inspector what he wants to know and have done with it?" She turned to Chan. "We arrived about seven-thirty, and after a little chat with Miss Fane, stepped out on the beach to watch the bathers. It was about a quarter to eight when we went out there, I imagine."

"You were engaged in this manner how long?"

"Answering for myself, I was on the beach until Jessop came out at eight-thirty. About ten minutes before that, Mr Van Horn joined us, and my husband got up and strolled toward the house."

"At two minutes past eight, then, yourself and husband were seated side by side on sand. You heard no cry or other indication of disturbance?"

"None at all. The two girls in the water were doing more or less screaming—you know how people will. But that's not the sort of thing you mean?"

"Not precisely," replied Chan. "Thank you so much. We drop you for the present."

Julie O'Neill came slowly into the room. The new pink evening gown she had looked forward to wearing at the party was back on its hanger, and she had donned a simple little dress of gray chiffon. Her face was still decidedly pale, but she seemed calm and collected now. Chan turned to her.

"Good evening. I am so sorry to be here. Not until this moment have I encountered the pleasant thrill of seeing you. Would you mind informing me just who you are?"

Bradshaw came forward. He introduced Julie to Chan, and went on to explain the girl's place in the household.

"My heart's deepest sympathy," Charlie remarked. "As mere matter of form, I must ask about your actions during this most tragic evening."

"I can tell you all about that," Bradshaw informed him, "and kill two birds—oh, sorry—I mean to say, give you my own story at the same time. I arrived at the house early for a swim with Miss O'Neill. The last time we saw Miss Fane was in this room when we came down dressed for the water—that was about seven-forty. She was here with Mr and Mrs Ballou, and Mr Jaynes."

"You went immediately to the beach?"

"We did—and on into the water. It was marvelous—pardon me if I put in a small advertisement for the local bathing beach. What I mean to say is, Miss O'Neill and I were together from the time we saw Miss Fane until about eight-thirty, when Jessop rang the gong calling us in. It was soon after that we made our unhappy discovery."

"You remained in water at all times?"

"Oh, no—we came back to the beach now and then. Mrs Ballou was there from the start, as she says. Mr Ballou disappeared toward the last and Mr Van Horn showed up."

"At two minutes past eight, then, you and Miss Julie were either in water or making brief excursion to shore?"

"One or the other—we had no means of knowing the time, of course. It went very quickly. We were surprised when Jessop called us in."

Chan turned to the girl. "Miss Fane was wearing tonight pretty nice bouquet of orchids on shoulder?"

Julie nodded. "Yes."

"Fastened with pin, no doubt?"

"Of course."

"Did you by any chance note the pin?"

"No, I didn't. But I remember her saying she was going to her room to get one. Perhaps her maid can tell you about that."

"Are you in position to know who it was sent those orchids?"

"I am," Julie replied. "There was no name, but Miss Fane recognized the writing on the card. She said they came from her ex-husband, Bob somebody—he's an actor playing with a stock company in Honolulu."

"Bob Fyfe," explained Rita Ballou. "He's in the company down at the Royal. They were married when Shelah was quite young, and I believe she was always very fond of him, even after their divorce."

Alan Jaynes rose and, taking a small cigar from a case, lighted it, then walked nervously about the room, seeking a place to throw the match.

"A discarded husband," mused Charlie. "Ah, yes, I would expect at least one of those. This man should be notified at once, and arrive here with all speed possible."

"I'll attend to it, Charlie," offered Jimmy Bradshaw.

"Warmest thanks," Chan remarked. As the boy left the room, he turned to the others. "We now resume somewhat rude questioning. Mr Van Horn, you are actor, perhaps?"

"Perhaps?" laughed Van Horn. "Well, that's flattering. The reward of ten years' hard work."

"You have, then, been in Hollywood for the past ten years?"

"Ten years and a half—lost in what the amiable Mr Mencken calls the sewers of Hollywood."

"And before that?"

"Oh, before that I led a most romantic life—ask my press-agent."

"I seek to determine facts," Charlie said.

"In that case I shall have to tell you that I came there, wide-eyed and innocent, from an engineering school. I planned to build bridges, but my fatal beauty intervened."

"You have appeared with Miss Shelah Fane in other pictures before this one?"

"No." Van Horn grew more serious. "I scarcely knew her until I was engaged for this part."

"I do not need to ask where you were at two minutes past eight tonight?" Chan continued.

"No, you don't," the actor agreed. "I was in the same room with you. You'll remember I looked at my watch and remarked that it was eight o'clock, and that I was toddling along down here. At two minutes past the hour I was still where you could see me—if you cared to avail yourself of the privilege."

"You came to this house immediately?"

"Yes—I walked. Exercise—that's how I keep in trim. I got here about eight-fifteen—I didn't hurry. Jessop let me in, we had a little chat, and at about eight-twenty I joined Mrs Ballou on the beach, as you've already heard."

Jimmy Bradshaw returned. "I got that man Fyfe at the theater," he announced. "My news just about bowled the poor fellow over. He said he would be through after the second act, and would come right along."

"Thank you most warmly," Chan nodded. "You have most helpful nature." He turned to Martino. "You are what they call a director, I think."

"Yes, they call me that," replied Martino grimly. "Among other things."

"You have been engaged in this work a long time?"

"Not very long. I was formerly an actor, on the English stage. Got interested in the pictures, you know, and eventually went to Hollywood."

"Could you mention date of arrival?"

"Surely. I landed there two years ago last March."

"At that date, you saw the place for the first time?"

"Yes—of course."

Charlie nodded. "With regard to this evening, I can also omit to ask from you your exact location at two minutes past eight."

"Naturally. I was with you and these other chaps at the hotel. As I believe I told you, when I left you just after eight o'clock, I went with Mr Jaynes on to the terrace. I tried to calm him a bit, but he broke away and wandered down the beach. I sat there on the beach walk for some twenty-five minutes, admiring the set. When I saw you again, I had just been upstairs to get my hat, intending to come down here."

Charlie looked over at Alan Jaynes, nervously smoking his small cigar in a distant corner. "Mr Jaynes," he said.

The Britisher rose and approached him, consulting his watch as he did so. "Yes?" he remarked.

Charlie regarded him gravely. "You are, I believe, one of the people who suffer most from this death tonight?"

"What do you mean by that?"

"It is reported that you loved Shelah Fane."

"Reported—by whom?" The man looked angrily at Tarneverro.

"No matter," said Chan. "You had asked her to marry you?"

"I had."

"Then you loved her?"

"Look here—must you make a public inquisition of this?"

"So sorry. It is, I perceive, somewhat indiscreet on my part. Mr Bradshaw has told me you were in this room at seven-forty tonight."

"I was. I had come to dinner."

"And to have, first of all, a private conversation with Miss Fane?"

"Yes. But the nature of that conversation is none of your business."

Charlie smiled. "Alas! I know so much that is none of my business. You ask for her final decision in the matter of marriage. She rejects you, and you suspect Mr Tarneverro here is responsible for the action. You tramp angrily back to hotel, seeking to make quarrel with this same Tarneverro. So, at two minutes past eight, you stand in hotel lounge, glowering. Which, dear sir, is fortunate affair for you."

"I take it," Jaynes said, "that you have fixed the moment of this—this murder, at two minutes after eight?"

"I have," Chan replied.

Jaynes tossed his cigar into an ash-tray with a gesture of deep relief. "Thank God for that. Have you any more questions?"

"You saw Miss Fane for final time when you left this room at about fifteen minutes before eight?"

"That was the last time I saw her—yes."

"Then you did not return here between eight-five and eight-thirty-five?"

"I did not."

"Have you ever been in Hollywood, Mr Jaynes?"

The Britisher laughed bitterly. "I have not—and I'm not likely to go there."

"That is all, sir," Chan nodded.

"Thank you. I'll say goodbye. I happen to be sailing on the *Oceanic* at midnight."

Charlie looked at him in sudden surprise. "You are leaving Hawaii tonight?"

"I am."

The detective shrugged. "I am so sorry to disappoint you. The matter is impossible."

"Why should it be?" Jaynes demanded.

"You are somewhat deeply involved in this affair."

"But you say you've fixed the moment of the murder—and at that moment I was standing in your presence. It's a perfect alibi."

"Perfect alibis have way of turning imperfect without warning," Charlie informed him. "I regret that I cannot allow you to sail. The *Oceanic* will be carefully watched, and no one connected with this affair will be permitted to leave the island aboard her. Or on any other ship, for the present."

An angry flush spread over the Britisher's face. "On what grounds do you keep me here?"

"As an important witness in present case," Chan replied. "I will go to extreme length of swearing out warrant, if necessary."

"I can at least go back to the hotel," Jaynes suggested.

"When I permit it," Charlie said gently. "Meanwhile, I hope you will find for yourself a comfortable chair."

Jaynes glared at him, then receded into the background. The doorbell rang, and Jessop admitted two men. One was a tall angular American with a deputy sheriff's badge, the other a small anxious-looking Japanese.

"Ah, Mr Coroner," Chan greeted the deputy, who doubled in that rôle. "And Kashimo. As usual, Kashimo, you are demon for speed to get on job. Is it too much to assume that you arrive here with horse and carriage?"

The deputy spoke. "They sent him to fetch me, and he finally managed it. Where did this thing happen, Charlie?"

"In a moment I lead you to the place," Charlie said.

"Maybe I search house," suggested Kashimo.

Chan regarded him sadly. "It would appear that there was great shortage of detectives at station house tonight," he said. "No, Mr Kashimo, please do not search house—at least, not until somebody tells you what you are searching for." He turned to the deputy. "If you will follow me—"

Diana Dixon came into the room. She wore a white evening gown, and her elaborate make-up was sufficient explanation of the long delay in her appearance. Chan looked at her with interest.

"Here is someone about whom I have not heard before," he said.

"Who in the world—" began Diana, staring at him.

"Do not be alarmed," smiled Charlie. "I am Inspector Chan, of Honolulu police. You are in Hawaii now."

"Oh, I see," she answered.

"Your name, please?"

She gave it.

"You are guest in house, perhaps?"

"I am. Miss Fane was kind enough to take me in. You know, I've just come up from the South Seas with her—I acted in her last picture."

"An actress," nodded Chan. "I find myself dazzled by so much fame and beauty. All the same, I collect myself to inquire—what have you been engaged in doing this evening?"

"Why, I've been in swimming," she told him.

"When did you last see Miss Fane?"

"When I went upstairs to put on my bathing-suit—I don't know what time that was. Mr Bradshaw had just come, and Miss Julie and he and I went up to change. We left Miss Fane standing here in the hall. Someone was ringing the doorbell."

"You came down and entered the water with these young people?"

"Oh, no—it took me a lot longer to change. It was eight o'clock when I was finally ready—I noticed the clock on my dressing-table just before I left my room. I'd no idea it was so late—so I hurried down—"

"You did not see Miss Fane?"

"No, I didn't. This room was empty when I came through it. I crossed the lanai and stepped out on the lawn—"

"At a little time past eight?"

"Yes—it must have been three or four minutes past the hour. As I ran over the lawn, I saw a man come hurriedly away from the pavilion—"

"You saw a man leaving the pavilion? Who was he?"

"I don't know. I couldn't see his face. I thought he was one of the guests, and I shouted hello. But he didn't answer."

"You are able to describe him?" Chan asked.

"Not his face—that was in shadow, as I told you. But he was wearing a coat—an overcoat—I thought it odd on a night like this. The coat was open, and a streak of light from the kitchen window fell on his shirt-front. He was dressed in evening clothes, you see, and across his white shirt—" Suddenly she turned pale and sat down weakly in the nearest chair. "Oh, my God," she cried, "I never thought of it before."

"You never thought of what before?" Charlie prompted.

"That stain on his shirt—that long, narrow, bright red stain," she gasped. "It—it must have been blood."

VI

FIREWORKS IN THE RAIN

For a moment, stunned by the picture Miss Dixon's words presented, the assemblage was silent. Then a low murmur, a buzz of amazed comment, filled the room. Charlie Chan stood looking at his newest witness speculatively, as though he asked himself whether her statement could possibly be true.

"Most interesting," he said at last. "There has been, then, on these grounds tonight, a gentleman whose presence was up to this moment unsuspected by me. Whether or not he carried blood-soaked shirt bosom—"

"But I tell you I saw it," the girl protested.

Chan shrugged. "Perhaps. Oh, most humble pardon—I do not question your truth. I merely mention overwrought nerves, or maybe optic illusion. You must excuse if I say I might admit murderer would be so clumsy at his work as to inundate himself, but reason totters on pedestal to add that such a man would rush from scene of crime with coat flapping open on his error. Rather I would picture him with garment wrapped close to hide away this crimson evidence. But what does it matter? We must at any rate pursue thought of man with overcoat. The idea in itself presents portrait of queer human being. Overcoat in smiling tropics, even over evening dress, is unaccustomed garb." He turned to Julie. "And what, please, is name of man servant in this house?"

"You mean Jessop?" she inquired.

"I mean the butler. Will you summon him—if I am not getting too obnoxious?"

Julie went into the hall, and Charlie turned to the deputy sheriff. "I find it impossible to accompany you to scene of crime just yet. Same took place in small beach house at right of lawn—please accept this key. You may begin examination, and I will join you when I have interrogated servants here."

"Did you find the weapon, Charlie?" asked the coroner.

"I did not. That was, I think, carried off by the assailant. He was person, you will find, who had wits in good control." Charlie turned to the Japanese. "Kashimo, you may enjoy yourself by keen observation of the neighborhood. But if you repeat one former performance and spoil any footprints for me, I will at once arrange for you to return to former position as janitor of fish market."

The coroner and the little Japanese went out. At the same moment Jessop held open the curtains and followed Julie into the room. The butler was pale and agitated.

"The name is Jessop?" Charlie inquired.

"Yes—ah—sir."

"You understand who it is that I am?"

"I take it you represent the local constabulary, sir."

Chan grinned. "If it will help you to endure society of person like me, Jessop, I offer statement that my humble efforts on one occasion met with the complete approval of a gentleman from Scotland Yard."

"Really, sir?" answered Jessop. "The memory must be most gratifying to you."

"It is, indeed. How long is it now that you have been Miss Fane's butler?"

"Two years, sir."

"You were in Hollywood before that, maybe?"

"For about eighteen months, I was."

"A butler, always?"

"Always a butler, sir. I had a number of berths before I went with Miss Fane. I am bound to say that I was unhappy in all of them."

"The work was, perhaps, too difficult?"

"Not at all, sir. I objected to the familiarity of my employers. There is a certain reserve that should exist between servant and master. I found that lacking. The ladies I worked for would often weep in my presence and tell me stories of unrequited love. The gentlemen who engaged me were inclined to treat me like some long-lost brother. One in particular was accustomed to address me as 'old pal' and when a bit under the influence, would embrace me in the presence of guests. A man has his dignity, sir."

"It has been well said, without dignity there can be no stature," Charlie assured him. "You found Miss Fane of a different type?"

"I did indeed, sir. A lady who knew her place as I knew mine. There was never any undue informality in her treatment of me."

"Relations were, then, of the happiest?"

"That they were. I should like to add that I am quite heart-broken by this evening's business, sir."

"Ah, yes—coming to this evening—did any of the gentlemen whom you admitted here tonight wear an overcoat, Jessop?"

"An overcoat, sir?" Jessop's white eyebrows went up.

"Yes. With dinner costume, you understand."

"No, sir," replied Jessop firmly. "No such gaucherie of dress was evident, Constable."

Chan smiled. "Kindly look about the room. Do you recall admitting any visitor with exception of those now visible to your view?"

"No, sir," returned Jessop, surveying the party.

"Thank you. When did you last see Miss Fane?"

"It was in this room, at about twenty minutes after seven, when I brought her a box of flowers. I heard her voice after that, but I did not see her."

"Please detail your activities from hour of twenty minutes past seven onward," Chan requested.

"I was engaged with my duties, sir, in the dining-room and the kitchen. I may add that it has been a rather trying evening, in my department. The Chinese cook has exhibited all the worst qualities of a heathen race—I'm sure I beg your pardon."

"A heathen race," repeated Charlie gravely, "that was busy inventing the art of printing at moment when gentlemen in Great Britain were still beating one another over head with spiked clubs. Pray excuse this brief reference to history. The cook has been in uproar?"

"Yes, Constable. He has proved himself sorely deficient in that patience for which his people have long been noted. Then, too, the—er—the bootlegger, to use one of your—or their—American phrases, has been unforgivably late."

"Ah—you already possess bootlegger?"

"Yes, sir. Miss Fane was a temperate woman herself, but she knew her duties as a hostess. So Wu Kno-ching, the cook, arranged with a friend to deliver a bit of liquor just out of the laboratory, and a wine of the most recent vintage."

"I am deeply shocked," Chan replied. "Wu's friend was late?"

"He was indeed, sir. As I say, I was busy with my duties from the moment I gave Miss Fane the flowers. At two minutes past eight—"

"Why do you make selection of two minutes past eight?"

"I could not help but overhear your questions to these others, sir. At that moment I was in the kitchen—"

"Alone?"

"No, sir. Wu was there, of course. And Anna, the maid, had dropped in for a cup of tea to sustain her until dinner. I called

Wu's attention to the fact that it was already past eight o'clock, and we had a few words about the bootlegger's tardiness. The three of us remained there together until ten after eight, when Wu's friend made a rather sheepish appearance, and I immediately set about to do what I could with the ingredients he brought. At fifteen past eight, I came out to admit Mr Van Horn. From that point on I was in and out of this room, sir, but I did not leave the house until I went to the beach and sounded the dinner gong."

"I am obliged to you for a most complete account," Charlie nodded. "That is all, Jessop."

The butler hesitated. "There is one other matter, Constable."

"Ah, yes. What is that?"

"I do not know whether or not it has any significance, sir, but it came back to me when I heard this terrible news. There is a small library upstairs, and today, when I had cleared away the luncheon things, I went in there to secure a book, planning to take it to my room as a recreation during my siesta. I came suddenly upon Miss Fane. She was looking at a photograph and weeping most bitterly, sir."

"A photograph of whom?"

"That I couldn't say, sir, save that it was of some gentleman. She held it so I could not obtain a better view of the face, and hurriedly left the room. All I can tell you is that it was a rather large photograph, and was mounted on a mat that was Nile green in color."

Chan nodded. "Thank you so much. Will you be kind enough to dispatch heathen cook into my presence, Jessop?"

"I will indeed, sir," replied Jessop, and withdrew.

Charlie looked about the circle. "The matter lengthens itself out," he remarked kindly. "I observe beyond windows a cool lanai crowded with nice Hong Kong chairs. Any who wish to do so may stroll to more airy perch. One thing only I ask—please do not leave these grounds."

There followed a general movement, and amid a low buzz of comment all save Bradshaw, Julie, Tarneverro and Chan went out on the dim lanai. The fortune-teller looked keenly at Charlie.

"What have you accomplished?" he wanted to know.

Charlie shrugged. "Up to the present moment, I seem to have been setting off fireworks in the rain."

"That's precisely what I thought," Tarneverro said impatiently.

"Do not lose heart," Chan advised. "Changing the figure, I might add that to dig up the tree, we must start with the root. All this digging is routine matter that does not fascinate, but at any moment we may strike a root of vital importance."

"I sincerely hope so," Tarneverro remarked.

"Oh, you trust Charlie," Bradshaw said. "One of Honolulu's first citizens, he is. He'll get his man."

Wu Kno-ching came in, mumbling to himself, and Charlie addressed him sharply in Cantonese. Looking at him with sleepy eyes, Wu replied at some length.

The high-pitched, singsong exchange of words between these two representatives of the oldest civilized nation in the world grew faster and louder, and on Wu's part, seemingly more impassioned. The three outsiders stood there deeply interested; it was like a play in some dead language; they could not understand the lines but they were conscious of a strong current of drama underneath. Once Chan, who had up to that point been seemingly uninterested, lifted his head like a bird-dog on the scent. He went closer to the old man, and seized his arm. One recognizable word in Wu's conversation occurred again and again. He mentioned the "bootleggah."

Finally, with a shrug, Chan turned away.

"What's he say, Charlie?" asked Bradshaw eagerly.

"He knows nothing," Chan answered.

"What was all that about the bootlegger?"

Charlie gave the boy a keen look. “The tongue of age speaks with accumulated wisdom, and is heard gladly, but the tongue of youth should save its strength,” he remarked.

“Yours received and contents noted,” smiled the boy.

Chan turned to Julie. “You have spoken of Miss Fane’s maid. She alone remains to be interviewed. Will you be so good as to produce her?”

Julie nodded and went out. Wu Kno-ching still lingered at the door, and now he burst into a tirade, with appropriate gestures. Charlie listened for a moment, and then shooed the old man from the room.

“Wu complains that no one eats his dinner,” he smiled. “He is great artist who lacks appreciation, and his ancient heart cracks with rage.”

“Well,” remarked Jimmy Bradshaw, “I suppose it’s an unfeeling thing to say, but I could put away a little of his handiwork.”

Chan nodded. “I have thought of that. Later, perhaps. Why not? Do the dead gain if the living starve?”

Julie returned, followed by Anna, the maid. The latter was a dark thin woman who moved gracefully.

“The name, please?” Chan inquired.

“Anna Rodderick,” she answered. There was just a trace of defiance in her tone.

“You have been with Miss Shelah Fane how long?”

“Something like a year and a half, sir.”

“I see. Before that you were perhaps employed elsewhere in Hollywood?”

“No, sir, I was not. I went with Miss Fane the day after my arrival there, and I have never been employed by anyone else in the picture colony.”

“How did you happen to go to California, please?”

“I was in service in England, and a friend wrote me of the higher wages that prevailed in the States.”

"Your relations with Miss Fane—they were pleasant?"

"Naturally, sir, or I wouldn't have remained with her. There were many other positions available."

"Did she ever admit you into her confidence regarding personal affairs?"

"No, sir, she did not. It was one of the things I liked about her."

"When did you last see your mistress?"

"At a bit before seven-thirty. I was about to go down to the kitchen for a cup of tea, for I saw that my dinner was likely to be long delayed. Miss Fane came to her room—I was in the one adjoining. She called to me and said she wanted a pin for some orchids she had in her hand. I went and got it for her."

"Kindly describe the pin."

"It was a rather delicate affair, set with diamonds. About two inches long, I should say. I fastened the flowers to the shoulder-strap of her gown."

"Did she remark about those flowers?" Charlie inquired.

"She said they were sent to her by someone of whom she was once very fond. She seemed a bit excited."

"What happened next?"

"She sat down at the telephone," Anna told him. "There is an extension in her room. She looked up a number in the telephone book and then busied herself with the dial, sir."

"Maybe you heard subsequent conversation?" Chan suggested.

"I am not accustomed to spying, sir. I left her at once and went down to the kitchen."

"You were in the kitchen at two minutes past eight?"

"Yes, sir. I recall the hour because there was a great deal of talk between Jessop and the cook about the bootlegger."

"You were still in the kitchen when this bootlegger came, at ten minutes past eight?"

"I was, sir. A little later I went back to my room."

"You did not see your mistress again?"

"No, sir, I did not."

"One other thing." Chan looked at her thoughtfully. "Kindly speak of her manner during the day. Was it same as always?"

"I noticed nothing unusual."

"You did not note that she was seen with a portrait—the portrait of a gentleman—during the afternoon?"

"I was not here this afternoon. It was our first day ashore, and Miss Fane kindly gave me a few hours off."

"Have you ever seen, among Miss Fane's possessions, portrait of gentleman mounted on Nile-green mat?"

"Miss Fane always carried with her a large portfolio, containing many pictures of her friends. It may be such a one is among them."

"But you never saw it?"

"I have never opened the portfolio. That would seem too much like prying—if I may say so, sir."

"Do you know where portfolio is now?" Charlie asked.

"I believe it is lying on a table in her room. Shall I fetch it for you?"

"A little later, perhaps. Just now I would inquire—you are familiar with jewelry usually worn by Miss Fane on occasion of evening party? Aside from diamond pin fastening orchids, I mean?"

"I think so, sir."

"Will you come with me, please?"

Leaving the others in the drawing-room, he led the maid across the moonlit lawn in the direction of the pavilion. They went in, and Anna lost her composure for a moment at sight of Shelah Fane. She gave a strangled little cry.

"Kindly conduct thorough search," Chan said to her, "and inform me if all jewelry is at present time in place."

Anna nodded without speaking. The coroner came over to greet Chan.

"I've made my examination," he said. "This is a pretty big thing, Charlie. I'd better send somebody to help you out."

Chan smiled. "I have Kashimo," he answered. "What more could any man ask? Tell Chief I will report entire matter to him at earliest convenience." They stepped out on the lanai of the pavilion, and at the same moment Kashimo crept like a correspondence-school sleuth from a cluster of bushes at the corner of the building.

"Charlie—come quick," he whispered hoarsely.

"Kashimo has discovered essential clue," Charlie said. "Please join us, Mr Coroner."

They followed the Japanese through the bushes and out upon a public beach that bounded the property on the right. On that side of the pavilion, which stood flush with the dividing line, was a single window. Kashimo led them to this, and swept a flash-light over the sand.

"Footprints-s-s!" he hissed dramatically.

Charlie seized the light and knelt on the sand. "True enough, Kashimo," he remarked. "These are footprints, and peculiar ones, too. Shoes were old and battered, the heels are worn down unevenly, and in sole of one shoe was most unfashionable hole." He stood up. "I fear that fortune has not been smiling on owner of that footwear," he added.

"I am one to find things," remarked Kashimo proudly.

"You are," smiled Charlie, "and for once you do not destroy clue the moment you come upon it. You are learning, Kashimo. Warm congratulations."

They returned to the lawn of Shelah Fane's house. "Well, Charlie, this is up to you," the deputy said. "I'll see you early in the morning—unless you want me to stay."

"Your duty is accomplished," Chan answered, "or will be when you have made proper arrangements in city. Body will of course be taken at once to mortuary."

"Certainly," the deputy replied. "Well, goodbye—and good luck."

Chan turned to Kashimo. "Now great opportunity arises for you to perform your specialty," he said.

"Yes-s-s," Kashimo answered eagerly.

"Go to house, inquire for bedroom of Miss Shelah Fane, and search—"

"I go now," cried Kashimo, leaping away.

"Stop!" commanded Charlie. "You are one grand apprentice detective, Kashimo, but you never pause to inquire what it is you sleuth for. On table of that room you will find large portfolio of photographs. I very much desire to see portrait of gentleman mounted on mat that is colored Nile green—"

"Nile is new word to me," the Japanese complained.

"Yes—and I have no time for geography lesson now," sighed Chan. "Bring me all photographs in room mounted on cardboard colored green. If none such is in portfolio, search elsewhere. Now be off. The portrait of a gentleman, remember. If you return with pretty picture of Fujiyama I will personally escort you back to private life."

Kashimo sped across the lawn, and Charlie again entered the pavilion. Anna was standing in the center of the room.

"You made investigation?" he inquired.

"I did," she said. "The pin that fastened the flowers is nowhere about."

"A matter already known to me," he nodded. "Otherwise the ornamental equipment is complete?"

"No," she replied. "It isn't."

He regarded her with sudden interest "Something is missing?"

"Yes—an emerald ring—a large emerald that Miss Fane usually wore on her right hand. She told me once that it represented quite a bit of money. And—it has disappeared."

VII

THE ALIBI OF THE WATCH

Charlie sent the maid back to the house, and then sat down in the straight-backed chair before the dressing-table. The sole illumination in the little room came from two pink-shaded lamps, one on either side of the mirror. Thoughtfully he stared into the glass where, dimly reflected, he caught occasional glimpses of an ivory satin gown. Shelah Fane now lay on the couch where the coroner had placed her. All the loves and the hates, the jealousies, the glittering triumphs of this tempestuous career were ended tonight. A woman of flame, they had called her. The flame had flickered and died like a candle in the wind—in the restless tradewind blowing from the Koolau Range.

Chan's small eyes narrowed in an intense effort at concentration. In one of her more indiscreet moments, Shelah Fane had seen Denny Mayo murdered. For three years she had carried the secret about with her until—and this moment was even more indiscreet—she poured it into the willing ears of Tarneverro the Great, a crystal-gazer—a charlatan, no doubt. That same night, the black camel had knelt before her gate.

Carefully in his mind, the detective began to go over the points his investigation had so far revealed. He was not one to carry a note-book, but he took an envelope from his pocket, and with a pencil began to write a list of names on the back. He was thus engaged when he heard a step behind him. Looking over his shoulder, he saw the lean mysterious figure of Tarneverro.

The fortune-teller came forward and dropped into a chair at Chan's side. He stared at the detective, and there was disapproval in that stare.

"Since you have asked me to work with you in this affair," he began, "you will perhaps pardon me if I say I think you have been extremely careless."

Charlie's eyes opened wide. "Yes?" he said.

"I refer to Miss Fane's letter," continued Tarneverro. "It may have been the answer to all our questions. In it the poor girl may have written the name we so eagerly seek. Yet you made no move to search the people in that room—you even pooh-poohed the idea when I offered it. Why?"

Chan shrugged. "You think, then, we have to deal with a fool? A miscreant who would take pretty complete pains to obtain the epistle, and then place it on his own person where a search would instantly reveal it? You are wrong, my friend. I had no taste for revealing how wrong you were, at the expense of further embarrassment for myself. No, the letter is hidden in that room, and sooner or later it will be found. If not—what of it? I have strong feeling that it contains nothing of the least importance."

"On what do you base that feeling?" Tarneverro inquired.

"I have plenty as a base. Would Shelah Fane have written big secret down and then given it to servant who must pass it along to you? No, she would have awaited her opportunity and then delivered it to you with her own hand. I do not reprove you, but I believe you attach undue importance to that probably innocent epistle."

"Well, the murderer certainly thought it important. You can't deny that."

"Murderer was in state of high excitement and took unnecessary risk. If he takes few more like that, we are at trail's end."

Tarneverro, with a gesture, dismissed the matter. "Well, and what have you discovered from all your questions?" He glanced at Chan's notes.

"Not much. You perceived that I was curious to learn who was in Hollywood three years ago last month. Assuming that the story is true—the story you say Shelah Fane told you this morning—"

"Why shouldn't it be true? Does a woman make a confession like that as a joke?"

"Never," answered Chan, somewhat sharply for him. "And for that reason I am remarking I assume it to be true. It is, then, important to locate our many suspects in June three years ago. I have written here the names of all who were in Hollywood at that time, and consequently may have slain Denny Mayo. They are Wilkie Ballou, Rita his wife, Huntley Van Horn. And—ah, yes—Jessop, the butler. I regret that, overwhelmed by account of bloody shirt, I neglected to make inquiries of Miss Dixon."

"She has been in Hollywood six years," the fortune-teller informed him. "I know from what she has told me during the readings I have given her."

"One more." Charlie wrote down the name. "I may, I presume, add Miss Julie—though very young at the time. Of these, for the hour of two minutes past eight tonight, two have been accounted for. Jessop presents plenty good alibi and Huntley Van Horn has perfect one, to which I myself can swear. Other things I learned—not very important—but it struck my mind, as it must have struck yours, that Mr Alan Jaynes was breathless with anxiety to leave Hawaii tonight. Do not forget—it is within grounds of possibility that Denny Mayo murder had nothing to do with death of Shelah Fane. This Jaynes was in overwrought state; his may be fiercely jealous nature; he may have looked at those orchids, the gift of another, on the lady's shoulder, and—"

"But he, too, has the alibi of the watch," Tarneverro suggested.

"Alas! yes," Chan nodded.

For a moment they sat in silence. Then Tarneverro rose, and walked slowly toward the couch. "By the way," he said casually, "have you made a thorough examination of this watch?"

"So sorry." Chan rose and followed him. "You now call my attention to fact that I have neglected most obvious duty." Tarneverro was bending over, but Chan stopped him. "I will remove it at once and have careful look at it—though I am so dense I do not quite grasp your meaning."

Taking a linen handkerchief from his pocket, he spread it over his left hand. With his other hand he unfastened the narrow black ribbon from Shelah Fane's wrist, and lifting the costly little watch, laid it on the handkerchief. He went back and stood directly under one of the lights, staring down at the timepiece.

"*Haie*, I seem in stupid mood tonight," he sighed "I am still at sea. Crystal is broken, watch has ceased to function at precisely two minutes past eight—"

"Permit me," said Tarneverro. "I will be more explicit." He took both handkerchief and watch, and with the linen always between his fingers and the metal, turned the stem of the fragile timepiece. At his touch, the minute hand moved instantly.

A flash of triumph shone in the fortune-teller's eyes. "That," he cried, "is more than I dared to hope for. The murderer has been guilty of a small error—it was very kind of him. He adjusted the stem so that the time shown on the face of the watch could be altered at will—and in his haste he forgot to readjust it. Surely I needn't tell you what that means."

Charlie gave him a look of enthusiastic approval. "You are detective of the first class yourself—give me credit that I noted same this morning. I can never cease to be grateful to you. Of course I grasp meaning now."

Tarneverro laid the watch down on the glass top of the dressing-table. "I think we may be sure of one thing, Inspector," he remarked. "At whatever hour the murder took place, it was certainly not at two minutes past eight. We are dealing with a clever man. After he had killed Shelah Fane he removed her watch, set the time back—or perhaps forward—to two minutes past eight, and then smashed the thing as though to indicate a struggle." The fortune-teller's eyes lighted; he pointed to the corner of the dressing-table. "That's the explanation of the nick in the glass. He banged the watch against that corner until he had stopped its running."

Chan was instantly on the floor. "There is no glass beneath," he said.

"No, no," Tarneverro continued. "There wouldn't be. The broken glass was naturally found where Miss Fane fell. And why? Because this unknown person removed the watch with a handkerchief, as you have done; he swung it against the table in that handkerchief to catch the bits of crystal, and carried the wrecked remains intact to the spot where he wanted them. A bright boy, Inspector."

Charlie nodded. Obvious chagrin was in his manner. "But you are brighter boy. Almost I am on verge of resigning in disgust at my own stupidity. You should take my badge, Mr Tarneverro, for you are the smart detective on this case."

Tarneverro gave him an odd look. "You think so, do you? I'm afraid you exaggerate—the matter was really simple enough. It came into my mind that too many of us had alibis in this affair. I thought how easy it would be to change the time on the face of a watch. That is what happened here. The murderer set it at a moment then past, for which he had already established an alibi—or at a future time for which he proposed to get an alibi forthwith. However, when a man is excited he is likely to slip up somewhere—and this chap stumbled when he forgot to push down that little stem before he left."

Chan sighed. "I am, as I remarked, bubbling with gratitude toward you, and yet I am appalled. Whole flock of alibis is now quite ruined, and the field broadens like some boundless prairie. Van Horn's alibi is gone, the alibis of Martino and of Jaynes, they are gone too, and—begging humble pardon, Mr Tarneverro—you have likewise destroyed the alibi you yourself possessed."

The fortune-teller threw back his head and laughed. "Do I need an alibi?" he cried.

"Perhaps not," Charlie grinned. "But when a tree falls, the shade is gone. Who knows? Even you might regret the loss of that shade in time."

"It may happen that I have another tree," suggested Tarneverro.

"If that is true, I congratulate you." Charlie glanced around the room. "I must have poor unfortunate lady removed now to house, then lock this place until finger-print expert can do work early in morning. You will observe we do not move with vast speed here in Hawaii. It is our lovely climate." He put the watch in the dressing-table drawer, and he and Tarneverro went out, Chan again locking the door. "We will now continue to living-room, which we will seek to obtain to ourselves. Perhaps there you will deign to keep on with remarkable research. I travel in luck tonight. What could I do without you?"

A little group of chairs on the lawn indicated the whereabouts of most of the guests. In the living-room they came upon Julie and Jimmy Bradshaw, seated close together. The girl had evidently been crying, and Mr Bradshaw's manner suggested that he played the rôle of comforter. Chan gave Julie the key to the pavilion, and told her gently what must be done. She and the boy went out to seek the aid of the servants.

When they had gone, Charlie walked thoughtfully up and down the big room. He peered into receptacles that held flowers and plants, opened the few books he came upon and ruffled the pages.

"By the way," Tarneverro remarked, "have you made an inspection of Miss Fane's bedroom?"

"Not yet," Chan answered. "So much to do, and only you and I to do it. I have sent Kashimo, our Japanese sleuth hound, on an errand, from which he will doubtless return in course of week or two. As for myself—" He was walking across a rug, and paused. "As for myself—" he repeated. He rubbed his thin-soled shoe back and forth over a spot in the rug. "As for myself," he added a third time, "I have plenty good business here."

He stooped and threw back the rug. There on the polished floor lay the big envelope that had been snatched from his hand earlier in the evening. One corner was missing, but otherwise the letter was intact.

"Fortunate that Miss Fane preferred such thick note-paper," Charlie said. He picked up the envelope. "I fear I cannot offer my unknown friend warm congratulations on his originality this time. But he was very hurried gentleman when this matter engaged his attention—I must remember that."

Tarneverro came close, his dark eyes gleaming. "By gad—Shelah's letter. And addressed to me, I believe?"

"I remind you again that the police are in charge," Chan said.

"They were in charge before," Tarneverro answered.

"Ah, yes. But history will not repeat just yet." Charlie removed the note from the envelope, and read. He shrugged his shoulders, and passed the missive to the fortune-teller. "Once I was right," he remarked.

Tarneverro looked down at the huge sprawling handwriting of one who was generous of note-paper as of all things. He frowned at what he saw.

"Dear Tarneverro:

"Please forget what I told you this morning. I must have been mad—mad. I intend to forget it—and so must you—oh, Tarneverro, promise me you will. Pretend that I never said it. I shall refuse poor Alan tonight—it will break my heart—but I'll do it. I am going on alone—perhaps in the end I may even find a little happiness. I want it so much.

"Yours ever

"Shelah Fane."

"Poor Shelah!" The fortune-teller stood for a moment, staring at the letter. "She hadn't the courage to go through with it—I might have known. A pitiful letter—I don't believe I would have insisted, after all." He crushed the paper in his hand fiercely. "The murderer of Denny Mayo was safe—she wasn't going to tell on him—he killed her for nothing. She's gone, and she might be here. By heaven—I'll get him if it's the last act of my life!"

Chan smiled. "I have a similar ambition, though I trust the accomplishment will not finish off my existence." His Japanese assistant came stealthily into the room. "Ah, Kashimo, have you enjoyed pleasant weekend upstairs?"

"Pretty hard job, but I got him," Kashimo announced proudly. "Found in jar under potted plant."

Chan reached out his hand. To his surprise Kashimo proffered, not the photograph Charlie expected, but a handful of torn bits of glazed paper and of heavy green cardboard. Someone had ripped the portrait on the green mat to bits, and then attempted to conceal the wreckage.

"What have we now?" Chan said. He stood looking in wonder at the handful of scraps that he held. His eyes sought Tarneverro's. "Here is a matter worthy of consideration. Person unknown does not wish me to look upon the photograph over which Shelah Fane wept this afternoon. Why? Is it the portrait of the man you had asked her to betray?"

"It may have been," Tarneverro agreed.

"Course now becomes clear," Charlie announced. "I must view this photograph, so with all patience at my command, I propose to fit these scraps together again." He pulled a small table up before the windows that faced the street.

"I investigate outside the house," Kashimo remarked.

"Much the safest place to have you," Chan returned. "By all means investigate very hard."

The Japanese went out.

Charlie removed the table cover, and sat down. On the smooth top he began carefully to lay together the pieces of the photograph. The task, he saw, was going to be long and arduous. "I never was bright man with jigsaw puzzle," he complained. "My daughter Rose was pride of family at that work. I would enjoy to have her at my side."

He had made scant progress when the door of the lanai opened, and a group of the guests entered the living-room. Wilkie Ballou walked at the head, and after him came Van Horn, Martino, Jaynes and Rita Ballou. Diana Dixon followed; she seemed detached from the crowd, which had the air of a delegation.

A delegation it was, evidently. Ballou began to speak, in his most commanding tone.

"See here, Inspector—we've talked it over and there's no earthly reason why you should keep us here any longer. We've all been questioned, we've told you what we know, and now we propose to leave."

Charlie tossed down the as yet unplaced bits of the photograph and rose. He bowed politely.

"I recognize you are impatient with good reason," he said.

"Then you're willing for us to go along?" inquired Ballou.

"I am—and I say it with extreme pain—quite unwilling," Chan replied. "Unfortunately, new developments keep popping off like firecrackers on New Year holiday, and I have something still to talk about with you."

"An outrage!" Ballou cried. "I'll have your badge for this."

Charlie rewarded him with a maddening smile. "That may happen—tomorrow. But looking only at tonight, I am placed in charge of this case, and I say—you will remain here until I tell you to depart."

Jaynes pushed forward. "I have important business on the mainland, and I intend to sail at midnight. It is now long past ten. I warn you that you must call out your entire force if you propose to keep me here—"

"That also can be done," answered Charlie amiably.

"Good lord!" The Britisher looked helplessly at Wilkie Ballou. "What kind of place is this? Why don't they send a white man out here?"

A rare light flared suddenly in Charlie's eyes. "The man who is about to cross a stream should not revile the crocodile's mother," he said in icy tones.

"What do you mean by that?" Jaynes asked.

"I mean you are not yet safely on the farther bank."

"You know damn' well I've got an alibi," cried the Britisher angrily.

Chan's little eyes surveyed him from head to foot "I am not so sure I do," he remarked calmly.

"You said yourself you had fixed the time of this affair—"

"How sad," cut in Charlie, "that we pass through this life, making so many errors as we go. Me, I am stupid blunderer. Your alibi, Mr Jaynes, has been punctured like bubble with a pin."

"What!" cried Jaynes.

Van Horn and Martino stirred with sudden interest.

"Back off and cool down," Chan continued. "And accepting my advice, speak no more of alibis. You have already said too much."

Like a man dazed, Jaynes almost literally obeyed Chan's orders. Charlie turned to Rita Ballou.

"Madam, my humblest apologies and regrets. I hold you here with the utmost grief. It has occurred to me that there is a dinner long prepared—I fear the passage of time has wrecked most of it now. But if I might suggest—"

"Oh, I couldn't eat a thing," Rita told him.

"No, of course, the very thought is horrifying," Chan nodded. "Such heartlessness would be quite out of place." Julie and Bradshaw came in. "Nevertheless I urge that you all go out to your positions at the table and at least partake of one cup of coffee. The event will shatter strain, and make easier the period of waiting. Coffee, as you know, stimulates and fortifies the mind."

"Not a bad idea," said Huntley Van Horn.

"Miss Julie—" Chan suggested.

The girl smiled wanly. "Yes, of course. I'll tell Jessop to get things ready. You must forgive me. I'd quite forgotten we had guests tonight."

She turned and went out. Charlie walked back to the small table where his task lay uncompleted. At that instant a French window facing the street was thrust suddenly open, and the tradewind swept into the room like a miniature hurricane. Instantly the air was filled with torn bits of photograph, swirling about like snow in a Minnesota blizzard.

Kashimo stuck his head into the room. "S-s-s," he hissed. "Charlie!"

"Splendid work, Kashimo," said Chan through his teeth. "What is it now?"

"I find window unlocked," announced the Japanese triumphantly, and withdrew, closing the aperture behind him.

Concealing his disgust, Charlie moved around the room, retrieving the bits of photograph from most unlikely places. Tarneverro and some of the others came promptly to his aid. In a few moments, he again held a little packet of scraps in his hand. He walked about, still seeking, but no more were in sight.

He resumed his place at the table, and for a few moments he worked hard. Then he shrugged his shoulders, and stood up.

"What's the trouble?" Tarneverro asked.

Charlie looked at him. "No use. I have now little more than half the pieces I had before." For a moment he stood staring about that innocent-appearing little group. It was in his mind to search everyone of them, but a glance at Ballou reminded him that such action would mean a hot battle, and he was ever a man of peace. No, he must reach his goal by some other path. He sighed, and placed what he had left of the photograph in his pocket, as Kashimo dashed in. More in sorrow than in anger Charlie regarded his ambitious confrère.

"Detectives were practically extinct at station house when they sent you out tonight," he said.

The doorbell rang, a loud, insistent peal. Jessop being in the distant kitchen, Jimmy Bradshaw went to the door. Those in the living-room heard a few sharp quick words in the hall, and a man strode into their midst. He was a handsome fellow of forty, gray at the temples, with great poise of manner and a keen eye. The grease-paint of the theater was still on his face. He stood, looking about him.

"Good evening," he said. "I am Robert Fyfe—at one time the husband of Miss Shelah Fane. This is terrible news someone telephoned me a short time ago. I came the instant my part in the piece was finished—without stopping to remove my make-up or change my costume. Most unprofessional—but I must ask you to overlook it."

"Shall I take your overcoat?" Jimmy Bradshaw asked.

"Thank you so much." He stepped to the curtains and handed Jimmy the coat. As he turned back toward the room, Diana Dixon's scream rang out, shrill and unexpected. She was pointing at Robert Fyfe's shirt-front.

Diagonally across that white expanse lay the bright red ribbon of the Legion of Honor. Startled, Fyfe looked down at it.

"Ah, yes," he said. "I came in my stage costume, as I told you. This week, you see, I happen to be playing the rôle of a French ambassador."

VIII

THE BEACH-COMBER'S SHOES

During the long silence that followed, Charlie stood gravely regarding this handsome actor who had, all unknowing, made the best entrance of his career. The actor looked back at him with a cool level stare. Still no one spoke, and Fyfe began to realize that the gaze of everyone in the room was upon him. Accustomed though he was to the scrutiny of crowds, he found something a bit disconcerting in this situation. He stirred uneasily, and sought for words to break the spell.

"What is all this about Shelah? I came at the earliest possible moment, as I say. Though I had not seen her for many years—"

"How many years?" cried Chan quickly.

Fyfe looked him over casually. "You must pardon me," he said, "if I do not at once grasp your position here—"

Nonchalantly Charlie pushed back the left side of his coat, revealing his badge of office. It was a gesture of which an actor could approve—business, not words.

"I am in charge," Chan said. "You were, you say, at one time husband of Miss Shelah Fane. You have not seen her for many years. How many?"

Fyfe considered. "It was nine years ago, in April, when we parted. We were both playing in New York—Miss Fane in a Ziegfeld revue at the New Amsterdam, and I was doing a mystery play at the Astor. She came home one night and told me she had a splendid offer to go to Hollywood for a picture—she was so excited, so keen for the idea, that I hadn't the heart to oppose her. A week later, on an April evening, I said goodbye to her at the Grand Central Station, wondering how long I could hold her love. Not very long, as it turned out. Within a year she went to Reno, and it was all quite painless—for her, I fancy. Not quite so painless for me—although I had felt it coming, that night at the station. Something had told me then that I was seeing her for the last time."

"You no doubt appeared in Los Angeles in later years," Chan suggested, "at moments when Miss Fane was in Hollywood?"

"Oh, yes—of course. But we never met."

"Do you happen to recall—were you playing in Los Angeles three years ago, in June?"

Charlie was struck by the look that came into the actor's eyes. Was it, perhaps, a look of understanding? "No," said Fyfe firmly. "I was not."

"You are plenty positive," Chan commented.

"I happen to be—yes," Fyfe replied. "Three years ago I was touring with a company that did not reach the coast."

"It is a matter that can easily be verified," the detective reminded him slowly.

"Certainly," agreed Fyfe. "Go ahead and verify it."

"Then you assert," Chan continued, "that you have not seen Shelah Fane since that moment in New York station, nine years ago?"

"I do."

"You did not see her in Honolulu today?"

"No."

"Or tonight?"

A pause. "No."

Julie entered. "The coffee is ready," she announced. "Please, all come into the dining-room."

"I make haste to endorse that suggestion," Chan put in.

Reluctantly they filed out, assuring one another that they could eat nothing, that the idea was unthinkable, but that perhaps a cup of coffee—Their voices trailed away beyond the curtains. Of the dinner guests, only the fortune-teller lingered.

"Please go, Mr Tarneverro," Chan said. "Small stimulant will increase action of that fine brain on which I lean so heavily."

Tarneverro bowed. "For a moment only," he replied, and left the room.

Charlie turned to Kashimo. "As for you, I suggest you travel out to lanai, sit upon a chair and think about your sins. When you appeared a moment ago like Jack of the box, you scattered precious evidence to the winds."

"So sorry," Kashimo hissed.

"Please be sorry on the lanai," Charlie advised, and hurrying him out, closed the windows after him. Turning, he came back to Robert Fyfe. "I am happy to be alone with you," he began. "Though you may not have guessed, you are most interesting figure who has yet popped into this affair."

"Really?" The actor dropped into a chair and sat there, a striking figure in his ambassadorial costume. His manner was calm, unperturbed, and seemingly he was in the frankest of moods.

"Very interesting indeed," Charlie continued. "I gaze at you, and I ask myself—why is he lying to me?"

Fyfe half rose from his chair. "Look here. What do you mean?"

Chan shrugged. "My dear sir—what is the use? When you visit lawn pavilions to call on ex-wives, how careless to flaunt distinctive red ribbon on chest. It might even be mistaken by excitable young women for—blood. Matter of fact—it was."

"Oh," said Fyfe grimly. "I see."

"The truth—for a change," went on Chan gently.

The actor sat for a moment with his head in his hands. Finally he looked up.

"Gladly," he answered. "Though the truth is a bit—unusual. I hadn't seen Shelah Fane since that night in the station—until tonight. This morning I heard she was in town. It was quite startling—what the news did to me. You did not know Miss Fane, Mr—er—Mr—"

"Inspector Chan," Charlie informed him. "No, I had not the pleasure."

"It was really that—a pleasure." Fyfe half smiled. "She was a remarkable girl, aflame with life. I'd once been very fond of her and—I never got over it. No other woman ever meant anything to me after Shelah left. I couldn't hold her—I don't blame her for that—no man could hold her long. She wanted romance, excitement. Well, as I say, I learned this morning she was in town, and the news thrilled me—it was as though I heard her voice again after nine years' silence. I sent her flowers, with a message—love from someone you have forgotten. Have I said she was impetuous? Wild, unreasoning, sudden—and irresistible. My flowers had barely reached this house when she called me on the telephone. She caught me at the theater, made up, ready to go on. 'Bob,' she said, 'you must come at once. You must. I want so much to see you. I am waiting.'"

He glanced at Chan, and shrugged. "Any other woman, and I would have answered: 'After the show.' Somehow, that was never the way one replied to Shelah. 'Coming'—that was always the answer when Shelah spoke.

"It was a rather mad idea, but possible. I had arrived at the theater early, I needn't go on for forty-five minutes. I had a car and could drive out here, if I rushed it a bit, in fifteen minutes each way. So, at seven-thirty, I went into my dressing-room on the ground floor of the building, locked the door on the inside, and stepped through a window into the alley that runs along beside the theater.

"Shelah had told me about the pavilion, she said she was giving a dinner party, but that I needn't meet any of the guests—my make-up, you know, and all that. She wanted to see me alone, anyhow. I reached here about seven-forty-five. Shelah met me on the lawn, and we went to the pavilion. She looked at me in a strange way—I wondered if she still cared for me. I was shocked at the change in her—when I knew her she was fresh and lovely and so very gay. Hollywood had altered her greatly. Oh, well—none of us grows younger, I suppose. We wasted precious time in reminiscences, living over the past—somehow, it seemed to make her happy, just to remember. I was nervous about the time—I kept looking at my watch. Finally I said that I must go."

He was silent. "And then—" Chan prompted.

"Well, it was odd," Fyfe continued. "I'd got the impression over the telephone, and even more so after I saw her, that she wanted my advice about some terribly pressing matter. But when I told her I was going, she only stared at me in a sort of pitiful way. 'Bob,' she said, 'you still care for me a little, don't you?' She was standing close to me, and I took her in my arms. 'I adore you,' I cried, and—but I needn't go into that. I had that moment—no one can take it from me. Thoughts of the happy past came back—I was torn between my love for Shelah and that damn' watch ticking in my very brain. I told her hurriedly that I would return after the play, that I would see her daily during her stay here, that we would swim together—I had a wild idea that perhaps I could win her all over again. And perhaps I could have done it—but now—now—" His voice broke. "Poor Shelah! Poor girl!"

Chan nodded gravely. "It has been well said, those who live too conspicuously tempt the notice of Fate."

"And I suppose no one ever lived more conspicuously than Shelah," Fyfe added. He gave Charlie a quick penetrating glance. "Look here, Inspector—you mustn't fail me. You must find out who has done this awful thing."

"Such is my aim," Chan assured him. "You departed at once?"

"Yes, I left her standing there—standing there smiling, alive and well. Smiling, and crying too. I dashed out of the pavilion—"

"It was now what time?"

"I know only too well—it was four minutes past eight. I rushed down the drive, found my car where I'd left it before the house, and motored back to town as quickly as I could. When I stepped through the window of my dressing-room, they were hammering like wild men on my door. I opened it, said I'd been having a nap, and went out with the stage manager to the wings. I was five minutes late—the stage manager showed me his watch—eight-twenty. But that wasn't serious—I went on and played my rôle—and I was just coming off after the first act when some young man telephoned me the terrible news."

He stood up. "That, Inspector Chan, is my story. My visit out here tonight may prove embarrassing for me, but I don't regret it. I saw Shelah again—I held her in my arms—and for that privilege I stand ready to pay any price you can name. Is there anything more I can tell you?"

Chan shook his head. "For the present, no. I ask that you remain on scene a brief time. Other matters may arise later."

"Of course," nodded Fyfe.

The bell rang, and Charlie himself went to the door. Peering into the night, he beheld a burly dark-skinned man in the khaki uniform of the Honolulu police.

"Ah, it is Spencer," he said. "I am very glad to have you here."

The officer came into the hall, dragging after him a figure that, anywhere save on a tropic beach, would have been quite unbelievable.

"I picked this up on Kalakaua Avenue," the policeman explained. "I thought you might like to see him. He's a little mixed on what he's been doing tonight."

The man to whom he referred shook off the officer's grip and stepped toward Charlie. "I trust we're not too late for dinner," he remarked. He stood for a moment looking about the hall and then, as though prompted by old memories, removed from his head a limp and tattered hat of straw. "My chauffeur is really rather stupid. He lost his way."

His manner was jaunty and debonair, no mean triumph considering his costume. Aside from the hat, which he now clutched in a thin freckled hand, that costume consisted of a badly soiled pair of white duck trousers, a blue shirt open at the throat, a disreputable velvet coat that had once been the color of Burgundy and the remnants of a pair of shoes, through the holes of which peered the white of his naked feet.

The buzz of conversation from the dining-room had died, the group in there appeared to be listening, and Charlie hastily held open the curtains to the living-room. "Come in here, please," he said, and they entered to find Fyfe waiting there alone. For a moment the man in the velvet coat stared at the actor, and under the yellow ragged beard that had not known barber's scissors for a month, a slow smile appeared.

"Now," Chan said. "Who are you? Where do you live?"

The man shrugged. "The name," he replied, "might be Smith."

"It might also be Jones," Charlie suggested.

"A mere matter of taste. Personally, I prefer Smith."

"And you live—"

Mr Smith hesitated. "To put it crudely, Officer, I'm afraid I'm on the beach."

Charlie smiled. "Ah, you uphold noble tradition. What would Waikiki be without beach-comber?" He went to the window that led to the lanai and summoned Kashimo. "Kindly search this gentleman," he directed.

"By all means," the beach-comber agreed. "And if you find anything that looks like money, in heaven's name let me know about it at once."

Kashimo's search revealed little—a piece of string, a comb, a rusty pocket-knife, and an object which at first glance looked like a coin, but which turned out to be a medal. Charlie took this and studied it.

"Temple bronze medal, Third Prize, Landscapes in Oils," he read. "The Pennsylvania Academy of Fine Arts." He looked inquiringly at Smith.

The beach-comber shrugged. "Yes," he said. "I see I shall have to confess it all now—I'm a painter. Not much of a one at that—the third prize only, you will observe. The first medal was of gold—it might have come in handy of late, if I'd won it. But I didn't." He came a bit nearer. "If it's not asking too much—just what is the reason for this unwarranted intrusion into my affairs? Can't a gentleman go about his business in this town without being pawed by a fat policeman, and searched by a thin one?"

"We are sorry to inconvenience you, Mr Smith," Charlie replied politely. "But tell me—have you been on the beach tonight?"

"I have not. I've been in town. I walked out—for reasons which we needn't take up now. I was going along Kalakaua when this cop—"

"Where downtown have you been?"

"In Aala Park."

"You talked with someone there?"

"I did. The company was not select, but I made it do."

"Not on the beach tonight." Chan was staring at the man's feet "Kashimo, you and Spencer will kindly escort this gentleman out to spot below window where you discovered footprints, and make careful comparison."

"I know," cried the Japanese eagerly. He went out with the other policeman and the beach-comber.

Chan turned to Fyfe. "Long arduous task," he commented. "But man, without work, becomes—what? A Mr Smith. Will you be seated at your ease?"

The others entered from the dining-room, and to them also Charlie offered chairs, which most of them accepted with poor grace. Alan Jaynes was consulting his watch. Eleven o'clock—he sought Chan's eyes. But the detective looked innocently the other way.

Tarneverro came close to Charlie. "Anything new?" he inquired, under his breath.

"The inquiry widens," Chan answered.

"I'd rather it narrowed down," replied the fortune-teller.

The two policemen and the beach-comber returned through the lanai. Spencer again had the latter firmly in his grip.

"O.K., Charlie," said the uniformed man. "The footprints under the window could have been made by only one pair of shoes in Honolulu." He pointed at the beach-comber's battered footwear. "Those shoes," he added.

Smith looked down, smiling whimsically. "They are a shocking bad pair, aren't they?" he inquired. "But Hawaii, you know, seems to have no appreciation of art. If you've noticed the paintings they buy to hang in their parlors—the wooden waves put on canvas by the local Rembrandts—I may be a third-rater, but I couldn't bring myself to do stuff like that. Not even for a new pair of—"

"Come here!" cut in Charlie sharply. "You lied to me."

Smith shrugged. "You put things bluntly for one of your race, Officer. It may be that I distorted the situation slightly in the interests of—"

"The interests of what?"

"The interests of Smith. I observe that there is something wrong here, and I much prefer to keep out of it—"

"You are in it now. Tell me—did you enter that beach house tonight?"

"I did not—I'll swear to that. True, I stood beneath the window for a few minutes."

"What were you doing there?"

"I was planning to make the sand in the shelter of the pavilion my lodging for the night. It's a favorite place of mine—"

"Go back to beginning," cut in Chan. "The truth this time."

"I hadn't been out to the beach for three days and nights," the man told him. "I got a little money, and I've been stopping downtown. When I was out here last, this house was unoccupied. Today my money was gone—I'm expecting a check—it hasn't come." He paused. "Rotten mail service out here. If I could only get back to the mainland—"

"Your money was gone," Charlie interrupted.

"Yes—so I was forced back to my old couch under the palm trees. I walked out from town, and got to the beach—"

"At what time?"

"My dear sir,—you embarrass me. If you will take a stroll along Hotel Street, you will see my watch hanging in a certain window, I often go and look at it myself."

"No matter. You got to the beach."

"I did. It's public, you know—this one out here. It belongs to everybody. I was surprised to see a light in the pavilion. Somebody's rented the house, I thought. The curtain of that window was down, but it was flapping in the wind. I heard voices inside—a man's and a woman's—I wondered whether it was such a good place to sleep, after all."

He paused. Charlie's eyes were on Robert Fyfe. The actor was leaning forward with a fierce intensity, staring at the beachcomber, his hands clenched until the knuckles showed white.

"I just stood there," Smith continued. "The curtain flopped about—and I got a good look at the man."

"Ah, yes," Charlie nodded. "What man?"

"Why, that fellow there," Smith said. He pointed at Fyfe. "The chap with the red ribbon across his shirt-front. I haven't seen one of those ribbons since the time when I was studying at Julien's, in Paris, and our ambassador invited me round for dinner. It's a fact. He came from my town—an old friend of my father—"

"No matter," Charlie cut in. "You stood there, peeping beneath the curtain—"

"What do you mean?" cried the beach-comber. "Don't judge a man by his clothes, please. I wasn't spying. If I caught a glimpse, as I did, it was unavoidable. They were talking fast, those two—this man, and the woman."

"Yes. And perhaps—equally unavoidable, do not misunderstand me—you heard what they said?"

Smith hesitated. "Well—as a matter of fact—I did. I heard her tell him—"

With a little cry, Robert Fyfe leaped forward. He pushed the beach-comber aside and stood before Charlie. His face was deathly pale, but his eyes did not falter.

"Drop it," he said hoarsely. "I can put an end to your investigation here and now. I killed Shelah Fane, and I'm willing to pay for it."

A shocked silence greeted his words. Calm, unmoved, quite motionless, Chan stared into the man's face.

"You killed Miss Fane?"

"I did."

"For what reason?"

"I wanted her to come back to me. I couldn't live without her. I pleaded and begged—and she wouldn't listen. She laughed at me—she said there wasn't a chance. She drove me to it—I killed her. I had to do it."

"You killed her—with what?"

"With a knife I carried as one of the props in the play."

"Where is it now?"

"I threw it into a swamp on my way to town."

"You can lead me to the spot?"

"I can try."

Chan turned away.

Alan Jaynes was on his feet. "Eleven-ten," he cried. "I can just make the boat if I hurry, Inspector. Of course, you're not going to hold me now."

"But I do hold you," Charlie answered. "Spencer, if this man makes another move, kindly place him beneath arrest."

"Are you mad?" Jaynes cried. "You have your confession, haven't you—"

"With regard to that," said Charlie, "wait just a moment, please." He turned back to Fyfe, who was standing quietly beside him. "You left the pavilion, Mr Fyfe, at four minutes past eight?"

"I did."

"You had already killed Shelah Fane?"

"I had."

"You drove to the theater and were in the wings of same at twenty minutes past eight?"

"Yes—I told you all that."

"The stage manager will swear that you were there at twenty minutes past eight?"

"Of course—of course."

Chan stared at him. "Yet at twelve minutes past eight," he said, "Shelah Fane was seen alive and well."

"What's that!" Tarneverro cried.

"Pardon—I am speaking with this other gentleman. At twelve minutes past eight, Mr Fyfe, Shelah Fane was seen alive and well. How do you account for that?"

Fyfe dropped into a chair and covered his face with his hands.

"I do not understand you," Charlie said gently. "You wish me to believe you killed Shelah Fane. Yet, of all the people in this room, you alone have unshakable alibi."

IX

EIGHTEEN IMPORTANT MINUTES

No one spoke. Outside what Jimmy Bradshaw had called the silken surf broke once again on the coral sand. The crash died away, and inside that crowded room there was no sound save the ticking of a small clock on a mantel beneath which fires were rarely lighted. With a gesture of despair, Alan Jaynes stepped to a table and, striking a match, applied it to one of his small cigars. Charlie crossed over and laid his hand on Fyfe's shoulder.

"Why have you confessed to a deed you did not perform?" he. asked. "That is something I warmly desire to know."

The actor made no answer, nor did he so much as look up. Charlie turned to face Tarneverro.

"So Shelah Fane was seen alive at twelve minutes past eight?" the fortune-teller remarked suavely, "Would you mind telling me how long you have known that?"

Charlie smiled. "If only it happened you understood Chinese language," he replied. "I would not find it necessary to elucidate." He went to the door, and called Jessop. When the butler appeared, Chan asked that he send in Wu Kno-ching at once. "I am doing something now for your benefit alone, Mr Tarneverro," he added.

"You are a considerate man, Inspector," the fortune-teller answered.

The old Chinese shuffled into the room; he was, evidently, in a rather peevish frame of mind. His carefully prepared dinner had been ruined by the events of this tragic evening, and he was in no mood to accept the philosophy of the patient K'ung-fu-tsze.

Chan talked with him for a moment, again in Cantonese, and then turned to Tarneverro. "I request that he verify story he told me in native language when I interrogated him in this room some while ago," he explained. "Wu, you have said you lingered in kitchen with Jessop and Anna when clock was speaking the hour of eight. You fretted because dinner was seemingly movable feast, and also because bootlegger of your choice had not shown up and was causing you to lose much face. Am I correct so far?"

"Bootleggah velly late," nodded Wu.

"But at ten minutes past hour, erring friend of yours makes panting appearance with hotly desired liquids. While Jessop begins task of making this poison palatable, you wander away in search of mistress." Chan glanced at the fortune-teller. "Wu informal type servant who pops up anywhere on place with great bland look. Characteristic of the race." He resumed his remarks to the Chinese. "You discover Miss Shelah Fane alone in pavilion. Vindicating your honor, you announce bootlegger friend has finally appeared. What did Missie say?"

"Missie look-see watch, say twelve minutes aftah eight plitty muchee time bootleggah come. I say plitty muchee time dinnah gets on table. Mebbe that can happen now if not new cook needed heah *wikiwiki*."

"Yes. Then she ordered you to get out and not annoy her with your bothers. So you went back to kitchen. That's what you told me before, isn't it?"

"Yes, boss."

"All same true, eh, Wu?"

"Yes, boss. Wha' foah my tell lie to you?"

"All right. You can go now."

"My go, boss."

As the old man moved silently away on his velvet slippers, Charlie turned to meet the penetrating gaze of Tarneverro. "All of which is very interesting," the fortune-teller said coldly. "I perceive that when I pointed out to you the matter of the watch, I was merely wasting my breath. You already knew that Shelah Fane had not been murdered at two minutes past eight."

Charlie laid a conciliatory hand on Tarneverro's arm. "Pray do not take offense. I knew Miss Fane had been seen at that later hour, yes; but I was still uncertain of how watch had been manipulated. I listened, curious and then entranced, to your logical explanation. Could I, at its finish, rudely cry thanks for nothing? A gentleman is always courteous. Much better I shower you with well-deserved words of praise, so you go forward with vigorous and triumphant mood of heart."

"Is that so?" remarked Tarneverro, moving off.

Charlie stepped up to the beach-comber. "Mr Smith," he said.

"Right here, Officer," Smith answered. "I was afraid you were going to forget me. What can I do for you now?"

"A moment ago you began interesting recital of conversation overheard between this gentleman with ribbon-bedecked shirt-front and lady he met in pavilion tonight. At crucial point you suffered very blunt interruption. I am most eager that you return to subject at once."

Fyfe rose to his feet, and stared hard at the derelict in the velvet coat. Smith looked back at him, and a speculative, cunning look flashed into his pale gray eyes.

"Oh, yes," he said slowly. "I was interrupted, wasn't I? But I'm used to that. Sure—sure, I was telling you that I heard them talking together. Well, there's no need to go on with it now. I've nothing to add to what the gentleman has already told you." Fyfe turned away. "He was pleading with her to come back to him—said he loved her, and all that. And she wouldn't listen to him. I felt rather sorry for him—I've been in that position myself. I heard her say: 'Oh, Bob—what's the use?' He went on insisting. Every now and then he looked at his watch. 'My time's up,' he said at last. 'I've got to go. We'll thrash this out later.' I heard the slam of the door—"

"And the woman was alone in the room—alive and well. You are sure of that?"

"Yes—the curtain was flapping—I saw her after he left. She was there alone—moving about."

With a puzzled frown, Charlie glanced at Robert Fyfe. "You are not content with one alibi. You have now a second. I do not understand you, Mr Fyfe."

The actor shrugged. "I find it hard to understand myself, Inspector. A fit of temperament, perhaps. We stage people are inclined to be overly dramatic."

"Then you withdraw your confession?"

"What else can I do?" Chan did not overlook the glance that passed between the immaculate actor and the battered beach-comber. "Others have withdrawn it for me. I did not kill Shelah—that's quite true. But I thought it would be better if—"

"If what?"

"Nothing."

"You thought it would be better if my investigation went no further."

"Oh, not at all."

"Something came out in that conversation with your ex-wife which you feared this man had overheard. Something you want suppressed."

"You have a keen imagination, Inspector."

"Also, I have a custom to discover facts which some people want to hide. Your move has been to this moment successful—but you and I have not finished with each other, Mr Fyfe."

"I am at your service at any time, sir."

"Thank you so much, but I hope the next time we meet your service will be of more value to my humble self." He looked at Smith. "As for you, though I am desolated by acute pain to make so rude a remark, I believe you mix plenty falsehood with your truth."

The beach-comber shrugged. "There you go—judging a man by his clothes again."

"Not by your clothes, which are silent, but by your tongue, which speaks," Charlie told him. "Mr Spencer, will you kindly take this man to station house and make record of his fingerprints."

"So many attentions," Smith put in. "I only hope they don't turn my head."

"After which," Chan continued, "you may release him—for time being."

"All right, Charlie," Spencer said.

"One other thing. Pause a moment while I introduce to you all people in this room." Gravely he went through that somewhat lengthy ceremony. "You have also seen butler and cook. There is in addition a maid, whom I ask that you pause and make note of on your way out. You will speed from station without delay to Pier Seven, from which the boat *Oceanic* sails for coast at midnight. No person you have seen in this house is to sail on that boat. You understand?"

"Sure, Charlie—I'll attend to it," Spencer nodded.

Jaynes stepped forward. "I'd like to remind you that my luggage is aboard that ship—some of it in the hold—"

Charlie nodded. "How fortunate you spoke of that. Mr Spencer, kindly see that all effects in state-room belonging to Mr Jaynes are put ashore in your care. Arrange for such as lie in hold to be guarded for the gentleman at San Francisco dock. Explain he is detained by important business and may be in Honolulu for some time. Is that satisfactory, Mr Jaynes?"

"It's damned unsatisfactory," the Britisher growled, "but I presume I shall have to make the best of it."

"All you can do," nodded Charlie. "Kashimo, you will accompany Mr Spencer downtown. Your passionate labors in this house are ended for the night. You retire in glory—and if you come back through unexpected window, you retire for ever. Keep same in mind."

The apprentice detective nodded, and went out after Spencer and the beach-comber. Robert Fyfe stepped forward.

"Is there any necessity for my staying any longer?" he inquired.

Charlie studied him thoughtfully. "I think not. You may go along. You and I will talk together when I have more leisure."

"Any time, Inspector." Fyfe went to the curtains, and held them open. "I am stopping at the Waioli Hotel, on Fort Street," he added. "Drop in at your convenience, won't you? Good night." He went into the hall, where Spencer could be heard talking with the maid. The door slammed behind him, and a second later, the two policemen and Smith also departed.

Charlie stood regarding the tired group in the living-room. "Accept my advice and take heart," he said. "We give Mr Spencer generous handicap on journey to pier, and then I find great joy releasing this company at last. While we are waiting, there are one or two matters. Since first I spoke with you, it has been found necessary to alter views. Then hour of tragedy was thought certain at two minutes past eight. Now we must advance and say, dreadful event happened some time between twelve minutes past eight and the half-hour. Eighteen minutes there—eighteen important minutes. Each of us must ask himself: What was I doing in those eighteen minutes?"

He paused. His eyes were bright, his manner quite keen and alive—for him. The Chinese are at their best at night; it is their favorite time. But he was alone in his vigor, the others were exhausted and drooping, the make-up of the women stood out, unnatural and far from pleasing, against the pallor of their weariness.

"Eighteen important minutes," Chan repeated. "Miss Dixon, Miss Julie and Mr Bradshaw disported gaily in breakers, visiting beach occasionally. On that beach Mrs Ballou sat and idly passed time until dinner. For final ten of those minutes, Mr Ballou wandered about, no one can say where—"

"I can say where," Ballou cut in. "I came into this room—the butler will verify that. I strolled in here and smoked a cigarette he gave me."

"He remained with you while you smoked it?"

"No—he didn't. He lighted it for me, and went out. When he returned, I was sitting in the same chair—"

"You wish me to note that, eh?" Charlie smiled.

"I don't care whether you note it or not."

Charlie took out a handkerchief and wiped the perspiration from his brow. The tropic night was beginning to live up to its reputation.

"I turn now to the four gentlemen whose alibis have been so rudely shattered. I know where they were at two minutes past eight, but after that—"

"Take me first," said Tarneverro. "You saw me go to join those two people in the lounge of the hotel—they are old friends of mine from Australia. We remained there for a few minutes after you left, and then I suggested that we go out on the lanai that faces the palm court. We did so, and for a time sat and chatted. When I finally looked at my watch, it was precisely eight-thirty. I remarked on the hour and said I was sorry, but I had to go along. We all went inside, I ran up to get my hat, and when I came back to the lobby, I happened on you near the door."

Charlie studied his face. "Your old friends will be willing to swear to all this?"

"I can see no reason why they shouldn't. They know it's true."

Chan smiled. "I congratulate you, Mr Tarneverro."

"I congratulate myself, Inspector. You may recall that I told you I had another tree."

"Mr Jaynes," said Chan, turning to the Britisher.

Jaynes shrugged hopelessly. "I have no alibi," he said. "During those eighteen minutes, I was wandering along the beach, alone. Make what you wish of it. I didn't come down here."

"Mr Van Horn—you did come down here?" Charlie addressed the picture actor.

"I did, worse luck," shrugged Van Horn. "The first time in a long and honorable career that I ever got to a party ahead of the hour set. It will be a lesson to me—I can tell you that."

"It was, I believe, eight-fifteen when Jessop admitted you?"

"About that time—yes. He told me that the party—or what there was of it—had moved to the beach. I went out on the lawn. I saw a light in a building which Jessop told me was a summer-house, and I thought of going there. I wish to heaven I had. But I heard voices down by the water, so I went there instead. I sat down by Rita Ballou—but you know all that."

Chan nodded. "Only one remains. Mr Martino?"

The director frowned. "Like Huntley and Mr Jaynes," he said, "I have no alibi worth mentioning. You wrecked me along with them when you smashed that eight-two theory." He took a handkerchief from a side pocket and mopped his forehead. "After Jaynes left me and started down the beach, I sat in one of the hotel swings near the water. I should have been busy getting myself a good alibi, I suppose, but I'm not so clever as Mr Tarneverro here." He gave the fortune-teller an unfriendly look. "So I just sat alone—the scene looked rather good to me. I wished I could get it into a picture—the purple starry sky, the yellow lamps along the waterfront, the black hulk of Diamond Head. A picture in color—we'll have 'em that way before long. I amused myself thinking up a possible story—you can't depend on authors for anything. Presently I looked at my watch. It was eight-twenty-five, so I went to my room to brush up and get my hat. When I came down I met you and Tarneverro here, and heard the news of Miss Fane's murder."

Charlie stood looking thoughtfully at the director. Suddenly he was pushed aside as Tarneverro strode forward.

"That's a nasty scratch on your forehead, Martino," the fortune-teller cried.

Startled, the director put his hand to his brow, and on one finger, as he took it away, he noted a trace of red.

"By jove," he said, "that's odd—"

"You'd better turn over to Inspector Chan the handkerchief you just replaced in your pocket."

"What handkerchief?" Martino produced the one which he had recently passed across his forehead. "Oh, this!"

"I will take it, please," said Charlie. He spread the white square of silk on a table and brought out his magnifying-glass. For a moment he studied the center of the square, then ran his fingers lightly across it. He looked up.

"A queer thing, Mr Martino," he remarked. "There exist, caught in mesh of this cloth, a few thin splinters of glass. How would you explain that?"

Martino rose quickly, and with a serious face bent over the table. "I can't explain it," he said. "I can't even explain how that handkerchief came to be in my pocket."

Chan regarded him intently. "It is not your property?" he inquired.

"It certainly isn't," the director replied. "I carry two handkerchiefs with my evening clothes. One here"—he indicated his breast pocket above which the ends of a handkerchief were showing—"and another in my hip pocket." He produced a second. "Certainly I'd have no use for a third. I just happened to reach into my side pocket, my hand touched this, and I used it. But I never put it there, and it isn't mine."

"A likely story," Tarneverro sneered.

"My dear Tarneverro," the director said, "when you've made as many pictures as I have, you'll realize that the truth often sounds less probable than fiction." He picked up the little square of silk and handed it to Charlie. "By the way, there's a laundry mark in one corner of that."

"I know," Chan nodded. He stood for a moment, looking at the tiny letter *B* done with black ink on the silk border. He glanced over at Wilkie Ballou. The planter stared back at him, and taking a handkerchief from his own pocket, casually mopped his brow.

X

SHELAH FROM DENNY

Shrugging his broad shoulders, Charlie turned back to Martino. The director's face was even more crimson than usual, and he was breathing hard.

"Do you wish to make statement," Chan asked, "as to moment when you think this object was placed on your person?"

Martino considered. "When we were leaving the dining-room a while back," he said, "we were all crowded together round the door. I thought then that I felt a little tug at my pocket."

"Just who was near you at that instant?"

"It's hard to say. Everybody was there together. The matter is serious, and I don't like to guess." He paused, and glanced at the fortune-teller. "I do recall that Mr Tarneverro wasn't far away."

"Is that an accusation?" asked Tarneverro coldly.

"Not precisely. I can't be sure—"

"You'd like nothing better than to be sure," the fortune-teller suggested.

Martino laughed. "You've hit it there, my friend. I haven't much love for you, and you know it. If I'd had my way, you'd have been run out of Hollywood long ago."

"Failing that, you've gone about secretly warning the women against me."

"What do you mean, secretly? I've done it openly, and you know it. I've told them to keep away from you—"

"Why?"

"I don't like the look in your eyes, my friend. What was it you told poor Shelah this morning? What did she tell you?"

"That is something I'd not be likely to discuss with you. So you sat on the beach by the water, did you?"

"Oh, don't get too cocky over that alibi of yours," Martino cried. "How did you happen to have it so pat and ready? Reading the future again, eh?"

"Gentlemen, gentlemen," Charlie protested. "We are arriving precisely nowhere by this. I perceive that nerves are very much up on edge, and I am glad to push open doors and put quick end to investigation. You are all free to depart."

There was an instant dash for the hall. Chan followed.

"Just one word to add," he said, "though I am certain that by now the buzz of my voice in your ears must be most tiresome sound. But please remember—you rest on small island in the midst of broad Pacific Ocean. Attempt by anyone of you to go aboard ship will be instantly known to us, and regarded with dark suspicious eye. Stay on, I beg of you, and enjoy beauties of spot, on which subject Mr Bradshaw will be happy to make oration for you any time, any place."

"That's right," the boy nodded. "Loaf on a palm-fringed shore and forget your troubles. Somewhere winter is raging—"

"In July?" Van Horn inquired.

"Sure—at the South Pole, for example. Put Hollywood out of your thoughts. Remember—Hawaii has the climate California thinks it has."

The door closed behind Ballou and his wife. Van Horn, Martino and Jaynes followed promptly. Bradshaw returned to the living-room, where Julie and Diana had remained, leaving the fortune-teller and Charlie in the hall. Tarneverro picked up his hat.

"Inspector," he remarked, "you have my sympathy. You are up against a puzzling case."

"Also I have your help," Chan reminded him. "The thought consoles me."

Tarneverro shook his head. "I'm afraid you overestimate my powers. But whatever they are, they are ranged on your side. When am I to see you again?"

"I will call on you tomorrow morning," Chan answered. "We will have good long talk. Perhaps, thinking deeply into matter over night, each of us will have new ideas to offer."

"I shall try to supply my share," nodded Tarneverro, and went out. For a moment Charlie stood looking at the door through which he had gone, then turning, he went into the living-room.

"Miss Dixon," he said, "may I make further request of you? Will you ascend stairs with me and point out various rooms, naming the persons to whom they have been assigned? I still have a little searching to do before repose."

"Of course," nodded the actress, "and speaking of repose, I hope you'll search my room first. I feel all in after this dreadful evening."

She and Charlie disappeared. With a forlorn gesture, Julie sank into a chair.

"Poor kid!" said Mr Bradshaw.

"Oh, Jimmy—it *has* been a dreadful evening, hasn't it?"

"It surely has. Think, Julie, think. You were closer to Shelah Fane than anyone else. Have you no idea who did—this terrible thing?"

She shook her head. "I can't imagine. Of course, Shelah had enemies—all successful people have—she was envied, perhaps even hated. But I never dreamed anyone hated her as much as this. It's just unbelievable, that's all."

The boy sat down beside her. "Let's forget it for a while. How about you? What are you going to do now?"

"Oh—I suppose I'll go back where I came from."

"Where did you come from? You haven't told me.

"From a theatrical boarding-house in Chicago—I was traveling with my mother when she—she left me. Stage people, you see, all my folks—father too. Mother called San Francisco home, though she seldom saw it. But she was born there—so many good actors were, you know. And she—"

"She was one of the best, I guess," said Jimmy Bradshaw.

"I thought so. I've got a grandmother there now—seventy-two, but she goes trouping occasionally—she's such a darling, Jimmy. I think I'll go to her, and get some sort of job—I could make good in an office, I believe. Grandmother would be glad to have me; we're all that's left of—us."

Bradshaw pulled himself together. "If no one else wants to speak, may I say a few words about Hawaii? Everywhere we have poetry and glamour. The climate breeds happiness and laughter, a natural reflection of the sunlight, the rainbows and the purple hills. Here there are no sunstrokes and no snow. Honolulu has its message of beauty for every heart. As for—"

"Jimmy, what in the world—"

"As for the people, where nature is kind man cannot help but be. You will find—"

"I don't get you, Jimmy."

"It's simple enough. I've sold this place to fifty thousand tourists, and now I want to sell it to you. As a substitute for grandmother, you see. No doubt she's a darling, as you say. Maybe I'm not, but I'm young yet. For of course it isn't just Honolulu I'm selling. I'm thrown in, you know. How about it, Julie? A little bungalow nestling under two mortgages and a bougainvillea vine—"

"You—you mean you love me, Jimmy?" the girl asked.

"Oh, lord—did I omit that line? I shall have to rewrite the whole darn piece. Naturally, I love you. Who wouldn't? It may not be the most fitting time for me to say all this, but I don't want you to think that I've fallen into the habit of putting things off, just because I live in the lazy latitudes. I'm crazy about you, and before you write grandmother to come down and meet your boat—she might be away trouping anyhow—I want you to give a thought to Hawaii—and to me. Will you do it, Julie?"

She nodded. "I will, Jimmy."

"That's good enough for me," he smiled.

Chan came silently into the room, and the boy stood up. "Well, Charlie, you ready to go along? I let my brother have my car tonight, so I'm honoring you with my presence in that famous flivver of yours."

"You will be remarkably welcome," Chan told him. "Yes—I travel townward almost at once. There remains one little matter—"

Anna, the maid, came hurriedly into the room. "Miss Dixon said you wanted to see me," she remarked to Chan.

He nodded. "A trifling affair. You told me earlier this evening that a certain ring was missing from Miss Fane's finger after the homicide. An emerald ring."

"I did, sir."

Julie O'Neill was leaning forward, breathless, her eyes wide.

"Is this the ring?" Chan suddenly produced a platinum band decorated with a surprising stone that flashed green in the brightly lighted room.

"That is it, sir," Anna nodded.

Chan turned to Julie. "So sorry to drag you in. But will you kindly tell me—how does it happen I find this bauble in the drawer of your dressing-table?" The girl gasped, and Jimmy Bradshaw looked at her in amazement. "I am very sorry this question comes out, which disappoints me sadly," Charlie continued. "But I should say, things need explanation."

"It's very simple," answered Julie in a low voice.

"Naturally," bowed Chan. "Just how simple, according to your story?"

"Well." She hesitated. "There are only a few of us here—I can speak frankly. Shelah was always hard up. Somehow money meant nothing to her, it slipped through her fingers, it was gone a moment after she got it. She came back from the South Seas in her usual state—more or less broke. Everyone was always cheating her, stealing from her—"

"Everyone?" Chan repeated. "You mean her servants, perhaps?"

"Some of them, yes—when they had a chance. But that doesn't matter. Shelah arrived here in need of money, as always. She'd drawn all the advance she could get from the company—they haven't been as generous of late as they used to be. Today, just after she reached the house, she sent for me and said she must have ready money at once. She gave me this ring and told me to sell it for her, if I could. I was to make a round of the jewelers immediately—this afternoon. But I put it off. I wasn't keen for the job. However, I fully intended to go in the morning—if this thing hadn't happened tonight. That's how I chanced to have the ring."

Chan considered. "She gave it to you just after she reached house. At what time, precisely?"

"At eight o'clock this morning."

"You have had it ever since?"

"Yes, of course. I put it in that drawer—I thought it would be safe there."

"That is all you wish to tell me?"

"That is all." The girl seemed on the point of tears.

Charlie turned to the maid. "You may go, Anna," he said.

"Very good, sir." Anna glanced at the girl, and then went out.

Charlie sighed heavily. Even though he came of a nocturnal race, the night was beginning to wear on him. He took the ring beneath a light and examined it with his magnifying-glass. There was, he noted, an inscription inside. "Shelah from Denny." So Denny Mayo came back into the case? Chan shrugged.

When he turned about, he perceived that Julie was weeping silently. Bradshaw had put his arm about her shoulder. "That's all right, honey," the boy said. "Charlie believes you. Don't you, Charlie?"

Chan bowed from the waist. "In the presence of so much charm, could I have brutal doubts? Miss Julie, I am sorrowed to perceive your overwrought state. Mr Bradshaw and I depart at once, leaving to you the solace of slumber. You have youth, and sleep will come. I bid you most sympathetic good night."

He disappeared through the curtains, and with a few whispered words to the girl, Bradshaw followed. Jessop, restraining a yawn but firmly polite as always, saw them out. On the steps Charlie stood for a moment, staring at the sky and drawing in a deep breath of the open air.

"It is something to recall," he said, "that during long painful ordeal in that house, stars were still shining and soft tropic night progressed as usual. What have I not been through? A brief respite will be lovely as soft music in the rain."

They got into his car, waiting alone and lonely in the drive.

"Pretty much up against it, eh, Charlie?" the boy suggested.

Chan nodded. "Dizzy feeling causes my head to circulate. I have upearthed so much, and yet I have upearthed nothing." They bowled along, past the Moana Hotel, in unaccustomed darkness now. The pink walls of the Grand glowed with a new splendor in the moonlight. "When you telephoned me," Chan added, "I was about to begin serious operation on a small fish. One taste I had was excellent. Alas! little fish and I will never meet again."

"A shame to spoil your dinner," Bradshaw replied.

"I will be content if your news does not also spoil my reputation," Charlie told him. "How am I going to emerge from the affair? In shining garments of success, or in sackcloth with ashes?"

"I called up the morning paper," the boy told him. "Used to work there, you know. They were short of men at the moment, and I landed the job of covering the story so far. Got to go back now and write it. I'll say that the police haven't a notion just at present—is that correct?"

Charlie barely avoided a collision with the curb. "Have you no better understanding of your task than that? Say nothing of the sort. Police have many clues and expect early arrest."

"But that's the same old bunk, Charlie. And judging from your talk, it isn't true in this case."

"Seldom true in any case," Chan reminded him. "You should know that."

"Well, I'll say it—to please you, Charlie. By the way, did I hear Tarneverro intimate he was working with you?"

"Yes—he fancies himself as bright assistant."

"He may be bright all right—but are you keen for his help?"

Charlie shrugged. "The bird chooses the tree, not the tree the bird," he remarked.

"Well, Tarneverro's a queer bird, all right. He gives me a funny sensation when I look at him." They rode on in silence for a time. "Anyhow, one thing's certain," the boy said at last.

"Is that really so?" Chan inquired. "Name it, please. I seem to have overlooked it in my haste."

"I mean—Julie had nothing to do with this affair."

Charlie grinned in the dark. "I have recollections myself," he said.

"Of what?"

"Being young—and muddled by love. Since I am now the father of eleven children, it is necessarily some time since I went about with head in clouds and warmly beating heart. But memories remain."

"Oh, nonsense," protested Bradshaw. "I'm looking at this thing coldly—as a rank outsider."

"Then I humbly suggest you have old Hawaii moon overhauled at once," commented Chan. "For it must be losing magic power you write about so glowingly."

He drew up before the newspaper office, the sound of his brakes grating noisily in the deserted street. On the lower floor of the building one lonely light burned dimly, but the upstairs windows were bright yellow with activity. There men sat sorting the cable news that was flowing in from the far corners of the world, from Europe, Asia, the mainland—brief bits of information thought worthy of transmission to this small island dreaming in the midst of the great Pacific.

Jimmy Bradshaw moved as though to alight, then paused. Out of the corner of his eye he glanced at Charlie. "I don't suppose I can have it now, can I?" he inquired.

"You cannot," Chan replied firmly.

"What are you talking about?" asked the boy innocently.

"Same thing you are," Charlie grinned.

"I was referring to that handkerchief you took away from the picture director."

"So was I," answered Charlie blandly.

"Then you knew it was mine?"

"I gathered that, yes. Small initial *B* was on it. Also I perceived you perspiring with no means to quench it. I was greatly moved to admiration by your restraint—not once did you make use of coat sleeve. You are going to tell me that it was taken from your pocket?"

"It must have been—yes."

"At what moment?"

"I don't know, but I suppose someone took it when I was in swimming."

"You are sure of that?"

"Well, it seems the only possible explanation. But I didn't notice it was gone until a long time afterward."

"And a still longer time after that—you mention the affair to me."

"It's my confounded modesty again, Charlie," the boy laughed. "I just couldn't stand the limelight. Let me look at the thing, anyhow."

Charlie handed it over, and Bradshaw examined it carefully in the dashboard light. "Mine all right." He pointed at the mark. "That's my alias at the laundry. This is pretty sinister, if you ask me."

Charlie took back the handkerchief. "I have very good notion to put you in jail," he remarked.

"And trifle with the power of the press?" the boy reminded him. "Think twice, Charlie. I didn't do away with our distinguished visitor. That's not the sort of Hawaiian hospitality I go in for." He hesitated. "I could use that handkerchief tonight."

"So could I," Chan answered.

"Oh, well, then I'll just have to drip perspiration on this immortal story I'm about to write. So long, Inspector."

"So long," Chan returned. "And please keep handkerchief out of that same story, and out of your conversation, or you will hear from me."

"O.K., Charlie. It stays a big secret. Nobody in on it but you and me—and the laundry."

XI

MIDNIGHT IN HONOLULU

Chan drove slowly on to Halekaua Hale, at the foot of Bethel Street, the home of the police. Parking his car, he ascended the worn stone steps. A light was burning in the detectives' room, and going in, he encountered his Chief.

"Hello, Charlie," that gentleman said. "I've been waiting for you. Drove over to Kalaua tonight, or I'd have been with you down the beach. This is a pretty mix-up, isn't it? Got anything yet?"

Sadly Chan shook his head. He glanced at his watch. "The story has length," he suggested.

"Guess I'd better hear it, anyhow," replied the Chief. In him, there was no lack of vigor. The ride in the moonlight to Kalaua had been restful and refreshing.

Charlie sat down and began to talk, while his Chief listened intently. He took up first the scene of the murder, the absence of any weapon, the unsuccessful attempt of the murderer to fix the moment of the crime at two minutes past eight. Coming to the question of clues, he mentioned the loss of the diamond pin which had held the orchids.

"That's something," nodded the Chief, lighting a cigar.

Chan shrugged. "Something we do not possess," he pointed out. He went on to repeat Shelah Fane's story of her presence at the murder of Denny Mayo—the tale she had told Tarneverro, according to the fortune-teller, that morning.

"Fine—fine," cried the Chief. "That gives you the motive, Charlie. Now if she had only written down the name, as this Tarneverro wanted her to—"

With acute distaste, Charlie added the incident of the letter's loss. His Chief looked at him with surprise and a marked disapproval.

"Never knew anything like that to happen to you before. Losing your grip, Charlie?"

"For a moment, I certainly lost grip and letter too," Chan replied ruefully. "As the matter turned out, it did not have much importance." His face brightened as he added the later discovery of the letter under the rug, proving that it was of no value save as a corroboration of Tarneverro's story. He went on to the destruction of the portrait over which Shelah Fane had been seen weeping bitterly in the afternoon.

"Someone didn't want you to see it," frowned the Chief.

"I arrived at the same deduction myself," Charlie admitted. He pictured the arrival of Robert Fyfe on what was obviously his second visit to Waikiki within a few hours, and then turned to the subject of the beach-comber.

"We took his fingerprints and let him go," put in the Chief. "He hasn't nerve enough to kill a fly."

Chan nodded. "You are no doubt correct in such surmise." His report of Fyfe's subsequent, easily punctured confession, evidently puzzled his superior. He mentioned the handkerchief with the telltale slivers of glass found in Martino's pocket, and Jimmy Bradshaw's somewhat belated claim to its ownership. He was by this time rather out of breath. "So matter stands at present," he finished.

His Chief was looking at him with an amused smile. "Well, Charlie, sometimes I've thought you weren't entirely satisfied here since your return from the mainland," he said. "Pretty quiet, you thought it. No big cases like over there. Just chasing a few scared gamblers down an alley—not very thrilling, was it? Honolulu didn't seem to be big enough for you any more. I guess it's big enough tonight."

"I experience uncomfortable feeling maybe it is too big," Chan admitted. "How will I come out of this? Considerable puzzle, if inquiry is made of me."

"We mustn't let it stump us," replied the Chief briskly. He was an intelligent man, and he knew where to lean. He foresaw that he was going to do some heavy leaning in the next few days. With an appraising glance, he surveyed his assistant. Charlie looked sleepy and somewhat worn—nothing alert, nothing clever in his appearance now. The Chief consoled himself with memories. Chan, he reflected, was ever keener than he looked.

He considered. "This Tarneverro, Charlie,—what sort of fellow is he?"

Chan brightened. "Ah, perhaps you go to heart of the matter. Tarneverro appears dark as rainy night, but it is his business to act so. He owns a quick mind. And he seems fiercely eager to assist poor policeman like me."

"A bit too eager, maybe?"

Charlie nodded. "I have thought of that. But consider—he offers to produce testimony of old couple with whom he sat until moment murder was discovered. Truth of that will be examined tomorrow, but I do not doubt it. No—I am plenty certain he did not visit house of Shelah Fane until I took him there. Other points absolve him."

"What, for example?"

"I have told you he spoke to me before murder was done, hinting we would tonight make arrest in famous case. That would have been strangely foolish move if he contemplated murder himself. And Tarneverro is not foolish—he goes far the other way. Then, too, indicating he has earnest desire to assist he points out the matter of the watch. It was bright act—not very necessary since I already knew facts from Wu Kno-ching—but all same plenty good proof he sincerely aims to help. No, I do not believe him guilty killer, and yet—"

"Yet what, Charlie?".

"I prefer to hold that safe in mind for the present. It may mean much, and it may mean nothing."

"You've got something on Tarneverro?" asked the Chief, looking at him keenly.

"With regard to killing—not one solitary thing. At moment when that took place, I believe he was most decidedly elsewhere. Gazing in another direction—kindly permit that I gaze that way a few hours longer before I divulge my thoughts." The plump detective put one hand to his head. "*Haie*, just now I wander, lost in maze of doubts and questionings."

"You'll have to cut that out, Charlie," his Chief told him in a kindly but somewhat worried tone. "The honor of the force is at stake. If these people are going to come over here to our quiet little city and murder each other at Waikiki, we've got to prove to them that they can't get away with it. I rely on you."

Chan bowed. "I'm afraid you do. Appreciate the distinction, and will do all my humble talents permit. Now I will wish you good night. The evening has worn on me like some prolonged dispute."

He went out into the battered old hall, just as Spencer entered from the street. Chan looked at his watch.

"The *Oceanic* has sailed?" he inquired.

"Yeah—she's out."

"With none of our friends aboard, I trust?" Chan said.

"None that I saw goin' aboard—and I guess I was there first. One of 'em showed up, though."

"Which one?"

"That Alan Jaynes. He came in a car from the Grand Hotel, an' collected his baggage. I heard him swearin' under his breath when the ship backed away from the pier. I helped him load up, an' he went back to the beach. He give me a message for you."

"What was that?"

"He said he was sailing on the next ship, and all hell couldn't stop him."

Charlie smiled. "None the less, I shall see that the province he mentions breaks loose at the dock if he tries it."

He went down the flight of steps to the street. Through the moonlight he saw approaching him the jaunty figure of Smith, the beach-comber.

"This is a pretty idea, Officer," that gentleman said. "You give me a nice ride down to the station, and then you kick me out. How am I going to get back to my bedroom? I've walked it once tonight."

Charlie reached into his pocket and held out one hand in which lay a small coin. "You may make the distance by trolley," he suggested.

Smith looked down at the coin. "A dime," he remarked. "Ten cents. I can't get on a street-car and offer the conductor a dime. A gentleman has to have the prestige of a dollar."

Tired as he was, Chan laughed. "So sorry," he answered. "There may be much in what you say. But I believe it wiser at this time to proffer you the ride and no more. The hour is late, and you should be able to maintain your dignity on very little prestige tonight."

Stubbornly Smith shook his head. "I've got to have the prestige of a dollar," he insisted.

"You mean you've got to have a drink," shrugged Chan. "If the coin is unsatisfactory, I regretfully withdraw it." He moved toward his car. "So sorry that I travel in opposite direction from your couch beneath the palm."

Smith followed him. "Oh, well," he said, "perhaps I'm a bit too sensitive. I'll take the dime." Charlie gave it to him. "Just a loan, Inspector. I'll make a note of it."

He hurried away down Bethel Street in the direction of King. With one foot on the running-board of his little car, Charlie stared after him. Finally he abandoned the flivver and followed. The empty streets were as bright as day, the risk was great, but Chan was an old hand at the game. Smith's battered shoes flopped noisily on the deserted sidewalk, but the detective moved as though on velvet slippers.

The beach-comber turned to the right on King Street and, dodging in and out of doorways, Chan followed. As his quarry neared the corner of Fort, Charlie waited anxiously in a shadowed nook. Would Smith pause at that corner for a Waikiki car? If he did, this pursuit came to nothing.

But Smith did not stop. Instead he crossed over and hastened down Fort Street. The moon shone brightly on his enormous flapping hat, on the shoulders of his absurd velvet coat. Charlie's interest revived at once. On what errand did the beach-comber set forth at this hour of the night?

Selecting the opposite side of the thoroughfare from that which Smith traveled—it was darker and better suited to his purpose—Chan trailed his man down Fort. Past the principal shops of Honolulu, in each of which a dim light burned, they moved along. Smith came to the entrance of the Waioli Hotel, and stopped there. Hiding in a dark doorway across the street, Chan saw him peer into the hotel lobby. The place was deserted save for a watchman who dozed in a chair behind the great glass window. For a moment the beach-comber hesitated and then, as though changing his mind, turned and retraced his steps. Charlie squeezed his great bulk against the door behind him, in a panic lest he be discovered.

But he was safe. All unsuspecting, Smith hurried back to the corner of King, there to await the Waikiki car. Charlie remained in hiding until the car arrived. He saw the beach-comber mount to a seat and ride away—without the prestige of a dollar.

Slowly Chan walked back to the station house. What did this mean? Evidently when Robert Fyfe announced his address to the detective, he was also proclaiming it to the battered Mr Smith. And Smith desired to see the actor at once, on urgent business.

Charlie was getting into his flivver when the Chief came down the steps of Halekaua Hale.

"Thought you'd gone home, Charlie," he said.

"I was for a moment delayed," Chan explained.

His superior came up eagerly. "Anything new?"

"I remain just where I always have been," the detective sighed.

"You're not really as much in the dark on this case as you say you are?" asked the Chief anxiously.

Chan nodded. "The man who sits in a well, sees little of the sky."

"Well, climb out, Charlie, climb out."

"I am planning swift ascent," the detective answered, and starting his engine, sped off at last in the direction of his house on Punchbowl Hill.

XII

NOBODY'S FOOL

The night was breaking, and a gray mist lay over Waikiki. Smith, the beach-comber, shivered slightly and stirred on his bed of sand. He put out his hand, as though to draw up over his thin ill-clad body a blanket that was not there. Turning over, he muttered in his sleep, then lay motionless again.

The gray mist turned to pink. Above the mountains to the east a small segment of sky became a deep gold in color, against which a few scattered clouds stood out, black as the recent night. Smith opened his eyes, and gradually came back to a recognition of his surroundings. He did not choose to sleep on the beach, but for some reason the usual bitterness with which he awoke to the realization that he was broke again was missing today. Something pleasant had happened—or was about to happen. Ah, yes. He smiled at the hau tree above him, and the tree showered him with mahogany-red blossoms that had been yellow when he retired for the night. He would have preferred grapefruit and coffee, but flowers were more in keeping with the scene.

He sat up. The gold in the eastern sky was spreading, and now the rim of the sun appeared. The snow-white beach was lapped by water that had in it a glint of gold to match the sky. At his left stood Diamond Head, that extinct volcano. He had always a sort of fellow feeling for Diamond Head, being a bit on the extinct side himself. His mind went back to the events of the preceding night. Good fortune had taken him by the hand and led him to that pavilion window. Too often in these last years he had been blind to opportunity. He was resolved that he would not be blind now.

He got to his feet and, removing his scanty clothing, revealed underneath a frayed pair of bathing trunks. Gathering all his courage, he ran down to the water and plunged in. The shock revivified him. He struck out boldly; one thing at least he had learned on tropic beaches, and that was the art of the swimmer. As he cut through the water the wasted years fell away from him, old ambitions returned, he made plans for the future. He would win back to his former self, he would leave this languorous spot where he had never intended to stay anyhow, he would be a man again. The money that would put his feet back on the high-road was finally within his grasp.

The sun, warm and friendly, crept up the eastern sky. Smith plunged far under the waves, swam there, felt more energetic with every exploit. Finally he returned to shallow water, and walking carefully to avoid the coral, came from his bath back to his bedroom. For a time he sat, leaning against the abandoned hulk of a boat in the shelter of which he had spent the night. The hot sun served as his towel, and he rested, at peace with the world. A delicious feeling of laziness spread over him. But no, no—this wouldn't do.

He donned his clothes, took a broken piece of comb from his pocket, and applied it to his yellow beard and hair. His toilet was completed, and breakfast was now the order of the day. Above him hung clusters of coconuts; often these had been forced to serve. But not this morning, he told himself with a smile. Through a scene of brightness and beauty, he walked slowly toward the Moana Hotel. It was a scene that had, in its way, contributed to Mr Smith's downfall, for every time he sought to paint it, he threw down his brush in disgust and bemoaned the inadequacy of his talent.

On the sand outside the hotel, an early beach-boy lay strumming a steel guitar and singing a gentle song. Smith went promptly to join him.

"Good morning, Frank," he said.

Frank turned his head. "Hello," he answered dreamily. The beach-comber sat down beside him. Suddenly Frank looked at him, his dark eyes wide and earnest. "I'm not going to sing for tourists today," the beach-boy announced. "I'm just going to sing for the blue sky."

Smith nodded. Coming from any other race, this would have been a stilted and theatrical remark, but the beach-comber knew his Hawaiians better than that. He had watched them arrive each morning on their beloved beach, staring at it as though its beauty were brought to their attention for the first time, diving into its familiar waters with cries of delight that betokened a happiness rare in this modern world.

"That's the ticket, Frank," Smith nodded approvingly. He suddenly introduced a more practical note. "Got any money?" he inquired.

The boy frowned. What was this money all the *haoles* seemed so interested in, so vocal about? It meant nothing to him, and never would.

"I guess so," he replied casually. "Dollar in my coat, I think."

Smith's eyes glittered. "Lend it to me. I'll pay it back before night. All the rest I owe you, too. How much do I owe you, anyhow?"

"Can't remember," Frank answered, and sang again.

"I'll have lots of money before the day's out," Smith continued, a note of excitement in his voice.

Frank sang softly. A queer thing to get excited about, money, when the sky was so blue, the water so warm, and there was such a deep satisfaction just in lying on the white beach and humming a song.

"In your coat, you say?" Smith persisted.

Frank nodded. "Go and get it. The locker door's open."

Smith went at once. When he returned he held a dollar bill in one hand, and in the other a small canvas.

"I'm taking that picture I left with you, Frank," he explained. "Something tells me there's a market for my work at last." He stared at the painting critically. A dark-skinned, black-eyed girl stood against a background of cool green. She held a crimson flower between her lips, and she had the look of the tropics, of lazy islands lost in southern seas. "You know," the beach-comber added with almost reluctant admiration, "that's not half bad."

"Yeah," said Frank.

"Not bad at all," Smith continued. "But then, they told me I had talent, Frank. I heard it in New York—and in Paris too. Talent—maybe a touch of genius—but not much else. No backbone—no character—nothing to back it up. You've got to have character, my boy."

"Yeah," repeated Frank idly.

"You know, Frank, painters without half my skill—oh, hell, what's the use? Why should I complain? Look at Corot, Frank. Not one of his pictures was sold during his lifetime. Look at Manet. You know what the critics did to Manet? They laughed at him."

"Yeah," continued Frank. He threw down his guitar, leaped to his feet and, running across the sand, dove like a fish into two feet of water. Smith looked after him. He shook his head.

"No interest in painting," he muttered. "Just music. Well, that's something." He put the bill in his pocket, tucked the canvas under his arm, and went out to the street.

A trolley was approaching, bound for the city, and Smith swung aboard. He offered the dollar proudly—after this, perhaps, the conductor would not judge everyone by his clothes. Once or twice, on the way into town, he looked again at his painting. His opinion of it grew even better.

At a lunch room in town he treated himself to a breakfast such as he had not known in several days, then moved on to the Waioli Hotel. His entrance there evoked no great enthusiasm. The clerk stared at him with open disapproval. "What do you want?" he inquired coldly.

"Mr Fyfe stopping here?" the beach-comber asked.

"He is—but he sleeps late. I can't disturb him."

"You'd better disturb him." There was a sudden note of authority in Smith's voice. "I've an appointment—very important. Mr Fyfe wants to see me more than I want to see him."

The clerk hesitated, and then took up a telephone. In a moment he turned to the beach-comber. "Be down right away," he announced.

Boldly Smith dropped into a chair and waited. Fyfe appeared almost at once; evidently he had not slept late today. There was a worried look in his eyes. He came over to the beach-comber. "You wanted to see me?" he said. "I'm on my way to the theater. Come along."

He left his key at the desk and strode toward the door, Smith struggling to keep up with him. They walked in silence. Finally the actor turned.

"Why be so indiscreet?" he inquired. "You could have telephoned me and I'd have met you."

Smith shrugged. "Telephoning costs money," he replied. "And I haven't much money—yet."

There was a world of meaning in that last word. Fyfe led the way from the more modern quarter of the city into the Oriental district. They moved on past shops crammed with silks, linens, embroideries, jade and porcelains. Bales and baskets filled with the food-stuffs of the Orient encroached upon the sidewalk.

"I take it you expect to have money soon?" Fyfe said at last.

Smith smiled. "Why not? Last night I did you a favor. Oh—I'm nobody's fool. I know why you made that fake confession.

You were afraid I was going to repeat what I heard when I was standing outside that window. Weren't you?"

"Just what did you overhear?"

"Enough, believe me. I heard that woman—the woman somebody killed later on—I heard her tell you that she—"

"Never mind!" The actor looked nervously about. Nothing but flat expressionless faces, dark eyes that avoided his.

"I think I fell in with your plan very neatly," Smith reminded him. "When that Chinese detective, after he'd punctured your confession, asked me again what I'd heard—well, I said what you wanted me to, didn't I? I backed up what you'd been saying. I could have exploded a bomb right then and there—but I didn't. Please remember that."

"I do remember it. And I rather expected you'd be around this morning to blackmail me—"

"My dear sir"—Smith raised a thin freckled hand—"you might have spared me that. I have some shreds of respectability left, and—er—what you said is scarcely in my line. It just occurred to me that as an intelligent man, a practitioner of one of the allied arts, you might possibly be interested in my work." He indicated the canvas. "I happen to have a sample with me," he added brightly.

Fyfe laughed. "You're a rather subtle person, Mr Smith. Suppose I did buy one of your paintings—what would you do with the money?"

Smith licked his lips. "I'd get out of this place for ever. I'm fed up here. For the past year I've been thinking about going home—to my folks in Cleveland. I don't know whether they'd be glad to see me—if I had decent clothes and a bit of money in my pocket—that might help."

"How did you get here in the first place?" the actor inquired.

"I went down to the South Seas to paint. Might be a good place for some people—but for me—well, the first thing I knew I was on the beach. After a long time, my people sent me money to come home. I managed to get aboard a boat, but unfortunately it stopped for a day at this port. And—have you tried any of the *okolehau* they call a drink in this paradise?"

Fyfe smiled. "I understand. You forgot to go back to your ship."

"My dear sir," Smith shrugged, "I forgot the world. When I woke up, my boat was two days out. Oddly enough, my father seemed annoyed. A rather impatient man."

They reached the river and, crossing a narrow stone bridge, entered Aala Park where, because of its convenient location, the dregs of the town congregate. Fyfe indicated a bench. They sat down together, and Smith handed over his canvas.

The actor glanced at it, and a look of surprise crossed his face. "By jove," he cried, "that's damned good."

"Glad to hear you say so," beamed Smith. "A bit unexpected, too, eh? I'm not what you'd call a born salesman, but I can't help pointing out that the thing might be valuable some day. There's just a chance. Think of the pride you could take in saying to your friends: 'Ah, yes—but I recognized his talent long ago. I was his first patron.'"

"Is this your real name—down here in the corner?"

The beach-comber hung his head. "My real name—yes," he replied.

Fyfe laid the canvas on his knee. "Just—what is the price?" he inquired.

"What am I offered?" Smith countered.

"If you're really sincere about wanting to go home," said the actor, "I'll be happy to arrange it for you. Not now, of course—the police wouldn't let you go at present. But when this has blown over a bit, I'll buy you a ticket—and give you something besides. In return for this canvas, you know."

"How much besides?"

"Two hundred dollars."

"Well, I don't know—"

"Make it two fifty. Look here, you're not dealing with a millionaire. I'm an actor on a salary, and it's none too big. I've had a long engagement in Honolulu, and I've saved a bit. I'm offering you about all I've got. If it's not enough, I'm sorry."

"It's enough," said the beach-comber slowly. "I don't mean to be hard on you. I'm not very proud of this, you know. But it's my chance—my chance to get away—lord, I've got to take it. We'll call it a bargain—a ticket to the mainland as soon as they'll let me go, and two fifty in my jeans. But say—how about meantime—I need a small advance now."

"For *okolehau*, eh?"

Smith hesitated. "I don't know," he said frankly. "I hope not. I don't want to touch it. I might talk, and spoil everything. I'm not thinking so much of you—spoil everything for myself, I mean." He stood up. "I won't touch it," he cried suddenly. "I'll fight, and I'll win. I give you my word of honor as a gentleman."

Fyfe looked him over, wondering what that was worth. He took out his wallet.

"I'll have to trust you, I suppose. I'll give you fifty now." Smith's eyes gleamed. "It's all I've got on me. Wait a minute!" He pushed away the beach-comber's eager hand. "Remember—you must be careful. If the police find that you've suddenly got money, they're bound to look into it."

"I was thinking of some new clothes," returned Smith wistfully.

"Not now," Fyfe warned. "Before you sail, yes—we'll attend to that. But now—just as you are for a while—and lie low." The actor was standing too, and he stared hard into the other's face. "I'm depending on you. A man who can paint as you can—don't be a fool. Go straight."

"By heaven, I will!" Smith cried, and hurried off across the park. For a moment Fyfe looked after him, then, with his recent purchase under his arm, walked slowly in the direction of the theater.

Smith went on to Beretania Street, and entered a small low-ceilinged room through a doorway that bore above it the faint sign: "Nippon Hotel." Behind the narrow desk stood a polite little Japanese. On the wall at his back hung the picture of a great liner cleaving the waves, under the words: "*Nippon Yusen Kaisha*."

"Hello, Nada," Smith said jauntily. "My old room vacant?"

"So sorry," hissed the Jap.

Smith threw a bill on to the counter. "Here's ten in advance," he remarked.

"So sorry you stay away such long time," hastily amended the clerk. "Room all ready—yes-s."

"I'll go and brush up a bit," Smith told him. "My baggage will be along later."

"You have money from home, I think," Nada smiled.

"Money from home, nothing," Smith responded airily. "I've sold a picture, Nada. You know, that's more than Corot ever did." He leaned across the counter confidentially. "Poor old Corot, Nada, never got on to himself. It's all in being outside the right window at the right time."

"Mebbe so," agreed Nada. "Much better you go along now. Room numba seven, like always."

"It's great to be home," Smith answered, and went out, whistling a merry tune.

XIII

BREAKFAST WITH THE CHANS

An hour after Smith took his morning swim, Charlie Chan rose and, stepping to his bedroom window, looked down on the bright panorama of town and sea. From Punchbowl Hill the view was one to stir the heart with beauty: green valleys and gleaming water, at this season the crimson umbrellas of the poinciana, golden shower trees blooming in generous profusion, here and there a brick-red bougainvillea vine. Charlie's lot was cast in a pleasant setting, and he loved to stand thus of a morning and reflect on his good fortune.

Today, however, he preferred to reflect on the problem that lay before him. Insoluble it had appeared when he went to bed, but he had slept soundly in the knowledge that what is to be will be, and now he felt a new energy stirring within him. Was he, then, a mainland policeman to be stumped and helpless in the face of a question that had, no doubt, some simple answer? It was a matter, however, that called for prompt and intelligent action on his part. He thought of the crane who, waiting for the sea to disappear and leave him dry fish to eat, died of starvation. Chan had no intention of emulating that stupid bird.

It was a far from silent house that lay about him. Eleven children in one family make of early morning something of a bedlam. He heard their voices here, there and all about, shouting, expostulating, laughing and, in one case at least, weeping bitterly. With a comfortable feeling that the day had begun as usual, he prepared himself for his tasks.

In the dining-room he found that his three eldest children were lingering about the table, and as he entered, he saw them regarding him with a keen interest he had not aroused in that quarter for a long time. They all spoke at once, and he realized the cause of their interest. One of their heroines, according to the morning paper, was murdered, and they were going to see the miscreant punished or know the reason why.

"Quiet!" Charlie cried. "Can a man think beneath a tree filled with myna birds?" He turned to his oldest son, Henry, dapper in college-cut clothes and engaged in lighting a cigarette. "You should be at the store."

"Going right along, Dad," Henry replied. "But say—what's all this about Shelah Fane?"

"You have read it in the paper. Someone most unkindly stabbed her. Now, get on to your work."

"Who did it?" said Rose, the oldest girl. "That's what we want to know."

"A few others languish in same fix," her father admitted.

"You're on the case, aren't you, Dad?" Henry inquired.

Charlie looked at him. "In Honolulu, who else would be summoned?" he asked blandly.

"Well, what's the dope?" went on Henry, who had been Americanized to a rather painful extent. "When do you grab the guilty party, and what's his name?"

Charlie again looked at him, and sighed. These children were his link with the future—what sort of future, he often wondered.

"As I have frequent reason to point out, your language is sadly lacking in dignity," he reproved. "I have not yet apprehended the wrong-doer, and as a consequence, I do not know his name."

"But you will, won't you, Dad?" Rose put in. "You're not going to fall down on it, are you?"

"When have I ever so much as stumbled?" he wanted to know.

She was smiling at him mischievously. "Now, Dad—"

"When I was youthful," Chan broke in hastily, "it was regarded deadly sin to question all-pervading wisdom of father. He was honored and respected by children. Such a hint of failure as you have just offered would have been impossible."

She got up and came round to him, still smiling. "Times have changed. You're not going to fail, of course. We all know that. But this is one case your family is really interested in. So move fast, won't you? Don't take too much time out for Oriental meditation."

"Should I pause to think deeply," he replied, "I would be plenty lonesome man in this new world."

Rose kissed him and went out on her way to the bank where she was employed during the summer vacation. Henry stood up languidly.

"Will you be wanting the car tonight, Dad?" he inquired.

"If I ever wanted it, tonight will be the time," his father answered.

Henry frowned. "I guess I'll have to buy one," he said. "I can get a good second-hand bus on the instalment plan—"

Charlie shook his head. "Work—and pay your way as you go," he advised. "Then you need fear no midnight knock upon the door."

"Old stuff," replied Henry, and made a leisurely exit.

Chan shrugged, and attacked his breakfast. Evelyn, aged fifteen, was addressing him. "Gee—I thought Shelah Fane was swell. I saw her in some swell parts."

"Enough!" cried Charlie. "Vast English language is spread out before you, and you select for your use the lowliest words. I am discouraged."

His wife appeared with his oatmeal and the tea. She was a jolly-looking woman, nearly as broad as Chan, with a placid smiling face. If her children and her husband had far outdistanced her in the matter of adjustment to a new land, she was, judging from her calm eyes, not at all distressed. "Heah about Shelah Fane," she remarked. "Plitty tellible thing."

"What do you know about Shelah Fane?" Charlie asked, surprised.

"All time chillun make talk, Shelah Fane, Shelah Fane," his wife said. "I think mus' be velly fine woman. I want you catch bad man plenty quick."

Chan choked on his hot tea. "If I do not, I perceive I am expelled from my own household. May I respectfully ask that you give me time. Much work to be done on this case."

"Mebbe you have moah tea," his wife suggested.

He drank a second cup, and then rose from the table. Evelyn brought his hat; they all seemed eager to speed him on his way. At the door he barely avoided falling over a round-faced little boy with keen black eyes that recalled those of his father. "Ah—the small Barry." He lifted the child and gave him an affectionate kiss. "Every day you grow more handsome, like fine namesake, Mr Barry Kirk. Be good boy, now, and do not eat the plaster."

He went out and got his car, and as he drove down the hill he thought about his children. He had always been proud of the fact that they were all American citizens. But, perhaps because of this very fact, they seemed to be growing away from him—the gulf widened daily. They made no effort to remember the precepts and the odes; they spoke the English language in a manner that grated on Charlie's sensitive ear.

He passed the Chinese cemetery, with its odd headstones scattered down the sloping hillside. There lay his mother, whom he had brought from China to spend her last years in the house on Punchbowl Hill. What would she think if she could see her descendants now: see Henry in his dapper clothes; see Rose, brisk and efficient, planning to go to a university on the mainland in the autumn; hear Evelyn speaking that shabby, out-moded slang she picked up on the school grounds? His mother would not have approved, Charlie knew. She would have mourned for the old ways, the old customs. He mourned for them himself—but there was nothing he could do about it.

Reaching the business district of the city, he turned his attention to the tasks that lay before him. These were many, and he planned in what order he should attack them. Robert Fyfe was uppermost in his thoughts, so he drove at once to the Waioli Hotel.

Mr Fyfe, the clerk said, had gone out with a man. What man? The description left no doubt as to the identity of Fyfe's caller, and Charlie frowned. What did Smith want of the actor? What had he overheard when he stood outside that pavilion window? Why had Fyfe confessed to a crime he had not committed? He couldn't have committed it, obviously. Not if his story of his actions on the previous night was correct—ah, yes, Charlie reflected, he must look into that.

"I think I heard Mr Fyfe say he was going to the theater," the clerk remarked.

Chan was not up on the drama. "What theater, please?" he inquired.

"The Royal," the clerk told him, and Charlie went there.

He entered from the street, passing from a tiled lobby into the dark auditorium. On the stage the members of the stock company were rehearsing next week's piece. A few old kitchen chairs represented exits and entrances, and the players stood about, waiting for their cues. At the moment Fyfe was delivering a long speech; he gave it languidly, as though it were something with which he had no personal concern.

Charlie walked down the dim aisle. A man with a green velour hat pulled low over his eyes, who sat at a small table on the stage with the play script in his hand, looked down at the detective with evident annoyance. "What do you want?" he barked.

"Just one word, please, with Mr Fyfe," Chan replied.

The actor stepped forward and, shading his eyes from the glare of the footlights, peered into the auditorium.

"Oh, yes—Inspector Chan," he said. "Won't you come up, please?"

Panting from the effort, Charlie boosted his heavy bulk on to the stage.

Fyfe was smiling and cordial. "What can I do for you this morning, Inspector?" he inquired.

Charlie regarded him through half-shut eyes. "Not much, I fear, unless maybe mood has altered overnight. You will recall I arranged for you, somewhat against your wish, a very nice alibi, I am here now to verify myself. A mere matter of form."

"Surely," nodded Fyfe. "Oh, Wayne," he called. Reluctantly the man in the green hat got up and came over to them. "This is Mr Wayne, our stage manager—Inspector Chan, of the Honolulu police. The Inspector is here regarding that affair last night. Wayne—what time was it when you rang up last evening?"

"Eight-twenty," growled Wayne. "Five minutes late."

"I was standing beside you when you rang up?"

"Yes—you were. Though where you were when we were hammering on your door, I'm damned if I know."

"The Inspector, however, does," Fyfe returned. "Was that all you wanted, Mr Chan?"

"One other thing." Chan addressed the stage manager. "In play which you perform this present week, does Mr Fyfe in actor capacity indulge in use of knife?"

"A knife?" repeated Wayne. "Why, no—there's no knife in this play. It's a polite drawing-room comedy."

"Thank you so much," Charlie said, bowing. "That is all." He turned on Robert Fyfe a speculative eye. "Will you come with me, please?"

He led the way down into the auditorium, thinking deeply as he did so. Shelah Fane was seen alive at eight-twelve. Robert Fyfe was in the wings of the theater, ready to go on, at eight-twenty. Just eight minutes—no one could possibly travel the distance from Waikiki to town in that time. Fyfe's alibi was perfect. And yet—

In the darkened foyer back of the last row Charlie paused, and the two leaned on the rail.

"I am still wondering, Mr Fyfe," the detective remarked, "why you made false confession that you killed Shelah Fane."

"I'm inclined to wonder a bit myself, Inspector."

"Obviously you did not kill her."

"I'm afraid you must think me a fool," Fyfe said.

"Other way about, I think you very smart man."

"Do you, really? That's flattering, I'm sure."

"There was reason for that confession, Mr Fyfe."

"If there was, it has quite escaped my memory at this time, Inspector."

"Much better you tell me. Otherwise you place obstacle in path of justice."

"I must be the judge of that, Mr Chan. I do not wish to hinder you. On the contrary I am eager for your success."

"Under such a circumstance, I find that difficult to believe." Chan was silent for a moment. "You have seen our friend the beach-comber this morning?"

Fyfe hesitated. He regretted more than ever the public nature of his meeting with Smith. Then he threw back his head and laughed—a laugh too long delayed, as Charlie noted.

"I certainly have," the actor admitted. "He called on me almost before I was up."

"For what purpose?"

"To get money, of course. I imagine he is making the rounds of the people he met last night. He seemed to think that the mere meeting gave him a sort of claim on us all."

"You are too busy with plural words," Chan protested. "His claim, I think, was on you alone." The actor said nothing. "You gave him money?" Charlie persisted.

"Why—yes—a few dollars. I was rather sorry for him. He is not a bad painter—" Fyfe stopped suddenly.

"How do you know he is not a bad painter?" Chan was quick to ask.

"Well—he—he left a canvas with me—"

"This canvas?" Charlie stepped down the aisle, and picked up something from a vacant seat. "I noted it as we came back here together," he explained. "If you do not mind, I will take it to light and examine it."

"By all means," the actor agreed.

Charlie walked to the door, and pushing it open, gazed for a moment at the painting. The eyes of that girl, posed against green shrubbery, seemed strangely alive. He came back to Fyfe's side.

"You are correct," he remarked, dropping the canvas into one of the chairs. "The man has talent. Pity such a one must resort to—blackmail."

"Who said it was blackmail?" demanded Fyfe.

"I say so. Mr Fyfe, I could place you beneath arrest—"

"Isn't my alibi satisfactory?"

"Quite. But you hamper my work. For the last time—what was it Smith, the beach-comber, heard your ex-wife say to you?"

The stage manager came to the footlights, and called.

"I'm so sorry," said Fyfe, "but I'm keeping the company. I really must go along—"

Chan shrugged. "The inquiry is young, as yet. Before I am through, I will know, Mr Fyfe."

"Drop in any time," said Fyfe blandly, holding out his hand. "Too bad I must leave you now, but an actor's life, you know—"

Chan gravely shook hands, and the actor hurried up the aisle. As he returned to the bright street, Charlie wore a puzzled frown. He knew that behind Fyfe's suave manner there lurked something of vital importance—something that might, indeed, solve his problem. Yet he would never get it from Fyfe. The beach-comber—ah, perhaps. He made a mental note of the beach-comber.

Climbing back into his flivver, Chan drove over to King Street and turned in the direction of Waikiki. As he passed the public library, set well back from the street amid great trees, he was tempted to stop. It occurred to him that he ought to read, in a Los Angeles paper, the story of Denny Mayo's murder. Buried in the yellowed columns describing that spectacular moment in the movie colony's history, he might discover a line that would at once put him on the true scent in his search for Shelah Fane's assailant.

With quick decision he swung about and returned to the library. In another moment, he was addressing the woman at the library desk.

"Is it possible that I obtain at once Los Angeles paper for June, three years ago?" he inquired.

"Certainly, Mr Chan," she answered. "Just fill out the card."

He filled it hastily, and saw it passed to a young assistant. The girl started to move toward the files, glancing at the card as she did so. She turned and came back.

"I'm sorry," she said. "I just happened to remember. That volume of the *Los Angeles Times* is in use just now."

"In use?" Chan was surprised.

"Yes. A gentleman took it out half an hour ago."

"Can you describe this gentleman?"

The girl nodded toward the reading-room. "He's still there. By that farther window."

Chan went over and peered round the corner of a bookcase. Seated bent over a huge gray-bound volume, he saw Huntley Van Horn. The picture actor did not look up; he seemed grimly intent on what he was doing. With a gesture toward the desk, meant to convey the fact that he dropped the whole matter, Chan walked softly out of the building.

XIV

THE PAVILION WINDOW

Charlie went to the street, got into his flivver, and in another moment was traveling rapidly toward Waikiki. It was good to feel the faithful little car shuddering under him again; so often in the past it had carried him along on the trail of innumerable clues. Many of these clues had led him, as he put it, "into presence of immovable stone wall." Thereupon he had swung the car about, seeking a new road. And the road that ended in victory had, in most cases, stretched before him at last.

As he sped through the brilliant morning, he thought of Huntley Van Horn. He pictured the cinema actor on the night before, walking across the lawn at the very moment when the black camel must have been kneeling at Shelah Fane's gate. No one was with the actor, no one saw him; he could easily have stepped into the pavilion, silenced the woman for ever and then calmly joined the two people on the beach.

What sort of man was Van Horn? Charlie wished he had read a few of the movie gossip magazines his children were always bringing into the house. Not the sleek, pretty boy type of film favorite, that was evident. Cynical, aloof, well-poised, he was the type who could keep his own counsel and turn an expressionless face on anyone who sought to pry into his affairs.

Ah, yes—Mr Van Horn would bear thinking about. Such thinking might yield a rich reward.

But it was not with Van Horn that Chan was immediately concerned. He was on Kalakaua Avenue now, and though the sun was still shining above him, he had entered a zone where rain was falling. He saw, as he approached the hotels, tourists who wore rain-coats and carried umbrellas; evidently they took this liquid sunshine with a seriousness that amused a *kamaaina* like Charlie. He turned sharply to the right and, moving on past the lovely gardens of the Grand Hotel, parked his car in the drive at the rear. Walking unconcerned through the drizzle, he went over and ascended the hotel steps.

The head bell-man, a Chinese boy with a winning smile, greeted him in Cantonese. Chan paused to chat for a moment. No, he explained, he was not looking for anyone in particular; he would, with kind permission, stroll about a bit. He crossed the high cool lobby, returning the jovial greeting of a young assistant manager.

He walked down the long corridor, toward the lounge. Unlike many of his fellow citizens of Honolulu, he had no feeling of somewhat resentful awe in this impressive interior. Having been to the mainland he regarded himself as a traveled man, a judge of hotels, and he approved heartily of this recent addition to the charms of Waikiki. He nodded affably at the flower girl, and stood for a moment in the entrance to the lounge. This room always inspired him. Through the great archways opening on the terrace he caught the shimmer of the sea, breath-taking fragments of a scene no coast in the world can surpass.

The huge room was empty of guests, but a few silent Oriental servants were busy arranging the floral decorations for the day. On tiny slivers of bamboo stuck in bowls of sand, they mounted innumerable hibiscus flowers, beautiful and fragile blossoms that would fade when evening came. Chan passed through to the terrace facing the ocean, and luck was with him. The only occupants of the place at that moment were the two old people with whom he had seen Tarneverro talking the previous evening. He stepped over to the Hongkong chairs where they sat, and stood looking down at them. The man put aside his morning paper; the woman glanced up from her book.

Chan bowed low. "May I wish you good morning," he said.

"Good morning, sir," the old man replied courteously. There was a pleasant Scotch burr to his words, and his face, lined by hard work under a hot sun, was as honest as any Charlie had ever seen.

Chan pushed back his coat. "I am Inspector Chan, of the Honolulu police. You have, I think, perused in the morning paper story of quick finish of noted actress. I am sorry to intrude my inspeakable presence between you and this charming view, but gentleman you know was friend of the departed lady. It therefore becomes unevitable that I speak to you for short moment."

"Happy to meet you," said the old gentleman. He rose, and pulled up a chair. "Be seated, Inspector. I am Thomas MacMaster, of Queensland, Australia, and this is Mrs MacMaster."

Chan achieved a notable bow, and the old lady gave him a quick kindly smile. A bit of idle chatter seemed in order.

"You are enjoying nice holiday?" the detective inquired.

"That we are," returned MacMaster. "And we've earned it, eh, Mother? Aye, after long years on a sheep ranch, we're off to revisit old Scotland at last. A very leisurely journey, Inspector; we mean to miss nothing along the way. And delighted we are"—he waved toward the beach—"that we did not miss this bonny spot."

His wife nodded. "Aye, bonny it is. We're very much afraid we'll no have the strength of character to move on."

"Speak for yourself, Mother," MacMaster said. "When the moment comes, I'm sure I'll have strength for two. Do not forget that Aberdeen is waiting."

"In behalf of Honolulu," beamed Chan, "my warmest thanks for all these treasured compliments. I recognize they come from honest lips, and my heart feels itself deeply touched. But reluctantly I must approach subject of last night's homicide. May I open my remarks by pointing out that some *malihini*—some stranger—must be responsible for this cruel event? Here people are kind, like climate. We seldom murder," he added feelingly.

"Of course," murmured the old lady.

Looking up, Charlie saw Tarneverro in the doorway. The fortune-teller's dark face lighted with satisfaction when he saw the group on the terrace, and he came rapidly down the steps. Chan sighed. He would have preferred to do this thing himself.

"Ah, good morning, Inspector," Tarneverro said. "Good morning, Mrs MacMaster. And how are you, sir?"

"A wee bit lost," answered the old man. "I cannot feel just right and not be at my work. But Mother tells me I must learn to rest."

"You certainly must—you have it coming to you," Tarneverro smiled. "Inspector, I am happy to see you on the job at this early hour. You are no doubt here to verify my alibi, and that is quite fitting and proper. Have you asked these two friends of mine the important question?"

"I was approaching it with suitable preparation."

"Ah, yes," the fortune-teller continued. "Mr MacMaster, in the matter of that unfortunate affair last night—I happen to have been one of the few people in the Islands acquainted with the poor girl, and it is important that I establish to the Inspector's satisfaction the fact that I was elsewhere at the moment of her death. Luckily I can establish it—with your help." He turned to Charlie. "After I left you in the lounge last night, you saw me return to my conversation with Mr and Mrs MacMaster. Mr MacMaster will tell you what happened after that."

The old man frowned thoughtfully. "Mr—er—Tarneverro suggested that we go out on the veranda—I believe you call it a lanai—that looks across the palm court. We did so, and for the matter of a half-hour sat talking about the old days in Queensland. Finally Mr Tarneverro had a look at his watch. He said it was thirty minutes after eight and that he must leave us, as he had a dinner engagement down the beach. We stood up—"

"Begging humblest pardon," Chan cut in, "did you by any chance consult own timepiece?"

"Aye, that I did," returned the old man. His manner was very earnest and there was an unmistakable ring of truth to his words. "I took out my watch—" He removed an old-fashioned timepiece from his pocket. "'I'm a wee bit fast,' I said. Eight-thirty-five, I make it. Mother, it's time old folks like us went upstairs.' You see, on the ranch we were always early abed, and well-established habits are hard to break. So we came into the hotel. Mother and I stopped at the elevators, and Mr Tarneverro went round the corner to his own room on the first floor. While we waited for the lift, I stepped to the desk to set my watch the correct time. Eighty-thirty-two it was then, and I made the change. Those are the facts, Inspector, and Mother and I will swear to them."

Chan nodded. "The speech of some is like wind in empty space," he said. "But blind man could see your word is good."

"Aye, it always has been. From Aberdeen to Queensland no one has ever questioned it, Inspector."

"You have known Mr Tarneverro long time?" Charlie asked.

Tarneverro answered. "Ten years ago," he remarked, "I was playing in a Melbourne theater. I was an actor in those days, you know. Our company stranded, and I went out to Mr MacMaster's ranch, a few miles from Brisbane, to work for him. I stayed a year—the happiest year of my life. For as you may see by looking at them, these two are the kindest people in the world, and they were like father and mother to me—"

"We did nothing," the old lady protested. "It was a joy to have you and—"

"Alone and lonely as I was," Tarneverro interrupted, "it was great luck to come upon people like these. You can imagine my delight when I ran across them again at this hotel the other day." He rose. "I take it that is all you wanted to know, Mr Chan. I'd like to have a talk with you."

"That is all," remarked Chan, rising too. "Lady,—sir,—may vacation continue as happy as it is this bright morning on undescribably lovely beach. I am so pleased that our paths met here at famous crossroads."

"We share that pleasure, sir," MacMaster replied. His wife nodded and smiled. "We'll be thinking of ye as we travel on to Aberdeen. Our very best wishes for success."

Charlie and the fortune-teller went inside, and sat down on a sofa. "You are favorite of the gods," Chan remarked. "If I needed alibi I would ask nothing better than word from honest people such as those."

Tarneverro smiled. "Yes—they're a grand pair. Simple and wholesome and addicted to all the old virtues." He paused. "Well, Inspector, you know where I was during those vital eighteen minutes. How about the others?"

"I know also, where Robert Fyfe was," Charlie replied, "though much about his actions puzzles me. Speaking of the rest, they have no such luck. Not one has offered alibi."

Tarneverro nodded. "Yes—and one among them may need an alibi badly before this affair is ended. You had, I take it, no flash of inspiration in the night?"

Chan sadly shook his head. "I had nothing but plenty good sleep. And you?"

The other smiled. "I'm afraid I weakly fell into a dreamless slumber too. No—I have thought hard, but I'm afraid I can't help you much. There are so many possibilities. Shall we go over them? Rita and Wilkie Ballou. Both in Hollywood at the time of Denny Mayo's death. Mayo was said to be a bit careless with the ladies—and it is clear that Ballou is a notably jealous man."

"I think about Ballou," remarked Chan slowly.

"It might pay," Tarneverro agreed. "He was wandering about—came into the living-room to get a cigarette—claims he stayed there. Turning from him for the time being, there's Alan Jaynes. His state of mind was rather emotional last night. Who knows anything about him? Suppose that like that of Ballou, his is a wildly jealous nature. He saw those flowers—not his—on the shoulder of the woman he loved. We found them trampled under foot, as though in rage. The Mayo affair, as I believe you pointed out, may have had nothing to do with Miss Fane's murder, after all. Perhaps it was just a case of mad unreasoning jealousy—"

"Perhaps," answered Chan calmly. "There is also Martino."

"Yes—Martino," repeated the fortune-teller. A black look swept across his handsome face. "It would give me great pleasure to help you pin this thing on him. He has made some very rude remarks about me—"

"What sort of man you call him?" Charlie asked.

"Oh, he seems to have brains," Tarneverro admitted. "And a kind of rude strength—a queer combination, the esthete and the brute in one package. He wasn't in Hollywood when Mayo was killed, but once again—perhaps we are on the wrong trail there. Martino's been a bit of a ladies' man—there may have been some unsuspected relationship between him and Shelah Fane. Certainly that handkerchief in his pocket had a fishy look to me. Of course he denied he owned it—who wouldn't? But if anyone placed it on Martino's person, he was taking a tremendous and unnecessary risk. Why not throw it into the bushes—drop it on the lawn? Why attempt the difficult, the dangerous? The handkerchief, Inspector, may have been Martino's own property. He may have gone on carrying it after the murder, quite innocent of the fact that it contained those splinters of glass. Unless—" the fortune-teller paused— "unless you have evidence that it belonged to someone else?"

Chan regarded him with sleepy eyes. "I have so little evidence," he sighed. "Languishing in such a state, how gladly I hear you talk. Continue, please, to dispense logic and eloquence, those twin blossoms of speech. I now bring up the name of Huntley Van Horn."

Tarneverro regarded him keenly. "Have you anything on Van Horn?"

"I regret to note that he has no alibi. Also, he was at proper place at proper time to do the deed." Chan paused, and decided he would keep some matters to himself. "Aside from that, I have nothing of importance. Deign to state your opinion of the man."

"Well," said Tarneverro, "I haven't thought much about Van Horn. He's an odd, rather bitter sort of chap—a notorious bachelor—the despair of all the women. No breath of scandal has ever touched him. I have always admired the fellow, though heaven knows he has never been any too friendly to me. He's an intelligent chap, with excellent taste—a bit conceited, perhaps, but no man could receive the adulation he does, and escape that." He considered a moment. "No, Inspector," he added with sudden decision, "in spite of the fact that his opportunities were excellent, as you point out, I cannot see Huntley Van Horn as our quarry in this affair."

Charlie rose. "Thank you for this little conversation." He glanced at his watch. "Now I must haste to home of Shelah Fane. You will accompany me?"

"I'm sorry," Tarneverro replied, "but I am not at liberty to do so just at present. You'll let me know of any new developments, won't you? It isn't mere curiosity on my part. If we are to work together I must, of course, know what you are doing."

"We will encounter from time to time," Chan assured him. They walked to the hotel door.

The head bell-man said something to Tarneverro in Cantonese, and the fortune-teller regarded him with a blank uncomprehending look. "What does he say?" he inquired of Charlie.

"He makes most respectful inquiry after your health this splendid morning," Chan translated.

"Oh, I'm fine, Sam," Tarneverro smiled. There was a puzzled expression on Sam's broad face. "So long, Inspector," the fortune-teller continued. "Ring me up if you strike anything new. I'll be hunting about myself—anything I can do—well, I'm with you to the finish, as I told you."

"You are so extremely kind," bowed Chan, and returned to his car.

The front lawn of Shelah Fane's house, when Charlie arrived there, lay peaceful and serene in the shade of its ancient banyan tree. Jessop answered the door, perfect in manner and attire, as always.

"How are you, Constable?" he said. "The morning is rather on the gorgeous side, is it not?"

"Presume so," agreed Chan. "It is matter we do not notice here. All mornings much the same."

"Which must, if I may say so, sir, grow a trifle monotonous in time." The butler followed Chan into the living-room. "Now in England, Constable, drawing back the curtains of a morning is something of a sporting proposition."

Charlie stood looking about the great room, where so much had happened the night before. It was calm, quiet and sunny now.

"Miss Julie and Mr Bradshaw are in the neighborhood of the beach, sir," Jessop remarked. "One of your officers—a Mr Hettick, I believe—is busily engaged in the pavilion."

"Ah, yes—Hettick is our finger-print expert," Charlie explained. "I will go outside at once." On the lawn he encountered the two young people, who greeted him warmly. "So sorry to develop into pest," he said to Julie. "But path of duty is often rocky one."

"Why, you could never be that," she smiled. "We've been expecting you."

He glanced at her, so fresh and lovely, her blue eyes wide and innocent. He thought of the emerald ring.

"Well, how did you like my story in the paper this morning?" Bradshaw wanted to know.

"My perusal was of a necessity hurried," Chan replied. "Imagine it covered the ground."

"Is that the best you can say for it?" the boy complained.

Charlie shrugged. "Always think twice before you scatter tributes," he answered. "If no one had praised the donkey's song, he would not still be singing." He grinned. "The comparison is, of course, unhappy one. I take it you enjoy a pleasant morning?"

"Oh, I just ran out to help Julie," the boy told him. "I've been acting as a shock-absorber between her and the reporters. The fellows on the evening paper weren't very polite. They seem a bit miffed the story didn't break right for them."

"A natural feeling," Chan replied.

"What are you going to do now?" asked Bradshaw.

"Propose to look about in bright light of day," Charlie answered.

"I'll help you," Bradshaw said. "Julie, you just sit down and relax. Close your eyes and try not to think. Nobody ever has at Waikiki, and you can't tell—it might be dangerous."

The girl smiled at him and dropped on to a beach chair.

"Want to keep the poor kid cheered up," Bradshaw explained, as he and Chan walked toward the pavilion. "This has been a pretty tough shock for her. But in time I think I can convince her that all her troubles are over. That is—if she'll marry me."

"You possess excellent opinion of yourself," Charlie smiled.

"Why shouldn't I? I know myself so well."

As they reached the pavilion, Hettick came out. He had been brought over from the mainland at the time of the reorganization to strengthen the force, and he had never been very cordial to Charlie, whom he had replaced in the rôle of finger-print expert.

"Good morning, Mr Hettick," Chan said politely. "Have you had successful time of it?"

"Not very," the man replied. "Plenty of prints, but mostly those of the murdered woman. All the others can be accounted for, I guess. Come inside, and I'll show you—"

"One little moment," interrupted Charlie. "First I take careless stroll about outside of place."

Followed by Bradshaw, he made his way through some bushes at the side of the cottage, and came out on the public beach that bounded the grounds on the west. Beneath the single pavilion window which opened on that beach—the one under which Smith had stood the previous night—he paused.

A great many footprints were there now, and those of the beach-comber barely distinguishable. Charlie stooped down and carefully sifted the sand. With a little cry of satisfaction, he stood erect again.

"Important discovery," he announced.

Bradshaw came nearer. He saw in Charlie's palm the remains of a small cigar, the size of a cigarette.

"Trampled into the sand," Charlie added. "I would never have expected to find this here."

"Why—I know only one man who smokes these," the boy cried. "I saw him—last night—"

"You are quite correct," Chan beamed. "One man, and who would believe he could act so careless? I am consumed with wonder. When did Mr Alan Jaynes stand outside this window—and why?"

XV

TWO JUICES OF THE ORANGE

Charlie took an empty envelope from his pocket and carefully placed his latest discovery inside it. He and the boy again penetrated the bushes and entered the pavilion. Hettick was sitting idly by the dressing-table, with the paraphernalia of his calling spread out before him.

Dropping down on a wicker chair, Chan glanced around the room where, only the night before, he had encountered tragedy. The detective's face was placid and serene; he might have been awaiting the luncheon bell untroubled by any problem. Through an enormous plate-glass window he watched a liner from the coast move slowly into port.

"You have enjoyed no luck here, Mr Hettick?" he inquired.

"Not much," replied Hettick. "The things on the table are covered with prints—all those of the murdered woman herself. I got her record at the mortuary this morning. By the way, the coroner asked me to tell you he has postponed the inquest until tomorrow. He expects you to have something by then."

Chan shrugged. "Thank him for the compliment. Also inform him I will exchange places with him at any moment." His gaze returned to the room; the woodwork, he noted, had recently been painted white. Suddenly he rose and stepped to the small window opening on the beach. "You have not tested this sill, I believe," he remarked.

"No—as a matter of fact, I haven't," Hettick answered. "I meant to, but it slipped my mind."

Chan grinned. "Mind gets so slippery in warm climate. May I humbly suggest you do so now?"

Hettick came over and covered the sill with his lamp black. With practised hand he applied the camel's-hair brush.

Charlie and the boy crowded close. "Ah!" cried Chan. On the smooth white surface of the sill were the marks of someone's fingers and thumb.

"These were not made by Shelah Fane?" Charlie inquired

"No," answered Hettick. "Those were left by a man's hand."

Chan stood, deep in thought. "Recent, too. We achieve some progress now. A man's hand. A man opened that screen, climbed up on sill. Why? To enter room, of course. When? Last night, when murder was in atmosphere. Yes, we move, we advance." He paused. "What man?" In his coat pocket, his fingers touched the envelope containing the cigar stub. He turned with sudden decision. "One thing is certain. I must without delay obtain thumb prints of Alan Jaynes." Smiling at Jimmy Bradshaw, he added: "Police have fine clue and promise early arrest. But if you publish one word of this, I recall matter of your laundry and put you in jail at once."

"I won't use it, Charlie," promised the boy. "What are you going to do now?"

"I propose to leave you with nobody for company—except Miss Julie. And who is she?"

"Wait a minute, and I'll tell you. She's the most—"

"Later," cut in Chan. "Much later. Mr Hettick, I request that you remain here until my return. Your keen eye will be required. I am off for session at Grand Hotel."

He left the pavilion, and the boy followed. As Charlie passed out of sight around the corner of the house, Bradshaw went over to where Julie sat. He dropped down beside her.

"Has that funny policeman gone?" she asked eagerly.

"For a few minutes. He'll be back before he's missed." Looking up at her, the boy thought he saw an expression of fear cross her delicate face. He wondered. "Charlie has just made an important discovery outside the pavilion window," he added.

"W-what?" she inquired.

"I don't believe he'd like to have me tell you," Bradshaw answered. "Not just yet, at any rate. But—what about this Alan Jaynes? You don't know him very well, do you?"

"Scarcely at all," the girl replied. "I never saw him until yesterday morning. Shelah met him in Tahiti—I believe she was very fond of him. But Shelah was fond of—so many people. She was even—fond of me." Without warning Julie turned away her head and burst into tears.

Bradshaw got up and laid a hand on her heaving shoulder. "Now—now," he said uncomfortably. "You mustn't do that. You're ruining all my press stuff. Waikiki, the abode of peace, the crescent beach where happiness rules supreme. Suppose one of these tourists who took me at my word should see you."

"I—I'm sorry," she sobbed. "I'm not happy; I can't be."

"No, of course you can't—not at this moment, I mean. But why not look ahead to all the happiness that's coming, and draw a little advance on that?"

"I'll—I'll never be happy again," she told him.

"Nonsense. I'm going to make the world as glamourous for you as I've made this town in the Tourist Bureau ads. When we're married—"

She pushed him away. "We'll never be married. Oh, it's terrible. I'm horrid, really—and you don't suspect. You'll hate me—when you know."

"Do tell! Look at me." He leaned over and kissed her.

"You mustn't," she cried.

"I've got to," he smiled. "It's my duty. I've advertised this place for its romance, and romance there must be if I have to attend to it myself. Now listen to me—inside a week or less all this will be over, and you can begin to forget. Charlie Chan is going to solve the puzzle at any minute—"

"Oh—do you think so?"

"He's sure to. You can't keep anything from Charlie."

"I wonder," said the girl.

"I know," Bradshaw replied firmly.

Scarcely sharing Bradshaw's confidence, Chan was at that moment entering the lobby of the Grand Hotel. He waved a hand toward the bell-man, and went at once to the desk.

"I arrive again," he remarked to the clerk. "For a non-paying guest, I am plenty much in evidence around this place. Will you give me number of room occupied by Mr Alan Jaynes, if you will be so good?"

The clerk smilingly gave it to him, and pointed out the house telephones at the right of the desk. Charlie was relieved to hear the Britisher's answering voice. He politely requested a moment's conversation, and Jaynes replied that he would come down immediately.

Charlie walked with unaccustomed speed to the lounge. A small Filipino bell-boy was there alone, and the detective summoned him.

"I wish to be served with two of your delicious orange-juice drinks," he announced.

"Yes, sir," replied the boy.

"I will also accompany you while you secure same." The boy appeared taken back, but it was not his rôle to argue. From out of the jungle he had come to learn that the guest is always right.

Charlie followed his small guide to the serving pantry, where they encountered a man in a white apron.

"Inspector Chan, of the Honolulu police," Charlie explained briefly. "I have just engaged to purchase two juices of the orange. Will you hand me the glasses in which you propose to place same, please?"

The servant was too weary to be surprised. The climate, as he often explained to his wife, had got him. He produced the glasses and Charlie, removing an immaculate handkerchief from his pocket, began to polish them briskly.

"This action, I hasten to say, involves no criticism of you," he remarked. "But I am reading lately about germs." He grinned. "A very dangerous form of animal life." It could be noted, however, that it was only the outside of the tumblers that concerned him. He completed the task, set the objects of his attention carefully down on the tray the boy had brought, and reaching into his pocket, handed a quarter to the serving man. "You will do me great favor if you will fill these receptacles without placing fingers on same." He turned to the boy. "That also applies to you. Do you understand? You are not to touch those glasses. Set tray on table as it is. Otherwise, when moment arrives for your tip, I develop far-away look in eye and cannot see you."

Returning to the lounge, Charlie found the Britisher already there. "Ah—Mr Jaynes," he said. "I am happy to see you again. You had good night's rest, I hope?"

Jaynes stared at him. "No," he replied, "I didn't; but what of it?"

"So sorry," Chan cried. "Waikiki is famous sleeping place, and being old resident of Honolulu, I experience deep pain when it fails to live up to reputation. Will you do me the honor to join me on this sofa?"

He dropped down on the seat, which creaked protestingly beneath him.

"Harsh voice of furniture proclaims to world my excessive avoirdupois," he continued affably. "I diet and I fast, but to no avail. What is to be, will be. Man—who is he to fix own weight upon the scales? All that is determined elsewhere."

Jaynes sat down beside him. "What can I do for you this morning, Inspector?" he inquired.

"You can accept, if you will be so kind, renewed apologies for detaining you on this island. Some people pronounce it Paradise, but even Paradise, I can appreciate, looks not so good when one is panting to travel elsewhere. Again my warm regrets. I assure you I apply myself with all possible speed to task of clearing up mystery, so that you may make quick exit."

"I'm glad to hear that," nodded Jaynes. He took out a case and offered Charlie one of his little black cigars. "No?" He lighted one himself. "You are making progress, I hope?"

"I encounter difficulties," Charlie admitted. "Those who know, don't talk; those who talk, don't know. But that is always to be expected in my work. Within last hour I think I see faint glimmer of light ahead. Ah—" The Filipino boy had arrived with the tray; he set it down on a small table before them. "I should have said, Mr Jaynes, that I am on orange-juice diet, and the hour of the drink is here. I have ventured to order same for you."

"Oh, no, thanks," replied the Britisher. "I don't believe—"

"Same is all prepared," Charlie protested, and a note of imminent offense crept into his voice. "The beverage is harmless. You are not going to refuse?"

"Well—thank you," said Jaynes. At the moment he wanted nothing less, but he knew how easily the feelings of a Chinese may be hurt, and he could not risk any further offense to this particular representative of the race. "You are very good." He reached for a glass.

Beaming, Charlie lifted his own. "We will drink to my quick success, since you desire it equally with me." He imbibed heartily, and set the glass down. "Presume mild nature of the liquid gives you hearty pain. I have noted how bitterly men from your country resent this prohibition."

"What prohibition?" Jaynes inquired.

"Ah, you mock and jeer. Well, it is noble experiment, but it is not new, as many think. The Emperor Yü, who came to the throne of China in year 2205 B.C., said when he tasted liquor for the first time, this will do my people much harm, and forbade its use. His edict had good effect for a while, but later got lost in dim pages of history. China," added Chan, drinking again, "like the purse of a generous man, has endured much. But it still survives."

Jaynes was looking at him with a deep curiosity. Had this odd policeman dropped in merely to discuss prohibition? Charlie noted the look.

"But to return to our mutton broth," he said. "I desire to make inquiries of you regarding last night. You are most unfortunate man not to possess nice alibi for motions during time of homicide. You were, as I understand things, wandering about plenty mad at fatal hour?"

"I'm afraid I was," Jaynes admitted.

"From the moment when you left Martino on beach until he went out and found you with announcement of murder, you exist quite alone?"

"Yes."

"Making your walk, how far down beach did you penetrate?"

"Only as far as the Moana Hotel. I sat there under the banyan tree and tried to think what I had better do."

"You did not—will you join me in another quaffing—ah, yes—you did not travel on to property of Shelah Fane?"

"I've just told you," replied Jaynes, "that I went only as far as the Moana. As I say, I sat down there to try to figure things out. When I had grown a bit calmer, it occurred to me that perhaps I was making a big row about nothing. A woman who could be so easily influenced by a silly fortune-teller—I asked myself whether she would, after all, make a satisfactory wife. Her life was far removed from mine—I began to feel that the whole affair might turn out to have been a mere passing infatuation with both of us. I resolved to take the boat at midnight and, if possible, forget the entire business. After that was decided, I felt better. I came back here, past the Outrigger Club, and just outside the hotel Martino met me with the appalling news of the poor girl's murder."

"No one noted you at Moana under banyan tree?"

"I fancy not. I sat in a dark corner."

"Were you ever in pavilion where Shelah Fane encountered finish?"

"No—I never saw the place."

"Then you could not have been in the neighborhood at any time? Hovering about window, for example?"

"Well, hardly." Without prompting, Jaynes took up his glass and drained it. Suddenly he stared at Charlie. "I say—why do you ask me that?"

"I seek only to narrow search," Chan explained. "That will be all, thank you. Can you name hour of next boat to mainland?"

"I certainly can," answered the Britisher. "There's one tomorrow at noon. I hope to heaven—"

"I will extend myself to the utmost," smiled Chan. "Though, to look at me, many might remark that I had already done so."

Jaynes laughed. "Don't let that thought deter you," he said. "You'll do your best, I know. By the way, I'm afraid I was a bit rude to you last night—but I was very anxious to get away. For many reasons—not only my business in the States—but this whole terrible affair—I wanted to be out of it. I still do. You understand?"

"I understand," nodded Chan gravely. His left hand, in the side pocket of his coat, touched a certain envelope. "I will say good morning," he added.

He stood watching the Britisher cross the terrace and stroll toward the sea. Sensing someone at his back, he turned just in time. An old bent Chinese who continually paraded the lounge in his native costume, armed with a brush and dust-pan, was reaching out for the glasses.

"*Haie!*" Chan seized the withered hand. "Do not touch, or the wrath of the seven watchful gods descends upon you." He took out his handkerchief and tenderly wrapped it round the glass from which Jaynes had drunk. "I am removing this, and the affair does not concern you."

But evidently the old man thought it did concern him, for he followed Charlie to the desk. There Chan encountered one of the managers. "I should like to purchase this object," he said, revealing what the handkerchief held. "Kindly name price."

The manager laughed. "Oh, that's all right. Take it along. What are you doing, Charlie? Collecting fingerprints from our harmless guests?"

"You are close to truth," nodded Chan. "Save perhaps with that word harmless. Thank you so much. And now will you kindly call off this aged gentleman who thinks he has captured one of the forty thieves?"

The manager said something to the servant, who moved away, muttering to himself. His comments, Chan knew, were not complimentary, but he gave no heed. He hurried through the door to his car.

Deep in thought, he drove back to Shelah Fane's house. Were the fingerprints on this glass identical with those on the window-sill in the pavilion? If they were, then he was approaching journey's end.

Hettick was waiting, and to him Charlie entrusted his precious cargo, still redolent of orange juice. The expert set quickly to work. Presently he stood by the window, the tumbler in one hand, a magnifying-glass in the other. Chan came close, awaiting the verdict.

Hettick shook his head. "Nothing like it," he announced. "You've been on the wrong trail this time, Inspector."

Keenly disappointed, Chan sat down in a chair. So it had not been Alan Jaynes who entered this room last night? It had all seemed to fit in so neatly that up to this minute he had not had a doubt of it. On the wrong trail, eh? He hadn't cared for the way in which Hettick had said that. The men at the station had been in a rather unfriendly mood since Charlie's return from the mainland. They had expected to find him in a haughty and triumphant state of mind since his exploits there, and the fact that he had shown no trace whatever of such an attitude, had done nothing to lessen their envy. He had been forced to endure many joking remarks that held an undercurrent of hostility.

On the wrong trail, eh? Well, who didn't take the wrong path occasionally in this business? Where was the superman so good that he never erred?

On the wrong trail. Chan sat deep in thought. Jaynes had been outside that window—the stub of the small cigar, which he had evidently forgotten, was proof enough. But it was not he who had pushed up the screen and entered, leaving the imprint of fingers on the white sill. Someone else had done that. Who? Who else had been—

Suddenly Charlie smote his forehead a resounding blow. "*Haie*—I have been complete and utter idiot. I move too fast, without proper thought. Everybody seeks to hurry me—even my own family. And I was not built for hurry. Hurry is the wind that destroys the scaffolding." He turned to Hettick. "What has become of finger-print record of beach-comber, taken at station last night?"

"Oh," replied Hettick. "I've got that here." He produced a manila envelope from his pocket and removed a glass plate. "Do you think—"

"I think, yes—a little late, but still I think," said Charlie. He took the plate from the unresisting hand of his brother officer and hurried to the window. "Come quickly," he called. "Your glass—look! What is your decision?"

"They are the same," Hettick announced.

Triumph shone brightly in Charlie's little eyes. "At last I arrive somewhere," he cried. "Smith, the beach-comber, was in this room last night! Am I for ever on wrong trail, or do I have my lucific moments?"

XVI

A WORD OF WARNING

Chan's air of calm detachment had vanished for the moment, and he walked the floor as though inspired by his latest discovery.

"Smith, the beach-comber," he said once more. "Dreary bit of human wreckage cast up on shore of splendid island. Ragged remnant of a man—how busy he was around this building last night. A big evening, I think, in the life of Smith."

Hettick was gathering up the tools of his trade. "Well, I believe I'll go back to the station now," he remarked. "I've given you boys something to work on. Go out and make the most of it."

"Ah, you are clever detective," Chan grinned. "Things slip from mind sometimes, but when humble fellow worker recalls them, then you move on like avenging demon. You have given us material indeed. Yes, please return to station at once. I will arrive later, and in meantime I respectfully suggest that you send out alarm call for Smith. Tell Chief beach-comber must be pulled into station with no delay. Let all low dives be explored. Put Kashimo on it. He is our most passioned searcher, and what is better, he knows all cracks and crannies of modest little underworld."

Hettick promised he would deliver the message, and departed. Charlie followed at his heels. He saw Julie and Bradshaw on the lawn, and paused beside them. "You wish ride to town?" he inquired of the latter.

"No, thanks," Bradshaw replied. "I've got my car today. Besides, Julie has just persuaded me to stay for lunch."

"May life hold for her no sterner task than such persuasion," smiled Chan. "I do not wish to cloud your future, Miss Julie, but must warn you that I return here soon."

He was skirting the house when Jessop appeared at the lanai door, "Ah—er—Constable," he said. "May I ask you to step inside just a moment?"

Struck by the seriousness of the butler's manner, Charlie passed through the door which the servant held open. "You have something to say to me?" he asked.

"I have, sir. Kindly come with me." Jessop led the way into a small reception-room near the front of the house. He entered it first—evidence of unusual abstraction on his part. "Oh—I beg your pardon, sir. I'll just close this door, so we may have an undisturbed tête-à-tête."

"Time is none too plentiful with me—" Chan began, somewhat surprised by these elaborate preparations.

"I know that, Constable, I will—er—plunge in at once." In spite of this promise, he hesitated. "My old father, who was for more than forty years the trusted employee of a rather exacting duke, remarked to me in my youth: 'A good servant, Cedric, sees all, knows all, but tells nothing.' It is only after prolonged and mature consideration, Constable, that I have determined to ignore that excellent counsel."

Chan nodded. "Circumstances," he remarked, "upset cases."

"Precisely, sir. I have always been a law-abiding man, and what is more, I am eager to see you get to the bottom of this matter without—if I may say so—further delay. Last evening I chanced to be busy in the hall at the moment when you were engaged in interviewing Miss Julie regarding the emerald ring. This may suggest to you that I was eavesdropping, but I can assure you that such duplicity was farthest from my thoughts. I heard the young lady tell you that Miss Fane had given her that ring early in the morning, and that she—Miss Julie, I mean—had held it in her possession from that moment on, until you discovered it in her room."

"Such was Miss Julie's story," Charlie agreed.

"I am at a complete loss to understand it, sir. I don't know what she meant by her testimony—but I do know this. At about seven last night, Miss Fane called me to her room and gave me the letter which I was to deliver to Mr Tarneverro immediately on his arrival at the house. As she passed over the missive, I distinctly saw, gleaming on her right hand, the ring in question. I am positive on that point, Constable, and prepared to offer a sworn statement along those lines."

Chan was silent for a moment. He thought of Julie O'Neill, so young, so innocent-looking. "Thank you very much," he said at last. "What you say seems of vast importance."

"I only hope it may not be so important as it appears," Jessop replied. "I tell you this, Constable, with considerable reluctance. I have nothing against Miss Julie—a charming young woman—indeed she is, sir. I was tempted for a long time to remain silent, but it struck me that my duty lay, most decidedly, in the opposite direction. Like yourself, I desire to see the miscreant in this affair adequately punished. Miss Fane was always extremely kind to me."

Chan moved toward the door. "I shall act upon your information at once," he announced.

Jessop looked uncomfortable. "If my name could only be kept out of it, sir—"

"Same may not be possible," Charlie told him.

Jessop sighed. "I recognize that, Constable. I can only say again that I am quite positive I saw the ring. My eyesight is excellent, which, to a man of my age, is a matter of deep satisfaction."

They went out into the hall. Anna, the maid, was slowly coming down the stairs. Chan turned to Jessop.

"Thank you again," he said. "You may go now."

The butler disappeared toward the kitchen, and Charlie waited for Anna at the foot of the stairs.

"Good morning," he remarked pleasantly. "I desire one word with you, please."

"Of course," replied Anna, and followed him into the living-room.

"You recall story of Miss Julie regarding the ring?"

"Naturally, sir."

"Same was given her by Miss Fane in early morning and remained in her possession. Have you anything to say regarding that?"

"Why—why what do you mean, sir?" the maid returned.

"You did not yourself see the ring on Miss Fane's finger during the day? Or when she came to you to procure pin for orchids?"

"If I did, it made no impression on me, sir."

"You see things, yet they make no impression?"

"You know how it is, sir. Things become familiar and you don't really notice. What I mean is—the ring may or may not have been there. I'm afraid I can't say, sir."

"You wish the matter to stand at that?"

"I fear it must, as far as I am concerned."

Chan bowed. "Thank you—that is all."

He stepped through a French window, and walked slowly across the lanai. He had no heart for the task that faced him now, but many such tasks had confronted him in the past, and he had never faltered. Stepping out on the lawn, he went over to a beach swing where Bradshaw and the girl were sitting.

"Miss Julie," he began. The girl looked up at him, and at sight of his grave face, her own paled.

"Yes, Mr Chan," she said in a low voice.

"Miss Julie, you have told me Miss Fane gave you that emerald ring soon after her arrival yesterday morning. Why did you tell me that?"

"Because it's the truth," Julie answered bravely.

"Then how do you account for fact that ring was seen on her finger last evening at seven?"

"Who says it was?" the girl cried.

"Is that important?"

"It is very important. Who says it was?"

"I learn it from what I think reliable source."

"You have no means of knowing how reliable, Mr Chan. Who made that statement? Not Miss Dixon—she isn't up yet. It must have been one of the servants. Jessop, perhaps. Was it Jessop, Mr Chan?"

"What does it matter—"

"But I assure you it matters very much. Because, you see, I don't stand very well with Jessop. There's an old grudge between us—on his part, at least."

"You will, please, explain what you mean by that?"

"Of course. As I told you last night, Miss Fane's servants were always cheating her. When I first became her secretary I shut my eyes to it, because I'm no tale-bearer. But about a year ago, her finances became terribly involved, and I began an investigation. I discovered that Jessop had a most shameless arrangement with the tradespeople—all the bills were padded outrageously and Jessop was getting a share of the profits.

"I said nothing to Miss Fane—I knew what that would mean—a temperamental outburst, tears and recriminations, and probably a grand scene of forgiveness in the end. She was always so kind-hearted. Instead I went to Jessop, told him I knew what he was doing and that the thing must stop. He was most indignant. All the other servants in Hollywood, he told me, were doing the same, and he seemed to consider it a sort of royal prerogative. But when I threatened to tell Miss Fane, he backed down and agreed to put an end to the practise. I fancy he did, too, but since that time he has always been very cool to me, and I know that I have never been forgiven. So you see why I asked you if it was Jessop who told that—falsehood about the ring."

"Just where do you stand—as you say it—with Anna?"

"Oh, Anna and I have always been on the most friendly terms," Julie answered. "A good steady girl who saves her money and buys bonds with it. It's money honestly come by—I'm sure of that because"—Julie smiled faintly—"the poor thing has never had a chance to pad bills. None of them passes through her hands."

Chan looked at Julie's flushed face for a long moment. "Then you desire to repeat that Miss Fane herself gave you the ring yesterday morning?"

"I certainly do. It's the truth, Mr Chan."

Charlie bowed. "I can only accept your word, Miss Julie. It is quite possible—the person who told me of seeing the ring last night may have been moved by ancient grudge—I thought of it at the time. Miss Julie, I say to myself, too fine and sweet for underhand work. You will note, Jimmy, that you and I have tastes in common."

"Which does you credit," smiled Bradshaw.

"Which credits us both," amended Chan. "I will no longer hang about, a blot on this lovely scene. My kindest goodbye—until we meet again."

He walked thoughtfully to his car, and drove away through the hot noon sunshine. "So many roads that wind and wind—" He had read that somewhere. He sighed. So many roads—would the little car finally leap down the right one?

As he approached the Grand Hotel, Huntley Van Horn was again in his thoughts. He was reluctant to reappear so soon at the hotel's main entrance so, parking his car in the street, he entered the grounds and walked toward the palm court. A group of excited tourists was gathered beneath the tallest of the coco-palms, and looking aloft, Charlie saw one of the beach-boys, in a red bathing-suit, climbing the tree with the agility of a monkey. He stood for a moment, admiring the boy's skill.

"The kid's clever, eh, Inspector?" remarked a voice at his elbow.

He turned and looked into the smiling gray eyes of Van Horn. They were standing a little apart from the others, and the picture actor was the recipient of many awed, adoring glances from young women who were ostensibly there to watch the beach-boy.

"Ah, Mr Van Horn," Chan said. "This meeting is indeed most fortunate. I am calling here for the sole purpose of seeing you."

"Really?" The actor looked up at the tree. "Well, he seems to have traveled as far as he can on that one. Shall we go on the veranda—pardon me, the lanai—and have a chat?"

"The idea is most suitable," Charlie agreed. He followed Van Horn and they sat down in a secluded corner. The boy had descended the coco-palm and stood now the center of an admiring group, hugely enjoying the limelight. Chan watched him.

"Sometimes in my heart," he remarked, "arouses hot envy of the beach-boys. To exist so happily—to have no cares and troubles, no worries—ah, that must be what men mean by Paradise. All they ask of life is one bathing-suit, slightly worn."

Van Horn laughed. "You have worries, I take it. Inspector?"

Charlie turned to him; he had decided to be frank. "I have." He paused. "You are one of them," he added suddenly.

The picture actor was unperturbed. "You flatter me," he answered. "Just how am I worrying you, Inspector?"

"You worry me because in this matter of Miss Shelah Fane's murder you are quite defenseless. Not only do you possess no alibi, but of all those concerned, you were nearest to the scene of her death. You walked across lawn at very important moment, Mr Van Horn. I could not worry about you more if you were own son."

Van Horn grinned. "That's kind of you, Inspector, I appreciate it. Yes—I am rather badly cast in the story of the crime. But I rely on you. As an intelligent man, you must realize that I could have had absolutely no motive for killing the poor girl. Until I joined her company to make this picture, I scarcely knew her, and all through our journey and the work together, we were on the friendliest terms."

"Ah, yes." Chan watched the actor's face eagerly. "Were you likewise on friendly terms with Denny Mayo?" he inquired.

"Just what has Denny Mayo to do with all this?" Van Horn asked. Despite his best efforts, his expression was not quite so casual as he wanted it to be.

"May have much to do with it," Charlie told him, "I seek to upearth facts. Maybe you assist me. I repeat—were you on friendly terms with Denny Mayo?"

"I knew him fairly well," Van Horn admitted. "A most attractive chap—a wild Irishman—you never could tell what he was going to do next. Everyone was very fond of him. His death was a great shock."

"Who killed him?" Charlie asked blandly.

"I wish I knew," Van Horn replied. "Last night, when I heard you asking everybody about three years ago last June, in Hollywood, I sensed that you thought his death involved in this somehow. I'm curious to know the connection."

"That, no doubt," said Charlie, "is why you haste to library early this morning to do hot reading about Mayo case?"

Van Horn smiled. "Oh—so you found me among my books, eh? Well, Inspector, as my press-agent will tell you, I'm of rather a studious type. There's nothing I like better than to curl up in a corner with a good book—real literature, mind you—"

Charlie raised a protesting hand. "The wise man, knowing he is under suspicion," he remarked, "does not stoop to tie his shoe in a melon patch."

Van Horn nodded. "An old Chinese saw, eh? Not bad either."

"You will," said Chan sternly, "before we leave these chairs, tell me the reason for your visit to library this morning."

Van Horn did not reply. He sat for a moment with a frown on his handsome face. Then he turned with sudden decision.

"You've been frank with me, Inspector. I'll be the same with you. Though when you've heard my reason for that visit, I fear you'll be more puzzled than ever." He took from his pocket an envelope bearing the crest of the Grand Hotel, and drew out a single sheet of note-paper. "Will you please read that?"

Chan took the paper. It bore a brief note, type-written and unsigned. He read:

> "Just a word of warning from a friend. You should go at once to the Honolulu Public Library and remove from the bound volumes of all Los Angeles papers carrying the Denny Mayo murder story, certain rather damaging references to your own part in that affair."

Charlie looked up. "Where did you get this?"

"I found it under my door when I awoke this morning," the actor told him.

"You went to library at once?"

"Directly after breakfast. Who wouldn't? I couldn't recall that I'd ever been mentioned in connection with the case—there was no reason why I should have been. But naturally—my curiosity was aroused. I went down and read every word I could find regarding Mayo's murder in the *Los Angeles Times*—the only paper they had. And oddly enough—"

"Yes?" Chan prompted.

"It was just as I thought. My name wasn't mentioned anywhere. I've had a rather puzzled morning, Inspector."

"Natural you should." nodded Charlie. "A queer circumstance, indeed. Have you any idea who wrote this note?"

"None whatever," returned Van Horn. "But the purpose of it seems to be clear. Somebody has sought to cast suspicion in my direction. It's a delicate little attention, and I appreciate it. He—or possibly she—figured that I would go to the library and sign for that volume, and that of course you would soon find it out. After that, you would fancy me deeply involved in this affair, and would spend precious time sleuthing in the wrong direction. Fortunately, you took the unusual course of coming to me at once with your suspicion. I'm glad you did. And I'm damned glad I kept the letter."

"Which, after all, you may have written to yourself," Chan suggested.

Van Horn laughed. "Oh, no—I'm not so deep as all that, Mr Chan. The letter was under my door when I rose. Find out who wrote it, and you may find the murderer of Shelah Fane."

"True enough," agreed Charlie. "I will keep it now, of course." He stood up. "We have had a good talk, Mr Van Horn, and I am grateful for your confidence. I go my way with one more puzzle burning in my pocket. Add a few more, and I collapse from mental strain. I trust I have not held you away from luncheon."

"Not at all," the actor replied. "This has been a very lucky interview for me. Goodbye, and all my best wishes for success."

Chan hastened through the palm court, and at last set his flivver on the road to the city. As he moved along, he thought deeply about Huntley Van Horn. Despite his airy manner, the actor had seemed to be open and sincere. But could he, Charlie wondered, be sure of that? Could he ever be sure in this world? Deceit sprouted everywhere and thrived like a weed.

Suppose Van Horn was sincere? Who put that note under his bedroom door while he slept? Chan began to realize that he was engaged in a duel—a duel to the death. His opponent was quick and wary, cleverer than any person he had yet encountered in a long career. How many of these clues were false, dropped but to befuddle him? How many real?

An inner craving told him that lunch would be a pleasant diversion; he was never one to put such promptings aside. But as he approached the public library an even greater craving assailed him—a keen desire to read for himself the story of Denny Mayo's murder. With a sigh for the business man's lunch that must languish without him a little longer, he stopped the car and went inside.

The desk was deserted for the moment, and he turned into the reading-room at his right. There was just a chance that the big volume taken out by Van Horn early that morning was not yet restored to its place on the shelves. Yes—there it lay, on the table at which he had seen the picture actor sitting. Save for one or two children, the place was deserted. Charlie rapidly crossed the room and opened the book.

It happened that he knew the date of the Mayo tragedy, and he sought immediately the issue of the subsequent morning. His eyes opened wide. Under an eight-column head, "Movie Actor Found Murdered in Home," a great torn gap stared up at him.

Quickly he examined the pages, and then sat back, dazed and unbelieving. Every picture of Denny Mayo had been ruthlessly cut from the book.

XVII

HOW DENNY MAYO DIED

Chan sat motionless for a long time, deep in thought. Some desperate person was determined that he should not look upon the likeness of Denny Mayo. The captions to the pictures were for the most part intact. "Denny Mayo When He First Came to Hollywood." And here again: "Denny Mayo as He Appeared in *The Unknown Sin*." But in every instance the reproduction of the actor's face was destroyed.

Who had done this thing? Huntley Van Horn? Perhaps. Yet if that were so, Van Horn's methods were crude and raw for so suave a gentleman. To go boldly to the library, ask for this volume, sign his name to the slip as he claimed to have done, and then mutilate the yellowed pages, would be unbelievably naive. It invited swift and inevitable detection. It certainly did not sound like Van Horn.

With a ponderous sigh, Charlie applied himself to the story that had surrounded Denny Mayo's pictures. The actor had come to Hollywood from the English stage, and had won immediate success. He had lived with one servant in a detached house on one of the best Los Angeles streets. On the night of the murder the servant, after completing his usual duties, took the evening off. He went out at eight o'clock, leaving Mayo in excellent spirits.

Returning at midnight, the man let himself in through the kitchen door. Seeing a light in the living-room, he went there to ask if anything further was required of him before he went to bed. On the floor of the room he discovered the actor, dead some two hours. Mayo had been shot at close range with his own revolver, a delicate weapon which he was accustomed to keeping in the drawer of his desk. The revolver was lying at his side, and there were no fingerprints on it—neither his own nor those of any unknown person. No one had been seen entering or leaving the house which occupied a dark position under its many trees.

Unfortunately, the following morning—and Charlie's eyebrows rose at this—the police had permitted the general public to swarm through the house. Actors, actresses, directors, producers—all friends, they claimed, of the dead man—had paraded through the rooms, and if any vital clue was still lying about it could easily have been destroyed. In any case, no vital clue was ever found. Those the police discovered led nowhere.

Little was known about Mayo's past; he had come from far away, and no member of his family stepped forward during the investigation. It was rumored that he had a wife in England, but he had not seen her for several years, never mentioned her to his friends—might, possibly, have been divorced. His life in Hollywood had not been spectacular; women admired him, but if he returned this admiration in any instance, he had been most discreet about it. If anyone had a grudge against him—

Further along in the story, a name caught Charlie's eye, and he sat up with sudden interest. Hastily he read on until he came to it. Mayo had been working in a picture, and as his leading woman he had had an actress named Rita Montaine. Miss Montaine was engaged to marry a certain Wilkie Ballou, a prominent figure in Honolulu, scion of an old family there. Some obscure person testified that he had overheard a quarrel between Mayo and Ballou—it concerned a party to which

Mayo had taken Miss Montaine. But the witness had heard Ballou make no threats against the actor.

Nevertheless, Ballou had been questioned. His alibi was complete, sworn to by Miss Montaine herself. On the night of Mayo's death the actress said that she and Ballou had been together from six o'clock until after midnight. They had taken a long ride in Ballou's car and danced together at a roadhouse far from the scene of the crime. She admitted that she was engaged to Ballou and intended to marry him soon.

These two faded from the limelight. Charlie read on, through the helpless meanderings of a completely baffled police. He turned page after page, no new developments arose, and amid a frantic sputtering on the part of the reporters, the story gradually died out.

How about that alibi of Ballou's? Sworn to by the woman who was going to marry him. Was she also ready to lie for him?

Chan picked up the heavy volume and returned to the main room of the library. He laid his burden down on the desk, behind which stood a bright young woman. Without speaking, he opened the book and indicated the mutilated pages.

If his aim had been to annoy the young woman, he could have found no better means. Her cry of dismay was immediate and heartfelt. "Who did this, Mr Chan?" she demanded.

Charlie smiled. "Thanks for touching faith in my ability," he remarked. "But I cannot tell you."

"It was taken out by Mr Van Horn, the actor. This sort of thing is prohibited by law, you know. You must arrest him at once."

Chan shrugged. "It was also lying on table from time Mr Van Horn left it, early today, until well past noon. What proof have we that Van Horn mutilated it? I know him well, and I do not think him complete fool."

"But—but—"

"I will, with your kind permission, speak to him over wire. He may be able to cast little light."

The young woman led him to the telephone, and Chan got Van Horn at the hotel. He explained at once the condition in which he had found the book.

"What do you know about that!" Van Horn remarked.

"Alas! very little," Charlie returned. "The volume was in the intact state when you saw it?"

"Absolutely. Perfectly O.K. I left it on the table about nine-thirty and went out."

"Did you see anyone known to you about place?"

"Not a soul. But I say, Inspector, this throws new light on that note I got this morning. Perhaps the intention of my unknown friend was not so much to involve me, as to get that volume out of the files. He—if it was a he—may have hoped that the thing would happen just as it has happened—that I would take it out and leave it where he could find it without himself signing a slip. Have you thought of that?"

"So much to think of," Chan sighed. "Thank you for the idea." He went back to the desk. "Mr Van Horn left the volume in original state. He is certain of that. Was it noted that anyone else examined it this morning?"

"I don't know," the young woman replied. "The librarian in charge of that room is out to lunch. Look here, Mr Chan, you've got to find who did this."

"Plenty busy with murder just now," Charlie explained.

"Never mind your murder," she answered grimly. "This is serious."

Chan smiled, but the young woman was in no mood to join him. He promised to do his best and departed.

A glance at his watch told him that he had no time for his usual leisurely lunch. He had instead a sandwich and a glass of milk, then went to the station. The Chief was pacing the floor of the detectives' room.

"Hello, Charlie," he cried. "I've been wondering where you were. Pretty busy this morning, I take it?"

"Like fly on hot griddle," Chan answered. "And just as eager to get off."

"Haven't got anything yet, eh?"

"Have so much I am worn out," Charlie told him. "But no idea who killed Shelah Fane."

"That's what we want," the Chief insisted. "The name—the name. Good lord, we ought to get somewhere pretty soon."

"Maybe we will," replied Chan, with just the slightest inflection on the "we." He sat down. "Now I will relate morning's adventures, and it can happen that your keen brain will function where mine wanders lonely in the dark."

He began at the beginning: his visit to the theater, Robert Fyfe's cast-iron alibi, his admission that he had given the beachcomber money in exchange for a painting. He mentioned his call at the library and his discovery there of Huntley Van Horn, then went on to the two old people on the terrace of the hotel, who had accounted so readily for Tarneverro's actions on the previous night.

"They may be lying," said the Chief.

Charlie shook his head. "You would not say that if you saw them. Honesty gleams like unceasing beacon from their eyes."

"I'll judge of that for myself," remarked his superior. "What was their name? MacMaster? I'll talk with them later. Go on."

Charlie continued. He told of finding the stub of the small cigar of a sort smoked only by Alan Jaynes, beneath the pavilion window.

"Oh, lord," sighed the Chief. "They can't all be in it. Somebody's kidding you, Charlie."

"You go back to singular pronoun," smiled Chan. "A moment ago it was we. But that was only in regard to approaching moment of success, I think."

"Well, somebody's kidding us, then. Have it your own way. You got Jaynes' fingerprints?"

"I slyly obtained same. But it was print of Smith, the beachcomber, we discover on window-sill."

"Yes—that was something we can really act on. I sent out the word to pick him up right away. They'll bring him in any minute now. What have you been doing since then?"

Charlie repeated Jessop's story about the ring, which, he pointed out, might mean merely the repayment of an old grudge. He showed his Chief the letter which Van Horn had offered in explanation of his visit to the library. Finally he told of the mutilation of the bound volume of the newspaper, and ended with the mention of Ballou and his wife in the story of the Denny Mayo murder case.

For a long time, when he had finished, his Chief sat in silence. "Well," he said at length, "according to your investigation, they're all in it, I guess. Good heavens, can't you draw any deductions from all this?"

"Kindly state what are your deductions," answered Chan with gentle malice.

"Me? I don't know. I'm stumped. But you—the pride of the force—"

"Kindly recall—I have never been demon for speed. While I stumble about this way, I am fiercely thinking. Large bodies arrive late. Grant me time."

"What do you propose to do now?"

"I consider a little social visit with Mrs Ballou."

"Great Scott, Charlie,—watch your step. Ballou's an important man in this town, and he's never been very friendly to me."

"I plan to use all possible diplomacy."

"You'll need it, and then some. Don't offend him, whatever you do. You know—these old families—"

Charlie shrugged. "I have not lived in Honolulu all these years in state of blindness. Do not worry. I move now on feet shod with velvet, and my voice drips oil and honey."

Kashimo came in. He walked with a dragging step and had a discouraged air.

"Well, where's this fellow Smith?" demanded the Chief.

"No place, sir," said Kashimo. "Melted like ice."

"Melted, hell! You go out again, and don't come back without him."

"Look everywhere," Kashimo complained. "All funny joints, up-stair, in cellar. Comb town. No Smith."

Charlie went over and patted him on the back. "If at first you have drawn blank, resume the job," he advised. He took a slip of paper from a desk and began to write. "I give you list of unsavory places," he explained. "Maybe you overlook some. Perhaps, after all, I have better knowledge of city's wickedness than honored member of Young Men's Buddhist Association like yourself."

He handed his list to the Japanese, who took it and left, followed by Charlie's kindly encouragement.

"Poor Kashimo," Chan remarked. "When there is no oil in the lamp, the wick is wasted. In dealing with such a one, friendly words bring best results. Now I go forth to wallow some more in bafflement."

"I'll be waiting to hear from you," his Chief called after him.

Charlie set out for the Manoa Valley home of the Ballous. The business district disappeared behind him, and he traveled a street lined with great houses set on rolling lawns. Above his head flamed flowering trees, now in the last weeks of their splendor. He sped past Punahou Academy, and as he penetrated farther into the valley, he left the zone of sunshine for one of darkness. Black clouds hung over the mountains ahead and suddenly, borne on the wind, came a wild gust of rain. It beat fiercely on the top of the little car and blurred the windshield.

Yet a mile away, at Charlie's back, Honolulu sparkled in the midday sun.

He reached the handsome house of Wilkie Ballou, and Rita received him in the dark drawing-room. Her husband, she explained, was upstairs dressing for his afternoon golf. In Honolulu a real golfer pays no attention to rain; it may be pouring on his street, but bright and sunny round the corner. Rita's manner was cordial, and Chan took heart.

"I am so sorry to obtrude my obnoxious presence," he apologized. "If you never saw me again, I feel sure you would like it well enough. But—mere matter of form—I must inflict little talk on everyone present at sad affair last night."

Rita nodded. "Poor Shelah! How are you getting on, Inspector?"

"I make splendid progress," he informed her blithely. There was, he felt, no occasion to go into that. "Would you speak with me little while about days when you were famous Hollywood figure?"

With bored eyes, Rita looked out at the rain lashing against the window. "I certainly will," she said.

"May I add that you broke heart of my eldest daughter, who is great film fan, when you retired from silvery sheet? No one, she moans, is ever so good as you were."

Rita's face brightened. "She remembers me? That's sweet of her."

"Your fine skill will never be forgotten anywhere," Chan assured her, and knew that he had made a friend for life.

"How can I help you?" she inquired.

Chan considered. "You knew Miss Fane in Hollywood?"

"Oh, yes, quite well."

"It is wisely forbidden to speak ill of those who have ascended the dragon, but sometimes we must let old rules go down the board. Was there at any time scandal in the lady's life?"

"Oh, no, none whatever. She wasn't that sort, you know."

"But she had what you call love-affairs?"

"Yes, frequently. She was emotional and impulsive—never without a love-affair. But they were all harmless, I'm sure."

"Did you hear that once she loved a man named—Denny Mayo?" Charlie watched Rita's face closely, and he thought she looked a little startled.

"Why, yes—Shelah was rather wild about Denny at one time, I believe. She took it rather hard when he was—killed. You knew about that, perhaps?"

"I know all about that," answered Chan slowly. But to his disappointment, the words seemed to leave the woman quite calm. "You had acquaintance with this Denny Mayo yourself, I think?"

"Yes—I was in his last picture."

Chan had an inspiration. "It may be you have photograph of Mayo somewhere among possessions?"

She shook her head. "No—I did have some old stills, but Mr Ballou made me burn them. He said he wouldn't have me mooning about over the dear, dead past when I was—" She stopped, her eyes on the door.

Charlie looked up. Wilkie Ballou, in a golf suit, was in the doorway. He strode grimly into the room.

"What's all this about Denny Mayo?" he demanded.

"Mr Chan was simply asking me if I knew him," Rita explained.

"Mr Chan should mind his own business," her husband growled. He walked over and faced Charlie. "Denny Mayo," he said, "is dead and buried."

Chan shrugged. "I am so sorry, but he does not stay buried."

"He stays that way as far as my wife and I are concerned," Ballou answered, and there was a certain dignity about him as he said it.

For a moment Chan looked sleepily into the hostile eyes of the millionaire. "Your alibi for the night of Mayo's murder," he ventured, "seems to have enjoyed a fine success."

Ballou flushed. "Why not? It was the truth."

"So naturally, it prevailed." Chan moved toward the door. "I am sorry if I have disturbed you—"

"You haven't disturbed me in the least," Ballou snapped. "Just what did you expect to find here, anyhow?"

"I thought I might chance upon photograph of Denny Mayo."

"And why should you want his photograph?"

"Some unknown person objects to my looking at it."

"Is that so?" said Ballou. "Well, you won't find Mayo's picture here. Or anything else that will interest you, for that matter. Good day, Inspector; and I must ask you not to call again."

Charlie shrugged. "I travel where duty takes me. Would much prefer to loll in station house—but can you study swimming on a carpet? No—you must go where waters are deep. Good day, Mr Ballou."

Rita followed him into the hall. "I'm afraid we haven't been able to help you," she remarked.

"Thanks all same," bowed Chan.

"I'm so sorry," the woman said. "I want to see you succeed. If there was only something I could do—"

Chan's eyes caught the flash of rings on her fingers. "There might be," he remarked suddenly.

"Anything," she replied.

"Last night you saw Miss Shelah Fane after long separation. Quick glance of women catches points men despise to notice. You recall all she was wearing, no doubt?"

"Why, of course. She had on a stunning gown—ivory satin, it was—"

"I speak mostly of jewels," Chan told her. "What woman is so blind she fails to note other woman's jewelry?"

Rita smiled. "Not I. She had on a gorgeous string of pearls, and a diamond bracelet—"

"And her rings?"

"Only one. A huge emerald I remember seeing in Hollywood. It was on her right hand."

"This was when you last encountered her? The young people were already in the water enjoying warm swim?"

"Julie and that boy were—yes."

Charlie bowed low. "My gratitude has no bounds. Now I must go on with my work. Goodbye."

He went out into the perpetual valley rain, and turned his car toward the sunlit beach.

XVIII

THE BELL-MAN'S STORY

Julie and Jimmy Bradshaw sat on the white sand of Waikiki and gazed at an ocean that stretched, apparently empty of life, from this curving shore all the way to the atolls of the South Seas.

"Well, I suppose I'd better be getting along downtown," remarked the boy. He yawned, and dropping on his back, watched the white clouds drift lazily across a cobalt sky.

"Picture of a young man filled with pep and energy," Julie smiled.

He shuddered. "Very poor taste, my girl, introducing words like that into a conversation at Waikiki beach. It must be that, after all, I have given you a very imperfect idea of the spirit of this place. Here we loaf, we dream—"

"But you'll never get anywhere," Julie reproved.

"I'm there already," he answered. "Why should I bestir myself? When you're in Hawaii you've no place to go—you've reached heaven, and a change couldn't possibly be an improvement. So you just sit down and wait for eternity to end."

Julie shrugged. "Is that so? Well, I'm afraid I'm not built that way. Great for a vacation, yes—this place is all you say of it. But as a permanent residence—well—"

He sat up suddenly. "Good lord, you mean I haven't sold you on it? Me—the greatest descriptive writer in history—and

I've failed to put over the big deal of my life. James J. Bradshaw strikes a snag—meets failure face to face—it seems incredible. Where have I slipped up, Julie? Haven't I made you feel the beauty of this island—"

"Beauty's all right," the girl replied. "But how about its effect on character? It seems to me that when you've stopped moving, you're going back."

"Yeah," he smiled. "I went to a Rotary Club luncheon once myself—over on the mainland. Boys, we gotta progress or perish. Last year we turned out ten million gaskets, this year let's turn out fifteen. Make America gasket-conscious. Take it from me—"

"What were you saying about getting back to the office?"

He shook his head. "I thought I'd cast you for the role of Eve in this paradise, and what a serpent you turn out to be. Getting back to the office is something we never do over here. We don't want to wake the poor fellows who didn't go out."

"That's just what I've been saying, Jimmy."

"But dear Mrs Legree, you don't need to be chained to an office desk in order to accomplish things. You can work just as well lying down. For instance, a minute ago I was well started on a new appeal to tourists. 'Come—let the laughing lei girl twine her garlands of flowers about your shoulders. Try your skill at riding Waikiki's surf, or just rest in lazy luxury—'"

"Ah, yes—that's what you prefer to do—"

"'Under the nodding coco-palms.' Don't you like our coco-palms, Julie?"

"They're interesting, but I think I prefer the redwoods. You draw a deep breath in a redwood forest, Jimmy, and you feel like going out and licking the world. Can't you see what I mean? This place may be all right for people who belong here—but you—how long have you been in Hawaii?"

"A little over two years."

"Did you intend to stay here when you came?"

"Well, now—let's not go into that."

"You didn't, of course. You just took the line of least resistance. Don't you ever want to go back to the mainland and make something of yourself?"

"Oh—at first—" He was silent for a moment. "Well, I've failed to make the sale on Hawaii, I guess. That will always leave a scar on my heart, but there's something more important. Have I sold myself? I'm keen about you, Julie. If you'll say the word—"

She shook her head. "Don't let's go into that, either, Jimmy. I'm not what you think me—I'm horrid, really—I—oh, Jimmy, you wouldn't want to marry a—a liar, would you?"

He shrugged. "Not a professional one—no. But a clumsy amateur like you—why, you do it as though you'd had no experience at all."

She was startled. "What do you mean?"

"All that about the ring. Why, in heaven's name, do you go on with it? I've been wise ever since this morning, and as for Charlie Chan—say, I admire the polite way he's treated you. I don't believe you've fooled him for a minute."

"Oh, dear—I thought I was rather good."

"What's it all about, Julie?" the boy inquired.

Tears were in her eyes. "It's about—poor Shelah. She took me in when I was broke and without a friend—she was always so good to me I'd—I'd have done anything in the world for her—let alone tell a little lie."

"I won't ask you to continue," Bradshaw remarked. "I don't have to. Don't look around. Inspector Chan of the Honolulu police is approaching rapidly, and something in his walk tells me that this is the zero hour for you. Brace up. I'm with you, kid."

Charlie joined them, amiable and smiling. "Not too welcome, I think. But anyhow I attach myself to this little group." He sat down, facing the girl. "What is your opinion of our beach, Miss Julie? Here you are deep in the languid zone. How do you like languor, as far as you have got with it?"

Julie stared at him. "Mr Chan, you have not come here to talk to me about the beach."

"Not precisely," he admitted. "But I am firm believer in leading up. Suitable preparation removes the sting of rudeness. Making an example, it would have been undecently abrupt for me to stride up and cry: 'Miss Julie, why do you lie to me about that emerald ring?'"

Her cheeks flushed. "You think I have been—lying?"

"More than think, Miss Julie. I know. Other eyes than Jessop's saw the ring on Miss Fane's finger long after you immersed in waters of Waikiki last night."

She did not reply. "Better own up, Julie," Bradshaw advised. "It's the best way. Charlie will be your friend then—won't you, Charlie?"

"Must admit feeling of friendship would suffer a notable increase," Chan nodded. "Miss Julie, it is not true that Miss Fane gave you that ring yesterday to obtain cash for it?"

"Oh, yes, it is," the girl insisted. "That much is true."

"Then she took it back later?"

"Yes—just after she returned from her interview with Tarneverro, about noon."

"Took it back, and wore it when she died?"

"Yes."

"After the tragedy, you again obtained possession?"

"I did. When Jimmy and I found her, I went in and knelt beside her. It was then I took the ring."

"Why?"

"I—I can't tell you."

"You mean you won't."

"I can't, and I won't. I'm sorry, Mr Chan."

"I also get deep pain from this." Charlie was silent for a moment. "Can it happen you removed the ring because name of 'Denny' was engraved inside?"

"Wh—what do you know about Denny?"

Chan sat up with sudden interest. "I will tell you, and perhaps you will grow frank. I have learned that Shelah Fane was in Los Angeles house the very night Denny Mayo was murdered there. Consequently, she knew name of killer. It was scandal in her past she was eager to conceal. Perhaps, to aid that concealment, you yourself wished name of Denny Mayo kept out of all discussions. A natural desire to shield your friend's reputation. But as you see, your actions have not availed. Now you may speak, with no injury to your dear benefactor."

The girl was weeping softly. "Yes, I guess I might as well tell you. I'm so sorry you know all that. I'd have given anything to keep Denny Mayo out of this."

"You were aware, then, of that scandal in Miss Fane's past?"

"I suspected that something was terribly wrong, but I didn't know what. I was quite young—I had just come to Shelah—at the time of Denny's—accident. On the night it happened, Shelah arrived home in a state of hysteria, and I was there alone with her. I took care of her the best I could. For weeks she wasn't herself. I knew that in some way she was connected with Mayo's murder, but until this moment, I never learned the facts. I was young, as I say, but I knew better than to ask questions."

"Coming to yesterday—" Chan prompted.

"It was just as I told you—yesterday morning she said she must get hold of money at once, and she gave me the ring to sell. Then she went down to the Grand Hotel to see Tarneverro, and when she came back she was sort of hysterical again. She sent for me to come to her room—she was walking the floor. I couldn't imagine what had happened. 'He's a devil, Julie,' she cried. 'That Tarneverro's a devil—I wish I had never sent for him. He told me things about Tahiti and on the boat—how could he know—he frightened me. And I've done something terribly foolish, Julie—I must have been mad.' She became rather incoherent then. I asked her what it was all about. 'Get the emerald,' she told me. 'We mustn't sell it, Julie. Denny's name is inside it, and I don't want any mention of that name now.'"

"She was hysteric, you say?"

"Yes. She was often that way, but this was worse, somehow. 'Denny Mayo won't die, Julie,' she said. 'He'll come back to disgrace me yet.' Then she urged me to get the ring, and of course I did. She told me we'd find something else to sell later. Just then she was too upset to discuss it. In the afternoon, I saw her crying over Denny Mayo's picture."

"Ah," cried Chan, "that was portrait of Denny Mayo mounted on green mat?"

"It was."

"Continue, please."

"Last night," Julie went on, "when Jimmy and I made our terrible discovery in the pavilion, I thought at once of what Shelah had said. Denny would come back to disgrace her yet. Somehow, I thought, his death must be connected with Shelah's. If only his name could be kept out of it—otherwise I didn't know what scandal might be revealed. So I slipped Denny's ring from her finger. Later, when I heard mention of the photograph, I ran upstairs and tore it into bits, hiding them under a potted plant.'"

Chan's eyes opened wide. "So it was you who performed that act? And later—when pieces of photograph scattered into wind—was it you who concealed large number of them?"

"Oh, no—you've forgotten—I wasn't in the room when that happened. And even if I'd been there, I wouldn't have been clever enough to think of that. Someone came to my aid at a critical moment. Who? I haven't the least idea, but I was grateful when I heard about it."

Chan sighed. "You have made everything a delay," he remarked, "and caused me to waste much precious time. I can admire your loyalty to this dead woman—" He paused. "*Haie*, I would enjoy to know such a woman. What loyalty she inspired. An innocent girl obstructs the police in defense of her memory, a man who could not have been guilty pleads to be arrested as her murderer, doubtless from same motive."

"Do you think Robert Fyfe took those lost bits of the photograph?" Bradshaw inquired.

Charlie shook his head. "Impossible. He had not yet arrived on scene. Alas! it is not so simple as that. It is not simple at all." He sighed. "I fear I will be worn to human skeleton before I disentangle this web. And you"—he looked at the girl— "you alone have melted off at least seven pounds."

"I'm so sorry," Julie said.

"Do not fret. Always my daughters tell me I am too enormous for beauty. And beauty is, of course, my only aim." He stood up. "Well, that is that. Jimmy, do not let this young woman escape you. She has proved herself faithful one. Also, she is most unexpert deceiver I have ever met. What a wife she will make for somebody."

"Me, I hope," Bradshaw grinned.

"I hope so, too." Charlie turned to the girl. "Accept him, and all is forgiven between you and me. The seven pounds is gladly donated."

She smiled. "That *is* an offer. Oh, Mr Chan, I'm so happy that everything is settled between us. I didn't like to deceive you—you're so nice."

He bowed. "Even the aged heart can leap at talk like that. You give me new courage to go on. On to what? Alas! the future lies hidden behind a veil—and I am no Tarneverro."

He left them standing together beneath a hau tree, and walked slowly to his car. Emerging from the drive, he narrowly escaped collision with a trolley. "Wake up, there!" shouted the motorman in rage, and then, recognizing a member of the Honolulu police force, sought to pretend he'd never said it. Charlie waved to him and drove on.

The detective was lost in a maze of doubt and uncertainty. The matter of the emerald ring was clear at last—but still he was far from his goal. One point in Julie's story interested him deeply. It had been Denny Mayo's picture that he had sought to put together the previous night.

Up to now he had thought himself balked in that purpose by someone who did not wish him to know the identity of the man over whose portrait Shelah had wept so bitterly. But might the motive not have been the same that prompted the destruction of the pictures at the library? The same person, undoubtedly, had been busy in both instances, and that person was bitterly determined that Inspector Chan should not look upon the likeness of Denny Mayo. Why?

Charlie resolved to go back and relive this case from the beginning. But in a moment he stopped. Too much of a task for this drowsy afternoon. "Much better I do not think at all," he muttered. "I will cease all activity and put tired brain in receptive state. Maybe subconscious mind sees chance and leaps on job during my own absence."

In such a state of suspended mental effort he turned his car into the drive of the Grand Hotel and, parking it, walked idly toward the entrance. A stiff breeze was blowing through the lobby, which was practically deserted at this hour of the day.

Sam, the young Chinese who rejoiced in the title of head bell-man, was alert and smiling. Charlie paused. There was a little matter about which he wished to question Sam.

"I hope you are well," he said. "You enjoy your duties here, no doubt?" Leading up, he would have called it.

"Plenty fine job," beamed Sam. "All time good tips."

"You know man they call Tarneverro the Great?"

"Plenty fine man. Good flend to me."

Charlie regarded the boy keenly. "This morning you spoke to him in Cantonese. Why did you do that?"

"Day he come, he say long time ago he live in China, knows Chinese talk plitty well. So he and I have talk in Cantonese. He not so good speaking, but he knows what I say allight."

"He didn't seem to understand you this morning."

Sam shrugged. "I don't know. This moahning I speak all same any othah day he has funny look an' say don' unnahstand."

"They are peculiar, these tourists," Chan smiled.

"Plenty funny," admitted Sam. "All same give nice tips."

Charlie strode on to the lounge, and through that to the terrace. He sat down there.

His vacation from thinking had been brief indeed, for now he was hard at it again. So Tarneverro understood the Cantonese dialect. But he did not wish Charlie Chan, whom he was so eager to assist in the search for Shelah Fane's murderer, to know that he understood it. Why was that?

A smile spread slowly over Charlie's broad face. Here at last was a fairly simple question. Tarneverro's initial act in helping to solve the murder had been the pointing out of the fact that the watch had been set back, and that the alibis for two minutes past eight were consequently worthless.

But would he have done that if he had not first overheard and understood Charlie's conversation with the cook—if he had not known that Wu Kno-ching had seen Shelah Fane at twelve minutes past eight and that the gesture with the watch was, accordingly, useless? His prompt display of detective skill had seemed, at the time, to prove his sincerity. But if he understood Cantonese, then he was simply making a virtue of necessity and was not sincere at all.

Charlie sat for a long time turning the matter over in his mind. Was his eager assistant, Tarneverro the Great, quite so eager as he appeared to be?

XIX

TARNEVERRO'S HELPING HAND

Val Martino, the director, came down the steps from the hotel lounge, a dashing figure in his white silk suit and flaming tie. He might have been the man on the cover of some steamship folder designed to lure hesitating travelers to the tropics. His gaze fell on Charlie, lolling at ease in a comfortable chair and looking as though he had not a care in the world. The director came over immediately.

"Well, Inspector," he remarked, "I scarcely expected to see you in such a placid mood just now. Unless you have already solved last night's affair?"

Chan shook his head. "Luck is not so good as that. Mystery still remains mystery, but do not be deceived. My brain moves, though my feet are still."

"I'm glad of that," Martino replied. "And I hope it gets somewhere soon." He dropped into a chair at Charlie's side. "You know that thing last night just plain wrecked two hundred thousand dollars' worth of picture for me, and I ought to hurry to Hollywood on the next boat and see what's to be done about it. Whoever killed Shelah certainly didn't have the best interests of our company at heart, or he'd have waited until I finished my job. Oh, well—it can't be helped now. But I must get away as soon as possible, and that's why I'm plugging for you to solve the problem at once."

Chan sighed. "Everybody seems to suffer from hurry complex. An unaccustomed situation in Hawaii. I am panting to keep in step. May I ask—what is your own idea on this case?"

Martino lighted a cigarette. "I hardly know. What's yours?" He tossed the match on to the floor, and the old Chinese with the dust-pan and brush came at once, casting a look at Charlie which seemed to say: "This is exactly the sort of person I would expect to find in your company."

"My ideas do not yet achieve definite form," Chan remarked. "One thing I do know—I am opposed in this matter by some person of extreme cleverness."

The director nodded. "It looks that way. Well, there were several clever people at Shelah Fane's house last night."

"Yourself included," Charlie ventured.

"Thanks. Naturally, that had to come from you. But it's true enough." He smiled. "I am speaking, of course, in confidence when I say there was another man present of whose cleverness I have never had the slightest doubt. I don't like him, but I've always thought him pretty smooth. I refer to Tarneverro the Great."

Chan nodded. "Yes, he is plenty quick. One word with him, and I had gathered that."

The director flicked the ash from his cigarette on to the floor. The old Chinese brought an ash-tray and set it close beside him on the small table.

"There are all kinds of seers and crystal-gazers fattening on the credulity of Hollywood," Martino continued. "But this man is the ace of the lot. The women go to him, and he tells them things about themselves they thought only God knew. As a result—"

"How does he discover these things?" Charlie asked.

"Spies," the director answered. "I can't prove it, but I'm certain he has spies working for him night and day. They pick up interesting bits of news about the celebrities, and pass them along to him. The poor little movie girls think he's in league with the powers of darkness, and as a result they tell all. That man knows enough secrets to blow up the colony if he wants to do it. We've tried to run him out of town, but he's too smart for us. You know, I'm rather sorry I stopped Jaynes last night when he wanted to beat Tarneverro up. I believe it would have been a grand idea. But on the other hand, Shelah's name would have been dragged into it, and remembering that, I broke up the row. The pictures are my profession, there are lots of fine people in the colony, and I don't like to see them suffer from harmful publicity. Unfortunately the decent ones must share the disgrace when the riffraff on the fringe misbehaves."

"Was it your intention," Chan inquired, "to hint that Tarneverro the Great may have killed Shelah Fane?"

"Not at all," responded Martino hastily. "Don't get me wrong. I was only trying to point out that if you sense a clever opponent in this affair, you should remember that there are few men cleverer than the fortune-teller. Further than that, I say nothing. I don't know whether he did it or not."

"For the time between eight and eight-thirty last night," Chan informed him, "Tarneverro has most unshakable alibi."

Martino stood up. "He would have. As I told you, he's as slick as they come. Well, so long. Good luck to you—and I mean that with all my heart."

He strolled off toward the glittering sea and left Chan to his thoughts. In a few moments the detective arose with sudden decision and went to the telephone booth in the lobby. He got his Chief on the wire.

"You very much busy now?" he asked.

"Not especially, Charlie. I've got a date with Mr and Mrs MacMaster here at five-thirty, but that's an hour away. Is anything doing?"

"Might be," Chan answered. "I cannot tell. But I will shortly require backing of your firm authority for little investigation at Grand Hotel. Pretty good idea if you leaped into car and rode out here at once."

"I'll be right with you, Charlie," the Chief promised.

Going to the house phone, Charlie called the room of Alan Jaynes. The Britisher answered in a sleepy tone. The detective informed him that he was coming up immediately to talk with him and then stepped to the hotel desk.

"Without calling room, can you ascertain if Mr Tarneverro is in residence?" he asked.

The clerk glanced at the letter box. "Well, his key isn't here," he said. "I guess that means he's in."

"Ah, yes," nodded Chan. "If you will be so kind, do this big favor for me. Secure Mr Tarneverro on wire, and say that Inspector Chan passed through here in too great rush to bother himself. But add that I desire to see Mr Tarneverro soon as can be in lobby of Young Hotel downtown. Say it is of fierce importance and he must arrive at once."

The clerk stared. "Downtown?" he repeated.

Chan nodded. "The idea is to remove him from this hotel for a brief space of time," he explained.

"Oh, yes," smiled the clerk. "I see. Well, I suppose it's all right. I'll call him."

Charlie went up to the room occupied by Alan Jaynes. The Britisher admitted him, yawning as he did so. He was in dressing-gown and slippers, and his bed was somewhat disheveled.

"Come in, Inspector. I've just been having forty winks. Good lord—what a sleepy country this is!"

"For the *malihini*—the newcomer—yes," Chan smiled. "We old-timers learn to disregard the summons. Otherwise we would get nowhere."

"You are getting somewhere, then?" Jaynes asked eagerly.

"Would not want to say that, but we are traveling at good pace—for Hawaii," responded Charlie. "Mr Jaynes, I have come to you in spirit of most open frankness. I am about to toss cards down flat on table."

"Good," Jaynes said heartily.

"This morning you told me you had never been in pavilion, never even loitered in neighborhood of place?"

"Certainly I did. It's the truth."

Charlie took out an envelope, and emptied on to a table the stub of a small cigar. "How, then, would you explain the fact that this is found just outside window of room in which Shelah Fane met sudden death?"

Jaynes looked for a long moment at this shabby bit of evidence. "Well, I'll be damned," he remarked. He turned to Chan, an angry light in his eyes. "Sit down," he said. "I can explain it, and I will."

"Happy to hear you say that," Chan told him.

"This morning, when I was in my bath," the Britisher began, "about eight o'clock, it must have been, someone knocked on my door. I thought it was the house-boy, and I called to him to come in. I heard the door open, and then the sound of footsteps. I asked who it was, and—why the devil didn't I break his neck last night?" he finished savagely.

"You have reference to the neck of Tarneverro the Great?" Charlie inquired with interest.

"I have. He was here in this room, and said he wanted to see me. I was rather taken aback, but I told him to wait. I stood up in the tub and began a brisk rub-down—will you come with me to the bathroom, Mr Chan?"

Surprised, Chan rose and followed.

"You will observe, Inspector, that there is a full-length mirror affixed to the bathroom door. With the door slightly ajar—like this—a person standing in the bath has a view of a portion of the bedroom—the portion which includes the desk. I was busy with my rub-down when I suddenly saw something that interested me keenly. A box of those small cigars was lying on the desk, with a few gone. I saw, in the mirror, Mr Tarneverro walk over and help himself to a couple of them. He put them in his pocket."

"Good," remarked Chan calmly. "I am much obliged to the mirror."

"At first I thought it was merely a case of petty pilfering. Nevertheless, I was deeply annoyed, and I planned to go out and order him from my room. But as I finished drying myself and got into my dressing-gown, it occurred to me that something must be in the air. I decided to say nothing, lie low, and try to find out, if possible, what the beggar was up to. I didn't guess—I'm a bit dense, I'm afraid—it never popped into my mind that he wanted to involve me in Shelah's murder. I knew he had no love for me, but somehow—that's not the sort of thing—"

"Well, I came out and asked him what he wanted. He looked me boldly in the eye and said he had just dropped in to urge that I let bygones be bygones, and shake hands on it. No reason why we shouldn't be friends, he thought. Felt that Miss Fane would wish it. Of course, I was aching to throw him from the window, but I controlled myself. Out of curiosity, I invited him to have one of my cigars. 'Oh, no, thanks,' he said. 'I never use them.'

"He ran on about Miss Fane, and how it would be best if we dropped our enmity of last night. I was cool but polite—I even shook hands with him. When he had gone, I sat down to think the thing out. What could have been his purpose in taking those cigars? As I say, I couldn't figure it. Now, of course, the matter is only too clear. He proposed to scatter a few false clues. By gad, Inspector—why should he take the trouble to do that? There's just one answer, isn't there? He murdered Miss Fane himself."

Chan shrugged. "I would be happy to join you in thinking that, but first several matters must be wiped away. Among others—an air-tight alibi."

"Oh, hell—what's that?" Jaynes cried. "A clever man always has an alibi." His heavy jaws snapped shut. "I appreciate what Mr Tarneverro tried to do for me—I do, indeed. When I see him again—"

"When you see him again, you will make no noise," Charlie cut in. "That is, if you wish to be of help."

Jaynes hesitated. "Oh—very good. But it won't be easy. However, I'll hold my tongue if you say so. Was there anything else you wanted?"

"No, thanks. You have supplied me with plenty. I go on my way with renewed energy."

Waiting for the elevator, Chan thought about Jaynes' story. Was it true? Perhaps. It seemed a rather glib explanation, but was the Britisher clever enough to concoct such a tale on the spot? He appeared to be a stolid, slow-thinking man—always going somewhere to be by himself and figure things out. Could such a man—Charlie sighed. So many problems!

He stepped cautiously from the elevator and peered round the corner. The coast seemed to be clear and he went to the desk. "Has Mr Tarneverro departed?" he inquired.

The clerk nodded. "Yes—he went out a moment ago, in a great hurry."

"My warmest thanks," Charlie said.

His Chief was coming up the hotel steps, and he went to greet him. Together they sought out a secluded corner.

"What's up?" the Chief wanted to know.

"Number of things," Chan replied. "Mr Tarneverro bursts into investigation and demands our strict attention."

"Tarneverro?" The Chief nodded. "That fellow never has sounded good to me. What about him?"

"For one point," Charlie answered, "he understands Cantonese." He told of making that discovery, which had served to turn his thoughts toward the fortune-teller. "But since I called you, even more important evidence leaps up," he added. Briefly he repeated Jaynes' story about the cigars.

The Chief whistled. "We're getting there, Charlie," he cried.

Chan shrugged. "You overlook Tarneverro's alibi—"

"No, I don't. I'll attend to that later. By the way, if you see that old couple from Australia about, keep out of their way. I've arranged for them to come to my office, as I told you, and I don't want to talk with them here. We can handle them better amid the proper surroundings. Now, what is it you want to do?"

"I desire," Chan answered, "to make complete search of Tarneverro's apartment."

The Chief frowned. "That's not quite according to Hoyle, Charlie. I don't know. We have no warrant—"

"Which is why I asked you to come. Big man such as you are can arrange it. We leave everything as we found it, and Tarneverro will not know."

"Where is he?"

Charlie explained the fortune-teller's present whereabouts. The Chief nodded. "That was a good idea. Wait here, and I'll have a talk with the management."

He returned presently, accompanied by a tall lean man with sandy hair. "It's all fixed," the Chief announced. "You know Jack Murdock, don't you, Charlie? He's going with us."

"Mr Murdock old friend," Chan said.

"Well, Charlie, how you been?" Murdock remarked. He was an ex-policeman, now one of the house detectives for the hotel.

"I enjoy the usual good health," Charlie replied, and with the Chief, followed Murdock.

After the house detective had unlocked the door and admitted them to Tarneverro's sitting-room, he stood looking at Chan with a speculative eye.

"Not going to rob us of one of our most distinguished guests, are you, Charlie?" he inquired.

Chan smiled. "That is a matter yet to be determined."

"Quite a little affair down the beach last night," Murdock continued. "And you're in the limelight, as usual. Some people have all the luck."

"Which they pay for by having also all the worry," Chan reminded him. "You are in soft berth here. Fish course last night was excellent. Did you taste it?"

"I did."

"So did I—and that was as far as I got," sighed Chan. "Limelight has many terrible penalties." He glanced about the room. "Our object is to search thoroughly and leave no trace. Fortune favors, however, for we have plenty time."

He and the Chief went to work systematically, while the house detective lolled in a comfortable chair with a cigar. The closets, the bureau drawers and the desk were all gone over carefully. Finally Charlie stood before a trunk. "Locked," he remarked.

Murdock got up. "That's nothing. I've a skeleton key that will fix it." He opened the trunk, which was of the wardrobe variety, and swung it wide. Chan lifted out one drawer, and gave a little cry of satisfaction.

"Here is one thing we seek, Chief," he cried, and produced a portable typewriter. Placing it on the desk, he inserted a sheet of note-paper and struck off a few sentences. "Just a word of warning from a friend. You should go at once to the Honolulu Public Library and—" He finished the note, and taking another from his pocket, compared the two. With a pleased smile he carried them to his Chief.

"Will you kindly regard these missives and tell me what they suggest to you?" he said.

The Chief studied them for a moment. "Simple enough," he remarked. "Both were written on the same machine. The top of the letter *e* is clogged with ink, and the letter *t* is slightly out of alignment."

Chan grinned and took them back. "Long time confinement in station house does not cause you to grow rusty. Yes—it is just as you say. Two notes are identical, both being written on this faithful little machine. Happy to say our visit here is not without fruit. I must now put typewriter in place so our call will go unsuspected. Or would go that way, if it was not for lingering odor of good friend Murdock's cigar.'"

The house detective looked guilty. "Say, Charlie—I never thought of that."

"Finish your weed. Damage is now done. But take care luxury of present job does not cause brain to stagnate."

Murdock did not smoke again, but let the cigar go out in his hand. Charlie continued to explore the trunk. He had about completed his search without further good fortune, when in the most remote corner of the lowest compartment, he came upon something which seemed to claim his interest.

He walked up to his Chief. In the palm of his hand lay a man's ring, a large diamond in a heavy-setting of gold. His superior stared at it. "Take good look," Chan advised, "and fix same in your mind."

"More jewelry, Charlie?"

Chan nodded. "Seeking to solve this case, it seems we wander lost in jewel store. Natural, perhaps, since we deal with Hollywood people." He restored the ring to its place, closed the trunk and locked it. "Mr Murdock, that will end business here."

They returned to the lobby, where the house detective left them. Chan accompanied the Chief out to the drive.

"What did you mean about the ring, Charlie," asked the latter.

"Little story which I have been perhaps too reluctant to repeat," smiled Chan. "Why? Perhaps because it concerns most distasteful moment of my long career. You will recall that last night, in house down the beach, I stood in middle of floor with letter written by Shelah Fane held firmly in my hand. Suddenly light goes out. I am most rudely struck in the face—struck and cut on the cheek, proving the assailant wore a ring. Lights go on, and the letter is gone."

"Yes, yes," cried the Chief impatiently.

"Immediately I make a survey—of the men in the room, who wears ring? Ballou and Van Horn—yes. Others do not. Mr Tarneverro, for example, does not. Yet yesterday morning, when I visited him in room, I noted that ring I have called to your attention, on his finger. What is more, when we rode down to Shelah Fane's house after news of murder, I perceived the diamond gleaming in the dark. I saw it again when he helps me make investigation in pavilion. Yet when lights flash on after theft of letter, ring is no longer in evidence. What would be your reaction to that, Mr Chief?"

"I should say," the Chief returned, "that Tarneverro struck that blow in the dark."

Charlie was thoughtfully rubbing his check. "Oddly enough," he remarked, "such was my own reaction."

XX

ONE CORNER OF THE VEIL

They went over and stood by Charlie's car. A puzzled frown wrinkled the Chief's brow. "I don't get this, Charlie."

"On which point," returned Chan placidly, "we are like as two reeds bending beside stream."

"Tarneverro hit you. Why?"

"Why not? Maybe he feels athletic."

"He'd just been telling you about that letter—hoping that the two of you would run across it somewhere—and when you got it he knocked you down and took it away from you."

"No doubt he wished to examine it in private."

The Chief shook his head. "Beyond me—way beyond me. He stole a cigar from Jaynes, hurried down and dropped the butt outside the pavilion window. He wrote a note to Van Horn, sending him off to the library on a fool's errand. He—he—what else has he done?"

"Perhaps he has murdered Shelah Fane," Charlie suggested.

"I'm sure he did."

"Yet he owns fine alibi."

The Chief looked at his watch. "Yes—I'll attend to that alibi at five-thirty, if those old people show up as they promised. What are you going to do now?"

"I follow you to join in that interview, but first I make stop at public library."

"Oh, yes, of course. Come as soon as you can. I—I think we're getting somewhere now."

"Where?" inquired Chan blandly.

"Lord knows—I don't," replied the Chief, and hurried to his own car. He got away first, and Charlie followed him through the big gates to Kalakaua Avenue.

It was nearly five o'clock, the bathing hour at Waikiki was on, and along the sidewalk passed a perpetual parade of pretty girls in gay beach robes and stalwart tanned men in vivid dressing-gowns. Other people had time to enjoy life, Charlie reflected, but not he. The further discoveries of the afternoon baffled him completely, and he had need of all his Oriental calm to keep him firmly on the pathway of his investigation. Tarneverro, who had sworn that his dearest wish was to assist in finding the murderer of Shelah Fane, had been impeding the search from the start. The fortune-teller's dark face, with its deep mysterious eyes, haunted Chan's thoughts as he flivvered on to town.

Stopping at the public library, he again appeared at the desk.

"Would you kindly tell me if the young woman in charge of reading-room is now on scene?" he asked.

The girl appeared, upset and indignant over the morning's events. She would never again leave a newspaper file idle on a table, but the Japanese boy whose work it was to return such items to the shelves was taking the day off. She remembered Van Horn, of course; she had seen him in the films.

"Were other striking personalities present in reading-room during the morning?" Charlie inquired.

The girl thought. Yes—she remembered one. A rather peculiar-looking man—she recalled especially his eyes. Chan urged her to a further description, and was left in no doubt as to whom she referred.

"Did you perceive him examining newspaper file left by actor?"

"No, I didn't. He came in soon after Mr Van Horn left, and stayed all morning, reading various papers and magazines. He seemed to be trying to pass the time."

"When did he leave?"

"I don't know. He was still here when I went out to lunch."

"Ah, yes," Chan nodded. "He would be."

"You think he cut the book?"

"I have no proof, and never will have, I fear. But I am sure he mutilated the volume."

"I'd like to see him in jail," said the girl warmly.

Charlie shrugged. "We have tastes in common. Thank you so much for significant information."

He drove quickly to the police station. The Chief, alone in his room, was gruffly talking over the telephone. "No—no—nothing yet." He slammed the receiver on to its hook. "Good lord, Charlie, they're hounding me to death. The whole world wants to know who killed Shelah Fane. The morning paper's had over a hundred cables. Well, what about the library?—Wait a minute."

The telephone was ringing again. The Chief's replies were none too gentle.

"That was Spencer," he announced, hanging up. "I don't know what's got into the boys—they seem to be helpless. They can't find a trace of that confounded beach-comber anywhere. He's of vital importance, Charlie; he was in that room last night—"

Charlie nodded. "He must assuredly be found. I am plenty busy man, but it seems I must go on his trail myself. As soon as interview with old people is ended—"

"Good! That's the ticket. You go out the first chance you get. What was I saying?—Oh, yes—the library. What did you find there?"

"No question about it," Charlie replied. "Tarneverro is man who destroyed pictures of Denny Mayo."

"He is, eh? Well, I thought so. Doesn't want you to know what this Mayo looked like. Why? I'll go mad if this keeps up. But there's one thing sure, and I'm clinging to it. Tarneverro's our man. He killed Shelah Fane, and we've got to pin it on him." Chan started to speak. "Oh, yes—I know—his alibi. Well, you watch me. I'll smash that alibi if it's the last act of my life."

"I was going to name one other objection," Chan told him gently.

"What's that?"

"If he contemplated killing of Shelah Fane, why did he announce first to me that we are about to arrest killer of Denny Mayo? Why, as my boy Henry would say, bring that up?"

The Chief put his head in his hands. "Lord, I don't know. It's a difficult case, isn't it, Charlie?" A plain-clothes man appeared at the door, announcing Mr Thomas MacMaster and wife. "Show them in," cried the Chief, leaping to his feet. "We can do one thing, anyhow, Charlie," he said. "We can smash that alibi, and when we've done that, maybe things will clear up a bit."

The old Scotch couple entered, and at the guileless and innocent look of them, the Chief received a severe shock. The old man approached Chan with outstretched hand.

"Ah, good evening, Mr Chan. We meet again."

Charlie got up. "Would you kindly shake hands with the Chief of Detectives. Mrs MacMaster, I would also present my superior officer to you. Chief desires to ask a few polite questions." He stressed the polite ever so slightly, but his superior got the hint.

"How do you do, madam," he said cordially. "Mr MacMaster—I am sorry to trouble you."

"No trouble at all, sir," replied the old man, with the rolled *r* of Aberdeen. "Mother and I have never had much to do wi' the police, but we're law-abiding citizens and glad to help."

"Fine," returned the Chief. "Now, sir, according to what you told Inspector Chan here, you are both old friends of the man who calls himself Tarneverro the Great?"

"Aye—that we are. It was in his younger days we knew him, and a splendid lad he was. We're deeply fond of him, sir."

The Chief nodded. "Last night you say you sat with him on one of the lanais of the Grand Hotel from a few minutes after eight until half past the hour."

"That is what we said, sir," MacMaster returned, "and we will swear to it in any court you put us in. It is the truth."

The Chief looked him firmly in the eye. "It can't be the truth," he announced.

"Why—why, what do you mean, sir?"

"I mean there's a mistake somewhere. We have indisputable evidence that Mr Tarneverro was elsewhere during that time."

The old man drew himself up proudly. "I do not like your tone, sir. The word of Thomas MacMaster has never been questioned before, and I have not come here to be insulted—"

"I don't question your word. You've made a mistake, that's all. Tarneverro left you at eight-thirty, you claim. Did you verify that by your own watch?"

"I did."

"The watch might have been wrong."

"It was wrong."

"What!"

"It was a wee bit fast—a matter of three minutes. I compared it with the hotel clock, which stood at eight-thirty-two."

"You're not—pardon me—a young man, Mr MacMaster?"

"Is that also forbidden by law in the States, sir?"

"What I mean is—your eyes—"

"My eyes, sir, are as good as yours, and better. Mr Tarneverro left us at eight-thirty—the correct time. He had been with us since we came out from our dinner, save for a brief period when he talked with a gentleman at the far end of the lounge. And during that time he did not leave our sight. That I say—and that I'll stand by"—he banged a great fist on the desk—"until hell freezes over!"

"Father—don't get excited," put in the old lady.

"Who's excited?" cried MacMaster. "You have to be emphatic wi' a policeman, Mother. You have to talk his language."

The Chief considered. In spite of himself, he was impressed by the obvious honesty of the old man. He had planned to bully him out of his testimony, but something told him such tactics would be useless. Hang it all, he reflected, Tarneverro did have an alibi, and a good one.

"You second what your husband says, madam?" he inquired.

"Every word of it," the old lady nodded.

The Chief made a helpless gesture, and turned toward MacMaster. "All right," he remarked. "You win."

Charlie stepped forward. "May I have honor to address few remarks to these good friends of mine?" he inquired.

"Sure. Go ahead, Charlie," replied the Chief wearily.

"I make simple inquiry," Chan continued gently. "Mr Tarneverro was young man starting career when he visited your ranch, I believe?"

"He was that," agreed MacMaster.

"An actor on theatrical stage?"

"Aye—and not a very successful one. He was glad of the work wi' us."

"Tarneverro very odd name. Was that what he called himself when he worked with you?"

The old man glanced quickly at his wife. "No, it was not," he said.

"What name did he offer at that time?"

MacMaster's jaw shut hard, and he said nothing.

"I repeat—what name did he offer when he worked with you?"

"I'm sorry, Inspector," the old man replied. "But he has asked us not to refer to the matter."

Chan's eyes flashed with sudden interest. "He requests that you do not mention his real name?"

"Yes. He said he had done wi' it, and asked us to think of him as Mr Tarneverro."

Charlie felt his way carefully. "Mr MacMaster, a serious situation looks us hard in the face. Murder was done last night. Tarneverro is not guilty man. You prove same yourself by offer of alibi, which is accepted by us in sincere spirit, because we know it is spoken same way. You have performed that favor for him. You do it gladly because you love truth. But more even dear friend has no right to ask of you. You have said you are law-abiding, and no one exists who is stupid enough to doubt that. I wish to know Mr Tarneverro's name when he was with you in Australia."

The old man turned uncertainly to his wife. "I—I don't know. This is a difficult position, Mother."

"You will not prove him murderer by giving it," Charlie continued. "Already you have saved him from that. But you will impede our work if you withhold same—and I am plenty certain you are not kind of man to do that."

"I don't understand," the Scotchman muttered. "Mother, what do you think?"

"I think Mr Chan is right." She beamed upon Charlie. "We have done enough when we swear to his alibi. If you won't tell, Father, I will. Why should a man be ashamed of his real name?—And it was his real name, I'm sure."

"Madam," said Chan. "You have proper view of things. Deign to mention the name."

"When we knew Tarneverro on the ranch," continued the old lady, "his name was Arthur Mayo."

"Mayo!" cried Chan. He and the Chief exchanged a triumphant glance.

"Yes. He told you this morning he was alone when he came to work for us. I can't think why he said that—it wasn't true. You see, he and his brother came to us together."

"His brother?"

"Yes, of course—his brother, Denny Mayo."

XXI

THE KING OF MYSTERY

Chan's breath came a little faster as he listened to this unexpected bit of news. Tarneverro was Denny Mayo's brother! No wonder, then, that the fortune-teller had been so eager to learn from Shelah Fane the name of Mayo's murderer. No wonder he had offered to help Chan to the limit of his ability in the task of finding out who had silenced Shelah just as she was, supposedly, on the point of telling.

And yet—had he carried out that promise to assist? On the contrary, he had evidently been placing in Chan's way every obstacle possible. Puzzles, puzzles—Charlie put his hand to his head. This man Tarneverro was the king of mystery.

"Madam, what you say is very interesting," the detective remarked. His eyes brightened. On one point, at least, light was breaking. "Will you be kind enough to tell me—was there resemblance in features between those two men?"

She nodded. "Aye, there was, though many people might not have noticed, because of the difference in age and coloring. Denny was blond, and Arthur very dark. But the first time I saw them, standing side by side in my kitchen, I knew they were brothers."

Chan smiled. "You have contributed something to our solution, madam, though up to moment of present speaking, only the gods know what. I think that is all we now require of you. Do I speak correctly, Chief?"

"Yes, that's right, Charlie. Mr MacMaster, I'm obliged to your wife and you for this visit."

"Not at all, sir," the old man answered. "Come, Mother. I—I'm not quite comfortable about this. Perhaps you've talked a wee bit too much."

"Nonsense, Thomas. No honest man is ashamed of his name—and I'm sure Arthur Mayo is honest. If he's not, he's sore changed from what he was when we knew him." The old lady rose.

"As for the alibi," her husband said stubbornly, "we stick to that—through thick and thin. Tarneverro was with us from eight to eight-thirty, and if the murder was done in that half-hour, he didn't do it. To that I'll swear, gentlemen."

"Yes, yes—I suppose you will," the Chief replied. "Good evening, sir. Madam—a great pleasure to meet you."

The old couple went out, and the Chief looked at Charlie. "Well, where are we now?" he inquired.

"Tangled in endless net, as always," Chan answered. "One thing I know—Tarneverro waits for me at Young Hotel. I will call him at once and request his presence here."

When he had done so, he came back and sat down beside his superior. His brows were contracted in thought.

"The case spreads itself," he remarked. "Tarneverro was Denny's brother. That ought to give us big boost toward our solution, but other way about, it only increases our worry. Why did he not tell me that? Why has he, as matter of fact, fiercely struggled to keep it from me? You heard what lady said about resemblance. That explains at once why all pictures of Mayo were torn to bits. Tarneverro was willing to travel long length to make sure we do not discover this fact just related to us." He sighed. "Anyhow, we have learned why portraits were destroyed."

"Yes, but that doesn't get us anywhere," the Chief replied. "If it was his brother who was killed, and he was on the point of asking you to arrest the murderer as soon as Shelah Fane revealed the name, I'd think that he would naturally tell you of his connection with Mayo—especially after the news of Miss Fane's death. It would have been a logical explanation of his interest in the case. Instead of telling you, he tries desperately to keep the relationship hidden." The Chief paused. "Strange none of these Hollywood folks ever noticed a resemblance between Mayo and the fortune-teller."

Chan shook his head. "Not likely they would. The two visit town at widely separated times, and were not seen together there. Many people, Mrs MacMaster said, would not note the resemblance, but Tarneverro flatters me by assuming I am one who would. As for others, he knows well it is the kind of likeness almost no one sees until it is pointed out. Then everybody sees it. Human nature is like that."

"Human nature is getting to be too much for me," growled the Chief. "What course do you propose to take with this fortune-teller when he gets here?"

"I plan to walk softly. We will say nothing about his many misendeavors, but we will speak of this thing we have just learned. What reasons will he give for his silence? They may have vast significance."

"Well, I don't know, Charlie. It might be better to keep him in the dark even on that point."

"Not if we pretend we hold no suspicion whatever. We will assume instead a keen delight. Now we know he has every reason to help us, and the skies brighten above our weary heads."

"Well, you handle him, Charlie."

A few moments later Tarneverro strode debonairly into the room. His manner was aloof and a bit condescending, as though he found himself in quaint company but was man of the world enough to be at home anywhere. He nodded at Charlie.

"Ah, Inspector, I waited for you a long time. I'd about given you up."

"A thousand of my humblest apologies," Chan returned. "I was detained by heavy weight of business. May I present my honored Chief?"

The fortune-teller bowed. "A great pleasure. How are you getting on, Inspector? I've been very eager to know."

"Natural you should be. Only a moment ago did we upearth fact which makes us realize how deep your interest is."

Tarneverro glanced at him keenly. "What do you mean by that?"

"I mean we discover that Denny Mayo was your brother."

Tarneverro stepped over and laid his walking-stick on a desk. The act, it seemed, gave him a moment for thought.

"It's true, Inspector," he remarked, facing Chan again. "I don't know how you found it out—"

Charlie permitted himself a quiet smile of satisfaction. "Not many things remain buried through investigation such as we are making," he remarked gently.

"Evidently not." Tarneverro hesitated. "I presume you are wondering why I didn't tell you this myself?"

Chan shrugged. "Undoubtedly you possessed good reason."

"Several reasons," the fortune-teller assured him. "For one thing, I didn't believe that such knowledge would help you in any way in solving the case."

"Which is sound thinking," Chan agreed readily. "Still—I must confess slight hurt in my heart. Frankness between friends is like warm sun after rain. The friendship grows."

Tarneverro nodded and sat down. "I suppose there's a great deal in what you say. I'm rather sorry I kept the relationship to myself, and I apologize most humbly. If it's not too late, Inspector, I will give you the whole story now—"

"Not at all too late," Chan beamed.

"Denny Mayo *was* my brother, Inspector, my youngest brother. The relationship between us was more like that of father and son. I was intensely fond of him. I watched over him, helped his career, took pride in it. When he was brutally murdered, the shock was a terrible one for me. So you can easily understand why I say"—his voice trembled with sudden passion— "that to avenge his death has been for three years my chief aim—indeed my only aim. If the person who killed Shelah Fane is the same man or woman who murdered Denny—then, by heaven, I cannot rest until justice is done."

He rose and began to pace the floor.

"When I heard the news of Denny's murder, I was playing in a London production. There was nothing I could do about it at the moment—I was too far away. But at my earliest opportunity I went to Hollywood, determined to solve the mystery of his death. I thought that the chances of my doing so would be better if I did not arrive in the picture colony as Denny's brother, but under an assumed name. At first I called myself Henry Smallwood—it was the name of a character I had lately played.

"I looked around. The police, it was evident, were completely at sea on the case. Gradually I became impressed by the number of seers and fortune-tellers of various sorts in Hollywood. They all seemed to be prospering, and it was rumored that they were the recipients of amazing confidences and secrets from the lips of the screen people.

"A big idea struck me. In my younger days I had been an assistant to Maskelyne the Great, one of a long line of famous magicians, and a man of really remarkable powers. I had some talent in a psychic way, had told fortunes as an amateur and had the nerve to carry the thing through. Why not, I thought, take an impressive name, set myself up as a crystal-gazer, and by prying into Hollywood's secrets, seek to solve the mystery of poor Denny's death? The whole thing looked absurdly simple and easy."

He sat down again.

"So for two years, gentlemen, I have been Tarneverro the Great. I have listened to stories of unrequited love, of overwhelming ambition, of hate and intrigue, hope and despair. It has been interesting, many secrets have been whispered in my ear, but until recently the one big secret I longed to hear was not among them. Then, out of a blue sky, yesterday morning at the Grand Hotel, my moment came. I finally got on the trail of Denny's murderer. It took all my will power to control myself when I realized what was happening. Shelah Fane told me she was in Denny's house that night—she saw him murdered. I had difficulty restraining myself—I wanted to leap upon her then and there and wring the name of his killer from her reluctant lips. Three years ago I would have done it—but time—well, we grow calmer with the passage of time.

"However, once I discovered she knew, I would never have left her until she told. When you saw me last night, Inspector, my hopes were running high. I proposed to take you with me to her home after the party, and between us I felt certain we could drag out that name at last. I intended to hand the guilty person over to you immediately, for"—he looked at the Chief—"I need hardly tell you that I have never thought of avenging the crime in any other manner. From the first, I proposed to let the courts deal with Denny's killer. That was, of course, the only sane way."

The Chief nodded gravely. "The only way, of course."

Tarneverro turned toward Chan. "You know what happened. Somehow this person discovered that Shelah was on the verge of telling, and silenced her for ever. On the very threshold of triumph, I was defeated. Unless you find out who killed poor Shelah, my years of exile in Hollywood will very likely go for nothing. That's why I'm with you—that's why I want"—his voice trembled again—"the murderer of Shelah Fane more than I've ever wanted anything in all my life before."

Charlie looked at him with a sort of awe. Was this the man who had been scattering all those false clues about the place?

"I am glad of this frankness, lately as it arrives," the detective said, with an odd smile.

"I should have told you at once, I presume," Tarneverro continued. "I was, as a matter of fact, on the point of explaining my relationship to Denny as we rode down to Shelah's house. But, I reflected, the information would not help you in the least. And I did not want it to become known why I was telling fortunes in Hollywood. If it did, of course my career there would be ended. Suppose, I said to myself, Inspector Chan fails to find Shelah Fane's murderer. In that case I must go back to Hollywood and resume my quest. They are still coming to me with their secrets. Diana Dixon consulted me today. That is why, until Denny's murderer is found, I do not want my real name made public. I rely on you gentlemen to be discreet."

"You may do so," Chan nodded. "Matter remains buried as though beneath Great Wall of China. Knowing how firmly you are with us in this hunt adds on new hope. We will find Shelah Fane's murderer, Mr Tarneverro—and your brother's all same time."

"You are making progress?" asked the fortune-teller eagerly.

Charlie regarded him fixedly. "Every moment we are approaching nearer. One or two little matters—and we are at journey's end."

"Good," said Tarneverro heartily. "You know now my stake in the affair. I hope you will forgive me that I didn't reveal it fully at the start."

"Explanation has been most reasonable," smiled Chan. "All is forgiven. I think you may now be excused."

"Thank you." Tarneverro glanced at his watch. "It is getting on toward the dinner hour, isn't it? I'm sorry that what I have told you is of no vital importance in your search. If there were only some really valuable contribution that I could make—"

Chan nodded. "Understand your feeling plenty well. Who knows? Your opportunity may yet arise." He escorted Tarneverro from the room, and out the front door of the station house.

When he returned, the Chief was slumped down in his chair. He looked up with a wry smile. "Well," he remarked, "what was wrong with that picture?"

Charlie grinned. "Pretty much everything," he responded. "Tarneverro plenty queer man. He wants to help—so he robs cigar from Mr Jaynes and drops same outside pavilion window. He thirsts for my success—so he writes note that causes me to waste time on innocent Mr Van Horn. He has mild little reason, of no importance, for not telling me he is Denny Mayo's brother—but he rages about destroying pictures of Denny as though he would keep matter from me or die in the attempt. He beholds letter in which may be written name of Denny's killer, and when I am about to open it, he kicks out light and smashes me in face." Chan rubbed his cheek thoughtfully. "Yes, this Tarneverro plenty peculiar man."

"Well, where do we go from here?" the Chief inquired. "It begins to look like one of your stone walls, Charlie."

Chan shrugged. "In which case, we circle about, seeking new path. Me, I get renewed interest in beach-comber. Why was he in pavilion room last night? More important yet, what was conversation he overheard between Shelah Fane and Robert Fyfe, for suppression of which Fyfe pays handsome sum?" He moved toward the door. "Kashimo has now played his game of hide-and-seek long time enough. I go to bestow inside small quantity of provisions, and after that I myself will do a little scouring of this town."

"That's the talk," his Chief cried. "You go after that beach-comber yourself. I'll eat downtown too, and come back here as soon as I've finished. You'll find me here any time after seven."

Charlie went to the telephone and called his house, getting his daughter Rose on the wire. He announced that he would not be home for dinner. A sharp cry of protest answered him.

"But, Dad,—you must come home. We all want to see you."

"Ah—at last you begin to feel keen affection for poor old father."

"Sure. And we're dying to hear the news."

"Remain alive a small time longer," he advised. "There are no news as yet."

"Well, what have you been doing all day?" Rose wanted to know.

Chan sighed. "Maybe I should put my eleven children on this case."

"Maybe you should," she laughed. "A little American pep might work wonders."

"That is true. I am only stupid old Oriental—"

"Who says you are? I never did. But Dad, if you love me, please hurry."

"I will speed," he answered. "If I do not, I perceive I cannot come home tonight."

He hung up the receiver and went to a nearby restaurant, where he ate a generous dinner.

Refreshed and fortified, he was presently strolling down King Street toward Aala Park. Dusk was falling over that littered stretch of ground, the campus of the undergraduates in the hard school of experience. They lolled about on the benches, some of them glancing up at Charlie with hostile eyes under discreetly lowered lids. There was muttering as he passed, an occasional curse from the lips of someone who had met the detective under circumstances none too pleasant. He paid no attention to any of them—he was seeking a man in a velvet coat and duck trousers that had once been white.

The Park yielded nothing. He crossed to a street of mean shops and shabby business. Above his head, on a fragile balcony, an enormous Filipino woman in a faded kimono puffed on an after-dinner cigar. Charlie moved along into a section of Honolulu quite unknown to tourists who breathed the pure air of the beach and raved about the beauty of these islands.

There was no beauty in the River District, only squalor and poverty; seven races jumbled together in an international slum. He heard voices raised in bitter argument, the weeping of children, the clatter of sandals, and, even here, the soft whine of Hawaiian music. *The Song of the Islands* floated lazily on the fetid air. Over a doorway that led to a dark and dirty stair, he saw the sign: "Oriental Cabaret."

He paused for a moment in the glare of the lights that formed this sign. A girl was approaching, dark-skinned, slender, graceful. He stood aside to let her pass, and saw her face. The tropics, lonely islands lost in vast southern seas—a lovely head against a background of cool green. Quickly he followed her up the stairs.

He came into a bare room with a sagging roof. There were many tables with blue and white checkered cloths; painted girls were eating at the rear. A suave little proprietor came forward, rubbing his hands with outward calm, but somewhat disturbed inside.

"What you want, Inspector?"

Charlie pushed him aside and followed the girl he had seen below. She had taken off her hat and hung it on a nail; evidently she worked here.

"Begging your pardon," Chan began.

She looked at him, fear and defiance mingling in her smoldering eyes. "What you want?"

"You are acquainted with *haole*—white man—Smith, the beach-comber?"

"Maybe."

"He painted your portrait—I have seen it. A beautiful thing."

The girl shrugged. "Yes, he come here, sometimes. I let him make the picture. What of it?"

"Have you seen Mr Smith lately?"

"Not for long time—no."

"Where does he live?"

"On the beach, I think."

"But when he has money—where then?"

The girl did not reply. The proprietor came forward. "You tell him, Leonora. Tell Inspector what he asks you to."

"Oh, well. Sometimes he live at Nippon Hotel, on Beretania Street."

Chan bowed. "Thank you so much." He wasted no time in that odorous cluttered room, but hastened down the dark stair. In a few moments he entered the Nippon Hotel. The sleek little Japanese behind the desk greeted him with a cordiality Chan knew was rankly insincere.

"Inspector, you honor my house."

"Such is not my purpose. *Haole* named Smith—he stops here?"

The clerk took a register from beneath the desk. "I look see—"

Charlie reached out and took the book from his slightly resisting hands. "I will see. Your eyes are notably bad. Archie Smith, room seven. Lead me there."

"Mr Smith out, I think."

"We will discover if he is. Please make haste."

Reluctantly the Japanese led him across an open courtyard, filled with a neglected tangle of plants and flowers. The Nippon Hotel was a cluster of shabby sheds, antiquated outbuildings. They stepped on to a lanai; a Japanese woman porter, bent low under a heavy tin trunk, staggered by. The clerk moved on into a musty hallway, and pointed to a door. The numeral seven—or what was left of it—hung by one nail on the panel.

"In there," said the Jap, and with a hostile look, disappeared.

Chan opened the door of number seven, and entered a dim low-ceilinged room. One dirty bulb was burning over a pine table, and at that table sat Smith, the beach-comber, with a canvas on his knees. He looked up, startled.

"Oh," he said. "So it's you?"

Chan regarded him sleepily. "Where you been all day?"

Smith indicated the canvas. "The evidence is right here, Inspector. I've been sitting in my palatial studio painting that courtyard outside. Glad you dropped in—it's been a bit dull since I finished." He leaned back in his chair and critically surveyed his work. "Come and look at this, Inspector. Do you know, I believe I've got something into it—a certain miasmic quality. Did you ever realize before that flowers can look mean and sinister? Well, they can—in the courtyard of the Nippon Hotel."

Chan glanced at the painting and nodded. "Yes, plenty good, but I have no time to be critic now. Get your hat and come with me."

"Where are we going—to dinner? I know a place on the Boulevard St.-Germain— "

"We go to the station house," Charlie replied.

"Wherever you say," nodded Smith, and putting aside the canvas, picked up his hat.

They crossed Aala Park to King Street. Chan regarded the derelict with an almost affectionate gaze. Before he and Smith parted company again, the beach-comber was going to tell him much—enough, perhaps, to solve his problem and put an end to all his worries.

The Chief was alone in the detectives' room. At sight of Charlie's companion, he brightened visibly. "Ah, you got him. I thought you would."

"What's it all about?" Smith asked jauntily. "I'm flattered, of course, by all these attentions, but— "

"Sit down," said the Chief. "Take off that hat." Thank heaven, here was someone who needn't be handled any too gently. "Look at me. A woman was killed last night at Waikiki, in a separate building on the grounds of her home. What were you doing in the room where she was killed?"

Beneath the yellow beard, Smith's face paled. He wet his lips with his tongue. "I was never in that room, Chief."

"You lie! We found your fingerprints on the window-sill. Look at me. What were you doing in that room?"

"I—I—"

"Come on, brace up. You're in a tight place. Tell the truth, or you'll swing for this. What were you doing—"

"All right," said Smith in a low voice. "I'll tell you about it. Give me a chance. I didn't kill anybody. It's true, I was in that room—in a way—"

"In a way?"

"Yes. I opened the window and climbed up on the sill. You see—"

"Kindly start at beginning," Chan cut in. "We know you arrived at window of pavilion to hear man and woman talking inside. What was said we pass over for the minute. You heard the man leaving the room—"

"Yes—and I went after him. I wanted to see him—but he got into a car and drove away down the avenue. I couldn't catch him. So I ambled back and sat down on the beach. Pretty soon I heard a cry—a woman's cry—from that pavilion. I didn't know what to do. I waited a while, and then I went over and looked through the window. The curtain was down, but it flapped about. Everything was quiet—I thought the place was empty. And then—well, really—I'm a little embarrassed about this. I'd never done such a thing before. But I was desperate—strapped—and when you're that way you get the feeling, somehow, that the world owes you a living—"

"Get on with it," barked the Chief.

"Well, just inside the window I caught a glimpse of—of a diamond pin. I thought there was no one inside, so I pushed up the screen and climbed on to the sill. I stooped over and picked up the pin—and then I saw her—the woman—lying over there by the table—stabbed, dead. Well, of course I realized at once that was no place for me. I lowered the screen, hid the pin in a little secret safety-deposit box of mine on the beach, and strolled as casually as I could to the avenue. I was still moving when that cop picked me up, an hour later."

"Is pin still on beach?" Chan inquired.

"No—I got it this morning." Smith reached into his trousers pocket and produced it. "Take it quick—I don't want it—don't let me ever see it again. I must have been crazy, I guess. But as I say—when you're down and out—"

Charlie was studying the pin. It was a delicate affair, a row of fine diamonds set in platinum. He turned it over. The pin itself was broken midway, and the end of it was lost.

The Chief was looking sternly at the beach-comber. "Well," he said, "you know what this means. We'll have to lock you up—"

"One moment, please," broke in Charlie. "Finding of pretty pin is good enough, but it is not vital to us. Vital matter is, what did this man hear Shelah Fane and Robert Fyfe saying to each other while he lingered outside pavilion window? Something of great importance—something Mr Fyfe made false confession to quiet—something he has paid Mr Smith nice sum to conceal. But now Mr Smith changes mind. He will not conceal it any longer."

"Oh, yes, I will," cried Smith. "I mean—it was nothing—nothing—"

"We hold you for theft," cut in Charlie. "Do you enjoy prisons? I think not. Neither does territory enjoy supporting you there. Under a certain circumstance, memory of theft might fade from our minds for ever. Am I speaking correctly, Chief?"

The Chief was dubious. "You think it's as important as that, Charlie?"

"It is of vast importance," Chan replied.

"All right." He turned to the beach-comber. "Tell us the truth of what you heard last night, and you can go. I won't press the charge. But—it's got to be the truth, this time."

Smith hesitated. His rosy dream of the mainland, decent clothes, respectability, was dying hard. But he shuddered at the thought of Oahu Prison.

"All right," he said at last. "I'll tell you. I hate to do it, but—oh, well—there's Cleveland. My father—a most punctilious man. Easily annoyed—growing old, you know. I've got to get out of this jam for his sake, if not for my own. When I came up to that window, Inspector—"

Chan raised his hand. "A moment, please, I have keen desire to see Robert Fyfe in this room when you tell the story." He looked at his watch. "I can reach him at hotel, I think. Excuse me." He took up the telephone and summoned Fyfe. Then he went over and sat down in a chair at the beach-comber's side. "Now we will rest as comfortable as may be. You, Smith, explore your mind and arrange story in advance. Kindly remember—the truth."

The beach-comber nodded. "You're on, Inspector. The truth this time." He looked down at his battered shoes. "I knew it was too good to last. Got a cigarette? No? Neither have I. Oh, well, life's like that."

XXII

WHAT THE BEACH-COMBER HEARD

They sat in silence, and the minutes dragged by. Smith's pale gray eyes stared hopelessly into the future, a future where he walked for ever, broke and forlorn, along a curving beach. Lighting a big cigar, the Chief picked up the evening paper. Charlie Chan took the diamond bar pin from his pocket and studied it, deep in thought.

Ten minutes passed, and then Robert Fyfe entered the room. He came in as though he were stepping on to a stage: suave, smiling, sure of himself. But as his gaze fell upon Smith the smile faded suddenly, and a frown replaced it.

"Good evening," the actor said. "I can give you about twenty minutes, Mr Chan, and then I must run. It wouldn't do to be late at the theater again tonight."

"Twenty minutes will be ample plenty," nodded Charlie. "Mr Smith and yourself have met before. Over here sits my Chief."

Fyfe bowed. "Ah, yes. I take it you have called me here for some important reason, Inspector?"

"Seems important to us," Chan answered. "I will squander no words. Last night you hold famous conversation with ex-wife in beach pavilion. The true contents of that talk have not yet been revealed. First when matter is discussed, you confess to crime you did not do, in order to change subject. Then, this morning, you discover yourself sudden lover of art, and buy picture from Smith, hoping to keep him quiet." He looked fixedly at the actor. "I rejoice you got nice painting, Mr Fyfe. Because that will be all you get. Smith cannot longer keep quiet. Smith is about to speak."

A look of distress crossed the actor's face, and was succeeded by one of anger. He wheeled about and faced the beachcomber. "You contemptible—"

Smith raised a protesting hand. "I know—I know. What a broken reed I've turned out to be. I'm as sorry about this as you are, old man. But these keen lads here have got something on me—something rather serious—it means prison unless I ditch you. And I've slept in the pure open air so much—somehow a prison cot doesn't appeal to me. Frightfully sorry, as I said, but I'm going to throw you over. By the way, have you got a cigarette?"

Fyfe glared at him for a moment, and then, shrugging his shoulders, opened a silver case and held it out. Smith helped himself.

"Thanks. It's a wretched affair, Mr Fyfe, and—no, that's all right, I've got a match—the sooner we get it over with, the better." He lighted the cigarette, and took a long pull at it. "To return to our favorite subject—last night on the beach—I went up to that pavilion window and they were in there together—this man and Shelah Fane. She was doing most of the talking—I got a look at her—lovely, even more so than in the films. I'd rather like to have painted her—wearing that cream-colored gown—"

"Come, come," cried the Chief. "Get on with it."

"That's what I'm trying to do. I just wanted to point out how beautiful she was—a woman like that ought to be allowed at least one—shot."

Chan stood up. "What is your meaning now?"

"I mean she'd taken it, anyhow. She was telling Mr Fyfe all about it—how three years ago, in Hollywood, she killed a man—"

With a groan Fyfe sank into a chair, and covered his face with his hands.

"Killed what man?" the Chief demanded.

"Ah, yes—the name." Smith hesitated. "Denny, I think she called him. Yes, that was it—Denny Mayo."

There was a moment's tense silence, and then Fyfe leaped to his feet. "Let me tell this," he cried. "It will sound dreadful, if he tells it. Let me explain about Shelah—she was emotional, impetuous. I'll try to make you understand—"

"I don't care who tells it," said the Chief. "But I want it told, and quick."

Fyfe turned to Chan. "You heard, Inspector, how she called me at the theater—a distracted, pitiful call—and said she must see me at once. I answered that I'd come after the show, but she said no, that might be too late. If I'd ever loved her, I must come at once. She had something to tell me, she wanted my advice, she was desperate. So—I went.

"I met her on the lawn; she seemed overwhelmed with anxiety and fear. We went to the pavilion and she burst at once into her story. Some years after our divorce, she told me, she met this Denny Mayo—she fell madly in love with him—I could picture it. I knew how Shelah loved. Wildly, unreasonably. Mayo seemed to care for her; he had a wife in London, a dancer in musical comedies, but he promised to divorce her and marry Shelah. For a time Shelah was happy—and then one night Mayo asked her to come to his house.

"That was three years ago—a night in June. She went to his place at the hour he had suggested. He told her that he was through; that his wife had had an accident and was unable to work any longer; that he believed he owed a duty to this woman—at any rate he was going to write her to join him in

Hollywood. Poor Shelah went a little mad then. Quite out of her senses. There was a revolver in the drawer of Mayo's desk, she got it, pointed it at him, threatened to kill him and herself. I have seen her in such moments; she was not responsible, I know. They struggled over the weapon, it went off in her hand. She stood looking down at Mayo, dead at her feet.

"She came to her senses then, I fancy. At any rate, she took her handkerchief and removed her fingerprints from the gun. She stole out of the house and went home unobserved. She was safe. Not once did the investigation point to her. Safe—but never happy again. From that day she lived in torment.

"A few weeks ago, in Tahiti, she met Alan Jaynes. She wanted to marry him, but she was haunted by that memory of the past. She'd fallen into the habit of consulting this fellow Tarneverro about everything; he had impressed her deeply with his cleverness. She sent for him to meet her here, and yesterday morning she went to his apartment.

"When she went there, she had no intention of telling him anything about Denny Mayo. She merely wanted him to read her future, to advise her as to whether a marriage with Jaynes would turn out happily. But he—he seemed to exert some mysterious power over her. Perhaps he hypnotized her. In any case, the first thing she knew, she found herself confessing the whole terrible story to the fortune-teller—"

"Stop!" cried Chan, with unaccustomed bruskness. "Ah, pardon me—one moment, please. You mean to say she told Tarneverro that she herself killed Denny Mayo?"

"Of course she did. I—"

"But Tarneverro relates different story."

"Then he lies. Shelah confessed to him that she had killed Denny—don't you understand—that's why she was so frightened, why she sent for me. I was the only one she could turn to, she said. She hadn't liked the light she saw in Tarneverro's eyes when she made her confession. She was deathly afraid of the man. She was sure he planned to use that confession in some way that would do her infinite harm. She clung to me, pleaded for my help. But what could I do? What was there to be done?"

Fyfe sat down as though exhausted by his story. "I tried to reassure her, promised to help her all I could—but I pointed out to her that I must get back to the theater at once. She begged me to stand by, stay with her—but you know, gentlemen, the show must go on. I had never disappointed an audience in my life—I refused to do it then. I left her and returned to town."

Again Fyfe buried his face in his hands. "If I had only stayed with her—but I didn't. The next thing I heard, poor Shelah was—murdered. I intended to tell the police the whole story at once, but somehow—when it came right down to it—I couldn't. Shelah, who had always been so straight and fine, such a good pal, so generous and kind. I pictured that blot on her past, that wild thing she had done in one irresponsible moment, cabled to the ends of the earth. She was gone. To find her murderer would never bring her back. No, I thought, keep Shelah's name unsullied. That's your job now.

"Then this accursed beach-comber came in and started his story. I went a little mad myself. I'd always loved Shelah—I loved her still—more than ever when I saw her last night. So I made my melodramatic confession to shut off the investigation. I don't know whether I'd have gone through with it or not—this morning when I woke up it seemed that I had carried chivalry a bit too far. Fortunately for me, I didn't have to go through with it—Mr Chan disproved my confession on the spot. But I had succeeded in my purpose, I had given Smith here a tip, and when he came to me today I was ready and willing to pay all I had to keep him quiet. I couldn't bear the thought of Shelah disgraced before the world that had so greatly admired her."

Charlie got up and laid his hand on the actor's shoulder. "You have caused me much trouble, but I forgive freely, for you are gallant gentleman. Pardon me if I grow tiresome with much pounding on one point, but it is of vast importance. You are quite sure that Miss Fane told her story to Tarneverro exactly as she told it to you?"

"Absolutely," Fyfe replied. "And if you can find any connection between Tarneverro and Denny Mayo, then the fortune-teller killed her. That's certain."

Charlie exchanged a long look with his Chief. The latter turned to Smith. "You can go along," he said. "And don't let me see you here again."

The beach-comber rose quickly. "You won't—not if it's left to me," he remarked. "Of course, if you keep dragging me in—" He walked over to Fyfe. "I really am sorry, old man. I want you to know—in one respect at least I kept my word—I haven't had a drink all day. I sat in my room—money in my pocket—sat there and painted a lot of wicked-looking flowers, with my throat as dry as the Sahara. It was a tough assignment, but I came through it. Who knows—maybe I've got a chance yet. Here"—he took a roll of bills from his pocket—"this is yours."

"Why, what is it?" Fyfe asked.

"Thirty-two bucks—all I've got left of the fifty. Sorry it isn't more, but I bought a bit of canvas and some brushes—a chap can't just sit in a room, you know."

Fyfe stood up, and pushed the money away. "Oh, that's all right. It was a rather good painting—that's how I feel about it. Keep the money and get yourself some decent clothes."

Smith's pale gray eyes shone with gratitude. "By heaven—you're a gentleman. It does a fellow good to meet you. I feel something stirring within me—can it be a great resolve? They tell me there's a scarcity of stewards on the boats. Tomorrow morning I'll buy myself some new things, and sign on for the trip to the coast. San Francisco—it's only a short walk from there to Cleveland. Yes—by the lord—I'll do it."

"Good luck to you," Fyfe answered,

"Thanks. May I trouble you—one more cigarette? You're very kind." He moved to the door, stopped and came back. "Somehow, Chief, I don't like to leave you. Will you do me a favor?"

The Chief laughed. "I might," he said.

"Lock me up until morning," the beach-comber went on. "Don't let me go into the street with all this money on me. I might be held up, or possibly—possibly—What I mean is, put me in a safe place overnight, and the chances of getting rid of me tomorrow will be a lot better than they look right now."

"With pleasure," nodded the Chief. "Come with me."

Smith waved a hand at Charlie Chan. "Remind me in the morning, Inspector, I owe you a dime—ten cents." He followed the Chief from the room.

Charlie turned to Fyfe. "You are now in demand at playhouse. I am deeply grateful for all you have told."

"Mr Chan—if you could only keep this thing about Shelah from reaching the public—"

Charlie shook his head. "I am so sorry, but I fear same cannot be done. The matter has vital connection with her murder."

"I suppose it has," Fyfe sighed. "Well, anyhow, you've been mighty decent to me, and I appreciate it."

Chan bowed him out.

Left alone, the detective stared thoughtfully into space. He was standing thus when the Chief strode again into the room. For a moment they regarded each other.

"Well," the Chief said, "so Tarneverro's story was a lie. And you've based your whole investigation on it. It's not like you, Charlie, to be tricked like that."

Chan nodded. "If I had time to do so, I would droop my head in shame. However, I choose now to forget the past. From this point on, my investigation takes new turn—"

"What do you mean—from this point on?" his Chief demanded. "The case is ended—don't you know that?"

"You think so?"

"I'm sure of it. In the morning Shelah Fane tells Tarneverro she killed Denny Mayo. Mayo was his brother. In the evening, she's found murdered. What could be simpler than that? I'm going to arrest the fortune-teller at once."

Charlie raised his hand. "No, no—I advise against that. You forget his alibi, solid as stone wall, not to be shaken."

"We'll have to shake it. It's evidently false. It must be. Either those old people are lying to save him, or else he tricked them as he tricked you—"

"I do not think so," Chan said stubbornly.

"What's the matter with you, Charlie? Losing your grip? We never had a clearer case than this. The little matter of the alibi—"

"Something else, too," Chan reminded him. "Why did Tarneverro say he would call me down the beach to arrest a murderer? His words stick in my mind and will not be unlodged. I tell you firmly, this problem not yet solved."

"I can't understand you, Charlie."

"Only one thing made clear by Mr Fyfe's interesting story. I know now why Mr Tarneverro did not wish me to open letter written by Shelah Fane. He feared I would learn at once his tale of seance with the lady was false in details, and house of cards would tumble about his ears. Fortunate for him, letter when finally opened was so worded as to add strength to his lie. 'Please forget what I told you this morning. I must have been mad—mad.' Then he knew that blow struck in the dark was not needed, after all. Must have wished to give himself a few resounding kicks." Chan paused. "Yes, Mr Tarneverro has muddled me with his deceit from very start, Still, I do not believe him guilty of murder."

"Well, what do you propose to do?" the Chief demanded. "Just sit here and twiddle your thumbs, with me to help you?"

"I am no thumb-twiddler," replied Chan with spirit. "I propose to act."

"On what? We have no more clues."

Charlie took the diamond pin from his pocket. "We have this." He handed it over. "Will you kindly oblige by making study of same?"

The Chief examined it. "The pin itself is broken in the middle, isn't it? Half of it seems to be gone."

Chan nodded. "Undubitably gone. And when we find that missing end, our case is solved."

The Chief looked puzzled. "What do you mean?"

"How was pin broken? When watch was smashed, murderer wished to provide further evidence of struggle that might make smashing of watch more probable. So he tore off orchid flowers and trampled them beneath foot. When he ripped off flowers, pin unfastened and came with them. No doubt it lay on floor, point uppermost. Perhaps that point drove deep into heel of murderer's shoe, and broke off there. Did this happen, and did it go unnoticed by killer? It might. If so, there may be tell-tale scratches on polished floors of house at Waikiki. I speed there at once to look for same."

The Chief pondered. "Well, there might be something in it, at that. I'll give you a chance to find out. Go along, and I'll wait here for news."

In the doorway, Charlie encountered Kashimo. The little Japanese was worn and dispirited. "Have combed town twenty, maybe fifty, times. Mr Smith no longer exists."

"A fine detective you are," growled the Chief. "Smith is out there in a cell now. Charlie found him."

Disappointment and distress showed in the eyes of the Japanese. Charlie paused at the door and came back. He patted the little man's shoulder.

"Cheer yourself up," he said kindly. "Be good boy, attend all meetings of Y. M. B. A., and you will yet win success. Nobody is perfect. Take look at me. Twenty-seven years on force, and I am nowhere near so clever as I thought I was."

He walked slowly from the room.

XXIII

THE FATEFUL CHAIR

Charlie rode out to the beach for what he hoped would be his final call at Shelah Fane's house. The moon had not yet risen, the sky was purple velvet pierced by ineffectual stars, the flowering trees hid their beauty somewhere in the calm breathless dark. Twenty-four hours ago, in this same period of impenetrable night before the coming of the moon, the black camel had knelt at Shelah Fane's gate.

Though he knew now the secret in the woman's past, knew that she had done a grievous wrong, he still thought of her with the deepest sympathy. She had never stood in court to answer for her crime, but she had suffered none the less. What torture those three years must have been! "Perhaps in the end I may find a little happiness. I want it so much"—thus she had written in her last pitiful note. Instead she had found—what? The black camel waiting to carry her away into the unknown.

Whatever the motive behind her murder may have been, Chan reflected, the act itself was heartless and cruel. He was firmly resolved that the person who had killed her should be found and made to pay. Found—but how? Would the little pin resting in his pocket come nobly to his aid? He hoped desperately that it would, for it was his sole reliance now.

The banyan tree's shade was like ink on the front lawn of the huge rambling building that had been the famous star's last home. Chan parked his car, switched off its lights, and leaped nimbly to the ground.

Jessop, serene and dignified as ever, let him in. "Ah, Constable, I was rather expecting you. What a pleasant evening to be abroad. Mild and fragrant, I should call it, sir."

Chan smiled. "I am too busy man, Jessop, to have concern with perfumes of the night."

"Ah, yes, I presume your time is fairly well occupied, Constable. Is there—if I may make bold to inquire—any news regarding the homicide?"

Chan shook his head. "Not up to present moment."

"I regret to hear that, sir. The young people are on the beach—Miss Julie and Mr Bradshaw, I mean. Whom did you wish to interrogate?"

"I wish to interrogate the floors of this house," Chan told him.

Jessop raised his white eyebrows. "Indeed, sir. My old father used to say that walls have ears—"

"Floors, also, may repeat a story," Charlie returned. "If you have no inclination for objecting, I will begin in living-room."

He pushed through the heavy curtains. Diana Dixon was sitting at the piano, softly playing. She got up.

"Oh, hello," she said. "You want somebody?"

"I want somebody very much," Chan nodded. "At end of trail I hope to find him—or her."

"Then you haven't yet discovered who killed poor Shelah?"

"I have not. But subject is unhappy one. Why are you not on beach? That is place for youth at this hour?"

Diana shrugged. "What's the beach without a man? And there aren't enough to go round, evidently."

"A situation rare in your neighborhood, I will wager," Charlie smiled.

"Oh, a change does us all good." She watched him as he stood there, looking impatiently about the room. "What are you going to do now? I'm so thrilled by all this—"

"Now, I am going to be unbearably rude," he replied. "I find myself in uncredible position of wanting to dispense with your company. Will you kindly wait on the lanai?"

She pouted. "I hoped you were going to ask me to help you."

"In such charming company as yours, I fear I could not keep mind on work." He held open the French window. "As a very great favor, please—"

With obvious reluctance she went out, and he closed the window after her. He did not wish to appear undignified in the presence of a witness, and it was his intention now to be undignified indeed. He turned on all the lights in the room and with some difficulty, got down on his knees. Taking a magnifying-glass from his pocket, he began a close scrutiny of the highly polished floor wherever it was uncovered by rugs.

For a long time he crept about, until his knees ached. But he did not mind that, for his efforts were richly rewarded. Here and there he encountered numerous little scratches which had been, without doubt, recently made. He breathed hard, and his black eyes shone with satisfaction.

Suddenly a brighter idea struck him. He scrambled to his feet and hurried to the dining-room. The table, he was happy to note, was the same size it had been on the previous evening. Jessop was putting away silver in the sideboard. He turned.

"I observe," Chan remarked, "that you have not yet reduced size of dining table."

"I couldn't, sir," replied the butler. "All the leaves are already out. The former occupants of this house, it would appear, were of a most hospitable temperament."

"Just as well," nodded Chan. He was pleased to see that the big table stood on the bare floor; the room was without rugs save for a small one that lay in the doorway. "Do me a great favor, if you will, Mr Jessop. Kindly place ten chairs about this board, in identical positions they occupied last night."

Puzzled, Jessop obeyed. When he had finished, Charlie stood for a moment in deep speculation.

"They now stand just as they did when you served dinner guests with coffee, some twenty-two hours ago?"

"Precisely," the butler assured him.

Without a word, Charlie pulled back a chair and disappeared beneath the table. One by one, mute evidence of his activity there, the chairs were pushed away, while Jessop stared with an amazement rarely seen on his imperturbable face. With a flash-light added to his equipment, Chan made the long circuit. Finally he came up as though for air.

"Were place-cards used for last night's dinner?" he inquired.

"No, sir. It was a rather informal affair, and Miss Fane told me she would seat the guests herself."

"Then when they came in here for coffee, they sat in no prearranged order?"

"Oh, no, sir. They just sat anywhere their fancy dictated."

"Is there chance you happen to remember who sat in which place?"

Jessop shook his head. "I'm sorry, Constable. It was a somewhat disturbing evening. I was a bit—unnerved, I fear."

Charlie laid his hand on the chair at the right of the one the hostess would no doubt have occupied. "You cannot, then, tell me who it was reclined here?"

"I'm afraid not, Mr Chan. One of the gentlemen, I fancy. But—I—I really don't know."

Charlie studied a moment. "Thank you so much. The telephone is in the hall closet, I believe?"

"Yes, sir. I will show you—"

"No need to trouble," Chan told him. "I will find it."

He went out to the hall and shutting himself in the hot cubby-hole under the stairs, made numerous calls. Finally he rang up his Chief.

"Inspector Chan speaking," he said. "May I humbly suggest that you bring one other good man with you, and come immediately to house of Shelah Fane?"

"Something doing, Charlie?" asked the Chief.

Chan pulled the door shut as far as it would go. Little beads of perspiration began to pop out on his forehead.

"Pin is about to lead us to success," he replied in a low voice. "On floor of living-room repose plenty fresh scratches. What is more, during time of investigation last night, guests who expected to enjoy dinner sat down round dining table for abbreviated repast. Floor is bare beneath table, and in front of one chair—and only one—more scratches are in evidence."

"Who sat in that chair?" the Chief demanded.

"The murderer of Shelah Fane," Chan answered. "The name I do not yet know. But I have just now summoned to house six guests, who, with three already here, make up complete list. When all are assembled we lead them to dining-room and ask them, please, to sit where they did last night. Chair of dead hostess was at head of table, facing door to hall. Note who sits down in chair at right of hostess. Same will be person we so hotly seek."

The Chief laughed. "Going to make a big drama out of it, eh, Charlie? Well, that's all right with me, so long as it means success. I'll be with you pronto."

Chan returned to the hall, mopping his brow. He caught a glimpse of the coat-tails of Jessop, hastily disappearing through the curtains of the dining-room door. With an idle step he moved along, and came finally to the lanai where he encountered Miss Dixon.

"Living-room is again at your disposal," he bowed.

She rose and came toward him. "Did you find what you were looking for?" she asked eagerly.

He shrugged. "Who in this world finds what he looks for? Success—what is it? A bubble that explodes when touched by human hand." And he strolled off toward the beach.

At his right, as he crossed the lawn, lay the pavilion, dark and empty tonight. Close by the sea, seated together in a beach chair intended for one person only, he came upon Julie and Jimmy Bradshaw. The boy rose.

"Why, it's good old Charlie," he cried. "Honolulu's noted sleuth. How are you, and what's the news?"

"News seems to be that spell of Waikiki Beach is still intact," Chan answered. "I am so sorry to interrupt this touching scene."

Bradshaw held out his hand. "Shake, Charlie. You're the first to hear about it. I'm going to be married. And oh, yes,—Julie is too."

"Plenty good news," returned Chan heartily. "May you have half the happiness I wish you—the full amount would be impossible."

"Oh, thank you, Mr Chan," Julie said.

"You're a great old scout," Bradshaw remarked. "I'll miss you. I'll miss this beach, too—"

"What is that? You leave Honolulu?"

"Oh—sure."

"You depart from this lovely spot, about which you have written one million words—"

"I've got to, Charlie. Have you ever stopped to think about the effect of all this languid beauty on a young man's character? Devastating, that's what it is. On this crescent beach, fanned by the warm breath of the south, and so on—what happens to him? He droops, he stagnates, he crumbles. No more coco-palms for me. Redwoods, Charlie. Do you know about the redwoods? They brace you up. They're my trees hereafter. A big lumber and sap man from the West—that's going to be my rôle."

Chan grinned. "You have failed to win Miss Julie to your views on Hawaii?"

"It looks that way. Sold it to fifty thousand tourists, but not to the girl I love. That's life, I suppose."

"When you go from here, you will leave much beauty behind," Charlie said. "But you will also take much beauty with you, since Miss Julie goes along."

"Which remark, Mr Bradshaw," Julie laughed, "should have come from you."

"It would have, presently," he answered.

Chan stood staring at the rising moon, the curve of lights along the whispering shore. The sad music of Hawaii came drifting up from the Moana courtyard, "To be young, in love, and on this beach," he said. "What greater happiness than that? Taste it to the full. It happens once, then time moves on. Moment comes when gold and pearls cannot buy back the raven locks of youth."

"Why, Charlie,—you're getting sentimental," Bradshaw cried.

Chan nodded. "I think of my own courtship on this shore—so long ago. How long, you wonder? I am now father of eleven children—judge for yourself."

"You must be very proud of them," Julie ventured.

"As proud as they will permit," Chan answered. "At least I have done my part to link past with future. When I move on, leaving eleven offspring, can any man say I have not been here? I think not."

"You're certainly right on that," Bradshaw assured him.

"May I speak with you in private for a moment?" Charlie said. He walked with the boy back toward the lights of the house.

"What's doing?" Bradshaw wanted to know.

"Plenty will be doing at any moment now. Within the hour I tell you who killed Shelah Fane."

"Good lord!" the boy gasped.

"First, I suggest a task for you. Miss Julie was Shelah Fane's dear friend. Go back and break news gently to her that it was Miss Fane who shot Denny Mayo. Same is now established beyond all doubt."

"You don't mean it?"

"I do. Impart news gently, as I request. Then blow will not hit her with such cruel force as in crowd of people. It will be unhappy shock for her, but she will soon forget. She has your love."

"All I've got, Charlie. Say—this is pretty considerate of you. But then—you think of everything."

"Within my limitations, I try to do so. When news is broken, both of you are to come at once to living-room."

"We'll do that, Charlie. Thanks."

As Chan entered the great room, Diana Dixon was greeting Martino, Van Horn and Jaynes, who had come down from the hotel together. The detective noted with satisfaction that all three were in dinner clothes—was it too much to hope they wore the same shoes as on the previous evening?

"Hello, Inspector," Martino said. "We came as soon as we could make it. What's in the air?"

"A little experiment," Chan answered. "Perhaps our case is *pau* tonight."

Jaynes was lighting a small cigar. "*Pau*—you mean finished? By jove, I hope so. They're holding a cabin for me on tomorrow's boat. I rely on you, Inspector."

"We all do," added the director. "I want to get off myself. Huntley—you and I might take that boat too."

Van Horn shrugged. "Oh—I don't care if I never leave. I was looking at that beach-comber last night. Shouldn't be surprised if he were the happiest man among us."

"Going primitive, eh?" Martino smiled. "I suppose it's the influence of that part you played down in Tahiti."

"It's the thought of Hollywood," responded Van Horn. "Of all the artificial places I've seen, that town wins the embossed medallion."

"Spoken like a true Californian," remarked Jimmy Bradshaw, entering with Julie. "Would you mind if I quoted you on that?

Famous picture actor prefers Honolulu's simple ways to the fevered swank of the film colony."

"You do," returned Van Horn grimly, "and I'll deny I ever said it."

"Alas!" grinned Bradshaw. "All the movie actors' best lines have to be left out of their interviews."

Wilkie Ballou and his wife came in. The former wore a linen suit, with white shoes, and Charlie was troubled. If Ballou took the chair that was waiting for someone in the dining-room, then his case might be far from proof even now.

"What's it all about?" Ballou demanded. "I was going to bed early tonight."

"Poor old Wilkie can't stand excitement," Rita remarked. "As for me, I love it. Hello, Diana,—what have you been doing today?"

The curtain parted, and Tarneverro stepped noiselessly into the room. He stood for a moment, staring about, a rather worried look in his dark eyes.

"Ah, yes," he said. "We're all here, aren't we?"

Jaynes got slowly to his feet, walked over and proffered a case. "Good evening," he remarked. "Will you have one of my cigars?"

"No, thank you," Tarneverro answered blandly. "I don't use them."

"So sorry," replied the Britisher. "I rather thought you did."

Charlie stepped hastily between them. "Will you be seated, please? We are all here, yes—except my Chief. We wait few minutes for him."

They sat down. Rita, Diana and Julie chatted together in low tones. The men were silent, staring into space.

Presently there was a clatter in the hall, and the Chief strode in. After him came Spencer, big and competent-looking. Chan leaped up.

"Ah, Chief,—now we may go forward. I have explained that we desire to make small experiment. You know some of these people—"

Wilkie Ballou shook the Chief's hand. "I'm glad to see you here," he remarked, with a glance toward Charlie.

"Mr Tarneverro is also known to you," Chan continued, oblivious. He introduced the others. "Now we will all proceed to dining-room," he finished.

"What! Another dinner party?" cried Rita Ballou.

"A peculiar dinner party," Chan told her, "at which no food will be served. Come this way, please."

They filed out, solemn and ill-at-ease now. The presence of the Chief and the burly policeman in uniform had served to impress them with the seriousness of the situation. Not unnaturally, they were asking themselves what all this meant? Was it a trap?

Jessop was on duty in the dining-room, grave and dignified. He waited, ready to seat them at the barren table with the same poise as though it had gleamed with silver, been snowy with linen.

"We are now about to make request," Chan said slowly. "I would remind you that this is important moment and you must think deep before acting. No mistake must be made. Will you kindly sit down at same places you occupied at this table last night?"

A little chorus of dismay greeted his words. "But I was so excited, I don't remember," cried Diana, and the others echoed her. For a moment they milled about, puzzled and uncertain. Then Jimmy Bradshaw dropped down at the foot of the table, opposite the empty chair of the hostess.

"I sat here," he announced. "I recall it perfectly. Julie, you were at my right. Mr Van Horn, you sat at my left."

Julie and the picture actor, with Jessop officiating, took their places.

"Mr Ballou, you were here beside me," Julie said, and Chan heaved a sigh of relief as the Honolulu man sank into his chair.

"So I was," Ballou remarked. "Thank you for remembering, my dear. Diana, you were at my right."

"True enough," Miss Dixon agreed, and Jessop held her chair. "And, Val, you were at my right."

"Of course," the director nodded, and sat down.

One side of the table was now completely filled—but it was not the side that interested Charlie.

"You were across from me, Rita," said Diana.

Mrs Ballou took her place.

Two chairs, aside from the one at the head of the table, remained vacant, with Jaynes and Tarneverro left to occupy them.

"I believe, Mrs Ballou, that I had the honor of sitting beside you," remarked Tarneverro, and took the chair at her right.

"So you did," Rita agreed. "And Mr Jaynes was on the other side." She indicated the chair at her left—the portentous chair before which were tiny scratches such as might have been made by a broken pin protruding slightly from the heel of a shoe.

"I fancy we have it now," smiled Jaynes innocently, and sat down.

There was a moment's silence. "You are seated just as you were last night?" Chan inquired slowly.

"We are not," said Huntley Van Horn suddenly.

"Something is wrong?" Charlie asked.

"It is. Mr Tarneverro is at my left now, but last night Mr Jaynes was in that position."

"Why, of course," Rita Ballou cried. She turned to Tarneverro. "You and Mr Jaynes have exchanged places."

"Perhaps we have," the fortune-teller answered amiably. He rose. Jaynes also got up, and took the chair at Rita's right. After a moment's hesitation, Tarneverro dropped into the fateful chair. "I fancy we're all set now," he remarked calmly. "Jessop, you may serve the soup."

Charlie and the Chief exchanged a look, and moved away from the neighborhood of the table. They went into the hall.

"Tarneverro," said the Chief softly. "I knew it. Take a look at his shoes—"

But Chan stubbornly shook his head. "Something is very wrong here," he insisted.

"Wrong, nonsense! What's got into you, anyhow, Charlie?"

"Extremely wrong," Chan continued. "You cannot convict a man with an alibi such as his. All broken pins in world would not avail."

"Then the whole thing's a flop, according to you?"

"So far—yes. But I do not despair. Permit me that I think a moment. There is some explanation of this. Ah, yes—come with me."

They returned to the dining-room. The group about that barren table looked at them expectantly.

"Kindly hold positions just as at present," Chan said. "I come back before I am missed."

He stepped through a swinging door into the kitchen, and they heard his voice in low converse with Wu Kno-ching, the cook. They waited in silence; even the obviously innocent appeared anxious and uneasy. Presently Charlie returned, walking with unwonted briskness and with a grim look on his face.

"Jessop," he said.

The butler stepped forward with a rather startled air.

"Yes, Constable?"

"Jessop, after these people departed last night, others sat at this table?"

The butler had a guilty look. "I'm extremely sorry, sir. It was not quite in order—I would not ordinarily countenance it in a well-run house, but things were rather at sixes and sevens—and we had had no dinner—so we just sat down for a bit of coffee; we needed it badly—"

"Who sat down?"

"Anna and I, sir."

"You and Anna sat down at this table, after the guests had gone? Where did you sit?"

"Over there—where Mr Martino is now seated, sir."

"And Anna—where did Anna sit?"

"She sat here, sir." And Jessop laid his hand on the back of Tarneverro's chair.

For a moment Chan was silent, staring at the butler with unseeing eyes. He sighed heavily, as one who after a long journey sights the end of the trail at last.

"Where is Anna now?" he asked.

"She is in her room, I fancy, sir, Upstairs."

Charlie nodded at Spencer. "Bring this woman at once," he ordered, and the policeman disappeared. Chan turned to the table. "Our little experiment is ended. Please step back to living-room."

They got up and filed silently across the hall. Charlie and the Chief waited at the foot of the stairway. The Chief said nothing, and Charlie also seemed disinclined to speak. Presently Spencer appeared at the head of the stairs, accompanied by Anna. They descended slowly. His eyes like black buttons in the half-light, Chan faced the woman. With cool unconcern, she returned his stare.

"Come with me," he said. He led her into the living-room, and stood for a moment looking at her feet. She wore high, black shoes, in keeping with her sober uniform. The right one, Charlie noted, seemed somewhat thick about the ankle.

"Anna, I must make very odd request of you," he said. "Will you be good enough to remove right shoe?"

She sat down, and began slowly to unlace it. Tarneverro came forward and stood at Chan's side. The detective ignored him.

He took the heavy shoe from Anna's hand, turned it over, and with his penknife slit the rubber heel. A little half-inch length of gold pin lay exposed, and with a gesture of triumph he lifted it out and held it up.

"You are all witnesses," he reminded them. He turned to Anna. "As for you, I fear you have been grossly careless. When you stamped those orchids under foot, you failed to note this telltale evidence of your act. Ah, well—but for such brief moments of neglect, we would get nowhere in this business." He gave his attention to the shoe. "I note braces built along the sides," he continued. "Meant to protect weak ankle, I think. You have had an accident, madam?"

"My—my ankle was broken—long ago," she replied, in a voice barely audible.

"Broken?" cried Charlie quickly. "When? How? Was it dancing on the stage you broke that ankle? Ah, yes—it was. Madam—I think you were once the wife of Denny Mayo."

The woman took a little step toward him. Her eyes were hard and defiant, but her usually dark face was white as Waikiki's sands.

XXIV

THE VEIL IS LIFTED

Charlie turned to Tarneverro. In the deep-set eyes of the fortune-teller he saw a reluctant admiration. He smiled.

"I have been plenty dense," he said. "This woman is on the scene by no coincidence. When you set up as lifter of the veil in Hollywood, you needed—what? Spies—spies to scatter about the place, and bring you morsels of gossip regarding film people. Your brother's wife had suffered accident, she was no longer able to work at profession, she was penniless and alone. You sent for her. What more natural than that action? You helped her to position, that she might help you."

Tarneverro shrugged. "You have a remarkable imagination, Mr Chan."

"No, no—you flatter me," Charlie cried. "It has just been proved I have not imagination enough. Only one claim I make for myself—when light at last begins to stream in, I do not close the shutters. Light is streaming in now. Anna's task was not alone to bring you trivial information—she was also to assist you in solving matter of Denny Mayo's murder. Was that why you placed her with Shelah Fane? Had you already some suspicion of Miss Fane? I think so. Yesterday morning in your apartment, actress confessed her misdeed to you. At once you inform Anna that victory has come. You are in high spirits.

Your own intention is honest one, you plan to hand Miss Fane to police. Otherwise you would not say to me what you did in Grand Hotel lounge last night. Then—what happened?"

"You tell me, Inspector."

"Such is my purpose. You learn that Shelah Fane is murdered. Without being told, you know who did the deed. The position is hard one for you, but mind works fast as usual. You invent false story about your seance with Shelah Fane, and boost me off on wrong trail at once. You talk about mythical letter Miss Fane was to write for you. Then, to your surprise and dismay, you find real letter was written. It may wreck plans at once, so you strike me down and obtain epistle. Needless act, as it turns out. You rage about, destroying photographs of Mayo to conceal relationship with him. You seek to befuddle me by involving innocent parties. Oh, you have been busy man, Mr Tarneverro. I might forgive you, but I find it difficult to forgive myself. Why have I been so stupid?"

"Who says you've been stupid, Charlie?" the Chief asked.

"I do, and I remark same with bitter force," Chan answered. "My little duel with this fortune-teller should have been finished long hours ago. Matter was clear enough. I knew he employed spies. I gathered—though I paid not enough attention to fact—that someone had been spying on Miss Fane in Tahiti and on returning boat. I learned that Anna here bought bonds—matter which might indicate more income than simple wage as maid. I listen to Tarneverro's alibi and feel certain he did not do murder himself. What, then, explains his actions? Natural inference for good detective would have been that he protects someone else. Who? I read in newspaper that Denny Mayo had wife. I discover Mayo was Tarneverro's brother, and I hear that Mayo was slain by hand of Shelah Fane. Later—crowning touch—I am told Mayo's wife encountered accident and can no longer follow profession. Do I put two and two together? Do I add up simple sum and get result? No—I fumble around—

I flounder like decrepit fish—finally I slide into happy harbor of success." He turned suddenly on Anna, standing pale and silent before him. "For I am in that harbor. It is true, is it not, madam? You killed Shelah Fane!"

"I did," the woman answered.

"Don't be a fool, Anna," Tarneverro cried. "Fight it out."

She gestured hopelessly. "What's the use? I don't care. I've nothing to live for—it doesn't matter what becomes of me. Yes, I killed her. Why not? She—"

"Just a moment," the Chief broke in. "Anything you say, you know, may be used against you."

"You're a little late with that, Chief," Tarneverro said. "She should have a lawyer—"

"I don't want one," Anna went on sullenly. "I don't want any help. I killed her—she robbed me of my husband—she wasn't content to take his love—she ended by taking his life. I've had my revenge, and I'm willing to pay for it. I intend to plead guilty, and get it over with at once."

"Fine," approved the Chief. He saw the territory saved the expense of a long trial.

"You're mad, Anna," cried the fortune-teller.

She shrugged. "Don't mind me. I wrecked all your plans, I fancy. I spoiled everything for you. Forget me and go your way alone."

Her tone was bitter and cold, and Tarneverro, rebuffed, turned away from her. Charlie offered her a chair. "Sit down, madam. I desire to make brief interrogation. It is true that Tarneverro brought you to Hollywood?"

"Yes." She accepted the chair. "I'll take it from the beginning, if you like. While Denny was acting in the pictures. I continued to dance in London music-halls. I was doing well, when I had that accident—I broke my ankle—I couldn't dance any more. I wrote to Denny about it, and asked if I could come to him.

I didn't receive any answer—and then I heard he had been killed.

"Arthur—Denny's brother here—was also playing in London at that time. He was kind to me—loaned me money—and then he told me he was going out to the States to learn who had killed poor Denny, if he could. After a time he wrote that he had set up in Hollywood as a fortune-teller, calling himself Tarneverro. He said he needed—help—that he could use me if I was willing to go into service. I had taken a position as wardrobe mistress with a manager for whom I used to dance. It was hard work—and the memories—I longed to get away from it all."

"So you went to Hollywood," prompted the Chief.

"I did, and I met Tarneverro secretly. He said he would place me with Miss Fane. He advised her to get rid of the maid she had, and sent me round the same day to apply for the position. He had discovered that Miss Fane and Denny were once—very close friends—and he thought I might be able to get on the trail of something in her house. He suggested that I change my appearance as much as possible—my way of doing my hair—he feared that Denny might have shown her pictures of me. I followed his instructions, but it was an unnecessary precaution. Denny—he must have lost my pictures—lost them or thrown them away. Miss Fane engaged me, and I was successful in the post. You see—I'd had maids myself. For a year and a half I was with her—helping Tarneverro. But I could discover nothing. Nothing about Denny, I mean.

"Yesterday afternoon Tarneverro and I met on the beach. He told me Shelah Fane had confessed to killing Denny—confessed it in his apartment that morning. He wanted to get a repetition of that confession with a witness to overhear—he planned it for last night in the pavilion. He would talk with her there alone, and I was to be hiding somewhere about. Then he proposed to send for an officer.

"I returned to this house, almost beside myself with hatred for the woman who had wrecked Denny's life—and mine. I got to thinking—sitting alone in my room. Tarneverro's plan began to look so very foolish to me. The police? I knew what one of your American juries would do with a woman like Shelah Fane—a beautiful, famous woman. They would never convict her—never. There were better ways than the police. I—I kept on thinking. I'm rather sorry I did."

Her eyes flashed. "No—I'm not. I'm glad. I planned it all out. Last night—during the party—that was the time. Plenty of people about—plenty of people who might have done it. I planned the alibi of the watch—I remembered it from a play in which Denny once acted. I was in the kitchen from twenty minutes before eight until ten after the hour. Jessop and the cook were there too. At eight-fifteen I located Shelah Fane in the pavilion—she was waiting there—waiting to make a good entrance on her party—as she always did. She was like that.

"I went to her room and got a knife—one she had bought in Tahiti. I wanted something to wrap it in—handkerchief—a big one. The door of the blue room was open—I saw a man's clothes. I went in and took the handkerchief from the pocket of the coat—Mr Bradshaw's coat, I think."

"As, yes," remarked Jimmy Bradshaw grimly. "Thanks for the ad."

"I went to the pavilion," Anna continued. "She didn't suspect. I came close to her—" The woman buried her face in her hands. "You won't make me tell that part. Afterward I broke the watch in the handkerchief, put it back on her wrist. But there was no other evidence of a struggle, so I tore off the orchids and trampled them under foot. I went out and buried the knife deep in the sand—I heard voices on the beach—I was frightened. I ran to the house, and went up to my room by way of the back stairs."

"And the handkerchief?" Charlie inquired. "You gave that to Mr Tarneverro when he arrived?"

"Just a moment," said the fortune-teller. "Anna—when did you and I last talk together alone?"

"On the beach, yesterday afternoon."

"Have we communicated with each other since that moment?"

She shook her head. "No."

"Have I heard you say before that you killed Shelah Fane?"

"No, you have not."

The fortune-teller looked at the Chief. "A little matter," he remarked, "that I am rather keen to bring out."

"But the handkerchief—?" The Chief turned to Anna.

"I dropped it on the lawn. I—I wanted it to be found there." She glanced at Bradshaw. "It wasn't mine, you know."

"Very thoughtful of you," bowed the boy.

"On the lawn, precisely," said Tarneverro, "where I picked it up."

"And put it in my pocket," remarked Martino. "By the way, I haven't thanked you for that."

"Do not trouble," Chan advised him. "You were not the only one Mr Tarneverro honored with his attentions."

The Chief went over to the woman's side. "Go upstairs," he said sternly. "And get ready. You'll have to go downtown with us. You can tell that story again—at the station." He nodded to Spencer to accompany her.

The woman rose, her manner sullen and defiant, and went from the room, with the policeman at her side.

"Well," said Ballou, "I guess we can all go now."

The Chief gave a sign of acquiescence. Wilkie and Rita left first, followed by Martino, Van Horn and Jaynes. The latter stopped to shake Charlie's hand.

"Thanks," he remarked in a low voice. "I shall make my boat. And on this boat—and all others in the future—I shall try to keep my head."

Diana went quietly up to her room. Chan turned to Julie.

"Go back to beach," he said gently. "Look up at stars, breathe clean fresh air and think of future happiness."

The girl gazed at him, wide-eyed. "Poor Shelah," she whispered.

"Shelah Fane's troubles over now," Chan reminded her. "Do poor lady great kindness, and forget. Jimmy here will help you."

Bradshaw nodded. "I certainly will." He put his arm about the girl. "Come on, Julie. One more look at the coco-palms, and then we're off for the coast, where trees are trees." They moved toward the French window. Bradshaw smiled at Chan over his shoulder. "So long, Charlie. I've got to go now and tone down my adjectives so they'll fit California."

They went out, and Chan turned back into the room to find his Chief staring speculatively at Tarneverro. "Well, Charlie," he remarked. "What are we going to do with our friend here?"

Chan did not answer, but thoughtfully rubbed his cheek. Tarneverro, seeing the gesture, smiled.

"I'm so sorry," he said. "I've made you a lot of trouble, Inspector. But I was in a horrible position—you can realize that. Should I have handed Anna over to you at once? Perhaps; but as I told you last night, I saw immediately that I was responsible for the whole affair. Innocently so, of course, but none the less responsible. I ought never to have told her—but I wanted a witness. If only I had kept my discovery to myself."

"The man who looks back sees his mistakes piled up behind," Chan nodded.

"But I never dreamed Anna would lose her head like that. These women, Inspector."

"They are primitive creatures, these women."

"So it would seem. Anna has always been a strange, silent, unfriendly person. But there was one bond between us—we both loved Denny. When she proved last night how desperately she loved him—well, I couldn't betray her. Instead I fought my duel with you. Fought to the limit of my ability—and lost." He held out his hand.

Chan took it. "Only the churlish are mean-spirited in victory," he remarked.

The policeman in uniform looked through the curtains.

"Right with you, Spencer," said the Chief. "Mr Tarneverro, you'd better come along. I'll talk to the Prosecutor about you. But you needn't be alarmed. We're not inclined to spend much money over here on chance visitors from the mainland."

Tarneverro bowed. "You're very encouraging."

"You got your car, Charlie?" the Chief asked.

"I have it," Chan told him.

The Chief and Tarneverro went into the hall, and presently Charlie heard the front door slam.

He stood for a moment looking about him at the bright room where his work was *pau* at last. Then, sighing ponderously, he stepped through the curtains and picked up his hat from a table in the hallway. Wu Kno-ching appeared suddenly from the dining-room.

Charlie gazed into the beady eyes, the withered yellow face of his compatriot.

"Tell me something, Wu," he said. "How was it I came upon this road? Why should one of our race concern himself with the hatreds and the misdeeds of the *haoles*?"

"Wha's mallah you?" Wu inquired.

"I am weary," sighed Chan. "I want peace now. A very trying case, good Wu Kno-ching. But"—he nodded, and a smile spread over his fat face— "as you know, my friend, a gem is not polished without rubbing nor a man perfected without trials."

The door closed gently behind him.

Charlie Chan Carries On

CONTENTS

I

RAIN IN PICCADILLY

Chief Inspector Duff, of Scotland Yard, was walking down Piccadilly in the rain. Faint and far away, beyond St. James's Park, he had just heard Big Ben on the Houses of Parliament strike the hour of ten. It was the night of February 6, 1930. One must keep in mind the clock and the calendar where chief inspectors are concerned, although in this case the items are relatively unimportant. They will never appear as evidence in court.

Though naturally of a serene and even temperament, Inspector Duff was at the moment in a rather restless mood. Only that morning a long and tedious case had come to an end as he sat in court and watched the judge, in his ominous black cap, sentence an insignificant, sullen-looking little man to the scaffold. Well, that was that, Duff had thought. A cowardly murderer, with no conscience, no human feeling whatever. And what a merry chase he had led Scotland Yard before his final capture. But perseverance had won – that, and a bit of the Duff luck. Getting hold of a letter the murderer had written to the woman in Battersea Park Road, seeing at once the double meaning of a harmless little phrase, seizing upon it and holding on until he had the picture complete. That had done it. All over now. What next?

Duff moved on, his ulster wrapped close about him. Water dripped from the brim of his old felt hat. For the past three hours he had been sitting in the Marble Arch Pavilion, a cinema theater, hoping to be taken out of himself. The story had been photographed in the South Seas – palm-fringed shores, blazing skies, eternal sunshine. As he watched it Duff had thought of a fellow detective, encountered some years before in San Francisco. A modest chap who followed the profession of man-hunting against such a background. Studied clues where the trade winds whispered in flowering trees and the month was always June. The inspector had smiled gently at the recollection.

With no definite destination in mind, Duff wandered along down Piccadilly. It was a thoroughfare of memories for him, and now they crowded about him. Up to a short time ago he had been divisional detective-inspector at the Vine Street station, and so in charge of the C.I.D. in this fashionable quarter. The West End had been his hunting preserve. There, looming in dignified splendor through the rain, was the exclusive club where, with a few quiet words, he had taken an absconding banker. A darkened shop front recalled that early morning when he had bent over the French woman, murdered among her Paris gowns. The white façade of the Berkeley brought memories of a cruel blackmailer seized, dazed and helpless, as he stepped from his bath. A few feet up Half Moon Street, before the tube station, Duff had whispered a word into a swarthy man's ear, and seen his face go white. The debonair killer wanted so badly by the New York police had been at breakfast in his comfortable quarters at the Albany when Duff laid a hand on his shoulder. In Prince's restaurant, across the way, the inspector had dined every night for two weeks, keeping a careful eye upon a man who thought that evening clothes concealed successfully the sordid secret in his heart. And here in Piccadilly Circus, to which he had now come, he had fought, one memorable midnight, a duel to the death with the diamond robbers of Hatton Garden.

The rain increased, lashing against him with a new fury. He stepped into a doorway and stared at the scene before him. London's quiet and restrained version of a Great White Way. The yellow lights of innumerable electric signs blurred uncertainly in the downpour, little pools of water lay shining in the street. Feeling the need of companionship, Duff skirted the circle and disappeared down a darker thoroughfare. A bare two hundred yards from the lights and the traffic he came upon a grim building with iron bars at the ground floor windows and a faintly burning lamp before it. In another moment he was mounting the familiar steps of Vine Street Police Station.

Divisional Inspector Hayley, Duff's successor at this important post, was alone in his room. A spare, weary-looking man, his face brightened at sight of an old friend.

"Come in, Duff, my boy," he said. "I was feeling the need of a chat."

"Glad to hear it," Duff answered. He removed the dripping hat, the soggy ulster, and sat down. Through the open door into the next room he noted a group of detectives, each armed with a halfpenny paper. "Rather quiet evening, I take it?"

"Yes, thank heaven," Hayley replied. "We're raiding a night club a bit later – but that sort of thing, as you know, is our chief diversion nowadays. By the way, I see that congratulations are again in order."

"Congratulations?" Duff raised his heavy eyebrows.

"Yes – that Borough case, you know. Special commendation for Inspector Duff from the judge – splendid work – intelligent reasoning – all that sort of thing."

Duff shrugged. "Yes, of course – thanks, old man." He took out his pipe and began to fill it. "But that's in the past – it will be forgotten tomorrow." He was silent for a moment, then he added: "Odd sort of trade, ours, what?"

Hayley gave him a searching look. "The reaction," he nodded. "Always feel it myself after a hard case. What you need is work, my boy. A new puzzle. No period for reflection between. Now, if you had this post—"

"I've had it," Duff reminded him.

"So you have – that's true. But before we dismiss the past from our minds – and it's a good plan, I agree with you – mayn't I add my own humble word of praise? Your work on this case should stand as an example—"

Duff interrupted him. "I had luck," he said. "Don't forget that. As our old chief, Sir Frederic Bruce, always put it – hard work, intelligence and luck, and of these three, luck is the greatest by far."

"Ah, yes – poor Sir Frederic," Hayley answered.

"Been thinking about Sir Frederic tonight," Duff continued. "Thinking about him, and the Chinese detective who ran down his murderer."

Hayley nodded. "The chap from Hawaii. Sergeant Chan – was that the name?"

"Charlie Chan – yes. But he's an inspector now, in Honolulu."

"You hear from him then?"

"At long intervals, yes." Duff lighted his pipe. "Busy as I am, I've kept up a correspondence. Can't get Charlie out of my mind, somehow. I wrote him a couple of months ago, asking for news of himself."

"And he answered?"

"Yes – the reply came only this morning." Duff took a letter from his pocket. "There are, it appears, no news," he added, smiling.

Hayley leaned back in his chair. "None the less, let's hear the letter," he suggested.

Duff drew two sheets of paper from the envelope and spread them out. For a moment he stared at those lines typed in another police station on the far side of the world. Then, a faint smile still lingering about his lips, he began to read in a voice strangely gentle for a Scotland Yard inspector:

"Revered and Honorable Friend:

"Kindly epistle from you finished long journey with due time elapsed, and brought happy memories of past floating into this despicable mind. What is wealth? Write down list of friends and you have answer. Plenty rich is way I feel when I know you still have space in honorably busy brain for thoughts of most unworthy C. Chan.

"Turning picture over to inspect other side, I do not forget you. Never. Pardon crude remark which I am now about to inscribe, but such suggestion on your part is getting plenty absurd. Words of praise you once heaped upon me linger on in memory, surrounded always by little glow of unseemly pride.

"Coming now to request conveyed in letter regarding the news with me, there are, most sorry to report, none whatever. Water falls from the eaves into the same old holes, which is accurate description of life as I encounter it. Homicides do not abound in Honolulu. The calm man is the happy man, and I offer no hot complaint. Oriental knows that there is a time to fish, and a time to dry the nets.

"But maybe sometimes I get a little anxious because there is so much drying of the nets. Why is that? Can it be that Oriental character is slipping from me owing to fact I live so many years among restless Americans? No matter. I keep the affair hidden. I pursue not very important duties with uncommunicative face. But it can happen that I sit some nights on lanai looking out across sleepy town and suffer strange wish telephone would jangle with important message. Nothing doing, to quote my children, who learn nice English as she is taught in local schools.

"I rejoice that gods have different fate waiting for you. Often I think of you in great city where it is your lot to dwell. Your fine talents are not allowed to lie like stagnant water. Many times the telephone jangles, and you go out on quest. I know in heart that success will always walk smiling at your side. I felt same when I enjoyed great privilege of your society. Chinese, you know, are very psychic people.

"How kind of you to burden great mind with inquiry for my children. Summing up quickly, they number now eleven. I am often reminded of wise man who said: To govern a kingdom is easy; to govern a family is difficult. But I struggle onward. My eldest daughter Rose is college student on mainland. When I meet for first time the true cost of American education, I get idea much better to draw line under present list of offspring and total up for ever.

"Once more my warmest thanks for plenty amiable letter. Maybe some day we meet again, though appalling miles of land and water between us make thought sound dreamy. Accept anyhow this fresh offering of my kind regards. May you have safe walk down every path where duty leads you. Same being wish of

"Yours, with deep respect,

"Charlie Chan."

Duff finished reading and slowly folded the missive. Looking up, he saw Hayley staring at him, incredulous.

"Charming," said the divisional inspector. "But – er – a bit naïve. You don't mean to tell me that the man who wrote that letter ran down the murderer of Sir Frederic Bruce!"

"Don't be deceived by Charlie's syntax," Duff laughed. "He's a bit deeper than he sounds. Patience, intelligence, hard work – Scotland Yard has no monopoly on these. Inspector Chan happens to be an ornament to our profession, Hayley. Pity he's buried in a place like Honolulu." The palm-fringed shore he had seen at the cinema flitted before his eyes. "Though perhaps, at that, the calm man is the happy man."

"Perhaps," Hayley answered. "But we'll never have a chance to test it, you and I. You're not going, are you?" For Duff had risen.

"Yes – I'll be getting on to my diggings," the chief inspector replied. "I was rather down when I came in, but I feel better now."

"Not married yet, eh?" Hayley inquired.

"Married no end," Duff told him. "Haven't time for anything else. Married to Scotland Yard."

Hayley shook his head. "That's not enough. But it's no affair of mine." He helped Duff on with his coat. "Here's hoping you won't be long between cases. Not good for you. When the telephone on your desk – what was it Chan said? – when it jangles with an important message – then, my boy, you'll be keen again."

"Water," Duff shrugged, "dropping from the eaves into the same old holes."

"But you love to hear it drop. You know you do."

"Yes," nodded the chief inspector. "You're quite right. As a matter of fact, I'm not happy unless I do. Goodby, and luck at the night club."

At eight o'clock on the following morning, Inspector Duff walked briskly into his room at Scotland Yard. He was his old cheery self; his cheeks were glowing, a heritage of the days on that Yorkshire farm whence he had come to join the Metropolitan Police. Opening his desk, he ran through a small morning mail. Then he took up his copy of the *Telegraph*, lighted a good cigar, and began a leisurely perusal of the news.

At eight-fifteen his telephone jangled suddenly. Duff stopped reading and stared at it. It rang again, sharply, insistently, like a call for help. Duff laid down his paper and picked up the instrument.

"Morning, old chap." It was Hayley's voice. "Just had a bit of news from my sergeant. Sometime during the night a man was murdered at Broome's Hotel."

"At Broome's," Duff repeated. "You don't mean at Broome's?"

"Sounds like an incredible setting for murder, I know," Hayley replied. "But none the less, it's happened. Murdered in his sleep – an American tourist from Detroit, or some queer place like that. I thought of you at once – naturally, after our chat last evening. Then, too, this is your old division. No doubt you know your way about in the rarified atmosphere of Broome's. I've spoken to the superintendent. You'll get your orders in a moment. Hop into a car with a squad and join me at the hotel at your earliest."

Hayley rang off. As he did so, Duff's superior came hastily into the room.

"An American murdered in Half Moon Street," he announced. "At Broome's Hotel, I believe. Mr Hayley has asked for help, and suggested you. A good idea. You'll go at once, Mr Duff—"

Duff was already in the doorway, wearing hat and coat. "On my way, sir."

"Good," he heard the superintendent say as he dashed down the stairs.

In another moment he was climbing into a little green car at the curb. Out of nowhere appeared a fingerprint expert and a photographer. Silently they joined the party. The green car traveled down the brief length of Derby Street and turned to the right on Whitehall.

The rain of the night before had ceased, but the morning was thick with fog. They crept along through an uncertain world, their ears assailed by the constant honking of motor horns, the shrill cries of police whistles. To right and left the street lamps were burning, pale, ineffectual blobs of yellow against a gloomy gray. Somewhere back of the curtain, London went about its business as usual.

The scene was in striking contrast with that the inspector had witnessed at the cinema the night before. No blazing sunlight here, no white breakers, no gently nodding palms. But Duff was not thinking of the South Seas. All that was swept from his mind. He sat hunched up in the little car, his eyes trying vainly to pierce the mist that covered the road ahead – the road that was to lead him far. He had completely forgotten everything else – including his old friend, Charlie Chan.

Nor was Charlie at that moment thinking of Duff. On the other side of the world this February day had not yet dawned – it was, in fact, the night of the day before. The plump inspector of the Honolulu police was sitting on his lanai, serenely indifferent to fate. From that perch on Punchbowl Hill he gazed across the twinkling lights of the town at the curving shore line of Waikiki, gleaming white beneath the tropic moon. He was a calm man, and this was one of the calmest moments of his life.

He had not heard the jangle of the telephone on Inspector Duff's desk at Scotland Yard. No sudden vision of the start of that little green car had flashed before him. Nor did he see, as in a dream, a certain high-ceilinged room in Broome's famous London hotel, and on the bed the for ever motionless figure of an old man, strangled by means of a luggage strap bound tightly about his throat.

Perhaps the Chinese are not so very psychic after all.

II

FOG AT BROOME'S HOTEL

To speak of Broome's Hotel in connection with the word murder is more or less sacrilege, but unfortunately it must be done. This quaint old hostelry has been standing in Half Moon Street for more than a hundred years, and it is strong in tradition, though weak in central heating and running water. Samuel Broome, it is rumored, started with a single house of the residential type. As the enterprise prospered, more were added, until today twelve such houses have been welded into a unit, and Broome's not only has a wide frontage on Half Moon Street, but stretches all the way to Clarges Street in the rear, where there is a second entrance.

The various residences have been joined in haphazard fashion, and a guest who walks the corridors of the upper floors finds himself in a sort of mystic maze. Here he mounts three steps, there he descends two more, he turns the most eccentric corners, doors and archways bob up before him where he least expects them. It is a bit hard on the servants who carry coals for the open fires, and hot water in old-fashioned cans for the guests who have not been able to secure one of the rare bathrooms, installed as a half-hearted afterthought.

But do not think that because it lacks in modern comforts, a suite at Broome's is easily secured. To be admitted to this hotel is an accolade, and in the London season an impossible feat for an outsider. Then it is filled to overflowing with good old county families, famous statesmen and writers, a sprinkling of nobility. Once it accommodated an exiled king, but his social connections were admirable. Out of the season, Broome's has of late years let down the bars. Even Americans have been admitted. And now, this foggy February morning, one of them had got himself murdered above-stairs. It was all very distressing.

Duff came through the Half Moon Street entrance into the dim, hushed interior. He felt as though he had stepped inside a cathedral. Taking off his hat, he stood as one awaiting the first notes of an organ. The pink-coated servants, however, who were flitting noiselessly about, rather upset this illusion. No one would ever mistake them for choir-boys. Almost without exception they seemed to date back to the days when Samuel Broome had only one house to his name. Old men who had grown gray at Broome's, thin old men, fat old men, most of them wearing spectacles. Men with the aura of the past about them.

A servant with the bearing of a prime minister rose from his chair behind the porter's desk and moved ponderously toward the inspector.

"Good morning, Peter," Duff said. "What's all this?"

Peter shook a gloomy head. "A most disturbing accident, sir. A gentleman from America – the third story, room number 28, at the rear. Quite defunct, they tell me." He lowered his quavering voice. "It all comes of letting in these outsiders," he added.

"No doubt," Duff smiled. "I'm sorry, Peter."

"We're all sorry, sir. We all feel it quite keenly. Henry!" He summoned a youngster of seventy who was feeling it keenly on a nearby bench. "Henry will take you wherever you wish to go, Inspector. If I may say so, it is most reassuring to have the inevitable investigation in such hands as yours."

"Thanks," Duff answered. "Has Inspector Hayley arrived?"

"He is above, sir, in the – in the room in question."

Duff turned to Henry. "Please take these men up to room 28," he said, indicating the photographer and the fingerprint man who had entered with him. "I should like a talk first with Mr Kent, Peter. Don't trouble – he's in his office, I presume?"

"I believe he is, sir. You know the way."

Kent, the managing director of Broome's, was resplendent in morning coat, gray waistcoat and tie. A small pink rose adorned his left lapel. For all that, he appeared to be far from happy. Beside his desk sat a scholarly-looking, bearded man, wrapped in gloomy silence.

"Come in, Mr Duff, come in," the manager said, rising at once. "This is a bit of luck, our first this morning. To have you assigned here – that's more than I hoped for. It's a horrible mess, Inspector, a horrible mess. If you will keep it all as quiet as possible, I shall be eternally—"

"I know," Duff cut in. "But unfortunately murder and publicity go hand in hand. I should like to learn who the murdered man was, when he got here, who was with him, and any other facts you can give me."

"The chap's name was Hugh Morris Drake," answered Kent, "and he was registered from Detroit – a city in the States, I understand. He arrived on last Monday, the third, coming up from Southampton on a boat train after crossing from New York. With him were his daughter, a Mrs Potter, also of Detroit, and his granddaughter. Her name – it escapes me for the moment." He turned to the bearded man. "The young lady's name, Doctor Lofton?"

"Pamela," said the other, in a cold, hard voice.

"Ah, yes – Miss Pamela Potter. Oh, by the way, Doctor Lofton – may I present Inspector Duff, of Scotland Yard?" The two men bowed. Kent turned to Duff. "The doctor can tell you much more about the dead man than I can. About all the party, in fact. You see, he's the conductor."

"The conductor?" repeated Duff, puzzled.

"Yes, of course. The conductor of the tour," Kent added.

"What tour? You mean this dead man was traveling in a party, with a courier?" Duff looked at the doctor.

"I should hardly call myself a courier," Lofton replied. "Though in a way, of course I am. Evidently, Inspector, you have not heard of Lofton's Round the World Tours, which I have been conducting for some fifteen years, in association with the Nomad Travel Company."

"The information had escaped me," Duff answered dryly. "So Mr Hugh Morris Drake had embarked on a world cruise, under your direction—"

"If you will permit me," interrupted Lofton, "it is not precisely a world cruise. That term is used only in connection with a large party traveling the entire distance aboard a single ship. My arrangements are quite different – various trains and many different ships – and comparatively a very small group."

"What do you call a small group?" Duff inquired.

"This year there are only seventeen in the party," Lofton told him. "That is – there were last night. Today, of course, there are but sixteen."

Duff's stout heart sank. "Plenty," he commented. "Now, Doctor Lofton – by the way, are you a medical doctor?"

"Not at all. I am a doctor of philosophy. I hold a large number of degrees—"

"Ah, yes. Has there been any trouble on this tour before last night? Any incident that might lead you to suspect an enmity, a feud—"

"Absurd!" Lofton broke in. He got up and began to pace the floor. "There has been nothing, nothing. We had a very rough crossing from New York, and the members of the party have really seen very little of one another. They were all practically strangers when they arrived at this hotel last Monday. We have made a few excursions together since, but they are still—Look here, Inspector!" His calmness had vanished, and his face was flushed and excited beneath the beard. "This is a horrible position for me. My life work, which I have built up by fifteen years of effort – my reputation, my standing – everything is likely to be smashed by this. In heaven's name, don't begin with the idea that some member of the party killed Hugh Drake. It's impossible. Some sneak thief – some hotel servant—"

"I beg your pardon," cried the manager hotly. "Look at my servants. They've been with us for years. No employee of this hotel is involved in any way. I'd stake my life on it."

"Then someone from outside," Lofton said. His tone was pleading. "I tell you it couldn't have been anyone in my group. My standards are high – the best people, always." He laid his hand on Duff's arm. "Pardon my excitement, Inspector. I know you'll be fair. But this is a serious situation for me."

"I know," Duff nodded. "I'll do all I can for you. But I must question the members of your party as soon as possible. Do you think you could get them together for me in one of the parlors of the hotel?"

"I'll try," Lofton replied. "Some of them may be out at the moment, but I'm certain they'll all be in by ten o'clock. You see, we are taking the ten-forty-five from Victoria, to connect with the Dover-Calais boat."

"You *were* taking the ten-forty-five from Victoria," Duff corrected him.

"Ah, yes, of course – we were leaving at that hour, I should have said. And now – what now, Inspector?"

"That's rather difficult to say," Duff answered. "We shall see. I'll go upstairs, Mr Kent, if I may."

He did not wait for an answer, but went quickly out. A lift operator who was wont to boast of his great-grandchildren took him up to the third floor. In the doorway of room 28, he encountered Hayley.

"Oh, hello, Duff," the man from Vine Street said. "Come in."

Duff entered a large bedroom in which the odor of flashlight powder was strong. The room was furnished in such fashion that, had Queen Victoria entered with him, she would have taken off her bonnet and sat down in the nearest rocking chair. She would have felt at home. The bed stood in an alcove at the rear, far from the windows. On it lay the body of a man well along in years – the late sixties, Duff guessed. It did not need the luggage strap, still bound about the thin throat of the dead man, to tell Duff that he had died by strangulation, and the detective's keen eyes saw also that the body presented every evidence of a frantic and fruitless struggle. He stood for a moment looking down at his newest puzzle. Outside, the fog was lifting, and from the pavement below came the notes of *Silver Threads among the Gold*, played by one of the innumerable street orchestras that haunt this section of London.

"Divisional surgeon been here?" Duff inquired.

"Yes – he's made his report and gone," Hayley replied. "He tells me the chap's been dead about four hours."

Duff stepped forward and removed, with his handkerchief, the luggage strap, which he handed to the fingerprint man. Then he began a careful examination of all that was mortal of Mr Hugh Morris Drake, of Detroit. He lifted the left arm, and bent back the clenched fingers of the hand. As he prepared to do the same with the right, an exclamation of interest escaped him. From between the lean stiff fingers something glittered – a link from a slender, platinum watch-chain. Duff released the object the right hand was clutching, and it fell to the bed. Three links of the chain, and on the end, a small key.

Hayley came close, and together they studied the find as it lay on Duff's handkerchief. On one side of the key was the number "3260" and on the other, the words: "Dietrich Safe and Lock Company, Canton, Ohio." Duff glanced at the blank face on the pillow.

"Good old boy," he remarked softly. "He tried to help us. Tore off the end of his assailant's watch-chain – and kept it, by gad."

"That's something," Hayley commented.

Duff nodded. "Perhaps. But it begins to look too much American for my taste, old chap. I'm a London detective, myself."

He knelt beside the bed for a closer examination of the floor. Someone entered the room, but Duff was for the moment too engrossed to look up. When he finally did so, what he saw caused him to leap to his feet, giving the knees of his trousers a hasty brush in passing. A slender and attractive American girl was standing there, looking at him with eyes which, he was not too busy to note, were something rather special in that line.

"Ah – er – good morning," the detective said.

"Good morning," the girl answered gravely. "I'm Pamela Potter, and Mr Drake – was my grandfather. I presume you're from Scotland Yard. Of course you'll want to talk to one of the family."

"Naturally," Duff agreed. Very composed and sure of herself, this girl was, but there were traces of tears about those violet eyes. "Your mother, I believe, is also with this touring party?"

"Mother is prostrated," the girl explained. "She may come round later. But just at present I am the only one who can face this thing. What can I tell you?"

"Can you think of any reason for this unhappy affair?"

The girl shook her head. "None whatever. It's quite unbelievable, really. The kindest man in the world – not an enemy. It's preposterous, you know."

Up from Clarges Street came the loud strains of *There's a Long, Long Trail A-Winding*. Duff turned to one of his men.

"Shut that window," he ordered sharply. "Your grandfather was prominent in the life of Detroit?" he added, to the girl. He spoke the name uncertainly, accenting the first syllable.

"Oh, yes – for many years. He was one of the first to go into the automobile business. He retired from the presidency of his company five years ago, but he kept a place on the board of directors. For the past few years he has been interested in charitable work – gave away hundreds of thousands. Everybody honored and respected him. Those who knew him loved him."

"He was, I take it, a very wealthy man?"

"Of course."

"And who—" Duff paused. "Pardon me, but it's a routine question. Who will inherit his money?"

The girl stared at Duff. "Why, I hadn't thought of that at all. But whatever isn't left to charity will, I suppose, go to my mother."

"And in time – to you?"

"To me and my brother. I fancy so. What of it?"

"Nothing, I imagine. When did you last see your grandfather? Alive, I mean."

"Just after dinner, last evening. Mother and I were going to the theater, but he didn't care to go. He was tired, he said, and besides he couldn't, poor dear, enjoy a play."

Duff nodded. "I understand. Your grandfather was deaf."

The girl started. "How did you know – oh—" Her eyes followed those of the inspector to a table where an ear-phone, with a battery attached, was lying. Suddenly she burst into tears, but instantly regained her self-control. "Yes – that was his," she added, and reached out her hand.

"Do not touch it, please," Duff said quickly.

"Oh, I see. Of course not. He wore that constantly, but it didn't help a lot. Last night he told us to go along, that he intended to retire early, as he expected today would be tiring – we were all starting for Paris, you know. We warned him not to oversleep – our rooms are on the floor below. He said he wouldn't, that he had arranged with a waiter to wake him every morning just before eight. We were down in the lobby expecting him to join us for breakfast at eight-thirty, when the manager told us – what had happened."

"Your mother was quite overcome?"

"Why not – such horrible news? She fainted, and I finally got her back to her room."

"You did not faint?"

The girl looked at Duff with some contempt. "I don't belong to a fainting generation. I was naturally terribly shocked."

"Naturally. May I step out of character to say that I'm frightfully sorry?"

"Thank you. What else can I tell you?"

"Nothing now. I hope very much that you can arrange for me to see your mother a moment before I go. I must, you understand. But we will give her another hour or so. In the meantime, I am meeting the other members of your travel party in a parlor below. I won't ask you to come—"

"Nonsense," cried the girl. "Of course I'll come. I'm no weakling, and besides, I want a good look at the members of this party. We haven't had time to get acquainted – the trip across was rather trying. Yes, I'll be there. This thing is too meaningless, too cruel. I shan't rest until I know what is behind it. Anything I can do, Mr—"

"Inspector Duff," he answered. "I'm glad you feel that way. We'll hunt the answer together, Miss Potter."

"And we'll find it," she added. "We've got to." For the first time she glanced at the bed. "He was so – so kind to me," she said brokenly, and went quickly out.

Duff stood looking after her. "Rather a thoroughbred, isn't she?" he commented to Hayley. "Amazing how many American girls are. Well, let's see. What have we? A bit of chain and a key. Good as far as it goes."

Hayley looked rather sheepish. "Duff, I have been an ass," he said. "There was something else. The surgeon picked it up from the bed – it was lying beside the body. Just carelessly thrown there, evidently."

"What?" Duff asked tersely.

"This." Hayley handed over a small, worn-looking bag of wash leather, fastened at the top with a slip cord. It was heavy with some mysterious contents. Duff stepped to a bureau, unloosed the cord, and poured the contents out on the bureau top. For a time he stared, a puzzled frown on his face.

"What – what should you say, Hayley?"

"Pebbles," Hayley remarked. "Little stones of various shapes and sizes. Some of them smooth – might have been picked up from a beach." He flattened out the pile with his hand. "Worthless little pebbles, and nothing else."

"A bit senseless, don't you think?" murmured Duff. He turned to one of his men. "I say – just count these, and put them back in the bag." As the officer set about his task, Duff sat down in an old-fashioned chair, and looked slowly about the room. "The case has its points," he remarked.

"It has indeed," Hayley answered.

"A harmless old man, making a pleasure trip around the world with his daughter and granddaughter, is strangled in a London hotel. A very deaf, gentle old soul, noted for his kindnesses and his benefactions. He rouses from sleep, struggles, gets hold of part of his assailant's watch-chain. But his strength fails, the strap draws tighter, and the murderer, with one final gesture, throws on to the bed a silly bag of stones. What do you make of it, Hayley?"

"I'm rather puzzled, I must say."

"So am I. But I've noted one or two things. You have too, no doubt?"

"I was never in your class, Duff."

"Rot. Don't be modest, old chap. You haven't used your eyes, that's all. If a man stood beside a bed, engaged in a mortal struggle with another man, his shoes would disturb the nap of the carpet to some extent. Especially if it were an old thick carpet such as this. There is no indication of any such roughing of the carpet, Hayley."

"No?"

"None whatever. And – take a look at the bed, if you please."

"By Jove!" The eyes of the Vine Street man widened. "I see what you mean. It's been slept in, of course, but—"

"Precisely. At the foot and at one side, the covers are still tucked into place. The whole impression is one of neatness and order. Was there a struggle to the death on that bed, Hayley?"

"I think not, Duff."

"I'm sure there was not." Duff gazed thoughtfully about him. "Yes – this was Drake's room. His property is all about. His ear-phone is on the table. His clothes are on that chair. But something tells me that Hugh Morris Drake was murdered elsewhere."

III

THE MAN WITH A WEAK HEART

After this surprising statement, Duff was silent for a moment, staring into space. Kent, the hotel manager, appeared in the doorway, his round face still harassed and worried.

"I thought perhaps I might be of some help here," he remarked.

"Thank you," Duff replied. "I should like to interview the person who first came upon this crime."

"I rather thought you might," the manager answered. "The body was found by Martin, the floor waiter. I have brought him along." He went to the door and beckoned.

A servant with a rather blank face, much younger than most of his fellows, entered the room. He was obviously nervous.

"Good morning," said Duff, taking out his notebook. "I am Inspector Duff, of Scotland Yard." The young man's manner became even more distressed. "I want you to tell me everything that happened here this morning."

"Well, sir, I – I had an arrangement with Mr Drake," Martin began. "I was to rouse him every morning, there being no telephones in the rooms. He preferred to breakfast below, but he was fearful of oversleeping. A bit of a job it was, sir, to make him hear, him being so deaf. Twice I had to go to the housekeeper for a key, and enter the room.

"This morning, at a quarter before eight, I knocked at his door. I knocked many times, but nothing happened. Finally I went for the housekeeper's key, but I was told it had disappeared yesterday."

"The housekeeper's key was lost?"

"It was, sir. There was another master key below-stairs, and I went for that. I had no thought of anything wrong – I had failed to make him hear me on those other mornings. I unlocked the door of this room and came in. One window was closed, the curtain was down all the way. The other was open and the curtain was up, too. The light entered from there. Everything seemed to be in order – I saw the ear-telephone on the table, Mr Drake's clothes on a chair. Then I approached the bed, sir – and it was a case of notifying the management immediately. That – that is all I can tell you, Inspector."

Duff turned to Kent. "What is this about the housekeeper's key?"

"Rather odd about that," the manager said. "This is an old-fashioned house, as you know, and our maids are not provided with keys to the rooms. If a guest locks his door on going out, the maids are unable to do the room until they have obtained the master key from the housekeeper. Yesterday the lady in room 27, next door, a Mrs Irene Spicer, also a member of Doctor Lofton's party, went out and locked her door, though she had been requested not to do so by the servants.

"The maid was forced to secure the housekeeper's key in order to enter. She left it in the lock and proceeded about her work. Later, when she sought the key, it had disappeared. It is still missing."

"Naturally," smiled Duff. "It was in use, no doubt, about four o'clock this morning." He looked at Hayley. "Deliberately planned." Hayley nodded. "Any other recent incidents around the hotel," he continued to Kent, "about which we should know?"

The manager considered. "Yes," he said. "Our night-watchman reports two rather queer events that took place during the night. He is no longer a young man and I told him to lie down in a vacant room and get a little rest. I have sent for him, however, and he will see you presently. I prefer that you hear of these things from him."

Lofton appeared in the doorway. "Ah, Inspector Duff," he remarked. "I find a few of our party are still out, but I am rounding up everybody possible. They will all be here, as I told you, by ten o'clock. There are a number on this floor, and—"

"Just a moment," Duff broke in. "I am particularly interested in the occupants of the rooms on either side of this one. In 27, Mr Kent tells me, there is a Mrs Spicer. Will you kindly see if she is in, Doctor Lofton, and if so, bring her here?"

Lofton went out, and Duff stepped to the bed, where he covered over the face of the dead man. As he returned from the alcove, Lofton reentered, accompanied by a smartly dressed woman of about thirty. She had no doubt been beautiful, but her tired eyes and the somewhat hard lines about her mouth suggested a rather gay past.

"This is Mrs Spicer," Lofton announced. "Inspector Duff, of Scotland Yard."

The woman stared at Duff with sudden interest. "Why should you wish to speak with me?" she asked.

"You know what has happened here this morning, I take it?"

"I know nothing. I had breakfast in my room, and I have not until this moment been outside it. Of course, I have heard a great deal of talking in here—"

"The gentleman who occupied this room was murdered in the night," said Duff, tersely, studying her face as he spoke. The face paled.

"Murdered?" she cried. She swayed slightly. Hayley was quick with a chair. "Thank you," she nodded mechanically. "You mean poor old Mr Drake? Such a charming man. Why – that's – that's terrible."

"It seems rather unfortunate," Duff admitted. "There is only a thin door between your room and this. It was locked at all times, of course?"

"Naturally."

"On both sides?"

Her eyes narrowed. "I know nothing of this side. It was always locked on mine." Duff's little stratagem had failed.

"Did you hear any noise in the night? A struggle – a cry, perhaps?"

"I heard nothing."

"That's rather odd."

"Why should it be? I am a sound sleeper."

"Then you were probably asleep at the hour the murder took place?"

She hesitated. "You're rather clever, aren't you, Inspector? I have, of course, no idea when the murder took place."

"Ah, no – how could you? At about four this morning, we believe. You have heard no one talking in this room within – say – the last twenty-four hours?"

"Let me think. I went to the theater last night—"

"Alone?"

"No – with Mr Stuart Vivian, who is also in our party. When I returned about twelve everything was very quiet here. But I did hear talking in this room – last evening, while I was dressing for dinner. Quite loud talking."

"Indeed?"

"It seemed, as a matter of fact, to be almost – a quarrel."

"How many people were involved?"

"Only two. Two men. Mr Drake and—" She stopped.

"You recognized the other voice?"

"I did. He has a distinctive voice. Doctor Lofton, I mean."

Duff turned suddenly to the conductor of the party. "You had a quarrel with the dead man in this room last evening before dinner?" he asked sternly. Distress was evident on the doctor's face.

"Not precisely – I wouldn't call it that," he protested. "I had dropped in to acquaint him with today's arrangements, and he began at once to criticize the personnel of the party. He said some of our members were not of the sort he had expected."

"No wonder he said that," put in Mrs Spicer.

"Naturally, my reputation is dear to me," Lofton went on. "I am not accustomed to that kind of criticism. It is true that this year, owing to bad business conditions at home, I have been forced to accept two or three people who would not ordinarily be taken. But whatever their station in life, they are quite all right, I'm certain. I resented Mr Drake's remarks, and no doubt the conversation became a bit heated. But it was hardly the type of misunderstanding that would lead to anything" – he nodded toward the bed – "like this."

Duff turned to the woman. "You heard none of that conversation?"

"I couldn't make out what was said, no. Of course I didn't particularly try. I only know they seemed quite intense and excited."

"Where is your home, Mrs Spicer?" Duff inquired.

"In San Francisco. My husband is a broker there. He was too busy to accompany me on this tour."

"Is this your first trip abroad?"

"Oh, no, indeed. I have been over many times. In fact, I've been around the world twice before."

"Really? Great travelers, you Americans. I am asking the members of Doctor Lofton's party to gather in a parlor on the ground floor at once. Will you be good enough to go down there?"

"Of course. I'll go immediately." She went out.

The fingerprint man came over and handed the luggage strap to Duff. "Nothing on it, Mr Duff," he remarked. "Wiped clean and handled with gloves after that, I fancy."

Duff held up the strap. "Doctor Lofton, have you ever noted this strap on the luggage of any of your – er – guests? It appears to be—" He stopped, surprised at the look on the conductor's face.

"This is odd," Lofton said. "I have a strap identically like that on one of my old bags. I purchased it just before we sailed from New York."

"Will you go get it, please," the inspector suggested.

"Gladly," agreed the doctor, and departed.

The hotel manager stepped forward. "I'll go see if the watchman is ready," he said.

As he left the room, Duff looked at Hayley. "Our conductor seems to be getting into rather deep water," he remarked.

"He was wearing a wrist-watch," Hayley said.

"So I noticed. Has he always worn it – or was there a watch on the end of a platinum chain? Nonsense. The man has everything to lose by this. It may wreck his business. That's a pretty good alibi."

"Unless he is contemplating a change of business," Hayley suggested.

"Yes. In that case, his natural distress over all this would be an excellent cloak. However, why should he mention that he owns a similar strap—"

Lofton returned. He appeared to be slightly upset. "I'm sorry, Inspector," he remarked. "My strap is gone."

"Really? Then perhaps this one is yours." The detective handed it over.

The doctor examined it. "I'm inclined to think it is," he said.

"When did you last see it?"

"On Monday night, when I unpacked. I put the bag into a dark closet, and haven't touched it since." He looked appealingly at Duff. "Someone is trying to cast suspicion on me."

"No doubt about that. Who has been in your room?"

"Everybody. They come in and out, asking questions about the tour. Not that I think any member of my party is involved. The whole of London has had access to my room the past five days. The maids, you will recall, asked us not to lock our doors on going out."

Duff nodded. "Don't distress yourself, Doctor Lofton. I don't believe you would be such a fool as to strangle a man with a strap so readily identified. We'll drop the matter. Now tell me – do you know who has that room there?" He indicated the connecting door on the other side. "Room 29, I fancy."

"That is occupied by Mr Walter Honywood, a very fine gentleman, a millionaire from New York. One of our party."

"If he is in, will you please ask him to step here, and then return to the task of gathering up your people below?"

After the doctor had gone, Duff rose and tried the door leading from Drake's room into number 29. It was locked from the side where he stood.

"Great pity about the strap," Hayley commented softly. "It lets Doctor Lofton out, I fancy."

"It probably does," Duff agreed. "Unless the man's remarkably subtle – it's my strap – naturally I wouldn't use it – it was stolen from my closet – no, men aren't as subtle as that. But it's rather unfortunate, for I don't feel like making a confidant of the conductor now. And we shall need a confidant in that party before we are finished—"

A tall handsome man in his late thirties was standing in the doorway leading to the hall. "I am Walter Honywood, of New York," he said. "I'm frightfully distressed about all this. I have, you know, room 29."

"Come in, Mr Honywood," Duff remarked. "You know what has happened, I perceive."

"Yes. I heard about it at breakfast."

"Please sit down." The New Yorker did so. His face was a bit florid for his age, and his hair graying. He had the look of a man who had lived hard in his short life. Duff was reminded of Mrs Spicer – the deep lines about the mouth, the weary sophisticated light in the eyes.

"You knew nothing about the matter until you were told at breakfast?" the detective inquired.

"Not a thing."

"That's odd, isn't it?"

"What do you mean?" An expression of alarm flashed across Honywood's face.

"I mean – in the next room, you know. You heard no cry, no struggle?"

"Nothing. I'm a sound sleeper."

"You were sleeping, then, when this murder took place?"

"Absolutely."

"Then you know when it took place?"

"Well – well, no, of course not. I was merely assuming that I must have been asleep – otherwise I should no doubt have heard—"

Duff smiled. "Ah, yes – I see. Tell me – the door between your room and this was always locked?"

"Oh, yes."

"On both sides?"

"Absolutely."

Duff lifted his eyebrows. "How do you know it was locked on this side?"

"Why – why, the other morning I heard the floor waiter trying to rouse the old gentleman. I unlocked the door on my side, thinking we could reach him that way. But his side was locked."

Honywood's man-of-the-world air had deserted him. He was perspiring, and his face had turned a sickly gray. Duff watched him with deep interest.

"I seem to have heard your name somewhere."

"Perhaps. I'm a theatrical producer in New York, and I've done a little of that sort of thing in London. No doubt you have heard also of my wife – Miss Sybil Conway, the actress. She has appeared on your side."

"Ah, yes. Is she with you?"

"She is not. We had a slight disagreement about two months ago, and she left me and came over to San Remo, on the Italian Riviera. She is there now. Our tour touches there, and I am hoping to see her, smooth over our difficulties, and persuade her to go the rest of the way around the world with me."

"I see," Duff nodded. The New Yorker had taken out a cigarette, and was holding a lighter to it. His hand trembled violently. Looking up, he saw the detective staring at him.

"This affair has been a great shock to me," he explained. "I got to know Mr Drake on the boat, and I liked him. Then too, I am not in the best of health. That is why I came on this tour. After my wife left me, I had a nervous breakdown, and my doctor suggested travel."

"I'm sorry," said Duff. "But it's rather odd, isn't it, Mr Honywood, that a man who has just had a nervous breakdown should be such – a sound sleeper?"

Honywood appeared startled. "I – I have never had any trouble that way," he replied.

"You're very fortunate," Duff told him. "I am meeting all the members of your party on the ground floor." He explained this again, and sent the New Yorker below to await him. When the man was out of hearing Duff turned to Hayley.

"What do you make of that, old chap?" he inquired.

"In a frightful funk, wasn't he?"

"I don't believe I ever saw a man in a worse," Duff agreed. "He knows a lot more than he's telling, and he's a badly rattled lad. But confound it, that's not evidence. Slowly, old man – we must go slowly – but we mustn't forget Mr Honywood. He knew when the murder took place, he knew that the door was locked on both sides. And he has been suffering from a nervous breakdown – we'll have to admit he looks it – yet he sleeps as soundly as a child. Yes, we must keep Mr Honywood in mind."

Kent came in again, this time accompanied by an old servant who was built along the general lines of Mr Pickwick.

"This is Eben, our night-watchman," the manager explained. "You'll want to hear his story, Inspector?"

"At once," Duff answered. "What have you to tell, Eben?"

"It's this way, sir," the old man began. "I make my rounds of the house every hour, on the hour, punching the clocks. When I came on to this floor last night, on my two o'clock round, I saw a gentleman standing before one of the doors."

"Which door?"

"I'm a bit confused about it, sir, but I think it was number 27."

"Twenty-seven. That's the Spicer woman's room. Go on."

"Well, sir, when he heard me, he turned quickly and came toward where I was standing, at the head of the stairs. 'Good evening,' he said. 'I'm afraid I'm on the wrong floor. My room is below.' He had the air of a gentleman, a guest, so I let him pass. I fancy I should have questioned him, sir, but here at Broome's we have never had any queer doings – up to now – so I didn't think of it."

"You saw his face?"

"Quite clearly, sir. The light was burning in the corridor. I saw him, and I can identify him if he is still about."

"Good." Duff rose. "We'll have you look over the members of Doctor Lofton's party immediately."

"One moment, sir. I had another little adventure."

"Oh, you did? What was that?"

"On my four o'clock round, when I reached this floor, the light was no longer burning. Everything was black darkness. 'Burnt out,' I thought, and I reached for my electric torch. Suddenly, as I put my hand to my pocket, I was conscious of someone standing at my side. Just felt him there, sir, breathing hard in the quiet night. I got the torch out and flashed it on. I saw the person was wearing gray clothes, sir – and then the torch was knocked from my hand. We struggled there, at the top of the stairs – but I'm not so young as I once was. I did get hold of the pocket of his coat – the right-hand pocket – trying to capture him and he trying to break away. I heard the cloth tear a bit. Then he struck me and I fell. I was out for a second, and when I knew where I was again, he had gone."

"But you are certain that he wore a gray suit? And that you tore the right-hand pocket of his coat?"

"I'd swear to those two points, sir."

"Did you get any idea at this time that you were dealing with the same man you had encountered on your two o'clock round?"

"I couldn't be sure of that, sir. The second one seemed a bit heavier. But that might have been my imagination, as it were."

"What did you do next?"

"I went downstairs and told the night porter. Together we searched the entire house as thoroughly as we could without disturbing any of the guests. We found no one. We debated about the police – but this is a very respectable and famous hotel, sir, and it seemed best—"

"Quite right, too," the manager put in.

"It seemed best to keep out of the daily press, if possible. So we did nothing more then, but of course I reported both incidents to Mr Kent when he arrived this morning."

"You've been with Broome's a long time, Eben?" Duff inquired.

"Forty-eight years, sir. I came here as a boy of fourteen."

"A splendid record," the inspector said. "Will you please go now and wait in Mr Kent's office. I shall want you later on."

"With pleasure, sir," the watchman replied, and went out.

Duff turned to Hayley. "I'm going down to meet that round the world crowd," he remarked. "If you don't mind a suggestion, old chap, you might get a few of your men in from the station and, while I'm holding these people below-stairs, have a look at their rooms. Mr Kent will no doubt be happy to act as your guide."

"I should hardly put it that way," said Kent gloomily. "However, if it must be done—"

"I'm afraid it must. A torn bit of watch-chain – a gray coat with the pocket ripped – it's hardly likely you'll succeed, Hayley. But of course we dare not overlook anything." He turned to the fingerprint expert and the photographer, who were still on the scene. "You lads finished yet?"

"Just about, sir," the fingerprint man answered.

"Wait for me here, both of you, and clear up all odds and ends," Duff directed. He went with Hayley and Kent into the hall. There he stood, looking about him. "Just four rooms on this corridor," he remarked. "Rooms 27, 28 and 29, occupied by Mrs Spicer, poor Drake and Honywood. Can you tell me who has room 30 – the only one remaining? The one next to Honywood?"

"That is occupied by a Mr Patrick Tait," Kent replied. "Another member of the Lofton party. A man of about sixty, very distinguished-looking – for an American. I believe he has been a well-known criminal lawyer in the States. Unfortunately he suffers from a weak heart, and so he is accompanied by a traveling companion – a young man in the early twenties. But you'll see Mr Tait below, no doubt – and his companion too."

Duff went alone to the first floor. Doctor Lofton was pacing anxiously up and down before a door. Beyond, Duff caught a glimpse of a little group of people waiting amid faded red-plush splendor.

"Ah, Inspector," the doctor greeted him. "I haven't been able to round up the entire party as yet. Five or six are still missing, but as it's nearly ten, they should be in soon. Here is one of them now."

A portly, dignified man came down the corridor from the Clarges Street entrance. His great shock of snow-white hair made him appear quite distinguished – for an American.

"Mr Tait," said Lofton, "meet Inspector Duff, of Scotland Yard."

The old man held out his hand. "How do you do, sir?" He had a deep booming voice. "What is this I hear? A murder? Incredible. Quite incredible. Who – may I ask – who is dead?"

"Just step inside, Mr Tait," Duff answered. "You'll know the details in a moment. A rather distressing affair—"

"It is, indeed." Tait turned and with a firm step crossed the threshold of the parlor. For a moment he stood, looking about the group inside. Then he gave a strangled little cry, and pitched forward on to the floor.

Duff was the first to reach him. He turned the old man over, and with deep concern noted his face. It was as blank as that of the dead man in room 28.

IV

DUFF OVERLOOKS A CLUE

The next instant a young man was at Duff's side, a good-looking American with frank gray eyes, now somewhat startled. Removing a small, pearl-like object from a bottle, he crushed it in his handkerchief, and held the latter beneath the nose of Mr Patrick Tait.

"Amyl nitrate," he explained, glancing up at the inspector. "It will bring him around in a moment, I imagine. It's what he told me to do if he had one of these attacks."

"Ah, yes. You are Mr Tait's traveling companion?"

"I am. My name's Mark Kennaway. Mr Tait is subject to this sort of thing, and that is why he employed me to come with him." Presently the man on the floor stirred and opened his eyes. He was breathing heavily and his face was whiter than his shock of snowy hair.

Duff had noted a door on the opposite side of the room and crossing to it, he discovered that it led to a smaller parlor, among the furnishings of which was a broad and comfortable couch. "Best get him in here, Mr Kennaway," he remarked. "He's still too shaky to go upstairs." Without another word, he picked the old man up in his arms and carried him to the couch. "You stay here with him," Duff suggested. "I'll talk to you both a little later." Returning to the larger room, he closed the door behind him.

For a moment he stood looking about the main lounge of Broome's Hotel. Plenty of red plush and walnut had been the scheme of the original decorator, and it had remained undisturbed through the years. There was a bookcase with a few dusty volumes, a pile of provincial papers on a table, on the walls a number of sporting prints, their once white mats yellowed by time.

The group of very modern people who sat now in this musty room were regarding Inspector Duff with serious and, it seemed to him, rather anxious eyes. Outside the sun had at last broken through the fog, and a strong light entered through the many-paned windows, illuminating these faces that were to be the chief study of the detective for a long time to come.

He turned to Lofton. "Some of your party are still missing?"

"Yes – five. Not counting the two in the next room – and of course, Mrs Potter."

"No matter," shrugged Duff. "We may as well get started." He drew a small table into the middle of the floor, and sitting down beside it, took out his notebook. "I presume everyone here knows what has happened. I refer to the murder of Mr Drake in room 28 last night." No one spoke, and Duff continued. "Allow me to introduce myself. I am Inspector Duff, of Scotland Yard. I may say, first of all, that this entire group, and all the other members of your party, must remain together here at Broome's Hotel until released by the authorities at the Yard."

A little man, with gold-rimmed eyeglasses, leaped to his feet. "Look here, sir," he cried in a high shrill voice, "I propose to leave the party immediately. I am not accustomed to being mixed up with murder. In Pittsfield, Massachusetts, where I come from—"

"Ah, yes," said Duff coldly. "Thank you. I scarcely knew where to begin. We will start with you." He took out a fountain pen. "Your name, please?"

"My name is Norman Fenwick." He pronounced it Fennick.

"Spell the last name, if you will."

"F-e-n-w-i-c-k. It's an English name, you know."

"Are you English?"

"English descent, yes. My ancestors came to Massachusetts in 1650. During the Revolution they were all loyal to the mother country."

"That," smiled Duff grimly, "was some time ago. It will hardly enter into the present case." He stared with some distaste at the little man who was so obviously eager to curry favor with the British. "Are you traveling alone?"

"No, I'm not. My sister is with me." He indicated a colorless, gray-haired woman. "Miss Laura Fenwick."

Duff wrote again. "Now tell me, do either of you know anything about last night's affair?"

Mr Fenwick bristled. "Just what do you mean by that, sir?"

"Come, come," the inspector protested. "I've a bit of a job here and no time to waste. Did you hear anything, see anything, or even sense anything that might have some bearing on the case?"

"Nothing, sir, and I can answer for my sister."

"Have you been out of the hotel this morning? Yes? Where?"

"We went for a stroll through the West End. A last look at London. We are both quite fond of the city. That's only natural, since we are of British origin—"

"Yes, yes. Pardon me, I must get on—"

"But one moment, Inspector. We desire to leave this party at once. At once, sir. I will not associate—"

"I have told you what you must do. That matter is settled."

"Very well, sir. I shall interview our ambassador. He's an old friend of my uncle's—"

"Interview him by all means," snapped Duff. "Who is next? Miss Pamela, we have had our chat. And Mrs Spicer – I have seen you before. That gentleman next to you—"

The man answered for himself. "I am Stuart Vivian, of Del Monte, California." He was bronzed, lean, and would have been handsome had it not been for a deep scar across the right side of his forehead. "I must say that I'm quite in sympathy with Mr Fenwick. Why should we be put under restraint in this affair? Myself, I was a complete stranger to the murdered man – I'd never even spoken to him. I don't know any of these others, either."

"With one exception," Duff reminded him.

"Ah – er – yes. With one exception."

"You took Mrs Spicer to the theater last evening?"

"I did. I knew her before we came on this tour."

"You planned the tour together?"

"A ridiculous question," the woman flared.

"Aren't you rather overstepping the bounds?" cried Vivian angrily. "It was quite a coincidence. I hadn't seen Mrs Spicer for a year, and imagine my surprise to come on to New York and find her a member of the same party. Naturally there was no reason why we shouldn't go on."

"Naturally," answered Duff amiably. "You know nothing about Mr Drake's murder?"

"How could I?"

"Have you been out of the hotel this morning?"

"Certainly. I took a stroll – wanted to buy some shirts at the Burlington Arcade."

"Make any other purchases?"

"I did not."

"What is your business, Mr Vivian?"

"I have none. Play a bit of polo now and then."

"Got that scar on the polo field, no doubt?"

"I did. Had a nasty spill a few years back."

Duff looked about the circle. "Mr Honywood, just one more question for you."

Honywood's hand trembled as he removed the cigarette from his mouth. "Yes, Inspector?"

"Have you been out of the hotel this morning?"

"No, I – I haven't. After breakfast I came in here and looked over some old copies of the *New York Tribune*."

"Thank you. That gentleman next to you?" Duff's gaze was on a middle-aged man with a long hawk-like nose and strikingly small eyes. Though he was dressed well enough and seemed completely at ease, there was that about him which suggested he was somewhat out of place in this gathering.

"Captain Ronald Keane," he said.

"A military man?" Duff inquired.

"Why – er – yes—"

"I should say he is a military man," Pamela Potter put in. She glanced at Duff. "Captain Keane told me he was once in the British army, and had seen service in India and South Africa."

Duff turned to the captain. "Is that true?"

"Well—" Keane hesitated. "No, not precisely. I may have been – romancing a bit. You see – on board a ship – a pretty girl—"

"I understand," nodded the detective. "In such a situation one tries to impress, regardless of the truth. It has been done before. Were you ever in any army, Captain Keane?"

Again Keane hesitated. But the Scotland Yard man was in too close touch with records to make further lying on this point advisable, "Sorry," he said. "I – er – the title is really honorary. It means – er – little or nothing."

"What is your business?"

"I haven't any at present. I've been – an engineer."

"How did you happen to come on this tour?"

"Why – for pleasure, of course."

"I trust you are not disappointed. What do you know about last night's affair?"

"Absolutely nothing."

"I presume that you, too, have been out for a stroll this morning?"

"Yes, I have. I cashed a check at the American Express Office."

"You were supposed to carry only Nomad checks," put in Doctor Lofton, his business sense coming to the fore.

"I had a few of the others," Keane replied. "Is there any law against that?"

"The matter was mentioned in our agreement—" began Lofton, but Duff cut him off.

"There remains only the gentleman in the corner," said the detective. He nodded toward a tall man in a tweed suit. This member of the party had a heavy walking-stick, and one leg was stiff in front of him. "What is your name, sir?" Duff added.

"John Ross," the other replied. "I'm a lumber man from Tacoma, Washington. Been looking forward to this trip for years, but I never dreamed it would be anything like this. My life's an open book, Inspector. Give the word, and I'll read aloud any page you select."

"Scotch, I believe?" Duff suggested.

"Does the burr still linger?" Ross smiled. "It shouldn't – Lord knows I've been in America long enough. I see you're looking at my foot, and since we're all explaining our scars and our weaknesses, I'll tell you that when I was down in the redwoods some months ago, I was foolish enough to let a tree fall on my right leg. Broke a lot of bones, and they haven't knitted as they should."

"That's a pity. Know anything about this murder?"

"Not a thing, Inspector. Sorry I can't help you. Nice old fellow, this Drake. I got pretty well acquainted with him on the ship – he and I both had rather good stomachs. I liked him a lot."

"I imagine that you, too—"

Ross nodded. "Yes – I went for a walk this morning. Fog and all. Interesting little town you've got here, Inspector. Ought to be out on the Pacific Coast."

"Wish we could bring the coast here," Duff replied. "Climate especially."

Ross sat up with interest. "You've been there, Inspector?"

"Briefly – a few years ago."

"What did you think of us?" the lumber man demanded.

Duff laughed, and shook his head. "Ask me some other time," he said. "I've more pressing matters to occupy me now." He stood up. "You will all wait here just for a moment," he added, and went out.

Fenwick went over to Doctor Lofton. "See here – you've got to give us our money back on this tour," he began, glaring through his thick glasses.

"Why so?" inquired Lofton suavely.

"Do you suppose we're going on after this?"

"The tour is going on," Lofton told him. "Whether you go or not rests with you. I have been making this trip for many years, and death is not altogether an unknown occurrence among the members of my parties. That it happens to be a murder in this case in no way alters my plans. We shall be delayed for a time in London but that is, of course, an act of God. Read your contract with me, Mr Fenwick. Not responsible for acts of God. I shall get the party around the world in due course, and if you choose to drop out, there will be no rebate."

"An outrage," Fenwick cried. He turned to the others. "We'll get together. We'll take it up with the Embassy." But no one seemed to be in a mood to match his.

Duff returned, and with him came Eben, the night-watchman.

"Ladies and gentlemen," the inspector began, "I have asked this man to look you over and see if he can identify a certain person who, at two o'clock last night, was a trifle confused as to the whereabouts of his room. A person who, in point of fact, was wandering about the floor on which the murder took place."

He turned to Eben, who was grimly studying the faces of the men in that old-fashioned parlor. The servant stared at Lofton, then at Honywood, at Ross, the lumber man, and at Vivian, the polo player. He gave the weak face of Fenwick but a fleeting glance.

"That's him," said Eben firmly, pointing at Captain Ronald Keane.

Keane sat up. "What do you mean?"

"I mean it's you I met on my two o'clock round. You told me you'd got on to that floor by mistake, thinking it was your own."

"Is this true?" Duff asked sternly.

"Why—" Keane looked anxiously about him. "Why, yes – I was up there. You see, I couldn't sleep, and I wanted a book to read."

"That's pretty old – that wanted-a-book-to-read-stuff," the detective reminded him.

"I fancy it is," returned Keane with a sudden show of spirit. "But it happens occasionally – among literate people I mean. I knew Tait had a lot of books – that young fellow reads to him until late at night. I found it out on the boat. I knew, too, that he was on the third floor, though I wasn't sure of the room. I just thought I'd go up there and listen outside the doors, and if I heard anyone reading, I'd go in and borrow something. Well, I didn't hear a thing, so I decided it was too late. When I met this watchman here, I was on my way back to the floor below."

"Why the statement about being confused as to the location of your room?" Duff wanted to know.

"Well, I couldn't very well take up the subject of my literary needs with a servant. He wouldn't have been interested. I just said the first thing that came into my head."

"Rather a habit with you, I judge," Duff remarked. He stood for a moment staring at Keane. A mean face, a face that he somehow didn't care for at all, and yet he had to admit that this explanation sounded plausible enough. But he resolved to keep an eye on this man. A sly wary sort, and the truth was not in him.

"Very good," the detective said. "Thank you, Eben. You may go now." He thought of Hayley, still searching above. "You will all remain here until I release you," he added, and ignoring a chorus of protest, walked briskly over and stepped into the smaller parlor.

As he closed the connecting door behind him, he saw Patrick Tait sitting erect on the couch, a glass of spirits in his hand. Kennaway was hovering solicitously about.

"Ah, Mr Tait," Duff remarked. "I am happy to see you are better."

The old man nodded his head. "Nothing," he said. "Nothing at all." The booming voice was a feeble murmur now. "I am subject to these spells – that is why I have this boy with me. He will take good care of me, I'm sure. A little too much excitement, perhaps. Murder, you know – I hardly bargained for that."

"No, of course not," the inspector agreed, and sat down. "If you're quite well enough now, sir—"

"Just a moment." Tait held up his hand. "You will pardon my curiosity, I'm sure. But I still don't know who was killed, Mr Duff."

The detective gave him a searching look. "You're sure you are strong enough—"

"Nonsense," Tait answered. "It means nothing to me, one way or the other. To whom did this appalling thing happen?"

"It happened to Mr Hugh Morris Drake, of Detroit," said Duff.

Tait bowed his head, and was silent for a moment. "I knew him, very slightly, for many years," he remarked at last. "A man of unsullied past, Inspector, and with the most humanitarian impulses. Why should anyone want to remove him? You are faced by an interesting problem."

"And a difficult one," Duff added. "I should like to discuss it with you for a moment. You occupy, I believe, room 30, which is near the spot where the unfortunate affair occurred. At what time did you retire for the night?"

Tait looked at the boy. "About twelve, wasn't it, Mark?"

Kennaway nodded. "Or a few minutes after, perhaps. You see, Inspector, I go to Mr Tait's room every evening and read him to sleep. Last night I began to read at ten, and at a few minutes past twelve he was sleeping soundly. So I slipped out, and went to my own room on the second floor."

"What do you read, mostly?" asked Duff, interested.

"Mystery stories," Kennaway smiled.

"To a man with a bad heart? I should think the excitement—"

"Bah," put in Tait. "There's little enough excitement in the things. I have been a criminal lawyer for many years back home, and as far as the word murder goes—" He stopped suddenly.

"You were about to say," suggested Duff gently, "that murder is not, where you are concerned, an exciting topic."

"What if I was?" demanded Tait, rather warmly.

"I was only wondering," continued Duff, "why this particular murder brought on such a serious spell this morning?"

"Oh, well – meeting it in one's own life is quite different from reading about it in books. Or even from talking about it in a courtroom."

"Quite, quite," agreed Duff. He was silent, drumming with his fingers on the arm of his chair. Suddenly he turned, and with the speed and precision of a machine-gun began to fire questions at the lawyer.

"You heard nothing on that third floor last night?"

"Nothing."

"No outcry? No call for help?"

"Nothing, I tell you."

"No scream from an old man brutally attacked?"

"I have told you, sir—"

"I am asking you, Mr Tait. I meet you in the hallway, and you appear to be strong and well. You have heard rumors of a murder, but you do not know who was killed. You walk with a firm step to the doorway of the parlor. You glance around the faces inside, and in another moment you are on the floor, in what seems a mortal attack—"

"They come like that—"

"Do they? Or did you see someone in that room—"

"No! No!"

"Some face, perhaps—"

"I tell you, no!"

The old man's eyes were blazing, the hand that held the glass trembled. Kennaway came forward.

"Inspector, I beg your pardon," he said quietly. "You are going too far. This man is ill—"

"I know," admitted Duff softly. "I'm sorry. I was wrong, and I apologize. I forgot, you see – I have my job to do, and I forgot." He arose. "None the less, Mr Tait," he added, "I think that some surprising situation dawned upon you as you stood in that doorway this morning, and I intend to find out what it was."

"It is your privilege to think anything you please, sir," replied the old man, and as Duff went out he carried a picture of the great criminal lawyer, gray of face and breathing heavily, sitting on a Victorian sofa and defying Scotland Yard.

Hayley was waiting in the lobby. "Been through the rooms of every man in the party," he reported. "No fragment of watch-chain. No gray coat with a torn pocket. Nothing."

"Of course not," Duff replied. "Practically every mother's son of 'em has been out of the hotel this morning, and naturally any evidence like that went with them."

"I really must get back to my duties at Vine Street," Hayley went on. "You'll drop in after you've finished, old man?"

Duff nodded. "Go along. What was it that street orchestra was playing? *There's a Long, Long Trail A-Winding*. It's true, Hayley. Damned true."

"I'm very much afraid it is," the other answered. "See you at the station."

As Duff turned, his worried frown disappeared. Pamela Potter was beckoning to him from the parlor doorway. He went over to her at once.

"I was wondering, Inspector," she said, "if you want to see mother now, I believe I can arrange it."

"Good," he answered. "I'll go up with you in a moment." He stepped inside the parlor, and with one final warning against leaving Broome's Hotel for the present, he dismissed the assembled crowd. "I shall want to see the five remaining members of your party," he said to Lofton.

"Of course. The moment they come in, I'll let you know," Lofton agreed. He went on down the lobby, with Fenwick still arguing at his heels.

At the door of the suite occupied by Pamela Potter and her mother, Duff waited while the girl went inside. After several moments, during which he heard the sounds of a discussion going on beyond the door, the young woman returned and admitted him.

The shades were all drawn in the sitting-room where he now found himself. Gradually accustoming his eyes to the gloom, he perceived, on a *chaise longue* in the darkest corner, the figure of a woman. He stepped nearer.

"This is Inspector Duff, Mother," said Pamela Potter.

"Oh, yes," answered the woman faintly.

"Mrs Potter," remarked the detective, feeling rather ill at ease, "I am extremely sorry to trouble you. But it cannot be avoided."

"I fancy not," she replied. "Won't you be seated? You won't mind the curtains being down, I hope. I'm afraid I'm not looking my best after this terrible shock."

"I have already talked with your daughter," continued Duff, moving a chair as close to the couch as he dared, "so I shan't be here more than a moment. If there is anything you can tell me about this affair, I assure you that it is very important you should do so. Your knowledge of the past is, of course, a trifle more extensive than that of Miss Pamela. Had your father any enemy?"

"Poor father," the woman said. "Pamela, the smelling salts." The girl produced a green bottle. "He was a saint, Mr – er – what did you say his name was, my dear?"

"Mr Duff, Mother."

"My father was a saint on earth if ever there was one. Not an enemy in the world. Really, I never heard of anything so senseless in all my life."

"But there must be sense in it somewhere, Mrs Potter. It is for us to find out. Something in your father's past—" Duff paused, and took from his pocket a wash leather bag. "I wonder if we might have that curtain up just a little way?" he added to the girl.

"Certainly," she said, and raised it.

"I'm sure I look a fright," protested the woman.

Duff held out the bag. "See, Madam – we found this on the bed beside your father."

"What in the world is it?"

"A simple little bag, Mrs Potter, of wash leather – chamois, I believe you call it." He poured some of the contents into the palm of his hand. "It was filled with a hundred or more pebbles, or small stones. Do they mean anything to you?"

"Certainly not. What do they mean to you?"

"Nothing, unfortunately. But – think, please, Mrs Potter. Your father was never, for example, engaged in mining?"

"If he was, I never heard of it."

"These pebbles could have no connection with automobiles?"

"How could they? Pamela – this – pillow—"

"I'll fix it, Mother."

Duff sighed, and returned the bag to his pocket. "You did not mingle, on the boat, with the other members of the travel party?"

"I never left my cabin," the woman said. "Pamela here was constantly wandering about. Talking with all sorts of people, when she should have been with me."

The detective took out the fragment of watch-chain, with the key attached. He handed it to the girl. "You did not, I suppose, happen to notice that chain on anyone with whom you talked?"

She examined it, and shook her head. "No. Who looks at a man's watch-chain?"

"The key means nothing to you?"

"Not a thing. I'm sorry."

"Please show it to your mother. Have you ever seen that chain or key before, Madam?"

The woman shrugged. "No, I haven't. The world is full of keys. You'll never get anywhere that way."

Duff restored this clue to his pocket and stood up. "That is all, I fancy," he remarked.

"The whole affair is utterly senseless, I tell you," the woman said complainingly. "There is no meaning to it. I hope you get to the bottom of it, but I don't believe you ever will."

"I shall try, at any rate," Duff assured her. And he went out, conscious of having met a vain and very shallow woman. The girl followed him into the hall.

"I thought it would be better for you to see mother," she said. "So you might understand that I happen to be spokesman for the family, sort of in charge, if you care to put it that way. Poor mother has never been strong."

"I understand," Duff answered. "I shall try not to trouble her again. It's you and I together, Miss Pamela."

"For grandfather's sake," she nodded gravely.

Duff returned to room 28. His two assistants were waiting, their paraphernalia packed.

"All finished, Mr Duff," the fingerprint man told him. "And very little, I fear, sir. This, however, is rather odd." He handed to the inspector the ear-phone of the dead man.

Duff took it. "What about this?"

"Not a print on it," the other said. "Not even that of the man on the bed. Wiped clean."

Duff stared at the instrument. "Wiped clean, eh? I wonder now. If the old gentleman and his ear-phone were in some other part of the hotel – if he was killed there, and then moved back here – and the ear-phone was carried back too—"

"I'm afraid I don't follow you, sir," the assistant remarked.

Duff smiled. "I was only thinking aloud. Come on, boys. We must be getting along." He returned the ear-phone to the table.

Though he did not suspect it at the moment, he had just held in his hand the key to his mystery. It had been Hugh Morris Drake's deafness that led to his murder in Broome's Hotel.

V

LUNCHEON AT THE MONICO

When they reached the ground floor, Duff directed his two assistants to return to the Yard at once with their findings, and then send the chauffeur back with the green car to await his own departure from Broome's. He began a round of the corridors, and came presently upon Doctor Lofton, who still had an upset and worried air.

"The other five members of the party are here," the doctor announced. "I've got them waiting in that same parlor. I hope you can see them now, as they are rather restless."

"At once," answered Duff amiably, and together with Lofton, entered the familiar room.

"You people know what has happened," the conductor said. "This is Inspector Duff, of Scotland Yard. He wants to talk with you. Inspector, Mr and Mrs Elmer Benbow, Mr and Mrs Max Minchin and Mrs Latimer Luce."

The inspector stood regarding this oddly assorted group. Funny lot, these Americans, he was thinking: all types, all races, all classes of society, traveling together in apparent peace and amity. Well, that was the melting-pot for you. He was reaching for his notebook when the man named Elmer Benbow rushed up and pumped enthusiastically at his hand.

"Pleased to meet you, Inspector," he cried. "Say, this will be something to tell when we get back to Akron. Mixed up in a murder – Scotland Yard and all that – just like I've been reading about in your English mystery novels. I read a lot of 'em. My wife tells me they won't improve my mind, but when I get home from the factory every night, I'm just about done up, and I don't want any of the heavy stuff— "

"Really?" broke in Duff. "Now, just a moment, Mr Benbow." Benbow waited, his flow of talk momentarily checked. He was a plump, genial soul; the naïve, unsophisticated sort the British so love to think of as a typical American. In his hand he carried a motion-picture camera. "What was the name of that place you expect to return to one day?" Duff asked.

"Akron. You've heard of Akron, haven't you? Akron, Ohio."

"I have now," Duff smiled. "On a pleasure trip, I presume?"

"Sure. Been talking about it for years. Business wasn't so good this winter, and my partner he says to me: 'Elmer, why don't you dig down into the old sock and take that trip around the world you've been boring me with for the past five years? That is,' he says, 'if there's anything in the sock after this Wall Street crash.' Well, there was plenty, for I'm no speculator. Good safe investment – that's my motto. I wasn't afraid to spend the money, because I knew that business was fundamentally sound and would turn the corner in time. I look for a return to normalcy – Harding came from Ohio, too – about the time we get back to Akron. You take the rediscount rate— "

Duff glanced at his watch. "I got you here, Mr Benbow, to ask if you could throw any light on that unfortunate affair in room 28?"

"Unfortunate is right," Benbow replied. "You said it. As nice an old gentleman as you'd want to meet. One of the big men of the country, rich as all get out, and somebody goes and murders him. I tell you, it's a slap at American institutions— "

"You know nothing about it?"

"I didn't do it, if that's what you mean. We make too many tires in Akron to go round killing off our best customers, the automobile men. No, sir, this is all a big mystery to Nettie and me. You've met the wife?"

The detective bowed in the direction of Mrs Benbow, a handsome, well-dressed woman who, not being needed at the factory, had evidently had more time for the refinements of life than had her husband.

"A great pleasure," he said. "I take it that you have been out this morning for a walk about London?"

Mr Benbow held up the camera. "Wanted to get a few more shots on the good old film," he explained. "But say – the fog was terrible. I don't know how some of these pictures will turn out. It's my hobby, you might say. When I get back from this tour I expect to have enough movies to make a fool of contract bridge at our house for months to come. And that will be O.K. with me."

"So you spent the morning taking pictures?"

"I sure did. The sun came out a while ago, and then I really went to it. Nettie, she says to me: 'Elmer, we'll be late for that train,' so I finally tore myself away. I was out of film by that time, anyhow."

Duff sat studying his notes. "This Akron," he remarked. "Is it near a town called" – he flipped the pages of his notebook – "is it near Canton, Ohio?"

"Just a few miles between 'em," Benbow answered. "McKinley came from Canton, you know. Mother of presidents – that's what we call Ohio."

"Indeed," murmured Duff. He turned to Mrs Latimer Luce, a keen-eyed old woman of indefinite age and cultivated bearing. "Mrs Luce, have you anything to tell me about this murder?"

"I'm sorry, Inspector," she replied, "but I can tell you nothing." Her voice was low and pleasing. "I've been traveling most of my life, but this is a new experience."

"Where is your home?"

"Well – Pasadena, California – if I have one. I keep a house there, but I'm never in it. I'm always on the go. At my age, it gives one something to think about. New scenes, new faces. I'm so shocked over this Drake affair. A charming man."

"You've been out of the hotel this morning?"

"Yes – I breakfasted with an old friend in Curzon Street. An English woman I knew when I lived in Shanghai, some twenty years ago."

Duff's eyes were on Mr Max Minchin, and they lighted with interest. Mr Minchin was a dark stocky man with close-cropped hair and a protruding lower lip. He had shown no such enthusiasm as had Mr Benbow at meeting a man from Scotland Yard. In fact, his manner was sullen, almost hostile.

"Where is your home, Mr Minchin?" Duff inquired.

"What's that got to do with the case?" Minchin inquired. With one hairy hand he fingered a big diamond in his tie.

"Oh, tell him, Maxy," said his wife, who overflowed a red plush chair. "It ain't nothing to be ashamed of, I guess." She looked at Duff. "We're from Chicago," she explained.

"Well, Chicago, it is," her husband remarked harshly. "And what of it, hey?"

"Have you any information about this murder?"

"I ain't no dick," said Maxy. "Do I look it? Dig up your own info. Me – I got nothing to say. My lawyers – well, they ain't here. I ain't talking. See what I mean?"

Duff glanced at Doctor Lofton. Some queer characters had certainly crept into Lofton's Round the World Tour this year. The doctor looked the other way obviously embarrassed.

Mrs Minchin also appeared rather uncomfortable. "Come on, Maxy," she protested. "There's no use nursing a grouch. Nobody's accusing you."

"Patrol your own beat," he said. "I'll handle this."

"What have you been doing this morning?" Duff inquired.

"Buying," answered Minchin tersely.

"Look at that sparkler." Sadie held out a fat hand. "I seen it in a window, and I says to Maxy – if you want me to remember London, that's what I remember it by. And he come across, Maxy did. A free spender – ask the boys in Chicago—"

Duff sighed, and stood up. "I won't detain you any longer," he remarked to the little group. He explained again that no one must leave Broome's Hotel, and the five went out. Lofton turned to him.

"What's to be the outcome of this, Mr Duff?" he wanted to know. "My tour is on schedule, of course, and a delay is going to tangle things frightfully. Boats, you understand. Boats all along the line, Naples, Port Said, Calcutta, Singapore. Have you any information that will entitle you to hold any of my party here? If so, hold them, and let the rest of us go on."

A puzzled frown was on Duff's usually serene face. "I'll be honest with you," he said. "I've never encountered a situation like this before. For the moment, I'm not quite certain about my future course of action. I must consult my superiors at the Yard. There'll be a coroner's inquest in the morning, which will no doubt be adjourned for a few weeks."

"A few weeks!" cried Lofton, in dismay.

"I'm sorry. I'll work as fast as I can, but I may tell you that until I've solved this thing, I'll be very reluctant to see your tour resume."

Lofton shrugged. "We shall see about that," he remarked.

"No doubt," Duff answered, and they parted.

Mark Kennaway was waiting in the hallway. "May I see you a moment, Inspector?" he said. They sat down on a nearby bench.

"You have information?" the detective inquired rather wearily.

"Of a sort – yes. It probably means nothing. But when I left Mr Tait last night and went down to the second floor, I saw a man lurking about in the shadows opposite the lift."

"What man?"

"Oh, don't expect any big surprise, Inspector. It was no one but our old friend, Captain Keane."

"Ah, yes. Hoping to borrow a book, perhaps."

"Might have been. The night lift man is a great reader. I've caught him at it. But his library is not extensive."

Duff studied the young man's face. He rather liked Kennaway. "Tell me," he said, "how long have you known Mr Tait?"

"Only since we started on this tour. You see, I'd just left Harvard Law School last June, and there didn't seem to be any great public clamor for my services. A friend told me about this job. I wanted to travel, and it seemed like a good chance to pick up pointers on the law – from a man like Tait."

"Picking any up?"

"No. He doesn't talk much. He demands a lot of attention, and if he's going to have many more attacks like that this morning, I may wish I was back in Boston."

"That was your first experience with one of Mr Tait's attacks?"

"Yes – he's seemed perfectly all right up to now."

Duff leaned back on the hard bench, and began to fill his pipe. "How about giving me a few of your impressions about this crowd?" he suggested.

"Well, I'm not sure that I'm a particularly bright-eyed boy," Kennaway smiled. "I got to know a few of them on the boat. Variety seems to be the keynote of the expedition."

"Take Keane, for example."

"A four-flusher – and a snooper, too. I can't figure out where he got the cash for this. It's an expensive tour, you know."

"Was the dead man – Drake – in evidence on the boat?"

"Very much so. A harmless old gentleman. Sociably inclined, too, which made it a little hard for the rest of us. His deafness, you understand. However, I used to be a cheer leader at college, so I didn't mind."

"What do you think of Lofton?"

"He's a rather remote sort of person. An educated man – he knows his stuff. You should have heard his little talk on the Tower of London. He's worried and distrait most of the time. No wonder. With this outfit on his hands."

"And Honywood?" Duff lighted his pipe.

"Never saw him on the boat, until the last morning. I don't believe he ever left his cabin."

"He told me he got to know Mr Drake quite well during the crossing."

"He was kidding you. I stood between them when we were drawing up to the pier at Southampton, and introduced them. I'm certain they'd never spoken to each other before."

"That's interesting," said Duff thoughtfully. "Did you take a good look at Honywood this morning?"

"I did," nodded Kennaway. "Like a man who'd seen a ghost, wasn't he? I was struck by it. Not well, I thought. But Lofton tells me these tours of his are very popular with the sick and the aged. I'm expecting to have a merry time of it."

"Miss Potter's a very charming girl," Duff suggested.

"So she is – and this is where she gets off. That would happen to me. It's the famous Kennaway luck."

"How about this fellow Minchin?"

The young man's face lighted. "Ah – the life of the party. Oozes money at every pore. He gave three champagne suppers on the way over. Nobody came but the Benbows, Keane and myself – and old Mrs Luce. She's a good sport – never misses anything, she tells me. That is, we all went to the first soirée. After that, it was just Keane, and some terrible passengers Maxy picked up in the smoking-room."

"Party was too gay, eh?"

"Oh, not that. But after a good look at Maxy – well, even champagne can't atone for some hosts."

Duff laughed. "Thanks for the tip about Keane," he said, rising.

"Don't imagine it means anything," Kennaway answered. "Personally, I don't like to tell tales. But poor old Drake was so nice to everybody. Well – see you later, I imagine."

"You can't help yourself," Duff told him.

After a few words with the managing director of the hotel, the detective went out to the street. The little green car was waiting. As he was about to step into it, a cheery voice sounded behind him.

"Say, listen, Inspector. Just turn around and face me, will you?" Duff turned. Mr Elmer Benbow was on the sidewalk, smiling broadly, his motion picture camera leveled and ready for action.

"Atta-boy," he cried. "Now, if you'll just take off the benny – the hat, you know – the light isn't so good—"

Cursing inwardly, Duff did as directed. The man from Akron held the machine before his eyes, and was turning a small crank.

"Let's have the little old smile – great – just for the folks back in Akron, you understand – now, move about a little – one hand on the door of the car – I guess this won't give them a kick back home – famous Scotland Yard inspector leaving Broome's Hotel in London, England, after investigating mysterious murder in round the world party – now, get into the car – that's the stuff – drive off – thanks!"

"Ass!" muttered Duff to his chauffeur. "Go around to Vine Street, please."

In a few moments they drew up before the police station that is hidden away in the heart of the West End, on a street so brief and unimportant it is unknown to most Londoners. Duff dismissed the car, and went inside. Hayley was in his room.

"Finished, old man?" he inquired.

Duff gave him a weary look. "I'll never be finished," he remarked. "Not with this case." He glanced at his watch. "It's getting on toward twelve. Will you come have a spot of lunch with me, old chap?"

Hayley was willing, and presently they were seated at a table in the Monico Grill. After they had ordered, Duff sat for some moments staring into space.

"Cheerio!" said his friend at last.

"Cheerio, my hat!" Duff answered. "Was there ever a case like this before?"

"Why the gloom?" Hayley wanted to know. "A simple little matter of murder."

"The crime itself – yes, that's simple enough," Duff agreed. "And under ordinary conditions, no doubt eventually solved. But consider this, if you will." He took out his notebook. "I have here the names of some fifteen or more people, and among them is probably that of the man I want. So far, so good. But these people are traveling. Where? Around the world, if you please. All my neat list of suspects, in one compact party, and unless something unexpected happens at once, that party will be moving along. Paris, Naples, Port Said, Calcutta, Singapore – Lofton just told me all about it. Moving along, farther and farther away from the scene of the crime."

"But you can hold them here."

"Can I? I'm glad you think so. I don't. I can hold the murderer here, the moment I have sufficient evidence of his guilt. But I'll have to get that immediately, or there will be international complications – the American consulate – perhaps the Ambassador himself – a summons for me from the Home Office. On what grounds do you hold these people? Where is your evidence that one of them committed the crime? I tell you, Hayley, there's no precedent for this situation. Such a thing has never happened before. And now that it's decided to happen at last, I'm the lucky lad it has happened to. Before I forget it, I must thank you for that."

Hayley laughed. "You were longing for another puzzle, last night," he said.

Duff shook his head. "The calm man is the happy man," he murmured, as his roast beef and bottle of stout were put before him.

"You got nothing from your examination of the party?" Hayley asked.

"Not a thing that's definite. Nothing that links any one of them with the crime, even remotely. A few faint suspicions – yes. A few odd incidents. But nothing that I could hold anybody on – nothing that would convince the American Embassy – or even my own superintendent."

"There's an unholy lot of writing in that book of yours," commented the Vine Street man. "Why not run over the list you talked with? You might get a flash – who knows?"

Duff took up the notebook. "You were with me when I interviewed the first of them. Miss Pamela Potter, a pretty American girl, determined to find out who killed her grandfather. Our friend Doctor Lofton, who had a bit of a row with the old man last evening, and with whose strap the murder was committed. Mrs Spicer, clever, quick, and not to be trapped by unexpected questions. Mr Honywood—"

"Ah, yes, Honywood," put in Hayley. "From a look at his face, he's my choice."

"That's the stuff to give a jury!" replied Duff sarcastically. "He looked guilty. I think he did, myself, but what of it? Does that get me anywhere?"

"You talked with the others downstairs?"

"I did. I met the man in room 30 – a Mr Patrick Tait." He told of Tait's heart attack at the door of the parlor. Hayley looked grave.

"What do you make of that?" he inquired.

"I suspect he was startled by something – or someone – he saw in that room. But he's a famous criminal lawyer on the other side – probably a past master of the art of cross-examination. Get something out of him that he doesn't want to tell, and you're a wonder. On the other hand, he may have nothing to tell. His attacks, he assured me, come with just that suddenness."

"None the less, like Honywood, he should be kept in mind."

"Yes, he should. And there is one other." He explained about Captain Ronald Keane. "Up to something last night – heaven knows what. A fox in trousers, if I ever met one. Sly – and a self-confessed liar."

"And the others?"

Duff shook his head. "Nothing there, so far. A nice young chap who is Tait's companion. A polo player with a scar – a Mr Vivian. Seems somehow connected with Mrs Irene Spicer. A lame man named Ross, in the lumber trade on the West Coast. A brother and sister named Fenwick – the former a pompous little nobody who has been frightened to death, and seems determined to leave the tour."

"Oh, he does, does he?"

"Yes, but don't be deceived. It means nothing. He hasn't nerve enough to kill a rabbit. There are just four, Hayley, – four to be watched. Honywood, Tait, Lofton and Keane."

"Then you didn't see the remaining members of the party?"

"Oh, yes I did. But they don't matter. A Mr and Mrs Benbow from a town called Akron – he runs a factory and is quite insane about a motion picture camera he carries with him. Going to look at his tour around the world when he gets home, and not before. But stop a bit – he told me Akron was near Canton, Ohio."

"Ah, yes – the address on the key?"

"Quite so. But he wasn't in this, I'm sure – he's not the type. Then there was a Mrs Luce, an elderly woman who's been everywhere. An inevitable feature, I fancy, of all tours like Lofton's. And a pair from Chicago – quite terrible people, really – a Mr and Mrs Max Minchin—"

Hayley dropped his fork. "Minchin?" he repeated.

"Yes, that was the name. What about it?"

"Nothing, old chap, except that you have evidently overlooked a small item sent out from the Yard several days ago. This man Minchin, it seems, is one of Chicago's leading racketeers, who has recently been persuaded to interrupt – perhaps only temporarily – a charming career of violence and crime."

"That's interesting," nodded Duff.

"Yes, isn't it? In the course of his activities he has been forced to remove from this world, either personally or through his lieutenants, a number of business rivals – 'to put them on the spot,' I believe the phrase goes. Recently, for some reason, he was moved to abdicate his throne and depart. The New York police suggested we keep a tender eye on him as he passes through. There are certain friends of his over here who, it was felt, might attempt to pay off old scores. Maxy Minchin, one of Chicago's first citizens."

Duff was thinking deeply. "I shall have another chat with him after lunch," he said. "Poor old Drake's body wasn't riddled with machine-gun bullets – but then, I fancy the atmosphere of Broome's might have its chastening effect even on a Maxy Minchin. Yes – I shall have a chat with the lad directly."

VI

TEN-FORTY-FIVE FROM VICTORIA

When they had finished luncheon, Duff went with Hayley back to the Vine Street station. Together they unearthed a dusty and forgotten atlas of the world, and Duff turned at once to the map of the United States.

"Good lord," he exclaimed, "what a country! Too big for comfort, Hayley, if you ask me. Ah – I've found Chicago. Max Minchin's city. Now, where the deuce is Detroit?"

Hayley bent over his shoulder, and in a moment laid a finger on the Michigan city. "There you are," he remarked. "No distance at all, in a country the size of that. Well?"

Duff leaned back in his chair. "I wonder," he said slowly. "The two cities are close together, and that's a fact. Was there some connection between the Chicago gangster and the Detroit millionaire? Drake was an eminently respectable man – but you never can tell. Liquor, you know, Hayley – liquor comes over the border at Detroit. I learned that when I visited the States. And liquor has been, no doubt, at least a side-line with Mr Minchin. Was there some feud – some ancient grudge? How could the pebbles figure in it? They may have been picked up from a lake shore. Oh, it all sounds devilish fantastic, I know – but in America, anything is possible. This angle will bear looking into, old chap."

With Hayley's encouragement, Duff set out for Broome's Hotel to look into it. Mr Max Minchin sent down word that he would receive the inspector in his suite. The detective found the celebrated racketeer in shirt sleeves and slippers. His hair was rumpled, and he explained that he had been taking his afternoon siesta.

"Keeps me fresh – see what I mean?" he remarked. His manner was more friendly than it had been earlier in the day.

"I'm sorry to disturb you," Duff said. "But there are one or two matters—"

"I get you. The third degree for Maxy, hey?"

"Something which is not practised over here," Duff told him.

"Yeah?" remarked Maxy, shrugging. "Well, if it ain't, that's another thing you got on us Americans. Oh, we think we're on the up and up in our country, but I guess we got a few things to learn. Well, what's the dope, Officer? Make it snappy. We was just talking about going to a pitcher."

"There was a murder in this hotel last night," the detective began.

Maxy smiled. "And who do you think I am? Some hick that just got in from Cicero? I know they was a murder."

"From information received, I believe that murder is one of your avocations, Mr Minchin."

"Try that again."

"One of your pastimes, if I may put it that way."

"Oh, I get you. Well, maybe I have had to rub out a few guys now and then. But they had it coming, get me? And them things don't concern you. They happened in the good old U.S.A."

"I know that. But now that there has been a killing in your immediate vicinity, I am – er – forced to—"

"You gotta prowl around me a little, hey? Well, go ahead. But you're wasting your breath."

"Had you ever met Mr Drake before you took this journey?"

"Naw, I useta hear about him in Detroit – I went over there now and then. But I never had the pleasure of his acquaintance. I talked with him on the boat – a nice old guy. If you think I put that necktie on him, you're all wet."

"Kindest man in the world, Maxy is," his wife interposed. She was slowly unpacking a suitcase. "Maybe he has had to pass the word that put a few gorillas on the spot in his day, but they wasn't fit to live. He's out of the racket now, ain't you, Maxy?"

"Yeah – I'm out," her husband agreed. "Can you beat it, Officer? Here I am, retired from business, trying to get away from it all, just taking a pleasure trip like any other gentleman. And right off the bat a bird is bumped off almost in my lap, you might say." He sighed: "It just seems a guy can't get away from business, no matter where he goes," he added gloomily.

"At what time did you retire last night?" Duff inquired.

"When did we go to bed? Well – we went to a show. Real actors, get me? But slow – boy, I couldn't keep awake. When I take a chance and go to a theater, I want action. This bunch was dead in their tracks. But we didn't have nothing else on, so we stuck it out. Come back here about eleven-thirty, and hit the hay at twelve. I don't know what happened in this hotel after that."

"Out of the racket, like he told you," added Sadie Minchin. "He got out for little Maxy's sake. That's our boy. He's at a military school, and doing fine. Just seemed to take naturally to guns."

Despite the fact that he was getting nowhere, Duff laughed. "I'm sorry to have troubled you," he said, rising. "But it's my duty to explore every path, you know."

"Sure," agreed Maxy affably. He stood up too. "You got your racket, just like I got mine – or did have. And say – listen. If I can help you any way, just hoist the signal. I can work with the bulls, or against 'em. This time I'm willing to work with 'em, get me? There don't seem no sense to this kick-off, and I ain't for that sort of thing when it don't mean nothing. Yes, sir." He patted Duff's broad back. "You want a hand on this, you call on Maxy Minchin."

Duff said goodby, and went out into the corridor. He was not precisely thrilled over this offer of assistance from Mr Minchin, but he reflected that indeed he seemed to need help from some quarter.

On the ground floor he encountered Doctor Lofton. With the conductor was a strikingly elegant young man, who carried a walking-stick and wore a gardenia in the buttonhole of his perfectly fitting coat.

"Oh, Mr Duff," Lofton greeted him. "Just the man we want to see. This is Mr Gillow, an under-secretary at the American Embassy. He has called about last night's affair. Inspector Duff, of Scotland Yard."

Mr Gillow was one of those youthful exquisites who are the pride of the embassies. They usually sleep all day, then change from pajamas to evening clothes and dance all night for their country. He gave Duff a haughty nod.

"When is the inquest, Inspector?" he inquired.

"Tomorrow at ten, I believe," Duff replied.

"Ah, yes. And if nothing new is disclosed at that time, I presume the doctor may continue his tour as planned?"

"I don't know about that," muttered the detective.

"Really? You have some evidence then, that will enable you to hold the doctor here?"

"Well – not precisely."

"You can hold some of his party, perhaps?"

"I shall hold them all."

Mr Gillow lifted his eyebrows. "On what grounds?"

"Well – I – I—" For once the capable Duff was at a loss.

Mr Gillow gave him a pitying smile. "Really, my dear fellow, you're being rather absurd," he remarked. "You can't do that sort of thing in England, and you know it. Unless you have more evidence after the inquest than you have now, your hands are tied. Doctor Lofton and I have been over the entire case."

"Someone in that party killed Hugh Drake," protested Duff stubbornly.

"Yes? And where is your proof? What was the motive behind the killing? You may be right, and on the other hand you may be talking nonsense. Perhaps some hotel prowler—"

"With a platinum watch-chain," Duff suggested.

"Someone who had no connection with the party – just as probable, my dear sir. Even more so, I should say. Evidence – you must have evidence, as you well know. Otherwise I am sorry to tell you that Doctor Lofton and his group will continue their tour at once."

"We'll see about that," Duff answered grimly. He left Mr Gillow's presence with ill-concealed annoyance. He did not approve of elegant young men, and he disliked this one all the more because he foresaw that unless light broke quickly, Mr Gillow's prediction would undoubtedly come true.

The inquest on the following morning revealed nothing that was not already known. The hotel servants and the members of the Lofton party repeated all they had told Duff on the previous day. The little bag of stones roused considerable interest, but since no explanation of it was available, the interest quickly died. There was obviously no evidence sufficient to hold anyone on, and the inquest was adjourned for three weeks. Duff saw Mr Gillow smiling at him from across the room.

For the next few days, Duff worked like a mad man. Had someone in that travel party purchased a watch-chain to replace the one torn in the struggle at Broome's? He visited every jeweler's shop in the West End, and many in the City. Had the gray suit with a torn pocket been disposed of through a pawn shop or a second-hand clothing emporium? These, too, were thoroughly combed. Or had the suit been made up into a bundle and carelessly tossed away? Every lost package that turned up in that great city was personally examined by Duff. Nothing came of his efforts. His face grew stern, his eyes weary. Rumblings from the region above him warned him that his time was short, that Lofton was preparing to move on.

Mrs Potter and her daughter were planning to sail for home on Friday, just one week after the morning when Drake's body was discovered in that room at Broome's. On Thursday evening Duff had a final talk with the two women. The mother seemed more helpless and lost than ever; the girl was silent and thoughtful. With a feeling of chagrin such as he had never known before, the inspector bade them goodby.

When, after a fruitless day of it, he came back to his office at the Yard late Friday afternoon, he was startled to find Pamela Potter waiting for him. With her was Mrs Latimer Luce.

"Hello," Duff cried. "Thought you'd sailed, Miss Potter?"

She shook her head. "I couldn't. With everything unsolved – up in the air – no answer to our question. No – I engaged a maid for mother, and sent her home without me. I'm going on with the tour."

The detective had heard that American girls did pretty much as they pleased, but he was none the less surprised. "And what did your mother say to that?" he inquired.

"Oh – she was horrified, of course. But I'm sorry to tell you I've horrified her so often, she's rather used to it now. Mrs Luce here agreed to take up the old-fashioned rôle of chaperon – you've met Mrs Luce?"

"Of course," Duff nodded. "I beg your pardon, Madam. I was so taken back at seeing Miss Pamela—"

"I understand," smiled the old lady. "The girl's got spirit, hasn't she? Well, I like spirit. Always did. Her mother and I happened to have mutual friends, so I helped put it over. Why not? Naturally the child is curious. So am I. Give five thousand dollars right now to know who killed Hugh Drake, and why."

"Two questions that are not going to be so easy to answer," Duff told her.

"No, I judge not. Sorry for you. Hard case. I don't know whether you're aware of it or not, but Lofton's round the world party is moving on next Monday morning."

Duff's heart sank. "I expected it," he said. "And I can assure you that it's a bit of bad news for me."

"Cheer up," the old lady answered. "Nothing's as bad as it seems to be – I know. I've tested that out pretty well in the past seventy-two years. Pamela and I will go along – with eyes and ears open. Wide open – eh, my dear?"

The girl nodded. "We must get to the bottom of this. I shan't rest until we do."

"Bravo!" Duff said. "I'll appoint you both to my staff. The entire party's going, I presume?"

"Every last one of them," Mrs Luce replied. "We had a meeting at the hotel this morning. That little Fenwick creature tried to start a mutiny, but it failed. It ought to fail. Never had any use for anyone who can't see a thing through. Speaking for myself, I'd go on if they'd all been murdered but me."

"So Fenwick kicked up a row?" Duff reflected aloud. "I should have been invited to that meeting."

"Lofton didn't want you," the woman told him. "Funny man, Lofton, I can't understand him. And I don't like men I can't understand. Well, anyhow, Fenwick tried to wreck the tour, but when he saw he was alone, he let the rest shame him out of it. So we're all going on – just one great big happy family – and a murderer right in the middle of it, or I miss my guess."

Duff smiled at her. "You don't usually miss your guess, I fancy," he said.

"Not as a rule. And I'm not missing it this time, am I?"

"I'm inclined to think you're not," he assured her.

She stood up. "Well, I've been traveling all my life. Getting a little sick of it, but this is like a tonic. I expect to enjoy Doctor Lofton's tour to the hilt – oh, I'm sorry, my dear."

"It's quite all right," smiled Pamela Potter, rising too. "I'm not going along as a skeleton at the feast. I'm going along to help solve a mystery if I can, and I mean to be cheerful despite the nature of that mystery."

Duff regarded her with keen approval, "You're a sportsman, Miss Potter," he remarked. "It's put new heart in me to know that you are continuing with the tour. I shall see you both before you leave on Monday – and I'll be in touch with you after that too, no doubt."

When the two women had gone, the inspector found a memorandum on his desk, requesting him to see his superior at once. He went to the superintendent's office, knowing in advance the reason for the summons.

"It couldn't be avoided, Mr Duff," the superintendent said. "The American Ambassador himself took an interest in the matter. We have been forced to grant that party permission to go on. Don't look so disappointed, my boy. There are, you know, such things as treaties of extradition."

Duff shook his head. "The case that isn't solved promptly is likely to go unsolved," he remarked.

"An exploded theory. Look over the records of the Yard. Think of the months spent on many important cases. For example – the Crippen affair."

"All the same, sir, it's hard to stand aside and watch that crowd wander off heaven knows where."

"I appreciate your position, my boy. You wouldn't care to hold this fellow Keane? We might arrange for a warrant."

"There'd be nothing in that, sir, I'm sure. I'd rather have Honywood, or even Tait. But of course I have nothing to take them on."

"How about Mr Max Minchin?"

"Poor chap. Trying to put all this sort of thing behind him."

The superintendent shrugged. "Well, there you are. You will, of course, secure from the conductor a complete itinerary of the tour, with the understanding that he must notify you at once of any change. Also, he must let you know immediately if any members of the party drop out en route."

"Of course, sir," nodded Duff. "A fat lot of good that will do," he reflected.

"For the present, you had better pursue your inquiries in London," his superior continued. "If they come to nothing, we shall send a man to keep an eye on the party – someone who is unknown to them. I'm afraid that bars you, Mr Duff."

"I know it does, sir," the inspector replied.

He went back to his desk, baffled and in despair. But he did not let his state of mind interfere with his activities, which were many and varied. All through Saturday, and even under the handicap of Sunday, when all shops were closed, he searched and questioned and studied his problem. Hayley lent his staff and his cheery comment. It was all to no avail. The murder in Broome's Hotel remained as far from solution as it had been on the foggy morning when the little green car first drew up before that respectable door.

On Monday morning, Duff went to Victoria Station on as odd a mission as a Scotland Yard detective had ever been called upon to perform. He was there to say goodby to a round the world party, to shake hands with them all and wish them a pleasant journey. And among the hands he must shake, he was quite certain in his mind, was one of the pair that had strangled Hugh Morris Drake in Broome's Hotel on the early morning of February seventh.

As he came on to the platform beside the ten-forty-five train for Dover, Doctor Lofton greeted him cordially. There was elation in the conductor's bearing; he was like a schoolboy off on a long vacation. He gripped Duff warmly by the hand.

"Sorry we must tear ourselves away," he remarked, with what was for him a near approach to levity. "But a tour is a tour, you know. You have our schedule, and any time you care to join us, we'll make you welcome. Eh, Mr Benbow?"

Duff had heard a grinding sound at his back, and turned to find Benbow busy with his eternal camera. The man from Akron shifted it quickly to his left hand, and gave Duff his right.

"Sorry you fell down on the case," he said, with amiable tactlessness. "Never knew a Scotland Yard man to do that – in the books. But this isn't a book, and I guess things are different in real life, eh?"

"I think it's a bit early to give up hope," Duff replied. "By the way, Mr Benbow—" He took a key and three links of a chain from his pocket. "Have you seen this before?"

"Saw it at the inquest – but from a distance," Benbow told him. He took the key and examined it. "Do you know what I think this is, Inspector?"

"I should be happy to learn."

"Well, it's a key to a safety-deposit box in some American bank," the man from Akron explained. "The only kind of key, except for luggage, that a fellow would be likely to carry on a tour like this. A bank over on our side usually gives a depositor two keys, so maybe there's a duplicate floating about somewhere."

Duff took the clue and studied it with new interest. "And this name – the Dietrich Safe and Lock Company, Canton, Ohio – that ought to mean the bank is somewhere in your neighborhood?"

"No, not at all. It's a big concern. They sell lockboxes and keys all over the States. Might be San Francisco, or Boston, or New York – anywhere. But if I were you, I'd think about that key."

"I shall," Duff told him. "Of course, it may have been placed in the dead man's hand to mislead me."

Benbow was busy with his camera, and looked up quickly. "Never thought of that," he admitted.

His wife came up. "Oh, for pity sake, Elmer," she said. "Put that camera away. You're getting on my nerves."

"Why?" he answered plaintively. "There's nothing I have to look at here, is there? I thought it was just a railroad station. Or is it a ruined castle or a museum, or something? I'm getting so I don't know one from the other."

Patrick Tait and his young companion strolled up. The old man appeared to be in glowing health, his step was firm, his cheeks ruddy. Somehow, a bit of Lofton's elation seemed to be reflected in his face.

"Well, Inspector," he remarked, "this is goodby, I imagine. Sorry you haven't had better luck. But of course, you won't give up."

"Hardly," Duff returned, looking him steadily in the eye. "It's not our habit, at the Yard."

Tait met the gaze for a moment, then his eyes wandered up and down the platform. "Ah, yes," he murmured. "That's what I've always understood."

The detective turned to Kennaway. "Miss Potter is going with you, after all," he said.

Kennaway laughed. "So I hear. More of the famous Kennaway luck. We have all kinds – good and bad."

The detective crossed the platform to where Mrs Spicer and Stuart Vivian were standing. Vivian's goodby was cool and unfriendly, and the woman was not very cordial, either. A lack of cordiality, however, was not evident in the farewell of Captain Ronald Keane, who stood near by. He rather overdid the handshaking, Duff thought. So did John Ross, the lame man, but in the latter instance Duff did not so much mind the enthusiasm.

"Hope to see you on the Pacific coast some day," Ross told him.

"Perhaps," nodded the inspector.

"A little more interest, please," smiled the other. "I certainly would like to introduce you to our redwoods. Finest trees in the world."

Honywood appeared on the platform. "It isn't every party that is seen off by a Scotland Yard inspector," he said. His tone attempted lightness, but there was an odd look in his eyes, and the hand he gave to Duff was damp and clammy.

The detective had a few final words with Mrs Luce and Pamela Potter, and then with the Minchins. He looked at his watch, and walked over to Lofton. "Three minutes," he remarked. "Where are the Fenwicks?"

The doctor looked uneasily down the platform. "I don't know. They agreed to be here."

A minute passed. All save Lofton were now aboard the train. Suddenly, at the far end of the station, the Fenwicks appeared, running. They arrived quite out of breath.

"Hello," said Duff. "Afraid you weren't coming."

"Oh – we're – coming," panted Fenwick. His sister climbed aboard. "Going a little way, anyhow. But if there's any more funny business, we leave the party" – he snapped his fingers – "like that."

"There will be no more funny business," Lofton assured him firmly.

"I'm glad you're going along," Fenwick said to Duff.

"But I'm not," the detective smiled.

"What – not going?" The little man stared at Duff, open-mouthed. "You mean you're dropping the whole matter?" Doors were slamming all along the platform.

"Get in, Mr Fenwick," Lofton cried, and half lifted him aboard. "Goodby, Inspector."

The train began to move. For as long as he could see it, Duff stood there on the platform staring after it. Someone in that party – that party moving on to Paris – to Italy – to Egypt – to India – to the ends of the earth—

The detective turned away with a sigh. For one imaginative moment he wished he might be aboard the express, invisible, watching the expressions of those various faces that interested him so much.

If he had been there, he might have come upon Walter Honywood, alone in a compartment, his face pressed close to the window as he watched the drab backyards of London drift by. His lips were parted, his eyes staring, and little beads of moisture were on his forehead.

The door of the compartment opened – almost noiselessly, but not quite. Just enough sound so that Honywood turned in a flash, and on his face was a surprising look of terror. "Oh, hello," he said.

"Hello," returned Fenwick. He advanced into the compartment, followed by his silent colorless sister. "May we come in here? We were late – all the seats taken—"

Honywood wet his lips with his tongue. "Come in, by all means," he said.

The Fenwicks sat down. The unlovely side of the great gray city continued to glide by the windows.

"Well," remarked Fenwick at last, "we're leaving London. Thank God for that."

"Yes, we're leaving London," Honywood repeated. He took out a handkerchief and mopped his brow. The look of terror was gradually fading from his face.

VII

AN ADMIRER OF SCOTLAND YARD

On the following Thursday night, Inspector Duff again walked into Hayley's room at the Vine Street station. The divisional inspector took one look at his old friend, and smiled sympathetically.

"I don't need to ask," he remarked.

Duff took off coat and hat and tossed them on to a chair, then slumped into another beside Hayley's desk.

"Do I show it as plainly as that?" he said. "Well, it's true, old chap. Not a thing, Hayley, not a blessed thing. I've hung round Broome's Hotel until I'm beginning to feel a hundred years old myself. I've scoured the shops until my feet ache. A clever lad, the murderer of Hugh Morris Drake. The trail is cold."

"You're about done up," Hayley told him. "Relax a bit, my boy, and try some entirely different method of approach."

"I'm thinking of taking a new tack," Duff nodded. "There's this key we removed from the dead man's hand." He repeated to his friend what Benbow had told him about its probable nature. "There was, very likely, a duplicate, and the murderer may have that with him now. I might follow up the party, and search the luggage of everyone in it. But they know who I am – the difficulties would be enormous. Even if we sent someone unknown to them, his task would be a tremendous one. I might go to the States, and visit the home town of every man in the party, seeking to ascertain if anyone of them has a safety box at his bank numbered 3260. Difficulties there, too. But I talked it over with the chief this afternoon, and he favors it."

"Then you'll be leaving soon for America?" Hayley inquired.

"I may. We'll decide tomorrow. But good lord – what a job that looks."

"I know," Hayley nodded. "But it seems to me the wise course. If the murderer did have a duplicate key, he has long since thrown it away."

Duff shook his head. "Not at all," he objected. "I don't believe he has. To do so would be to arrive back at his bank and report the loss of both keys. That would be inviting a dangerous amount of attention to an affair he no doubt wants kept very dark. No, I am certain – if he is the man I think he is – that he will hold on to the duplicate through thick and thin. But he will hide it, Hayley. It's a small object and can be cleverly concealed. So cleverly, perhaps, that a search for it on our part would be hopeless. The chief is right – the American journey is clearly indicated – though I dread the whole idea. However, I've reached the end of my string here, and I'm damned if I'll give up."

"It wouldn't be like you if you did," Hayley replied. "Take heart, old man. I never knew a case to get on your nerves before. Why worry – you're certain to win out in the end. What was it Inspector Chan said? Success will always walk smiling at your side. He sensed it, and according to him, the Chinese are psychic people."

A slow smile spread over Duff's face. "Good old Charlie. I wish I had him with me on this case." He stopped. "I noticed Honolulu on the itinerary of the tour," he added thoughtfully. "However, that's a long time yet. And much may happen before Doctor Lofton's none too select group comes into Honolulu harbor." He rose with a sudden air of determination.

"Going already?" Hayley asked.

"Yes. Much as I enjoy your society, old chap, it just flashed into my mind that I'm getting nowhere sitting here. Perseverance – that was Chan's method. Patience, hard work and perseverance. I'm going to make one more stab at Broome's Hotel. There may be something there – something I haven't got – and if there is, I'm going to get it or die in the attempt."

"Spoken like your old self," his friend answered. "Go to it, and the best of luck."

Once again Inspector Duff was walking down Piccadilly. The cold drizzle of the afternoon had turned into a fitful snowfall. Just enough to make his footing on the pavement uncertain, to penetrate down his collar and annoy him. Under his breath he cursed the English climate.

The night porter was on duty at the desk just inside the Half Moon Street entrance of Broome's Hotel. He put aside his evening paper and regarded the inspector benevolently over his spectacles.

"Good evening, sir," he said. "My word – is it snowing?"

"It's trying to," Duff answered. "Look here, you and I haven't seen much of each other. You recall the night when the American was killed in room 28?"

"I am not likely to forget it, sir. A most disturbing occurrence. In all my years at Broome's—"

"Yes, yes, of course. Have you thought much about that night lately? Have you recalled any incident about which you haven't told me?"

"There was one thing, sir. I meant to speak to you about it if I saw you again. I'm afraid that so far there has been no mention of the cablegram."

"What cablegram?"

"The one that came in about ten o'clock, sir. Addressed to Mr Hugh Morris Drake."

"There was a cablegram addressed to Mr Drake? Who received it?"

"I did, sir."

"And who took it up to his room?"

"Martin, the floor waiter. He was just going off for the night, and none of the bellboys was available. So I asked Martin if he would kindly take it up to Mr Drake—"

"Where is Martin now?"

"I don't know, sir. Perhaps he is still at supper in the servants' dining-room. I can send a messenger, if you wish—"

But Duff had already beckoned to a venerable bellboy who was resting comfortably on a bench farther down the hall. "Quick," he cried. He handed the old man a shilling. "Get Martin, the floor waiter, for me before he leaves the hotel. Try the servants' dining-room."

The old man disappeared with surprising speed, and Duff again addressed the night porter. "I should have heard of this before," he said sternly.

"Do you really think it's important, sir?" inquired the porter blandly.

"Everything is important in a matter of this sort."

"Ah, sir, you've had so much more experience with such matters than we have. I was naturally a bit upset and—"

The detective turned away, for Martin had arrived. His jaws were still moving, so suddenly had he left the table. "You want—" He swallowed. "You want me, sir?"

"I do." Duff was all action now; his words crisp and clear. "About ten o'clock on the night Mr Hugh Morris Drake was murdered in room 28, you delivered a cablegram to his room?"

He stopped, surprised. For the usually ruddy Martin had gone white and seemed about to collapse on the spot.

"I did, sir," he managed to say.

"You took it up, I presume, and knocked at Mr Drake's door? Then what happened?"

"Why – why, Mr Drake, sir, he came to the door and took the envelope. He thanked me, and gave me a tip. A generous one. Then I came away."

"That is all?"

"Yes, sir. Yes, sir. Quite all."

Duff seized the young man rather roughly by the arm. He meant it to be rough – all the authority of Scotland Yard behind it. The waiter cringed.

"Come with me," Duff said. He pushed the servant along to the manager's office, deserted and in semi-darkness. Thrusting Martin into a chair, he fumbled for the switch of the lamp on the manager's desk, and turned it on. Moving the lamp so that the full glare of it fell on the servant, he slammed shut the door and sat down in a chair facing the young man.

"You're lying, Martin," he began. "And by heaven, I'm in no mood to stand it. I've dilly-dallied over this case as long as I mean to. You're lying – a blind man would know it. But you've finished now. The truth from you, my boy, or by gad— "

"Yes, sir," muttered the waiter. He whimpered a little. "I'm sorry, sir. My wife has been telling me I ought to give you – the whole story. She's been nagging me. 'Tell him,' she says. But I – I didn't know what to do. You see, I'd taken the hundred pounds."

"What hundred pounds?"

"The hundred pounds Mr Honywood gave me, sir."

"Honywood gave you money? What for?"

"You won't send me to prison, Inspector— "

"I'll lock you up in a minute if you don't talk, and talk fast."

"I know I've done wrong, sir – but a hundred pounds is a lot of money. And when I accepted it, I didn't know anything about the murder."

"Why did Honywood give you a hundred pounds? Stop a bit. Take it from the beginning. The truth, or I'll arrest you at once. You went upstairs with that cablegram for Mr Drake. You knocked on the door of room 28. Then what?"

"The door opened, sir."

"Yes, of course. Who opened it? Drake?"

"No, sir."

"What! Who, then?"

"Mr Honywood opened it, sir. The gentleman who had room 29."

"So Honywood opened Drake's door? What did he say?"

"I gave him the envelope. 'It's for Mr Drake,' I told him. He looked at it. 'Oh, yes,' he said, and handed it back, 'You will find Mr Drake in room 29, Martin. We have changed rooms for the night.'"

Duff's heart leaped at the words. A feeling of exultation, so long in coming, swept over him. "Yes," he remarked. "Then what?"

"I knocked on the door of room 29 – Mr Honywood's room – and after a time Mr Drake came to the door. He was wearing his pajamas, sir. He took the cablegram, thanked me, and gave me a tip. So I came away."

"And the hundred pounds?"

"At seven in the morning when I went on duty, Mr Honywood rang for me. He was back in room 29 again, sir. He asked me not to say anything about the change of rooms the night before. And he handed me two fifty-pound notes. Fair took my breath away, he did. So I promised – gave him my word. At a quarter before eight, I found Mr Drake murdered in room 28. I was frightened, and no mistake. I – it seemed I couldn't think, sir – I was that frightened. I met Mr Honywood in the hall. 'I have your word,' he reminded me. 'I swear I had nothing to do with the murder. You stick to your promise, Martin, and you won't regret it.'"

"So you stuck to your promise," said Duff accusingly.

"I'm – I'm sorry, sir. No one asked me about the cablegram. If they had, things might have been different. I was afraid, sir –

it seemed best just to keep mum. When I got home, my wife said I'd done wrong. She's been begging me to tell."

"You follow her advice in the future," Duff advised. "You've disgraced Broome's Hotel."

Martin's face paled again. "Don't say that, sir. What are you going to do to me?"

Duff rose. In spite of all the delay this weak young man had caused him, he found it difficult to view the matter as sternly as he should. This was the sort of news he had been waiting for, praying for, and now that it had come, his heart was light and he was extremely happy.

"I have no time for you," he said. "What you have told me here you are not to repeat unless I ask you to do so. Is that understood?"

"Perfectly, sir."

"You are not to leave your present position or home without advising me of your whereabouts. With these restrictions, things go on as usual. Tell your wife she was right, and give her my compliments."

He left the waiter wilted and perspiring in the manager's office, and walked with jaunty air to the street. Pleasant, a bit of snow after so much rain. Just what London needed. Pretty good climate, the English. The very sort to keep a man on his toes, full of vim and energy. Martin's story, it will be seen, had completely altered Inspector Duff's outlook on life.

He walked along, considering what the waiter had told him. "Mr Drake is in room 29, Martin. We have changed rooms for the night." In that case, Drake must have been murdered in room 29. But in the morning, he was back in his own bed in room 28. Well, it all fitted in with what Duff had thought at the time. "Something tells me that Hugh Morris Drake was murdered elsewhere," he had said. That something had been right. Duff had been right. Not such a fool, if you came right down to it. The inspector's spirits soared.

Back in his own bed in the morning. Who had put him there? Honywood, of course. Who had murdered him? Who but Honywood?

But stop a bit. If Honywood intended murder, why the change in rooms? A ruse, perhaps, to get the door open between them and free access to the person of Hugh Morris Drake. Yet he had already stolen the housekeeper's key. Such a ruse was hardly necessary. And if he was intending murder, would he have calmly involved himself by telling Martin of the change of rooms?

No, he wouldn't. Duff came down a bit from the clouds. The matter didn't work out quite so neatly as he had thought it would. Puzzles still. But one thing was certain, Honywood was mixed up in it somehow. Martin's story would bring the New York millionaire back from the Continent in a hurry. And once they had him again at the Yard, the skein would begin to unravel.

Duff went back and tried again. It didn't appear likely that Honywood had intended murder when he changed rooms with Hugh Morris Drake, and then told Martin what had been done. No – the resolution must have come later. Perhaps that cablegram –

Going to the nearby cable office, the detective found it about to close for the night. After a show of authority he was handed a copy of the message Drake had received on the evening of February sixth. It was merely a business communication. "Directors voted price increase in effect July first hope you approve." The cablegram was not the answer, evidently. But Duff blessed that cablegram none the less.

Taking a taxi to the Yard, he called the home of his superior. That gentleman, torn away from a game of bridge, was inclined at first to be short and crisp. But as Duff's story unrolled, he began to share the excitement of his subordinate.

"Where is the travel party now?" he inquired.

"According to the schedule, sir, they are leaving Paris for Nice tonight. They will be in Nice for three days."

"Good. You will take the regular Riviera Express from Victoria in the morning. Nothing to be gained by starting sooner. That will bring you into Nice early on Saturday. I shall see you tomorrow before you leave. Congratulations, my boy. We appear to be getting somewhere at last."

And the superintendent went back to play four hearts, doubled.

After a happy chat with Hayley over the telephone, Duff went to his rooms and packed a bag. At eight in the morning he was in the superintendent's office. His superior took a package of bank-notes from the safe, where money was kept for just such occasions, and handed it over.

"You have your ticket booked, I presume?"

"Yes, sir. I'll pick it up on my way to the station."

"Have the French police hold Honywood for us in Nice until I can get the necessary papers. I'm taking the matter up with the Home Office at once. Goodby, Mr Duff, and the best of luck."

Action was what Duff had wanted, and he rode down to Dover in high spirits. The channel crossing was rough, but that meant nothing to him. By evening they were on the outskirts of Paris, and the train began its slow journey round the ceinture, with many interminable stops. Duff was relieved when they finally reached the Gare de Lyon, and the road to the Riviera stretched straight before them.

As he sat enjoying an excellent dinner, and watching the last walls of Paris disappear into the dusk, he thought deeply about Mr Walter Honywood. No wonder the man had been in such a funk the morning after the murder. If only, Duff reflected, he might have arrested him then, saved himself this long journey. But things were going to come out all right in the end. Silly to worry – they usually did. Soon he would be coming back along this same route, and Honywood would be with him. Perhaps the man's confession would be in the detective's pocket. Not a strong character, Honywood. Not the sort to hold out in the face of all Duff knew now.

The next morning, at a little before ten, Duff's taxi drew up before the gateway leading to the Hotel Excelsior Grand in Nice. This was the name of the hostelry he had found on the detailed itinerary left with him by Lofton. The Excelsior Grand was an enormous rambling affair, set high on a hill overlooking the city and the aquamarine sea, in the midst of extensive grounds. Duff noted orange and olive trees, with here and there a tall cypress, gloomy even under the gracious Riviera sun. The taxi man sounded his asthmatic horn, and after some delay a bellboy appeared and took the detective's bag. Duff followed the servant up the gravel walk that led to the hotel's side entrance. Giant palms were overhead, and bordering the walk were beds of fragrant Parma violets.

The first person the inspector saw when he entered the hotel lobby was the bearded Doctor Lofton. The second person he noted gave him a distinct shock. This was a Frenchman, also bearded, and as resplendent in gold lace and gorgeous uniform as the doorman of a Ritz hotel. The two men were in close converse, their beards almost touching, and Lofton looked worried. He glanced up and saw Duff.

"Ah, Inspector," he remarked, and a shadow crossed his face. "You made quick time. I scarcely expected you so soon."

"You expected me?" Duff returned, puzzled.

"Naturally. If you please, Monsieur le Commissaire. May I present Inspector Duff, of Scotland Yard, Monsieur Henrique?" He turned to Duff. "This gentleman, as you have no doubt gathered from his uniform, is the local commissary of police."

The Frenchman rushed over to Duff and grasped his hand. "I am so happy for this meeting. Me, I am a fond admirer of

Scotland Yard. I beg of you that you will not judge harshly in this case, Monsieur Duff. Consider if you will the stupidity with which we have been faced. Is the body left as it fell? No. Is the pistol permitted to lie in peace where it was? Not for a moment. All – all have touched it – the concierge, two bellboys, a clerk – five or six people. With what result? In the matter of fingerprints we are helpless. Is it possible that you can picture such stupidity—"

"One moment, please," Duff broke in. "A body? A pistol?" He turned to Lofton. "Tell me what has happened."

"You don't know?" Lofton asked.

"Of course not."

"But I thought – however, it is too soon. I understand now. You were already on your way. Well, Inspector, you arrive most opportunely. Poor Walter Honywood killed himself in the grounds of this hotel last night."

For a moment Duff said nothing. Walter Honywood had killed himself – while Scotland Yard moved forward to take him. A guilty conscience, no doubt. Killed Drake, and then himself. The case was over. But Duff felt no elation; he felt instead an unpleasant sensation of being let down. This was too easy. Too easy altogether.

"But did Monsieur Honywood finish himself?" the commissary was saying. "Alas, Inspector Duff, we cannot be certain. The fingerprints on the pistol – destroyed by the stupidity of the hotel employees, as I have related to you. True – it lay by his side, as though fallen from a dying hand. No one was seen near that vicinity. But even so, I welcome eagerly the opinion of a man from Scotland Yard."

"You have found no note of farewell? No message of any sort?"

"Alas, no. Last night we searched his apartment. Today I am here to repeat the process. I should be overjoyed if you would be kind enough to join me."

"I'll be with you in a moment," Duff said, with an air of dismissal. The commissary bowed and retired.

Duff turned at once to Doctor Lofton. "Please tell me all you know about this," he directed. They sat down together on a sofa.

"I gave the party only three days in Paris," Lofton began. "Trying to make up for the time lost in London, you see. We arrived here yesterday morning. In the afternoon Honywood decided to drive over to Monte Carlo. He invited Mrs Luce and Miss Pamela Potter to go with him. At six o'clock last evening I was here in the lobby talking with Fenwick – the prize pest of the tour, between you and me – when I saw Mrs Luce and the girl enter that side door over there. I asked them about their drive, and they said they'd enjoyed it immensely. Honywood, they told me, was out at the gate paying off the driver of the car – he would be in in a moment. They went on upstairs. Fenwick continued to pester me. There was the sound of a sharp report from outside, but I paid no attention. I thought it the exhaust of a car, or possibly a bursting tire – you know how they drive over here. In another moment Mrs Luce came rushing from the lift. She's the calmest of women ordinarily, and I was struck by her appearance. She seemed to be in a state of high excitement—"

"One moment," Duff put in. "Have you told any of this to the commissary of police?"

"No. I thought it better to save it for you."

"Good. Go on. Mrs Luce was upset—"

"Extremely so. She hurried up to me. 'Has Mr Honywood come in yet?' she demanded. I stared at her. 'Mrs Luce – what has happened?' I cried. 'A great deal has happened,' she replied. 'I must see Mr Honywood at once. What can be keeping him?' The memory of that sharp report – like a shot, I realized it now – came back to me. I rushed out, followed by Mrs Luce. We found the gardens in darkness, dusk had fallen, these economical French had not yet lighted the lamps. About half-way down the walk we came upon Walter Honywood, lying partly on the walk, partly on the floral border. He was shot unerringly through the heart, the pistol lay at his side, near his right hand."

"Suicide?" said Duff, giving the doctor a searching look.

"I believe so."

"You want to believe so."

"Naturally. It would be better—" Lofton stopped. Mrs Luce was standing just back of the sofa.

"Suicide, your grandmother," she remarked briskly. "Good morning, Inspector Duff. You're wanted here. Murder again."

"Murder?" Duff repeated.

"Absolutely," returned the old lady. "I'll tell you in a moment why I think so. Oh, you needn't look so shocked, Doctor Lofton. Another member of your party has been killed, and what worries me is, will there be enough of us to supply the demand? It's still quite some distance around the world."

VIII

FOG ON THE RIVIERA

Lofton was standing, and he began to pace nervously back and forth over a patch of bright sunlight that lay on the Persian rug. He was chewing savagely at the ends of his mustache, a habit he had when perturbed. Mrs Luce wished he wouldn't do it.

"I can't believe it," the conductor cried. "It's incredible. One murder in the party I might admit – but not two. Unless someone is trying to wreck my business. Someone with a grudge against me."

"It seems more likely," the old lady said dryly, "that someone has a grudge against the members of your party. As for your believing that this second affair is murder too, listen to what I have to say, and then tell me what you think." She sat down on the sofa. "Come," she went on, "draw up that chair and stop pacing. You remind me of a lion I used to see at the Hamburg Zoo – I got to know him quite well – but no matter. Inspector Duff, won't you sit here beside me? I think you will both find my story interesting."

Duff meekly took his place, and Lofton also obeyed orders. Somehow, this was the type of woman who doesn't have to speak twice.

"Mr Honywood, Miss Pamela and I drove to Monte Carlo yesterday afternoon," Mrs Luce continued. "Perhaps you already know that, Inspector. Mr Honywood has been rather distraught and worried on this tour, but during our jaunt over to Monaco he seemed to relax – he was quite charming, really. More, I imagine, like his real self. He was not contemplating suicide – I am confident of that. There was a man once at the hill station of Darjeeling, in India – it happened I was the last person to see him alive – but I needn't go into it. Mr Honywood was light-hearted, almost gay. He returned here at dusk last night still in that mood. We left him out at the gate paying off the driver of the car and, coming in, went to our rooms."

"I saw you," Lofton reminded her.

"Yes, of course. Well, as I was unlocking my door, it came over me in a flash that the lock had been tampered with. Once, in Melbourne, Australia, my hotel room was entered – I'd had experience, you see. The doors here have shrunk, the cracks are wide, and I saw about the lock the marks of some sharp instrument, probably a knife. A simple matter to force the spring. I went inside and turned on the light. Instantly my impressions were verified. My room was in the utmost confusion, it had been searched from top to bottom. My trunk was broken open, and in a moment I made sure that what I had feared had happened. A document that had been entrusted to my keeping was missing."

"What sort of document?" Duff inquired with interest.

"We must go back to London, and the period following the murder of Hugh Drake. On the Saturday afternoon just two days before our departure from your city, Mr Duff, I had a message from Mr Walter Honywood asking me to meet him at once in the lounge of Broome's Hotel. I was puzzled, of course, but I did as he asked. He came into the room in what seemed a very perturbed state of mind. 'Mrs Luce,' he said without preamble, 'I know you are a woman of wide experience and great discretion. Though I have no right to do so, I am going to ask a favor of you.' He took a long white envelope from his pocket. 'I wish you to take charge of this envelope for me. Keep it well guarded, and if anything should happen to me on this tour, please open it and read the contents at once.'"

"And that is the document which was stolen?" Duff demanded.

"Let's not get ahead of our story," the old lady replied. "Naturally I was somewhat taken aback. I hadn't said two words to him thus far on the tour. 'Mr Honywood,' I inquired, 'what is in this envelope?' He looked at me in a queer way. 'Nothing,' he replied. 'Nothing save a list of instructions as to what must be done in case I – in case I am not here any more.' 'Certainly Doctor Lofton is the person with whom this should be left,' I told him. 'No,' he said. 'Doctor Lofton is decidedly not the person to hold that envelope.'

"Well, I just sat there, wondering. I asked him what he thought was going to happen to him. He murmured something about being ill – one never could tell, he said. He looked so spent, so utterly weary, I felt sorry for him. We were all rather on edge. I knew that Mr Honywood was supposed to be suffering from a nervous breakdown, and I told myself that this was perhaps the whim of a sick and troubled mind. It seemed to me a small thing he was asking, and I told him I would take the envelope. He appeared to be delighted. 'It's so good of you,' he said. 'I would keep it locked up, if I were you. We had better not leave this room together. I will wait here until you have gone. And if you don't mind, I suggest we keep as far apart as possible when we are with the other members of the tour.'

"All that was rather queer, too. But I had an engagement with some friends in Belgravia that afternoon, and I was already late. I patted the poor man on the back, told him not to worry, and hurried out. When I got to my room, I glanced at the envelope. On it was written in a small script: 'To be opened in case of my death. Walter Honywood.' I hastily locked it in my trunk, and went out."

"You should have communicated with me at once," Duff reproved her.

"Should I? I couldn't decide. As I say, I thought it the notion of a sick mind, and of no importance. And I was very busy those last few days in London. It wasn't until I got on the train for Dover on Monday morning that I really began to think about Mr Honywood and the document he had given into my care. For the first time I wondered if it could have any connection with the murder of Hugh Drake. When I walked on to the deck of the channel boat at Dover, I determined to find out.

"I saw Mr Honywood leaning against the starboard rail, and I went over and joined him. He seemed very reluctant to have me do so. All the while we talked he kept glancing up and down the deck with a sort of hunted and terrified look in his eyes. I was quite uncomfortable about the whole affair by this time. 'Mr Honywood,' I said, 'I have been thinking about that envelope you left with me. I feel the moment has arrived for a frank talk between us. Tell me – have you any reason to believe that your life is in danger?'

"He started at that, and gave me a searching look. 'Why – no,' he stammered. 'Not at all. No more than anyone's life is in danger in this uncertain world.' His reply didn't satisfy me. I decided to put into words a thought that had come to me in the train. 'If you should meet the same fate as Hugh Morris Drake,' I said, 'would the name of your assailant be found inside that envelope?'

"It seemed for a moment that he wasn't going to answer me. Then he turned, and his eyes were so sad that again I pitied him. 'My dear lady,' he remarked, 'why should you think I would put such a burden on you? That envelope contains just what I said it did – instructions to be carried out in case of my death.' 'If that is true,' I answered, 'why wasn't it left with Doctor Lofton? Why must I guard it so carefully? Why do you object to our being seen together?' He nodded. 'Those are fair questions,' he admitted, 'and I'm frightfully sorry I can't answer them. But I give you my word, Mrs Luce – I am not letting you in for anything. Please – I beg of you – hold that envelope just a little longer, and say nothing. The matter will soon be settled. And now – if you don't mind' – he was still looking up and down in that frightened, anxious way – 'I don't feel very well and I am going inside to lie down.' Before I could say another word, he had gone.

"Well, I went on to Paris, still worried. I'm sorry to say I didn't believe what the poor man had told me. I thought that with my usual perspicacity I had hit upon the true situation, I was certain that Walter Honywood expected to be murdered, just as Hugh Morris Drake was murdered, and by the same person. And I was almost as certain that he had written the name of that person in the letter he left with me. That would make me a sort of accomplice in the Drake murder or something like it. I had no fear on that score. Once, in Japan, where I lived three years, I protected – oh, well, I had right on my side, there's nothing more to be said. But in this case I didn't want to protect anybody. I wanted the man who had killed Drake discovered and punished. I was upset – and I'm not often upset. I didn't know what to do."

"There was just one thing to do," remarked Duff sternly. "And I am disappointed in you that you didn't do it. You had my address—"

"Yes, I know. But I'm not accustomed to calling in some mere man to help me solve my difficulties. There was one other thing to do, and I'm disappointed in you that you haven't thought of it. Have you never heard of the old trick of opening an envelope by the use of steam?"

"You steamed open that envelope?" Duff cried.

"I did, and I make no apologies. All's fair in love and murder. That night in Paris I released the flap, and took out the sheet of paper the envelope contained."

"And what was on it?" Duff asked eagerly.

"Just what poor Mr Honywood had told me was on it. A brief note that ran something like this:

"'Dear Mrs Luce: I am so sorry to have troubled you. Will you be kind enough to ask Doctor Lofton to communicate at once with my wife, Miss Sybil Conway? She is at the Palace Hotel, San Remo, Italy.'"

"Meaning precisely nothing," Duff sighed.

"Precisely," agreed Mrs Luce. "I felt rather small when I read it. And puzzled. I had never been so puzzled in all my seventy-two years. Why couldn't he have left that message with the doctor? There was no need of it in the first place. Doctor Lofton knew the name and whereabouts of Mr Honywood's wife. A number of us did – he had mentioned her several times, and said that she was in San Remo. Yet here he had written this unnecessary bit of information on a slip of paper and given it to me, intimating that I must guard it with my life."

Duff stared thoughtfully into space. "I don't get it," he admitted.

"Nor I," said Mrs Luce. "But can you wonder I believe Mr Honywood was murdered? I am sure he saw it coming – the look in his eyes. And the murderer thought it necessary to get possession of that slip of paper in my trunk before going on with his plans. Why? Heaven knows. Who told him there was such a paper? Did Walter Honywood? It's all too obscure for me. You must unravel it, Mr Duff. I hand the whole matter over to you."

"Thanks," answered Duff. He turned to Doctor Lofton. "Is it true you already knew that Honywood's wife was in San Remo?"

"I certainly did," Lofton replied. "Honywood told me so himself. He asked me to stop over there a day, at the Palace Hotel, in the hope that he might persuade her to join our tour."

Duff frowned. "The fog increases," he sighed. "You've notified the lady, I presume?"

"Yes, I called her on the telephone last night, and when she heard my news, I believe she fainted. At least, it sounded that way – I heard her fall, and I lost the connection. This morning her maid telephoned me and said that Mrs Honywood – or Sybil Conway, as she calls herself – was unable to come to Nice, and that she wanted me to bring her husband's body to San Remo."

Duff considered. "I must have a talk with the lady at my earliest. Well, Doctor, now that we have heard Mrs Luce's story, what have you to say about Honywood's death?"

"What should I say? I must admit that it begins to look like something more than a simple case of suicide. As a matter of fact, I shall have to tell you that my own room was searched repeatedly while we were in Paris. Yes, it was probably murder, Inspector – but can you think of any good reason why anyone save the three of us here should know it? If the French police find it out – well, you understand what red tape is over here, Mr Duff."

"There's a lot in what you say, Doctor," Duff agreed. "I must admit I wouldn't care to have the Paris Sûreté enter the case now – much as I respect their intelligence and their record. No, it's my job, and I want to do it."

"Precisely," said Lofton, with evident relief. "Consider this, too. Shall we tell the remaining members of the party what we suspect? They're a bit on edge already. Fenwick has tried to stir up mutiny before, and this would certainly start him off again. Suppose the party broke up and scattered to the four winds? Would that help your investigation? Or would you prefer that we stick together until your case is solved?"

Duff smiled grimly. "You put it all most logically and convincingly, Doctor. If you'll get your party together, I'll have another chat with them, and then I'll see what I can do with that commissary of police. I don't believe he'll prove difficult."

Lofton departed, and Duff stood staring after him. He looked down at Mrs Luce.

"Honywood thought Lofton was decidedly not the person to hold the envelope," he remarked.

She nodded vigorously. "He was very firm on that point," she said.

Pamela Potter and Mark Kennaway had entered the side door of the hotel. Duff nodded and waved to them. They came over at once.

"Why, it's Inspector Duff," the girl cried, with every evidence of pleasure. "How nice to see you again."

"Hello, Miss Pamela," the detective said. "And Mr Kennaway. Been out for a stroll?"

"Yes," answered the girl. "We managed to evade the eagle-eyed chaperon and took a walk along the beach. It was heavenly – at least I thought it was. But I'm given to understand that the air is nowhere near so invigorating as on the North Shore, in Massachusetts."

Kennaway shrugged. "I'm afraid I'm in wrong," he remarked. "I ventured to say a good word for my native state, and I hear that in Detroit it isn't even regarded as a good market for automobiles. And how could we sink lower than that? However, I do approve of Nice—"

"Fine," laughed the girl. "They won't have to tear it down just yet. Why – what's wrong with Mr Tait?"

The famous lawyer was approaching rapidly, his face a purplish red that boded ill for a man with a heart like his.

"Where the devil – oh, hello, Mr Duff," he began. "Where the devil have you been, Kennaway?"

The young man flushed at his tone. "I have been for a walk with Miss Pamela," he said in a low voice.

"Oh, you have, have you?" Tait went on. "Leaving me to shift for myself. Did you think of that? To tie my own necktie." He indicated the polka-dot bow he affected. "Look at the damn' thing. I never could tie them."

"I wasn't aware," Kennaway said, his voice rising, "that I was engaged as a valet."

"You know perfectly well what you were engaged for. To be my companion. If Miss Potter wants a companion, let her hire one—"

"That is a service," began the young man hotly, "for which some people do not have to—"

"Just a moment." Pamela Potter stepped forward with a conciliating smile. "Do let me fix that tie, Mr Tait. There. That's better. Go look in a mirror and see." Tait softened a bit – he couldn't very well help it. But he continued to glare at the boy. Then he started to walk away.

"Pardon me, Mr Tait," Duff said. "The members of Doctor Lofton's party are asked to meet in that parlor over there—"

Tait wheeled. "What for? More of your damned silly investigation, eh? You may waste the time of the others, but not mine, sir, not mine. You're a fumbler, Inspector, an incompetent fumbler – I saw that in London. Where did you get there? Nowhere. To hell with your meetings." He took a few steps then turned and came back. His face was contrite. "I beg your pardon, Inspector. I'm sorry. It's my blood pressure – my nerves are all shot to pieces. I really didn't mean what I said."

"Very good," Duff answered quietly. "I quite understand. In that parlor across the way, please."

"I will wait there," Tait replied humbly. "Are you coming, Mark?"

The young man hesitated a second, then shrugged his shoulders and followed. Mrs Luce and the girl accompanied him. Duff went to the desk of the hotel to register at last. He arranged with a bellboy to take his bag above-stairs. As he turned away, he encountered Mr and Mrs Elmer Benbow.

"Rather expected to see you," Benbow said, after a genial greeting. "But you got here sooner than I thought you would. Too bad about Honywood, isn't it?"

"A great pity," Duff agreed. "What do you think of that affair?"

"Don't know what to think," Benbow told him. "But – well, I guess I'd better tell him, Nettie."

"Of course you'd better tell him," Mrs Benbow advised.

"I don't know whether it has anything to do with all this or not," Benbow continued. "But one night Nettie and I went to one of those hot shows in Paris – boy, did I need my smoked glasses? – and when we got back to the hotel, our room was a wreck. Every bit of baggage ripped open and searched, but not a thing taken. I didn't know what to make of it. Wasn't Scotland Yard, was it?"

Duff smiled. "Hardly. Scotland Yard is not so clumsy as that, Mr Benbow. So your room was searched. Tell me – have you been seeing much of Mr Honywood since you left London?"

"Well, yes – we have. His room was near ours, in Paris. I went around a little with him there. He knew the town like I know Akron. Say – do you believe he killed himself?"

"It looks that way," Duff replied. "Will you wait for me in that parlor, please?"

"Sure," Benbow answered, and he and his wife walked to the room Duff had indicated. The detective followed. As he crossed the threshold, the Minchins appeared in his path. Maxy gave him a friendly greeting.

"Well, another guy has been put on the spot," the racketeer remarked, in a hoarse whisper. "Looks like they was something doing in this mob. What do you make of it, Officer?"

"What do you?" Duff inquired.

"Too deep for this baby," Maxy assured him. "No, I don't get it. But that guy Honywood didn't rub himself out, you can gamble your roll on that. I been watching. I see other birds get the news their number was up, and believe me, he had it. You could tell it from his eyes. Looked like he was praying to know which way the hot lead was coming from."

"Mr Minchin," Duff said, "I'm going to ask a favor of you. When we discuss the affair here this morning, will you be good enough to keep that opinion to yourself?"

"I'm wise," Minchin replied. "It's just like I told you – I trail along with the bulls this time. Sealed like a coffin – that's my lips."

Lofton arrived at that moment with Mrs Spicer and Stuart Vivian. While they were finding chairs, Ross came limping in. He was followed by Keane, whose sly little eyes traveled everywhere about the room before he sat down.

"All here but the Fenwicks," Lofton remarked to Duff. "They seem to be out, and I didn't make much effort to find them. If we can get everything settled before that little fool shows up, so much the better."

Duff nodded, and faced the group. "Here I am again," he began grimly. "I want to say a few words to you about your future plans, in view of last night's unhappy affair. I refer to the suicide of Mr Walter Honywood."

"Suicide?" inquired Mrs Spicer languidly. She looked very smart in a white frock, with a trim little hat pulled far down over her brilliant eyes.

"Suicide is what I said," Duff went on. "Has anyone of you anything to tell me about the unfortunate occurrence?"

No one spoke. "Very good," Duff continued. "In that case we will—"

"Just a moment," Vivian broke in. The scar on his forehead stood out with appalling clarity in that bright room. "Merely a little incident, Inspector. It may mean nothing. But Mr Honywood and I came down here in the same sleeping compartment. I'd got to know him rather well in Paris – I liked him. We went to the dining-car together for dinner. When we returned to our compartment, both of my bags had been broken into and obviously searched. Nothing belonging to Honywood had been touched. It seemed a bit odd – and odder still when I looked at his face, after I had made my discovery. He was deathly pale, and trembling like a leaf. I asked him what was wrong, but he turned my questions aside. None the less, he was obviously alarmed – if that is a strong enough word."

"Thanks," Duff said. "Interesting, but it doesn't upset the suicide theory."

"You think, then, he committed suicide?" Vivian asked, with just a faint note of incredulity.

"That is what the French police believe, and I am inclined to agree with them," Duff told him. "Mr Honywood had suffered a nervous breakdown. His wife, of whom he appeared very fond, was estranged from him. The stage was all set for a tragedy of that sort."

"Perhaps it was," Vivian replied, but there was a question in the words.

"You have had a most distressing tour so far," Duff continued. "But I am inclined to think your troubles are now over. It is possible the secret of Mr Drake's – er – accident has died with Honywood. I may tell you that certain of my discoveries in London would indicate that it has. Better let them think so, anyhow. It might put the murderer off his guard. I should like to see you, as soon as the police investigation here is finished, resume your tour. I feel sure that it will be without unpleasant incident from here on. Is there any reason why you shouldn't?"

"None whatever," said Mrs Luce promptly. "I'll go on as long as there's a tour."

"That's the way we feel, lady," Maxy Minchin added.

"I knew you would," Mrs Luce assured him.

"Well, I don't see any reason for stopping," Captain Keane announced.

"I couldn't go back to Akron without the pictures I promised 'em," Benbow remarked. "I'd be the laughing stock of the town.

Around the world – that was my order, and when I turn in an order, I want to see it filled."

"Mr Ross?" Duff inquired.

The lumber man smiled. "By all means," he said, "let's go on with the tour. It's taken me a long time to get started, and I'd hate to drop it now."

"Mrs Spicer?"

That lady took out a long holder, and inserted a cigarette. "I'm no quitter," she remarked. "Who's got a match?"

Vivian leaped into action. It was evident he would follow where she led.

"Who began all this, anyhow?" Tait wanted to know. His temper appeared still uncertain. "No one has ever talked of stopping, except that little idiot Fenwick. Do I have to apologize? No – he isn't here, is he?"

"Good," Doctor Lofton said. "We shall leave here whenever the commissary of police gives the word. I'll let you know the time of the train later. Our next stop will be San Remo, over the border in Italy."

Amid a buzz of comment, the meeting broke up. Duff followed Mrs Luce from the room. He stopped her beside the sofa where they had talked before.

"By the way," he remarked, "when you came back last night, and entered the lobby with Miss Pamela, I believe Lofton was here talking with Fenwick?"

"He was – yes."

"When you hurried down again, after discovering the theft of that envelope, was Fenwick still with the doctor?"

"He was not. Doctor Lofton was alone."

"Lofton had asked you about Honywood when you came in?"

"Yes. He inquired about Mr Honywood in a rather anxious way."

"Be careful. I don't want editorial opinions, Mrs Luce. I want facts. So far as you know, Lofton and Fenwick may have separated the moment you went up in the lift to your room?"

"Yes. And Doctor Lofton may have rushed outside and fired that—"

"Never mind."

"But I don't like the man either," protested the old lady.

"What do you mean by that word either?" Duff inquired. "I don't have likes and dislikes, Mrs Luce. I can't afford to, in my business."

"Oh, I guess you're human, like the rest of us," said Mrs Luce, and went on her way.

Lofton came up. "Thank you, Inspector," he remarked. "You settled our future plans in short order. If you can have an equal success with the commissary of police, all will be well."

"I fancy it will. By the way, Doctor Lofton – last night, when you heard that shot outside, were you still talking with Fenwick?"

"Yes, of course. I couldn't shake the man."

"Do you think he also heard the sound of the shot being fired?"

"I imagine he did. He started a bit."

"Ah, yes. Then you and he both have a very good alibi."

Lofton smiled in a somewhat strained way. "I guess we have. Unfortunately, however, Mr Fenwick is not here to verify what I say."

"What do you mean, he's not here?" Duff cried.

"I didn't tell you in the parlor," Lofton answered, "but this note has been found, pinned to the pillowcase in the Fenwicks' room. You'll notice it is addressed to me." He handed it over. Duff read:

"Dear Doctor Lofton: I warned you that if there was any more funny business, we'd quit. Well, there has been more funny business, and we're off. I've arranged it with the concierge, and we're pulling out in a car at midnight. You can't stop us, and you know it. You have my Pittsfield address, and I shall expect to find a rebate on the price of the tour waiting for me there when I get back. That means you had better get it off at once.

"Norman Fenwick."

"Leaving at midnight," mused Duff. "I wonder which way they went."

"The hotel people tell me Fenwick was asking about the boats from Genoa to New York."

"Genoa, eh? Then they went east along the Riviera. They're over the border by now."

Lofton nodded. "Undoubtedly. Over the border in Italy."

"You appear rather pleased, Doctor Lofton," Duff remarked.

"I'm delighted," the doctor returned. "Why should I try to conceal it? In fifteen years of touring, I never met a worse pest than Fenwick. I'm glad he's gone."

"Even though your alibi went with him?" Duff suggested.

Lofton smiled. "Why should I need an alibi?" he inquired blandly.

IX

DUSK AT SAN REMO

Lofton stepped over to the desk, leaving the detective to ponder this somewhat disconcerting news. Two of his traveling group of suspects had broken away from the fold. Nothing had been discovered that connected the Fenwicks with the London murder in any way – or with that of Honywood either. None the less, Duff felt that every member of the Lofton party was under suspicion until the problem was solved, and the Fenwicks were not immune. The man did not look like a murderer, but experience had taught the inspector that few murderers do. He was exceedingly annoyed by the high-handed conduct of the pompous little chap from Pittsfield. Yet what could he do about it? He had no authority to dictate the actions of anyone in that party save Honywood – and Honywood was dead.

A commotion about the lift attracted his attention, and the next moment the resplendent commissary of police was marching toward him. How well that dazzling uniform fitted into the colorful background of the Riviera.

"Ah, Inspector, you do not arrive above," the commissary cried. "I wait, but you do not appear."

Duff shook his head. "There was no need, Monsieur le Commissaire. I know only too well the keen eyes of the French police. May I congratulate you on your conduct of this case?

I have investigated, and I am struck by the intelligence you have shown."

"That is so kind of you to say," the commissary beamed. "Me, I have learned much that I know from a study of Scotland Yard methods." His chest expanded. "Yes, I believe what you say is correct – I have done well here under the conditions. But what conditions! Impossible even for the most brilliant mind. The stupidity of the servants – Monsieur, I could easily weep. Footprints trampled upon, fingerprints destroyed. What is it there remains I can do?"

"Fortunately, there is nothing more you need to do," Duff assured him. "It is a case of suicide, Commissary. I can guarantee that."

The Frenchman's face lighted with relief. "It is a thing I am most 'appy to hear. A woman – she is in it, of course?"

Duff smiled. "Yes," he said, taking his cue neatly. "The dead man's wife. He loved her passionately, and she deserted him. Heart-broken he tried to go on alone. It was no use. Even here in your charming and cheerful city, he perceived it was no use. Hence the pistol, the body on the walk."

The commissary shook his head. "Ah, the woman, Monsieur. Always the woman! What suffering, what sorrow, is she not responsible for? Yet – could we do without her?"

"Hardly," ventured Duff.

"Never!" cried the commissary, with vehemence. "I shudder to think—" He paused. "But I fear we get beside the point. The Doctor Lofton tells me why you are here, Inspector. I accept your word of the suicide. Who should know better than you? So I will report it, and the affair closes itself."

"Very good," Duff nodded. "Then I take it that the party may continue its tour at once?"

The commissary hesitated. After all, one must not treat the affair too lightly. "Not quite so fast, Monsieur, if you please," he said. "I go now to the room of the Juge d'Instruction. With him rests the final decision. Presently I shall call you with the telephone and inform you what that is. The arrangement is satisfactory, Inspector?"

"Oh, quite," Duff answered. "Once more, my heartiest congratulations."

"You say too much, Monsieur."

"Not at all. I have been impressed – deeply impressed."

"How can I thank you? How indicate my pleasure at this meeting?"

"Do not attempt it, Monsieur."

"Again I accept your advice. *Bon jour*, Inspector."

"*Bon jour,*" repeated Duff, with a Yorkshire accent. The glittering commissary strode away.

Lofton came up to Duff at once. "Well?" he inquired.

The detective shrugged. "It will be all right, I fancy. The commissary was glad to be convinced. But he has to report the matter to the examining magistrate before a final decision can be made. I am to await a telephone call. I hope it comes soon, as I am eager to put through one myself for San Remo the moment I know what our plans are to be."

"I shall be somewhere in the hotel," Lofton told him. "Naturally I want to hear about it as soon as you get the call. There's a train de luxe at four-thirty this afternoon, and I hope very much we can be on it."

An hour passed before the word came through from the commissary that they could go on whenever they pleased. Duff hastily scribbled a note for Lofton, gave it to a bellboy, and then stepped up to the desk.

"Please get me the Palace Hotel at San Remo on the telephone," he said. "I wish to speak with Mrs Walter Honywood – or Miss Sybil Conway, as she sometimes calls herself."

This, it appeared, was viewed by the staff as considerable of an undertaking. An excited discussion took place behind the scenes. Duff sat down in a nearby chair and waited. After many minutes a bellboy came to him breathless with news. "A lady in San Remo has the wire," he said.

The detective hastened into the booth that was pointed out to him. "Are you there?" he cried. His deep distrust of Continental telephones moved him to shout at the top of his voice.

An answering voice faint, far-away, but musical, sounded in his ear. "Did someone wish to speak to Miss Conway?"

"Yes – I did. Inspector Duff, of Scotland Yard."

"I cannot hear you. Inspector what?"

"Duff. Duff."

"Perhaps you speak a little too loudly. I still can't hear you."

Duff was perspiring freely, and he suddenly realized that he had been bellowing. He spoke in a lower tone, and more distinctly.

"I am Inspector Duff, of Scotland Yard. It has been my duty to investigate the murder of Mr Hugh Drake, of the Lofton travel party, in London. I am now in Nice, where I have happened upon the unfortunate death of your husband, Mr Walter Honywood."

"Yes." The voice was very faint.

"Madam, I am deeply sorry."

"Thank you. What did you wish to say to me?"

"I am wondering if you know anything that may throw light on his death?"

"Doctor Lofton told me it was suicide."

"It was not suicide, Madam." Duff's voice was now very low. "Your husband was murdered. Are you still there?"

"I am here." Very faintly.

"I feel certain the murder has some connection with that of Mr Drake in London," Duff went on.

There was a pause. "I can assure you that it has, Inspector," said the woman.

"What's that?" Duff cried.

"I am telling you that the two are connected. They are, in a manner of speaking, the same murder."

"Good lord," the detective gasped. "What do you mean by that?"

"I will explain when I see you. The story is a long one. You will come to San Remo with the Lofton party?"

"I certainly will. We are leaving here at four-thirty this afternoon, and should reach your hotel about two hours later."

"Very well. The matter can wait until then. Mr Honywood wanted the whole affair kept quiet for my sake. I imagine he feared it would hurt my career in the theater, and that I'd be distressed on that account. But I have made up my mind. I mean to see justice done, at any cost to myself. You see – I know who murdered my husband."

Again Duff gasped.

"You know who—"

"I do, indeed."

"Then, for God's sake, Madam, don't let's take any chances. Tell me now – at once."

"I can only tell you that it was a man who is traveling with the Lofton party around the world."

"But his name – his name!"

"I do not know what he calls himself now. Years ago, when we met him in – in a far country, his name was Jim Everhard. Now he is traveling with the Lofton party, but under another name."

"Who told you this?"

"My husband wrote it to me."

"But he did not write you the name?"

"No."

"Did this same man kill Hugh Morris Drake?" Duff held his breath. It was Drake's murderer he had to find.

"Yes, he did."

"Your husband told you that, too?"

"Yes – it is all in the letter, which I shall give you tonight."

"But this man – who is he – that is what I must discover, Madam. You say you met him years ago. Will you recognize him if you meet him again?"

"I shall recognize him instantly."

Duff took out a handkerchief and mopped his brow. This was magnificent.

"Madam, are you still there? Mrs Honywood?"

"I am still here."

"What you have told me is – very satisfactory." Duff was always given to understatement. "I shall arrive at your hotel at about half past six this evening. I am not certain of the exact moment. With me will be the entire Lofton party." A thought of Fenwick dashed through his mind, but he dismissed it. "There must be no accident. I beseech you to stay in your rooms until I communicate with you again. I shall arrange for you to see every member of the party, preferably from a point where you yourself will remain unseen. When you have made your identification, the rest will lie with me. Everything will be made as easy for you as possible."

"You are very kind. I shall do my duty. I have made up my mind. At any cost to myself – and the cost will not be inconsiderable – I shall help you to bring Walter's murderer to justice. You may rely on me."

"I am relying on you, and I am eternally grateful. Until tonight, then, Mrs Honywood."

"Until tonight. I shall be awaiting your call in my rooms."

As Duff left the booth, he was startled to find Doctor Lofton standing just beside it.

"I got your message," Lofton remarked. "We're booked for the four-thirty express. There's a ticket for you, if you want it."

"Of course I want it," Duff answered. "I'll pay you for it later."

"No hurry." Lofton started to walk away, then paused. "Ah – er – you have talked with Mrs Honywood?"

"I just finished."

"Could she tell you anything?"

"Nothing," Duff replied.

"What a pity," Lofton said casually, and moved on toward the lift.

Duff went to his room as near to elation as he ever got. A difficult case – one of the most difficult he had ever been called upon to face – and another seven hours would solve it. As he sat in the dining-room at luncheon, he made a cautious study of the men in Lofton's travel party. Which one? Which one could smile and smile, and be a villain still? Lofton himself? Lofton was traveling with the party. With, the woman had said, not in. Was that significant? Possibly. Tait, who had experienced that terrific heart attack just as he entered the parlor at Broome's Hotel? Not out of it, not by a long shot. A man could have a weak heart, and still gather the strength to strangle another man of Drake's advanced age. And Tait had about him the look of far countries. Kennaway? A mere boy. Benbow? Duff shook his head. Ross or Vivian or Keane? All possible. Maxy Minchin? He hardly seemed to fit into the setting, but the affair was quite in his line. Fenwick? The detective's heart sank. Suppose it were Fenwick – well, what of it? He'd go after him, even to the ends of the earth – to Pittsfield, Massachusetts, wherever that was – he'd go after Fenwick and bring him back.

At four-thirty that afternoon they were all aboard the train de luxe, bound for San Remo. Duff had confided in no one, so he alone knew what was waiting ahead. He went from one compartment to another, making sure once more – though he had counted them at the station – that no one was missing. After chatting with a number of the others, he entered the compartment occupied by Tait and Kennaway.

"Well, Mr Tait," he began amiably, dropping into a seat, "I trust that for your sake the exciting part of your tour around the world is now ended."

Tait gave him an unfriendly look. "You needn't worry about me," he said.

"How can I help it?" Duff smiled. He sat for a moment in silence, staring out at the passing scene. Wooded hills and richly cultivated plains swept by, a tiny seaport with a chapel, a ruined castle. Beyond, the blue and sparkling Mediterranean. "Rather pretty country along here," the detective ventured.

"Looks like the movies," growled Tait, and picked up a copy of the *New York Herald*'s Paris edition.

Duff turned to the young man. "First trip abroad?" he inquired.

Kennaway shook his head. "No, I used to come over in college vacations. Had a grand time in those days – I didn't know my luck." He looked at the old man and sighed. "Nothing to worry me – nothing on my mind but my hair."

"This is different," Duff suggested.

"I'll sign a statement to that effect any time," smiled the boy.

Duff turned back to the old man with an air of determination. "As I was saying, Mr Tait," he remarked loudly, "how can I help worrying about you? I saw one of your attacks, you may recall, and my word – I thought you were gone, I did indeed."

"I wasn't gone," Tait snapped. "Even you must have noticed that."

"Even I?" Duff raised his eyebrows. "Quite true. I'm not much of a detective, am I? So many points I haven't solved. For example, I don't yet know what you saw inside Broome's parlor that brought on such a severe heart attack."

"I saw nothing, I tell you – nothing."

"I've forgotten," the inspector went on blandly. "Have I asked you this before? On the night Hugh Morris Drake was murdered, did you hear no sound – no cry – you know what I mean?"

"How should I? Honywood's room was between mine and Drake's."

"Ah, yes. So it was. But you see, Mr Tait" – the detective's eyes were keen on the old man's face – "Drake was murdered in Honywood's room."

"What's that?" Kennaway cried. Tait said nothing, but the inspector thought his face had grown a trifle paler.

"You understood what I said, Mr Tait? Drake was murdered in Honywood's room."

The old man tossed down his newspaper. "Perhaps you're a better detective than I thought you," he remarked. "So you've found that out, have you?"

"I have. And under the circumstances, don't you want to alter your story a bit?"

Tait nodded. "I'll tell you just what happened," he said. "I presume you won't believe it, but that won't matter a damn. Early on the morning of February seventh, I was awakened by the sounds of some sort of struggle going on in the room next to mine at Broome's Hotel. Honywood's room, it was. The struggle was extremely brief, and by the time I was fully awake, all indication of it had ceased. I debated with myself what I should do. I'd been trying for some months to rest, and the thought of becoming involved in a matter that did not concern me was very distasteful. No thought of murder, of course, came into my mind. Some sort of trouble – yes – I sensed that. But everything was quiet by that time, and I determined to go back to sleep and forget it.

"In the morning I rose at an early hour and decided to breakfast outside. After I'd had my coffee – it's forbidden but, dammit, no man can live forever – I went for a walk in St. James's Park. When I arrived back at Broome's I met a servant at the Clarges Street entrance who told me that an American had been murdered upstairs. He didn't know the name, but it came to me suddenly that I knew it. Honywood! That struggle! I had heard Honywood murdered and had made no move to help him, to apprehend his assailant.

"I had already had one great shock, you see, when I came to you at the parlor door. I stepped across the threshold, certain that Honywood was dead upstairs. He was the first person I saw. That shock, added to the previous one, was too much. My heart went back on me."

"I see," nodded Duff. "But you told me nothing of the struggle in Honywood's room. Was that sporting of you?"

"Probably not. But when I saw you again, I was weak and ill. My one thought was to keep out of the thing if I could. You had your job – you could do it. All I wanted was peace. That's my story. Believe it or not, as you like."

Duff smiled. "I am rather inclined to believe it, Mr Tait. Subject, of course, to what the future may reveal."

Tait's look softened. "By Jove," he remarked, "you *are* a better detective than I thought you were."

"Thank you very much," answered Duff. "I believe we are already at San Remo."

As the hotel bus rolled through the streets of the town in the dusk, Doctor Lofton spoke a few words to his charges. "We're leaving here tomorrow noon," he announced. "None of you will unpack any more than is absolutely necessary. You understand that we must go on to Genoa at the earliest possible moment."

Presently they drew up before the entrance of the Palace Hotel. Duff secured a room on the first floor, at the head of the stairs leading up from the lobby. There was a lift of the Continental type not far from his door, he noted, as he made a study of his surroundings. Though not a man given to moments of excitement, his heart was beating at a quite surprising rate. The Palace was a comparatively small establishment, not one of the huge show places of the town, but even so there was an air of spaciousness and comfort about it. Dinner, the detective discovered, was only half an hour away. About the lobby and the corridors hung that atmosphere of quiet characteristic of a resort hotel when the guests are dressing for the evening.

Duff had ascertained at the desk that Miss Sybil Conway – it was under that name she had registered – was on the fourth floor. His room, he was glad to discover, was equipped with a telephone. He called Miss Conway's apartment, and in another moment the low musical voice, which must have been so pleasing in the theater, was answering him.

"Inspector Duff, of Scotland Yard." He half-whispered it.

"I'm so glad. The wait has been terrible. I – I am ready to go through with it."

"Good. We must meet at once. The members of the party are all in their rooms, but they will reappear in the lobby presently for dinner. While we are waiting for them, you and I will have a chat."

"Of course. I shall bring you a letter my husband wrote me from London. It will explain many things. And after that—"

"After that, you and I will watch the members of Doctor Lofton's travel party go in to dinner. I have selected our hiding-place, behind a cluster of palms. For our chat, I have planned it this way. There is a small deserted public parlor just beside my room on the first floor. You understand what I mean by the first floor – the one above the lobby – I believe you would call it the second in America. The door of the little parlor can be locked on the inside. I suggest we meet there. Is your apartment near the lift?"

"A few steps only."

"Splendid. You will come down in the lift—Stop a bit. I have thought of a better way. I will come and fetch you. Number 40, I believe – your room?"

"Number 40, yes, I shall be waiting."

Duff went immediately into the hall. He was pleased to see that the corridor was in semi-darkness, illuminated only by such light as came up from below along the open elevator shaft.

He pressed the lift button. Occasional visits to modest hotels in Paris had made him familiar with the whims of the automatic Continental elevator. The cage rose slowly and majestically – thank heaven, for once it was not out of order. He got in, and pressed another button, this time for the fourth floor.

He knocked at the door of number 40, and it was opened by a tall graceful woman. A blaze of light at her back left her face in shadow, but he knew at once that she was beautiful. Her hair was gold, like her gown, and her voice, heard now over no telephone wire, thrilled even the stolid inspector.

"Mr Duff – I'm so glad." She was a little breathless. "Here – this is my husband's letter."

He took it and put it in his pocket. "Thanks a thousand times," he said. "Will you come with me? The lift is waiting."

He ushered her into the narrow cage, then followed and pushed the button for the first floor. Slowly, hesitantly, the unsteady car began its descent.

"I have been ill," Sybil Conway told him. "I am finding it difficult to go on with this. But I must – I must—"

"Hush!" admonished the detective. "Not now, please." They were slipping past the third floor. "In a moment, you must tell me everything—"

He stopped in horror. From slightly above his head came the sharp explosion of a shot. A small object hurtled through the air and fell at his feet. The woman's face appalled him. He caught her in his arms, for he had seen, on the bodice of her gold silk gown, a spreading, dull red stain.

"It's all over," Sybil Conway whispered. Duff could not speak. He reached out one hand and fought savagely with the locked door of the lift. The imperturbable invention of the French moved resolutely on. A great bitterness was in the detective's heart.

This was a situation that would haunt Inspector Duff to the end of his career. He had seen a woman murdered at his side, had held her dying in his arms, locked with her in a little cage, the door of which would open all in good time. He looked aloft into the darkness and knew that it was no use. When the lift released him, he would be too late.

It released him at the first floor. Doors were opening, half-clothed guests were peering out. He carried Sybil Conway to a sofa in the parlor. She was dead, he knew. Running back to the lift, he picked up an object that was lying there. A small bag of wash leather – he did not need to open it. He knew what it contained. Pebbles gathered from some beach – a hundred silly, meaningless little stones.

X

THE DEAFNESS OF MR DRAKE

As Duff left the elevator he closed the door behind him, and almost instantly the bell rang and the cage began to ascend. He stood for a moment watching it slowly rising, the only spot of light in that dark scene. Too late he noted what a target was presented by anyone who stood on the unprotected platform. Like most foreign lifts it moved along a shaft which was, save for a sparse iron grill work, open on all sides. The platform was surrounded by a similar grill, no higher than the average passenger's shoulder. What a shining mark that gold silk gown, how simple to kneel on the floor of the hallway and fire through the grill from above, just as the lift and its human freight passed slowly out of sight. It seemed so obvious now that it had happened, but it was one of those things that no honest man, lacking in imagination, would ever see in advance. As he turned away, the inspector was muttering savagely beneath his breath. In his heart was an unwilling respect for his antagonist.

The owner-manager of the Palace was puffing up the stairs. He was a man of enormous girth, innumerable yards of black frock coat encircled him. Mountains of spaghetti must have existed, ere he could be. After him came his clerk, also in a frock coat, but thin and with a chronically anxious look. The hallway was filled with excited guests.

Quickly the detective led the two men into the parlor, and locked the door. They stood staring at the sofa and its pathetic burden.

As briefly as possible, Duff presented the situation.

"Murdered in the lift? Who would do that?" The eyes widened in the owner's fat face.

"Who, indeed?" replied Duff crisply. "I was with her at the time—"

"Ah, you were? Then you will remain here and talk with the police when they arrive."

"Of course I will. I am Inspector Duff, of Scotland Yard, and this dead woman was to have been an important witness in the matter of a murder which took place in London."

"It becomes clearer," the big man nodded. "The poor, poor lady. But such things, you must know, are bad for my hotel. There is a doctor who lives here." He turned to his clerk. "Vito – you will fetch him at once. Though it is, I fear, too late."

He waddled to the door, unlocked it, and stood there facing the guests. As a screen, he was efficient.

"A small accident," he announced. "It concerns none of you. You will return to your rooms, if you please." Reluctantly the group melted away. As Vito was hurrying by him, the proprietor laid a hand on the clerk's arm. "Call also the City Guards. Not, you understand, the Carabinieri." He glanced at Duff. "They would bring Il Duce himself into the affair," he shrugged.

The clerk dashed down the stairs. Inspector Duff started to leave the room, but the fat man blocked his way. "Where do you go, Signore?" he demanded.

"I want to make an investigation," the detective explained. "I tell you I am from Scotland Yard. How many guests are at present in the hotel?"

"Last night there slept here one hundred and twenty," the owner answered. "It is the season's high point. Quite filled, Signore."

"One hundred and twenty," Duff repeated grimly. A bit of work for the City Guards. A bit of work even for him, who knew that of this great group, only the members of the Lofton party need be considered.

With some difficulty he edged by the owner, and went aloft by way of the stairs. The third-floor hallway was silent and deserted; he found no sign of any sort about the lift shaft. If ever there was a murder without a clue, he reflected, this was no doubt one. Dejectedly he went on up and knocked at the door of room 40.

A white-faced maid opened to him. Briefly he related what had happened. The woman seemed quite overcome.

"She feared this, sir. All afternoon she has been worried. 'If anything happens to me, Tina,' she said, over and over, and she gave me directions what I must do."

"What was that?"

"I was to take her body back to the States, sir. And that of poor Mr Honywood as well. There are cables I must send, too. To friends in New York."

"And relatives, perhaps?"

"I never heard her speak of any relatives, sir. Nor Mr Honywood, either. They seemed quite alone."

"Really? Later, you must give me a list of those to whom you are cabling. Now you had better go down to the parlor on the first floor. Tell the manager who you are. They will no doubt bring your mistress back here presently. I will stop in the rooms a moment."

"You are Inspector Duff?"

"I am."

"My poor mistress spoke of you. Many times in the past few hours."

The maid disappeared, and Duff passed through a small entrance hall into a pleasant sitting-room. The letter Sybil Conway had given him burned in his pocket, demanding to be read, but first he wanted to search these rooms. In a moment the Italian police would arrive and he would be too late. He went to work with speed and system. Letters from American friends – not many – telling nothing. Drawer after drawer – the open trunks – he hurried on. At last he was conscious, as he bent over a bag in Sybil Conway's bedroom, that someone was watching from the doorway. He swung about. A major of the City Guards was standing there, an expression of surprise and displeasure on his dark face.

"You search the rooms, Signore?" he inquired.

"Let me introduce myself," said Duff hastily. "I am Inspector Duff, of Scotland Yard. The British consul will vouch for me."

"From Scotland Yard?" The policeman was impressed. "I begin to understand. It was you who was with the lady when she was killed?"

"Yes," nodded Duff uncomfortably. "I did find myself in that unpleasant position. If you'll sit down—"

"I prefer to stand."

Naturally, in that uniform, Duff thought. "As you please," he went on. "I want to tell you something of this affair." As briefly as he could, he outlined the case on which he was engaged, and explained Sybil Conway's rôle in it. Not sure as yet just how much he wanted the Italian police to know, he was none too explicit. Especially was he careful to say nothing of Lofton's Round the World Tour.

The Italian listened with unruffled calm. When Duff had finished, he nodded slowly. "Thank you very much. I assume you will not leave San Remo without communicating with me?"

"Well, hardly." Duff smiled grimly, thinking of the innumerable times he had made a similar remark to other men.

"What did you find in your search of these rooms, Inspector?"

"Nothing," said the Scotland Yard man quickly. "Not a thing." His heart beat a little faster. Suppose this policeman, annoyed at his interference, ordered him searched, found Honywood's letter?

For a moment they stared at each other. It was an international crisis. But Duff's appearance of stolid respectability won out.

The Italian bowed. "I shall have the honor of meeting you later," he said. It was a dismissal.

Much relieved, Duff hastened to his room. Without delay he meant to read the letter Sybil Conway had handed him a few moments before her death. He locked his door, drew a chair up beneath a feeble light, and took out the already opened envelope. It bore in the upper left corner the crest of Broome's Hotel, London, and it was postmarked February fifteenth. Eight days after the murder of Hugh Drake, the detective reflected, and only a short time before the Lofton party started for the Continent.

He removed the bulky contents of the envelope. Walter Honywood wrote an unusually small hand, but even so this message to his wife covered many pages. With eager anticipation, Duff began to read:

"Dearest Sybil:

"You will see from the letterhead that I have now reached London on that tour around the world which, as I wrote you from New York, the doctors advised. It was to have been a rest for me, a release, a period of relaxation. Instead it has turned into the most terrible nightmare imaginable. Jim Everhard is also with the tour!

"I found this out on the morning of February seventh, a little more than a week ago. Found it out under the most frightful circumstances. Under circumstances so bizarre, so horrible – but wait.

"When I went aboard the boat in New York, even the names of the other members of the party were unknown to me. I had not so much as met the conductor. We were called together on the deck for a moment before sailing, and I shook hands with all of them. I did not recognize Jim Everhard. Why should I? I saw him, you will remember, only the once and the light was poor – a dim oil lamp in that little parlor of yours. So many years ago. Yes, I shook hands with them all – with Jim Everhard – the man who had sworn to kill me – and to kill you, too. And I never suspected – never dreamed—

"Well, we sailed. It proved a rough passage, and I did not leave my cabin, except for a few brief strolls on the deck after dark, until the morning we reached Southampton. We came on here to London, and still I had no inkling. There was much sightseeing during the first few days, but I kept out of it. That was not what I had come abroad for – and London was an old story, anyhow.

"On the night of February sixth I was sitting in the parlor of Broome's Hotel when another member of the party came in. A fine old fellow from Detroit, named Hugh Morris Drake, the kindest man alive, and very deaf. We got into conversation. I told him about my illness, and added that I had got very little sleep for the past few nights, owing to the fact that someone was reading aloud in the room on one side of me until a late hour. I said I was reluctant to go upstairs to bed, because I knew I could not rest.

"At that the dear old chap had an idea. He pointed out that, owing to his deafness, the sort of thing that was troubling me would mean nothing to him, and he offered to change rooms with me for the night. It developed that he had the room on the other side of me, so it seemed a simple matter to arrange. I accepted Mr Drake's offer gratefully. We went upstairs. It was agreed we would leave all our possessions just as they were, unlock the door between the rooms, and merely change beds. I closed the connecting door between us and retired – in Mr Drake's bed.

"The doctor had given me a package of sleeping powders to use as a last resort, and as an added guarantee of sleep, I had taken one of those. In the unaccustomed silence, and with the aid of the powder, I slept as I hadn't slept in months. But I was awake at six-thirty, and inasmuch as Mr Drake had told me he wanted to rise early – we were expecting to leave for Paris that morning – I went into the other room.

"I entered and looked about me. His clothes were on a chair, his ear-phone on a table; all the doors and windows were closed. I went over to the bed to wake him. He had been strangled with a luggage strap. He was dead.

"At first I didn't understand – early morning, only half-awake – you see how it was. Then, on the bed, I saw a little wash leather bag. You remember, my dear? One of those bags we gave Jim Everhard – there were two, weren't there? Am I wrong, or were there two wash leather bags, with the pebbles inside?

"I sat down and thought the matter out. It was simple enough. Jim Everhard was somewhere in Broome's Hotel. He had located me with the tour – he had made up his mind to carry out his old threat at last – he had stolen into my room to strangle me in the night and return the bag of stones. Into my room! But it wasn't my room that night. Hugh Morris Drake was in my bed in that dark corner where the light of the street lamps never penetrated. And Hugh Morris Drake had died; died because of his kindness to me; died – if you like irony – because he was deaf.

"It was horrible. But I knew I must pull myself together. There was nothing I could do for Drake. I would gladly have given my life to prevent what had happened – too late now. I must get through the thing somehow – I wanted to see you again – to hear your voice – I love you, my dear. I loved you from the moment I saw you. If I hadn't, all this would never have been. But I don't regret it. I never shall.

"I decided that I couldn't leave poor Drake there in my bed, among my things. How explain that? So I carried him to his own room and put him in his bed. There was the bag of stones. I didn't want that. I didn't know what to do with it. It would mean nothing to anyone – save to Jim Everhard – and to us. I tossed it down on the bed beside Mr Drake. I almost smiled as I did so – smiled at the thought of Everhard carrying it all those years, and leaving it at last in the wrong place, wreaking his vengeance on the wrong man. – Of course, he still has that other bag.

"I unlocked my door into the hall, then slipped back into Drake's bedroom and locked the door between the rooms on his side. The ear-phone caught my attention; I had been forced to move it, so I wiped it clean of fingerprints. Lucky I thought of that. Then I went from his room into the hall, springing his lock behind me, and so to my own room again. No one saw me. But I remembered a waiter who had brought up a cable for Drake the night before, and who knew about the change of rooms. As soon as he came on duty, I rang for him and bribed him. It was easy. Then I sat down to wait for the breakfast hour – another day. My meeting with Jim Everhard.

"I saw him. I knew him this time – the eyes – there is something about a man's eyes that never changes through the years. I was sitting in a parlor of the hotel waiting for the Scotland Yard inspector, and I looked up. He was standing there. Jim Everhard, with another name now. And traveling with the party, too.

"While the Scotland Yard man was asking questions, I tried to think what I had better do. I couldn't very well drop out of the party – I was already in a bad position. My nerves – I hadn't stood the questioning very well. If I dropped out, they might arrest me at once. The whole unhappy story might be revealed. No, for the present I must go on, travel side by side with a man who was no doubt now more determined than ever to kill me – who had, in fact, already killed me, after a manner of speaking.

"I decided that it must be done. For a week I slept every night with a bureau against my door – or tried to sleep. Gradually I evolved a scheme for my protection. I would go to Everhard, tell him I had left in a safe place a sealed envelope, to be opened in case anything happened to me. In that envelope, I would give him to understand was written his name – the name of my murderer, if murder had occurred. That, I thought, would stay his hand, for a time at least.

"I prepared such an envelope. But in the brief note inside I did not mention Everhard's name. Even if it happens – even if he gets me in the end – the old story must not come out. The old scandal. It would ruin your fine career, my dear. I couldn't have that. I have been so proud of you.

"I left the envelope only this afternoon with a member of the party I am certain no one would ever suspect of having it. A few moments ago I saw Jim Everhard in the lobby. I went and sat beside him, and in the most casual way, as though I were discussing the weather, I told him what I had done. He didn't speak. He just sat there looking at me. I told him of the envelope, with his name inside. The last part wasn't true, of course, but I think my plan will serve its purpose.

"So I am coming on with the party, as far as Nice. I am sure he will do nothing before we reach there. The whole affair appears to have shaken him badly – as well it might. The first night our party is in Nice, I propose to slip away in a car in the dark, to come to San Remo and get you. Scotland Yard has given up the chase for the moment, and I doubt if they could stop me in any case. We shall hide until the threat has passed. I am taking it for granted that in the face of this unexpected danger, our differences are buried.

"No, my dear – I am not going to tell you the name under which Jim Everhard travels with our party. You were always so impulsive, so quick to act. I am afraid if you knew it, and something happened to me, you could not remain silent. You would throw away your splendid career with one grand gesture, expose the whole situation – and no doubt live to regret bitterly what you had done. If something should happen to me, for God's sake get out of the path of the Lofton party at once. Disappear from San Remo – your own safety must be your first thought. Motor to Genoa and take the first boat for New York. For my sake – I beseech you. Don't spoil the remaining years of your life – what good would it do? Let the dead past bury its dead.

"But nothing will happen to me. You have only to keep calm, as I am doing. My hand is quite steady as I write this. Everything will come right in the end, I am sure. I shall wire you the date; be ready for me when I come. We'll go away for a second honeymoon. Everhard and the events of the long ago will fade back into the shadows where they have remained so many years.

"With all my love, forever,

"Walter."

Gravely Inspector Duff folded the letter and put it back into its envelope. An acute feeling of helplessness stole over him. Again he had been so close to knowing, again the hotly desired knowledge had been snatched away at the last moment. The news that the murder of Hugh Morris Drake had been pure accident did not greatly surprise him. He had suspected as much these past few days. But accident or not, its perpetrator must be seized and brought to justice. And all through this letter the name of that perpetrator – now a triple murderer – had seemed on the very point of Honywood's pen. Then – nothing. What name? Tait – Kennaway – Vivian? Lofton or Ross? Minchin, Benbow or Keane? Or perhaps even Fenwick. But no, Fenwick was no longer with the party. He could hardly have been concerned in this murder tonight.

Well, he would know in the end, Duff thought. Know, or after that scene in the elevator feel eternally disgraced. With his lips set in a firm line that betokened determination, he locked the letter securely away in his bag, and went downstairs.

Doctor Lofton was the only person in the lobby at the moment. He came to Duff at once, and the inspector was struck by his appearance. His face was white beneath his beard, his eyes staring.

"My God, what's this?" he demanded.

"Honywood's wife," answered Duff calmly. "Murdered by my side in the lift. Just as she was about to point out to me the killer of Drake and of Honywood. Point him out to me – in your party."

"In my party," Lofton repeated. "Yes, I believe it now. All along I've been telling myself – it couldn't be true." He shrugged his shoulders despairingly. "Why go on?" he added. "This is the end."

Duff gripped him firmly by the arm. People were coming out of the dining-room, and the detective led the way to a far corner.

"Of course you're going on," he insisted. "My word – you won't be the one to fail me, I hope. Listen to me – it wasn't a member of your party who was killed this time – you need tell your crowd little or nothing about the affair. I'm keeping you entirely out of the local investigation. Your people will perhaps be questioned – but along with all the other guests in the house. There isn't a chance these Italian police will get anywhere. Better men than they would be stumped. In a day or two you'll go on – go on as though nothing had happened. Do you hear me?"

"I hear you. But so much *has* happened."

"Only a few of us know how much. You will go on, and the murderer in your party will begin to think himself safe. He has finished his work now. Resume your tour, and leave the rest to me – and the Yard. Do you understand that?"

Lofton nodded. "I understand. I'll go, if you say so. But this last affair seemed almost too much. I was badly shaken for a moment."

"Naturally you were," answered Duff, and left him. As he sat down to dinner at a table just inside the dining-room door, the detective was thinking hard. For the first time, Lofton spoke of giving up the tour. At this moment – when the killer's work was finished.

The inspector was busy with an excellent soup, when Pamela Potter came in. She stopped beside his table.

"By the way," she said, "I've news for you. Mr Kennaway and I went for a stroll soon after we got here – Mr Tait was taking a nap. Just as we were leaving the hotel, a car drew up and waited. Something told me to stop a minute – just to see who it was waiting for."

"Ah, yes," smiled Duff. "And whom was it waiting for?"

"I get you," she nodded. "But there are finer things in life than who and whom – don't you think so, too? The car was waiting for some old friends of ours. They came hurriedly out of this very hotel, with all their baggage. The Fenwicks, I mean."

Duff's bushy eyebrows rose. "The Fenwicks?"

"None other. They seemed surprised to see Mr Kennaway and me. Said they thought we weren't due here until tomorrow. I explained that the schedule had undergone one of its usual changes."

"What time was this?" the inspector inquired.

"A few minutes past seven. I know, because it was just seven when Mr Kennaway and I met in the lobby."

"A few minutes past seven," Duff repeated thoughtfully.

The girl went on to join Mrs Luce at a distant table, and Duff sat down again to his soup. It had been just six-forty-five, he reflected, when that shot was fired into the lift.

XI

THE GENOA EXPRESS

All through the entrée – and it was really a pity, for a mind divided cannot truly appreciate a chef's masterpiece of the evening – Duff debated with himself over the Fenwicks. Should he look up that Italian policeman and suggest that the pair be apprehended and brought back to San Remo? The matter could be easily accomplished – but what then? There was absolutely no evidence against Norman Fenwick. To call attention to him would be to involve the Lofton travel party – a thing which Duff certainly didn't want to do. No, he determined over the inevitable roast chicken, he would make no mention to the Italian police of that somewhat precipitate departure.

When he saw the major of the City Guards again, Duff was glad he had decided not to complicate that gentleman's troubled existence with Fenwicks. Though the Italian had seemed serene enough during the interview in Miss Conway's suite, such a state of mind had evidently not long endured. As he got farther along with the case, the poor man had begun to realize the true nature of the situation which faced him, and now he was temperamental and Latin in the extreme. A murder without a clue, without a fingerprint or a footprint, with no weapon to be examined, no witness save Duff, who was from Scotland Yard and so, obviously, above suspicion. A hundred and twenty guests and thirty-nine servants in the house when the shot was fired. It was no wonder that the distracted policeman raged about, asking useless questions, and gradually drifted into a state of nervous excitement that led him into a long passionate argument about the case, in which his opponent was a small and emotional bellboy who knew nothing whatever about it.

At ten o'clock that night Duff came upon Pamela Potter and Kennaway seated in wicker chairs on the hotel terrace. "Heavenly spot for a chat," the detective remarked, sitting down beside them.

"Yes, isn't it?" said Kennaway. "Note the oversize moon, and the scent of orange blossoms drifting up from the grounds. We were just wondering if these were included in the rate, or if they'd be among the extras on our bills. Lofton's contract, you know. Not responsible for personal expenses such as mineral waters, wines and laundry. Moonlight and orange blossoms usually turn out to be rated a personal expense."

"I'm sorry to interrupt your romantic speculations," Duff smiled. "Miss Potter has told me that the two of you took a stroll just before dinner?"

Kennaway nodded. "We were trying to build up an appetite," he explained. "After you've been on a tour of this kind for a while, life seems just one long table d'hôte."

"When you told Mr Tait you were going out did he offer any opposition to the plan?"

"No, he didn't. As a matter of fact, he acted rather in favor of it. He said he didn't care to dine before eight, as he was very tired, and wanted to lie down for a while before eating. Our rooms are quite small, and possibly he figured I might disturb him if I stuck around."

"On what floor are your rooms?"

"On the third floor."

"Are you near the lift?"

"Just opposite it."

"Ah, yes. At six-forty-five this evening, I believe you had not yet left the hotel. Did you hear the sound of a shot about that time?"

"I did."

"Where were you at the moment?"

"I was down in the lobby, waiting for Miss Potter. We weren't supposed to meet until seven, but Mr Tait had sort of shooed me out."

"Who else was in the lobby? Any other member of the party?"

"No. Just myself and a few servants. I heard the shot, but I didn't realize what it was right away. You see, it came from the elevator shaft. Having ridden on the elevator, I wasn't surprised. I was expecting to see it blow up in a cloud of red smoke at any moment."

"Then when the shot was fired, Mr Tait was alone in your suite?"

"Undoubtedly. Alone, and probably sound asleep."

"Probably," nodded Duff.

At that instant, Tait appeared on the terrace. He stood there straight and tall, a handsome figure in evening dress under the Riviera moon. Duff had been thinking of him as an old man, but it suddenly occurred to the inspector that Tait was not so old as he seemed – illness, anxiety, in his face perhaps, but not age.

"I thought I'd find you here," the lawyer remarked to Kennaway.

"Sit down, Mr Tait," Duff suggested. "We've been admiring the view."

"I'm fed up on views," Tait snapped. "Wish I was back in New York. Active all my life, and this loafing is hell." Duff wondered. Was Tait thinking of dropping out of the party too?

"Come on, Mark, let's go upstairs," the lawyer went on. "I want to get to bed. You won't have to read to me very long tonight."

"Still mystery stories?" the detective inquired.

"Not a chance," Tait answered. "There's enough murder in real life without reading about it in books. We've taken up the Russians now. It was Mark's idea. He thought he was clever, but I'm on to him. I have to listen or go to sleep, so naturally I go to sleep. That gives him more time for the ladies." He turned and walked toward the lighted French window through which he had come. "Are you ready, Mark?" he said, over his shoulder.

Kennaway rose reluctantly. "When duty calls with clarion voice, the youth replies, I come," he remarked. "Sorry, Miss Potter. Mark Kennaway signing off. If the orange blossoms are an extra, you'll have to bear the expense alone from now on."

"Nice chap, isn't he?" Duff inquired, as the young man disappeared.

"Very nice," answered the girl. "At times. Tonight was one of the times."

"What do you mean, at times?" the detective inquired.

"Oh, he has his moments. At others, he looks at me as much as to say, how in the world did I ever come to speak to this person from the crude Middle West? It's Boston, you know. But there – you wouldn't understand."

"I'm afraid not," Duff replied. "Tell me – how are the members of the travel party taking our latest murder?"

"Calmly enough, I believe. I've always heard that one gets used to anything in time. I presume we'll be held up here for a while?"

"It's hard to say," Duff told her. "A murder investigation in Italy, you know, is likely to be a complicated affair. There are three branches of the police, the City Guards, the Carabinieri and the Municipal Force. The last are concerned only with minor crimes, but often the other two branches are called upon simultaneously to investigate a murder, and the result is a very pretty little row between them. So far, only the City Guards have come into this case, and I am hoping the Carabinieri stay out. If they do, I don't anticipate much difficulty. I believe I can convince that worried major that this is my affair, and that he mustn't trouble, really."

The girl leaned suddenly closer. "Tell me something, please?" she said gravely. "Is the murderer the same person every time? My grandfather, poor Mr Honywood, and now Mrs Honywood? All killed by the same man?"

Duff nodded slowly. "Undoubtedly, Miss Pamela. The same man."

"Who?" Her voice was low, tense. "Who?"

The detective smiled. "All in good time, we know," he replied. "I am quoting an old friend – a Chinese whom I want you to meet when you reach Honolulu. At present moment we are faced by stone wall. We swing about, seeking new path. Still quoting my friend." The girl did not speak. After a brief silence Duff continued. "I looked you up tonight because I have something to tell you, Miss Pamela. A part of our mystery at least has been solved. I have in my bag a letter which fully explains how your grandfather happened to be involved in this affair."

The girl leaped to her feet. "You have! I must see it."

"Of course." Duff also rose. "If you will come up with me I will give it to you. Take it to your own room and read it. I should like to have it back in the morning."

Without a word, she went with him into the brightly lighted lobby. They moved toward the lift. Duff regarded the little cage with marked distaste. "I'm on the first floor," he suggested hopefully.

"Then we won't bother with that thing," said the girl. "Let's walk."

She waited in his doorway while he brought the letter. He was frantically searching his mind for words of preparation and of sympathy, but none came to him. Words were not his forte. All he could say was: "At what hour shall we meet tomorrow?"

"At eight o'clock," the girl answered. "In the lobby." Seizing the thick envelope eagerly, she hurried away.

Duff returned below-stairs, where he had another chat with the baffled major of the City Guards. Subtly he planted in that official's mind the uselessness of further investigation. This particular murder, he pointed out, looked to be solution-proof, but fortunately it happened to be one of a series, and since the first had taken place in London, the whole matter was up to Scotland Yard. He intimated that the Yard stood ready to relieve the Italian police of a difficult and thankless task.

The major intimated that the Italian police stood ready to be relieved. When they parted, the local man seemed to be in a much happier frame of mind.

The next day proved to be the type which the Riviera does so well – deep blue sky, sparkling sea, and sunlight like a gold piece just from the mint. At eight o'clock, as they had planned, Duff met Pamela Potter in the lobby. The beauty of the morning was seemingly lost on the girl. Her violet eyes were clouded with the evidence of recent tears. She handed the letter back to Duff.

"I wanted to prepare you," he told her. "But I didn't know how. My methods are rather clumsy – I'm so sorry."

"Not at all," she answered in a low voice. "You took the very best course. Poor grandfather – dead for no reason whatever. Dead because he did another man a kindness."

"Who could ask a better epitaph?" the detective said gently.

Pamela Potter looked at him, and her fine eyes flashed. "Well, this doesn't end the matter with me," she cried. "I want that man – that man who killed him. I shan't rest until he's been found."

"Nor I," Duff replied. He thought of the lift. "No, by gad – nor I. I mean to run down Jim Everhard if it's the last act of my life. Have you any idea—"

She shook her head. "I lay awake nearly all night, thinking. Who of the men in our party? They all seem incapable of such a thing – even Maxy Minchin. Who – who? Mr Vivian – he appears to be interested only in Mrs Spicer. Captain Keane – such a sneaky air – I don't like him, but that's not enough, of course. Mr Tait – he's very disagreeable at times. But then, the poor man is ill. Mr Ross – there's not a thing to connect him with all this. As for Mr Benbow, I'm sure he'd never do anything he couldn't photograph and show the boys back in Akron. There's Doctor Lofton left. And that foolish little Fenwick man. But it would be absurd to think that he—"

"Nothing is absurd in this business," Duff broke in. "And by the way – you've forgotten one member of the party."

"Really?" She appeared surprised. "Who? Or should it be whom? I know how fussy you are about grammar."

"I was referring to Mark Kennaway."

She smiled. "Oh, don't be ridiculous."

"I never overlook anyone myself," he remarked. "And since I am about to take you in as my partner—"

"What do you mean by that?"

"I mean that I shall probably leave the party for a time. I don't expect any more – er – accidents, and there is little I could accomplish if I came along. As I told you last night, I am faced with stone wall, and I must swing about, seeking another path. Sooner or later I shall no doubt join you again. In the meantime, I should like to have you act as my representative. Please make a study of the men in this group, and write me occasionally from the various ports where your tour touches. Just tell me how things are going. If you come across anything that looks like a clue, let me have it. You know – nice gossipy letters – you're very good at that sort of thing, I'm sure. And a cable if anything important turns up – New Scotland Yard, London, will reach me. Will you do that?"

"Of course," the girl nodded. "I'm writing to some twenty boys already. The more the merrier."

"I'm flattered to be included on the list," Duff replied. "Thank you so much."

Mrs Luce came up. "Oh, there you are, Pamela," she said. "I'm glad to see you in such safe company. Oh, don't look at me like that, Inspector. Where matters of the heart are concerned, I presume you're just as dangerous as any man. There – I've probably made you very happy by saying that."

Duff laughed. "Gorgeous morning, isn't it?" he inquired.

"Is it?" she answered. "I'm from southern California myself, and I'm not impressed."

"I hope you slept well, my dear," the girl remarked pleasantly.

"I always sleep well – provided I change bedrooms often enough. Even a murder doesn't disturb me. I remember once at Maiden's Hotel, in Delhi – of course, he was only a bus boy – the victim, I mean. But I must save that for my reminiscences. What have you made of last night's affair, Inspector?"

"Nothing, as usual," Duff replied grimly.

"Well, I'm not surprised. You're no superman, and this friend of ours with the urge to kill begins to look like one. Clever, certainly. One reassuring thing – he's starting to operate outside the party. There may be enough of us to last him, after all. Are you breakfasting, Pamela?"

"I'm famished," said the girl, and followed Mrs Luce into the dining-room.

By noon it was apparent that the Italian authorities would attempt to hold none of the travelers in the hotel. The tourist business was no mean industry along the Riviera di Ponente, and not to be disturbed to satisfy a policeman's whim. Bags were piled up at the door of the hotel, and a number of guests departed. The word went around among the Lofton party that they were to take the two o'clock express for Genoa. All of them were eager to be off. Lofton himself had recovered from his despairing mood of the night before; he was everywhere at once, spreading information and advice.

As for the major of the City Guards, his spirits had risen noticeably. After a talk with his associates, and a telegram to Rome, it had been decided to hand the whole matter over to Scotland Yard, which left the major nothing to do but wear his uniform and impress the ladies. At both of these tasks he excelled, and he knew it.

Again, as on that morning in London, Inspector Duff found himself in the odd position of saying goodby to a group of people among whom was undoubtedly the quarry he so much wanted to capture. Of seeing them off on a long journey – Naples, Alexandria, Bombay, the far ports of the Orient. But by this time he was resigned to any turn which fate might take. With a cheery air he went with them to the station on the west bay, just outside the new town.

They gathered on the platform to await the train. Benbow with his camera, Sadie Minchin loaded down with recent purchases in the jewelry line. "Maybe Maxy won't have to come across when he meets a customs man," she predicted proudly.

Suddenly Mrs Spicer gave a little cry. "Good heavens – I never realized it before," she exclaimed.

"What is the trouble?" Doctor Lofton asked solicitously.

"There are thirteen of us," she replied, with a stricken look.

Maxy Minchin patted her on the back. "Don't mean a thing, lady," he assured her.

Doctor Lofton smiled wearily. "There are only twelve in the party now," he told her. "I'm not in it, really, you know."

"Oh, yes, you are," the woman persisted. "And you're the thirteenth."

"Nonsense, Irene," Stuart Vivian said. "Surely you're not superstitious?"

"Why not? Everybody is."

"Only the ignorant," he replied. "Oh – I'm sorry—"

He was sorry a bit too late. The woman had given him a look. Even those at whom it was not directed were startled to see it. There was a dangerous fire in her green eyes.

"I'm superstitious too," Mrs Luce put in diplomatically. "Not about thirteen, though. That's always been lucky for me. But when it comes to a black cat – one crossed before my rickshaw on the Bubbling Well Road in Shanghai ten years ago, and half an hour later an automobile struck us. I pulled through all right, but I always blamed the cat. Thirteen, as I was saying, Mrs Spicer—" But that lady had walked haughtily away.

The express thundered in, crowded as usual, and there began a hurried search for seats in the first-class compartments. Duff helped Mrs Luce and Pamela Potter to find places. Once more he spoke to the girl about the letters.

"Don't worry," she smiled. "I'm positively garrulous with a fountain pen."

The detective leaped back to the platform. Doors were slamming shut, one by one the Lofton travel party was disappearing from his ken. He noted Benbow, his camera hanging from a black strap across his shoulder, climbing into a compartment from which his wife had beckoned; noted Ross with his Malacca stick helped aboard by a porter, caught a last knowing smile from Captain Keane. The final face he saw was that of Patrick Tait, the lined, worried face of a man old before his time, white as death now in the dazzling Riviera sunshine.

"Well, that's that," shrugged Duff, and returned to the hotel to inquire about London trains.

The next morning but one he sat in the superintendent's office at Scotland Yard. His face was very red and he was perspiring freely, for he had just related the latter part of his story – the disturbing incident of the murder in the lift. His superior looked at him in a kindly way.

"Don't take it too hard, my boy. It might have happened to any of us."

"I shall take it just this hard, sir," Duff replied. "I shall go on searching for Jim Everhard until I find him. It may take months, but I mean to have him in the end."

"Naturally," the superintendent nodded. "I know how you feel. And every facility of the Yard will be put at your disposal. But don't forget this. Evidence in the matter of the killing of Honywood and his wife is of no value to us. Those cases could never be tried in London. No – it is the murder of Hugh Morris Drake that alone concerns us. We must capture Everhard and bring him here to answer for that, and our proofs must be unanswerable."

"I understand that, sir. It was why I didn't linger on in Nice or San Remo."

"Have you mapped out any future course of action?"

"No, I haven't. I thought I would consult with you about that."

"Precisely." The superintendent nodded his complete approval. "Will you please leave with me all your notes on the case? I shall look them over during the day. If you will come in at five this afternoon, we will decide at that time what we had better do. And once more – don't worry about that affair in the lift. Think of it only as a stronger incentive to get your man."

"Thank you, sir."

Feeling much better than when he had entered the room, Duff left it. A good egg, his superior.

He lunched with Hayley, who was even more sympathetic than the superintendent. At five that afternoon he returned to his superior's office.

"Hello," that gentleman said. "Sit down, please. I've read your notes. A puzzle, of course. But I was struck by one thing. No doubt you were, too."

"What was that?"

"This man Tait, Mr Duff."

"Ah, yes – Tait."

"Rather queer, my boy, rather queer. His story may be absolutely true, but doubts crept into my mind as I read. He thought Honywood had been murdered, he entered that parlor and saw Honywood alive, and the shock nearly finished him. Why should he take it so hard? Honywood and he were, it seems, practically strangers. Why should the matter have been such a shock, unless—" The superintendent paused.

"I quite understand, sir," Duff said. "Unless he supposed Honywood dead because he thought he himself had strangled the man in the night. Unless – in other words – Tait is Jim Everhard."

"Precisely," nodded the superintendent. "It is a matter to think about. Now, with regard to the future. As far as the travel party is concerned I believe, Mr Duff, that for the time being your usefulness in that quarter is ended." The inspector's face fell. "Don't misunderstand me, my boy. I merely feel that you are too well known among them to accomplish anything there. I have looked over the itinerary Lofton gave you. After Egypt, I note four boat trips – on a P. and O. liner from Port Said to Bombay, on a British India Steam Navigation Company ship from Calcutta to Rangoon and Singapore, then by way of another P. and O. boat from the latter place via Saigon to Hongkong. From Hongkong they are to take a Dollar liner bound for San Francisco. For the present I would leave the party in peace. Our quarry may think we have dropped the matter and be off his guard. In a few days I intend to dispatch a good man to Calcutta with instructions to get in touch with the party from that point on, in any manner that offers. I haven't definitely decided, but I am thinking of sending Sergeant Welby."

"One of the cleverest, Welby is, sir," Duff replied.

"Yes – and the type who could easily pass as a ship's steward, or something of the sort. Cheer up, my boy. If Welby hits on anything definite, you shall join him and make the arrest. In the meantime, there is work to be done in the States. An investigation of the Honywoods' past – the meaning of those wash leather bags – the search for a safety-deposit box with the number 3260. All that will be left to you. But there is no need for you to be off just yet. I want you to time your investigation in America so that you can conclude it on the west coast about the date when Lofton's travel party lands at San Francisco."

Duff was smiling again. "Very well planned, sir. But may I make one suggestion?"

"Of course. What is it?"

"I should like to meet the party at Honolulu, sir."

"And why at Honolulu?"

"It would give me that last run from Honolulu to the mainland, sir. Some of them may leave the party at San Francisco. And furthermore—"

"Yes?"

"I have a very good friend at Honolulu. A chap of whom I'm particularly fond. I believe I've spoken to you about him – Inspector Chan, of the Honolulu police."

The superintendent nodded. "Ah, yes. Charlie Chan – the Bruce case. Do you think Inspector Chan would like to see you, Duff?"

Duff was puzzled. "I'm sure he would, sir. Why do you ask?"

His superior smiled. "Because I have long wanted to do a favor for Mr Chan. Don't worry, my boy. Honolulu can undoubtedly be arranged."

XII

THE JEWELER IN CHOWRINGHEE ROAD

There followed for Duff weeks of restless waiting. He busied himself with minor tasks, but his heart was elsewhere. Welby was off on a P. and O. boat, his destination Calcutta. For several nights Duff had coached him, read aloud from his notes, speculated with him over the possibilities in the Lofton travel party. Sergeant Welby, he realized with mixed emotions, was a remarkably clever lad. Not, like most of the C. I. D. men, from some inland farm, but a London product, a little cockney born within sound of Bow-bells. Within sound of those bells most of his days had been passed, and the seven seas were to him an uncharted emptiness. He had never even read about them; he was having some difficulties with his geography now; but he faced the future with cool unconcern and unbounded confidence. He examined again and again the little bags of pebbles; they seemed to fascinate him. They formed, he said, the essential clue. He trembled to be off.

Well, he was off now. Duff had gone with him to Tilbury Docks, and had watched the cheerful face of his fellow detective until it faded from sight. Walking that same night across Vauxhall Bridge, with the tide out and the tang of salt sharp in the air, the inspector thought of Welby, some miles out at sea by this time on his great adventure. Would Welby solve the puzzle – the puzzle that was by all rights the special task of Duff? He would try to be broad-minded. He had wished Welby luck, and by gad, he meant it.

In a little more than two weeks came the first news of the Lofton party. It was contained in a letter from Pamela Potter, postmarked at Aden. The inspector opened it and read:

"Dear Inspector Duff:

"I'm so sorry. I meant to send in my first report from Port Said. But the days are so full and the nights are so wonderful – well, we just drift along. I'm afraid you'd be feeling a bit impatient if you were with us. A murderer in our party – and what of it? We've done all the bazaars, we've met the Sphinx – I did remember to ask her that question we so want answered, but she didn't reply.

"I've seen Port Said. It may be as wicked as it's reputed to be, but Mrs Luce wouldn't let me find out. She said she'd tell me all about it – and she did. Yes, she's as full of reminiscences as ever. You need an atlas of the world when she talks to you. But she's an old dear.

"We've put the Suez Canal behind us. Like a muddy river, with lonely people sitting at the stations beside the locks. I wanted to get off and tell them about Maurice Chevalier in the talkies. On each side, oceans of sand dotted with scrub acacias, and at night the nice light air of the desert blowing across the ship. We're nearly out of the Red Sea now, and the way I feel is, thank heaven that's attended to. Hot – my word! The flying fish flopped on to the deck with a sort of pleased-to-meet-you air. The sun is a huge red ball when we watch it go down every night, and we listen to hear it sizzle when it hits the water. At least I do. Mark Kennaway says it never touches the water at all, and that the sound I hear is eggs frying in the crow's-nest.

"Faithful to my orders, I've been cultivating the men in the party. The only result up to date is that I've got myself heartily disliked by the women. Even Sadie Minchin thinks I'm trying to steal her Maxy. Maybe I have overplayed Maxy a bit – but he's quite amusing. I've posed for Elmer Benbow so many times, I expect to see his wife take his camera away from him at any moment. As for the rest, well, I really believe I've got over big with Stuart Vivian.

"You remember that nice little row between Stuart and his lady friend at the San Remo station? About being superstitious? They didn't speak for days – that is, she didn't, and after a while he gave up trying. It was then I came into his life. I got to thinking we didn't know much about him, so I set to work. When the gentle Irene saw the speed I was making, she rose in her wrath and took him back. I'm not so sure he wanted to be taken. He squirmed considerably. A conceited man. As though I meant anything by my deep interest in his past. He's forty-five, if a day.

"All of which brings me – don't ask me how – to dear Captain Keane. I was going to my stateroom the other night at twelve – I'd been sitting up on deck with somebody or other – a man, I believe it was. I'm trying to follow out your instructions to the letter, you see. Well, when I entered the alleyway – that's authentic and nautical – leading to my room, there was Captain Keane snooping just outside Mr Vivian's door. He muttered something and hurried away. Still up to his old tricks, you will note. He's one of the slyest men I've ever met, but I'm afraid he's too obvious to mean anything, aren't you?

"As for the rest, I've listened to Doctor Lofton's erudite talks, to Mr Ross on the subject of Tacoma and why does anybody live in the Middle West now that the Pacific coast has been discovered, until my ears ache. There's Mr Tait, too – my one failure. Somehow, my charms seem to fall on barren ground when he is about. How would you explain it? Perhaps he's a bit miffed because I take up a little of Mark Kennaway's time. Did I say a little? Maybe that isn't quite accurate. You see, he is so young, and I am so beautiful—But as I was saying, I've cultivated them all. And so far, I must admit I haven't turned up a single clue. I wouldn't call that about Keane a clue. Would you?

"We have nearly reached Aden. Mrs Luce is taking me to luncheon there, at her favorite restaurant. Probably she will call the head waiter by his first name, and ask after all the little waiters. Aden, she tells me, is a melting-pot that somebody put on the stove and forgot to remove. According to her, I shall get my first smell of the East when we reach there. I believe I've had a whiff or two already. I don't much like it. But Mrs Luce claims you grow to love it in time. That when you're sitting in your patio at Pasadena you suddenly remember it, and then it's just a case of engaging a caretaker and locking the front door. Maybe. No doubt I shall be able to tell you more about that when I write again.

"Sadie Minchin has just stopped at my elbow, wondering about the jewelry shops in Aden. Maxy had better arrange to have her met by an armored truck at the San Francisco dock. He owns a limousine with bullet-proof glass – perhaps he'll have that there.

"Sorry I haven't proved more of a detective. Better luck from here on. I'll have lots of time in the Indian Ocean.

"Sincerely yours

"Pamela Potter."

That night, in the Vine Street station in London, Duff discussed this letter with Hayley. There wasn't much to discuss, as they both realized. Duff was inclined to be impatient.

"First time in my life," he muttered, "that I ever depended on a girl to keep me abreast of a case. And the last, I hope."

"A charming girl, at any rate," Hayley smiled.

"What of that? She's not so charming that one of those men will suddenly turn to her and say: 'Oh, by the way, I murdered your grandfather.' And that's all I want. Not charm, but the identity of Jim Everhard."

"When does Welby join the party?" asked the Vine Street man.

"Not for ages," sighed Duff. "There they are, just drifting along, with no one watching them but a girl. A big idea of the chief's."

"It will all come right in the end," Hayley answered. "Something tells me."

"Please ask your something to come and talk to me," said Duff. "I need it."

He needed it even more before he heard again. Every night he studied the itinerary Lofton had given him. In his thoughts he followed the little party across the Indian Ocean to Bombay, then by the long route – they would take the long route – to Mt. Abu, Delhi, Agra, Lucknow, Benares, Calcutta. It was while they were at Calcutta that he heard once more – a mysterious cable from the girl.

"If one of your men is in this neighborhood, have him get in touch with me at once. At the Great Eastern Hotel, Calcutta, until this evening, then aboard British-India liner *Malaya* bound for Rangoon, Penang, Singapore."

Feeling an unaccustomed thrill of anticipation, Duff cabled Welby in care of certain British agents in Calcutta. Then – silence again. One dreary day succeeding another, and not an atom of news. Confound the girl – didn't she realize that he, too, had a deep interest in this affair, wanted to know what was happening?

He heard at last. A letter came in, postmarked Rangoon. Eagerly the man in London tore it open:

"Dear Inspector Duff:

"I am rather a dud as a correspondent, aren't I? No doubt my cable left you in a little fever, and the explanation has been slow in coming. But the mails, Inspector – you really must blame it on the mails. I couldn't very well cable the contents of this letter. Spies, you know, in this mysterious East – spies back of every tamarind tree.

"Let me see – where was I? We were just steaming into Aden, I believe. We went on steaming after we got there, and all the way across the Indian Ocean to Bombay. Tempers began to get a little frayed about the edges. You know, a party of this sort starts out as one great, big, happy family. It was a bit delayed in our case by certain events at the beginning, but the peak of comradeship and mutual love and esteem was reached in Italy and Egypt. Everyone was very confidential. Then gradually, as the weather got hotter, our ardor for one another began to cool. It's got so now that nobody enters a room without a preliminary survey to make sure no other member of the party, thank God, is inside.

"Well, we did the Indian Ocean. We came into Bombay, said goodby to the dear old ship, and staggered up to the Taj Mahal Hotel. And who do you think was in the lobby? Mr Fenwick, and his silent sister, from Pittsfield, Massachusetts. It seems that after they left us at Nice they said to themselves, we've started out on a world tour, so why not go through with it? In Naples, it appears, they signed on for a cruise – you know, one of the big wonder ships that goes right on around without a change. At least, that's what they told us, and as we'd seen such a ship in the harbor, I presume it was the truth. Little Norman was insufferable. He asked us if we'd had any more murders, and gave us a long talk on the superiority of their method of travel over ours. We were so happy to see a comparatively new face – even one like Mr Fenwick's – that we listened meekly.

"We stayed in Bombay a couple of days, and then set out over the hills and far away in the direction of Calcutta. I got a good look at the Taj Mahal, and a terrible cold. Eventually we reached our destination, feeling a little sad about India and rather wishing there wasn't any such place. In Calcutta something happened – and so I come at last to my long delayed story of the cable.

"On our final morning in Calcutta, Doctor Lofton herded us into a jewelry shop on Chowringhee Road. I presume he gets a commission on sales, he was so passionate about having us go there. Imri Ismail, I believe, was the proprietor's name. Once I got inside, I was glad I'd come. Really, the most gorgeous jewels you ever saw in your life – star sapphires, rubies, diamonds – but of course you're not interested. Sadie Minchin went haywire on the spot. Even Maxy turned a bit pale to see her buying.

"Most of the others in the party just looked casually around and then drifted out. But I happened to see a necklace of diamonds, and my will-power certainly failed me. A little weathered clerk with a drooping eyelid and a most villainous expression saw the condition I was in, and fastened himself on me. While I was hovering on the brink, Stuart Vivian came up and advised me to wait a minute. He said he knew a little about diamonds, and that these were good stones, but not worth what my pirate friend was asking. After a bitter argument, the price began to drop amazingly, until finally Mr Vivian said it was a good buy. At that point Irene Spicer swept down on him, evidently after a long search, and carried him off.

"It was while the clerk was removing the fictional price tag from the necklace that a surprising thing happened. Another clerk came along behind him, and as my man pressed close to the counter to let the other pass, he said something in a foreign tongue. Right in the middle of that string of strange sounds, two English words stood out like a house afire. He said 'Jim Everhard' as clearly and distinctly as a radio announcer.

"My heart stood still. The other man paused, as though he were idly curious, and looked toward the door. No one was there. I had to get busy at once with travelers' checks, and when I handed them over, I said casually to the man with the drooping eyelid: 'You know Jim Everhard, too?' That was where I made my big mistake. I should have said it before he got his hands on the checks. Now it was all a closed incident as far as he was concerned. He calmly pretended he didn't understand English any longer, and bowed me out.

"I went for a walk in the Maidan and wondered what to do. I thought maybe I'd send you a postcard with the message: 'Wish you were here.' I certainly wished it. Then I evolved the brilliant idea of the cable.

"I didn't hear anything all day. Mr Kennaway and I went for a stroll in the Eden Gardens that afternoon, and then rode down to Diamond Harbor to get the British-India boat. We were quite late, and everybody else was aboard. As we started up the gangplank, which they were about to draw in, who should come rushing down it but my friend of the drooping eyelid? He'd evidently been aboard to see somebody off. Who? Jim Everhard? Or was this merely a last minute effort to make a few more sales?

"Late that night I was walking along the deck of the *Malaya* when a steward stopped me and told me someone in the second class wanted to see me. I was startled at first, then I remembered my cable, and so I followed the steward down a ladder to the lower deck. In the shadow of a life boat I met the queerest little man. I was a bit dubious about him at first, but he was all right. He was your friend, Mr Welby, of the C. I. D. I liked him. He was cute. And such a quaint cockney accent.

"I told him what had happened in the jewelry shop, and he was naturally interested. When I added that I had seen the clerk leaving the ship a few hours ago, he nodded. He said that he had been up in the first class about that time himself, talking with a friend among the stewards, and that the man from Imri Ismail's had attracted his attention. He had followed him and noticed which cabin he visited. 'And', added Mr Welby, 'it was a cabin occupied by two members of the Lofton travel party, Miss Potter.'

"Of course I wanted to know which two. Did I find out? You know better. Mr Welby just thanked me heartily for my information. 'You may have lightened my job considerably,' he said. Then he asked me how much Stuart Vivian seemed to know about diamonds. I said I couldn't tell, but that like all men he claimed to know everything about everything. Mr Welby nodded again, and intimated that I could run along now. He told me he was hoping to obtain a position as steward on the Dollar boat out of Hongkong, and that in the meantime he would be hovering about, but that I mustn't speak to him unless he spoke first. I assured him I was always the perfect lady in such matters, and we parted. I haven't seen him since.

"Well, there you are, Inspector. That's the situation on this hot April night in Rangoon, where our boat lays over two days. Speaking of the smell of the East, I know all about it now. The odor of fetid narrow streets, vegetables rotting in the tropic sun, dead fish, copra, mosquito lotions – and of too many people trying to be in one place at one time. I'm used to it. I can look forward to China and Japan with an unconquerable nose.

"I'll probably write again from Singapore – it will depend on what happens next. Please pardon this long letter, but I told you I was garrulous with a fountain pen. And I really had something to write about this time.

"Warmly yours – it's the climate –

"Pamela Potter."

An hour after reading this epistle, Inspector Duff was in conference with his chief. The superintendent read it too, and with an interest almost as great as Duff's.

"Welby appears to be playing a lone game," he remarked, and his tone suggested a certain lack of approval.

"He probably has nothing definite to report as yet, sir," Duff replied. "But if the girl has narrowed his search to one of two people, then there ought to be news very soon. Of course, it may all come to nothing. She may even be mistaken about what she heard in the jeweler's shop."

The superintendent considered. "Why did Welby ask her how much Vivian knew about diamonds?" he said at last.

"Couldn't say, sir," Duff answered. "He's deep, Welby is. No doubt he has a theory of some sort. We might cable to Calcutta and have that clerk questioned about Jim Everhard."

His superior shook his head. "No – I prefer to leave it to Welby. To do what you suggest might interfere with his game. A cable of warning from the clerk to Everhard, and Everhard might disappear from the party. Besides, I'm certain we should get nothing from Miss Potter's friend with the drooping eyelid. He doesn't sound like the sort who would be eager to assist Scotland Yard."

Duff had taken out a pocket calendar. "I figure that the Lofton party is in Hongkong today, sir. They're to stop at that port a week, I believe, making a side trip to Canton. If I'm to carry through the investigation you suggested, and then get on to Honolulu—" He waited.

"You want to be off, I suppose," the superintendent smiled. "How soon can you start?"

"Tonight – if there's a boat, sir," Duff answered.

"Tomorrow, at any rate," agreed his superior.

On the morrow Duff, radiantly happy that the moment for action had arrived at last, set out for Southampton. This time it was Hayley who sped the parting traveler, with many expressions of encouragement and hope. That night the inspector was aboard one of the swiftest of Atlantic liners. The steady turn of the screw was music in his ears; he stood at the starboard rail and watched the prow of the ship as it cut with amazing speed through the dark water. His heart was light. Every moment was carrying him nearer the puzzle that had so rudely left him to travel round the world.

His inquiries into the past of the Honywoods, which he pursued diligently once he had reached New York, got him nowhere. They had arrived in that confusing city some fifteen years ago, and none of the friends whose names Mrs Honywood's maid had given him appeared to know whence they had come. It was not, it appeared, customary to inquire, in New York. Today was all that mattered, yesterday was nobody's business. Blank looks met any mention of the wash leather bags. Duff found himself baffled, and somewhat resentful toward this teeming, heedless city.

In the matter of a safety-deposit box numbered 3260, he was equally helpless. With the aid of the New York police, he was able to ascertain the number of Tait's box at his bank, and also that of the one kept by Lofton. Neither meant anything. A helpful commissioner pointed out to the Britisher that a man might have any number of secret boxes at banks where he did not regularly do business. This part of it, Duff began to realize, was nothing but a wild goose chase.

Nevertheless he plodded on, patient to the end. He went to Boston and looked up Mark Kennaway's position there. An excellent family, he discovered, and even he, an outsider, sensed what that meant – in Boston. Next he visited Pittsfield, where the continued absence of the Fenwicks was deplored by a little circle of the best people. Painfully respectable, it seemed, the Fenwicks. At Akron the air was less rarified, but the situation appeared much the same. Duff was taken out to lunch by Benbow's partner, who told him to tell old Elmer to hurry home. Business, it was rumored, had definitely turned the corner, and was on the up grade.

In Chicago he found the friends of Maxy Minchin reticent in the extreme. Tight-lipped, they listened to the inspector and had nothing at all to say. Duff gathered that there was no great public demand for the gangster's return. He moved on to Tacoma. John Ross, he found, was an important figure in the lumber trade. Dropping down to San Francisco, he made inquiries about Stuart Vivian. The man was known to many of the leading citizens; they all spoke highly of him. A call at the office of Irene Spicer's husband revealed that he was away in Hollywood, and was not expected back for some time.

Sitting down one mild May evening in his room at the Fairmont Hotel, Duff summed up the results of his long trek. They were nil. He had looked into the home standing of every man in the Lofton travel party, and with the exception of Maxy Minchin, all appeared to be above reproach. As for Maxy, it seemed unlikely that he could be involved in any such affair as this. Every man in the party? Well, it was true he had found no track of Keane in New York, where the captain claimed to reside. The name was in no directory. But Duff gave this little thought. From the first, for some reason he couldn't quite define, he had refused to suspect Keane.

With that one exception, then, he was familiar with the home environment of all of them, and he was no nearer than ever to knowing which one was capable of murder. Yet there was a murderer in that group – there must be, if Honywood's letter spoke true. "Jim Everhard is traveling with the party. Jim Everhard, who has sworn to kill me – and you, too."

Duff got up and walked to the window. From his lofty perch he saw the lights of Chinatown, of the ferries in the harbor, of the tall buildings across the bay. Memories of his previous visit to this fascinating city came back to him. Memories of Charlie Chan.

A bellboy knocked at his door and handed him a cablegram. It was from his chief at the Yard.

"Cable from Kobe. Welby anticipates early success. Proceed to Honolulu. Luck."

A few words only, but Duff was mightily cheered. Welby, at least, was making progress. Would the little cockney solve the problem in the end? Not usually an imaginative man, Duff was able none the less to picture a gratifying scene. A meeting with Welby on the Honolulu dock, Welby with proofs such as would satisfy the most exacting jury, Welby pointing out some not quite – at this moment – clearly discerned figure. "Tyke him, Duff. He's guilty as hell." Not quite so gratifying, of course, as it would have been if Duff had gathered those proofs himself. But what of that? Scotland Yard always worked as a team. He would do something for Welby some day.

The next morning but one, Duff sailed for Honolulu on the *Maui*. It would bring him, he knew, into Honolulu harbor some twenty hours before that Dollar liner from Yokohama docked beneath the Aloha Tower. A brief time to renew old acquaintance with Charlie Chan, to tell him about this new case on which he had been working – and then, the Lofton travel party and action. Quick action, he hoped. He had decided not to cable Charlie of his coming. Why take the edge off the surprise?

For two days Duff loafed about the ship, at peace with the world. A glorious rest, this was. When the big moment arrived, he would be strong and ready. On the evening of the second day, a boy came up to him and handed him a radiogram. Tearing open the envelope, he glanced at the signature. The message was from his chief.

"Welby found murdered on dock at Yokohama shortly after sailing of liner carrying Lofton party. Get Everhard dead or alive."

Crushing the message savagely in his hand, Duff sat for a long time staring into the darkness beyond the rail of the ship. Before his eyes was a picture of Welby as he had seen him last in London, smiling, confident, serene. The little cockney who had never hitherto strayed beyond the sound of the bells of St. Mary le Bow, killed on a Yokohama dock.

"Dead or alive," said Duff through his teeth. "Dead, if I have my way."

XIII

A KNOCK AT CHARLIE'S DOOR

A few mornings later, in the police court on the second floor of Halekaua Hale at the foot of Bethel Street in Honolulu, three men were on trial – a Portuguese, a Korean and a Filipino. They were charged with gambling in the street, and on the witness stand at the moment sat a placid and serene Chinese. The East, we are told, has a deep respect for obesity; in China as a mandarin increases in weight, he gains in prestige; in Japan the wrestlers, heroes of the crowd, are enormous. The Oriental in the witness-box was equipped, on this count, for high standing among his own.

"All right, Inspector Chan," said the judge. "Let us have your story, please."

The witness sat, immobile as a stone Buddha. He opened his narrow black eyes a trifle wider, and spoke.

"I am walking down Pawaa Alley," he remarked. "With me is my fellow detective, Mr Kashimo. Before us, at the door of Timo's fish shop, we perceive extensive crowd has gathered. We accelerate our speed. As we approach, crowd melts gradually away, and next moment we come upon these three men, now prisoners in the dock. They are bent on to knees, and they disport themselves with dice. Endearing remarks toward these same dice issue from their lips in three languages."

"Come, come, Charlie," said the prosecuting attorney, a red-haired, aggressive man. "I beg your pardon – Inspector Chan. Your language is, as usual, a little flowery for an American court. These men were shooting craps. That's what you mean to say, isn't it?"

"I am very much afraid it is," Chan replied.

"You are familiar with the game? You know it when you see it?"

"As a child knows its mother's face."

"And you identify these men absolutely? They are the crap shooters?

"No question whatever," Charlie nodded. "They are, unfortunately for them, the three."

The lawyer for the defense, a slick little Japanese, was instantly on his feet. "Now I object," he cried. "Your Honor, I question propriety of that word 'unfortunately.' The witness speaks as though my clients had already been tried and found guilty. Mr Chan, kindly restrain such comment, if you will do so."

Chan bowed his head. "Overwhelmed with chagrin, I am sure," he replied. "Pardon me for assuming inevitable has already occurred." The lawyer gave a little cry of rebuke, but Charlie went blandly on. "To continue testimony, next moment the three look up and behold myself and the redoubtable Kashimo. At simultaneous moment, expressions of faces take on startling change. They leap up to feet to accomplish escape. Down the alley they race, myself after them. Before end of alley occurs, I have them."

The lawyer for the defense gave Charlie a hard look. He pointed to the three lean men, his clients. "Is it your purpose to tell the court that your avoirdupois conquered those thin legs?" he demanded.

Chan smiled. "He who runs with a light conscience makes the most speed," he answered gently.

"Meantime, how does Kashimo occupy himself?" inquired the lawyer.

"Kashimo knows his duty, and performs it. He remains behind to gather up abandoned dice. Such was the proper move." Chan nodded with grave approval.

"Yes, yes," broke in the judge, a bald-headed man with an air of infinite boredom. "And where are the dice?"

"Your Honor," Charlie answered, "unless I am much mistaken, the dice have only this moment entered the courtroom, in pocket of the active Mr Kashimo."

Kashimo had indeed come in. He was a nervous little Japanese, and at sight of the bleak look on his face, Charlie's heart sank. Stepping hastily inside the enclosure, the Japanese whispered excitedly into Charlie's ear. Presently Chan looked up.

"I *was* much mistaken, your Honor," he said. "Mr Kashimo has lost the dice."

A roar of laughter swept through the room, while the judge idly hammered on his desk. Charlie sat motionless and seemingly undisturbed, but his heart was bitter. Like all Orientals, he did not relish laughter at his own expense, and much of this was no doubt directed at him. As a matter of fact, he was now in a ridiculous position. The lawyer for the defense, grinning broadly, addressed the court.

"Your Honor, I move charge be dismissed. There is no material evidence. Even famous Inspector Chan will tell you there is no material evidence, when he regains composure and speaks again."

"Inspector Chan," said Charlie, with a grim look at the slant-eyed little attorney, "would much prefer to make oration on efficiency of Japanese race."

"That will do," cut in the judge. "Once more the time of this court has been wasted. Charge is dismissed. Call the next case."

With all the dignity he could muster, Chan left the witness-box and moved slowly down the aisle. At the rear of the room he encountered Kashimo, crouching on a bench. He took him gently by one brown ear, and led him into the hall.

"Again," he remarked, "you let me down with terrible tumble. Where do I obtain all this patience I squander on you? I astound myself."

"So sorry," hissed Kashimo.

"So sorry, so sorry," repeated Charlie. "Those words fall from your lips in never-ending stream. Can good intentions atone for so many blunders? Can the morning dew fill a well? Where were dice lost?"

The contrite Kashimo tried to explain. This morning, on his way to court, he had stopped at the barber shop of Kryimota, on Hotel Street, for hair cut. He had hung coat on rack.

"After first showing dice to entire shop, no doubt?" Chan suggested.

No – he had shown them only to Kryimota, an honorable man. While he submitted to the cut of the hair, various customers had come in and gone out of the shop. The operation finished, he had again donned his coat, and hastened to the courtroom. On his way up the stairs, he had made the unhappy discovery that he was bereft.

Charlie regarded him sadly. "You began work as supreme fumbler," he remarked, "but I think you improve as you go forward. What laughter there must have been among the gods when you were made detective."

"So sorry," Kashimo said again.

"Be sorry out of my sight," sighed Chan. "While you are in it, my vision blurs and I feel my self-control under big strain." He shrugged his broad shoulders and turned away down the stairs.

The police station was on the ground floor, just beneath the courtroom, and at the rear was a small private office that was Chan's pride and joy. It had been turned over to him by his chief after he had brought to a successful conclusion the case of Shelah Fane, more than a year ago. He went inside now, closed the door, and stood looking through the open window into the alleyway that ran along behind the building.

He was still smarting from the incident upstairs, but that was merely a climax to a year of frustration. "Oriental knows," he had written to Duff in the letter the Britisher had read aloud in the Vine Street station, "that there is a time to fish, and a time to dry the nets." But, as he had confessed further along in the same epistle, this eternal drying of the nets was beginning to distress him.

He had for some months past been troubled by a restlessness such as the Chinese are not supposed to know. He was troubled by it now as he stared out into the peaceful alley. Over a year since his last big case, and nothing of note had happened. Chasing slightly annoyed gamblers down obscure by-paths, invading odorous kitchens in search of stills, even sent to tag cars along King Street – was this the career for a Charlie Chan? Honolulu – he loved it – but what was Honolulu doing for him? A prophet is not without honor, save in his own country. Honolulu did not take him seriously – it had laughed at him only this morning. Like that alley out there, it was narrow – narrow as was his life.

With a ponderous sigh, he sat down at his roll-top desk. It was swept clean – clean as the desk of an old man who has retired from business. He swung slowly about in his chair, which creaked in alarm. Getting older every day – well, his children would carry on. Rose, for instance. A brilliant girl, Rose. Making a grand record at that mainland university—

There was a knock on Charlie's door. He frowned. Kashimo, perhaps, with more of his apologies? Or the chief, to learn what had happened upstairs?

"Come!" Chan called.

The door opened, and there on the threshold stood his good friend, Inspector Duff, of Scotland Yard.

XIV

DINNER ON PUNCHBOWL HILL

A Chinese does not, as a rule, register surprise, and a good detective learns early in his career the wisdom of keeping his emotions to himself. When you get the two in one package, as in the case of Charlie Chan, you are likely to have something pretty imperturbable. Yet now his eyes widened amazingly, and for a moment his mouth stood open. One would have said that he was, at the least, slightly taken aback.

In another moment he had leaped nimbly to his feet, and was moving swiftly toward the door. "My celebrated friend," he cried, "for an instant I question the reliability of my sight."

Smiling, Duff held out his hand. "Inspector Chan!"

Charlie took it. "Inspector Duff!"

The Britisher tossed a briefcase down on the desk. "Here I am at last, Charlie. Did I surprise you? I meant to."

"For a brief space the breath left me," grinned Charlie. "Putting it more forcefully, I might say I gasped." He held ready a chair for his visitor, and inserted himself again into the one behind the desk. "I had so long desired this tremendous honor and happiness that I feared I endured hallucination. First question is now in order. What is your opinion of Honolulu, as far as you have got with it?"

Duff considered. "Well, it seems to be a nice clean town," he admitted.

Chan was shaking with silent mirth. "Almost I am drowned in the flood of your enthusiasm," he remarked. "But with you it is deeds, not words, I know. Busy man like yourself has no time for tourist nonsense. I make the wager you are here on case."

The other nodded. "I certainly am."

"I wish you no bad luck, but I am hoping you must remain for a lengthy visit."

"Only a few hours," Duff replied. "I'm here to meet the *President Arthur* at this port tomorrow morning, and I expect to go out on her when she sails for San Francisco tomorrow night."

Chan waved a hand. "Too brief, my friend. I am desolate to hear it. But I too know call of duty. You have, no doubt, a suspect on the ship?"

"Seven or eight of them," Duff answered. "Charlie, I've had suspects on boats and trains and at railway stations and hotels until I feel like Thomas Cook, or at least like one of the sons. I'm on the strangest case – as soon as your work permits, I want to tell you about it."

Charlie sighed. "Even if story requires one week to relate," he replied, "I possess plenty time to listen."

"Not much happening in your line, you wrote me?"

"The Indian philosopher who sat under one tree for twenty years was offensive busybody compared with me," Chan admitted.

Duff smiled. "I'm sorry. But perhaps in that event you can think about my troubles a bit, and it may be you can make a few suggestions."

The Chinese shrugged. "Does the mosquito advise the lion?" he inquired. "But I burn to hear what brings you to this somnolent paradise."

"A murder, of course," Duff answered. "A murder in Broome's Hotel, in the city of London, on the morning of

February seventh. Other murders too along the way, but only the first concerns me." And he launched into his story.

Chan listened, paying the rare tribute of silence as he did so. A casual observer might have supposed his interest slight, for he sat like a statue, seemingly as somnolent as the paradise he had mentioned. The little black eyes, however, never left Duff's face. Though the hands of the British detective busied themselves from time to time with his briefcase, though he took out letters and notes and read from them, still Charlie's gaze remained riveted where it had been when the long tale began.

"And now it's Welby," Duff finished at last. "Poor little Welby, shot down in a dark corner of the Yokohama docks. Why? Because he had located Jim Everhard, no doubt. Because he had learned the identity of as cruel and ruthless a killer as I have ever been called upon to hunt. By gad, I'll get him, Charlie! I must. Never before have I wanted a man so badly."

"A natural feeling," agreed Chan. "I am a mere outsider, but I can understand. Would you deign to partake of a terrible lunch at my expense?"

Duff was slightly shaken at this abrupt dismissal of an affair that was, to him, the most important in the world. "Why – er – you lunch with me," he suggested. "I'm stopping at the Young Hotel."

"No debate, please," Chan insisted. "You arrive over eight thousand miles of land and water, and you think to buy me a lunch. I am surprised. This is Hawaii, land of excessive hospitality. We will go to the Young, but I will demand check in strident terms."

"About my notes, Charlie. And these letters. I see you have a safe."

Chan nodded. "Yes, station-house safe is in this room. We will lock up your valuable papers there."

They walked up Bethel Street to the main thoroughfare, King, and along that in the direction of the Young. The penetrating midday sun shone down upon them, taxi drivers slept fitfully at their wheels, a radio in a shop doorway was playing *My South Sea Rose*. Duff felt that some further comment was required of him.

"Hawaii's a sort of bright place, isn't it?" he said. "I mean the light's rather strong, you know."

Charlie shook his head. "My dear old friend," he replied, "please do not think that the matter must be attempted. Later I will hand you folders from Hawaii Tourist Bureau, and there you will find the words that now escape you. In the meantime, enjoy yourself. Here is the hotel, where inspeakably humble lunch awaits us."

When they were seated in the Young dining-room, Duff returned to the topic nearest his heart. "What did you think of my story, Charlie? Did you get a psychic wave about any of the members of that party? Chinese, I'm told, are very psychic people."

Chan grinned. "Yes – and psychic wave from unknown Chinese in Honolulu would rouse great sensation in London, I am sure. A locality where, if my reading is correct, more definite evidence of guilt is demanded than any other place in world."

Duff's face went grave. "You're right. That's the thought which haunts me constantly. I might discover to my own satisfaction which of those men is Jim Everhard, I might be positive I was right, yet I might still lack enough evidence for a warrant at home. They ask a lot of us at Scotland Yard, Charlie. Every man innocent until proved guilty, and we mean it on the other side. And that affair in Broome's Hotel on February seventh is a long way in the past now – slipping further away each minute, too."

"I do not envy you your task," Chan told him. "All the greater triumph, however, when you win success at last. Was the soup possible? Yes? That is good. One meets so much impossible soup in Hawaii." His eyes narrowed. "You seek evidently two men," he added.

"What do you mean – two men?" Duff was startled.

"Great writer who once lived in these islands wrote book named *Dr Jekyll and Mr Hyde*. The Jim Everhard who had some strange adventure with Honywood couple long ago is now, no doubt, stranger almost to himself. For years he has lived, under new name, respected life without violence. All time former self lies buried from sight, but it simmers there, nursing old grievance, promising to keep old vow. What wakes it – what brings it to life again – the bitter, half-forgotten self that throws off respectability with wild gesture and is able to strangle and to shoot – to shoot so straight without error? Ah, if we only understood queer twists and turns of human mind. But here is waiter with alleged chicken fricassee."

"It looks very good," remarked Duff.

"Looks," added Charlie, "are sometimes frightful liar. That is important thing for you to remember as you sail away tomorrow night with Lofton round world party. Jim Everhard looks good, I think. Looks respectable, without doubt, wearing disguise of new life so perfect from much use. But do not forget, my friend – many times honey in the mouth means poison in the heart."

"Of course," agreed Duff impatiently. He was bitterly disappointed to be met in this anxious hour with general moralizing. It meant nothing, and Charlie must know that himself. Almost the Chinese acted as though he were not interested in the problem. Was it that – or was it merely that Chan's talents were rusty from lying unused so long? Duff yawned. Wouldn't be surprising, here in this sunny land where life was so easy, so effortless. A detective needed constant activity, he needed too the tang of sharp winds, flurries of snow. Southern people were always languid, always slow.

"If respectability is, in this case, the mark of the criminal," the Englishman continued, seeking to draw the conversation on to more definite ground, "we have several suspects to offer. Maxy Minchin, of course, is out, and so, to my way of thinking, is Captain Keane. But we have Doctor Lofton, cool, aloof, the intellectual type. And we have Tait, a cultivated man of brilliant ability – oddly enough, in the criminal field himself; he has spent his life defending criminals. We have Vivian, Ross and Benbow, all men of unimpeachable standing in their own small worlds. And we have Fenwick, whom we mustn't forget – a man who holds a high position in a society that struck me as most select."

"You have interest in Fenwick?" inquired Charlie.

"Have you?" asked Duff quickly.

"I could not fail to note how he hovers about like brooding hawk above," Chan replied. "He leaves party at Nice, and you think you are finished with him. Yet there he is, at San Remo. In the hotel of the Taj Mahal at Bombay he still persists."

Duff sat up. The easy manner with which Charlie rattled off these names suggested that, after all, the matter was interesting him more than his sleepy eyes would indicate. Once again, Duff thought, he had been wronging the Honolulu policeman. Once again, as had frequently happened several years ago in San Francisco, he must hastily revise his opinion of this Chinese.

"But how about Yokohama?" he said. "How about the jeweler's shop in Calcutta? In neither of those places did anyone see Fenwick."

"You are certain of that?" Chan inquired.

"In point of fact, I'm not," Duff replied. "I must look further into the matter. Particularly if you fancy the man, Charlie—"

Chan grinned. "I have not said I fancied him. Maybe it was his name catches my attention. For a moment only. No – I have no fancies. Except, perhaps, chocolate ice cream. I make bold to suggest it as final course for this unworthy lunch."

"A bully good lunch," Duff assured him.

When they had finished, Charlie led his English friend back to the station and proudly introduced him to the force – to his chief, who was obviously impressed, and even to Kashimo, who showed no sign of any emotion, whatever.

"Kashimo studies to be great detective like you are," Chan explained to Duff. "So far fortune does not favor him. Only this morning he proved himself useful as a mirror to a blind man. But" – he patted the Japanese on the shoulder – "he perseveres. And that means much."

Later in the afternoon Charlie got out, with marked pride, a shining new flivver, and took Duff for a tour of Honolulu and the surrounding section of the island. The Britisher looked, struggled gallantly to express his admiration, proved indeed a perfect guest, but his mind was uneasy. He could not forget that his big problem was still unsolved; in the midst of a conversation about something entirely different, that fact would slip back into his thoughts to torment him. At dinner that night at the Royal Hawaiian, where Chan insisted on playing host, Duff was still in the same troubled frame of mind. He longed for the morrow and a return to action.

The next morning at ten he stood with Charlie on the dock and watched the *President Arthur* come in. For a time he had considered remaining in the background while the ship was in port, but he told himself there was nothing to be gained by that course; he must see them all again as soon as the liner sailed. He had insisted that Charlie come along and meet the members of the Lofton party. In the back of his head was a dim idea that the Chinese might have a sudden inspiration, a really helpful suggestion to offer. Overnight he had been thinking of Charlie on the trail of that other killer in San Francisco, and his confidence in his confrère had returned stronger than ever.

The big liner docked, and the gangplank was put down. There was a moment's confusion at the top and then a motley crowd began slowly to descend. There is always a strange variety to the throng that lands from a through boat at Honolulu – a feeling in the onlooker – who are these people? Salesmen who have carried the creed of pep and hustle to far corners, raw Australians, bowing little Orientals, Englishmen walking secure in the feeling that under their feet is always a little bit of England, pale missionaries, washed-out Colonials, and the eternal tourist. Duff watched eagerly, and at his side stood Charlie, as one who hears an oft-told story.

Finally Lofton, in a pith helmet, appeared at the top of the plank and then started slowly to walk down it. After him came the twelve members of his party, until at one time on that plank Duff knew the man he sought must be walking. The man who had struck down Welby – a sudden anger flamed in the inspector's heart. As Doctor Lofton reached the pier-shed, Duff stepped forward with outstretched hand. Lofton glanced up. It was not precisely an expression of hearty welcome that crossed the conductor's face. Rather a look of keen annoyance – almost of dislike. Chan was watching him closely. Was it merely that Lofton hated to be reminded of certain events now put far behind?

"Ah, Doctor," Duff cried. "We meet again."

"Inspector Duff," said Lofton, and managed a wan smile. But now Duff was busily shaking hands with the Benbows, then with the Minchins, with Mrs Spicer and Vivian, with Kennaway, Ross and the others – last of all with Tait, who looked more tired and ill than ever.

"Near the end of your journey, eh?" the Englishman said.

They all talked at once; it appeared that they were not sorry to step foot on U.S. soil again. Benbow did a little jig on the dock, his camera, hanging from the strap across his shoulder, flying wildly about him.

"Ladies and gentlemen, may I present my old friend, Inspector Chan, of the Honolulu Police?" Duff said. "I just dropped over for a little visit with the inspector, who happens to be the best detective in the Pacific Ocean. We once worked together on a case."

Vivian spoke. "Here for a long stay, Mr Duff?"

"Unfortunately, no," Duff told him. "I'm booked out on your ship tonight. I hope none of you will mind."

"Delighted," Vivian murmured. The scar on his forehead shone suddenly crimson in the dazzling light of Honolulu.

"There are supposed to be cars waiting for us," Lofton announced. "We're going out for a swim at Waikiki, and lunch at the Royal Hawaiian." He bustled about.

Duff's eyes fell on Pamela Potter who was standing, a lovely vision in white, a little away from the others. There was a question in her own eyes; he shook his head ever so slightly as he approached her.

"How did I come to overlook you?" he inquired, taking her hand. "You're more charming than ever. The tour must have agreed with you." And in a lower voice: "Stick to the party, I shall see you later today."

"We're taking rooms at the Young," she answered. "Where in the world is—"

"Tell you later," Duff murmured. He shook hands with Mrs Luce.

"Hello – we've missed you," the old lady said. "Well, here I am. Nearly around the world, and haven't been murdered so far."

"You're not home yet," he reminded her.

He refused Lofton's half-hearted invitation to join them for lunch. "You'll see plenty of me on the ship," he said jovially. The party entered waiting automobiles and was driven off in the direction of Waikiki. Duff and Charlie walked back to King Street.

"Well, there's my travel crowd," said the Englishman. "Did you notice a murderer among them?"

Chan shrugged. "Brand of Cain no longer legible," he returned. "Hasty glance such as I had then was not enough. Can you dispel fog with a fan? One matter I did note. Nobody boiled over with happiness to see you again. Except maybe beautiful young lady. That Doctor Lofton now—"

"He did seem annoyed, didn't he?" agreed Duff. "But, you see, I recall the unpleasant past, and I may also bring him some very unfortunate publicity before I'm through. He's worried about his business."

"No more terrible worry than that in modern world," Chan nodded. "Ask Chamber of Commerce."

They lunched together again, this time with Duff as host. Afterward Charlie was forced to return to the station to attend to some of the minor details of his work. At about two o'clock the Englishman was alone in the lobby of the Young, when Mrs Luce and Pamela Potter came in. The rest of the party, it appeared, had driven to the Pali, but Mrs Luce had seen it often, and the girl was eager for a chat with Duff. The two women went to the desk and engaged a sitting-room, bedroom and bath for the remainder of the day. Duff waited until he felt that they were comfortably settled in the suite, then went upstairs.

The girl was alone in the sitting-room. "At last," she greeted him. "I thought I was never going to be able to see you alone. Please sit down."

"Tell me your story first," Duff said. "When did you see Welby again?"

"What was the last letter you had from me?" she inquired.

"The one from Rangoon," he told her.

"I wrote another from Singapore, and still another from Shanghai."

"I'm sorry. They're probably following me about."

"Well, I hope they catch up with you. There wasn't any news in them, but they were masterpieces of descriptive writing. You'll do very wrong if you miss them."

"I shall read every word when they finally arrive. But no news, you say?"

"No – nothing much happened. I didn't see Mr Welby again until I went aboard the *President Arthur* at Hongkong. He was steward for my cabin, and several others. He told me he'd learned how to do the work on the British-India boat, and he was efficiency itself. I imagine he began to search the cabins at once, but nothing happened until we got to Yokohama."

"Something happened there?" asked Duff.

"Yes, it did. We spent the day ashore, but I was rather fed up on sightseeing. So I came back to the ship for dinner, though we weren't scheduled to sail until late that night. Mrs Luce came too. We—"

"Pardon me – just a moment. Did you note any other members of the party on the ship at dinner that evening?"

"Yes – Mr Tait was there. He'd been feeling quite badly and hardly ever made any shore trips. And – oh, yes – Mr Kennaway. If any of the others were aboard, I didn't see them."

"Very good. Go on, please."

"As I was leaving the dining salon, I saw Mr Welby. He motioned to me and I followed him up to the top deck. We stood by the rail, looking out at the lights of Yokohama. I saw he was very excited. 'Well, Miss,' he whispered, 'the fun's over.' I stared at him. 'What do you mean?' I asked. 'I mean I've got my man,' he told me. 'I've located that duplicate key – number 3260, and no other.'

"'Where is it?' I cried. I meant, of course, who has it, but he took me literally. 'It's right where I found it,' he said. 'I'm leaving it there until I can get my man to the States and into the hands of Inspector Duff. It's rather late now to make an arrest in Japan, and I think the other plan would be better. I know Mr Duff wants to get his hands on this lad himself, and I understand he's already in San Francisco. I'm going ashore now to send him a cable, care of the Yard, telling him to be on the Honolulu dock without fail. I'm not taking any chance beyond that point.'"

The girl stopped, and Duff sat in silence. Welby had taken too much of a chance as it was; he had blundered, that was all too plain now. But he had meant well. And he had paid for his blunder.

"I wish to heaven," said the English detective savagely, "you had made him tell you the name of the holder of that key."

"Well, I certainly tried," the girl answered. "I begged and pleaded, but Mr Welby simply wouldn't listen. He said it would be dangerous for me to know – and aside from that, I could see he had old-fashioned ideas about women. Never trust them with a secret – that sort of thing. He was a nice little man – I liked him – so I didn't nag. I told myself I would know all in good time. He went ashore to send that cable. And the next morning, when we were well out at sea, I discovered that he had never come back."

"No," said Duff quietly. "He never came back."

The girl looked at him quickly. "You know what happened to him?"

"Welby was found dead on the dock soon after your ship sailed."

"Murdered?"

"Of course."

Duff was startled to see that the girl, for all her sophistication, was weeping. "I – I can't help it," she apologized. "Such a nice little man. And – oh, it's abominable. That beast! Shall we ever find him? We must!"

"Indeed we must," returned Duff gravely. He got up and walked to the window. Honolulu was dozing in the blazing sun, under a palm tree in the little park across the way a brown-skinned, ragged boy was sprawled, his steel guitar forgotten at his side. That was the life, Duff thought, not a care in the world, nothing to do until tomorrow and perhaps not then. He heard a door open behind him, and turning, saw Mrs Luce enter from the bedroom.

"Just taking a nap," she explained. She noted the girl's tears. "What's wrong now?"

Pamela Potter told her. The old lady's face paled, and she sat down suddenly.

"Not our little steward," she cried. "I've had millions of stewards all over the world, but I'd taken a particular fancy to him. Well, I shall never make a long trip like this again. Maybe a little run over to China, or down to Australia, but that's all. I begin to feel old, for the first time in seventy-two years."

"Nonsense," said Duff. "You don't look a day over fifty."

She brightened. "Do you mean that? Well, as a matter of fact, I'll probably get over this soon. After I've had a good rest in Pasadena – I've never been to South America, you know. I can't think how I came to miss it."

"I've got an invitation for the two of you," Duff announced. "It sounds quite interesting. That Chinese you met on the dock this morning – he's a good fellow and a gentleman. He's invited me to his home for dinner tonight, and he told me to bring you along. Both of you. The honor, it appears, is all his."

They agreed to go, and at six-thirty Duff was waiting for them in the lobby. They drove up to Punchbowl Hill in the cool of the evening. The mountains ahead of them were wrapped in black clouds, but the town at their backs was yellow and rose in the light of the setting sun.

Charlie was waiting on his lanai, in his best American clothes, his broad face shining with joy.

"What a moment in the family history," he cried. "Over my threshold steps my old friend from London, in itself an honor almost too great to endure. Additions to the party make me proud man indeed."

With many remarks about his mean house and its contemptible furniture, he ushered them into the parlor. His unflattering picture of the hospitality he was offering was, of course, merely his conception of what was due his guests. The room was a charming one, a rare old rug on the floor, crimson and gold Chinese lanterns hanging from the ceiling, many carved teakwood tables bearing Swatow bowls, porcelain wine jars, dwarfed trees. On the wall was a single picture, a bird on an apple bough, painted on silk. Pamela Potter looked at Charlie with a new interest. She wished certain interior decorators she knew could see this parlor.

Mrs Chan appeared, stiff in her best black silk, and very careful about her English. A number of the older children entered and were ceremoniously presented.

"I will not burden you with entire roll-call," Chan explained. "The matter would, I fear, come to be an ordeal." He spoke of his eldest daughter, Rose, away at college on the mainland. His voice softened, and his eyes took on a look of sadness. If Rose were here – Rose, the flower of his flock – how well she would meet this situation, which had somewhat upset his wife's accustomed calm.

An aged woman servant appeared in the doorway and said something in a high shrill voice. They moved on into the dining-room, where Charlie explained that he was giving them a Hawaiian dinner, rather than a Chinese. The initial stiffness wore off, Mrs Chan finally ventured a smile, and after Mrs Luce had chatted breezily for a few moments, everybody felt at ease.

"My favorite race, the Chinese, Mr Chan," the old lady remarked.

Charlie bowed. "After your own, of course."

She shook her head. "Not at all. I've just been cooped up in close quarters with my own for nearly four months, and I repeat – the Chinese are my favorite race."

"On trip round world you see many of my people," Chan suggested.

"One certainly does – doesn't one, Pamela?"

"Everywhere," nodded the girl.

"The Chinese are the aristocrats of the East," Mrs Luce went on. "In every city out there – in the Malay States, in the Straits Settlements, in Siam – they are the merchants, the bankers, the men of substance and authority. So clever and competent and honest, carrying on among the lazy riffraff of the Orient. A grand people, Mr Chan. But you know all that."

Charlie smiled. "All I know, I do not speak. Appreciation such as yours makes music to my ears. We are not highly valued in the United States, where we are appraised as laundrymen, or maybe villains in the literature of the talkative films. You have great country, rich and proud, and sure of itself. About rest of world – pardon me – it knows little, and cares extremely less."

Mrs Luce nodded. "Quite true. And sometimes the most provincial among us we reward with a seat in the Senate. Have you visited China recently, Mr Chan?"

"Not for many years," Charlie told her. "I saw it last through sparkling eyes of youth. It was peaceful land in those days."

"But not any more," Pamela Potter said.

Chan nodded gravely. "Yes, China is sick now. But as someone has so well said, many of those who send sympathy to the sick man will die before him. That has happened in China's past – it will happen again." There was a rush of wind outside, followed by the terrific beating of rain upon the roof. "Now I think there is going to be a shower," Charlie added.

Through the remainder of the dinner, the rain continued. It was still pouring down with tropical fervor when they returned to the parlor. Duff consulted his watch.

"I don't mean to be rude, Charlie," he explained. "This evening will remain one of the happiest memories of my life. But the *President Arthur* goes at ten, you know, and it's past eight-thirty. I'm a bit nervous over the thought of missing that ship – as you can quite understand. Hadn't I better telephone for a car—"

"Not to be considered," Chan protested. "I possess automobile completely enclosed that will hold four with spacious ease – even four like myself, if there were such. I know the burden on your shoulders, and will convey you down Punchbowl Hill immediately."

With many expressions of their pleasure in the dinner, they prepared to leave. "It's the high spot of my trip around the world," Pamela Potter said, and Charlie and his wife both beamed with delight. In a few moments the new car was on its way down the hillside, the lights of the water front blurred and indistinct in the distance.

They stopped at the Young for Duff's luggage, and the two small bags the women had brought ashore. As they set out for the dock, Duff put his hand to his head.

"Good lord, Charlie," he remarked, "what's wrong with me, anyhow? I'd completely forgotten – all my notes about the case are in your safe at the station."

"I had not forgotten," Charlie answered. "I am taking you there now. I will drop you off, then I will transport ladies to the dock. When I return, you can have papers gathered up – chief or one of men will open safe for you. We will have last chat, and you shall smoke a final pipe."

"Very good," Duff agreed. He alighted in a torrent of rain before Halekaua Hale, and the other three went on.

At the dock, Charlie bade the women a polite farewell, then hurried back to the station. As he climbed those worn, familiar steps, his heart was heavy. Duff's coming had meant a happy break in the monotony, but the Englishman's stay was all too brief. Tomorrow, Chan reflected, would be like all the other days. The roar of tropic rain still in his ears, he crossed the hallway and pushed open the door of his office. For the second time within thirty-six hours, he encountered the unexpected.

Duff was lying on the floor beside the desk chair, his arms sprawled helplessly above his head. With a cry of mingled anger and alarm, Chan ran forward and bent over him. The English detective's face was pale as death, but placing a quick finger on his pulse, Charlie could feel a slight fluttering. He leaped to the telephone and got the Queen's Hospital.

"An ambulance," he shouted. "Send it to the police station at once. Be quick, in name of heaven!"

He stood for a moment, staring helplessly about. The single window was raised, as usual; out in the murky alley the rain was beating down. The window – ah, yes – and a sudden bullet from the misty darkness. Chan turned to the desk. On it lay Duff's open briefcase. Its contents appeared to be intact; some of the papers were still in the case; a few were strewn carelessly about, scattered, it was clear, by the wind.

Charlie called, and the chief came in from his office near by. At the same instant, Duff stirred slightly. Chan knelt by his side. The Englishman opened his eyes and saw his old friend.

"Carry on, Charlie," he whispered, and again lapsed into unconsciousness.

Chan stood erect, glanced at his watch, and began to gather up the papers on the desk.

XV

BOUND EAST FROM HONOLULU

The chief was bending over Duff. His face very grave, he rose from his knees and looked wonderingly at Chan. "What does this mean, Charlie?" he wanted to know.

The Chinese pointed to the open window. "Shot," he explained tersely. "Shot in back by bullet entering from there. Poor Inspector Duff. He comes to our quiet city in search of murderer in traveling party landing at this port today, and tonight murderer attempts to ply his trade."

"Of all the damned impertinence," cried the chief, suddenly enraged. "A man shot down in the Honolulu police station—"

Chan nodded. "Even worse than that. Shot down in my very office, of which I have been so proud. Until this killer is captured, I am laughing stock of world."

"Oh, I wouldn't put it that way," the chief said. Chan had restored all Duff's papers to the briefcase, and was strapping it up. "What are you going to do, Charlie?"

"What should I do? Can I lose face like this and offer no counter attack? I am sailing tonight on *President Arthur*."

"But you can't do that—"

"Who stops me? Will you kindly tell me which surgeon in this town is ablest man?"

"Well, I suppose Doctor Lang—"

In another second, Chan had the telephone book in his hand, and was dialing a number. As he talked, he heard the clang of an ambulance at the door of Halekaua Hale, and white-coated orderlies entered the hallway with a stretcher. The chief superintended the removal of the unfortunate Duff, while Charlie consulted with the surgeon. Doctor Lang lived at the Young Hotel, and he promised to be at the Queen's Hospital almost as soon as the ambulance. Charlie put the receiver back on the hook, then removed it and dialed once more.

"Hello," he said. "This is you, Henry? You are home early tonight. The gods are good. Listen carefully. Your father speaking. I sail in one hour for the mainland. What? Kindly omit surprised feelings – the matter is settled. I am off on important case. Pull self together and get this straight – to quote language you affect. Kindly pack bag with amazing speed, toothbrush, other suit, razor. Ask yourself what I shall require and bring same. Your honorable mother will assist. Come in your car to dock where *President Arthur*, Dollar boat, is waiting, bringing my bag and your mother. Boat departs at ten. You will gather that speed is essential. Thank you so much."

As he rose from the telephone, the chief faced him. "Better think this over, Charlie," he suggested.

Chan shrugged. "I have thought it over."

"What do you suggest – another leave of absence? I'd have to take that up with the commissioners – it would require several days—"

"Then call it my resignation," Chan answered briefly.

"No, no," protested the chief. "I'll fix it somehow. But listen, Charlie. This job is dangerous – this man is a killer—"

"Who knows that better than I? Is it important? My honor is assailed. In my office, you recall."

"I'm not suggesting that you shouldn't risk your life, provided it's in the legitimate line of duty. But I'd – I'd hate to lose you, Charlie. And this looks to me like Scotland Yard's affair—"

Stubbornly Chan shook his head. "Not any more. My affair, now. You would hate to lose me – from what? From pursuing fleet gamblers down an alley? From tagging cars on King Street—"

"I understand. Things have been rather slow—"

"Have been – yes. But not tonight. Things are plenty fast again. I am on that boat when she sails, and I will have my man before the mainland is reached. If not, I say goodby for all time to title of detective inspector, I retire for ever in sackcloth with ashes." He went to the safe. "I find here two hundred cash dollars. I am taking same. You will cable me more at San Francisco. Either it is necessary expense of catching criminal who performed black act on premises of Honolulu police station, or it is my money and I will repay it. Which does not matter. Now I am off for hospital. I am saying goodby—"

"No, you're not," replied his chief. "I'll be at the dock when you sail."

Clasping Duff's precious briefcase under his arm, Chan hurried to the street. With that sudden change of mood characteristic of Honolulu weather, the rain had ceased, and here and there amid the clouds the stars were shining. Charlie went to the lobby of the Young, and accosted the first man he met in the uniform of a ship's officer. Luck was with him, for the man proved to be one Harry Lynch, purser of the *President Arthur*.

Chan introduced himself, and persuaded Mr Lynch to get into the flivver with him. While he drove to Queen's Hospital, he hastily explained what had happened. The purser was deeply interested.

"The old man told me a Scotland Yard detective was coming aboard here," he remarked. "We knew all about Welby, of course. It was quite a shock when we lost him so abruptly. The word from Yokohama was simply that the man had been killed. And now Inspector Duff has been wounded, eh? Well, we'll be glad to have a police officer aboard. There seems to be plenty of work waiting for you, Mr Chan."

Charlie shrugged. "My talents are of the slightest," he protested.

"Yeah?" said Mr Lynch. "I heard different."

He said no more, but Chan's heart had warmed toward him. After his long period of inaction, it was good to know that he was remembered.

"I'll fix up the matter of your ticket," Lynch went on. "We're running light this crossing, and I can give you a good cabin to yourself."

They were at the hospital now, and Charlie went inside, a feeling of deep anxiety weighing him down. Doctor Lang was pointed out to him – a ghostly figure all in white, his face lost somewhere in the shadow of an eye shade.

"I've located the bullet," the surgeon announced, "and I'm operating at once. Fortunately it was deflected from its course by a rib. It's a ticklish business, but the man looks to be in remarkably good condition, and he ought to pull through."

"He must," Charlie said firmly. He told the doctor who Duff was, and why he had come to Honolulu. "If I could see him for one final moment—" he suggested, timid in this unfamiliar place.

"Come up to the operating-room," the surgeon invited. "The patient has talked a little, but it's delirious talk. However, maybe you can make something of it."

In the rather terrifying, odoriferous room upstairs, Charlie bent over the sheeted form of his friend. Had Duff caught a glimpse of the man who fired that shot? If he had, and spoke the name now, the case was finished.

"Inspector," said the Chinese gently. "This is Charlie Chan. Haie, what an awful thing has happened! I am so sorry. Tell me – did you behold face of assailant?"

Duff stirred slightly, and spoke in a thick voice. "Lofton," he muttered. "Lofton – the man with a beard—"

Charlie held his breath. Was it Lofton who had appeared at the window?

"There's Tait, too," Duff muttered. "And Fenwick. Where's Fenwick now? Vivian – Keane—"

Charlie turned sadly away. Poor Duff was only running over once again the list of his suspects.

"Better leave him now, Mr Chan," the surgeon said.

"I will go," Charlie replied. "But I must say this last thing. Tomorrow or whenever he awakes, you will have most restless patient on your hands. He will warmly desire to rise from bed and follow trail again. When that happens, soothe him with this word from me. Tell him Charlie Chan has sailed for San Francisco on *President Arthur*, and will have guilty man before boat reaches shore of mainland. Make it in form of promise, and say it comes from one who has never yet smashed promise to a friend."

The surgeon nodded gravely. "I'll tell him, Mr Chan. Thanks for the suggestion. And now – we're going to do our best for him. That's my promise to you."

It was nine-forty-five when Charlie and the purser drove on to the dock beside the *President Arthur*. Not far away, as he alighted, Chan saw his son Henry and with him a dumpy little figure in black silk – Mrs Chan, still in her party finery. He went over, and led them up the gangplank in the purser's company. An officer who stood at a little desk at the bottom of the plank eyed them curiously as they passed.

On the deck, Mrs Chan stood looking up at her inexplicable husband with timid eyes. "Wheh you go now, please?" she asked.

He gave her a kindly pat on the back. "Events break suddenly like fire-crackers in the face of innocent passer-by," he said. He told her what had happened in his office, and of the need for his immediate departure in order to save his face and regain his lost prestige.

The gentle little woman understood. “Plenty clean clo’es in bag,” she told him. She considered for a moment. “I think mebbe dangah wheh you go,” she added.

Charlie smiled reassuringly. “What the gods have decreed, man cannot alter,” he reminded her. “Can he dodge down by-path and avoid his fate? Do not fret. All will no doubt be well. And before many days I expect to see our Rose.”

In the dim light he saw sudden tears shining on her chubby cheeks. “Much love,” she said. “I send much love. She goes so fah away.” A quick pathetic little wringing of her hands. “I do not unnahstand why she go so fah away.”

“You will understand in the proud days to come,” Charlie promised.

Little groups of passengers straggled up the gangplank, lingered a moment on the deck, and then drifted off to their cabins. There was to be no excitement attending this sailing evidently. Chan’s chief appeared.

“Ah, here you are, Charlie,” he said. “I was able to dig up another sixty dollars for you.” He handed over a roll of bills.

“You overwhelm me with kindness,” Charlie answered.

“I’ll cable you more to bring you home – after you’ve got your man,” the chief went on. “You’ll get him, I’m sure.”

“Now that I have time to think it over, I am not so certain myself,” Chan responded. “Seems this is pretty hard task I have selected. I know from talk with Inspector Duff only one thing will make him happy. I must discover identity of man who committed murder more than three months ago in Broome’s Hotel, London. All time I have remained eight thousand miles away from scene of crime, and I must solve same when clues are cold, trail is covered, and no doubt the one vital point that might have brought about arrest is forgotten by all involved. It appears to me now that tonight I hotly elected myself to superman’s job without possessing necessary equipment. Maybe I come crawling home before long, defeated and expunged of all honor.”

"Yes, and maybe not," returned the chief. "It does look like a difficult task, that's true, but—"

He was interrupted by a small panting figure that appeared out of the night and faced Charlie. It was Kashimo.

"Hello, Charlie," the Japanese cried.

"Ah – this is kind of you to say goodby—" Chan began.

"Never mind goodby," Kashimo broke in. "I got important information, Charlie."

"Have you indeed?" Chan answered politely. "Of what nature, Kashimo?"

"I am going by end of alley soon after shot is fired injuring your honorable friend," went on the Japanese breathlessly. "I behold man coming out of alley into lighted street. He is tall man wrapped in big coat, hat over eyes."

"Then you didn't see his face?" Chan suggested.

"What's the matter," Kashimo replied. "Face not necessary. Saw something better. The man is very lame, like this—" With great histrionic vigor he gave an imitation of a lame man there on the deck. "He carries walking-stick, light-colored, maybe Malacca kind."

"I am very grateful," nodded Charlie, speaking in a voice such as he might have used to his youngest child. "You are observant, Kashimo. You are learning fast."

"Maybe some day I am good detective too," suggested the Japanese hopefully.

"Who can say?" Chan replied. A deep voice suggested that all who were going ashore had better do so. Charlie turned to his wife, and at that instant Kashimo burst into a torrent of words directed at the chief. The burden of it appeared to be that he should be sent to San Francisco as Chan's assistant.

"I am very fine searcher," the Japanese insisted. "Charlie says so himself."

"How about it, Charlie?" grinned the chief. "Could you use him?"

Chan hesitated for a second, then he went over and patted the little man on the shoulder.

"Consider, Kashimo," he remarked. "You do not weigh situation properly. Should you and I both be absent from Honolulu at identical moment, what an opportunity for the evil-doers! Crime wave might sweep over island, almost obliterating it. Run along now, and be good boy while I am gone. Always remember, we learn by our mistakes. First you know, you will be ablest man among us."

Kashimo nodded, shook hands and disappeared down the deck. Charlie turned to his son. "Please arrange that my car is taken up to garage on Punchbowl Hill at once," he said. "In my absence you will show your mother every deference, and guard whole family well."

"Sure," Henry agreed. "And say, Dad – can I use your bus until you come back? There's something wrong with that old flivver I inherited from you."

Chan nodded. "I foresaw that request. Yes, you may use my car, but please treat it with unusual kindness. Do not continually demand more than it has to give, like speed-mad young people you imitate. Good-by, Henry." He said a few low words to his wife, kissed her in Occidental fashion, and led her to the top of the gangplank.

"Good luck, Charlie," remarked his chief, and shook hands.

A chain clanked in the quiet night, and the plank was lowered, cutting Chan irrevocably off from the group on the dock. He saw them standing there looking up at him, and the sight touched him. There was, in their very attitudes, an expression of confidence in him and in his ultimate success. It was a confidence he did not share with them. What was this wild task he had set himself? He clutched Duff's briefcase tightly in his arms.

Slowly the big liner backed away, out into midstream. No orchestra playing *Aloha* tonight, no gaily colored streamers floating between ship and shore, none of the picturesque gestures that usually attended island sailings. Just the grim business of getting on with it, the old story of a ship putting out to sea.

The little group on the shadowy pier faded finally from his sight; still he did not move from his post by the rail. The throb of the engines became more pronounced; the ship was settling down to it. Presently Chan saw the circle of lights that marked Waikiki Beach. How many nights he had sat on his lanai staring across the town toward that beach, vaguely wishing for action, for something to happen. Well, it had happened at last – yes, something had certainly happened when he saw the lights of Waikiki from a ship at sea.

He turned and regarded the huge bulk of the liner, dark and mysterious behind him. He was in a new world now, a small world, and in it with him was a man who had killed in London through error, had killed again in Nice and San Remo through grim intention, and then again on the Yokohama dock, no doubt through necessity. A ruthless man who had only tonight sought to remove the relentless Duff from his trail. Not a squeamish person, this Jim Everhard. Now for six days Chan and he would be together in a limited space, prisoners on this brave contraption of steel and wood, each seeking to outwit the other. Which would win?

Charlie started. Someone had come up noiselessly behind him, and he had heard a sudden hissing in his ear. He turned.

"Kashimo," he gasped.

"Hello, Charlie," grinned the Japanese.

"Kashimo – what does this mean?"

"I am hide-away," Kashimo explained. "I go with you to assist on big case."

Chan cast a speculative eye at the breakers between the boat and Waikiki Beach. "Can you swim, Kashimo?" he inquired.

"Not a single stroke," replied the little man gleefully.

Chan sighed. “Ah, well. He who accepts with a smile whatever the gods may send, has mastered most important lesson in life’s hard school. Pardon me one moment, Kashimo. I am seeking to achieve the smile.”

XVI

THE MALACCA STICK

In another moment Chan's inherent good-nature triumphed, and the smile was accomplished.

"You will pardon, Kashimo, if for one instant I was slightly appalled. Can you blame me? I remember our last adventure together – the affair of the dice. But enterprise such as yours is not to be met with a sneeze. I welcome you into present case – which was a most difficult one, even before you arrived."

"Hearty thanks," replied the Japanese.

The purser emerged from a nearby doorway, and came rapidly along the deck.

"Oh, Mr Chan," he said, "I've been looking for you. Just had a chat with the captain and he told me to give you the best I've got. There's a cabin with bath – at the minimum rate, of course. I'm having one of the beds made up. If you'll bring your bag and follow me—" He stared at Kashimo. "And who is this?"

Chan hesitated "Er – Mr Lynch, condescend to meet Officer Kashimo, of Honolulu force. One of" – he choked a little – "our most able men. At last moment it was decided to bring him along in rôle of assistant. If you can find a place to lay him away for the night—"

Lynch considered. "He's going as a passenger, too, I suppose?"

A brilliant idea struck Charlie. "Kashimo is specialist, like everybody nowadays. He is grand searcher. If you could find him place in crew which would not consume too much brain power, he might accomplish brilliant results. In that way he could maintain anonymous standing, which I, alas, can not do."

"One of our boys was pinched in Honolulu tonight for bootlegging," Lynch replied. "What's getting into those Federal men, anyhow? It means a few changes in our assignments. We might make Mr Kashimo a biscuit boy – one of the lads who sit in the alleyways and answer the cabin bells. Of course, it's not a very dignified job—"

"But a splendid opportunity," Chan assured him. "Kashimo will not mind. His duty is first with him, always. Kashimo, tell the gentleman how you feel about it."

"Biscuit boys get tips?" inquired the Japanese eagerly.

Charlie waved a hand. "Behold – he pants to begin."

"Well, you'd better take him in with you tonight," Lynch, said. "Nobody will know about it but your steward, and I'll tell him not to say anything." He turned to Kashimo. "Report to the chief steward at eight tomorrow. I don't mind your searching, but you mustn't get caught, you understand. We can't have innocent people annoyed."

"Naturally not," agreed Chan heartily. But he wasn't so sure. Annoying innocent people, he reflected, was another of Kashimo's specialties.

"The captain would like to see you in the morning, Mr Chan," the purser remarked at the doorway of the cabin to which he led them. He departed.

Charlie and Kashimo entered the stateroom. The steward was still there, and Chan directed him to make up the other bed. While they waited, the detective looked about him. A large airy room, a pleasant place to think. And he would have to do much thinking during the next six days – and nights.

"I will return presently," he said to his assistant.

He went to the top deck and dispatched a radiogram. It was addressed to his chief, and in it he wrote:

"If you notice Kashimo has mislaid himself, I am one to do worrying. He is with me on ship."

Going back to his cabin, he found the Japanese there alone. "I have just broken news to chief about your departure," he explained. "This biscuit boy business is brilliant stroke. Otherwise question might have come up who pays your passage, and I have deep fear everybody would have declined the honor."

"Better go to bed now," Kashimo suggested.

Charlie gave him a pair of his own pajamas, and was moved to silent mirth at the resulting spectacle. "You have aspect of deflated balloon going nowhere," he said.

Kashimo grinned. "Can sleep in anything," he announced, and climbed into bed prepared to prove it.

Presently Charlie turned on the light above his pillow, put out all the others, and got into his own bed with Duff's briefcase in his hand. He undid the straps, and took out a huge sheaf of papers. Duff's notes were on numbered pages, and Chan was relieved to discover that none was missing. Honywood's letter to his wife, together with all other messages and documents pertinent to the case, remained intact. Either Jim Everhard had been afraid to enter the office after his shooting of Duff, or he had felt that there was nothing in these papers he need bother about.

"I trust I shall not disturb you, Kashimo," Chan remarked. "But stowaways must not be too particular. It is my duty now to read the story of our case, until I know it perfectly by the heart."

"Won't disturb me none," yawned the Japanese.

"Ah, all the fun and no responsibility," sighed Charlie. "You have happy life. While I read, I shall pay especial attention to lame man in the party. What was he doing at mouth of alley when poor Mr Duff lay shot in my office? You gave me point of attack on case with that news, and I am grateful."

He began to read and, in imagination, he traveled far. London, all his life a name and nothing more, became a familiar city. He saw the little green car set out from Scotland Yard, he stepped inside the sacred portals of Broome's Hotel, he bent above the lifeless form of Hugh Morris Drake as it lay on the bed in room 28. Descending to the musty parlor of the hotel, he witnessed Tait's heart attack on the threshold, noted Honywood's haunted look. Then on to Paris, and Nice: Honywood dead in the garden. San Remo, and that terrible moment in the lift. Carefully he read Honywood's epistle to his wife, which explained so much but left the vital question unanswered. Every detail in the long case burned itself into his mind now.

True, he had been all over it with Duff, but then the affair had seemed so remote, so little to concern him. It concerned him tonight. He was in Duff's shoes, the case was his; nothing must escape him; nothing could be safely overlooked. Last of all he perused the report of Duff's talk with Pamela Potter in Honolulu that very afternoon, in which she had told of Welby's discovery of the key. It was a matter of pride with Duff that he kept his notes up to the minute.

Chan finished reading. "Kashimo," he remarked thoughtfully, "that man Ross has intriguing sound. What about Ross? Always in the background, limping along, never a hint against him – until now. Yes, Kashimo, the matter of Mr Ross must be our first concern."

He paused. A loud snore from the bed across the way was his only answer. Charlie looked at his watch, it was past midnight. He turned back to the beginning and read it all again.

It was after two o'clock when he finally put out his light. Even then, he was not ready to sleep. He lay there, planning the future.

At seven-thirty he rudely dragged his small assistant out of slumberland. Kashimo was lost in the clouds, and had to be gradually brought back to earth and a realization of where he was. While he made his sketchy toilet Charlie told him a little of the case, with special emphasis on the part the Japanese was to play. He was to search among the possessions of the travel party for a key bearing the number 3260. He might find it, he might not – perhaps by this time it was at the bottom of the Pacific. But the effort must be made anyhow. The Japanese nodded in a dazed, uncomprehending sort of way, and at two minutes of eight was ready for his interview with the chief steward.

"Remember, Kashimo, too much haste may have fatal ending," was Chan's final admonition. "Take plenty of time and know what you are doing before you do it. You are biscuit boy from now on, and if we meet on ship, you have never seen me before. All talks between us are conducted with utmost secrecy in this cabin. Farewell, and best of luck."

"So long," Kashimo responded, and went out. Charlie stood for a moment at the port-hole, gazing at the sunlit sea and breathing in great drafts of the bracing air. There is something invigorating about the first morning on a ship, the cool peace, the feeling of security away from the land's alarms. A sense of well-being and confidence flooded Chan's heart. It was a glorious day, and the future looked promising.

He was shaving when a boy knocked at his door and handed him a radiogram from his chief. He read:

"Surgeon reports operation O.K. Duff doing fine. Sincere condolences on Kashimo."

Charlie smiled. Great news, that about Duff. In a cheerful frame of mind he stepped out on to the deck to face his problems. The first person he saw was Pamela Potter, who was taking a morning stroll, accompanied by Mark Kennaway. The girl stopped, and stared.

"Mr Chan," she cried. "What are you doing here?"

Charlie managed a low and sweeping bow. "I am enjoying a very good morning, thank you. You appear to be doing the same."

"But I'd no idea you were coming with us."

"I had no idea myself, until late hour last night. In me you behold quite worthless replacement for Inspector Duff."

She started. "He – you don't mean that he, too—"

"Do not be alarmed. Wounded only." Quickly he reported what had happened.

The girl shook her head. "There seems to be no end to it," she said.

"What begins, must finish," Chan told her. "Miscreant in this case is clever enough to play a fiddle behind his back, but ever the cleverest have been known to blunder. I believe I saw this young man on the dock yesterday. The name—"

"Oh, I'm sorry," the girl replied. "I was so startled to see you. Inspector Chan – this is Mr Kennaway. I've just been telling him what a wonderful party he missed last night. He's all upset. You know, he belongs to *such* a family in Boston, and he isn't accustomed to being left out."

"Nonsense," Kennaway said.

"He would have been very welcome," Charlie remarked. He turned to the young man. "I myself have keen interest in Boston, and some day we must enjoy small talk about same. Just now I will not further interrupt your perambulations. Since I was introduced to your entire party yesterday, full name and title, it will be useless for me to attempt dissemble of my identity. So I propose to meet all of you presently for little chat about last night."

"Same old story," Kennaway replied. "We've been gathered together to meet policemen at frequent intervals ever since the tour started. Well, you're bringing a new face into it, and that's something. I wish you luck, Inspector Chan."

"Thank you so much. I shall do my best. True, I am coming into the case through the back door. But I am encouraged when I remember old saying which remarks, the turtle that enters the house at the rear gate comes finally to the head of the table."

"Ah, yes – in the soup," Kennaway reminded him.

Chan laughed. "Ancient proverbs must not be taken too literally. Pardon me while I sample the cuisine of this vessel. At some later hour I shall sample your society more extensively."

He went to the dining saloon, where he was given a good table to himself. After a hearty breakfast, he rose to leave. In a seat near the door, he saw Doctor Lofton. He stopped.

"Ah, Doctor," he said. "Perhaps you do me the honor to recall my face?"

Lofton glanced up. Few people could look at Charlie without a friendly smile, but the doctor managed it. In fact, his expression was a rather sour one.

"Yes," he said. "I remember you. A policeman, I believe?"

"I am inspector of detectives, attached to Honolulu station," Charlie explained. "May I sit down, please?"

"I suppose so," Lofton growled. "But don't blame me if my feelings are none too cordial. I'm a bit fed up with detectives. Where is your friend Duff this morning?"

Charlie raised his eyebrows. "You have not heard what happened to Inspector Duff?"

"Of course not," snapped Lofton. "I've got twelve people to look after, and I can assure you that they keep me busy. I can't bother with every policeman who tags along. What's happened to Duff? Come on, man – speak! Don't tell me he's been killed, too?"

"Not entirely," Chan answered gently. He told his story, his little black eyes fixed on Lofton's face. He was amazed at the lack of shock or sympathy on that bearded countenance.

"Well, that's the end of Duff, as far as this tour is concerned," the doctor remarked, when Chan had finished. "And now what?"

"Now I replace poor Duff."

Lofton stared at him. "You!" he cried rudely.

"Why not?" asked Charlie blandly.

"Well, no reason, I suppose. You'll pardon me, but my nerves have been completely upset by the events of the last few months. Thank God, we break up at San Francisco, and it's a question in my mind if I ever go out again. I've been thinking of retiring, and this is as good a time as any."

"Whether you do or not is a private and personal matter," Chan told him. "What is not so private is, what is name of the killer who has honored you with his presence on this journey? It is an affair I am here to look into, with full authority to do so. If you will get your party together in the lounge at ten o'clock, I shall launch the campaign."

Lofton glared at him. "How long, O Lord, how long?" he said.

"I shall be brief as possible."

"You know what I mean. How long must I continue to gather my party together for these inquisitions? Nothing ever comes of them. Ever has, or ever will, if you ask me."

Charlie gave him a searching look. "And you would be sorry if anything did," he ventured.

Lofton returned the look. "Why should I try to deceive you? I am not longing for any final flare of publicity about this matter. That would mean the end of my touring days, and no mistake. An unpleasant end, too. No, what I want is a petering out of the whole business. You see, I intend to be frank with you."

"Quite refreshing, thank you," bowed Charlie.

"I'll get the party together, of course. But further than that, if you look for any help from me, you'll be looking in the wrong place."

"Looking in wrong place is always terrible waste of time," Chan assured him.

"I'm glad you realize that," Lofton answered, and rising, moved toward the door. Chan followed meekly at his heels.

Going up to see the captain of the ship, Charlie encountered a more cordial greeting. That old sea-dog heard the story of the chase with mounting indignation.

"All that I can say is, I hope you get your man," he remarked at last. "I'll give you every help possible. But remember this, Mr Chan. A mistake would be a serious thing. If you came to me and asked me to have someone put under restraint, and he proved to be the wrong person, I'd be in a hell of a hole. The line would probably never hear the end of it – lawsuits and all that. We'll have to be very sure what we are doing."

"Man who runs big ship like this should always be sure what he is doing," Chan suggested mildly. "I promise to use every care."

"And I know you will," smiled the captain. "I haven't been on the Pacific run these past ten years without hearing about you. I have every confidence in you, but I couldn't under the circumstances, fail to point out my position. If an arrest becomes necessary, let's try to have it made on the San Francisco dock. That would avoid many complications."

"You call up pretty picture," Chan remarked. "I hope it eventuates."

"So do I," nodded the captain, "with all my heart."

Charlie went back to the promenade deck. He saw Kashimo flit by, resplendent in a new uniform which fitted him only in spots. Pamela Potter was sitting in a deck chair, and waved to him. He joined her.

"Your friend Mrs Luce is not yet about?" he inquired.

"No – she sleeps late at sea, and has breakfast in her cabin. Did you want to speak with her right away?"

"I wished talk with the two of you. But you alone suffice in a very pleasant manner. Last night I set you down on dock at about nine o'clock. Tell me – what members of travel party did you encounter between that hour and moment of retiring?"

"We saw several of them. The stateroom was quite warm, so we went up and sat in steamer chairs near the top of the gangplank. The Minchins came aboard presently, and Sadie stopped to show us her day's loot. A ukulele for that boy of hers at military school, among other things. Then Mark Kennaway came on, but he didn't stop with us. He thought Mr Tait might want him for the eternal bedtime story. Then the Benbows, Elmer all loaded down with exposed film. That was all, I guess. Mr Kennaway came back to us in a few minutes. He said Mr Tait didn't seem to be aboard, and he appeared to think that rather surprising."

"Those were all. No man with a Malacca stick?"

"Oh – Mr Ross, you mean. Yes, he was one of the first, I think. He came limping aboard—"

"Pardon me – at about what time?"

"It must have been about nine-fifteen. He passed where we were sitting – I thought he was limping even more than usual. Mrs Luce spoke to him, but oddly enough, he didn't answer. He just hurried on down the deck."

"Can you tell me – is his the only Malacca stick in the party?"

The girl laughed. "My dear Mr Chan – we spent three days in Singapore, and if you don't buy a Malacca stick there, they won't let you leave. Every man in our party has one at least."

Charlie frowned. "Indeed? Then how can you be absolutely certain it was Mr Ross who passed you?"

"Well – this man was limping—"

"Simplest thing in the world to imitate. Think hard. Was there no other way in which you could identify him?"

The girl sat for a moment in silence. "How's this?" she remarked at last. "Getting to be some little detective myself. The sticks that were bought in Singapore all had metal tips –

I noticed that. But Mr Ross's stick has a heavy rubber tip on it. It makes no noise when he walks along the deck."

"And the stick of the man who passed you last night—"

"It made no sound. So the man must have been Mr Ross. Am I good? Just to show you how good I am, I'll give you a demonstration. Here comes Mr Ross now. Listen!"

Ross had appeared in the distance, and was swinging along toward them. He passed with a nod and a smile, and disappeared around the corner. Chan and the girl looked at each other. For accompanying the lame man like a chant they had heard the steady "tap-tap-tap" of metal on the hard deck.

"Well, of all things," cried the girl.

"Mr Ross's stick has lost its rubber tip," Charlie said.

She nodded. "What can that mean?"

"A puzzle," Chan answered. "And unless I am much mistaken, the first of many aboard this ship. Why should I worry? Puzzles are my business."

XVII

THE GREAT EASTERN LABEL

At a little before ten, Lofton appeared in front of the chair where Chan was sitting. He still had the air of a much-abused man.

"Well, Inspector," he announced, "I've got my people together in the smoking-room. I chose that spot because it's always deserted at this hour. A bit odoriferous, perhaps – I trust you won't hold them there long. I suggest you come at once. Keeping a touring party intact in one place for any length of time is, I have discovered, a difficult feat."

Chan rose. "Will you also come, Miss Pamela?" he suggested. As they walked along, he added to the doctor: "Am I to understand that all members of band are present?"

"All except Mrs Luce," Lofton told him. "She prefers to sleep late. But I'll have her roused, if you say so."

"Not at all," Chan replied. "I know where Mrs Luce was last evening. Matter of fact, she dined at my house."

"Not really?" cried the doctor, with unflattering surprise.

"You would have been welcome yourself," Charlie smiled.

They entered the thick atmosphere of the smoking-room, redolent of old, unhappy, far-off things, and bottles, long ago. The group inside regarded Chan with frank curiosity. He stood for a moment, facing them. A little speech seemed indicated.

"May I extend courteous good morning?" he began. "Would say I am as surprised to see you all again as you must be to behold me. I am reluctant to enforce my inspeakable presence upon you, but fate will not have it otherwise. Inspector Duff, as you know, was awaiting you at Honolulu, Paradise of Pacific, intending to travel eastward in your company. Last night in paradise history repeats and snake appears, striking down the worthy Duff. He is much better this morning, thank you. Maybe plenty soon he sees you all again. In meantime, a stupid substitute for Duff has been pushed into position for which he has not the brains, the wit, the reputation. Notably – myself."

He smiled pleasantly and sat down. "All mischief comes from opening the mouth," he continued. "Knowing this, I am still forced to operate mine to considerable extent from now on. Let us make the best of it. My initial effort will be to find out from each of you exact presence between hour of – may I say – eight last evening, and sailing of boat at ten. Pardon such outrageous hint, but any of you who fails to speak true may have cause to regret same later on. I have said I am dull and stupid, and that is the fact, but often the gods go out of way to take care of such. To recompense, they shower on me sometimes amazing luck. Look out I don't get shower at any moment."

Patrick Tait was on his feet. "My dear sir," he remarked irritably, "I question your authority to interrogate any of us. We are no longer in Honolulu—"

"Pardon interruption, but what you say is true," Charlie put in. "Legal side of matter is no doubt such as to give eminent lawyer bad attack of choleric. I judge from records of case same has happened before. Can only say captain of ship stands behind me firm as Gibraltar rock. We proceed on assumption everyone of you is shocked and grieved by attack on Duff, and eager to see the attacker captured. If this is wrong – if there is man among you has something to hide—"

"Just a minute!" Tait cried. "I won't let you maneuver me into that position. I've nothing to hide. I only wanted to remind you that there is such a thing as legal procedure."

"Which is usually the criminal's best friend," nodded Chan blandly. "You and I – we know. Do we not, Mr Tait?" The lawyer sank back into his chair. "But we are some miles off the point," continued Charlie. "You are all friends of justice, I feel certain. You have no interest in that poor relation of same, legal procedure. Let us go forward on such basis. Doctor Lofton, since you are conductor of party, I begin with you. How did you spend two hours mentioned by me?"

"From eight to about nine-thirty," said Lofton sourly, "I was at the Honolulu office of the Nomad Travel Company, which manages my tours for me. I had a lot of accounts to go over, and some typewriting to do."

"Ah, yes. Of course, others were with you at that office?"

"Not a soul. The manager was due to attend a country club dance, and he left me there alone. Since the door had a spring lock, I had only to close it after me when I went out. I returned to the ship at about nine-thirty."

"Nomad Travel Company office is, I believe, on Fort Street? Only few steps from mouth of alley wandering along rear of police station."

"It's on Fort Street, yes. I don't know anything about your police station."

"Naturally you don't. Did you encounter any members of travel party in neighborhood of alley?"

"I have no idea what alley you're talking about. I saw none of my people from the time I went to the office until I returned to the ship. I suggest you get on with this. Time is pressing."

"Whom is it pressing?" asked Chan suavely. "Speaking for myself, I have six days to squander. Mr Tait, do you cling to legal rights, or will you condescend to tell humble policeman how you spent last evening?"

"Oh, I've no objection," returned Tait, amiable with an effort. "Why should I have? Last night, about eight o'clock, we started a contract bridge game in the lounge. Aside from myself, Mrs Spicer, Mr Vivian and Mr Kennaway took part in it. It's a foursome that has had many similar contests as we went round the world."

"Ah, yes – travel is fine education," nodded Chan. "You played until the boat sailed."

"We did not. We were having a splendid game when, at about eight-thirty, Mr Vivian raised the most unholy row—"

"I beg your pardon," Vivian cut in. "If I broke up the game, I had an excellent reason. You have heard me tell my partner a thousand times that if I make an original two bid, I expect her to keep it open, even if—"

"So – you told me that a thousand times, did you?" flared Mrs Spicer. "A million would be more like it. And I've explained patiently to you that if I had a flat hand, I wouldn't bid – no, not even if Mr Whitehead was sitting beside me with a gun. The trouble with you is, a little knowledge is a dangerous—"

"Pardon me that I burst in," Charlie said, "but the matter becomes too technical for my stupidity to cope with. Let us seize on fact that game broke up."

"Broke up in a row, at eight-thirty," Tait continued. "Mr Kennaway and I went out on to the deck. It was raining hard. Mark said he thought he'd get his rain-coat and take a stroll up to the town. I saw him leave about ten minutes later. I told him I preferred to stay aboard."

"And did you?" Charlie asked.

"No, I didn't. After Mr Kennaway had gone, I remembered that I'd seen a copy of the *New York Sunday Times* hanging outside a news-stand on King Street yesterday morning. I'd meant to go back and get it. I hadn't seen one for ages, and I was keen to have it. The rain seemed to be letting up a bit. So I got a coat, my hat and stick—"

"Your Malacca stick?"

"Yes – I believe I carried the Malacca. At about ten minutes of nine I walked up-town, bought the paper, and returned to the ship. I'm a slow walker, and I suppose it was about twenty minutes past the hour when I came aboard again."

Chan took his watch from his left-hand vest pocket. "What time have you now, Mr Tait?" he asked quickly.

Tait's right hand went to his own waistcoat pocket. Then it dropped back to his lap, and he looked rather foolish. He extended his left wrist, and examined the watch on it. "I make it ten-twenty-five," he announced.

"Correct," smiled Charlie. "I make it the same, and I am always right."

Tait's bushy eyebrows rose. "Always?" he repeated, with a touch of sarcasm.

"In such matters – yes," nodded the Chinese. For a moment he and the lawyer stared at each other. Then Chan looked away. "So many changes of time as you peruse way around world," he said softly. "I merely wished to be certain your watch is up to date. Mr Vivian, what was your course of action after bridge table eruption?"

"I, too, went ashore," Vivian responded. "I wanted to cool off."

"With hat, coat and Malacca stick, no doubt?" suggested Charlie.

"We've all got Malacca sticks," snapped the polo player. "They're almost obligatory when you visit Singapore. I walked about the city, and got back to the ship a few minutes before it sailed."

"Mrs Spicer?" Charlie's eyes turned in her direction.

She looked weary and fed-up.

"I went to bed when I left the bridge table," she told him. "It had been a somewhat trying experience. Bridge is only fun when you happen to have a gentleman for a partner."

"Mr Kennaway, your actions have already been detailed by Mr Tait."

Kennaway nodded. "Yes – I took my little stick and went ashore. I didn't stay long, however. I thought Mr Tait might want me to read to him, so I came back to the ship soon after nine. But Mr Tait, to my surprise, wasn't aboard. He appeared about nine-twenty, as he told you, and he had the *Times* under his arm. We went to our cabin, and I read to him from the paper until he fell asleep."

Charlie looked around the circle. "And this gentleman?"

"Max Minchin, Chicago. And nothing to hide, get me?"

Charlie bowed. "Then you will be glad to detail your actions?"

"Yes – and it'll take just one minute – see?" Mr Minchin fondled an expensive, half-smoked cigar, from which he had failed to remove a shining gold band. "Me and Sadie – that's the wife – was doing the town, in the rain. Well, the evening wasn't so much on the up and up with me, so I dragged the frau into a pitcher show. But we seen that filum a year ago in Chi., and Sadie was itching to get back to the stores, so we made our get-away quick. After that, just buying right and left. We didn't have no truck with us, and when we couldn't handle no more, Sadie agreed to quit. We staggered back to the ship. I didn't have no gat on me, and I wasn't carrying no Malacca stick. When I carry a cane, it'll mean my dogs ain't no good no more – I told Sadie that in Singapore."

Charlie smiled. "Mr Benbow?" he suggested.

"Same story as the Minchins," that gentleman replied. "We did the stores, though they're not much after those Oriental bazaars. Sat a while in the Young lobby and watched it rain. I said I wished I was back in Akron, and Nettie practically agreed with me. First time we've been in accord on that point since the tour started. But we were on good old U.S. soil, even if it was pretty sloppy, and we came back to the ship walking high, wide and handsome. I think we stepped aboard about nine-fifteen. I was dead tired – I'd bought a motion picture projector in Honolulu, and the weight of one of those things is nobody's business."

"Miss Pamela," said Chan. "I already know how your evening was spent. Leaving, I think, only two yet to be inquisitioned. This gentleman – Captain Keane, I believe."

Keane leaned back, stifled a yawn, and clasped his hands behind his head. "I watched the bridge for a while," he replied. "Not as a kibitzer, you understand." He glanced at Vivian. "I never interfere in affairs that don't concern me."

Recalling the captain's record outside various doors, Charlie felt the remark was somewhat lacking in sincerity. "And after the bridge—" he prompted.

"When the battle broke," Keane went on, "I took to the open air. Thought some of getting my own little Malacca stick and going ashore, but the rain gave me pause. Never did care for rain, especially the tropical kind. So I went to my cabin, got a book, and returned here to the smoking-room."

"Ah," remarked Chan. "You now possess a book."

"What are you trying to do, razz me?" said the captain. "I sat here reading for a while, and about the time the boat sailed, I went to bed."

"Was anyone else in this room while you were?"

"Nobody at all. Everybody ashore, including the stewards."

Charlie turned to the man whom he had purposely saved until the last. Ross was sitting not far away, staring down at his injured foot. His stick, innocent of its rubber tip, lay beside him on the floor.

"Mr Ross, I believe you will complete the roster," Chan remarked. "You went ashore last evening, I have heard."

Ross looked up in surprise. "Why, no, Inspector," he replied. "I didn't."

"Indeed? Yet you were seen to come aboard ship at nine-fifteen."

"Really?" Ross lifted his eyebrows.

"On authority not to be impeached."

"But – I am sorry to say – in this case quite mistaken."

"You are sure you did not leave the ship?"

"Naturally I'm sure. It's the sort of thing I ought to know about, you must admit." He remained entirely amiable. "I dined aboard, and sat in the lounge for a while after dinner. I'd had a rather hard day – a lot of walking, and that tires me. My leg was aching, so I retired at eight o'clock. I was sound asleep when Mr Vivian, who shares my cabin, came in. That was in the neighborhood of ten, he told me this morning. He was careful not to wake me. He is always most considerate."

Chan regarded him thoughtfully. "Yet at nine-fifteen, as I have said, Mr Ross, two people of unreproachable honesty saw you come up the plank, and you passed them on deck."

"May I ask how they recognized me, Inspector?"

"You carried stick, of course."

"A Malacca stick," nodded Ross. "You have seen what that amounts to."

"But more, Mr Ross. You were walking with customary difficulty, owing to unhappy accident which is so deeply deplored by all."

For a moment Ross regarded the detective. "Inspector," he remarked at last, "I've watched you here. You're a clever man."

"You exaggerate shamelessly," Charlie told him.

"No, I don't," smiled Ross. "I say you're clever, and I believe that all I need do now is to tell you about a queer little incident that happened on this ship late yesterday afternoon." He picked up his stick. "This was not bought in Singapore, but in Tacoma some months ago just after I had my accident. After I bought it, I looked around until I found a rubber tip – a shoe, I believe it is sometimes called – to fit over the end of it. This made walking easier for me, and it did not scratch hardwood floors. About five yesterday afternoon, I returned to the ship and took a brief nap in my cabin. When I rose and went down to dinner, I was conscious of something – something wrong – at first I didn't know just what. But presently I realized. As I walked, my stick was tapping on the deck. I looked down in amazement. The rubber tip was gone. Someone had taken it." He stopped. "I remember Mr Kennaway came along at that moment, and I told him what had happened."

"That's right," Kennaway agreed. "We puzzled over the matter. I suggested somebody was playing a joke."

"It was no joke," remarked Ross gravely. "Someone, I now believe, was planning to impersonate me for the evening. Someone who was clever enough to recall that my stick made no sound when it touched a hard surface."

No one spoke. Mrs Luce appeared in the distant doorway, and came swiftly to Chan's side. The detective leaped to his feet.

"What's this I hear?" she cried. "Poor Inspector Duff!"

"Not badly injured," Charlie assured her. "Recovering."

"Thank heaven," she replied. "The aim is wavering. The arm is getting weak. Well, too much shooting is bad for anybody. I take it you are with us in Inspector Duff's place, Mr Chan?"

"I am unworthy substitute," he bowed.

"Unworthy fiddlesticks! You can't put that over on me. Known Chinese most of my life – lived among 'em. At last we're going to get somewhere. I'm sure of it." She glanced belligerently around the circle. "And about time, if you ask me."

"You arrive at good moment," Charlie said. "I will request your testimony, please. Last night, after I brought you to dock, you and Miss Pamela sat on deck near top of gangplank. You beheld several members of party return to ship. Among them, Mr Ross here?"

The old lady stood for a moment staring at Ross. Then she shook her head. "I don't know," she answered.

Chan was surprised. "You don't know whether you saw Mr Ross or not?"

"No, I don't."

"But, my dear," said Pamela Potter, "surely you remember. We were sitting near the rail, and Mr Ross came up the plank, and passed us—"

Again Mrs Luce shook her head. "A man who walked with a stick, and limped, passed us – yes. I spoke to him, but he didn't answer. Mr Ross is a polite man. Besides—"

"Yes?" Charlie said eagerly.

"Besides, Mr Ross carries his stick in his left hand, whereas that man last night was carrying his in the right. I noticed it at the time. That's why I say I don't know whether it was Mr Ross or not. My own feeling at the moment was that it was not."

Silence followed. Finally Ross looked up at Charlie. "What did I tell you, Inspector?" he remarked. "I did not leave the ship last evening. I had rather a hunch the matter would be proved in time, though I didn't expect the proof so soon."

"Your right leg is injured one," Charlie said.

"Yes – and anyone who has never suffered such an injury might suppose that I would naturally carry my stick in the right hand. But as my doctor pointed out to me, the left is better. I am more securely balanced, and I can move much faster."

"That's O.K., Officer," put in Maxy Minchin, "A few years back an old pal of mine winged me in the left calf. I found out then the dope was to carry the cane on the opposite side. It gives you better support – get me?"

Ross smiled "Thank you, Mr Minchin," he said. He glanced at Chan. "These clever lads always slip up somewhere, don't they?" he added. "Here is one who had brains enough to want my rubber shoe so his stick couldn't be distinguished on that score – and then, in his haste, forgot to notice in which hand

I carried mine. Well, all I can say is, I'm very glad he did." His eyes traveled questioningly about the little circle.

Charlie stood up. "Meeting now adjourns for time being," he announced. "I am very grateful to you all for kind cooperating."

They filed out, until Tait alone remained with the detective. He strolled over to Chan with a grim smile on his face.

"You didn't get much out of that session," he remarked.

"You believe not?" Chan inquired.

"No, but you did your best. And on one point, at least, you showed unusual acumen. That about the watch, I mean."

"Ah, yes – the watch," Charlie nodded.

"A man who has been accustomed all his life to carrying a watch in his vest pocket, and then switches to a wrist-watch, is inclined to put his hand to the old location when suddenly asked the time."

"So I noticed," the detective replied.

"I thought you did. What a pity you wasted that experiment on an innocent man."

"There will be more experiments," Chan assured him.

"I hope so. I may tell you that I purchased a wrist-watch just before I came on this tour."

"Before you came on the tour." The first word was accented ever so slightly.

"Exactly. I can prove that by Mr Kennaway. Any time at all."

"For the present, I accept your word," Charlie replied.

"Thank you. I trust I shall be present when you attempt those other experiments."

"Do not worry. You are plenty sure to be there."

"Good. I like to watch you work." And Tait strode debonairly from the room, while Chan stood looking after him.

The investigation was young yet, Charlie thought, as he walked toward his cabin to prepare for lunch. No great progress this morning, but a good beginning. At least he had now a pretty shrewd idea as to the character and capabilities of the people with whom he had to deal. Know them better tomorrow. No place like a ship for getting acquainted.

A boy appeared with a radiogram. Chan opened it and read:

"Charlie, as a friend, I implore you to drop the whole matter. I am getting on beautifully and can take up the trail soon myself. Situation is far too dangerous for me to ask such a service of you. Believe me, I was quite delirious when I suggested you carry on. Duff."

Charlie smiled to himself, and sat down at a desk in the library. After due deliberation, he composed an answering message:

"You were not delirious last night, but I have deep pain to note you are in such state now. How else could you think I would not pursue to very frontier of my ability this interesting affair? Remain calm, get back health promptly, and meantime I am willing replacement. Hoping you soon regain reason I remain your solid friend, C. Chan."

After lunch, Charlie spent several hours meditating in his cabin. This was a case after his own heart, six long days to ponder it, while the person he sought must stay within easy reach of his hand.

That evening after dinner the detective came upon Pamela Potter and Mark Kennaway having coffee in a corner of the lounge. At the girl's invitation, he joined them.

"Well, Mr Chan," she remarked, "one of your precious six days is gone."

"Yes, and where are you?" Kennaway inquired.

"Two hundred and fifty miles from Honolulu, and moving comfortably along," Chan smiled.

"You didn't learn much this morning?" the young man suggested.

"I learned that my friend the murderer still seeks to entangle the innocent, as he did when he stole Doctor Lofton's luggage strap in London."

"You mean that about Ross?" the girl asked.

Charlie nodded. "Tell me – you agree now with Mrs Luce?"

"I do," she answered. "I thought at the time that person was limping very weirdly – much more than Mr Ross ever had. Whom could it have been?"

"It might have been any of us," said Kennaway, looking at Chan over his cup.

"How right you are," returned the detective. "Any of you who wandered about rainy town, assisted on way by Malacca stick."

"Or it might even have been the lad who couldn't tear himself away from his book," the young man suggested. "Or claims he couldn't. I refer to jolly old Captain Keane, the irrepressible reader."

"Ah, yes – Keane," Chan said. "Has anyone ever determined cause of Keane's fondness for loitering outside wrong doors?"

"Not so far as I know," Pamela Potter replied. "As a matter of fact, he hasn't been doing it much lately. Mr Vivian caught him at it just after we left Yokohama, and the row could be heard for blocks. If there'd been any blocks, I mean."

"Mr Vivian has special talent for rows," Charlie noted.

"I'll say he has," Kennaway agreed. "That last night made bridge look like one of the more hazardous occupations. I thought Vivian started it with very little reason. It almost looked as though he wanted to break up the game."

Chan's eyes narrowed. "Mr Kennaway, I understand your employer, Mr Tait, bought a wrist-watch just before he left New York?"

The young man laughed. "Yes – he warned me you were going to ask that. He did. Thought it would be more convenient on a long tour. He has his old watch and chain in his trunk, I believe. Get him to show them to you."

"Chain is intact, of course?"

"Oh, naturally. Or was when I saw it last – in Cairo."

Tait came up to them. "Mrs Luce and I are getting up a bridge game," he announced. "You young people are elected."

"But I'm a terrible player," the girl protested.

"I know you are," the lawyer replied. "That's why I'm going to assign you to Mark as a partner. I feel I'm going to win. I love to win."

Kennaway and the girl got up. "Sorry to leave you, Mr Chan," the latter said.

"I would not interfere with your pleasure," he returned.

"Pleasure?" she repeated. "You've heard about the slaughter of the innocents. Haven't you an old Chinese proverb to comfort me?"

"I have one which might have warned you," Charlie told her. "The deer should not play with the tiger."

"That's the best bridge rule I ever heard," the girl answered.

After a time, Charlie rose and walked out on to the deck. He was standing in a dark corner by the rail when he heard a stealthy hiss out of the night. He had completely forgotten Kashimo.

His slim little assistant came close. Even in the dark it was evident that he bubbled over with mystery and excitement.

"Search all over," he whispered breathlessly.

"What!" breathed Charlie.

"I have discovered key," the Japanese replied.

Chan's heart leaped at the words. Welby, he recalled, had also discovered the key.

"You are quick worker, Kashimo," the Chinese said. "Where is it?"

"Follow me," directed Kashimo. He led the way into the corridor, and to a de luxe cabin on the same deck. At the door, he paused.

"Who occupies this room?" Charlie asked anxiously.

"Mr Tait and Mr Kennaway," the Japanese told him, and pushing open the door, flooded the cabin with light.

Remembering the bridge game with relief, Charlie followed, closing the door behind him. He noticed that the port-holes, which opened on the promenade deck, were safely shuttered.

Kashimo knelt, and dragged from beneath one of the beds a battered old bag. It was plastered with the labels of foreign hotels. The Japanese made no effort to open it, but lovingly ran his fingers over a particularly gorgeous label – that of the Great Eastern Hotel, Calcutta. "You do same," he suggested to Charlie.

Charlie touched the label. Underneath he felt the faint outline of a key, about the size of the one Duff had shown him.

"Good work, Kashimo," he murmured.

In gold letters near the bag's lock, he saw the initials "M. K."

XVIII

MAXY MINCHIN'S PARTY

After a few whispered instructions to Kashimo, Charlie returned to the deck and stood by the rail, staring thoughtfully out at the silver path of the moon on the dark waters. His chief feeling at the moment was one of admiration for his assistant. An ingenious place to hide an object like a key – it had made but the slightest protuberance on the rough leather of the case. The eye would never have detected it – only the fingers. Yes, Kashimo was undoubtedly a blunderer, but in this matter of searching, of meddling with the property of others, the boy was touched with genius.

Gradually Chan began to consider the larger aspects of the matter. How came this key, duplicate of the one found in the dead hand of Hugh Morris Drake that morning in a London hotel, to be on Kennaway's bag? Of course he had not seen it, but Charlie felt it safe to assume that it was the duplicate. The one Welby had located the night he told Pamela Potter: "The fun's all over." The fun had indeed been over for poor Welby. A dangerous object to discover.

Where had Welby found it? In the same place where it was now? He must have. For it was under the label of the Great Eastern Hotel, Calcutta, and the natural inference must be that it had been put there in the Indian city. A man couldn't pick up a Calcutta label anywhere save in Calcutta. Yes, it must have been in its present position in Yokohama, where Welby found it—

Wait a minute. Welby had spoken of this key to the girl as though he had actually seen it. Number and all. But had he? Perhaps he was merely assuming, as Chan was doing, that this was the duplicate key. It would have been a natural assumption. It might be that he had only run his fingers over the outline, as Chan had done. And someone had learned of his discovery, had followed him ashore and murdered him.

Who? Kennaway? Nonsense. It had without doubt been the same man who killed Honywood and his wife. Kennaway was a mere boy; what concern could he have with Jim Everhard and the Honywoods. With events that had happened long ago in some far place, and then remained in the shadows for many years?

Charlie put his hand to his head. Puzzles, puzzles. It couldn't have been Kennaway. The murderer's settled policy, evidently, was to implicate innocent men if he could. Witness the matter of the strap in London, the theft of the rubber tip from the stick belonging to Ross. Furthermore, he would hardly care to have this key discovered in his possession. What more natural than for him to attach it to the property of another man?

Who would have had the best opportunity to put that key on Kennaway's bag? Chan's eyes, fixed unseeing on the glittering water, narrowed suddenly. Who but Tait? Tait, who had been so prompt that morning to proclaim himself an innocent man, who had asserted that his change to a wrist-watch had been effected before the tour started. Tait, who had slept in the room next to that in which Drake died; Tait, who had fallen in a terrific heart attack when he discovered next morning that Honywood, the man Everhard meant to kill, was still alive. Certainly Tait was old enough to have been Everhard in his day, to have acquired those little bags of pebbles, to have carried them for years, determined to return them when opportunity offered. What more likely than that Tait had made use of his companion's suitcase?

Chan began a slow stroll about the deck. No, the key was never Kennaway's. Suddenly he stood still. If Welby had found it where it was now, and it did not belong to Kennaway, then the little detective from Scotland Yard had not discovered the murderer. Why, then, had he been killed on the Yokohama dock?

Again Chan put his hand to his head. "Haie, I wander amid confusing fog," he murmured. "Much better I go to my pillow, seeking to gain clarity for the morrow."

He took his own advice at once, and the second night aboard the *President Arthur* passed without incident.

In the morning Charlie cultivated the society of Mark Kennaway. It meant considerable moving about, for the young man seemed restless and distraught. He roamed the ship, and Charlie roamed with him.

"You are youthful person," the Chinese remarked. "You should study calm. I should say to look at you you have few more than twenty years."

"Twenty-five," Kennaway informed him. "But I seem to have added about ten by this tour."

"It has been difficult time?" inquired Chan sympathetically.

"Ever been a nurse maid?" asked the young man. "Lord – if I'd known what I was letting myself in for! I've read aloud at night until my eyes ached and my throat felt like the desert's dusty face. Then there's been the constant anxiety about poor Mr Tait's condition."

"There have been other attacks since the one in Broome's Hotel?" Charlie suggested.

Kennaway nodded. "Yes, several. One on the boat in the Red Sea, and a quite terrible one at Calcutta. I've cabled his son to meet us at San Francisco, and believe me I'll be glad to see that Golden Gate. If I can get him ashore there still alive, I'll consider that I'm a fool for luck. I'll heave a sigh of relief that will be reported in all the Eastern papers as another California earthquake."

"Ah, yes," agreed Chan. "You must have been under much strain."

"Oh, I had it coming to me," Kennaway returned gloomily. "I should have started to practise law and let the map of the world alone. None of my people in Boston were in favor of this trip. They warned me. But I knew it all."

"Boston," repeated Charlie. "As I told you yesterday, a city in which I have great interest. The diction of its people is most superior. Some years ago I did small favor for Boston family, and never in my life was I thanked in better language."

Kennaway laughed. "Well, that must have been something," he replied.

"A great deal," Chan assured him. "I am old-fashioned person who feels that choice of words proclaims the gentleman. Or, in the case of which I speak, the lady. My children regard me old fogy on this point."

"Children don't show their parents enough respect these days," the young man nodded. "I say that as an ex-child. Well, I hope my parents don't find out the hell I've been through on this trip. I'd hate to hear the familiar: 'I told you so.' Of course, it hasn't been only poor Mr Tait. I've had other troubles."

"I do not wish to penetrate any Boston reserve," Charlie remarked. "But could you name one, please?"

"I certainly could. That Potter girl – well, perhaps I shouldn't have said it."

Chan's eyes opened in surprise. "What is wrong with Potter girl?" he inquired.

"Everything," returned the young man. "She annoys me beyond words."

"Annoys you?"

"Yes. I've said it, and I'll stick to it. Doesn't she get on your nerves too? So damned Middle Western and competent? So sure of herself? She's got more poise than a great-aunt of mine who's lived on Beacon Hill for eighty-one years and met everybody worth while." He leaned closer. "You know, I actually believe the girl thinks I'll propose to her before this tour's over. Would I take that chance? Not I. And get her bank-book thrown in my face."

"You think that would happen?"

"I'm sure of it. I know these Middle Westerners – nothing matters but money. How much have you got? We don't feel that way in Boston. Money doesn't count there. Ours certainly doesn't. Uncle Eldred lost it all betting on the New York, New Haven and Hartford. I – I don't know why I've said all this to you. But you can see how I feel. Worn out acting as a nurse maid – and this girl on my mind all the time."

"Ah – then she is on your mind?"

"She certainly is. She can be mighty nice when she tries. Sweet, and – er – you know, sweet – and then all at once I'm run over by an automobile. One of the Drake brand. Millions at the wheel."

Chan consulted his watch. "I see her now at far end of deck. I presume you wish to flee?"

Kennaway shook his head. "What's the use? You can't get away from people on a boat. I've given up trying, long ago."

Pamela Potter came up to them. "Good morning, Mr Chan. Hello, Mark. How about some deck tennis? I think I can trim you this morning."

"You always do," Kennaway said.

"The East is so effete," she smiled, and led the captive Kennaway off.

Chan made a hasty tour of the deck. He found Captain Ronald Keane seated alone near the bow of the boat, and dropped into a chair beside him.

"Ah, Captain," he said, "a somewhat gorgeous morning."

"I guess it is," Keane replied. "Hadn't noticed, really."

"You have other matters that require pondering?" Charlie suggested.

"Not a thing in the world," yawned Keane. "But I never pay any attention to the weather. People who do are nothing but human vegetables."

The chief engineer came strolling along the deck. He paused at Charlie's chair. "About time for our tour of the engine room, Mr Chan," he remarked.

"Ah, yes," returned the Chinese. "You were kind enough to promise me that pleasure when we talked together last night. Captain Keane, I am sure, would enjoy to come along." He looked inquiringly at Keane.

The captain stared back, amazed. "Me? Oh, no, thanks. I've no interest in engines. Wouldn't know a gadget from a gasket. And care less."

Charlie glanced up at the engineer. "Thank you so much," he said. "If you do not object, I will postpone my own tour. I desire short talk with Captain Keane."

"All right," nodded the engineer, and moved away. Chan was regarding Keane grimly.

"You know nothing about engines?" he suggested.

"Certainly not. What are you getting at, anyhow?"

"Some months ago, in parlor of Broome's Hotel, London, you informed Inspector Duff you were one time engineer."

Keane stared at him. "Say, you're quite a lad, aren't you?" he remarked. "Did I tell Duff that? I'd forgot all about it."

"It was not the truth?"

"No, of course not. I just said the first thing that came into my head."

"A habit of yours, it seems."

"What do you mean by that?"

"I have been reading about you, Captain Keane. In Inspector Duff's notebook. Investigation of murder is serious business, and you will pardon me if I get plenty crude in my remarks. You are self-confessed liar, seemingly with no regrets. All through tour you have behaved strangely, listening outside doors. Not very lovable activity."

"No, I fancy it isn't," Keane snapped. "You must have found that out in your own work."

"I am not sneaky kind of detective," replied Chan, with dignity.

"Is that so?" replied Keane. "Then you can't be much good. I've been in the business six years, and I'm not proud of what I've done."

Charlie sat up. "You are detective?" he asked.

Keane nodded. "Yes – keep it under your hat. I represent a private agency in San Francisco—"

"Ah – private detective," nodded Chan, relieved.

"Yes, and don't be nasty. We're just as good as you are. I'm telling you this because I don't want you to waste your time on me. Mrs Spicer has a husband and he's eager to get rid of her. Wants to marry a movie actress, or something like that. So he sent me on this trip to see what I could see."

Chan studied Keane's mean face carefully. Was this the truth? The man certainly looked well-suited to the rôle of private detective. So he didn't want Chan to waste any time on him? Unexpected consideration, this was.

"You have had no success?" the Chinese remarked.

"No – the thing was a flop from the first. I believe Vivian suspected me the moment he saw me. I dread meeting Spicer when we land at San Francisco – all this has cost him a pretty penny. But it wasn't my fault if love's young dream blew up right in my face. If they only hadn't been partners at bridge – that finished it. They're not even speaking now, and Vivian has threatened to break my neck if I come near him again. I'm fond of my neck. So I'm at a loose end from here on home. By the way, all this is on the quiet."

Charlie nodded.

"Your secret is safe with me."

"I was wondering," continued Keane. "Couldn't I help you out on this murder thing? Is there any reward, or anything like that?"

"The reward of work well done," Charlie replied.

"Tripe! You don't mean to say you've come into this without having an understanding with the Potter girl? Say – you need a manager. I'll go and have a talk with her. The family's got wads of money, and they naturally want to find out who killed the old man. We'll go fifty-fifty—"

"Stop!" cried Chan. "You have already said too much. Kindly remember that I am not private detective. You have no authority from me for your low plan—"

"Wait a minute. Let's argue this out—"

"No. The ignorant are never defeated in argument. What is more, there is nothing to debate. You will kindly keep out of this affair, which does not concern you in the least. I am bidding you good day."

"You're a hell of a business man," growled Keane.

Charlie walked rapidly down the deck, his accustomed calm rudely disturbed. What a worm this fellow Keane was! All that about being a private detective – was it true? Possibly. On the other hand, it might be merely a blind, a tall story designed to put Charlie off his guard. Charlie sighed. Mustn't forget Keane. Mustn't forget any of them.

The creaking ship plowed on its way, making good time over the glassy sea. Kashimo reported the key still on Kennaway's bag. Long, leisurely talks with one member of the party after another yielded no result. The second day passed, and the third night. Not until the fourth night did Charlie begin to take hope again. It was on that evening that Maxy Minchin entertained – a grand party to celebrate the approaching end of the tour.

Maxy had passed about with his invitations and had been, much to his own surprise, cordially received. Familiarity had bred charity where he was concerned. The long weeks together had led the party to overlook his crudities. As Mrs Luce put it: "We mustn't forget there's someone in this crowd who's even worse than Mr Minchin."

Everyone accepted, and Maxy was delighted. When he brought the news to his wife she reminded him that, with Lofton, there would be thirteen at table.

"Don't let's take any chances, Maxy," she said. "You been gettin' all the breaks so far – don't trifle with your luck. You got to find a fourteenth."

Mr Minchin found the fourteenth in Charlie. "I ain't got nothing against the dicks," he explained to the Chinese. "I give a party once in Chicago for a table full of 'em. One of the nicest feeds I ever pulled off. You come along. Informal. I'm leaving my Tux in the trunk."

"Thank you so much," Chan answered. "And may I hope that you will not be offended if at this dinner I make bold to refer to the subject of murder?"

"I don't get you," said Maxy, startled.

"I mean I have unlimited yearning to mention there the unfortunate fate of Hugh Morris Drake in Broome's Hotel. It would make me happy to hear conversation regarding this affair from one and all."

Maxy frowned. "Well, I don't know about that. I was hopin' we wasn't going to talk business. Just a good time for all and no questions asked – get me? Some guy in this gang's got a lot on his mind, and I wouldn't like him to have no anxious minutes while he's my guest. After that, you can put the cuffs on him any minute – see what I mean? He ain't no pal of mine. But for the one evening—"

"I will be discreet," Chan promised. "No questions, of course."

Maxy waved his hand. "Well, have it your own way. Start the murder thing if you want to. They's no tags to my bids. It's Liberty Hall when Maxy Minchin is paying the check."

Liberty Hall turned out to be the deck café, where fourteen people sat down that evening around a lavishly decorated table. Knowing full well his duties as a sea-going host, Mr Minchin had provided a comic hat for everyone. He himself put on a Napoleonic tricorn with a scarlet cockade, and thus equipped, felt that the evening had begun auspiciously.

"Eat hearty, folks," he ordered. "And drink the same. It's all on the house. I told 'em to put out the best they got."

After the coffee, Maxy rose. "Well, here we are," he began, "near the end of the big hop. We seen the world together, and we had good times, and some not so good. Take it all and all, I'll say it's been a swell lay-out from the start. And if you're asking me, we had one dandy guide. Lift your glasses, people. To old Doc Lofton, the grandest guy afloat."

There were cries for a speech and Lofton arose, somewhat embarrassed.

"Thank you, friends," he said. "I have been conducting parties like this for many years, and I want to say that this has been in many ways one of my more – er – memorable experiences. You have given me very little trouble – this is, of course – most of you have. There have been differences, but they have been amicably settled. You have all been most reasonable, sometimes under great strain, and I am grateful. Of course, I would be foolish to overlook the fact that our tour began under very unusual and trying circumstances. If Miss Pamela will forgive me, I am referring to the unfortunate passing of – er – her grandfather that midnight at Broome's Hotel in London. That is to say, between midnight and morning – er – an occurrence that I regret more deeply than any of you – with, of course, the exception of the young lady I have mentioned. But that is now long in the past, and it seems best to forget it.

If it remains among the unsolved mysteries, we must accept that as the will of fate. I shall land you all in San Francisco very soon, and we shall part" – his manner brightened noticeably – "but I assure you that I shall always treasure memories of our companionship."

"Hear, hear," cried Mr Minchin, as the doctor sat down amid polite applause. "Well, folks, since the Doc's brought it up, I may say that we're all sorry about that kick-off at Broome's. And that brings me at this time to mention our special guest here tonight – the Chinese dick from Hawaii. Believe me, people, I seen all kinds, but this is a new one on me. Mr Chan, spill a few words."

Charlie rose with dignity, despite his introduction. He glanced calmly about the little room.

"The drum which makes the most noise is filled with wind," he said. "I remember this in time so I will not obtrude myself. But I welcome opportunity to bow to my gracious host, and to his delightful lady, obscured with plenty jewels. Fate is capricious stage manager. She has introduced you to policemen round the world. To my distinguished friend from Scotland Yard, to the officers of France and Italy. Now you get sample from melting-pot of Hawaii, you let your gaze for fleeting moment rest on humble Chinese who follows meager clues left behind by the few criminals who infest our paradise.

"I stand here before you in not entirely happy position. Wise man has said, do not follow on the heels of a sorrow, or it may turn back. Such would be my own advice to Miss Pamela. But while I remain thus in upright posture, old sorrow will not fade from your minds.

"You must recall that had it not occurred, I would not be here. You see pictures of Broome's Hotel, old incidents, now long forgotten, come back to you. It can happen they take on new meaning after extensive absence. I am desolate to know I recall these things, and I make haste to erase myself. First

I would add – Doctor Lofton has told you that if matter is never solved, it is will of fate. I am Chinese, I accept will of fate, but I have lived so long among American people I feel inclination to give fate small tussle before I offer my meek acceptance. By this time my broad bulk has cast plently shade on this gay feast. I am sitting down."

Mr Minchin's roving eye fell on Mr Tait. That gentleman rose with the manner of the experienced speaker.

"I am, perhaps, happier than any of you to be here," he began. "There have been times when it seemed I must leave you long before this. But the determination to live is strong, and I promise that I shall finish with you, as I began.

"In many ways, I feel that I am lucky. I have much to be grateful for. For example, referring again to my friend Mr Hugh Morris Drake, and the night of February sixth – the morning of the seventh – I might have been the occupant of the bed in room 28 – the innocent victim of a murder that was purely—"

He stopped, and looked helplessly about him. "Pardon me. I am off on the wrong tack there. We are, I fear, making this a rather unhappy evening for the charming Miss Pamela. I only meant to say that I am happy to have survived thus far on our tour around the world, and that it has been a great pleasure to meet you all. Thank you very much."

He sat down abruptly amid subdued applause. Mrs Luce obliged with a travelogue, and Pamela Potter said a few graceful words. Captain Keane arose.

"Well, it's been a great trip," he said. "However, I guess it's about over now, and those of us who have work to do can go and do it. We've had a lot of fun, and for my part I'd almost forgotten the incident at Broome's Hotel. That was a bit of a strain, and no mistake. Inspector Duff acted for a while as though he intended to spoil the tour – for some of us at least. His questions were pretty personal. I don't go in for murder myself, but I happened to be wandering about that night, as you may recall. I had my bad moments. And I guess some of the rest of us were on the anxious seat, too. I guess Mr Elmer Benbow was a little bit worried – eh, Mr Benbow? I haven't said a word to anybody about this before, but now we're all back in God's country and I guess we can take care of ourselves. I saw Mr Benbow at three o'clock the morning of the murder, just as he was slipping back into his room from the hall. I imagine you're glad you didn't have to explain that to Scotland Yard – eh, Benbow?"

Keane's air was one of light-hearted banter, but it deceived no one. Underneath was a cheap malice that was unpleasant to contemplate. Even Maxy Minchin, though he couldn't have defined the feeling, knew that here was an exhibition of bad taste that took the palm. The little gangster leaped to his feet.

"The way things is going you don't need no toastmaster here," he announced. "Mr Benbow, you been elected the next speaker."

The man from Akron got slowly to his feet. "I've been doing a lot of speaking the past few years," he began, "but I don't know that I ever had to make a speech like this before. It's quite true – I was out of my room that night at Broome's Hotel. After we got home and got to bed, I suddenly remembered that February sixth was my daughter's birthday. We'd been intending all day to send her a cable, but we'd been so busy we both forgot. Well, I was upset, and no mistake. Then I remembered the change of time – that it was six hours earlier in Akron. It came to me that maybe I could still get my cable to her that day – late at night, perhaps, but still on her birthday. I jumped out of bed, dressed, and hustled out. There were some scrubwomen in the hotel lobby, but I didn't meet any of the other servants, coming or going. Of course, I should have told the police about this, but I certainly didn't feel like getting mixed up in the affair. It was a foreign country – different – you know how it is. If I'd been at home – well, I'd have told the chief of police all about it. But England. Scotland Yard. I got cold feet.

"I'm glad Captain Keane brought the matter up here tonight. I'm glad to explain the thing, and I hope you believe me. Now – er – I had a speech ready, but it's clean gone. Oh, yes – one thing I do remember. I've been taking pictures all the way around, as I guess you know. You're all in 'em. I bought a projector in Honolulu and Friday night – our last night aboard – well, Mrs Benbow and I are entertaining then. We want you all to be our guests, and I'll run off the whole trip for you. That's – that's about all, now."

He sat down amid loud and friendly applause. Several rebuking looks were cast at Keane, who received them nonchalantly. Mr Minchin rose again.

"I guess it's up to me to make the next selection," he remarked. "Mr Ross, we ain't heard from you yet."

Ross stood up, and leaned heavily on his stick. "I have no belated accusations to offer," he remarked, and a little round of applause circled the table. "All I can say is, this has been an interesting tour. I've been looking forward to it for many years – how many, I wouldn't like to tell you. It has been somewhat more exciting than I'd bargained for, but I have no regrets. I'm glad I came on this party with Doctor Lofton – and with all of you. I only wish I had been as wise as Mr Benbow and made a record of my experiences, to solace the long hours when I get back to Tacoma. As for that unfortunate night in London, when poor Hugh Morris Drake lay dead in that stuffy room in Broome's Hotel, with Doctor Lofton's luggage strap about his throat—"

Suddenly from far down the table, Vivian spoke. "Who says it was Doctor Lofton's luggage strap?" he demanded bruskly.

Ross hesitated. "Why – why – I understood at the inquest," he replied, "that it was taken from the doctor's closet—"

"We're all telling our real names tonight," went on Vivian in a clear, cool voice. "That wasn't Lofton's luggage strap. In point of fact, it wasn't a luggage strap at all. It was a camera strap – the kind you use to carry a motion picture camera over your shoulder. And I happen to know that it was the property of Mr Elmer Benbow."

With one accord they all turned and stared at Benbow, sitting with a stricken look on his face near the foot of the table.

XIX

THE FRUITFUL TREE

In the tense silence Maxy Minchin got slowly to his feet. He removed the Napoleonic hat from his head, and with a gesture of abdication, cast it aside.

"Well, you bimbos are certainly making some dinner out of this," he remarked. "Sadie, I guess we never give one like it before, did we? Way I figure it, guys that put on the feed-bag together ought to act nice and friendly at the table, even if they do pull a gat on the stairs going out. Still, I ain't one to tell my guests how to behave. Mr Benbow, you spoke once, but it looks to me like you gotta speak again."

Benbow leaped to his feet. The stricken look had faded, and he appeared grim and determined.

"Well," he said, "I guess I made a mistake. When I was telling you that about the cablegram to my daughter, it flashed through my mind I ought to say something about the strap—"

"I suppose you sent her that as a birthday present," Keane sneered.

Benbow turned on him. "Captain Keane, I don't know what I have done to win this hostility from you. I've regarded you from the first as a cheap and contemptible light-weight, but I thought I had kept my opinion of you hidden. I did not send that strap to my girl as a birthday present. I wish I had. Then it would not have been put to the use it ultimately was."

He took a sip of water, and continued. "I heard about Mr Drake's murder early that next morning, and I went to his room to see if there was anything I could do. That's what I would have done in Akron – it seemed the neighborly and kindly thing. There was no one in the room at the moment but a hotel servant – the police hadn't come. I went over and looked at Drake. I saw the strap about his throat, and I thought it was almighty like my camera strap. It gave me a shock, I can tell you. I went to my room, hunted up my camera – and found that the strap was missing from the case.

"Well, we talked it over, Nettie and I. Our door was always unlocked – I didn't like to go out and leave it that way, but the maid had requested us to do it. The camera had been there all the previous afternoon, as well as in the evening, when we went to the theater. It had been easy enough for somebody to slip in and get that strap. My wife suggested that I go and talk things over with Doctor Lofton." He looked at the doctor. "I'm going to tell the whole business," he added.

Lofton nodded. "By all means," he remarked.

"Well, the doctor pooh-poohed my fears at first, but when I told him I had been out the previous night to send that cablegram, he began to look serious. I asked him if he thought I'd better tell Scotland Yard it was my strap, and also that I had been away from my room between two and three o'clock on the morning of the murder. Men have been hung on less than that. And there I was, in a strange country, first time I'd ever been out of the good old United States, and – well, I was scared stiff. 'It looks like I leave your party here and now,' I said to the doctor. He patted me on the shoulder. 'Say nothing,' he told me. 'Leave everything to me. I'm sure you didn't kill Drake, and I'll do all I can to keep you out of the investigation.' Believe me – it was a good offer. I took it. The next thing I heard about the strap, Doctor Lofton had claimed it as his own. That's all I've got to say. Oh, yes – Vivian asked me on the channel boat where my strap was. He asked in sort of a nasty way. When I bought another in Paris, he made some crack about it. I saw that he was on to the situation, but he didn't seem inclined to do anything about it."

For the first time in many moments, Chan spoke. He turned to Vivian with interest.

"Is this true, sir?" he inquired.

"Yes, it is," replied Vivian. "I knew from the first it was Benbow's strap. But there we were, in a foreign country – and I didn't really think Benbow was guilty. I didn't know what to do. So I consulted the one man in our party who ought to know about such things. A celebrated criminal lawyer. Mr Tait, I mean. I outlined the matter to him, and he advised me to say nothing."

"And now you disregard his advice?" Charlie said.

"Not precisely. He and I were speaking about it today, and he told me he thought it was about time to get to the bottom of the strap business. He suggested I tell you. He said he thought yours the best mind that had yet come into the case."

Chan bowed. "Mr Tait does me too much honor," he protested.

"Well, there's nothing more I can say," Benbow went on, mopping his perspiring brow. "Doctor Lofton claimed the strap, and that let me out." He sat down.

They all looked at Lofton. His manner showed that he was decidedly annoyed; his eyes were flashing.

"Everything that Mr Benbow has told you is true," he remarked. "But consider my position, if you will. There I was, with a murder in my party, and up against the most celebrated man-hunting organization in the world. My only object was to cut off their investigation at the earliest possible moment, and get out of England with my party intact. I felt that if Mr Benbow admitted those two damaging facts, he would certainly be held in London. One of them alone might not have sufficed, but both together – well, that would have been too much. I saw myself losing at the very start of the tour a couple of my best clients. And I was morally certain Mr Benbow was entirely innocent.

"When the matter of the strap was brought up by Inspector Duff, I saw my way out immediately. I had not left my room the night before, and no one could say I had. True, there had been a little matter of warm words between Mr Drake and myself, but that meant nothing, as the inspector was quick to see. I was not connected with the crime in any way. The strap was not unlike one I had about an old bag – not quite so wide, but the same color, black. I told Duff I possessed a strap similar to the one he was showing me. I went to my room, removed it from my bag, and hid it beneath a wardrobe that reached nearly to the floor. If my plan failed, I could pretend to discover it there and simply tell Duff I had been mistaken. Then I went back to Drake's room and told the inspector that I believed the strap used to strangle the old gentleman was mine.

"It worked like a charm. From that point on the matter of the strap was of no further interest to Scotland Yard. Mr Benbow was safe and—"

"And so were you," suggested Captain Keane, blowing a ring of smoke toward the ceiling.

"I beg your pardon, sir," glowered Lofton.

"I say, Benbow was safe, and so were you," Keane went on calmly. "If there had been any disposition on the part of Duff to suspect you of the crime, you rather took him aback by claiming that strap on the spot. He figured that if you'd been guilty, you'd hardly have committed the murder with your own strap, and then admitted the ownership immediately. Yes, my dear Doctor, it worked like a charm—"

Lofton's face was scarlet. "What the devil are you driving at—"

"Oh, nothing, nothing. Don't get excited. But nobody's been paying much attention to you in this affair. There you were – broken-hearted because such a thing had happened on a tour of yours. But were you? Mightn't there have been something more important to you than your tour—"

Lofton tossed aside his chair, and strode over to where Keane sat.

"Stand up," he cried. "Stand up, you dirty cur. I'm an old man, but by heaven—"

"Gentlemen, gentlemen," shouted Maxy Minchin. "Remember they's ladies present."

Charlie inserted his great bulk between Doctor Lofton and the captain. "Let the refreshing breeze of reason blow over this affair," he suggested gently. "Doctor Lofton, you are foolish man to listen to unresponsible talk of this plenty flippant person. He has no basis whatever for evil insinuations." He took the doctor by the arm and led him a few feet away.

"Well, folks," announced Maxy Minchin, "I guess the dinner's over. I was going to suggest we all join hands and sing *Auld Lang Syne* at the finish, but mebbe we better chop that. Open the doors. An' for the sake of my boy at school, I hope they won't be no rods drawn in the hallway."

Chan quickly escorted Lofton outside. Behind him, as he left, he heard the scraping of chairs, the breaking up of Maxy's interesting dinner party.

"Hot words will cool here on windy deck," he suggested. "Accepting my advice, you will abstain from presence of Keane until you feel less fiery."

"Yes, I fancy I'd better," the doctor admitted. "I've hated that sneering whelp from the moment I saw him. But of course, I mustn't forget my position." He gave Charlie a searching look. "I was happy to hear you say that he had no basis for his accusations."

"None whatever that I discover," answered Chan blandly.

"I don't know – now that I come to think of it, it was a rather silly move, my claiming that strap. I can't explain it except for the fact that after you've traveled with groups like this for a few years, you begin to look upon them as children. Somewhat stupid children, too, helpless and needing protection. My first instinct is always to furnish the protection. One of my people was in trouble so, as had happened many times before, I simply shifted his burden to my own shoulders, and carried on."

Charlie nodded. "I understand plenty well," he reassured the older man.

"Thank you, Mr Chan," Lofton replied. "You seem an understanding person. I'm inclined to think I underrated you when we met."

Charlie smiled. "That is customary. I do not let it distress me. My object is to arrange so people are not still underrating me when we part."

"I imagine your object is usually attained," the doctor bowed. "I think I'll go to my cabin now. I have a lot of work to do."

They parted, and Chan set out on a walk about the deck. His step was brisk, his manner serene and composed. Much had happened at Maxy Minchin's dinner. Charlie smiled to himself as he recalled how much had happened. Someone called to him from a steamer chair.

"Ah, Mr Tait," he remarked. "I will sit down at your side, if you have no inclination for objecting."

"I am delighted," replied Tait.

"Ah, yes. You were kind enough to speak to Mr Vivian in flattering terms of my poor brain power."

"I meant every word of it," the lawyer assured him.

"Then you judge on the smallest grounds."

"No, I never do that." Tait struggled with his rug, and Chan assisted him. "Thanks," he said. "Well, that was quite a little dinner, as it turned out. Was it, by any chance, another of your experiments?"

Chan shook his head. "No – it was idea of hospitable Mr Minchin. But who knows – I may be able to turn it to my purpose."

"I'm sure you can."

"Detective is in happy luck," Charlie continued, "when he can stand aside and hear murderer talk about incidents attending crime. Tonight many men spoke – possibly murderer among them. Was there some indiscreet admission?"

"Did you note any?" inquired Tait.

"I am much afraid I did. It came – you will pardon my rudeness – it came from you."

The lawyer nodded. "You justify my belief in you. I hardly expected you would overlook my indiscretion."

"We are talking, no doubt, about same thing?"

"Oh, no doubt at all."

"Will you tell me, then, of what we speak?"

"Gladly. It was rather a slip for me to admit that anyone of us might have been in Hugh Morris Drake's position that night in Broome's Hotel."

"It was, indeed. You knew, of course, that Honywood and Drake changed rooms that night. Inspector Duff told you same on train between Nice and San Remo."

"Yes – that was where he told me about the change. You know Duff's notes pretty thoroughly, I perceive?"

"I must. They are my only hope. I find no record that you ever read a letter written by late Mr Honywood to his wife."

"I didn't even know there was such a letter."

"Yet you knew that Drake was killed by someone seeking to kill Honywood. You understand that poor man's taking off was, as you started to say, purely accidental. That it might have happened to any man in the party."

"Yes – I'll have to admit that I knew that. I'm sorry I let it out, but it's too late now for regrets."

"How did you know it? Duff never told you."

"No, of course – Duff never told me."

"Then who did?"

Tait hesitated. "I suppose I shall have to confess. I got the information from Mark Kennaway."

"Ah, yes. And Mr Kennaway got it from—"

"According to his story, he got it from Pamela Potter."

A brief silence, then Charlie stood up. "Mr Tait, I congratulate you. You are out of that in neat fashion."

Tait laughed. "And in simple fashion," he added. "Just by telling the truth, Mr Chan."

"A pleasant evening," Charlie said. "I leave you to enjoy your no doubt interesting thoughts." He strolled away.

Seeking the dancers on the promenade deck, he noted Pamela Potter circling that restricted floor in Mark Kennaway's arms. He waited patiently until the music stopped, and then approached the couple.

"Pardon," he announced. "But this lady has next fox trotting with me."

"Just as you say," smiled Kennaway.

Gravely Chan offered his arm, and led the girl off. The music was beginning again.

"I spoke with metaphor," Charlie remarked. "My avoirdupois and dancing do not make good mixture."

"Nonsense," she answered. "I'll bet you've never tried."

"The wise elephant does not seek to ape the butterfly," he told her, and escorted her to a shadowy corner by the rail. "I have brought you here not only for the fragrance of your society, which is delectable, but also to ask a question."

"Oh – and I thought I'd made a conquest," she laughed.

"Surely same would be ancient story for you," he replied, "and hardly worthy of recording. Tell me this, if you will be so kind. You have related to others the matter you read in Mr Honywood's letter to his wife? You have told fellow members of tour that murder of grandfather was accident?"

"Oh, dear," she murmured. "Shouldn't I have done it?"

Chan shrugged. "Old saying has it, two ears, one mouth. Hear twice as much as you tell."

"I'm properly rebuked," she said.

"Do not fret. No harm may have been done. I merely wish to know whom you told."

"Well, I told Mrs Luce."

"That was natural. And how many more?"

"Just one more. Mark – Mr Kennaway."

"Ah, yes. You noted tonight, perhaps, that Mr Kennaway has passed information along to Mr Tait?"

"Yes, I did note it – and it made me rather angry. I didn't tell Mark it was a secret, but he should have known. He irritates me very much, that lad."

"Irritates you? I should have said—"

"Yes, I know – I'm with him a lot. But heavens – what have I to choose from? Vivian? Keane? It's hopeless. When there's anything doing that calls for a man – a dance, for instance – naturally I select Mark. But all the same, he irritates me."

"So you said."

"I meant it. You must have seen yourself how he acts. So frightfully superior – Boston and Harvard and all that. I can tell you – it gets on my nerves—"

"Suppose," smiled Chan, "that this irritating young man should ask you to marry him?"

"Do you think he will?" asked the girl quickly.

"In what way should I know?" Charlie said.

"Well – it's almost uncanny, Mr Chan, how you invite confidences. I may tell you that I hope he will ask me to marry him. As a matter of fact, I've been leading him on – a little. I want him to propose to me."

"And then?"

"Then I shall turn him down. What a triumph! The flower of Boston turned down by something crude and vulgar from the terrible Middle West."

Chan shook his head. "A woman's heart," he remarked, "is like a needle at the bottom of the sea."

"Oh, we're not so darned hard to fathom. My motives are perfectly clear. Of course, in a way, it will be a pity – he can be so nice when he wants to be—"

"Yes?"

"Yes, but he seldom wants to be. Usually he's just cold and lofty and Bostonian, and I know that he's sneering at my money." She laid a slender hand on Charlie's arm. "Can I help it," she added wistfully, "if my grandfather had brains enough to get rich?"

"No honorable man would hold you accountable," Charlie answered soothingly. "But if you are leading this young man on – a little – we should get back to the work."

They walked along the deck toward the music.

"He should never have told that to Mr Tait," the girl said. "I ought to call him down for it – but I don't think I will. The mood tonight is one of tenderness."

"Let it remain so," urged Chan. "I like it better that way myself."

Kennaway, he noted, showed no signs of annoyance when he saw the girl again. Nor did Pamela Potter seem especially irritated. As Charlie turned away, the purser faced him.

"Come with me, Mr Chan," Lynch said. He led the way to his office.

In a chair drooped Kashimo, evidently much depressed.

"What has happened?" Charlie inquired.

Kashimo looked up. "So sorry," he hissed, and Chan's heart sank.

"Your helper here has got himself into trouble," the purser explained.

"How do I know she will come back?" the Japanese said.

"You speak in riddles," Chan told him. "Who came back?"

"Mrs Minchin," the purser put in, "returned to her cabin a few moments ago and found this boy searching there. She's got a billion dollars' worth of knickknacks in her luggage, and her screams could be heard as far away as the Astor House bar, in Shanghai. I promised her I'd throw the lad overboard myself. We'll have to take him off those cabins and put him somewhere else. I'm afraid his usefulness to you is ended."

"So sorry," Kashimo repeated.

"One minute," Charlie said. "You will have plenty time to be sorry later. Tell me first – did you find anything of interest in Maxy Minchin's cabin?"

Kashimo leaped to his feet. "I think so, Charlie. I find – I search hard and I am good searcher – you said so—"

"Yes, yes. What did you find?"

"I find nice collection of hotel labels not pasted on to anything. Pretty labels from all hotels visited by these travelers – labels that say Grand Hotel, Splendid Hotel, Palace Hotel—"

"And was there one from the Great Eastern Hotel, Calcutta?" Chan inquired.

"No. I look twice. Label from that hotel is not among those present."

Chan smiled, and patted the little Japanese on the back. "Do not belittle own attainments any longer, Kashimo," he advised. "Stones are cast alone at fruitful trees, and one of these days you may find yourself in veritable shower of missiles."

XX

MISS PAMELA MAKES A LIST

Charlie turned to the purser, and within a few minutes the question of Kashimo's future status on the ship was settled. It was arranged that he was to be transferred to a series of cabins on a lower deck, and that he must keep out of the way of the loudly vocal Sadie Minchin as much as possible from that moment on to the end of the journey. The little Japanese, crestfallen, slipped away, and Chan returned to the deck. Standing once more by the rail, he considered this latest development.

If there were loose hotel labels available aboard the *President Arthur*, then it became more unlikely than ever that the key had been attached to Kennaway's bag at Calcutta, and had consequently been in its present position when Welby located it in Yokohama. No, it had unquestionably been elsewhere, in the possession of its owner. That person, not wanting to throw it away, but somewhat shaken by the Welby episode, had evolved the happy idea of planting it on Kennaway's suitcase, under the label of a hotel long since visited and left behind. He had known where such a label could be had. He might even have owned such a label himself. He might have been Maxy Minchin.

Chan smiled to himself, and after spending a few moments in the library, went to his cabin. His first act there was to take out Duff's notes, and study them once again. What he read seemed to please him, and he went cheerfully to bed, where he enjoyed the most complete rest he had yet encountered aboard the boat.

Early the next morning Charlie met Maxy Minchin pacing the deck, grimly determined on exercise. He fell into step beside the gangster.

"Hello, Officer," Maxy said. "Swell morning after the storm."

"Storm?" Chan inquired.

"I mean that snappy little party I give last night. Say, maybe them birds didn't mix it, hey? Hope you had a good time?"

"An excellent one," smiled the Chinese.

"Well, I was a little anxious myself," Maxy returned. "A guy that's host, he can't get much of a kick out of a rough-house like that. I thought for a minute it was going to end in a pair of bracelets for some bimbo. But after all was said and done, I guess you was just as far from a pinch as ever."

Chan sighed ponderously.

"I fear I was."

"It's sure some mystery," Maxy went on. "Me, I can't figure why any guy'd want to rub out that nice old gentleman. Something Tait said made me think mebbe it was all a mistake – mebbe Drake got took for a ride because they thought he was somebody else. Such things do happen. I remember once in Chicago – but why should I let a bull in on that? What I was going to say, we had a little excitement in our cabin last night."

"Yes? Of what nature?" Charlie was mildly curious.

"Us rich millionaires," Maxy continued, "we gotta keep our eyes peeled every minute. The word goes round we're rolling in jack, and after that, good night! I don't know what the world's coming to. No respect for property rights no more – it's disgusting. Sadie went back to the cabin, and there was a biscuit boy going through things like a Kansas cyclone."

"What a pity," Chan answered. "I trust nothing valuable was taken."

"That's the funny angle on it. There was all that jewelry Sadie's been copping on to – valuable stuff. I ought to know, I come across for it. And when Sadie went into the cabin, there was this Chink—"

"Ah – er – no matter—" cried Chan, catching himself in time.

"There was this Chink, with a bunch of old hotel labels in his hand."

"You have collection of such labels?" Charlie inquired.

"Yeah – I been picking 'em up from each hotel we been to. Going to take 'em home to little Maxy – that's my son – so he can paste 'em on his suitcase. He wanted to come along with us, but I tells him an education comes first. You stay here and learn to talk right, I says. Even a bootlegger's got to speak good language nowadays, associating with the best people the way he does. Not that I want Maxy in the racket – he'll have all he can do to manage the estate. I'll bring you the labels, I says to him. It'll be as good as taking the trip. And as I just been telling you, with all Sadie's valuables laying around, it was them labels that caught the Chink's eye. But he only had time to pinch one of 'em."

"Ah – one is missing?"

"Yeah. The wife noticed it right off the bat. The swellest one in the bunch – we both remembered speaking of it when we got it – how pleased little Maxy would be. A Calcutta hotel. But it was gone. We couldn't dig it up nowhere."

Charlie turned and stared at the gangster. The simple innocence of that dark face amazed him. Nothing there save the anxiety of an indulgent father.

"I tossed in a kick to the purser," Mr Minchin went on, "but he tells me he searched the Chink and he was clean. I guess he'd made away with the label. In Chi. in the old days he'd'a' got a pineapple in his soup for this. But – oh, well – let it ride. Little Maxy won't know what he missed – and that's something."

"I congratulate you," said Chan. "Life has made you philosopher, which means peaceful days ahead."

"That's the kind I got a yen for now," Minchin replied. They finished the walk in silence.

Early that afternoon Charlie met the unpleasant Captain Keane. The Chinese was inclined to ignore the encounter, but the Captain stopped him.

"Well?" Keane began.

"Yes?" returned Chan.

"That dinner last night. Quite a few developments."

"Plenty," nodded Charlie.

"Plenty for me," Keane replied. "As far as I can see, the matter begins to look pretty plain."

"You mean Mr Benbow?"

"Benbow, my hat! Don't try to kid me. Lofton's my choice, and has been from the start. Do you know, he told me at San Remo that the tour was off? Why? Elementary, my dear Mr Chan. Duff forced him to go on, but he didn't want to do it. He'd finished his job."

"You think that is proof enough to convict in English courts?"

"No – I know it isn't. I'm working on the case, though. Miss Potter has authorized me to go ahead, and she's promised to pay up if I make good."

Chan glared at him. "You did not mention my name?"

"Why should I? You're going to be on the outside looking in before this case is ended. Go ahead – look wise. I suppose you think I'm on the wrong track."

"Not at all," Chan answered.

"What?"

"Why should I think that? The stupidest man in the town may point out the road to the school."

"And just what do you mean by that?"

"Nothing. Old Chinese saying."

"I don't think much of it," answered Keane, and went on his way.

The afternoon passed swiftly, while the ship sailed on across a calm and sunlit sea. Evening came – the last of his evenings but one – and Chan was as calm as the sea. He prepared for dinner and, stepping out on to the deck, saw Tait about to enter the smoking-room.

"Won't you join me, Mr Chan?" the lawyer invited.

Charlie shook his head. "I am seeking Mr Kennaway," he replied.

"Still in the cabin when I left," Tait said.

"And the number is—" the Chinese inquired.

Tait gave him this quite unnecessary information, and Chan walked away. He found Mark Kennaway busy with a black tie.

"Oh, come in, Mr Chan," the young man greeted him. "Just trying to beautify the old façade."

"Yes – the time in Miss Pamela's society is growing brief," Charlie smiled.

"Why bring that up?" asked Kennaway. "Always look your best – that's my motto. There may be somebody about who wants to hire a lawyer."

Chan closed the door. "I have called for a private talk with you," he announced. "I must have your word of honor you will keep what is said in dark."

"Naturally." Kennaway seemed surprised.

Charlie dropped to his knees and dragged from beneath one of the beds the suitcase with the interesting label. He pointed to the latter.

"You will regard that, please."

"You mean the label from the Great Eastern Hotel in Calcutta? What about it?"

"Do you recall – was it there when you left Calcutta?"

"Why, of course. I noticed it after I got on the boat at Diamond Harbor. It's so striking one could hardly overlook it."

"You are certain this is the label you saw on that occasion?"

"Well – how could I be certain of that? I saw one just like it."

"Precisely," answered Chan. "You saw one just like it. But you did not see this one."

Kennaway came closer. "What do you mean?" he inquired.

"I mean that at some later date, second label was pasted neatly over the first. And between the two—Will you kindly run fingers over surface?"

The young man did so. "What's this?" he frowned. "Feels like a key."

"It is a key," Charlie nodded. "Duplicate of the one found in hand of Hugh Morris Drake one February morning in Broome's Hotel."

Kennaway whistled softly. "Who put it on my bag?" he asked.

"I wonder," said Chan slowly.

The young man sat down on the edge of his bed, thinking deeply. His eyes strayed across the room to another bed, on which lay a pair of pajamas. "I wonder, too," he said. He and Charlie exchanged a long look.

"I will put suitcase back in place," remarked the detective with sudden briskness. He did so. "You will say nothing of this to living soul. Keep eye on key. It will, I think, be removed before ship reaches port. Kindly inform me the moment it is gone."

The door opened abruptly, and Tait came in. "Ah, Mr Chan," he said. "Pardon me. Is this a private conference?"

"Not at all," Charlie assured him.

"I found I had no handkerchief," Tait explained. He opened a drawer and took one out. "Won't you join me for an appetizer – both of you?"

"So sorry not to do so," the Chinese answered. "What I require mostly is non-appetizer." He went out, smiling and serene.

After dinner, he found Mrs Luce and Pamela Potter seated together in deck chairs.

"May I intrude my obnoxious presence?" he inquired.

"Sit down, Mr Chan," the old lady said. "I'm not seeing much of you on this trip. But then, I suppose you're a busy man?"

"Not so much busy as I expected to be," he answered quietly.

"Really?" She gave him a questioning look. "Lovely evening, isn't it? This weather reminds me of the South African veldt. I spent a year there once."

"You have pretty well investigated the map."

"Yes – I've been about. Think now I'll settle down in Pasadena – but that feeling is usual with me just as I finish a long tour. Some day I'll pass a window filled with steamship folders – and then I'll be off again."

Charlie turned to the girl. "May I, with rude boldness, inquire about last evening? Maybe you led young man on – a little farther?"

"When I was a small girl," she smiled, "I used to build snow men. It's been interesting to meet one who can walk about."

"You have two more nights – with plenty good moon shining."

"It wouldn't help if they were Arctic nights, and six months long," she told him. "I'm afraid the last returns are in."

"Do not despair," Chan replied. "Perseverance wins. A matter I have proved in my own endeavors. By the way, did you promise Captain Keane reward if he finds slayer of your grandfather?"

"Why, no."

"But he has talked with you about it?"

"He hasn't talked with me about anything."

Chan's eyes narrowed. "The truth is not in him. We will say no more of that." He glanced at a sheet of paper and pencil in the girl's hand. "Pardon me – I think I interrupt. You are writing letter?"

She shook her head. "No, I – I – well, as a matter of fact, I was merely puzzling over our mystery. The time is getting rather short, you know."

"No one could know it better," he nodded gravely.

"And it doesn't seem to me that we're getting anywhere. Oh – I'm sorry – but you came into the case rather late. You really haven't had a chance. I was just making a list of the men in our party, and opposite the name of each, I've been putting down the things against him. So far as I can see, every single one of them except Mr Minchin and Mark Kennaway has been under a cloud at one time or another—"

"Your list is not correct. Those two, also, have no claim to clean record."

She gasped. "You mean every man in the party has been involved?"

Chan rose, and gently removed the paper from her hand. He tore it into tiny fragments and, walking to the rail, tossed them overboard.

"Do not worry pretty head over matter," he advised, coming back. "It is already settled."

"What do you mean?" she cried.

"Of course, there remains stern quest for proofs acceptable to English courts, but these will yet be found."

"You mean you know who killed my grandfather?"

"You yourself do not know?" inquired Charlie.

"Of course I don't. How should I?"

Charlie smiled. "You had same opportunities as I. But then, your mind was filled with young man who irritates you. As for me, I labored under no such handicap."

With a beautiful bow which included both of them, he strolled casually off down the deck.

XXI

THE PROMENADE DES ANGLAIS

Her eyes wide with amazement, Pamela Potter looked at Mrs Luce. "What in the world," she cried, "did Mr Chan mean by that?"

Mrs Luce smiled. "He meant that he knows who killed your grandfather, my dear. I rather thought he'd find it out."

"But how did he find it out? He said I ought to know, too. And I can't imagine—"

The old lady shrugged. "Even for your generation," she said, "you're a clever girl. I've noticed that. Bright as a dollar, as we used to say. But you're not so clever as Charlie Chan. Not many people are. I've noticed that, too." She stood up. "Here comes young Kennaway – I think I'll go into the lounge."

"Oh, please don't run away."

"I may be a chaperon, Pamela, but I was young once myself." And she moved toward a distant door.

Kennaway sat down tentatively on the foot of the deck chair the old lady had deserted.

"Well," he remarked. "Another day gone."

The girl nodded.

"You don't seem very talkative," the young man suggested.

"That should be a relief," she answered. "I – I was very busy thinking. Mr Chan has just told me the most surprising thing."

"What, for instance?"

She shook her head. "No, I mustn't repeat it to you. I told you something once – and you failed to keep it secret."

"I don't know what you mean."

"No matter. We needn't go into it now."

"Whatever I've done, I'm sorry," he said. "Really, I am." He looked quite contrite, and very handsome in the light of the newly risen moon. For a moment neither spoke. Then a sudden expression of concern crossed the young man's face. "I say – Mr Chan didn't tell you that – that he had his man?"

"Why should he?"

"I don't know – but something that happened tonight—" Again he was silent, staring into space. "I wonder," he added at last, and his voice was strained, even frightened.

Pamela Potter glanced at him. A boy in Detroit had once been the recipient of a similar glance, and had never been the same since. "Our next to the last night aboard the ship," she reminded him.

"I know," he replied gloomily.

"We shall miss this old war when it's over."

"I shall," he nodded. "But you – you'll be back in Detroit, having a grand time. The little princess of the automobiles. All the peasants bowing low."

"Nonsense. You'll be back in Boston – that's where the royal blood is. One of the Beacon Street Kennaways. I presume the Browning Society will call a special meeting when you arrive."

He shook his head. "Don't kid me, please. Somehow, I don't seem to enjoy it any more."

"What's the matter? I supposed you'd be in high spirits. The end of the tour so near, and all. Rid of poor Mr Tait at last – and of me."

"I know," he agreed. "I ought to be the happiest man in the world. But I'm not. Oh, well – that's life, no doubt."

"And that nice girl waiting for you in Back Bay."

"What girl?"

"The one you're engaged to."

"Me – engaged? Do I look as feeble as that? They're lots of nice girls in Boston, but I'm not engaged to any of them, thank heaven."

"You ought to try it some time. It's fun, rather."

"I suppose you've tried it?"

"Oh, yes – frequently."

"One of those fellows who's been writing to you?"

"One of them? I'm no piker. All of them, at various times."

"Well, make a selection," he suggested. "Get it over with. We're none of us as young as we used to be."

"I am – and I mean to stay so. Shall you write to me, after we part?"

"What for?"

"I love to get letters."

"I hate to write them. Besides, I'll be terribly busy. It will take me a lifetime of hard work to put by even a modest competence. We can't all manufacture automobiles."

"Heaven forbid! The roads are crowded enough now. Then – when we say goodby, it will be for ever?"

"And a day," he added, with forced cheerfulness.

"That will make it so much more romantic, don't you think? You'd better go in and play bridge. I imagine Mr Tait is waiting."

"No doubt he is," the young man agreed.

"Would you like me to play?"

"Suit yourself. You're pretty bad, you know."

"I guess I am," she sighed.

"But of course, you make poor old Tait happy. As long as you aren't his partner."

"It's tough on you – having me for a partner, I mean."

He shrugged, and stood up. "Oh, I don't mind. I realize that it isn't permanent."

She started to rise, and he gave her his hand. "Since you insist," she said, "I *will* join you."

"Thanks so much," he smiled grimly. They went inside.

Mrs Luce and Tait were seated at a bridge table, the latter looking wistfully about the room. His face lighted when he saw Kennaway.

"Ah, my boy," he cried. "Will you join us?"

"Surely," Kennaway answered.

"That's good of you. I didn't like to ask. I've taken so much of your time – and this is one of your last nights aboard."

"Quite all right," the young man assured him. "I have nothing else to do."

"God bless the man who invented bridge," remarked Pamela Potter. "Come on, old son – say it."

"Say what?" Kennaway inquired.

"Your proper come-back to that should have been: 'You ought to learn it some time.'"

He laughed. "I couldn't be so rude as that," he protested.

"Oh, couldn't you?" she answered.

Meanwhile Charlie, having gone to the library and selected a book, was sitting there reading with the air of a man who has joined a book club and hopes none of his friends will call him up for a year. He read until ten o'clock, and after a leisurely stroll around the deck, sought his cabin. Sleep came to him without delay, the dreamless sleep of one who hasn't a care in the world.

At eight o'clock the next morning, he was abroad on the sunlit deck. The final twenty-four hours of a most momentous journey were impending. If the realization of this was hanging over him, it evidently left him calm and undisturbed. From his manner it was clear he was one of those who feel that what is to be, will be.

Later that morning he had a long radiogram from Duff. He retired with it to his cabin. There, with the sun streaming over his shoulder, he read:

"Splendid news. How can I ever thank you? Get the proofs, Charlie. But I know you will. Cable from chief says investigation clerk jewelry shop Calcutta reveals him once I.D.B. in South Africa. Meaning illicit diamond buyer. Inquiries among diamond merchants Amsterdam brought out further fact another I.D.B. around Kimberley some fifteen years back by name Jim Everhard. May be help. Remember bags of stones. Scotland Yard man Sergeant Wales in New York time my accident now in San Francisco by chief's order. Will meet you at dock prepared to make arrest. With him our friend Flannery. Like old times. Sorry can't be there. Mending rapidly, be on coast soon, wait there for my thanks. Cheerio.

Best of luck.

"Duff."

Chan read the message a second time, and when he came to the mention of Captain Flannery, an amused smile spread over his broad face. Fate was a wonderful stage manager, he reflected. He would be happy to see Flannery again. He tore Duff's message to bits, and tossed them through the port-hole.

The day wore on without incident. Benbow came to him late in the afternoon.

"I don't know whether or not you understand, Mr Chan," he remarked, "but you're invited to that party of ours tonight. Couldn't get along without you. Policemen round the world – you said it."

Chan bowed. "I accept with unbounded pleasure. You will show your films?"

"Yes. I've arranged to have the sitting-room of one of the empty de luxe suites. We'll meet there about eight-thirty. I'll put up a screen I've borrowed from the purser. I must say nobody seems to be much interested."

"I am deeply interested," Charlie assured him.

"Yes – but the rest of them – you'd think they'd be keen to see those pictures. Their own trip." He sighed. "But that's the way it goes. A man with a camera never gets any encouragement.

I suppose I'll have to lock the doors when I try to show those films in Akron. At eight-thirty, then, in Cabin A."

"You are so very kind," Chan returned. "I am honored beyond words."

By eight o'clock the clear skies, that had for so long looked down on the *President Arthur* were lost behind an impenetrable curtain. The ship moved cautiously along through a thick fog that recalled London on the morning Hugh Morris Drake lay dead in Broome's Hotel. At intervals the voice of the fog horn, deep and sonorous, claimed for a moment the sole attention of everyone aboard.

When, at eight-thirty, Charlie pushed open the door of Cabin A, all the members of the party appeared to be already gathered inside. They were moving about, chatting aimlessly, but Mrs Benbow, an efficient woman, soon had them seated in a little semicircle facing a white screen. Before this Benbow labored, busy with the many details that oppress a man about to show his own motion pictures.

While they waited, Charlie spoke. "All life long," he remarked, "I have unbearable yearning to travel – to take same extended tour you people in this room are now completing. One thing I have unquenchable desire to learn. What sight envisioned on your long journey stands out in outline of fire amid great crowd of memories? Mrs Luce, you are agile traveler. On recent circle of world, what that you witnessed interests you most?"

"I can tell you in a minute," the old lady replied. "A troupe of trained cats I saw at a vaudeville theater in Nice. I'll never forget them. Greatest sight I ever saw in my life."

Doctor Lofton smiled. "You needn't look so surprised, Mr Chan," he said. "I always ask that same question at the close of a tour, and often the answers leave me breathless. Mrs Spicer – if I were to ask it of you—"

"Let me think." The San Francisco woman's eyes grew dreamy. "There was a gown I saw at the Opera in Paris. It wasn't just a gown – it was a little bit of heaven. Any woman could have looked young in that," she added wistfully.

"As far as I'm concerned," said Vivian, "the bright spot of this tour is still to come. When we pass the Farallones tomorrow morning, and Russian Hill rises out of the mist – well, ask me your question then, Mr Chan. I know it's impolite to point, but that's what I'll have to do."

Maxy Minchin took out a large cigar, looked about the crowded room, and then put it back in his pocket. "They was a kid drivin' an ox cart in Italy," he remarked. "Gee, I wish little Maxy coulda seen him. It woulda give him a new slant on that Straight Eight I bought him just before we left."

"Do any of you remember the trees in the Forest of Fontainebleau?" Ross inquired. "I'm very fond of trees. Something so solid and serene and comfortable about them. Great timber, that was."

"Miss Pamela, you have not spoken," Chan reminded her.

"I have so many memories," she answered. She was wearing a delphinium blue gown she had saved for this final evening. All the women had noticed it – and even a few of the men. It could have been the one that haunted Mrs Spicer's dreams. "I find it difficult to say what interested me most," the girl went on. "But there was one flying fish that hopped aboard our ship in the Red Sea. He had such sad, romantic eyes – I just can't forget him." She turned to the young man at her side. "You remember – I named him John Barrymore."

"He looked more like Eddie Cantor to me," smiled Kennaway.

"It's all been wonderful," Mrs Benbow said. "So different from Akron, and I wanted a change. I'll never forget the afternoon I was walking in Delhi, and a maharajah drove by in a Rolls-Royce. He had on the most wonderful clothes – gold brocade, they were—" She looked severely at her husband, busy with the projector. "You've got to go to your tailor the minute you get home, Elmer," she announced.

"A lot of things have interested me on this trip," Keane put in. "There's one night that sticks in my mind – the last in Yokohama. I was walking round the town, and I dropped into a cable office. Doctor Lofton was there – and that little steward named Welby. I asked the doctor if he was going back to the ship, but he put me off – I could see he wanted to be alone. So I went along by myself – down to the water front – dark and mysterious – the godowns – the funny little people running around in the dark – the lights of the sampans – picturesque, I'd call it. It sort of gave me the feel of the East." He stopped and looked meaningly at Lofton, a malicious light in his eyes. "That was the place where Welby was found dead, you know—"

"All ready, folks," cried Mr Benbow. "Mr Kennaway, will you snap off the lights? Thanks. The first pictures, as you can see, are the ones I took on the deck of the ship just as we were leaving New York harbor. We didn't know one another very well then. I think I got the Statue of Liberty – yes, here she is. Take off your hats, boys. Now we're coming to some I got on the way across the Atlantic. Not many of you people in these – I guess most of you had a date with the little old berth down below. Here's poor Mr Drake – lucky he didn't know what was coming."

He continued his prattle as the film unwound. They saw London again, and Broome's Hotel. They had a few moments with the Fenwicks, whom Benbow had met on a street corner and insisted on recording for posterity. The little man from Pittsfield was obviously somewhat resentful of the honor being done him. Then came the pictures of Inspector Duff, driving away from the doorway of Broome's, and evidently as unwilling an actor as Fenwick. Dover and the channel boat. Paris, and after that, Nice.

Mr Benbow's audience sat in attitudes that betokened an increasing interest. As the pictures of Nice were unrolled, Charlie suddenly uncrossed his plump legs and leaned forward. He was recalled to his surroundings by the voice of Tait, who sat by his side. The lawyer spoke in a low voice.

"I'm leaving, Mr Chan," he said. "I – I feel rather ill." Charlie saw, even in that dim light, that his face was like chalk. "I'll not say anything to Kennaway – it's his last night and I don't want to trouble him. I shall be all right when I've rested for a moment on my bed." He slipped out noiselessly.

Benbow was starting on a new reel. His pictorial record seemed endless, but now his audience was with him. Egypt, India, Singapore, China – the man had really shown remarkable intelligence in the scenes he had selected.

He came at last to the end, and after thanking him, the party drifted from the room, until only Chan and the Benbows were left. The detective was examining the little spools on which the film was wound. "A very interesting evening," he remarked.

"Thanks," Benbow replied. "I believe they did enjoy it, don't you?"

"I am certain they did," Charlie told him. "Mrs Benbow, it is not just that you should oppress frail self with that burden. Your husband and I will together transport this material to your cabin." He took up the many reels of film, and moved toward the door. Benbow carrying the projector, followed. They went below.

Once inside the Benbow stateroom, Charlie laid the film on the bed, and turned to the man from Akron.

"May I inquire who has cabins on either side of you?" he said.

Benbow seemed startled. "Why – Mrs Luce and Miss Pamela are on one side. The cabin forward is empty."

"One moment," Chan answered. He disappeared, but returned almost at once. "At this instant," he announced, "both cabins quite empty. Corridor also is entirely deserted by one and all."

Benbow was fumbling nervously with the projector. He got it into its case, and began to buckle up a long black strap. "What – what's it all about, Mr Chan?" he stammered.

"That is very valuable film of yours?" Charlie suggested blandly.

"I'll say it is."

"You have trunk with good strong lock?"

"Why, yes." Benbow nodded toward a wardrobe trunk in the corner.

"Making humble suggestion, would you be good enough to bestow all reels of film in that, and fasten lock securely?"

"Of course. But why? Surely nobody—"

Chan's little eyes narrowed. "Person never knows," he remarked. "It would grieve me greatly if you arrived in beloved home town lacking important reel. The reel, for example, that includes pictures taken at Nice."

"What is all this, Mr Chan?" Benbow asked.

"You noticed nothing about those particular pictures?"

"No, I can't say I did."

"Others were perhaps more observant. Please do not distress yourself. Merely lock pictures all away. They have told their story to me, and may never be required by Scotland Yard—"

"Scotland Yard!" cried Benbow. "I'd like to see them try to—"

"Pardon that I interrupt. I must ask just one question. Do you now recall exact date when the photographs of street in Nice were taken?"

"You mean of the Promenade des Anglais?" Removing a worn bit of paper from his pocket, Benbow studied it. "That film was exposed on the morning of February twenty-first," he announced.

"An excellent system," Chan approved. "I am grateful. Now, you will stow away all reels, and I will assist. This is snap lock, I perceive. There – it has nice strong appearance." He turned to go. "Mr Benbow, I am much in your debt, first, for taking so many pictures, second, for showing them to me."

"Why – why, that's all right," returned the dazed Benbow.

Chan departed. He went at once to the topmost deck and entered the radio room. For a moment he thought deeply, then he wrote a message:

"Sergeant Wales, care Captain Flannery, Hall of Justice, San Francisco: Without delay request Scotland Yard authorities obtain from Jimmy Breen, English Tailor, Promenade des Anglais, Nice, France, full description man who had work performed on or about February twenty-first, calling for same on morning of that date, also nature of work done. Expecting you without fail on dock tomorrow morning.

"Charlie Chan, Inspector."

With light heart, Charlie descended to a lower deck and began a thoughtful turn about it. Damp, dripping, clammy fog surrounded the ship on all sides. In marked contrast to previous nights he walked a deserted path, the passengers had with one accord sought the brightly lighted public rooms. Twice he made the circle, well-pleased with himself and the world.

For the third time he was crossing the after deck, which was shrouded in darkness. Suddenly, amid the shadows at his right, he saw a black figure moving, caught the faint glint of steel. It must be set down for ever to his credit that he was rushing in that direction when the shot was fired. Charlie dropped to the deck and lay there, motionless.

There followed the stealthy sound of quickly retreating footsteps, then a moment of grim silence. It was broken by the voice of the purser, leaning over Chan.

"In heaven's name, Inspector," he cried. "What has happened?"

Charlie sat up. "For a moment I found the recumbent position more comfortable," he remarked. "I am, you will observe, conservative by nature."

"Somebody shot at you?" the purser said.

"Briefly," replied the Chinese. "And missed – by one inch."

"I say – we can't have this sort of thing here," the officer objected plaintively.

Chan got slowly to his feet. "Do not fret," he advised. "The man who fired that shot will repose in arms of police tomorrow morning, moment ship docks."

"But tonight—"

"There is no occasion for alarm. Something tells me there was no real effort to hit target. Kindly note size of same. And that aim has never failed before."

"Just a warning, eh?" remarked the purser, relieved.

"Something of that nature," Charlie returned, and strolled away. As he reached the door leading to the main companionway, Mark Kennaway ran up to him. The young man's face was pale, his hair sadly rumpled.

"Mr Chan," he cried: "You must come with me at once."

Silently Charlie followed. Kennaway led the way to the stateroom he shared with Tait, and pushed open the door. Tait was lying, apparently lifeless, on his bed.

"Ah – the poor gentleman has had one of his attacks," Chan said.

"Evidently," Kennaway replied. "I came in here a moment ago and found him like this. But see – what does this mean? I heard that somebody had taken a shot at you – and look!"

He pointed to the floor beside the bed. A pistol was lying there.

"It's still warm," the young man added hoarsely. "I touched it, and it's still warm."

Charlie stooped and carelessly picked up the weapon. "Ah, yes," he remarked, "it remains overheated. And for good reason. It was only a moment ago discharged at my plentiful person."

Kennaway sat on the edge of his own bed, and put his face in his hands. "Tait," he muttered. "Good lord – Tait!"

"Yes," Charlie nodded. "Mr Tait's fingerprints will indubitably be found on bright surface of pistol." He stooped again, and drew Kennaway's bag from beneath the bed. For a moment he stared at that innocent-seeming Calcutta label. Then he felt it with his fingers. There was a slit little more than the length of a key just above the center, but the heavy paper was pasted back into place. One spot was still rather damp. "Plenty neat job," the detective commented. "It is just as I thought. The key is gone."

Kennaway looked wildly about. "Where is it?" he asked.

"It is where I want it to be," Charlie answered. "On the person of the man who fired this revolver a moment ago."

The young man stared at the other bed. "You mean he's got it?"

"No," replied Charlie, shaking his head. "It is not on Mr Tait. It is on the person of a ruthless killer – a man who was not above putting to his own uses the misfortune of our poor friend there on the bed. A man who came here tonight for his key, found Mr Tait unconscious, saw his chance. A man who rushed out, fired at me, then returned here and after pressing Tait's hand about revolver to attend to fingerprints, dropped weapon suggestively on floor. A clever criminal if ever I met one. I shall experience great joy in handing him over to my old friend Flannery in the morning."

XXII

TIME TO FISH

Kennaway stood up, a look of immense relief on his face. Charlie was putting the revolver away in his pocket.

"Thank heaven," the young man said. "That's a load off my shoulders." He glanced down at Tait, who was stirring slightly. "I think he's coming out of it now. Poor chap. All evening I've been wondering – asking myself – but I just couldn't believe it. He's a kind man, underneath his bluster. I couldn't believe him capable of – all those terrible things."

Chan was moving toward the door. "Your lips, I trust, are sealed," he remarked. "You will repeat no word of what I have told you, of course. We have yet to make our capture, but I am certain our quarry is unsuspecting. Should he feel that his little stratagem here has succeeded, I think maybe our future path becomes even smoother."

"I understand," Kennaway answered. "You may rely on me." He put his hand over the lawyer's heart. "It begins to look as though I'm going to get poor Mr Tait safely home, after all. And from then on – no more jobs like this for me."

Charlie nodded. "To supervise his own destiny is task enough for any man," he suggested.

"I'll say it is," Kennaway agreed warmly. Chan opened the door. "Er – just a moment, Inspector. If you should happen to run across Miss Potter, will you kindly ask her to wait up for me? I may be here for a half-hour or so, but as soon as Mr Tait falls asleep—"

"Ah, yes," smiled Chan. "I shall be happy to take that message."

"Oh – please don't go out of your way to find her. I merely thought – it's our last night, you know. I really ought to say goodby to her."

"Goodby?" Charlie repeated.

"Yes – and nothing more. What was that you just told me? To supervise his own destiny is task enough—"

"For the timid man," finished Chan quickly. "Mind is so filled with other matters, regret to say I stupidly misquoted the passage when I spoke before."

"Oh," said Kennaway blankly. Chan stepped into the corridor and closed the door behind him.

The ship's captain was waiting for him in the main companionway. "I've just heard what has happened," he remarked. "I have an extra berth in my cabin and I want you to sleep there tonight."

"I am immensely honored," Charlie bowed. "But there is no need for such sacrifice—"

"What do you mean, sacrifice? I'm doing this for myself, not for you. I don't want any accidents on my ship. I'll be expecting you. Captain's orders."

"Which must, of course, be obeyed," Chan agreed.

He found Pamela Potter reading in a corner of the lounge. She put down her book and looked at him with deep concern.

"What's all this about your being shot at?" she wanted to know.

Charlie shrugged. "The matter is of no consequence," he assured her. "I am recipient of slight attention from a shipmate. Do not give it thought. I arrive with message for you. Mr Kennaway requests you loiter up for him."

"Well, that's an offer," the girl replied.

"Mr Tait has suffered bad attack—"

"Oh, I'm so sorry."

"He is improving. When chance offers, Mr Kennaway will seek you out." The girl said nothing. "He is plenty fine young man," Charlie added.

"He still irritates me," she replied firmly.

Charlie smiled. "I can understand feeling. But as favor to me, please wait up and let him irritate you for final time."

"I might," she answered. "But only as a favor to you."

When Chan had gone, she picked up her book again. Presently she laid it aside, put on a wrap, and stepped out on to the deck. Tonight the Pacific belied its name, it was dark, angry and tempestuous. The girl went over to the rail and stared into the mist. The fog horn somewhere above her head spoke at frequent intervals in a voice that seemed hoarse with anxiety.

Kennaway appeared suddenly at her side. "Hello," he remarked "Mr Chan gave you my message, I see."

"Oh, it didn't matter," she replied. "I had no intention of going to my cabin. Never be able to sleep with that thing blowing."

They waited until the end of a particularly insistent blast.

"Jolly old horn, isn't it?" Kennaway went on. "Once when I was a kid I got a horn for Christmas. It's a pretty good world."

"Why the sudden cheerfulness?" asked the girl.

"Oh, lots of reasons. I've been worried about something all evening, and I've just found out there was nothing to worry about. Everything's fine. Going ashore in the morning – Mr Tait's son will be waiting – after that, freedom for me. I tell you, I—"

The horn broke in again.

"What were you saying?" asked the girl, when it stopped.

"What was I? Oh, yes. Only myself to take care of, beginning tomorrow."

"It will be a glorious feeling, won't it?"

"I'll say it will. If I shouldn't see you in the morning—"

"Oh, you'll see me."

"Just wanted to tell you that it's been fun knowing you – you're awfully nice, you know. Charming. Don't know what I'd have done without you on this tour. I'll think of you a lot – but no letters, remember—"

The horn shrieked above them. Kennaway continued to shout indistinguishable words. The girl was looking up at him, she seemed suddenly very lovely and appealing. He took her in his arms and kissed her.

"All right," she said. "If you insist."

"All right what?" he inquired.

"I'll marry you, if you want me to. That's what you were saying, wasn't it?"

"Not exactly."

"My mistake. I couldn't hear very well. But I did think I caught the word 'marry'—"

"I was saying I hoped you'd marry some nice boy, and be very happy."

"Oh. Excuse it, please."

"But look here. Do you mean you'd actually marry me?"

"Why bring that up? You haven't asked me."

"But I will. I do. I am."

The horn again. Kennaway wasted no time in words. He released her when the blast was over.

"You really do care for me, after all?" she asked.

"I'm crazy about you. But I was sure you'd turn me down. That's why I didn't like to ask you. You're not going to turn me down, I take it?"

"What a ridiculous idea," she answered.

"Wonderful night," the young man said, and so it seemed, to him. "I know where there are a couple of chairs – in a dark corner on the after deck."

"They've been there ever since Hongkong," the girl replied. They went to find them.

As they walked along through the dripping fog, the horn blared forth again. "The lad who's working that," Kennaway remarked, "is going to get a big surprise in the morning. I intend to tip him within an inch of his life."

Meanwhile, amid the unfamiliar surroundings of the captain's cabin, Charlie Chan lay wide awake. He wondered if all old sea-dogs snored as loudly as this one.

He was aroused next morning by a knock at the door, and leaping up, he discovered that his cabin-mate was already about and dressed for the day. The captain took a radiogram from a rather flustered boy, and handed it to Chan.

"From Captain Flannery, of the San Francisco police," Charlie announced when he had read it. "He and Sergeant Wales of Scotland Yard will be aboard immigration launch."

"Good," said the other. "The sooner the better, as far as I'm concerned. I've been wondering, Inspector. Hadn't I better put our friend under restraint until they come?"

Chan shook his head. "Not necessary, thank you. I prefer he remain unsuspecting to the end. Mr Tait will no doubt spend morning in cabin, and I shall spread underground word among Lofton party we have our man in him. Believe real quarry will assume extra carelessness when he hears that."

"Just as you say," the captain nodded. "I'm not keen about taking action myself, as you know, though after what you told me last night, I'd gamble a year's pay that you're right. I will instruct the second officer not to lose sight of your man until he's in the hands of the police. People have been known to disappear from boats, you know."

"A wise suggestion," Charlie agreed. "I am grateful for your help." He had been rapidly dressing while they talked, and now moved toward the door with his bag. "I will continue toilet in my own room, please. Many hearty thanks for lodging of the night."

"Not at all. By gad, Inspector, you've been on the job this time. Ought to get a lot of kudos for your work on this case."

Chan shrugged. "When the dinner is ended, who values the spoon?" he replied, and went out on to the bridge. The fog was rapidly dispersing, and a hint of sun was in the eastern sky.

Back in his own cabin, he went about his preparations for the day with characteristic deliberation. On his way to breakfast, he stopped at the stateroom occupied by Tait and Kennaway. Both were awake, and the lawyer looked to be much improved.

"Oh, I'm fine," he said, in answer to Chan's query. "I promised you I'd make San Francisco, didn't I? And I'll make a lot of other towns, too, before I'm through. Mark thinks I'd better stay in bed until we're ready to land. It's all nonsense, but I've agreed to do it."

"A splendid idea," nodded Chan. "Has Mr Kennaway told you of last night's happenings?"

Tait frowned. "He has. There's one criminal I wouldn't defend – not for a million dollars."

Charlie outlined his plan for the morning, and the lawyer readily agreed.

"All right with me," he said. "Anything to get him. But of course, you'll let the members of the party know the truth before we land?"

"Naturally," Chan answered.

"Then go to it. You say you've got your man? I don't suppose—"

"Later, please," smiled Charlie as he left.

After breakfast, he met the purser on the deck. "I've got a landing card for you," that gentleman said. "But as for Kashimo – well, I don't know. He's never been over here before, and of course he has no record of his birth in the islands. He came as a stowaway – he's admitted as much to me – and he'd better go back at once. One of our boats will be at the same pier, due to sail at two o'clock today, and I'll simply turn him over to her purser with instructions to return him to Honolulu."

Chan nodded. "I approve of plan, and so, no doubt, will Kashimo. His work is done – it was good work, too – and already he shows signs of yearning for home. I know he will be glad to hurry back and face the plaudits of his chief. Kindly arrange he goes as passenger. I will supply the money." The busy purser nodded, and hurried away.

Further down the deck, the detective came upon Stuart Vivian. The San Franciscan stood at the rail, a pair of glasses in his hand, the empty case from which they had been taken hanging from his shoulder.

"Good morning," he said. "Just had a glimpse of Russian Hill. By heaven, I was never so glad to see it before."

"There is no vision so restful to weary eyes as that of home," Charlie remarked.

"You've said it. And I've been fed up with this tour for weeks. I'd have dropped out long ago, but I was afraid you policemen might think—By the way, I hear a rumor that you've found out who the killer is?"

Charlie nodded. "A very distressing affair."

"It is, indeed. Ah – er – I presume the man's name is a secret?"

"Not at all. Mr Tait has granted full permission to make the matter public."

"Tait!" cried Vivian. He was silent for a moment. "That's interesting, isn't it?" He looked at his watch. "We're having a farewell meeting in the library in ten minutes. Lofton's giving out the tickets to those who travel beyond San Francisco – and his final blessing, I suppose. What a riot this news will stir up!"

"I think maybe it will," smiled Chan, and went on down the deck.

Twenty minutes later the ship's engines were stilled at last, and they waited on the gray, rolling sea for the launch bearing the customs men and the immigration officials.

When the small motor-boat arrived, Charlie was at the top of the ladder. Presently the crimson face and broad shoulders of Flannery hove in sight.

"Hello, there," the officer cried. "It's my old pal! Sergeant Chan, as I live."

They shook hands. "So happy to see you again," Charlie said. "But since the day, long time ago, when I stood by and noted your admirable work on Bruce case, there have been changes. For one thing, I am now promoted to inspector."

"Is that so?" Flannery answered. "Well, you can't keep a squirrel on the ground. An old Chinese saying."

Charlie laughed. "I perceive you have not forgotten me." Behind Flannery stood a solid mountain of a man. "This, I presume, is—"

"Excuse me," said Flannery. "Shake hands with Sergeant Wales, of Scotland Yard."

"Highly honored," Chan remarked.

"What's your latest word from Duff?" inquired the sergeant.

"Steady improvement has set in," Charlie told him. "And speaking of Duff, you have come for his assailant, of course. The murderer of Hugh Morris Drake in your London hotel?"

"I certainly have," Wales said.

"I am happy to hand him over to you," Chan replied. "So that the matter may not encounter too much publicity, I fix up little plan. Will you come with me, please?"

He led them to a stateroom, on the door of which was the number 119. Escorting them inside, he indicated a couple of wicker chairs. There were two beds, one on either side of the cabin, and beside each was a pile of luggage.

"If you will wait here, your quarry will come to you," he announced. He turned to Wales. "One thing I would inquire about. You had message from me last night?"

"Yes, I did," the sergeant replied. "And I got in touch with the Yard at once. It was morning over there, you know, and within a few hours they had an answer. The news arrived in San Francisco just before we left Captain Flannery's office. It's great stuff. Jimmy Breen told our representative your man brought him a coat to be repaired on February twentieth, and called for it the next morning. It was the coat of a gray suit, and the right-hand pocket was torn."

"Ah, yes," nodded Charlie. "Torn by hand of aged porter in hallway of Broome's Hotel on early morning of February seventh. Murderer should have discarded that coat. But it is not his nature to discard, and from the first, he has felt himself so safe. I would wager he shipped it from London to Nice, addressed to himself, and then engaged the able Mr Breen. It was excellent choice. I behold on many tailors' signs nowadays the words 'Invisible Repairing.' Screen was too small for me to note them on Breen establishment, but they should have been there. Many times I have examined that coat, but Mr Breen was evidently master of invisibility." He stepped to the door. "However, talk will not cook rice. You will await guilty man here," he added, and disappeared.

He found the Lofton party, with the single exception of Tait, gathered in the library, and evidently in a state of great excitement. At the only door leading into the room, Charlie met the second officer. With him the detective held a brief conversation.

"All right, people," shouted the officer. "The baggage is examined on the ship here, you know. The customs men are now ready. Go to your rooms, please."

Mark Kennaway and Pamela Potter were the first to emerge. They were both in high spirits.

"Just like Yale tap day," laughed the young man. "Go to your room. We'll see you later, Mr Chan. We've news for you."

"That has happy sound," Charlie replied, but his face was grave.

Minchin and his wife came out. "Should I fail to see you again," Charlie remarked, shaking hands, "my kindest regards to little Maxy. Tell him to be good boy and study hard. An idle brain is the devil's workshop."

"I'll tell him, Officer," the gangster said. "You're one bull I been glad to meet. So long."

Mrs Spicer passed, with a nod and a smile of farewell. Mrs Luce followed.

"You let me know when you reach southern California," she said. "The greatest country on God's footstool—"

"Hold back your judgment on that, Mr Chan," broke in Benbow, coming up. "Wait until we've shown you Akron—"

"Then forget them both and come and look at the Northwest," added Ross.

"You're all wrong," protested Vivian. "He'll be in God's country in half an hour."

Keane and Lofton were approaching, but Charlie did not wait. Leaving the second officer at the door, he hurried away.

Meanwhile, in cabin 119, Captain Flannery and the man from Scotland Yard were growing a bit restless. The latter got up, and moved anxiously about.

"I hope nothing goes wrong," he muttered.

"Don't you worry," said Flannery generously. "Charlie Chan is the best detective west of the Golden Gate—"

The door opened suddenly, and Flannery leaped to his feet. Vivian was standing in the doorway.

"What's all this?" he demanded.

"Come in," the policeman said. "Shut that door – quick – and step inside. Who are you?"

"My name is Vivian, and this is my cabin—"

"Sit down there on the bed."

"What do you mean – giving me orders—"

"I mean business. Sit down and keep still."

Vivian reluctantly obeyed. Wales looked at Flannery. "He would be the last, of course," the sergeant remarked.

"Listen." Flannery whispered.

Outside, on the hard surface of the alleyway, they heard the "tap-tap-tap" of a cane.

The door opened, and Ross stepped inside. For a moment he looked inquiringly about him. Then he glanced back at the door. Charlie Chan was standing there, and to say he filled the aperture is putting it mildly.

"Mr Ross," said Charlie, "you will shake hands with Captain Flannery, of San Francisco police." The captain seized Ross's unresisting hand. Stepping forward, Chan made a hasty search. "I perceive," he added, "that weapon supply, which you have replenished so many times along the way, is exhausted at last."

"What – what do you mean?" Ross demanded.

"I am sorry to say Captain Flannery has warrant for your arrest."

"Arrest!"

"He has been asked by Scotland Yard to hold you for the murder of Hugh Morris Drake in Broome's Hotel, London, on the morning of February seventh, present year." Ross stared about him defiantly. "There remain other matters," Chan continued, "but you will never be called upon to answer for those. The murder of Honywood in Nice, the murder of Sybil Conway in San Remo, the murder of Sergeant Welby in Yokohama. The brutal attack on Inspector Duff in Honolulu. Murder round the world, Mr Ross."

"It's not true," Ross said hoarsely.

"We will see. Kashimo!" Charlie's voice rose. "You may now emerge from your hiding-place."

A bedraggled little figure rolled swiftly from beneath one of the beds. The Japanese was covered with lint, stray threads and dust. Chan helped him to his feet.

"Ah, you are somewhat stiff, Kashimo," he remarked. "I am sorry I could not dig you out sooner. Captain Flannery, the Oriental invasion becomes serious. Meet Officer Kashimo, of the Honolulu force." He turned to the boy. "Is it too much to hope you know present whereabouts of precious key?"

"I know," the Japanese answered proudly. He dropped to his knees, and from the cuff of Ross's right trouser leg extracted the key, which he held aloft in triumph.

Charlie took it. "What is this? Looks like plenty good evidence to me, Sergeant Wales. Key to safety-deposit box in some bank, with number 3260. Ah, Mr Ross, you should have thrown it away. But I understand. You feared that without it you would not dare approach valuables again." He handed the key to Wales.

"That's the stuff to give a jury," remarked the Britisher, with satisfaction.

"The key was planted there," cried Ross. "I deny everything."

"Everything?" Charlie's eyes narrowed. "Last night we sat together, watching Mr Benbow's pictures. Flickering film revealed you emerging from doorway of a shop in Nice. Did you think that I failed to notice? I might have – but for days I have known you guilty—"

"What!" Ross was unable to conceal his surprise.

"I will explain in moment. Just now, I speak of Nice. Jimmy Breen, the tailor, remembers. He recalls gray coat with torn right pocket—"

Ross started to speak, but the detective raised his hand.

"Cards lie against you," Charlie went on. "You are clever man, you have high opinion of yourself, and it is difficult for you to believe that you have failed. Such, however, is the situation. Clever – ah, yes. Clever when you hid that key on Mr Kennaway's bag – a bag that would naturally be thrust under bed and forgotten until hour of landing was imminent once more. Clever when you discarded rubber tip from stick, then carried same in wrong hand, hoping some keen eye would notice. So many were under suspicion, you thought to gain by being suspected too, and then extricating yourself in convincing manner – which I must admit you did. You were clever again last night when you fired wild shot at me and dropped smoking revolver beside poor Mr Tait. It was cruel act – but you are cruel man. And what a useless gesture! For, as I remarked before, I have known for several days that you were guilty person."

"You don't tell me," Ross sneered. "And how did you know it?"

"I knew it because there was one moment when you were not quite so clever, Mr Ross. That moment arrived at Mr Minchin's dinner. You made a speech there. It was brief speech, but it contained one word – one careless little word. That word convicted you."

"Really? What word was that?"

Charlie took out a card and wrote something on it. He handed it to Ross. "Keep same as souvenir," he suggested.

The man glanced at it. His face was white, and suddenly very old. He tore the card into shreds and tossed them to the floor.

"Thanks," he said bitterly, "but I'm not collecting souvenirs. Well – what happens next?"

XXIII

TIME TO DRY THE NETS

What happened next was that a customs inspector knocked on the door, and in that strained atmosphere made his examination of the hand luggage belonging to both Vivian and Ross. He was followed by a steward who carried the bags below. Vivian slipped out, and Kashimo, after a brief word with Charlie, also departed.

Captain Flannery took out a handkerchief and mopped his brow. "Getting pretty hot down here," he remarked to Wales. "Let's take this bird up to the library and hear what he's got to say for himself."

"I have nothing to say," Ross put in grimly.

"Is that so? Well, I've seen men in your position change their minds." Flannery went first, then Ross, and Wales was close behind. Charlie brought up the rear.

They passed Mark Kennaway on the stairs. Chan stopped for a word.

"We have our man," he announced.

"Ross!" Kennaway cried. "Good lord!"

"I suggest you pass among members of travel party, clearing name of poor Mr Tait."

"Watch me," the young man replied. "I'll beat the time of Paul Revere – and he had a horse."

Coming out on to the open deck, Charlie realized for the first time that they were moving again. On the right were the low buildings of the Presidio, and up ahead the fortress of Alcatraz Island. All about him the ship's passengers were milling, in a last frenzy of farewell.

Flannery and Wales were sitting with their quarry in the otherwise deserted library. Charlie closed the door behind him, and the racket outside subsided to a low murmur.

As the Chinese went over to join the group, Ross gave him a look of bitter hatred. In the man's eyes there was now a light that recalled to Chan's mind a luncheon over which he had sat with Duff a week ago. "You seek evidently two men," he had said to the English detective on that occasion. This was no longer the gentle, mild-mannered Ross the travel party had known; it was the other man, hard, merciless and cruel.

"You'd better come across," Flannery was saying. Ross's only reply was a glance of contempt.

"The captain is giving you good advice," remarked Wales pleasantly. His methods were more suave than those of Flannery. "In all my professional career I never encountered a case in which the evidence was quite so strong as it is here – thanks, of course, to Inspector Chan. It is my duty to warn you that anything you say may be used against you. But my suggestion would be that you plan to plead guilty—"

"To something I didn't do?" flared Ross.

"Oh, come, come. We have not only the key, but the information from the tailor who—"

"Yes, and how about a motive?" The voice of the accused man rose. "I don't give a damn for all your keys and your coats – you can't prove any motive. That's important, and you know it. I never saw any of these people I'm supposed to have murdered before – I've lived on the west coast of the States for years – I—"

"You had a very obvious motive, Mr Ross," Wales answered politely. "Or perhaps I should say – Mr Everhard. Jim Everhard, I believe."

The man's face turned a ghastly gray, and for a moment he seemed about to collapse. He was fighting for the strength that had sustained him thus far, but he fought in vain.

"Ah, yes, Mr Everhard – or Ross, if you prefer," Wales went on evenly. "Judging by information that came in to the Yard only a few days ago, your motive is only too clear. We haven't worried recently about motive – we've worried only as to your identity. Inspector Chan has cleverly discovered that. When the jury asks for a motive, we have only to tell them of your days in South Africa – of how Honywood stole your girl—"

"And my diamonds," cried Ross. "My diamonds and my girl. But she was as bad as he was—" He had half risen from his chair, now he fell back, suddenly silent.

Wales glanced at Charlie. Their eyes met, but they were careful to conceal the elation with which they heard those words from Ross.

"You went out to South Africa some fifteen years ago, I believe," the sergeant continued, "as a violinist in a musical comedy company orchestra. Sybil Conway was leading woman in the troupe, and you fell in love with her. But she was ambitious, she wanted money, stardom, success. You came into a small inheritance, but it wasn't enough. It was enough, however, to launch you into a business – a shady business – the trade of the I.D.B. Buying diamonds from natives, from thieves. Inside a year you had two bags filled with these stolen stones. Sybil Conway promised to marry you. You went on one last tour to the vicinity of the diamond fields, leaving those two bags with your girl in Capetown. And when you came back to her—"

"I saw him," Ross finished. "Oh, what's the use – you're too much for me – you and this Chinese. I saw him the first night after I got back – Walter Honywood Swan, that was his name. It was in the little parlor of the house where Sybil Conway was living."

"A younger son," Wales suggested. "A ne'er-do-well at home – out there a member of the South African police."

"Yes, I knew he was with the police. After he'd gone, I asked Sybil what it meant. She said the fellow was suspicious, that he was after me, and that I'd better get away at once. She would follow when the show closed. There was a boat leaving at midnight – a boat for Australia. She hurried me aboard – in the dark on the deck just before I sailed, she slipped me the two little bags. I could feel the stones inside. I didn't dare look at them then. She kissed me goodby – and we parted.

"When the boat was well out, I went to my cabin and examined the bags. The little bags of stones. That's what they were – wash leather bags, each filled with about a hundred pebbles of various sizes. I'd been done. She preferred that policeman to me. She'd sold me out."

"So you went to Australia," Wales gently urged him on. "You heard there that Sybil Conway and Swan were married, and that he now called himself Walter Honywood. You wrote, promising to kill them both. But you were broke – it wasn't so easy to reach them. The years went by. Eventually you drifted to the States. You prospered, became a respectable citizen. The old urge for revenge was gone. And then – suddenly – it returned."

Ross looked up. His eyes were bloodshot. "Yes," he said slowly, "it returned."

"How was that?" Wales continued. "Did it happen after you hurt your foot? When you lay there, idle, alone, plenty of time to think—"

"Yes – and something to think about," Ross cried. "The whole affair came back to me as vividly as yesterday. What they'd done to me – do you wonder I thought? And I'd let them get away with it." He looked wildly about him. "I tell you, if ever a man was justified—"

"No, no," Wales protested. "You should have forgotten the past. You'd be a happy man today if you had. Don't expect any mercy on that score. Were you justified in killing Drake—"

"A mistake. I was sorry. It was dark in that room."

"And Sergeant Welby – as fine a chap as I ever knew?"

"I had to do it."

"And your attempt to kill Duff—"

"I didn't attempt to kill him. I'd have done it if I had meant to. No, I only wanted to put him out for the moment—"

"You have been ruthless and cruel, Ross," Wales said sternly. "And you will have to pay for it."

"I expect to pay."

"How much better for you," Wales went on, "if you had never attempted your belated vengeance. But you did attempt it. When your foot was better, I see you gathering up all your valuables, your savings, and leaving Tacoma for ever. You put all your property in the safety-deposit box of a bank in some strange town. Where? We shall know presently. You set out for New York to find the Honywood pair. Walter Honywood was about to make a tour around the world. You booked for the same party.

"In Broome's Hotel you attempted your first murder. It was a ghastly mistake. But you hung on. You sent that coat to Nice, where you had it repaired. You had lost part of your watch-chain, one of the keys to your safety-deposit box. You debated with yourself – should you throw the duplicate key away? You knew Scotland Yard would make every effort to find the owner of a safety-deposit box numbered 3260. Could you go into a bank where you were practically unknown and call undue attention to yourself by admitting you had lost both keys? No, your only hope of ever seeing your valuables again was to hang on to that other key.

"The party went on. Walter Honywood knew you now, but he was as eager to avoid publicity as you were. He warned you of a letter that would incriminate you if anything happened to him. You searched until you had it, and that same night, in the hotel gardens at Nice, you got him. You heard that Sybil Conway was in the next town. You didn't dare leave the party. You went along, hoping for the best – and that lift – it was made for your purpose.

"After that, it seemed smooth sailing. You began to think luck was with you. Duff was baffled, and you knew it. You moved on in peace, until Yokohama. There you learned that Welby had discovered the duplicate key. By the way, where did you have it then?" Ross made no reply. "Some clever place, I'll wager," the Scotland Yard man continued. "But it doesn't matter. You sensed somehow that Welby had gone ashore to cable. He'd sent the message before you could stop him, but on the chance that there was no mention of you in it – as indeed there wasn't – you shot him down on the dock when he returned.

"Again you began to feel safe. I don't know much about what has happened since Yokohama. But I judge that when you got to Honolulu and met Duff on the pier, you saw red again. Nearly at the end of your journey – only a few more miles – and all serene – save for Duff. How much had he learned? Nothing, that was clear. How much would he learn on that final lap of the tour? Nothing again, if you could prevent it. You removed him from your trail." Wales glanced at Charlie Chan. "And right there, Ross," the Englishman finished, "I think you made the big mistake of your life."

Ross stood up. The boat was now fast to the dock, and outside the window, the passengers were gathered about the top of the plank.

"Well, what of it?" Ross said. "How about going ashore?"

They waited a moment on the deck, until the crowd on the plank had diminished to a few late stragglers, then started down. A uniformed policeman appeared before Flannery. "The car's ready, Chief," he said.

Charlie held out his hand to Sergeant Wales. "Maybe we meet again," he said. "I have in bag Inspector Duff's briefcase, my study of which is now completed."

Wales shook hands warmly. "Yes, you've passed your examination on that, I fancy," he smiled. "With honors, too. I'll be in San Francisco until Duff comes. I hope you'll be here when he arrives. He'll want to thank you in person, I know."

"I may be – who can say?" Charlie returned.

"Good. In the meantime, you must dine with me tonight. There are still some details I'm curious about. Ross's speech at the Minchin dinner, for example. Can you meet me at the Stewart at seven?"

"Delighted," Charlie answered. "I stop at same hotel myself."

Wales walked away with Ross in the company of the uniformed policeman. The man whom Charlie had at last brought to justice was wrapped in sullen silence now. His eyes, in those final moments, had studiously avoided those of Chan.

"Be in San Francisco long, Charlie?" asked Flannery, coming up.

"Hard to answer," Chan replied. "I have daughter at college in south California, and I have unquenchable longing to visit her."

"That's the ticket," Flannery cried, relieved. "You go down and give a helping hand to the Los Angeles police. They need it, if anybody ever did."

Chan smiled gently to himself. "You have here no little matter on which I might assist?"

"Not a thing, Charlie. Everything's pretty well cleaned up around San Francisco. But then, we got a mighty able organization here."

Chan nodded. "Under a strong general there are no weak soldiers."

"You said it. Lot of truth in some of those old wheezes of yours. Well, Charlie – drop in and see me before you go. I'll have to run along now."

As Charlie walked over to get his bag, he met Kashimo and the purser.

"Taking this lad aboard the *President Taft*," the purser said. "He'll be on his way back to Hawaii at two."

Chan beamed upon his assistant. "And he goes covered with glory," he remarked. "Kashimo, you have suffused my heart with pride. Not only did you do notable searching on boat, but when you came aboard that night in Honolulu, your suspicious eye was already on the guilty man." He patted the Japanese on the shoulder. "Even a peach grown in the shade will ripen in the end," he added.

"Hope chief will not be angry that I ran away," Kashimo said.

"Chief will be at pier with loudly playing band," Charlie assured him. "I do not appear to make you understand, Kashimo. You are hero. You are, I repeat again, covered with glory. Do not continually seek to push it aside, like blanket on hot night. Go aboard other ship now and wait for my return. I go to city to purchase fresh linen for you. I am inclined to think six days are plenty for that present outfit."

He picked up his bag, and walked a few steps with them toward the plank of the *President Taft*.

"For the present, I say goodby," he announced. "Will see you again, maybe at one o'clock. You are going home, Kashimo, not only in the shining garments of success, but also in a more hygienic shirt."

"All right," said Kashimo meekly.

As Charlie was leaving the pier-shed, he encountered Mark Kennaway.

"Hello," the young man cried. "Pamela and I have been waiting for you. I've engaged a car, and you're riding up-town with us."

"You are too kind," Charlie replied.

"Oh, our motives are not entirely unselfish. Tell you what I mean in a minute." They went to the curb, where Pamela

Potter was seated in a large touring car. "Jump in, Mr Chan," the young man added.

Chan did no jumping, but climbed aboard with his usual dignity. Kennaway followed and the car started.

"Both are looking very happy," Charlie suggested.

"Then I suppose our news is superfluous," the young man said. "As a matter of fact, we're engaged—"

Chan turned to the girl. "Pardon my surprise. You accepted this irritating young man, after all?"

"I certainly did. About a minute before he proposed, at that. I wasn't going to let all my hard work go for nothing."

"My warmest congratulations to you both," Chan bowed.

"Thanks," smiled the girl. "Mark's all right, everything considered. He's promised to forget Boston, and practise law in Detroit."

"Greater love hath no man than that," nodded Kennaway.

"So it's turned out to be a pretty good tour, after all," the girl continued. "Even if it did start so badly." Her smile faded. "By the way, I can't wait another minute. I want to learn how you knew that Ross was guilty. You said that night on the deck that I ought to know, too, and I've wracked my slight brain until I'm dizzy. But it's no use. I'm no detective, I guess."

"Vivian told us a few minutes ago," Kennaway added, "that it was something Ross said at the Minchin dinner. We've been over that speech of Ross's a dozen times. There wasn't much to it, as I recall. He was interrupted before he'd fairly got started—"

"But not before he had spoken a most incriminating word," Chan put in. "I will repeat for you the sentence in which it occurred. I have memorized it. Listen carefully. 'As for that unfortunate night in London, when poor Hugh Morris Drake lay dead in that stuffy room in Broome's Hotel—'"

"Stuffy!" cried Pamela Potter.

"Stuffy," repeated Charlie. "You are now bright girl I thought you. Consider. Was the room in which your honorable grandfather was discovered lifeless on bed a stuffy room? Remember testimony of Martin, the floor waiter, which you heard at inquest, and which I read in Inspector Duff's notes. 'I unlocked the door of the room and went in,' Martin said. 'One window was closed, the curtain was down all the way. The other was open, and the curtain was up, too. The light entered from there.' Adding word of my own I would remark, so also did plenty good fresh air."

"Of course," cried the girl. "I should have remembered. When I was in that room, talking with Mr Duff, the window was still open, and a street orchestra was playing *There's a Long, Long Trail A-Winding* outside. The music came up to us quite loudly."

"Ah, yes – but it was not in same room that grandfather was slain," Chan reminded her. "It was in room next door. And when Ross mentioned matter at dinner, his memory played him sorry trick. His thoughts returned, not to room in which grandfather was finally discovered, but to that other room in which he died. You read Walter Honywood's letter to his wife?"

"Yes, I did."

"Recall how he said to her: 'I entered and looked about me. Drake's clothes were on a chair, his ear-phone on a table; all the doors and windows were closed.' You observe, Miss Pamela – that was the stuffy room. The room where your grandfather perished."

"Of course it was," the girl answered. "Poor grandfather had asthma, and he thought the London night air was bad for it. So he refused to have any windows open where he slept. Oh – I have been stupid."

"You were otherwise engaged," smiled Charlie. "I was not. Three men knew that Hugh Morris Drake slept that night in a stuffy room. One, Mr Drake himself – and he was dead. Two, Mr Honywood, who went in and found the body – and he too was dead. Three, the man who stole in there in the night and strangled him – the murderer. In simpler words – Mr Ross."

"Good work!" cried Kennaway.

"But finished now," added Chan. "The Emperor Shi Hwang-ti, who built the Great Wall of China, once said: 'He who squanders today talking of yesterday's triumph, will have nothing to boast of tomorrow."

The car had drawn up before the door of a hotel in Union Square, and when the young people had alighted, Charlie followed. He took the girl's hand in his.

"I see plenty glad look in your eyes this morning," he said. "May it remain, is vigorous wish from me. Remember, fortune calls at the smiling gate."

He shook hands with Kennaway, picked up his bag, and disappeared quickly around the corner.

Keeper of the Keys

To MY SON BOB

As Quietly as Possible

Since He Dislikes Publicity

CONTENTS

I

SNOW ON THE MOUNTAINS

The train had left Sacramento some distance behind, and was now bravely beginning the long climb that led to the high Sierras and the town of Truckee. Little patches of snow sparkled in the late afternoon sun along the way, and far ahead snow-capped peaks suddenly stood out against the pale sky of a reluctant spring.

Two conductors, traveling together as though for safety, came down the aisle and paused at section seven. "Tickets on at Sacramento," demanded the leader. The occupant of the section, a pretty blonde girl who seemed no more than twenty, handed him the small green slips. He glanced at them, then passed one to his companion. "Seat in Seven," he said loudly. "Reno."

"Reno," echoed the Pullman conductor, in an even louder tone.

They passed on, leaving the blonde girl staring about the car with an air that was a mixture of timidity and defiance. This was the first time, since she had left home the day before, that she had been so openly tagged with the name of her destination. All up and down the car, strange faces turned and looked at her with casual curiosity. Some smiled knowingly; others were merely cold and aloof. The general public in one of its ruder moments.

One passenger only showed no interest. Across the aisle, in section eight, the girl noted the broad shoulders and back of a man in a dark suit. He was sitting close to the window, staring out, and even from this rear view it was apparent that he was deeply engrossed with his own affairs. The young woman who was bound for Reno felt somehow rather grateful toward him.

Presently he turned, and the girl understood, for she saw that he was a Chinese. A race that minds its own business. An admirable race. This member of it was plump and middle-aged. His little black eyes were shining as from some inner excitement; his lips were parted in a smile that seemed to indicate a sudden immense delight. Without so much as a glance toward number seven, he rose and walked rapidly down the car.

Arrived on the front platform of the Pullman, he stood for a moment deeply inhaling the chilly air. Then again, as though irresistibly, he was drawn to the window. The train was climbing more slowly now; the landscape, wherever he looked, was white. Presently he was conscious of someone standing behind him, and turned. The train maid, a Chinese girl of whose guarded glances he had been conscious at intervals all afternoon, was gazing solemnly up at him.

"How do you do," the man remarked, "and thank you so much. You have arrived at most opportune moment. The need to speak words assails me with unbearable force. I must release flood of enthusiasm or burst. For at this moment I am seeing snow for the first time!"

"Oh – I am so glad!" answered the girl. It was an odd reply, but the plump Chinese was evidently too excited to notice that.

"You see, it is this way," he continued eagerly. "All my life I can remember only nodding palm-trees, the trade winds of the tropics, surf tumbling on coral beach—"

"Honolulu," suggested the girl.

He paused, and stared at her. “Perhaps you have seen Hawaii too?” he inquired.

She shook her head. “No. Me – I am born in San Francisco. But I read advertisements in magazines – and besides—”

“You are bright girl,” the man cut in, “and your deduction is eminently correct. Honolulu has been my home for many years. Once, it is true, I saw California before, and from flat floor of desert I beheld, far in distance, mountain snow. But that was all same dream. Now I am moving on into veritable snow country, the substance lies on ground all about, soon I shall plunge unaccustomed feet into its delicious cold. I shall intake great breaths of frigidair.” He sighed. “Life is plenty good,” he added.

“Some people,” said the girl, “find the snow boresome.”

“And some, no doubt, consider the stars a blemish on the sky. But you and I, we are not so insensible to the beauties of the world. We delight to travel – to find novelty and change. Is it not so?”

“I certainly do.”

“Ah – you should visit my islands. Do not think that in my ecstasy of raving I forget the charm of my own land. I have daughter same age as you – how happy she would be to act as your guide. She would show you Honolulu, the flowering trees, the—”

“The new police station, perhaps,” cried the girl suddenly.

The big man started slightly and stared at her. “I perceive that I am known,” he remarked.

“Naturally,” the girl smiled. “For many years you have been newspaper hero for me. I was small child at the time, but I read with panting interest when you carried Phillimore pearls on flat floor of desert. Again, when you captured killer of famous Scotland Yard man in San Francisco, I perused daily accounts breathlessly. And only three weeks ago you arrived in San Francisco with one more cruel murderer in your firm grasp.”

"But even so," he shrugged.

"Your pictures were in all the papers. Have you forgot?"

"I seek to do so," he answered ruefully. "Were those my pictures?"

"More than that, I have seen you in person. Two weeks ago when the Chan Family Society gave big banquet for you in San Francisco. My mother was a Chan, and we were all present. I stood only a few feet away when you entered building. True, I was seated so far distant I could not hear your speech, but I was told by others it was brilliant talk."

He shrugged. "The Chan family should have more respect for truth," he objected.

"I am Violet Lee," she went on, holding out a tiny hand. "And you – may I speak the name—"

"Why not?" he replied, taking her hand. "You have me trapped. I am Inspector Charlie Chan, of the Honolulu Police."

"My husband and I recognized you when you came aboard at Oakland," the girl went on. "He is Henry Lee, steward of club car," she added proudly. "But he tells me sternly I must not speak to you – that is why I cried 'I am so glad!' when you spoke first to me. Perhaps, said my husband, inspector is now on new murder case, and does not want identity known. He is often right, my husband."

"As husbands must be," Chan nodded. "But this time he is wrong."

A shadow of disappointment crossed the girl's face. "You are not, then, on trail of some wrong-doer?"

"I am on no trail but my own."

"We thought there might have been some recent murder—"

Charlie laughed. "This is the mainland," he remarked, "so of course there have been many recent murders. But I am happy to say, none of them concerns me. No – I am involved only in contemplation of snow-capped peaks."

"Then – may I tell my husband that he is free to address you? The honor will overwhelm him with joy."

Chan laid his hand on the girl's arm. "I will tell him myself," he announced. "And I will see you again before I leave the train. In the meantime, your friendly words have been as food to the famished, rest to the jaded. Aloha."

He stepped through the door of the car ahead, leaving his small compatriot flushed and breathing fast on the chilly platform.

When he reached the club car, the white-jacketed steward was bending solicitously over the solitary passenger there. Receiving the latter's order, he stood erect and cast one look in the direction of Charlie Chan. He was a small thin Chinese, and only another member of his race would have caught the brief flame of interest that flared under his heavy eyelids.

Charlie dropped into a chair and, for lack of anything better to do, studied his fellow traveler, some distance down the aisle. The man was a lean, rather distinguished-looking foreigner of some sort – probably a Latin, Chan thought. His hair was as black and sleek as the detective's, save where it was touched with gray over the ears. His eyes were quick and roving, his thin hands moved nervously about, he sat on the edge of his chair, as though his stay on the train was but a brief interlude in an exciting life.

When the steward returned with a package of cigarettes on a silver tray and got his money and tip from the other passenger, Chan beckoned to him. The boy was at his side in an instant.

"One juice of the orange, if you will be so good," Charlie ordered.

"Delighted to serve," replied the steward, and was off like a greyhound. With surprising speed he returned, and placed the drink on the arm of Charlie's chair. He was moving reluctantly away, when the detective spoke.

"An excellent concoction," he said, holding the glass aloft.

"Yes, sir," replied the steward, and looked at Chan much as the Chinese girl on the platform had done.

"Helpful in reducing the girth," Chan went on. "A question which, I perceive, does not concern you. But as for myself – you will note how snugly I repose in this broad chair."

The eyes of the other narrowed. "The man-hunting tiger is sometimes over-plump," he remarked. "Still he pounces with admirable precision."

Charlie smiled. "He who is cautious by nature is a safe companion in crossing a bridge."

The steward nodded. "When you travel abroad, speak as the people of the country are speaking."

"I commend your discretion," Charlie told him. "But as I have just said to your wife, it is happily unnecessary at this time. The man-hunting tiger is at present unemployed. You may safely call him by his name."

"Ah, thank you, Inspector. It is under any conditions a great honor to meet you. My wife and I are both long-time admirers of your work. At this moment you seem to stand at very pinnacle of fame."

Charlie sighed, and drained his glass. "He who stands on pinnacle," he ventured, "has no place to step but off."

"The need for moving," suggested the steward, "may not be imminent."

"Very true." The detective nodded approvingly. "Such wisdom, and such efficiency. When I met your wife, I congratulated you. Now I meet you, I felicitate her."

A delighted smile spread over the younger man's face. "A remark," he answered, "that will find place in our family archive. The subjects are unworthy, but the source is notable. Will you deign to drink again?"

"No, thank you." Chan glanced at his watch. "The town of Truckee, I believe, is but twenty-five minutes distant."

"Twenty-four and one-half," replied Henry Lee, who was a railroad man. The flicker of surprise in his black eyes was scarcely noticeable. "You alight at Truckee, Inspector?"

"I do," nodded Charlie, his gaze on the other passenger, who had evinced sudden interest.

"You travel for pleasure, I believe you intimated," the steward continued.

Chan smiled. "In part," he said softly.

"Ah, yes – in part," Henry Lee repeated. He saw Chan's hand go to his trousers pocket. "The charge, I regret to state, is one half-dollar."

Nodding, Charlie hesitated a moment. Then he laid the precise sum on the silver tray. He was not unaware of the institution of tipping. He was also not unaware of the sensitive Chinese nature. They would part now as friends, not as master and menial. He saw from the light in Henry Lee's eyes that the young man appreciated his delicacy.

"Thank you so much," said the steward, bowing low. "It has been great honor and privilege to serve Inspector Charlie Chan."

It chanced that at the moment the detective's eyes were on the foreign-looking passenger at the other end of the car. The man had been about to light a cigarette, but when he overheard the name he paused, and stared until the match burned down to his finger-tips. He tossed it aside, lighted another and then came down the car and dropped into the seat at Charlie's side.

"Pardon," he said. "Me – I have no wish to intrude. But I overhear you say you leave the train at Truckee. So also must I."

"Yes?" Chan said politely.

"Alas, yes. A desolate place, they tell me, at this time of year."

"The snow is very beautiful," suggested Charlie.

"Bah!" The other shrugged disgustedly. "Me, I have had sufficient snow. I fought for two winters with the Italian Army in the North."

"Distasteful work," commented Chan, "for you."

"What do you mean?"

"Pardon – no offense. But one of your temperament. A musician."

"You know me, then?"

"I have not the pleasure. But I note flattened, calloused finger-tips. You have played violin."

"I have done more than play the violin. I am Luis Romano, conductor of the opera. Ah – I perceive that means nothing to you. But in my own country – at La Scala in Milan, at Naples. And also in Paris, in London, even in New York. However, that is all finished now."

"I am so sorry."

"Finished – by a woman. A woman who – but what of this? We both alight at Truckee. And after that—"

"Ah, yes – after that."

"We travel together, Signor Chan. I could not help it – I heard the name. But that was lucky. I was told to look out for you. You do not believe? Read this."

He handed Charlie a somewhat soiled and crumpled telegram. The detective read:

"Mr Luis Romano, Kilarney Hotel, San Francisco: Delighted you are coming to Tahoe to visit me. Owing to very late spring, roads around lake in poor condition. Leave train Truckee, I will telephone local garage have car waiting, you will be driven to Tahoe Tavern. At Tavern pier my man will wait for you with motor-launch, bring you down to my place, Pineview. Other guests may join you in car at Truckee, among them Mr Charlie Chan, of Honolulu. Thanks for coming.

"DUDLEY WARD."

Chan returned the missive to the eager hand of the Italian. "Now I understand," he remarked.

Mr Romano made a gesture of despair. "You are more fortunate than I. I understand to the door of this place Pineview – but no further. You, however – it may be you are old friend of Mr Dudley Ward? The whole affair may be clear to you."

Charlie's face was bland, expressionless. "You are, then, in the dark yourself?" he inquired.

"Absolutely," the Italian admitted.

"Mr Dudley Ward is no friend of yours?"

"Not at all. I have yet to see him. I know, of course, he is a member of a famous San Francisco family, very wealthy. He spends the summers at his place on this high lake, to which he goes very early in the season. A few days ago I had a most surprising letter from him, asking me to visit him up here. There was, he said, a certain matter he wished to discuss, and he promised to pay me well for my trouble. I was – I am, Signor, financially embarrassed – owing to a circumstance quite unforeseen and abominable. So I agreed to come."

"You have no trace of idea what subject Mr Ward desires to discuss?"

"I have an inkling – yes. You see – Mr Ward was once the husband of – my wife." Chan nodded hazily. "The relationship, however, is not very close. There were two other husbands in between us. He was the first – I am the fourth."

Charlie sought to keep a look of surprise from his face. What would his wife, on Punchbowl Hill, think of this? But he was now on the mainland, with Reno only a few miles away.

"It will be perhaps easier for you to understand," the Italian went on, "if I tell you who is my wife. A name, Signor, known even to you – pardon – to the whole world. Landini, the opera singer, Ellen Landini." He sat excitedly on the edge of his chair. "What a talent – magnificent. What an organ – superb. And what a heart – cold as those snow-covered stones." He waved at the passing landscape.

"So sorry," Chan said. "You are not, then, happy with your wife?"

"Happy with her, Signor? Happy with her!" He stood up, the better to declaim. "Can I be happy with a woman who is at this very moment in Reno seeking to divorce me and marry her latest fancy – a silly boy with a face like putty? After all I have done for her – the loving care I have lavished upon her – and now she does not send me even the first payment of the settlement that was agreed on – she leaves me to—"

He sank into the chair again. "But why not? What could I expect from her? Always she was like that. The husband she had was never the right one."

Chan nodded. "Ginger grown in one's own garden is not so pungent," he remarked.

Mr Romano wakened to new excitement. "That is it. That expresses it. It was always so with her. Look at her record – married to Dudley Ward as a girl. Everything she wanted – except a new husband. And she got him in time. John Ryder, his name was. But he didn't last long. Then – another. He was – what does it matter? I forget. Then me. I, who devoted every waking hour to her voice, to coaching her. It was I, Signor, who taught her the old Italian system of breathing, without which a singer is nothing – nothing. If you will credit it – she did not know it when I met her."

He buried his head emotionally in his hands. Charlie respected the moment.

"And now," went on Mr Romano, "this boy, this singer – this what's his name. Will he command her not to eat pastries – seeking to save that figure once so glorious? Will he prepare her gargle, remind her to use it? Now I recall the name of the third husband – he was Dr Frederic Swan, a throat specialist. He has lived in Reno since the divorce – no doubt she flirts with him again. She will flirt with me, once she has hooked this boy. Always like that. But now – now she cannot even send me the agreed settlement—"

Henry Lee approached. "Pardon, Inspector," he announced. "Truckee three minutes."

Mr Romano dashed for the door, evidently bound for the Pullman and his baggage. Charlie turned to his compatriot.

"So happy to know you," he said.

"Same for you," replied Henry Lee. "Also, I hope you gain much pleasure from your journey. In part," he added, with a grin. "I am going to watch newspapers."

"Nothing about this in newspapers," Charlie assured him.

"If you will pardon my saying it," replied Henry Lee, "I watch newspapers just the same."

Charlie went on back to his Pullman. Swift dark had fallen outside the windows, the snow was blotted from view. He gathered up his bags, turned them over to the porter and proceeded to don the heavy overcoat he had purchased for this journey – the first such garment he had owned in his life.

When he reached the car platform, Mrs Lee was awaiting him. "My husband has told me of his happy moment with you," she cried. "This is notable day in our lives. I shall have much to tell my small man-child, who is now well past his eleventh moon."

"Pray give him my kind regards," said Charlie. He staggered slightly as his legs were struck from behind by some heavy object. Turning, he saw a tall man with a blond beard, who had just snatched up a bag from the platform – the object, evidently, which had struck Chan so sharp a blow. Expectantly Charlie waited for the inevitable apology. But the stranger gave him one cold look, pushed him ruthlessly aside and crowded past him to the car steps.

In another moment the train had stopped, and Charlie was out on the snowy platform. He tipped his porter, waved goodby to the Lees and took a few steps along the brightly lighted space in front of the station. For the first time in his life he heard the creak of frost under his shoes, saw his own breath materialized before his eyes.

Romano came swiftly up. "I have located our motor," he announced. "Come quickly, if you will. I secured a view of the town, and it is not even a one-night stand."

As they came up to the automobile waiting beside the station, they beheld the driver of it conversing with a man who had evidently just left the train. Charlie looked closer – the man with the blond beard. The latter turned to them.

"Good evening," he said. "Are you Dudley Ward's other guests? My name is John Ryder."

Without waiting for their response, he slipped into the preferred front seat by the driver's side. "John Ryder." Charlie looked at Romano, and saw an expression of vast surprise on the Italian's mobile face. They got into the rear seat without speaking, and the driver started the car.

They emerged into the main street of a town that was, in the dim light of a wintry evening, reminiscent of a moving picture of the Old West. A row of brick buildings that spoke of being clubs, but behind the frosted windows of which no gaiety seemed to be afoot tonight. Restaurants with signs that advertised only the softer drinks, a bank, a post-office. Here and there a dusky figure hurrying through the gloom.

The car crossed a railroad spur and turned off into the white nothingness of the country. Now for the first time Charlie was close to the pines, tall and stern, rooted deep in the soil, their aroma pungent and invigorating. Across his vision flitted a picture of distant palms, unbelievable relatives of these proud and lofty giants.

The chains on the tires flopped unceasingly, down the open path between the snow-banks, and Charlie wondered at the sound. On their right now was a tremendous cliff, on their left a half-frozen river.

The man on the front seat beside the driver did not turn. He said no word. The two on the rear seat followed his example.

In about an hour they came upon the lights of a few scattered houses; a little later they turned off into the Tavern grounds. A vast shingled building stood lonely in the winter night, with but a few lights burning on its ground floor.

Close to the pier entrance the driver stopped his car. A man with a boatman's cap came forward.

"Got 'em, Bill?" he inquired.

"Three – that's right, ain't it?" the garage man inquired.

"O.K. I'll take them bags."

Bill said good night and departed, strangely eager to get back to town. The boatman led them on to the pier. For a moment Chan paused, struck by the beauty of the scene. Here lay a lake like a great dark sapphire, six thousand feet above the sea, surrounded by snow-covered mountains. On and on they moved down the dim pier.

"But," cried Romano – "the lake – it does not freeze."

"Tahoe never freezes," the guide explained scornfully. "Too deep. Well, here's the launch." They paused beside a handsome boat. "I'll put your stuff aboard, but we'll have to wait a minute. They's one more coming."

Even as he spoke, a man came hurrying along the pier. He joined them, a bit breathless.

"Sorry," he said. "Hope I haven't kept you waiting, gentlemen. I stopped at the Tavern for a minute. Guess we might as well get acquainted. My name is Swan," he added. "Dr Frederic Swan."

One by one he shook hands with each of them, learning from each his name. As this newcomer and the man with the blond beard climbed aboard, Romano turned to Charlie and said softly:

"What is it? What is it you call it when you reach a town and all the hotel rooms are filled?"

"So sorry," Chan said blankly.

"All right – I will get it. It has happened to me so often. A – a convention. That is it. A convention. My friend, we are about to attend one of those. We are going to attend a convention of the lost loves of Landini."

He and Chan followed the others aboard, and in another moment they were skimming lightly over the icy waters in the direction of Emerald Bay.

II

DINNER AT PINEVIEW

The mountains were breathlessly still under the black sky, the wind blew chill from their snowy slopes and as the spray occasionally stung Charlie Chan's broad face, he reflected with deep inner joy upon the new setting to which fate had now transplanted him. Too long, he decided, had he known only the semi-tropics; his blood had grown thin – he drew his great coat closer: his energy had run low. Yes – no doubt about it – he was becoming soft. This was the medicine that would revive him; new life was coursing in his veins; new ambitions seethed within him; he longed for a chance to show what he could really do. He began to regret the obviously simple nature of the matter that had brought him to Tahoe; the affair was, on the face of it, so easy and uncomplicated that, as his son Henry might have phrased it, he had come just for the ride.

Though the moon had not yet risen, he could discern the nature of the lake shore on their starboard side. The dim outlines of one huge summer home after another glided by; each without a light, without a sign of life. Presently, in the distance, he saw a lamp burning by the water's edge; a little later and it multiplied into a string of them, stretched along a pier. The boat was swinging inshore now; they fought their way along against the wind. As they reached the wharf, the passengers in the launch looked up and saw a man of about fifty standing, hatless and without an overcoat, above them. He waved, then hurried to help the boatman with the mooring ropes.

Evidently this was their host, Dudley Ward, debonair and gracious even in a stiff wind. He greeted them as they came ashore. "John, old boy," he said to Ryder, "it was good of you to come. Doctor Swan, I appreciate your kindness. And this, no doubt, is Mr Romano – a great pleasure to welcome you to Pineview. The view is a bit obscured, but I can assure you the pines are there."

The boat was rocking violently as Charlie, always politely last, made a notable leap for the pier. Ward received him, literally, in his arms.

"Inspector Chan," he cried. "For years I have wanted to meet you."

"Desire has been mutual," Chan answered, panting a bit.

"Your native courtesy," Ward smiled. "I am sorry to remind you that you heard of me only – er – recently. Gentlemen – if you will follow me—"

He led the way along a broad walk from which the snow had been cleared toward a great house set amid the eternal pines. As their feet sounded on the wide veranda, an old Chinese servant swung open the door. They caught the odor of burning wood, saw lights and good cheer awaiting them, and crossed the threshold into the big living-room of Pineview.

"Sing, take the gentlemen's coats." The host was alert and cordial. Charlie looked at him with interest; a man of fifty, perhaps more, with gray hair and ruddy pleasant face. The cut of his clothes, and the material of which they were made, placed him at once; only a gentleman, it seemed, knew the names of tailors like that. He led the way to the tremendous fireplace at the far end of the room.

"A bit chilly on Tahoe tonight," he remarked. "For myself, I like it – come up here earlier every year. However – the fire won't go so badly – nor will those." He waved a hand toward a tray of cocktails. "I had Sing pour them when we sighted you, so there would be no delay."

He himself passed the tray. Ryder, Romano and Swan accepted with evident pleasure. Charlie shook his head and smiled, and Ward did not press him. There was a moment of awkward silence, and then the irrepressible Romano, posing with feet far apart in front of the blaze, raised his glass.

"Gentlemen," he announced. "I am about to propose a toast. No other, I believe, could be more appropriate at this time. However little she may mean to you now, whatever you may think of her at this late day—"

"One moment," Ryder spoke, with his accustomed cool rudeness. "I suggest you withdraw your toast. Because, as it happens, I want this drink."

Romano was taken aback. "Why, of course. I am so sorry. Me—I am too impetuous. No one, I am sure, has more to forgive than myself."

"Beside the point," said Ryder, and drained his glass.

Swan also drank, then laughed softly. "We have all much to forgive, I fancy," he remarked. "And to forget. Yes, it was always herself Landini thought of first. Her own wishes – her own happiness. But that, of course, is genius. We ordinary mortals should be charitable. I myself have supposed for many years that I hated the very name of Ellen Landini – and yet when I saw her a few moments ago—"

Dudley Ward paused in his task of refilling the glasses. "A few moments ago?" he repeated.

"Yes. I drove up from Reno to the Tavern, and dropped in there for a chat with my friend, Jim Dinsdale, the manager. When I came into the lobby I thought it was deserted, but presently I saw a woman's green scarf lying on a table. Then

I looked over to the fire and saw her – the woman – sitting there. I went closer – the light was poor – but even before my eyes told me, I knew that it was Ellen. I had known she was in Reno, of course, but I hadn't wanted particularly to see her. When we parted years ago – well, I needn't go into that. Anyhow, I've been avoiding her. Yet now we were meeting again – the stage all set, as though she'd arranged it, alone together in the dim-lighted lobby of a practically deserted hotel. She jumped up. 'Fred,' she cried—"

Romano came closer, his face glowing with excitement. "How was she looking, Signor? Not too much flesh? Her voice – how did her voice seem to you—"

Swan laughed. "Why – why, she seemed all right to me. In fact – and this is the point of what I started out to say – after all she'd done to me, I felt in that moment the old spell, the old enchantment. She seemed charming, as always. She held out both her hands—"

"She would," snarled Ryder. "May I have another drink?"

"She was lovely," Swan went on. "Just at that moment Dinsdale came in, and with him a young fellow named Beaton—"

"Hugh Beaton," Romano cried. "The infant she has snatched from the cradle. The callow child she would exchange for me across the counters of Reno. Bah! I, too, must drink again."

"Yes, it turned out that way," Swan admitted. "He was her latest flame. She introduced him as such, with all her old arrogance. Also his sister, quite a pretty girl. The romance was rather gone from our meeting."

"What was Landini doing at the Tavern?" Ward inquired.

"I gathered she was a friend of Dinsdale, and had just driven over for dinner. She's not stopping there, of course – she's served four weeks of her cure at Reno, and she's not staying out of the state more than a few hours. Naturally, I didn't linger.

I hurried away." He looked about the group. "But pardon me. I didn't mean to monopolize the conversation."

"It was Ellen who was doing that," smiled Dudley Ward, "not you. Up to her old tricks again. Dinner, gentlemen, is at seven. In the meantime, Sing will show you to your various rooms, though I'm afraid you'll have to sort out your own baggage in the upper hall. Doctor Swan, I've assigned you a room, even though, to my regret, you're not staying the night. Ah Sing – where is the old rascal?"

The servant appeared, and led the procession above.

Ward laid a hand on Charlie Chan's arm. "At a quarter to seven, in my study upstairs at the front of the house," he said softly. "For just a few minutes."

Chan nodded.

"One more thing, gentlemen," Ward called. "No one need dress. This is strictly stag, of course."

He stood and watched them disappear, an ironical smile on his face.

Presently Charlie entered a warm and pleasant bedroom, meekly following Ah Sing. The old man turned on the lights, set down Chan's bags, then looked up at his compatriot from Honolulu. His face was lean and the color of a lemon that has withered, his shoulders were hunched and bent. His eyes alone betrayed his race; and in them Chan detected an authentic gleam of humor.

"P'liceman?" said Ah Sing.

Charlie admitted it, with a smile.

"Some people say plitty wise man?" continued Sing. "Maybe."

"Maybe," agreed Charlie.

Sing nodded sagely, and went out.

Charlie stepped to the window, and looked down an aisle of tall pines at snow-covered hills and a bit of wintry sky. The novelty of this scene so engrossed him that he was three minutes late for his appointment with his host in the study.

"That's all right," Dudley Ward said, when Chan apologized. "I'm not going over the whole business here – I'll have to do it anyhow at the table. I just want to say I'm glad you've come, and I hope you'll be able to help me."

"I shall extend myself to utmost," Charlie assured him.

"It's rather a small matter for a man of your talents," Ward went on. He was sitting behind a broad desk, over which an alabaster lamp cast its glow. "But I can assure you it's important to me. I got you in here just to make sure you know why I invited these three men up here tonight – but now I've done it, I realize I must be insulting your intelligence."

Chan smiled. "On second thoughts, you changed original plan?"

"Yes. I thought when I wrote you, I'd just get in touch with them by letter. But that's a terribly unsatisfactory way of dealing with things – at least, I've always thought so. I like to see a man's face when I'm asking him questions. Then I heard this Romano was in San Francisco, and broke – I knew money would bring him here. Swan was already in Reno, and Ryder – well, he and I've been friends from boyhood, and the fact that he was Ellen's second husband never made any difference between us. So I resolved to bring them all together here tonight."

Charlie nodded. "A bright plan," he agreed.

"I'll ask all the questions," Ward continued. "What sort of replies I'll get, I don't know. None of them loves Landini any too much, I imagine, but because of one reason or another – perhaps in view of promises made long ago – the information we are after may be difficult to get. I rely on you to watch each one carefully, and to sense it if anyone of them fails to tell the truth. You've had plenty of experience along that line, I fancy."

"I fear you over-estimate my poor ability," Charlie protested.

"Nonsense," cried Ward. "We're bound to get a clue somewhere. We may even get all we're after. But whether we do or not, I want you to feel that you are here not just as an investigator, but as my guest, and an honored one." Before him on the desk stood twin boxes; one of bright yellow, the other a deep crimson. He opened the nearer one, and pushed it toward Chan. "Will you have a cigarette before dinner?" he invited. Charlie declined, and taking one himself, Ward rose and lighted it. "Cozy little room, this," he suggested.

"The reply is obvious," Chan nodded. He glanced about, reflecting that some woman must have had a hand here. Gay cretonnes hung at the windows; the shades of the several lamps about the room were of delicate silk; the rug was deep and soft.

"Please use it as your own," his host said. "Any work you have to do – letters and the like – come in here. We'll be getting on downstairs now, eh?" Charlie noted for the first time that the man's hands trembled, and that a faint perspiration shone on his forehead. "A damned important dinner for me," Ward added, and his voice broke suddenly in the middle of the sentence.

But when they reached the group downstairs before the fire, the host was again his debonair self, assured and smiling. He led his four guests through a brief passageway to the dining-room, and assigned them to their places.

That great oak-paneled room, that table gleaming with silver, spoke eloquently of the prestige of the family of Ward. Ever since the days of Virginia City and the Comstock Lode, the name had been known and honored in this western country. No boat around the Horn for the first Dudley Ward; he had trekked in with the gold rush, a member of that gallant band of whom it has been well said: "The cowards never started, and the weaklings died on the way." Now this famous family had dwindled to the polished, gray-haired gentleman at the head of the table, and Charlie, thinking of his own eleven children at home in Honolulu, glanced around the board and sighed over the futility of such a situation.

In its earlier stages, the dinner seemed a trifle strained, despite the urbane chatter of the host. Charlie alone knew why he was there; the others seemed inclined to silent speculation. Evidently Ward was not yet ready to enlighten them. As Ah Sing moved along with the main course, Charlie said a few words to him in Cantonese, and got a brief answer in the same dialect.

"Pardon, please," Chan bowed to his host, "I take the liberty of asking Ah Sing his age. His reply is not altogether clear."

Ward smiled. "I don't suppose the old boy really knows. In the late seventies, I fancy – a long life, and most of it spent in our service. I know it's not the thing to talk about one's servants – but Ah Sing years ago passed out of that category. He's been one of the family for as long as I can remember."

"I have heard, my heart bursting with pride," Chan said, "of the loyalty and devotion of old Chinese servants in this state."

Ryder spoke suddenly. "Everything you have heard is true," he said. He turned to Ward. "I remember when we were kids, Dudley. Great Scott, how good Sing was to us in those days. The stuff he used to cook for us – grumbling all the time. Huge bowls of rice with meat gravy – I dream of them yet. He'd been with you ages then, hadn't he?"

"My grandfather picked him up in Nevada," Ward replied. "He came to our house when I was just three years old. I remember, because I had a birthday party that day on the lawn, and Sing was serving – his first day. There were a lot of bees down in the meadow, and I imagine they were attracted by Sing's cooking, just as we kids were. Anyhow, I remember Sing – a young man then – marching toward us proudly bearing the cake, when a bee suddenly stung him on the leg. He dropped the cake, let out a yell and looked at my mother accusingly. 'Melican buttahfly too damn hot,' he complained. If I were to write my memoirs, I think I should have to begin with that – my first conscious recollection."

"I guess I missed that party," Ryder said. "It came a couple of years too soon for me. But I remember many a later one, in Sing's kitchen. Always a friend in need to us boys, Sing was."

Ward's face was serious. "They're dying out," he remarked. "The ones like Sing. Somebody ought to put up a statue in Golden Gate Park – or at least a tablet somewhere on one of the famous trails – to the best friends Californians ever had."

Sing came in at that moment, and the subject was dropped. A long silence ensued. Romano and Swan seemed to be getting rather impatient over the long delay in reaching the real business of the evening. Since the discussion that had broken out on their first entrance, Ellen Landini had not been so much as mentioned. Romano's cheeks were flushed, his white hands fluttered nervously over his plate, he fidgeted in his chair. Swan also showed various signs of restlessness.

Coffee was finally brought, and then a tray of cut-glass decanters was set before Dudley Ward.

"I have here, gentlemen," he remarked, "some Benedictine, crème de menthe, peach brandy. Also, some port wine. All pre-prohibition – you break no law in my house. What will you have? Just a moment – Sing! Where the devil is that boy?" He rang the bell, and the old Chinese hurriedly returned. "Sing – take the gentlemen's orders – and fill them. And now—"

He paused, and they all looked at him expectantly. "Now, gentlemen, you are wondering why you are here. You are wondering why Inspector Chan, of the Honolulu Police, is here. I have kept you waiting an intolerably long time, I know, but the truth is, I am loath to bring this matter up. To introduce it properly I shall have to go into a subject that I had hoped was for ever dead and forgotten – my life with Ellen Landini."

He pushed his chair back from the table, and crossed his legs. "Sing – you haven't overlooked the cigars? Ah, yes –

gentlemen, help yourselves. I – I married Ellen Landini nearly twenty years ago, in San Francisco. She had just come to town from the islands, a young girl of eighteen, with a voice – even then it was magical. But she had more than the voice, she had a freshness, a vivacity, a beauty – however, I needn't go into her charm, surely not in this company. She gave a little concert, I saw her, heard her sing. The courtship was brief. We were married, and went to Paris on our honeymoon.

"That year in Paris – I shall never forget it. I want to be fair. She was wonderful – then. She studied with the best teacher in Europe, and what he told her about her voice made her supremely happy. It made me happy, too – for a time.

"Only gradually did I come to see that this wonderful year had wrecked my dreams – my hopes for a home, for children. Domestic life was now impossible for us. She was determined to become a professional singer. I saw myself, the prima donna's husband, carrying a dog about Europe, waiting at stage doors, enduring for ever an artistic temperament. The career did not appeal to me. I said so.

"Perhaps I was unreasonable. I want, as I have said, to be fair to her. Men were not so complacent about careers for their wives in those days. At any rate, there began a series of endless quarrels. I brought her home from Paris, to San Francisco, and thence, since it was spring, up to this house. I could see she would never be reconciled to the life I wanted."

He was silent for a moment. "I apologize humbly," he went on, "for dragging you into affairs that should be private. I must add, however, that our quarrels became daily more bitter, that we began to say unforgivable things, to hate each other. I could see her hate in her eyes when she looked at me. One June day – in this very room – matters came to a climax and she left the house. She never returned.

"I refused to divorce her, but when, nearly a year later, she applied for a divorce in some middle-western state, on a false charge of desertion, I did not contest the suit. I still loved her – or rather, the girl I thought I had married – but I realized she was lost to me for ever. I balanced the account and closed the books."

He turned to the doctor. "Doctor Swan – won't you try that brandy again? Just help yourself, please. So far, gentlemen, you can see no reason for my story. But there is something more – and only within the past ten days have I come upon the trail of it.

"I have been told, by someone who ought to know, that when Ellen Landini left my house she carried with her a secret which she had not seen fit to divulge to me. I have heard, from a source I believe reliable, that less than seven months after she left this place, she gave birth to a child, in a New York hospital. A son. Her son – and mine."

He did not go on for a moment. All the men about the table were looking at him, some with pity, some with amazement.

"I have said," Ward went on, "that Ellen hated me. Perhaps with reason – oh, I want to be just. She hated me so much, evidently, that she was determined I must never have the satisfaction of knowing about – my boy. Perhaps she feared it would start the old argument all over again. Perhaps it was just – hate. I – I think it was rather cruel."

"She was always cruel," said Ryder harshly. He laid a sympathetic hand on Dudley Ward's arm.

"At any rate," Ward went on, "she gave this child for adoption to some wealthy friends of hers. It wasn't legal adoption, of course. But she agreed to give him up for ever, to let him be known by another name, never to try to see him. She could do that. Her career was everything.

"That, gentlemen, ends my story. You can see my position. I am not – not so young as I was. My brother and sister are both dead, childless. Somewhere in this world, if the story is true, and the boy lived, I have a son, now nearly eighteen. All this –

is his. I intend to find him." His voice grew louder. "By heaven, I will find him. As far as Landini is concerned, bygones are bygones. I have no more hatred. But I want my boy.

"That is why," he continued in a lower tone, "I have sent for Inspector Chan. I shall back him to the limit in this search. I've had only ten days – I've only started—"

"Who told you all this?" Ryder inquired.

"Ah – that's rather interesting," Ward replied. "It was Ellen's return to this part of the world that, indirectly, brought it out. It seems that about eight years ago, when Ellen came to Nevada to divorce – er – Doctor Swan, she was, at the moment, interested in – you will pardon me, Doctor—"

Swan smiled. "Oh, that's perfectly all right. We've all been victims – we can speak freely here. She wanted to divorce me because she had fallen in love – or thought she had – with her chauffeur, a handsome boy named Michael Ireland. I came out to fight the divorce – but she got it anyhow. She didn't, however, get Michael. It was one of her few defeats in that line. The day before her divorce, young Michael eloped with Ellen's maid, a French girl named Cecile. The maid just took him away from her. It was rather amusing. Michael and his wife are still living in Reno, and the former is a pilot for a passenger airplane company over there."

"Precisely," nodded Ward. "When I first came up here two weeks ago I sent to Reno for a couple of servants – a cook and an upstairs maid – and the latter happened to be Michael's wife. It seems they're not very prosperous, and she'd decided to go into service temporarily. She knew, of course, my connection with Ellen Landini when she came here, but for a time she said nothing. Naturally, I had never seen or heard of the woman before. But it appears that Ellen is doing a great deal of flying during her stay in Reno, and her favorite pilot is Michael Ireland. Cecile is wildly jealous, and that is no doubt what led her to come to me with the story about my son. She claims she went with Ellen as personal maid shortly before the baby was born, and that she had been sworn to eternal secrecy in the matter."

Ryder shook his head. "The story of a jealous woman," he remarked. "I'm sorry, Dudley, but aren't you building a bit too much on that? Not the best evidence, you know."

Ward nodded. "I know. Still, I can't well ignore a thing as important as this. And as the woman told it, I must admit it had the ring of truth. Also, I recalled certain little things that had happened, things that Ellen had said during her last mad weeks in this house – it is quite possible the story is true. And I mean to find out whether it's true or not."

"Have you questioned Landini?" asked Doctor Swan.

"I have not," replied Ward. "In the first excitement of the moment, I called her hotel in Reno, but before I got the connection, I had sense enough to ring off. Inspector Chan may have an interview with her later, if he sees fit, but I would expect nothing to come of it. I know her of old.

"No, gentlemen, it is to you three that, at the beginning of this hunt, I have seen fit to pin my hopes. You have all, like myself, been married to Landini. I do not believe that she would ever have deliberately told any of you about this child, but even so – these things sometimes come out. A telegram opened by mistake, a telephone call in some strange city, a chance meeting – by one or another of these methods, one of you may have come upon her secret. I am not asking you to be disloyal in any way. But I do contend that if Ellen deceived me in this matter, it was a piece of unwarranted cruelty, and as man to man I ask you, if you can, to relieve me of this horrible suspense. Nothing shall happen to Landini, or to the boy, save to his advantage. But – you can see – I am in hell over this – and I must know – I must know."

His voice rose to an almost hysterical pitch as he looked appealingly about the table. John Ryder spoke first.

"Dudley," he said, "no one would be happier to help you now than I would be – if I could. God knows I have no wish to spare the feelings of Ellen Landini. But as you know, my life with her was of the briefest – and that was the only lucky break I ever got where she was concerned. So brief and so hectic that I never heard of this matter you have brought up tonight – never dreamed of it. I – I'm sorry."

Ward nodded. "I was afraid of that." He looked toward Swan and Romano, and his expression changed. "Before we go any further, I may add that I am willing to pay handsomely – and I mean no offense – for any information that may be of help. Doctor Swan – you were married to Landini for several years—"

Swan's eyelids narrowed. He toyed with his coffee cup, took out his eye-glasses, put them on, restored them to his pocket.

"Don't misunderstand me," he said slowly. "Landini means nothing to me, despite what I said earlier about her charm when I saw her again at the Tavern. It isn't very pleasant to be thrown over for a chauffeur." Across his usually pleasant face shot a look of malevolence that was startling and unexpected. "No," he added harshly, "I have no wish to protect the woman – but I'm sorry to say that this is – well, it's all news to me."

Ward's face was gray and tired as he turned to Romano. The opera conductor shot his cuffs and spoke.

"The figures – er – the figures of the amount you wish to pay, Mr Ward – I leave them entirely to you. I rely on your reputation as a gentleman."

"I think you may safely do so," replied Ward grimly.

"Landini – she is still my wife – but what does she mean to me? In New York were drawn up terms of settlement by which I was to release her for this new divorce. Has she made the initial payment? She has not. I must live – is it not so? Once I had a career of my own – I was aimed high for success – all gone now. She has done that to me. She has wrecked my life –

and now she casts me off." He clenched his fist that lay on the table, and a sudden fire gleamed in his dark eyes.

"You were going to tell me—" suggested Ward.

"There was, sir, a telegram opened by mistake. I opened it. It held some news of that son of hers. She told me little, but enough. There was a son. That much I can say. I have, of course, no recollection of the signature to the telegram."

"But – the town from which it was sent?" Ward cried.

Romano looked at him – the sly anxious look of a man who needs money – needs it badly enough to lie for it, perhaps.

"The town I do not now remember," Romano said. "But I will think – I will think hard – and it will come to me, I am sure."

Ward looked hopelessly at Charlie Chan. He sighed. At that instant, from the big room beyond the passage, came the slamming of a door, and then, sharp and clear, the bark of a dog.

The four guests of Dudley Ward looked up in amazement, as though they found something sinister and disquieting in that bark. Sing came shuffling in and, leaning over the chair of the host, spoke in a low tone. Ward nodded, and gave a direction. Then, an ironical smile on his face, he rose to his feet.

"Gentlemen," he said, "I hope you will not be too much annoyed by my peculiar sense of humor. I have acted on impulse – and I may have been wrong. But it came to me when Doctor Swan spoke of his encounter at the Tavern – there was just one person lacking to make our party complete. And since she was so near—"

"Landini," cried Ryder. "You have invited Landini here?"

"For a very brief call – I have."

"I won't see her," Ryder protested. "I swore years ago I'd never see her again—"

"Oh, come on, John," Ward said. "Be modern. Landini will regard it as a lark – I didn't tell her you were all here, but I know she won't care. Doctor Swan has already seen her. Mr Romano has no objections—"

"Me?" cried Romano. "I *want* to talk to her!"

"Precisely. I am willing to forget the past. Come on, John."

Ryder's eyes were on the table. "All right," he agreed.

Dudley Ward smiled. "Gentlemen," he said, "shall we join the lady?"

III

THE FALLEN FLOWER

But when they stepped through the passage into the living-room the lady was not there. Two men were warming themselves before the fire: one, a round cheery, red-faced little man, the other a pale youth with black curly hair and a weak but handsome face. The older of the two stepped forward.

"Hello, Dudley," he said. "This is like old times, isn't it? Ellen back at the old house again and – er – ah – and all that."

"Hello, Jim," Ward replied. He introduced his guests to Jim, who was, it appeared, Mr Dinsdale, manager of the Tavern. When he had finished, the hotel man turned to the boy who accompanied him.

"This is Mr Hugh Beaton," he announced. "Ellen and Mr Beaton's sister have gone upstairs to leave their wraps, and—"

Mr Romano had leaped to the boy's side and was shaking his hand. "Ah, Mr Beaton," he cried, "I have wanted to see you. There is so much I must say."

"Y-yes," replied the boy with a startled air.

"Indeed – yes. You are taking over a very great responsibility. You, a musician, need not be told that. The talent – the genius – of Ellen Landini – it is something to guard, to watch over, to encourage. That is your duty in the name of Art. How does she behave with the pastries?"

"The – the what?" stammered the boy.

"The pastries? She has a wild passion for them. And it must be curbed. It is no easy matter, but she must be held back with a strong hand. Otherwise she will – she will expand – she will grow gross. And cigarettes. How many cigarettes do you permit her each day?"

"*I* permit her?" Beaton stared at Romano as at a madman. "Why – that's no affair of mine."

Romano looked toward high heaven.

"Ah – it is as I feared. You are too young to understand. Too young for this huge task. No affair of yours? My dear sir, in that case she is lost. She will smoke her voice into eternal silence. She will wreck her great career for ever—"

He was interrupted by a commotion at the head of the stairs, and Ellen Landini began to descend. The long stairway against one side of the room afforded her an excellent entrance. Of this she was not unaware; indeed, she had just sent her companion back on a trivial errand in order that she might have the stage to herself. Which of itself was a good description of Ellen Landini, once young and lovely and innocent, but now a bit too plump, a bit too blonde, and a bit too wise in the tricks of the trade.

She had decided on a dramatic entrance, and such was the one she made, holding in her arms a small Boston terrier who looked world-weary and old. Dudley Ward awaited her at the foot of the stairs; she saw him and him alone.

"Welcome home, Ellen," he said.

"Dudley," she cried. "Dear old Dudley, after all these years. But" – she held aloft the dog – "but poor Trouble—"

"Trouble?" repeated Ward, puzzled.

"Yes – that's his name – but you don't know. You wouldn't. From the baby in *Madame Butterfly*. My baby – my sweet poor baby – he's having a chill. I knew I shouldn't bring him – it's bitter cold on the lake – it always was on this lake. Where's Sing? Call Sing at once." The old man appeared on the stairs behind her. "Oh, Sing – take Trouble to the kitchen and give him some hot milk. Make him drink it."

"My take 'um," replied Sing with a bored look.

Landini followed him with many admonitions. A young girl in a smart dinner gown had come unostentatiously down the stairs, and Ward was greeting her. He turned to the others.

"This is Miss Leslie Beaton," he said. "I'm sure we're all happy to have her here—"

But Landini was back in the room, overflowing personality and energy and charm. "Darling old Sing," she cried. "The same as ever. I've thought of him so often. He was always—" She stopped suddenly, as her eyes moved unbelievingly about the little group.

Dudley Ward permitted himself a delighted smile. "I think, Ellen," he said, "you already know these gentlemen."

She wanted a moment, obviously, to get her breath, and she found it when her glance fell on Charlie Chan. "Not – not all of them," she said.

"Oh, yes – pardon me," Ward answered. "May I present Inspector Charlie Chan, of the Honolulu Police? On vacation, I should add."

Charlie stepped forward and bowed low over her hand. "Overcome," he murmured.

"Inspector Chan," she said. "I've heard of you."

"It would be tarnishing the lily with gilt," Charlie assured her, "to remark I have heard of you. Speaking further on the subject I once, with great difficulty, heard you sing."

"With – great difficulty?"

"Yes – you may recall. The night you stopped over for a concert in your home city, Honolulu. At the Royal Hawaiian Opera House – and they had but recently applied to it the new tin roof—"

The great Landini clapped her hands and laughed. "And it rained!" she cried. "I should say I do remember! It was my only night – the boat was leaving at twelve – and so I sang – and sang. There in that boiler-factory – or so it seemed – with the downpour on the tin above. What a concert! But that was – some years – ago."

"I was impressed at the time by your extreme youthfulness," Charlie remarked.

She gave him a ravishing smile. "I shall sing again for you some day," she said. "And it will not be raining then."

Her poise regained, sure of herself now, she turned to the odd party into which Dudley Ward had brought her. "What fun," she cried. "What wonderful fun! All my dear ones gathered together. John – looking as stern as ever – Frederic – I miss the reflector on your forehead. I always think of you wearing that. And Luis – you here – of all people—"

Mr Romano stepped forward with his usual promptness. "Yes, you may bet I am here," he replied, his eyes flashing. "I, of all people, and of all people I will be present at a good many places to which you travel in the future – unless your memory speedily improves. Must I recall to you an arrangement made in New York—"

"Luis – not here!" She stamped her foot.

"No, perhaps not here. But somewhere – soon – depend on that. Look at your shoes!"

"What is wrong with my shoes?"

"Wet! Soaking wet!" He turned hotly on young Beaton. "Are there, then, no rubbers in the world? Is the supply of arctics exhausted? I told you – you do not understand your job. You let her walk about in the snow in her evening slippers. What sort of husband is that for Ellen Landini—"

"Oh, do be quiet, Luis," Landini cried. "You were always so tiresome – a nurse. Do you think I want a nurse? I do not – and that is what I like about Hugh." She stepped toward the boy, who appeared to draw back a bit. "Hugh is more interested in romance than in arctics – aren't you, my dear?"

She ran her fingers affectionately through the young man's black hair, a theatrical gesture that was a bit upsetting to all who saw it. Dudley Ward, looking hastily away, caught on the face of Hugh Beaton's sister an expression of such bitter disgust that he sought to divert the girl's attention.

"Your first visit west, Miss Beaton?" he inquired.

"My very first," she answered. "I love it, too. All except—"

"Reno."

"Naturally – I don't like that. The place sort of puts a blight on one's outlook – don't you think? What price romance – after seeing Reno?"

"Pity you feel that way," Ward said. He looked at her admiringly. Hugh Beaton's sister was even prettier than he was. But there was a worried look about her brown eyes; the lips that should be always laughing were drawn and tired.

"Dudley – it's marvelous to be back here." Landini was drawing him again into the general conversation. "It's just as well you invited me, because I was coming anyway. Several times I've been on the point of descending on you."

"I should have been charmed," Ward replied.

"And surprised," she laughed, "because I mean that literally – descending on you. You see, I've flown over you often, and seen that flying field you've had cleared behind the house."

"Oh, yes," Ward nodded. "So many of my friends have planes – and I like to fly a bit myself."

"My pilot told me he'd land any time," Landini continued. "But somehow – the hour never seemed right – too late – too early – or we had to hurry back."

"You enjoy flying, I hear?" It was Doctor Swan who spoke, and there was an expression on his face that mingled malice and contempt.

"Oh – I adore it! It's the biggest thrill in the world. It's living – at last. Especially here, above the snow-capped mountains, and these marvelous lakes. And I've found such a wonder of a pilot—"

"So I've been told," Swan answered. "But as I recall, you found him some years ago—"

Landini walked quickly to where John Ryder was standing, as far apart from the others as he could get.

"John," she said, "I'm so happy to see you again. You're looking well."

"Unfortunately," Ryder said, "I'm looking better than I feel. Dudley, I'm afraid I shall have to be excused. Good night." He bowed to the room in general, and went hastily up the stairs.

Ellen Landini shrugged her generous shoulders and laughed. "Poor John," she said. "Always he took life so seriously. What is to be gained by that? But we are what we are – we cannot change—"

"Ellen," said Dudley Ward, "you enjoy seeing the old place again?"

"I adore it," she sparkled. "I'm simply wild with joy."

He looked at her in amazement – still sparkling, after all these years. Not since she came in had she let down for a minute. He thought back to the days of their marriage. It had been one of the things that had driven him mad. "Every day is Christmas with Landini," he had once complained to himself.

"Then perhaps you'd like to take a tour about," Ward continued. "There are a few changes – I'd like to show them to you. If my guests will be so very good as to excuse me."

There was a polite murmur, and Dinsdale raised his glass. "These highballs of yours, Dudley, excuse anything," he laughed.

"Good," smiled Ward. "Ellen, I want you to see the old study, I've just had it done over by a decorator. Probably all wrong. And as we can't afford any scandal, I'm taking along a chaperon. Inspector Chan – will you join us?"

"With great pleasure," smiled Charlie. "Everybody knows policeman always on hand when least needed."

Ellen Landini laughed with the others, but there was a deeply puzzled look in her blue eyes. Dinsdale came forward, looking at his watch.

"Just to remind you, Ellen," he said. "You'll have to be starting soon if you're to be back in Reno by midnight."

"What time is it, Jim?"

"It's twenty-five minutes to ten."

"I'm starting at ten, and I'll be back in Reno before eleven."

He shook his head. "Not tonight – over these roads," he said.

"Tonight," she laughed. "But not over these roads. Not for little Ellen."

Hugh Beaton looked up. "Ellen – what are you talking about?" he asked.

She gave him a loving glance. "Now, be a good boy. You and Leslie go back by car from the Tavern. It's a nasty old car, and you're liable to have a few blowouts just as we did coming over, but that won't matter to you. However, I must make better time. I had an inspiration when Dudley here called up and invited me to drop in on him. I telephoned to Reno for my favorite plane and pilot, and they'll be here at ten. Won't it be glorious? There's a gorgeous moon – I'm simply thrilled to death." She turned to Ward. "Michael told me you have lights on the field?"

Ward nodded. "Yes. I'll turn them on presently. Everything's in order – that's a grand idea of yours. But then – your ideas always were."

Romano, who had been talking violently with Hugh Beaton in a corner, rose quickly. "I will go to my room," he announced, "and I will make for you a list. The things she must do, and the things she must not do. It will be useful—"

"Oh, please don't trouble," Beaton protested.

"It is my duty," Romano said sternly.

Ward stood aside, and let his guests precede him up the stairs. Romano walked close to Landini's side, and as they came into the upper hall, he swung on her. "Where is my money?" he demanded.

"Luis – I don't know – oh, hasn't it been sent?"

"You know very well it has not been sent. How am I to live—"

"But, Luis, – there has been trouble – my investments – oh, please, please don't bother me now."

"I suggest, Mr Romano," Ward said, "that you comply with Madame Landini's wishes. This, I believe, is the door of your room."

"As you say," shrugged Romano. "But, Ellen, I have not finished. There must be an understanding before we part."

He disappeared, and the three others went into the study in front. Ward flashed on the floor lamps, and Landini dropped into the chair beside the desk. Both men saw that her face was suddenly drawn and haggard, all the vivacity gone. Then she *did* let down at times. It was not always Christmas, it was sometimes the morning after.

"Oh, the little beast," she cried. "I hate him. Dudley, you can see what my life has been – lived in a whirlwind, excitement, madness, filled all the time with noisy nothings. I'm so tired – so deathly tired. If only I could find peace—"

Charlie Chan saw that Ward's face was filled with genuine tenderness and pity. "I know, my dear," said the host, as he closed the door. "But peace was never for you – we knew that in the old days. It had to be the limelit highway – the bright parade. Come – pull yourself together." He offered her one of the colored boxes on the desk. "Have a cigarette. Or perhaps you prefer this other brand." He reached for the companion box.

She took one from the latter, and lighted it. "Dudley," she said, "coming here has taken me back to my girlhood. It has touched me deeply—" She looked toward Charlie Chan.

A sudden hardness came into Ward's eyes. "Sorry," he said. "Mr Chan stays. I was wondering why you accepted my invitation tonight. I see now – it was to pull this airplane stunt. The spectacular thing – the thing you would do. Has it occurred to you to wonder – why I invited you?"

"Why – I thought, of course – after all, you did love me once. I thought you would like to see me again. But when I saw John, and Frederic, and Luis – I was puzzled—"

"Naturally. I invited you, Ellen, because I wanted you to realize that I am in touch with your various husbands. I wanted you, also, to meet Inspector Charlie Chan who, as you know, is a detective. Inspector Chan and I have begun tonight an investigation which may take us many weeks – or which may end here and now. You have it in your power to end it. Ellen, I have no bitterness, no ill will for you at this late day. I have thought it over so long – perhaps I was wrong from the first. But I have brought you to Pineview to ask you, simply – where is my son?"

Charlie Chan, watching, reflected that here was either a great actress or a much maligned woman. Her expression did not change. "What son?" she asked.

Ward shrugged his shoulders. "Very well," he said. "We won't go any further with it."

"Oh, yes, we will," said Ellen Landini. "Dudley – don't be a fool. Someone has told you a lie, evidently. Don't you know they've been lying about me for years? I've got so I don't mind – but if you've heard something that's made you unhappy – that's sending you off on a wild-goose chase – well, I'd like to stop that, if I can. If you'll only tell me—"

"No matter," said Ward. "What's the use?"

"If you take that tone," she replied, "it's hopeless." She was surprisingly cool and calm. "By the way – hadn't you better turn on the lights on the field? And I should like a small blanket for Trouble – he'll need it, in addition to the robes in the plane. I'll send it back to you. He'll go with me, of course. He loves it."

"Very well," nodded Ward. "I'll see about it, and then I'll get down to those lights." He went to the door. "Cecile," he called. "Oh, Sing – send Cecile to me, please."

He stepped back into the room. "Cecile?" said Ellen Landini.

"Yes," Ward said. "An old servant of yours, I believe. The wife of your wonder pilot. You didn't know she was here?"

Landini lighted another cigarette. "I did not. But I might have guessed it these last few minutes. A liar, Dudley, always, with a temper like the devil. She stole from me, too, but naturally, one expects that. But the truth was not in her. I don't know what cock-and-bull story she has told you, but whatever it is—"

"What makes you think it was she who told me?"

"I have discovered that a lie has been told in this house, Dudley, and now I discover Cecile is here. It's effect and cause, my dear."

"You wanted me, sir?" The Frenchwoman at the door was about thirty, with lovely eyes, but an unhappy and discontented face. For a long moment she stared at Landini. "Ah, Madame," she murmured.

"How are you, Cecile?" the singer asked.

"I am well, thank you." She turned to Ward, inquiringly.

"Cecile," said her employer, "please go and get Madame Landini a small blanket of some sort – something suitable to wrap about a dog."

"A dog?" The eyes of the Frenchwoman narrowed. There was a moment's silence, and in the quiet they all heard, suddenly, a far-off but unmistakable sound – the droning of an airplane. Ward flung open the French windows that led on to a balcony, which was in reality the roof of the front veranda. The others crowded about him, and in the moonlit sky, far out over the lake, they saw the approaching plane.

"Ah, yes," cried Cecile, "I understand. Madame returns to Reno by air."

"Is that any affair of yours?" Landini asked coldly.

"It happens to be, Madame," the woman answered.

"Will you get that blanket?" Ward demanded.

Without a word, the Frenchwoman went out. Ward looked at his watch.

"Your pilot's ahead of time," he said. "I must hurry out to those lights—"

"Dudley – would you do something—" Landini cried.

"Too late. When the plane has landed—"

He hastened out. The singer turned to Charlie.

"Tell me," she said. "Do you know which is Mr Ryder's room?"

Charlie bowed. "I think I do."

"Then please go to him. Send him here at once. Tell him I must see him – he must come – don't take no for an answer! Tell him – it's life and death!"

She fairly pushed the detective from the room. He hurried down the hall and knocked on the door of the room into which he had seen Ryder ushered before dinner. Without awaiting an answer, he opened it and entered. Ryder was seated reading a book beside a floor lamp.

"So sorry," Charlie remarked. "The intrusion is objectionable, I realize. But Madame Landini—"

"What about Madame Landini?" asked Ryder grimly.

"She must see you at once – in the study at the front. She demands this wildly. It is, she tells me, life and death."

Ryder shrugged. "Rot! There is nothing to be said between us. She knows that."

"But—"

"Yes – life and death – I know. Don't be fooled by her theatrics. She was always that way. Kindly tell her I refuse to see her."

Chan hesitated. Ryder got up and led him to the door. "Tell her that under no circumstances will I ever see her again."

Charlie found himself in the hall, with Ryder's door closed behind him. When he got back to the study, Landini was seated at the desk, writing madly.

"I am so sorry—" the detective began.

She looked up. "He won't see me? I expected it. No matter, Mr Chan. I have thought of another way. Thanks."

Chan turned, and went down the hall toward the head of the stairs. As he passed the open door of Romano's room he saw the conductor, walking anxiously up and down. Ryder's door remained closed. The noise of the plane was momentarily growing louder.

In the living-room Dinsdale and Hugh Beaton were alone, evidently vastly uninterested in the spectacular approach of Landini's pilot. Charlie was not so callous and, stepping out the front door, he crossed the porch and walked a short distance down the path to the pier. He was staring up at the lights of the plane, when someone approached from the direction of the water. It was Doctor Swan.

"Went out on the pier to see it better," Swan said. "A beautiful sight, on a night like this. Wish I could go back in it myself." The aviator was turning in toward the house.

"Shall we find the landing field?" Charlie suggested.

"Not for me," Swan shivered. "It's somewhere at the back, God knows where. I'm going to get my things – I want to start for the Tavern as soon as Ellen has made her grand exit." He ran up the steps to the house.

Michael Ireland, it appeared, was planning a few stunts. Despite the tallness of the pines, he swept down on the house, dangerously near. Hurrying through the snow to the rear, Charlie was conscious that the plane was circling about above the roof of Pineview. Aviators never could resist the spectacular. Presently Chan came upon a cleared place, flooded with lights, and there, when the pilot had completed his exhibition, he finally brought the plane down, in a skilful landing.

"Pretty work," cried a voice at Chan's elbow. It was Dudley Ward. "By gad, that lad knows how to drive his old two-seater."

He hurried out to meet Ireland on the field, and led him back to where Charlie stood. All three went up the narrow path to the back door, and entered a long passage that led to the front of the house. As they passed the open door of the kitchen Chan saw a large woman, evidently the cook. With her was Landini's dog, whining and still shivering from its chill. Ward led on to the living-room.

"Nice night for it," he was saying to Ireland, a husky red-cheeked man of thirty or so. "I envy you – the way you brought her down." Dinsdale and Beaton rose to greet them, and the aviator, pulling off a huge glove, shook hands all round. "Sit down a minute," Ward continued. "You'll want a drink before you start back."

"Thank you, sir," Ireland replied. "And maybe I'd better be havin' a word with my wife—"

Ward nodded. "I fancy you had," he smiled. "I'll arrange that. But first of all – what will it be? A highball?"

"Sounds good to me," Ireland answered. He looked a bit apprehensive and ill at ease. "Not too much, Mr Ward, please—"

Ryder appeared on the stairs, lighting a cigarette. Half-way down, he paused. "Has Landini gone?" he inquired.

"Come along, John," Ward said genially. "Just in time for another little drink. Is that right for you, Ireland?"

"Just, thank you," the aviator replied.

From somewhere upstairs came a sharp report that sounded unpleasantly like the firing of a pistol.

"What was that?" asked Ryder, now at the foot of the stairs.

Ward set down the bottle he was holding and looked toward Charlie Chan. "I wonder," he said.

Charlie did not pause to wonder. Pushing Ryder aside, he ran up the stairs. He was conscious of figures in the upper hall as he passed, figures he did not pause to identify. Chinese, he had always contended, were psychic people, but he did not have to be particularly psychic on this occasion to know which door to seek. It was closed. He pushed it open.

The lights in the study were out, but for a first glance the moonlight sufficed. Landini was lying just inside the French windows that led on to the balcony. Charlie leaped across her and peered out the open window. He saw no one.

Black shapes crowded the doorway. "Turn on the lights," Charlie said. "And do not come too close, please."

The lights flashed on, and Dudley Ward pushed forward. "Ellen!" he cried. "What's happened here—"

Chan intercepted him and laid his hand on the host's arm. Beyond Ward he saw frightened faces – Romano, Swan, Beaton, Dinsdale, Ireland, Cecile. "You are psychic, Mr Ward," Charlie said gravely. "All same Chinese race. Three days before the crime, you summon detective."

"Crime!" repeated Ward. He sought to kneel beside the singer, but again Chan restrained him.

"Permit me, please," the Chinese continued. "For you, it means pain. For me, alas, a customary duty." With some difficulty, he knelt upon the floor, and placed his fingers gently on Landini's wrist.

"Doctor Swan is here," Ward said. "Perhaps – can nothing be done?"

Chan struggled back to his feet. "Can the fallen flower return to the branch again?" he asked softly.

Ward turned quickly away, and there was silence in the room. Charlie stood for a moment, staring down at the body. Landini lay on her back; those evening shoes whose dampness had so distressed Romano were but a few inches away from the threshold of the open windows. In her dead hands was loosely held a chiffon scarf, bright pink in color, contrasting oddly with her green gown. And just inside the windows, close to her feet, lay a dainty, snub-nosed revolver.

Charlie removed his handkerchief from his pocket and stooping over, picked up the weapon. It was still warm, he noted through the handkerchief. One cartridge had been fired. He carried it over and deposited it on the desk.

There for a long moment he stood staring, behind him the murmur of many voices. He appeared to be lost in thought, and indeed he was. For an odd thing had suddenly occurred to him. When he had last seen Landini sitting at this desk, the two boxes containing cigarettes had been close at her elbow, both open. Now they had been restored to their places, farther back on the desk. But on the crimson box rested the yellow lid – and on the yellow box, the crimson.

IV

UPWARD NO ROAD

As Charlie stood, silently regarding those boxes whose lids had become so strangely confused, he was conscious that some newcomer had pushed his way into the room. He swung around and beheld the shrunken figure of Ah Sing. The old Chinese held a blue bundle under his arm, which he now proffered to the room at large.

"Blanket," he announced, his high shrill voice sounding oddly out of place at that moment. "Blanket fo' lil dog."

Chan watched him closely as his beady eyes fell on the silent figure by the window. "Wha's mallah heah?" the old man inquired. His expression did not change.

"You can see what's the matter," Charlie replied sharply. "Madame Landini has been murdered."

The dim old eyes turned to Chan with what was almost a look of insolence. "P'liceman him come," he muttered complainingly. "Then woik fo' p'liceman him come plitty soon too." He glanced at Ward accusingly. "What my tell you, Boss? You clazy invite p'liceman heah. Mebbe some day you lissen to Ah Sing."

Somewhat nettled, Chan pointed to the blanket. "What are you doing with that? Who asked you to bring it?"

"Missie ask me," the old man nodded toward the figure on the floor. "Missie say she send Cecile fo' blanket, no catch 'um. She say, Sing, you catch 'um like goo' boy."

"When was this?"

"Mebbe half past nine, between ten."

"Where was the airplane at that time? Over the house?"

"Not ovah house no moah. Mebbe on field."

"I see," Chan nodded. "The blanket is no longer required. Take it away."

"Allight, p'liceman," nodded the old man, and did so.

Charlie turned back and addressed Dinsdale. "I have really no authority in this place," he remarked. "Those who are out of office should not meddle with the government. There is, I presume, a sheriff?"

"By gad, yes," Dinsdale said. "Young Don Holt – this will be a whale of a job for him. He was elected less than a year ago. His dad, old Sam Holt, has been sheriff of this county for fifty years, but he went blind a while back, and as a sort of tribute to him, they put up young Don. He'll be a puzzled kid over this. Horses are his specialty."

"Does it chance that he lives near by?" Charlie inquired.

"He lives down at the county-seat," Dinsdale answered, "but he has charge of the riding stables at the Tavern during the summer, and it happens he's over there tonight. I'll get him on the telephone, and he can reach here inside of twenty minutes by boat."

"If you will be so good," Charlie said, and Dinsdale went quickly out.

For a moment Charlie stared at the varied group gathered in that little room. How unfortunate, he reflected, that he could not have announced this killing to them suddenly, and watched their faces at the news. But alas, they had come upon him in the dark, they had known of the tragedy almost as soon as he, and whatever their reception of this knowledge, he was never to learn it now.

Nevertheless, their faces were an interesting study. That of Romano, the emotional, was pale and drawn, and there were tears in his brown eyes. Doctor Swan's was taut and excited. Dudley Ward had dropped into a chair beside the fire, and was shading his eyes with his hand. Beaton and his sister stood as far from the body as possible, the girl was crying, and the young man comforted her. The look on the face of Cecile was a mixture of fright and sullenness, while Michael's expression was dazed and puzzled, bespeaking an honest but somewhat stupid simplicity. As for John Ryder, his blue eyes were cold as usual, and they looked at the woman who had once been his wife with no sign of pity or regret.

"I think it much better," Chan said, "if you all returned to living-room below. You understand, naturally, sad state of affairs which makes it necessary you do not take departure now."

"But I've got to get back to Reno," Swan cried.

Charlie shrugged. "You must not place blame on me. Place it on guilty shoulders of one who fired this recent shot."

Dinsdale returned. "I got hold of the sheriff," he announced. "He's on his way."

"Thank you so much," Charlie said. "Mr Dinsdale, you will remain here with Mr Ward and myself, but I am inviting the others downstairs. Before you go," he added, as they started to file out, "I must inquire – though there is no stern necessity to answer, for I am stranger here myself – has anyone of you seen this before?" He lifted the snub-nosed revolver from the desk, and held it high in the handkerchief.

"I have," said Dinsdale promptly. "I saw it once before, only tonight."

"Where was that?" Charlie asked.

"At the Tavern," the hotel man continued. "Ellen Landini and I were engaged in a small financial transaction, and that revolver fell from her bag when she opened it. I picked it up, and handed it back—"

"Quite true," nodded Luis Romano, coming close and staring at the weapon. "It is Ellen's property. Some years ago there was an attempt to hold her up in a hotel room, and always since she has insisted on carrying that with her. I pleaded with her – I did not approve – and now she has been killed with her own revolver."

"Others, then, must have known she carried it," mused Chan. "Mr Beaton?"

The young man nodded. "Yes – I've seen it many times. It's hers, all right."

Suddenly, Charlie swung on the girl at Beaton's side. "And you, Miss Beaton?"

She shrank away from him as he held the weapon close. "Yes – yes – I've seen it too."

"You have known it was always in Madame Landini's bag?"

"I have known it – yes."

"For how long?"

"Ever since I met her – a week ago."

Chan's voice softened to its customary tone. "What a pity," he said. "You are trembling. It is too cold for you here, with these windows open." He restored the revolver to the desk. "You should have a scarf," he continued. "A pretty pink scarf to match that gown of yours."

"I – I have," she said. She was on her way toward the door.

"This one, perhaps," Charlie cried. He stepped to the side of the dead woman and lifted one corner of the chiffon scarf that lay in her lifeless hands. "This, perhaps, belongs to you," he continued. The girl's eyes had followed him, fascinated, and now her scream rang out sharply in the room. Her brother put his arm about her.

"My scarf," she cried. "What is it doing – there?"

Chan's eyebrows rose. "You had not noticed it before?"

"No – no, I hadn't. It was dark when I came in here – and after the lights went on – I never really looked in this direction."

"You never really looked," Chan went on thoughtfully. He dropped the corner of the scarf and rose. His eyes strayed to the boxes on the table. "I am so sorry – I cannot return your property just at this moment. Later, perhaps – when the sheriff of the county has beheld it – in a dead woman's hands. You will all go now – thank you so much."

When the last one had left, he closed the door and turned to Dinsdale and Ward. The latter had risen, and was anxiously pacing the floor.

"Confound it, Inspector," he cried. "That young woman is my guest. You don't for a moment think—" He paused.

"I think," said Chan slowly, "that one of your guests has tonight stooped to murder."

"Evidently. But a woman – a charming girl—"

Chan shrugged. "There is no such poison in the green snake's mouth as in a woman's heart."

"I don't know who said that first," Ward replied, "but I don't agree with him. No – not even after all that has – that I've been through." He stood for a moment, staring down at the dead woman on the floor. "Poor Ellen – she deserved better than this. I'll never forgive myself for inviting her over here. But I thought we might induce her to tell—" He stopped. "By heaven – I hadn't thought of it until now. Shall we ever find the truth about my boy – after this? Ellen was our best chance – perhaps, in the final analysis, our only one." He stared hopelessly at Charlie.

"Do not despair." Charlie patted his shoulder pityingly. "We will persevere – and we will succeed, I am sure. This event may really speed our search – for among the papers and effects of this lady we may find our answer. However, matter of even fiercer importance now intrudes itself. Who killed Ellen Landini?"

"What's your guess, Mr Chan?" Dinsdale inquired.

Charlie smiled. "Guessing is cheap, but wrong guess expensive. I cannot afford it, myself."

"Well, I'm a spendthrift. Sleuth all you like, but I can tell you now Romano killed her."

"You have evidence, perhaps—"

"The evidence of my eyes – I noticed he was sore at her about something. Money, I imagine. He's Latin, excitable—"

Charlie shook his head. "Ah, yes. But Latins do not become so excitable they forget where financial advantage lies. Landini alive was worth money to him, but with Landini dead – unless – unless—"

"Unless what?"

"No matter. We will look into that later. There is long torturous path to climb, and the wise man starts slowly, conserving his strength for a swift finish. By the way, you spoke of moment at Tavern tonight when Landini opened bag to pay you money?"

"Yes, so I did," Dinsdale replied. "I meant to explain it. Last week I called on Ellen in Reno to invite her over to the Tavern for dinner. While I was there, a C.O.D. package arrived – there was the usual wild hunt for cash, which ended in her borrowing twenty dollars from me. Tonight she insisted on repaying it – and that was when the revolver dropped out of her bag."

"She did repay it?"

"Yes, with a brand-new bill which she peeled from a great roll of them in her purse."

"Odd," Charlie said. "There are no bills in her purse now."

"Good lord," cried Ward. "Not only a murderer but a petty thief. I'm afraid I've carried hospitality too far."

"What did I tell you?" the hotel man said. "Romano."

Charlie rose. "When I came to mainland," he remarked, "I was engaged deep in puzzling case. Remnant of that effort, I have in my baggage lampblack and camel's-hair brush. Same are useful in matter of fingerprints, and while we await the sheriff, I may as well obtain them."

He went to his room. While he searched his luggage for the tools of his trade, he heard the sound of footsteps ascending the stairs. Presently he found what he was looking for, and returned to the study. A tall, black-haired young westerner in riding boots, breeches and leather coat was standing in the center of the room.

"Inspector Chan," said Dinsdale, "meet Don Holt."

"Hello, Inspector," the young man cried, and seized the hand of the Chinese in a grip that almost lifted him from the floor. "Pleased to meet you – and I'm telling you I never meant that so heartfelt before in all my born days."

"You have grasped situation?" inquired Charlie. He set down his burden and caressed his right hand with his left, seeking to restore the circulation.

"Well – in a way – at least I've gathered there is a situation. Coroner lives over to the county-seat, so he won't be able to see this lady till tomorrow. But I got a Tahoe doctor on the way to make a preliminary examination, and after that I guess we can move her down to town – what town there is. So far – am I right?"

"So far you appear to act with most commendable speed," Chan assured him.

"I know, but this is my first case of this – this sort of thing, and I can assure you, Inspector, I'm trembling all over like a roped yearling. Mr Ward was just telling me you was here, on a visit to him. He says he's got a little job for you, but it can wait while you give the county and me a helping hand. How's that sound to you?"

Charlie looked at Ward. "We are, of course, very lucky to be able to enlist the inspector's services," his host remarked. "My affair can wait."

"In which case," Charlie said, "my very slight talents are yours to command, Mr Holt."

"Fine," Holt answered. "I could speak a couple of volumes on the way that makes me feel, but action, not words, is my specialty. Let's get down to brass tacks. What happened here tonight, anyhow? Who was all them people downstairs? Where do we start, and how soon?"

They all looked at Charlie, and patiently he went over the events of the evening, up to the firing of the shot and the discovery of Landini's dead body. The young man nodded.

"I get you. At the time the shot was fired, who was unaccounted for?"

"Quite a number," Charlie told him. "Of the guests, Miss Leslie Beaton, whose scarf, oddly enough, is clutched in dead woman's hands. Also, Dr Frederic Swan and Mr Luis Romano. Of the servants, Cecile and – er – Ah Sing."

"Five of 'em," commented the sheriff. "Well, it could of been worse. It really is only four, because I've known Ah Sing since I was ten inches tall, and he wouldn't—"

"Pardon," said Chan.

Mr Holt laughed. "I know," he said. "That's no way for a sheriff to act. Getting ideas all set in advance – anything can happen, at that. Well, that's lesson number one. Just deal 'em out to me as we go along. And now, Inspector, you just go ahead and solve this case, and don't pay any attention to me."

"Ah, but I must pay attention to you. You are constituted authority in this place, and everything I do must be done with your approval and permission."

"Granted in advance," nodded Holt. "What I want is results, and I guess you can get 'em. You see, I got a sort of family reputation to uphold—"

Chan nodded. "Yes – I have heard of your honorable father. Maybe we also call him in. It has well been said – in time of severe illness summon three doctors. One might be good."

"Dad *was* good," the young man replied softly. "But he's blind now."

"A terrible pity," Charlie said. "But even a blind man, if he has been over the road before, may point out the way. Just now, however, you and I are in charge. You have spoken of lesson number one. May I, with all humility, now proffer the second lesson?"

"Shoot," said Holt.

"It has been my good fortune to know famous detectives, some from Scotland Yard. All these say, in case of homicide, first duty of detective is to examine position of body as it fell. What does that examination suggest to you?"

The boy considered. "I should say – well, she may have been shot from the balcony. Or at least by someone standing in the window."

"Precisely. The body is well arranged to present that effect. Let us now examine the room. Kindly come and view this desk. You observe upon it fine particles of – what?"

"Tobacco," Holt answered.

"Correct. Very fine tobacco, such as is contained in cigarettes. Observe these two boxes, in which cigarettes of two brands are kept. What strikes you?"

"Somebody got twisted and put the wrong lids on them."

"So it would seem," Chan nodded. "Somebody was in very great hurry, no doubt. The time for escape was brief, for the shot was heard instantly below. We will open boxes." He did so, using his handkerchief, which he pulled from under the weapon. "Behold. Cigarettes are not piled in neat order, but are in unsettled state. They were tossed back hurriedly. What shall we say to that? Was there a struggle at this desk? When last I saw Madame Landini she was seated here. Was the struggle here, and was she then dragged to window in hope to make it appear killing was done from balcony? Why else should there be this frantic effort to tidy desk? The time was brief, but there was just enough, perhaps – though great haste was needed, so great that wrong lids got on to boxes. The killer could have so performed, then fled through open window and escaped into another room that opens on balcony. I should have examined those rooms at once – it may be killer lurked there until all were crowded into this study, then moved away – perhaps crowded into study himself. You will perceive that your new assistant has sinking spells of stupidity."

"Ain't we all?" grinned Holt. "What you say's mighty interesting. I take it you think, then, that the lady was shot by someone who was with her in this room, and not from the balcony?"

Chan shrugged. "I am merely putting facts on parade. I find it wise not to draw conclusions too rapidly. We get answer too quick, we may be wrong, like my children who labor with algebra. I leave it open for present. Lady may, in spite of all I say, have been shot from balcony. She may even have been shot on balcony, and taken step back into room before falling. Perhaps doctor can tell us that. We will now travel to balcony, if you please."

All four stepped through the windows, past the dead Landini, and came into the bracing night air. The lake lay calm and chill under the full moon; the stars here were dim and remote, Chan noted, lacking the friendliness of those in the Hawaiian sky. Charlie took a deep breath.

"I regret there is no snow here," he said to Ward.

"Unfortunately, no," his host replied. "I had this balcony cleared off when we first came, and Sing has kept it swept and garnished ever since. Otherwise the snow piles against the windows and chills the rooms."

Charlie shrugged. "After many years I encounter snow, and the clue of the footstep is denied me. Such, I presume, is life." He examined the scene. "Two other rooms, I perceive, open on this veranda. This one is—"

"That," said Ward slowly, "is the room Landini used to have as a sitting-room. I have kept it – just as she left it."

Charlie tried the window. "Locked from the inside, of course. Naturally, if killer went that way, he – or she – would attend to that. We will study threshold in the morning." He led the way to the windows on the opposite side of the study. "And this room?" he inquired.

"It's my bedroom," Ward told him. "I believe Sing showed the ladies here with their wraps." He peered through the window into the room, where a dim light was burning. "Yes – there are coats on the bed—"

"And a woman's scarf," added Chan, at his side. "A green scarf. The one Landini should have been clutching in her hands. Her own."

Ward nodded. "I suppose so." Chan tried this window with the same result as before, and they returned to the study.

"Next step," said Chan to the sheriff, "fingerprints. Matter about which we hear so much, and from which we get so little."

"Oh, lord, I suppose so," the young man answered. "I've got a homicide squad, but he's sick in bed. Fingerprints are in his department – I wonder if he knows it. My Dad never took a fingerprint in his life."

"Ah, but we are more unfortunate – we live in age of science," Charlie smiled. "Great marvels happen all times, and world gets less human by minute. Sorry to say I possess utensils to get scientific here and now. I will proceed to examine fatal pistol and discover not a print on it. The suspense will be terrible. Humbly suggest you ease your mind by careful study of room."

He sat down at the desk and busied himself with his lampblack and brush. Don Holt began a careful survey of the room, as suggested. Dudley Ward picked up a log, and was about to place it on the fire, when a cry from Chan startled him.

"Please," Charlie called, "just a moment, if you will be so good."

"Why – er – what—" Ward was puzzled.

"The log, pardon me. Not just now," Chan explained.

Ward nodded and put the log back in the basket. Presently Charlie stood up.

"Suspense now over," he announced. "No print on pistol anywhere. Gloves, held in handkerchief, wiped clean – take your honorable choice. Something more suggestive, though – there are also no marks on lids of pretty colored boxes. I think we may go below—"

Holt approached him, holding out his great hand. In it Chan beheld a cheap little gold pin, with semi-precious stones.

"Ah – you make discovery," Charlie said.

"Bedded deep in the carpet," the sheriff explained. "Somebody stepped on it, I guess."

"Plenty ladies around here," Charlie remarked. "That was not Landini's – we know that much. It has not the rich look of prima-donna jewelry. Let us carry it below – and I suggest that you now remove pink scarf, so we may take that also. But one thing remains to be done here. Gentlemen – if you will do me the favor to await me one moment—"

He went briskly out, and walked part way down the stairs to a point where he had a clear view of the room below. The silent little party seated there looked up at him with interest. The detective's eye lighted on one who sat far from the others. "Mr Ryder," he said.

For a moment there was no reply. "Yes?" said Ryder finally.

"If you please – will you be so good as to return to the study?"

With annoying slowness, Ryder got to his feet. Chan waited patiently. When finally the bearded man reached him on the stairs, the Chinese bowed low. "You are quite right," he said. "He who hurries cannot walk with a stately step. Precede me, I beg of you."

They came again into the room where Landini lay. "I don't quite know," Ryder said, "why I should have the honor of a separate inquisition."

"You will yet learn," Chan assured him. "Have you met Mr Don Holt, sheriff of this county?"

"I've not had the pleasure," Ryder replied, shaking hands.

"Mr Ryder," Charlie began, "it is not my purpose to keep you here for long time. Before tragic passing of this lady, I visited your room with urgent message from her to you. A message which you belittled. You hurried me out, closing door almost against my back. And then—"

"Then – what?"

"Kindly detail your acts from that moment until lady's murder."

"A simple matter," Ryder said easily. "I sat down and resumed my reading. Shortly afterward I heard the airplane approaching. I went on reading. Then I heard it over the house."

"You went on reading?"

"Precisely. After a time, I thought the airplane must have landed. Ellen Landini, I decided, was leaving by plane. So – I went on reading."

"An interesting book," Charlie nodded. "But sooner or later – you put it down."

"Yes – I went to the door, opened it and listened. Everything was rather quiet – I couldn't hear Landini's voice – so I decided she must have gone out on the field. I went to the stairs—"

"One moment, please. From the time I left you, until I saw you again on the stairs, you did not visit any other part of house? This room, for example?"

"I did not."

"You are certain on that point?"

"Of course I am."

"Mr Holt," said Chan, stepping to the fireplace, "will you come here, please?" The sheriff did so. "Permit that I point out to you certain matters," Charlie continued. "We have here" – he took up the poker – "the completely consumed ashes of a letter, written, I may tell you, on paper similar to that on desk. And over here, in far corner, we have partly consumed envelope, burned but slightly at top. Will you be so kind as to rescue same?" Holt took it up in his fingers. "What would be address on envelope, Mr Sheriff?"

The young man examined it. "Why – it says: 'Mr John Ryder. Urgent. Private.' In a big bold hand – but it doesn't look like a man's writing, at that."

"Mr Ryder will tell you whose writing it is," Chan suggested.

Ryder glanced at it. "It is the writing," he said, "of Ellen Landini."

"Correct," cried Chan. "It was addressed to you as private and urgent. It was sealed. It was torn open, and the letter removed. Who would do that, Mr Ryder?"

"I'm sure I don't know," Ryder answered.

"Not many in this house," Chan continued. "No gentleman, surely – no lady. Such would not tear open the letter of another, marked private. No, it appears to me, Mr Ryder, there is only one person who could have opened that letter. Yourself."

Ryder stared at him coldly. "A natural inference, Mr Chan," he replied. "However, even if you were correct – and I can tell you at once that you're not – what of it? Surely you haven't forgotten that at the moment Landini was killed, I was standing at the foot of the stairs, in the living-room below."

Charlie turned to the sheriff. "You and I – we have long journey to take together," he remarked. "Often it will seem matter of upward, no road, downward, no door. But the man with a tongue in his head can always find the way. Let us go downstairs and exercise our tongues."

V

DOWNWARD NO DOOR

The five men descended to the living-room at once. A glance at the formidable company that awaited them there caused Charlie's heart to sink. He looked toward the sheriff. The young man nervously cleared his throat.

"This is sure too bad," he began. "It's going to be pretty unpleasant for all of us, I guess. I'm Don Holt, sheriff of the county, and I don't aim to cause no innocent person any unnecessary trouble. But I got to get to the bottom of this business, and the shorter the route, the better for all of us – well, most of us, anyhow. I've asked Inspector Chan, who's had more experience in this line than I have, to give me a hand here, an' I want to say right now, that when he asks, you answer. That's all, I reckon."

A diversion at the door interrupted the proceedings. Sing admitted a small gray-haired man with a black satchel, who proved to be the doctor from Tahoe Holt had mentioned. The young man took him aside for a brief talk, and then called to Sing, who led the newcomer upstairs.

"I guess we can get goin' now," said Holt, looking helplessly at Charlie.

Charlie nodded. "We begin with least important of the gathering," he announced. "When fatal shot was fired, terminating brilliant career of one who was much beloved, six men were present in this room. One of these, Mr Ryder, has already made statement. I would learn from remaining five all actions just before they met here, their conduct and locations, and when they last saw Landini. In this way, some light might be thrown. Since hour of the clock is uncertain, we can perhaps fix times by location of airplane over-head. I myself was one of these five. Answering my questions without asking same, I last saw Landini above in study while airplane was still over lake. She had requested I summon to her side Mr Ryder, and I reported back to her he refused to accede. She was then writing hurriedly at desk. I left her, came down here, and went outside, where I eventually met Mr Ward and Mr Ireland at edge of field." He turned to the aviator. "Mr Ireland, we can pass over you completely. You can scarcely be involved in this, or have any information of any sort."

The big Irishman nodded. "All I know is, Landini called me up to come and get her. And I came." He looked up, and his eyes met those of his wife. "I had to," he added. "That's my job. I'm workin' for others."

"Exactly," said Charlie. "Mr Ward – you last saw Landini —"

"You were with me, Inspector," Ward replied. "You remember I left the study to turn on the lights at the field, as soon as we saw the plane over the lake. The lights are worked from a small shed in back of the hangar. We keep it closed and locked. I had to get the keys, and the lock stuck – a bit rusty, I fancy. It was a hurry-up job, but I got them on in time."

Chan turned to Ireland. "When did lights blaze on?" he asked.

"It was while I was circling over the house, I think," the aviator said. "Thanks a lot," he added to Ward. "But it wouldn't have mattered if you hadn't made it – the moon was good enough."

"Leaving two of the five," Charlie persisted. "Mr Dinsdale and Mr Beaton. It is my impression that neither left this room during the evening, until after the shot was fired. Am I correct?"

"In my case, yes," Dinsdale said. "A good fire and a good drink – all the airplanes in the world landing in the back yard couldn't rout me out. Yes – I sat here, right from the time I came until we heard the shot and ran upstairs."

"And Mr Beaton was with you?"

"Well – not all the time—"

"No – no, I wasn't, that's true." Young Beaton stood up, fragile and pale and evidently very nervous. "You see – I went outside. You remember you went through the room, Mr Chan, and then we heard you talking with someone out there, and in a minute Doctor Swan came in. He said the airplane was a beautiful sight, or something like that, so I said I guessed I'd have a look at it too. I went out – it was just coming in from over the lake then. I stepped down on to the path, and suddenly I heard a voice up above me."

"Ah – you heard a voice," repeated Charlie with sudden interest.

"Yes – it – it was Ellen – I couldn't mistake that, of course. And I heard her say – she was calling to somebody, really – I heard her call: 'Oh, it's you, is it? I'm freezing – get me my scarf. It's on the bed in the next room. The green one.'"

Chan smiled with sudden understanding. "Ah – most interesting. You heard Miss Landini ask for her scarf?"

"Yes, yes," cried the boy eagerly. His manner was almost pathetically ingenuous. "It's true, Mr Chan. It really is. I know it sounds—"

"Let us not trouble how it sounds. Continue, please."

"I went a little farther along the path, and I saw Landini standing alone on the balcony just over the front door. She was looking up and waving her handkerchief. Then the airplane came down terribly close, and began to circle around the house. I started to cough and realized I didn't have my hat or overcoat – so I hurried inside. Anyhow – the picture sort of sickened me – Ellen standing there and waving like a mad woman—"

"That's O.K., Inspector," Dinsdale said. "He was out there only a few minutes."

"But long enough," shrugged Chan, "to hear Landini demand a scarf. Her green scarf. How much better, Mr Beaton, if you had not added that last."

The boy's face contorted. "But it's the truth," he cried. "I'm telling it to you just as it happened. Somebody came into that room, and she asked for her scarf. And – and—"

"And the person, intending murder and wishing to incriminate innocent girl, returned with your sister's scarf. You are asking me to believe that?"

"I'm not asking you to believe anything," the boy almost screamed. "I'm just telling you what happened. I'm just trying to help you – and you won't believe me – you won't believe me—"

"Never mind, Hughie." His sister got up and patted him on the back. "Please don't get so upset."

"It happened, I tell you."

"I know. I know."

"Thank you, my boy," Charlie said gently. "I have not said I do not believe you. As a matter of fact—" He paused, his eyes on the sheriff. Mr Holt was staring at Leslie Beaton with the most unsheriff-like look Chan ever remembered having seen in his long career. He sighed. A new complication, perhaps.

"As a matter of fact," Charlie continued, "this brings you, Mr Ireland, unexpectedly back into limelight. Though you had not yet arrived on the place, it must be that you, none the less, were one of the last people to see Landini alive."

Ireland shifted in his chair. "Maybe I was," he remarked. "It didn't strike me before. When I turned in over the house,

I looked down and seen some dame waving to me from the balcony. I dropped down to see who it was—"

"You knew well enough who it was," flashed his wife.

"How could I, dearie? I thought maybe it was you. So I got down as near as I dared, and I seen it was Landini—"

"So then you stunted around, risking your neck to give her a thrill—"

"Now, dearie, I just circled round a few times, to get my bearings and locate the field—"

"Did you, then, think the field was on the roof?" Cecile sneered.

Her husband shrugged. "I knew where it was, and I knew what I was doing. I don't need no back-seat drivers—"

"Pardon," Chan said. "How many times did you circle the house?"

"Three times."

"And three times you beheld Landini on that balcony."

"No – only the first. The last two times she'd gone inside."

"And could you see – were the windows open?"

"Well – I couldn't be sure of that."

"Thank you so much." Charlie walked off to a corner of the room with the sheriff. "Which concludes all those who were in this room when shot was fired," he said in a low tone. "Now we advance to more important sector of our attack."

"But say," demanded Holt. "Oughtn't we to be writing all this down in a book?"

Chan shook his head. "Not my method. Sight of paper and pencil sometimes has deleterious effect on speaker. I keep all this in mind, and at early opportunity, I make slight notes of it."

"My gosh – can you do that?" Holt answered. "I've forgot it already."

Charlie smiled. "Large empty place makes good storehouse," he remarked, tapping his forehead. "Now we proceed."

"Just a minute," Holt laid his hand on the detective's arm. "Who's that girl in the pink dress?"

"Owner of the pink scarf," Chan answered. "And I would humbly recall to you for the next few minutes the stern realities of lesson number one."

They went back to the other end of the room, and Chan again faced the assembly. "We come now," he said, "to members of this party who were not in view when death came to unfortunate lady above. One of these has already made at least partial statement. Sing, here, was probably last person to see Landini alive, having been dispatched for blanket, he says, after airplane landed. What you do, Sing, up to that time?"

"My don' know," shrugged Sing.

"You must know," replied Chan sternly.

"Mebbe my min' own business," suggested Sing slyly.

Charlie glared at him. He was finding his own compatriot a bit trying. "Listen to me," he said. "This is murder case, understand – murder case. You answer my questions, or maybe the sheriff here lock you up in big jail."

Sing stared at the young man. "Who – him?" he asked, incredulous.

"That's right, Sing," Holt said. "You answer. Understand."

"Allight," agreed Sing. "Why you no say so light away? My jes' go aloun' tendin' to own business."

"What was your business? What did you do?" Chan continued patiently.

"Boss see me in hall, say you catch 'um Cecile. My catch 'um. Then my go down-stair. Go out back step watch landing field. Boss come out, say to me, 'Sing, Landini want something, you catch 'um.'"

"Just a minute." Chan turned to Dudley Ward.

"That's right," Ward said. "I'd just passed Cecile on the back stairs and I gathered she had no intention of getting that blanket. I was in too much of a hurry about the lights to argue, so I just sent Sing to attend to it."

"My go in house," Sing continued when urged. "Heah lil dog bark in kitchen. Stop lissen. Plitty soon go up-stah, membah

Missie. Go to room, say, 'What you want, Missie?' She say, 'Sing, you catch 'um blanket like go' boy, covah up dog.' Dog, dog, dog all time when she 'lound. My go out—"

"The airplane had now landed on the field?" Charlie inquired.

"Yes."

"How you know that?"

"Damn noise quiet now. My go my loom—"

"On the third floor?"

"Yes. My catch 'um blanket. Plitty soon heah noise. Mebbe pistol. So my come down with blanket—"

"Very slowly, I judge," remarked Chan.

"Wha's th' mallah?" inquired Sing. "Plenty time. Plitty soon see Missie gits shot. Too bad," he added, without emotion.

"Thank you so much," said Chan, with obvious relief. "That will do, for the present." He glanced at Holt. "Probably the last person to see Landini alive. I'll talk with him later, alone." He turned to the conductor. "Mr Romano, so sorry to say I have somewhat warm interest in your actions for half-hour preceding this sad event."

"Me?" Romano gazed at him with innocent eyes.

"You, indeed. When I last saw you, airplane was still over lake, and you walked about room with panther tread. What next?"

"Ah, I recall," said the musician slowly. "I was engaged in making a list of rules for this young man – a list which, alas, will not now be required. I was no doubt at that moment seeking to determine whether or not I had fully covered the ground. I saw you pass my door on your way downstairs—"

"And continued with the list, maybe?"

"No," Romano answered, "not at all. It comes to me – now Landini must be alone. I hasten to the study, she is writing letter, she puts it in envelope, seals the flap. Now, I say, is come the time to talk about that settlement. I am – what you say –

broke. I am – am I right? – flat. Landini addresses the envelope. 'I am so sorry,' she say, 'but, Luis, I am in financial difficulty too. My investments do not pay proper dividends.'

"Then I say, impassioned, 'Ellen, you cannot afford a new husband at this time. Why not cling to the old? I am still fond of you' – but, Mr Chan" – his voice broke – "need I discuss that scene?"

"Not at all," Chan answered, "except to tell me her reply."

"It was," Romano bowed his head, "it was not flattering to me. Imagine, if you can – after all I had done for her – cared for her like a bambino. – The airplane was now approaching the house. She leaped to her feet, flung wide the windows. 'Come and see me in Reno,' she cried. 'I will do what I can.' And she ran on to the balcony."

"And you, Mr Romano?"

"Me – I was broken-hearted. I stared at her there on the balcony – it was to be my last sight of her alive – though of course I did not know that. Then I returned to my room, closed my door. I sat by the window, staring out at the snow, the dark trees, the sad night. Flung off, like an old coat, I sorrowed. But I was indignant, too. I remembered all I had done—"

"Ah, yes. And you sat there, brooding, until you heard the shot."

"It is true. I heard the shot, and for a time, I wondered. Then, I hear footsteps, voices, and I follow you in here to your sad discovery."

"Tell me this." Chan studied him keenly. "You were still the husband of Ellen Landini – at the least for two weeks more. As such, will you inherit any property she may leave?"

Romano shook his head. "Alas, no. At the time the settlement was drawn up – the one which she so cruelly ignored – she told me she was making a will, leaving everything she had to her future husband – to Mr Hugh Beaton here."

Surprised, Chan turned to the young man. "Did you know of this, Mr Beaton?"

Beaton looked up wearily. "Yes – she told me about it. Naturally, I didn't want her to do it."

"Do you know whether the will was made or not?"

"She told me one day it had been drawn up. Signed, too, I suppose. I didn't ask any questions. I hated the whole idea."

Charlie looked at Miss Beaton. "You, too, had heard of the affair?"

"I had," said the girl softly. "But I paid no attention. It didn't matter."

Chan turned back to Romano. "What a sad position for you. Wife, money, everything lost. Do you, may I ask, happen to have that list you drew up for Mr Beaton?"

"It is in my—" Suddenly he stopped. "It is in my room. I will get it for you."

"So sorry." Chan's eyes narrowed. "You were about to say, I think, that it is in your pocket."

"You are mistaken," Romano said, but his pale face had suddenly grown paler than ever. "What does it matter, at any rate?"

"It matters so much," Chan continued gently, "that unless you empty pockets here and now, I must reluctantly do same for you. Believe me, such a barbarous action would bring me pain."

Romano stood for a moment, considering.

"The story," he said finally, "of my interview with my wife was not quite complete. I – a man does not willingly speak of such things – but—" He reached into a trousers pocket and took out a roll of crisp new twenty-dollar bills, which he handed to Chan. "Just before Ellen rushed on to the balcony she removed these from her bag, flung them on the desk. I – I accepted them. My case – was – desperate." He dropped into a chair and covered his face with his hands. Chan looked down on him with real pity.

"I am so glad," the detective said, "that you saw way clear to amending own story. Unfortunately, these must remain with sheriff at present as evidence. But in meantime – we will see – way will be found – do not worry, Mr Romano." He turned with sudden grim determination on Doctor Swan. "And now, Doctor, your turn arrives. Where did you go after you left me in path before house?"

"I haven't much to tell," said Swan. "I came in here, had a word or two with Dinsdale and Beaton, and then went upstairs – to the room that had been assigned me before dinner. I was planning to leave at the earliest possible moment."

"Ah – and you had left something in that room you wished to obtain?"

"No – I had nothing up there. My coat and hat were in the closet down here. I had no luggage – it was not my intention to spend the night."

"You had nothing up there – then why did you go?"

Swan hesitated. "The windows of that room faced the back. I figured I could see the plane land – and—"

Charlie and the sheriff exchanged a look.

"Well, I'll be frank with you," Swan went on. "As a matter of fact, it occurred to me that after Ireland had landed his plane, he'd probably come inside for a moment. I didn't care to meet him. He knows what I think of him."

"And you know what I think of you," said Ireland sneeringly.

"No man," continued Swan, "can look forward to a social meeting with a greasy chauffeur who once made love to his wife behind his back—"

Ireland was on his feet. "Is that so—"

"Sit down," said Don Holt. "Now this is getting to be a case that I can handle. Sit down, Ireland, and shut up."

Big as he was, the aviator was not inclined to argue with the sheriff. He sat down, and Holt looked somewhat disappointed.

"Let us continue," said Chan, "peacefully. You went upstairs to avoid Mr Ireland, Doctor Swan?"

"Yes. I went into that room and closed the door. It was not my intention to come out of there until Ellen and the plane had gone. I watched it land, and I was standing by the window waiting to see it depart before returning downstairs. That is where I was when the shot was fired. It's not much of an alibi, I know, but—"

"I'll say it's not much of an alibi," growled Ireland. "A fat chance you've got putting that over. Especially when they find out you've been blackmailing poor Landini for seven years—"

"That's a lie," cried Swan, trembling with fury.

"Blackmailing," remarked Chan. He looked at Dudley Ward.

"Yeah – blackmailing," Ireland repeated. "She told me all about it. Two hundred and fifty a month for seven years, and the other day she told me she couldn't pay any more. I advised her to order this buzzard to scram. Did she tell you, Doctor? I guess she did – from the looks of tonight."

"You'd better be careful," said Swan through his teeth. "You're not out of the woods yet yourself."

"Me?" Ireland said. "Why – I was flying around in the sky, innocent as a bird. I had nothing to do with this—"

"But – your wife?" cried Swan. "How about your wife – or don't you care what happens to her? Poor Cecile – wandering about upstairs almost insane with jealousy – and with good reason, too, I imagine. Where was Cecile when that shot was fired – that's what I want to know."

"The proper authorities," Chan put in, "will resume the inquiry into this case – if you have no objection, Doctor Swan. Cecile – pardon, Mrs Ireland – we come now, with the doctor's kind assistance, to you. Courtesy has not ruled us, you will observe. It appears to be a matter of ladies last."

"I – I know nothing," the woman said.

"As I feared. But let us push questions, none the less. When last I saw you, you had been sent to obtain blanket for dog. You did not busy yourself with such task?"

Her eyes flashed. "I did not. I had no intention of doing so."

"Hot anger was in your heart?"

"Why not? I had just seen Michael's plane – I knew that woman had sent for him to take her home in the moonlight. And he, like a fool—"

"It was my job, I tell you," Ireland persisted sullenly.

"And how you hated it, eh? No matter. I thought, 'Let her find her own blanket for that accursed dog.' I was on my way down the back stairs, when Mr Ward hurried down after me. He asked about the blanket – I told him frankly I would not get it. 'I wonder where Sing is,' he said, and hastened past."

"And you—"

"Me – I went to the kitchen, where the cook was. I heard Michael risking his life above the house. I waited – I would have a word with him, I thought. The plane landed – and Michael came into the passageway, as I expected. But he was not alone – Mr Ward and Mr Chan were with him. I was too unhappy – 'I will have no scene here,' I said, so I let him pass. Then I started up the back stairs again – my place was above – and I figured how I would send Sing to bring Michael to me there. But on the stairs—"

"Ah, yes – on the stairs," nodded Charlie.

"I – I paused to weep, Monsieur. I was so very unhappy. I had known from the sound how close Michael had come to the house – reckless, a fool – to impress that woman, with whom he was always infatuated—"

"Bologny," interrupted her husband.

"You were – you know it. But I will say no more of the dead. I wept quietly for a moment, then I dried my eyes and started again up the stairs. It was then I heard the shot – loud, unexpected, clear. That – that is all."

Chan turned to Holt. "The little object, please, which you found embedded in study carpet."

"Oh – oh, yes." The sheriff found it and turned it over. Charlie held it out to the woman. "Have you, by any chance, ever seen this pin before?" he inquired.

She glanced at it. "Never, Monsieur."

Chan showed it to her husband, closely studying his face as he did so. "You – Mr Ireland. Have you seen it before?"

"Me? No. Why should I?"

Charlie put it in his pocket. "Long routine business," he remarked. "But it comes shortly now to a finish. One person alone remains—"

"I know." Leslie Beaton got up and stood, facing him. Tall, slender and appealing, she seemed at first glance quite helpless and lost. But – thought Chan – a competent look in those deep eyes of hers. Not for nothing had she cared for a spineless, artistic brother; she had learned, meanwhile, to take care of herself.

"I'm awful sorry about this," Don Holt said. And looked it.

"Don't worry," the girl replied. She flashed him a friendly smile. "These things will happen, I imagine, even to the kindest-looking of sheriffs. You will want to know of my actions here tonight, Mr Chan. I'll be as brief as I can—"

"But you needn't stand," Holt protested. He picked up a large chair in one hand, and tossed it casually into position for her.

"Thank you," she remarked. "Well, Mr Chan – when we heard the airplane over the lake, I was the first out of this room. I got my brother's overcoat, put it on and ran out to the pier. I went to the end and watched the plane approaching. It was a lovely thing – if I hadn't been – well, like Cecile – a bit unhappy, I could have been terribly thrilled. Doctor Swan appeared presently, and we watched it together. We had – a little chat, and then he went back to the house. I believe he met you just outside. I – I stayed where I was."

"Ah, yes," Chan nodded. "For how long?"

"I watched the airplane circle over the house—"

"You saw Landini on the balcony, perhaps?"

"No – the trees came together there – I couldn't see the study windows. But I saw Mr Ireland circling, and then I saw him come down somewhere in the rear. By that time I was thoroughly chilled, so I ran back to the living-room. Hugh and Mr Dinsdale were here together. I imagined we would be starting back to the Tavern as soon as Ellen had gone, so I ran up the stairs to the bedroom where our wraps were."

"One of the rooms next to the study where Landini died?" Chan suggested.

She shivered slightly, but went on. "Yes – of course. I sat down at the dressing-table to powder my nose – rearrange my hair – when suddenly, in that next room, I heard a shot—"

"One moment," Chan cut in, "pardon so much. But you heard first – what? A struggle?"

"No – nothing."

"But voices, perhaps?"

"Nothing at all, Mr Chan. You see, there is no door connecting the rooms."

"Ah, I see," Chan replied. "Continue, please."

"Well – I just heard this shot. And – I sat there. I couldn't quite comprehend what had happened. Then I heard people running along the hall, crowding into the study. And I followed them. That's – that's all."

"Alas," Charlie answered. "I wish very much that it were. But – Mr Holt – that pink scarf – one end of which I see hanging from your pocket—"

"Say – I'm sorry," Holt said. "I'm afraid I've mussed this up something terrible. You know – when I tucked it in there – I hadn't seen you—"

"It's all right, I'm sure," the girl replied.

"It is not all right – pardon me," cried Chan sternly, taking the scarf. "Excuse that I call attention to the fact, but we are not enjoying social hour of tea. This is your scarf, Miss Beaton?"

"As I told you, upstairs."

"It was found in dead hands of Ellen Landini? How do you account for same?"

"I cannot account for it, Mr Chan."

He took the pin from his pocket. "Have you seen this before?"

"It is mine."

"It is yours. It was found by the dead woman's side."

"It's a little old pin I used to fasten my scarf. When I left the scarf on that bed upstairs, I just carelessly stuck the pin in it. That's all."

"You are alone in room next to one in which murder occurs. Your scarf and your pin are in dead person's presence. And you cannot explain—"

"Perhaps, as my brother said—"

"Your brother made gallant effort to think up explanation. It is not enough, Miss Beaton. I have long experience in these matters, and never before have I encountered evidence so damaging—"

"But—" Suddenly the girl's face was stricken with fear. "Surely you don't think that I – that I could – kill Landini? What motive—"

"What motive?" cried Doctor Swan. "What motive, indeed?"

With one accord, they turned and looked at the doctor.

"I'm sorry, Miss Beaton," he said. "It's rather painful – such a charming girl, too. But under the circumstances, I should be shirking my duty shamefully if I did not recall our little conversation on the pier – what you said—"

"Very well," said the girl in a low voice. "What did I say?"

"Our little conversation about Landini," the doctor continued suavely. "Your last words to me, as I recall, were: 'I hate her! I hate her! I wish she were dead!'"

VI

THREE O'CLOCK IN THE MORNING

A tense silence followed in that big bright room, broken at last by the collapse of a burning log, which fell into a hundred pieces, sending sparks and embers in all directions. Sing moved forward to attend to it, and at that moment young Hugh Beaton faced Doctor Swan. He was livid with rage; an utterly unexpected transformation seemed to have taken place in the boy.

"You contemptible liar!" he cried hoarsely.

"Just a minute," Swan replied coolly. "It so happens I am telling the truth. Am I not, Miss Beaton?"

The girl's eyes were on the handkerchief which she twisted nervously in her hands. "You are," she said softly.

"So sorry," Charlie began. "But, Miss Beaton, it now becomes necessary for us to know—"

"Yeah – I suppose it does," said the sheriff. "But look here, there's no need of any more of this inquisition in front of everybody. Mr Ward – is there another room – "

Ward rose. "Yes," he answered. "You may use the dining-room, if you wish. If you'll come with me—"

"That's the idea," Holt approved. "The rest of you stick right here – understand? Now, Miss Beaton – yes, your brother too – and Doctor Swan – you come along with me and the inspector." As they followed Ward, he added to the girl: "I don't aim to make any public show of you. Some things is private."

"You're very kind to me," the girl said.

Ward ushered them into the dining-room, closed the door and disappeared. Doctor Swan was looking rather sheepish.

"Miss Beaton, believe me – I am very sorry that I was faced with such an unpleasant duty," he remarked. "Still – you understand my position—"

"Oh, we understand it, all right," her brother cried hotly. "Try to pin this terrible thing on someone else if you can. Your own situation is pretty shaky. Looking out the window when the shot was fired – enjoying the beautiful snow! Did you carry my sister's scarf into the study? Was it you Landini asked to—"

"Hughie," interrupted his sister, "please be quiet."

"Most admirable suggestion," Chan smiled. "It is Miss Beaton who should be talking now. So sorry, my dear young lady – but why did you cry out that you wished Landini dead?"

The girl sat down in the chair which Don Holt had placed for her near the fire.

"It's quite true," she began. "I did say that. I said I hated her, too. I did hate her. To explain I have to go back – a long way back – and even then – I doubt if you will quite understand. You don't know what it is to be poor – horribly poor – and to have someone in the family with a great gift, a gift you believe in – to slave and struggle and fight for that person's training and education. That's – that's what happened to us."

"Must you tell all this?" her brother protested.

"I have to, Hughie. You see, we knew very early that Hugh had a voice – and from then on, everything went for that. My father wearing the same old overcoat year after year – my mother going without, scrimping, saving – neither having any fun, any joy in life – just to pay for Hugh's education. New York – and then, Paris – and finally, after years of that sort of thing – Hugh giving a concert here and there, making a little money at last

– seemingly on the threshold of a great career. The moment we'd always dreamed about. And then this woman, pouncing on him, threatening to ruin everything—"

"You're wronging her, my dear," said the boy.

"Wronging her! She was fifteen years older than you. Had she any interest in your career? Would she have helped you to success – of course not. We all knew that. You knew it yourself. You said, only the other day—"

"Never mind. She's dead now."

"I know," the girl nodded. "I don't want to say anything – I just want to make clear my feeling about her." She turned to Chan and the sheriff. "It just seemed I couldn't let this marriage happen," she explained. "I mustn't. I came out here to try to stop it if I could. I talked with her – she laughed at me. I became desperate – I wanted to save Hugh from this terrible mistake. He was just a passing fancy with her, I felt. I was furious when she began going around with this Ireland person—"

"Stop it," put in the boy. "There was nothing in that. It was – Ellen's way." He was very white.

"It was not much of a way," the girl replied. "It sickened me. Tonight when she called him up, and left us to go home alone – I was furious. Hughie might weakly stand for that sort of thing—"

"Go on," the boy said. "Tell 'em I'm weak – no good – spineless. Tell 'em I always have been. That you've always had to care for me – mother me—"

"Have I said so?" the girl answered gently. "Don't be angry, Hughie. I'm only trying to explain the mood I was in when I went out on that pier. Soon Doctor Swan came out. I'd met him before in Reno. We got to talking about Landini, and I – I went a little wild, I guess. I told him what I thought about her marrying my brother – and as the plane came nearer, I burst into tears, and I – I said I hated her, and that I wished she was dead. And I did – I did – but I didn't kill her." She was weeping now. "I – I know it looks terrible," she went on. "I was in the next room. My scarf was in her hands, and my pin beside her. Why – how? I don't understand. I can't explain it. Someone – put them there. Someone who must have known how I felt toward her. For what other reason?"

She stopped suddenly, staring at Doctor Swan. Charlie and the sheriff were also looking at the doctor. Landini's third husband felt of his collar nervously, and his face flushed slightly.

"Yeah," nodded Don Holt. "Might be something in that theory, Miss Beaton. Well, we won't detain you in here any longer. I want to say right now, I understand exactly how—"

"Quite true, quite true," Charlie put in. "Yes, Miss Beaton, you may return to other room. But I would falsify facts if I hid from you you are for present moment in dangerous position. Later discoveries may clear same up. With deep sincerity I may say, I hope so." He smiled. "You see, I like the sheriff."

Holt stared at him. "What's that got to do with it?" he wanted to know.

"Another mystery which time, I trust, will solve," Charlie said. "Mr Sheriff, will you be good enough to remain in this room with me for one moment?"

After the others had gone, Charlie sat down and motioned Holt to a chair near by.

"Well?" said Holt rather gloomily.

"Feel somewhat same way myself," nodded Chan. "Well! A moment's summing up in order now. By this time we have questioned all those who were not present in my vision when the shot was heard. What have we got?"

"Not much, if you ask me," sighed Holt. "Swan and Romano were shut up in their rooms, looking out the windows. Oh, yeah? Cecile was climbing the back stairs, Sing was foraging for a blanket in his room, and Miss Beaton was right next door to the study, powdering her nose. Dog-gone it, I wish she'd been somewhere else. But anyhow, she was there when the shot was fired. And that accounts for the five. What's the answer?"

"Somebody is lying," Chan remarked.

"Sure – somebody is certainly lying. But which one? Romano?"

Charlie considered. "Romano had the money from her purse. Did she, then, give it to him? Or did he slip in to protest matter of settlement, lose temper, kill her, and himself remove money? Possible. No alibi."

"That fellow Swan," mused Holt. "I don't like him."

Charlie shook his head. "Again – please maintain neutral attitude. But – Swan – I cannot say I admire his looks myself. Did he kill the lady? Possible. No alibi."

"Cecile had a mighty good motive," the sheriff reflected.

"So far – absolutely nothing connects Cecile with murder," Charlie reminded him. "And yet, she is quite possible selection. She has no—" He paused, and a slow smile spread over his face. "Note the peculiar situation," he added. "Perhaps not so strange to you, but to me, with my experience, up to this minute unheard of. Five people not accounted for at time of shooting, and of the five not one has even offered alibi. I wonder—"

"What?" inquired Holt eagerly.

Chan shrugged. "No matter. It lightens work – we have no alibis to investigate. But it also adds heaviness – we have, alas, five healthy suspects. I have kept you here to remind you of one thing – we are near state line. It is your duty to see that no one of five departs across that line tonight."

"I know. I suppose there'll be an argument. Perhaps we could put some of them up at the Tavern."

"It is very late," Chan replied. "Romano, Cecile and Sing remain here naturally. You must persuade the good doctor and Miss Beaton to do the same – for tonight at least. There are plenty rooms. I will be responsible."

"Suppose one of them slips out in the night," suggested Holt.

"Only the thief oils his wheelbarrow," Chan said, as they rose. "And only the guilty flee. It would be a happy solution. I shall be sitting just inside my door all night. I shall try not to take nap – but I cannot guarantee. For I now realize suddenly that I have been napping all evening."

"How so?" Holt inquired.

"There were six, not five, unaccounted for at time of shot."

"Six?" Holt cried. "Good lord – another one. Who?"

"I forgot the cook," Chan explained. "Most impolite of me – for she is a very good cook. Perhaps very good witness, too. If you will arrange matter of overnight stay, I will visit kitchen. You might join me there, when able."

"Sure," said Holt. He paused. "I suppose I may as well let Ireland go back to Reno?"

"Why not?" Chan shrugged. "He could have had nothing to do with killing. Yes, Ireland, Dinsdale and young Beaton, if he wishes – these may go."

Separating from Holt, he followed the passageway toward the rear until he came to the kitchen door. Looking in, a homey scene greeted him. Beside an old-fashioned kitchen range, in a large easy chair, sat the ample figure of the cook, sound asleep. At her feet on a bit of old carpet, lay Trouble, the dog, also mercifully slumbering. Chan smiled and moved on to the back steps.

For a time he walked about outside, using a flashlight he had obtained from his luggage when he went for the fingerprint paraphernalia. He studied the path which led to the hangar, but the snow on that was packed hard, and no clear footprints were discernible. The lights on the field were still blazing, and Michael Ireland's plane stood like an actor in a spotlight.

The examination yielded him nothing, and he paused for a moment, staring at the clear beauty of the distant mountains, then went inside. Holt was standing beside the kitchen door.

"Sleeping, eh?" he said, nodding toward the cook.

"The slumber of innocence," Chan smiled. "Matters are now arranged for the night?"

Holt nodded. "All set. Swan put up a battle – got to get back to Reno – lot of appointments early in the morning. But he's staying all right – that bird's not putting anything over on me. I don't like – oh, yes, lesson number one. Anyhow, I hate the sight of him. Miss Beaton is staying – Cecile's fixing her up with the necessary feminine doodads. Her brother has decided to put up here for the night, too."

"We shall be a large party," Chan answered.

The cook was stirring in her chair, and the two stepped into the kitchen.

"So sorry to disturb you," Charlie apologized.

"Sure, I should be in me bed," the woman answered. "Why am I here – oh, yes – the poor lady. I was afther forgettin' —"

"Let me explain, Mrs. —" Holt began.

"O'Ferrell," she added.

"Mrs O'Ferrell. I am Don Holt, sheriff of the county."

"God have mercy on us," she cried.

"And this is Inspector Chan, of the Honolulu Police."

"Honolulu, eh? Sure, he got here quick."

Charlie smiled. "Honored, if I may say so. Earlier this evening I had great pleasure to sample your cooking, and I bow to you in humble congratulation."

"You talk very nice," she responded, pleased.

"But sterner topics now engage us," he continued. "You are evidently aware of what happened a short time ago?"

"Murder," she said. "I am. I don't hold with it."

"We none of us hold with it," he assured her. "That is why we seek the murderer. It becomes necessary to ask a few questions, which I know you will answer gladly."

"I will that. I'll not be at peace in this house, with a murderer havin' the run of it. But I'm afraid I can't help ye much. I been busy in this room all evenin', for a dinner like that is no joke, nor is washin' dishes afther it a picnic, ayether. I'm supposed to have the help of Sing, but like a will-o'-the wisp he's been this night, now here, now gone."

"He's been in and out occasionally, however?"

"In an' out is right."

"Well, Mrs O'Ferrell, let us take it from the time you heard the airplane. Where was the plane when you first heard it?"

"I couldn't tell you that exactly, Mr Chan, but it must have been some distance off, over the lake, ye might say. I heared it buzzin', an' I thinks, now what can that be, an' thin Cecile – no, wait a minute – thin Mr Ward himself stops in that door, an' asks me have I seen Sing. I says I think the Chink – begging yer pardon, sir, you're a gintleman, as annybody can see – I says I think Sing is on the back porch, an' Mr Ward is hardly gone, whin Cecile comes in mad as a hornet, with somethin' about her husband, an' a blanket, an' this opera singer, an' what-not. An' thin the plane comes over th' house, an' from that minute I have me hands full, what with Cecile ravin' and this poor lamb at me feet" – she indicated the dog – "scared near out of his wits be the noise."

"Ah – Trouble was frightened by the plane?"

"He was that, sir, an' no mistake, cryin' an' whinin' an' carryin' on until I had to take him on me lap, an' comfort him, an' him tremblin' all over like gelatine."

"And Cecile—"

"Cecile wint out in th' passage, like she was waitin' f'r someone. I see Mr Ward an' you an' the leather man come in, but I didn't hear anny talk from Cecile. I was too busy with th' dog to come to th' door. Look at him, th' poor little orphan, sleepin' there so peaceful an' not knowin' his loss."

Chan smiled. "We will leave him in your care for the present, Mrs O'Ferrell, and I'm sure he could not be in kinder hands. That is all. I suggest you retire for the night."

"Thank ye kindly, sir, but I'll not rest in me bed until this wild murderer is caught. Ye'll move as fast as ye can, I hope."

Charlie shook his head. "We must collect at leisure what we may use in haste," he explained. "The fool in a hurry drinks his tea with a fork." He and Holt went into the passage. At the foot of the back stairs, Holt stopped. "A lot we got out of that," he remarked glumly.

"You think so?" Chan asked.

The sheriff looked at him suddenly. "We didn't get anything, did we?"

Charlie shrugged. "He who fishes in muddy waters cannot tell the great catch from the small."

"Yeah. I guess this is the back stairway, isn't it? I told that doctor to wait for me upstairs – he'll think I've forgot him. Let's go up."

They found the doctor in the study, his work evidently completed, his bag closed on the desk, and himself with professional calm seated by the fire. He rose as they entered.

"Well," he said, when he had been introduced to Chan, "I've made the examination, although the coroner, of course, will want to make another in the morning. Poor Landini – I knew her as a young bride in this house, and she comes back to it to die. Um – er – that is, of course, beside the point. Nothing much to be said. The bullet entered about four inches below the shoulder, and pursued, I believe, a downward course. Perhaps the person who fired it was standing over her, and she was on her knees." He looked at Chan.

"Perhaps," Chan said. He seemed very sleepy, and not overly keen. The doctor turned to Holt.

"We can tell more about that tomorrow," he continued. "The caliber of the gun – that must wait until tomorrow, also."

Holt held out the small pearl-handled revolver. "We've found this," he said.

"One thing, Doctor," Charlie remarked. "Was death, in your opinion, instantaneous? Or could the lady have taken a step or two after the wound?"

The doctor considered. "I can tell you better after we have probed for the bullet," he said. "At present, all I can say is – there is a chance that she did move after the shot. But you must understand—"

He was interrupted by the loud whirring of an airplane engine, and then the steady drone of it moving off, evidently away from the house.

"It's Ireland," said the sheriff to Charlie. "I told him he could go."

"Naturally," nodded Chan. He stepped on to the balcony and watched the plane as it moved out over the sapphire lake. Much had happened, he reflected, since that machine had first been sighted in the still night sky.

"I'd like to be getting along," the doctor was saying. "I had a hard night last night."

"Sure," said Holt. "We can take this poor lady with us, I guess. I phoned Gus Elkins to wait up for us. We'll need some blankets, won't we? I hope everybody's out of that room downstairs – especially the women—"

Charlie took up his lampblack and brush from the desk. "While you busy yourself with unhappy task," he said, "I will make superficial investigation of room next door – that old sitting-room of Ellen Landini's – through which her slayer must have left the scene. Kindly visit me there before taking departure for the night."

"I'll do that," Holt promised.

Some fifteen minutes later he pushed open the door of the room in question. Chan was standing in the center of it, all the lights, both on the walls and in the ceiling, were blazing. The atmosphere of the place was faintly out-of-date, for the furnishings were those of twenty years before, though probably this made no impression on Holt.

"What luck?" the young man inquired.

"A little," Charlie shrugged.

Holt went over and examined the catch fastening the windows that opened on to the balcony. "Any prints on this?" he asked.

"None whatever," Chan answered. "There are also no prints on door-knob, either side."

"But there should be – shouldn't there?" Holt inquired. "I mean – if everything was O.K.?"

"There should be dozens," Charlie admitted. "But alas – too many people read detective stories now – get fingerprint complex. All have been rubbed away."

"Then Landini's murderer did come this way," Holt mused. "And probably went this way to reach her, too. Leaving the window unlocked so he could return through it."

Chan nodded. "You are learning fast. Pretty soon, your instructor must take lessons from you. Yes – the firing of that pistol must have been premeditated. Otherwise, the killer could not have come through here without smashing glass in window."

"Anything else to make you think he—"

"Or she," suggested Chan.

"Or she, escaped through this room?"

Chan pointed. There was a dressing-table against one wall of the room, and overturned on the floor in front of it was a heavy bench.

"Someone came, hurrying in the dark," he said. "Knee met sharp edge of plenty solid bench, which is turned on side. Maybe somebody have pretty sore knee."

Holt nodded. "I hope so. Even if a bad infection sets in, it will be all right with me. This room doesn't connect with any other, does it?"

"No – that is closet door over there," Chan told him.

"Well, I'd better be getting along," Holt said. "I'll be up early in the morning, of course. Poor Landini is in my launch, and the doctor has already taken his boat and gone. He was a candidate for coroner himself last election, and lost out, so he's not very keen about this job."

They went downstairs, through the living-room, which was now deserted. Chan stepped outside, and walked toward the pier with his new-found friend.

"I'm certainly glad to have you on this job with me," Holt remarked. "It just looks hopeless. I can't see any light ahead."

"Be cheerful," urged Charlie. "When the melon is ripe, it will fall of itself. I have always found it so."

"Have you got any clue?" asked the boy.

"Clue?" Chan smiled. "I have so many clues, I would sell some very cheaply. Yes," he mused, "if I was complaining man, and were asked for complaint against this case, I would say, bitterly, too many clues. Pointing all ways at once."

"I'll have to take your word for it," Holt sighed.

"But long experience shows," added Chan briskly, "that in time clues fall into place, false ones fade and wither, true ones cluster together in one unerring signboard. I may say I am interested in this case. Unusual event has roused itself and occurred here tonight, and one unusual clue may point our final path. – But I anticipate." They had come to the pier. Charlie held out his hand. "Good night. I enjoy knowing you, if you permit my saying so. I enjoy knowing cool fresh country like this. I am plenty happy."

"Fine," said Holt. "Let's all be happy. See you tomorrow, Mr Chan."

"Just one matter." Charlie laid a hand on his arm.

"What's that?"

"The bullet for which they probe in the morning – get it, and guard it well. It must on no account be lost."

"I'll hang on to it," Holt promised, and ran down the pier to his launch.

Charlie came back to the living-room to find Dudley Ward waiting there.

"Ah, Mr Chan," he said. "I fancy you're the last of my guests to retire."

"I will do so at once," Charlie assured him. "So sorry to delay your own rest."

"Not at all," Ward answered. He sank into a chair. "But I am rather weary, at that. Poor Ellen – I shall never forgive myself for inviting her here. However, I was so anxious – about my boy."

"How natural," Chan said.

"I am more anxious than ever, now," Ward continued. "I hope, in the terrible excitement of tonight, you won't forget why you have come here, Inspector. You must, of course, find who killed Landini if you can – but you must also find my boy. He needs me more than ever – with Landini gone."

"I am not forgetting same," Chan nodded.

"You heard what Ireland said about Doctor Swan's having blackmailed poor Ellen," Ward went on. "Did it occur to you that he might have known about the boy, and been threatening to tell me of him?"

"It did," Chan nodded gravely.

"Of course, he denied at dinner that he had ever heard of the child—"

"He was lying," Charlie said firmly.

"You thought so?" Ward inquired.

"I was certain of it. Just as I was sure Romano was lying when he said he had."

"Well, I am glad to have such expert confirmation of my own opinion," Ward went on. "I went to Swan's room a moment ago to loan him some things – and I told him what I thought.

I pleaded with him, if he knew anything of the boy, to tell me about him. He still denied any knowledge."

"Still lying," Chan suggested.

"I think so," Ward agreed. "Well, we must look elsewhere, perhaps. But as a last resort, we must not forget Doctor Swan."

"I shall not forget him," Chan promised. "And now – if you don't mind – I will go to my room."

"Ah, yes," said Ward, rising. "You know where it is. I have just remembered that I forgot to turn off the lights on the landing field. I must send Sing to attend to that – then perhaps I can retire for the night myself."

Charlie had been in his room but a few minutes, when Ward knocked on his door. "Just to say you must let Sing or me know if you want anything," he remarked. "Good night, Inspector."

"Good night, Mr Ward," Chan said.

There was, he noted, plenty of wood in the basket beside his fireplace. That would come in handy, if he was to keep his promise to Don Holt and sit up through the night. A rather silly promise, he reflected, as he began to undress. No one of these people would be so foolish as to attempt escape.

Nevertheless, he changed to pajamas, dressing-gown and slippers, put another log on the fire, opened his door a few inches and sat down in a comfortable chair just inside it. He looked at his wrist-watch. One-thirty. All was quiet in the hall outside, save for the sounds that afflict an ancient wooden house on a frosty night. Crackings, creakings, moanings. But the human company, Chan knew, were in their beds.

He settled more deeply into his upholstered chair, to think about this case upon which he was so unexpectedly engaged. Pictures flashed through his mind – the calm lake under the stars – Dudley Ward greeting his fellow-husbands on the pier – Landini lively and vivacious on the stairs, holding aloft the dog, Trouble, – Ireland circling the house in his plane – Landini lying on the study carpet – promised to sing for him some day – never would sing for him now – never—

Chan sat up with a start. He looked at his wrist-watch. Ten minutes to three. Too comfortable, that chair. But what had startled him? – ah, now he knew. A groan – a faint groan from somewhere outside his door. Not the groan of an old house in the night, but of a human being in pain.

Charlie slipped out into the hall, which was in utter darkness. Feeling his way along the wall, still somewhat confused by sleep, he approached the head of the stairs. His foot encountered some soft object on the floor.

Then at last he remembered his flashlight, and removed it from the pocket of his dressing-gown. Its glare fell on a supine figure at his feet – then on the face – the lined yellow face of Ah Sing.

The old man groaned again, and raising one thin hand, rubbed his even thinner jaw.

"No can do," he protested feebly. "No can do."

VII

THE BLIND MAN'S EYES

For a moment Chan stood looking down at the crumpled figure of Ah Sing, and a wave of pity for this loyal servant who had been with the house of Ward so many years swept through him. He bent over solicitously.

"What has happened here?" he asked. Gently he shook the old man. "Who has done this thing to you?"

Sing opened his eyes, sighed and closed them again.

Rising, Charlie found the switch on the wall with his flash, and turned on the light in the upper hall. He surveyed the many doors. With the exception of his own, all were closed; they seemed blind, uninterested, secretive. He walked down the hall and knocked softly on the door of Dudley Ward's room.

Presently it opened and Ward appeared, a weary gray-haired man in pajamas, looking older than Chan had thought him.

"Mr Chan!" he exclaimed. "Is anything wrong?"

"There has been," Chan explained, "an accident."

"An accident! Good lord! What now!" Ward ran into the hall and, seeing Sing, went with Charlie toward the recumbent figure.

"I find your servant unconscious from blow in face."

"A blow! Who the devil—"

At sound of the familiar voice, the old man sat up. He looked his master over disapprovingly.

"Wha's mallah you?" he demanded. "You clazy? You walk loun' heah no bathlobe, no slippahs, you catch 'um plenty col'. You mebbe die."

"Never mind that," Ward said. "Who hit you, Sing?"

Sing shrugged. "How my know? Plenty big man, mebbe. Plenty big fist. Jus' hide in dahk an' hit me. Tha's all."

"You didn't see him?"

"How my do that?" He struggled to get to his feet, and Charlie helped him. "No light nowheh." With a groan he pushed Chan aside, and tottered unsteadily into Ward's room. In a moment he returned with bathrobe and slippers. "Heah, Boss – you lissen to Sing. You go loun' like clazy man, you catch 'um all kin' col'."

Ward sighed and submitted meekly to the additions to his costume. "Very well," he said. "But what were you doing down here, anyhow?"

"What my always do?" Sing queried in a complaining voice. "Woik, woik, all time woik. Wake up, take look-see clock, think mebbe moah bettah my go down cellah fix fiah. People all ovah house, too many people, they wake up say too col'." He viewed his master as one who had been meaning to speak of this matter for some time. "Too much woik this house. Nevah no stop. Too much fo' me. No can do. No can do."

"He's been talking like that for fifty years," Ward explained to Chan, "and I have to battle him tooth and nail to get another servant on to the place. God knows I don't want him to get up at three in the morning and fix the furnace. Well" – he turned to Sing – "did you fix it?"

"My fix 'um," nodded the old man. "Put new logs down-steh, too. Then come up heah, fist come out f'om dahk, catch 'um my jaw. Tha's all."

Charlie patted him on the back. "You go to bed now," he suggested. "Too many people in this house – you have spoken truly there. Not very nice people, some of them. Aged men should not consort with ruffians. Eggs should not dance with stones."

"Goo' night," replied Sing, and departed.

Chan turned to his host. "I note you are shivering," he said. "Kindly step into my room for a moment. I have maintained my fire, which you will find welcome, I think." He led the way and indicated a chair. "Who, I would ask, has perpetrated this latest outrage?"

Ward sat down, and stared into the fire. "Don't ask me, please," he said wearily. "I'd like to get my hands on him, whoever he is. A harmless old man like Sing – but good lord – I'm all at sea."

"I am inclined to wonder," Chan mused. "In a way, the sheriff left me in charge here tonight. Can it be that one of my birds has flown? With your permission, I intend to make a brief survey."

"Maybe you'd better," Ward nodded.

"The rooms of Romano, Ryder and Swan I know," Charlie continued. "I will also, I think, investigate that of young Hugh Beaton, if you will acquaint me with his door."

Ward did so, and Chan went out. In less than ten minutes he returned.

"The loss of one night's sleep means ten days of discomfort," he smiled. "Happy to say none of the gentlemen we mentioned faces such a fate. I opened the door of each, flashed light on bed. One and all they appeared to slumber."

"Well – that gets us nowhere," Ward remarked.

"As far as I expected," Charlie replied. "Yes, they slumbered – and not one faced the door. The long arm of coincidence, I believe it is called. Speaking for myself, I was plenty glad to find them here at all, asleep or otherwise."

Ward rose. "I may as well go back to bed, I fancy. It is not easy for me to sleep tonight, Inspector. Ellen dead – in this old house where I had expected to spend a happy life with her. And tomorrow we must go over to Reno and look into her affairs." He laid his hand on Chan's arm. "I'm afraid," he added.

"Afraid?" Chan asked.

"Yes. Suppose – I have a son. A boy who has never heard of me – never seen me. It came to me tonight – after I went to bed. What will I mean to him? Less than nothing. Love – affection – never, under those conditions. Too late, Mr Chan. Always too late, for me."

"Go back and seek for sleep, at least," Charlie said gently. "As for the future – when you have reached the river, then is the time to take off your shoes."

After Ward had gone, Charlie put fresh logs on the fire and sat down – in front of it this time, but with his door open. He was thoroughly awake now, and four o'clock in the morning is an excellent time to think. What was behind this unprovoked attack on Sing? Or was it unprovoked? Did Sing know who it was that had struck him? If so – why should he hide it? Fear, no doubt, fear of the white man inspired in the old Chinese of mining-camp days by years of rough treatment and oppression.

A clue. Charlie eagerly searched his mind for a clue. "No can do," the old man had muttered, semi-conscious on the floor. But that was probably just the refrain that ran through all his days: "Too much woik this house. No can do." The complaint under which he hid his real devotion.

Chan sighed. It was too early, he decided, to place this attack in the scheme of things, too early to come to any real decision regarding the murder of Landini. For the present, the mere marshaling of facts must suffice, and so he sat and marshaled them in that mind which he had called "large, empty place that makes good storehouse." He marshaled them while the chill dawn crept across the lake, and somewhere behind the snow-capped peaks a yellow sun was rising. Doors began to slam, the voice of Mrs O'Ferrell was heard in the land, and from the distant kitchen came, faintly, the bark of a dog.

While Chan bathed and shaved, his mind was filled with Trouble. Trouble, the dog.

When finally Charlie was ready to go downstairs, the sun was on the lake, and a prospect of breath-taking beauty was spread before him. He opened his window and leaned far out enjoying the cool, fresh, bracing mountain air. In the darkness of the night he had had his doubts, but now he felt he could conquer the world. Problems, puzzles – he welcomed them.

He walked, with his chest well out, through the chilly hall and down the stairs. The delicious odor of bacon and coffee floated about him. He knew he would enjoy his breakfast, even though, at the same table, sat the murderer of Ellen Landini.

Reaching that table, he found Ward, Ryder and Swan already there. They greeted him with varying degrees of cordiality. At Chan's heels came Romano, his sartorial elegance a bit cheapened by the clean light of day. Scarcely had he and Charlie sat down when Leslie Beaton appeared, and all the men rose.

"Ah, Miss Beaton," said Ward. "So happy to have you here. And looking, if I may say so, as fresh and beautiful as the morning."

"I thought I'd have to appear in an evening gown," she smiled. "But Cecile saved the situation. She's really a brick." She turned upon her heel for inspection. "What do you think of it?"

She was referring to the morning frock in which she was garbed. Evidently it met with their approval.

"I think it's cute," the girl went on. "But why shouldn't it be? Cecile is French. Of course, there's not enough of me to fill it, quite. But I'm so hungry, I'm sure there will be – after breakfast." When she was seated, she looked suddenly at Chan. "I'll simply have to go over to Reno today and get my things—"

"That," said Charlie, "depends on the sheriff. Do not, I beg of you, squander such a charming smile on me."

"Oh, I have others," she assured him. "Plenty for the sheriff, too." For the first time, the shadow of the night before crossed her face. "Must – must we really stay here?"

"Come, come," said Ward with forced gaiety. "That's not exactly complimentary to me. And I'm trying so hard to be the perfect host."

"Succeeding, too," the girl replied. "But the conditions – they are unusual. One can't help feeling that underneath you may be – for all your kindness – an unwilling host."

"Never – to you," Ward murmured. And as Sing appeared at his elbow, he added: "What fruit will you have? We have all kinds – of oranges."

"I'll have the nicest kind," said the girl. "Good morning, Sing. Why – the poor man! He's hurt his face."

Chan had already noted that the left jaw of the servant was swollen and discolored. Sing shrugged his shoulders and departed.

"Sh," said Ward. "He's had an accident. We won't say anything about it – he's rather sensitive, you know."

"He's limping, too," the girl went on.

"It was rather a bad accident," Ward explained. "He fell on the stairs, you see."

"Poor Sing's getting old," Ryder remarked. "I was noticing it last night. He doesn't see very well. Shouldn't he have glasses, Dudley?"

Ward grimaced. "Of course he should – and has. Or had, rather. But he broke them about a month ago – and you know how stubborn he is. I've been pleading with him ever since to get them fixed – by George, I'll take them over to Reno with me this morning. An optician over there has his prescription."

Hugh Beaton came in, glum and in the mood of genius at breakfast. The repast continued, to the accompaniment of a conversation that was surprisingly cheerful, all things considered.

But in this Charlie took no part. He had several new facts to marshal in the storehouse of his mind. So Sing was limping this morning? It seemed impossible he could have hurt his leg in the fall that resulted from an encounter with an unknown fist. He had given no indication of such an injury at the time. And – there was that overturned dressing-table bench in the old sitting-room next to the study upstairs.

And Sing needed glasses. Usually wore them, in fact. Well, that fitted in, too. The confusion of the box lids. For a moment Charlie's appetite lost some of its keenness. But no – too early yet, he decided. Get all the facts in mind. Wait until you reach the river before you start to unlace your shoes.

After breakfast, Charlie visited the kitchen for a brief call on Mrs O'Ferrell and Trouble. He spoke enthusiastically of the former's coffee – so much so she never dreamed that he greatly preferred tea. The dog romped in a friendly fashion at his feet.

"Look at him – the little darlin'," Mrs O'Ferrell remarked. "Sure, I've only knowed him a few hours, an' he's like an old friend."

Charlie picked up the dog and stroked it musingly. "I have known him but a brief time myself," he said, "and yet I have for him a deep affection."

"I been thinkin'," the cook continued. "If no wan else wants him, couldn't you leave him here, Mr Chan? What with the lady gone, an' no wan to take care iv him—"

"As to that," Chan replied, "I cannot say. I can only tell you that at least once – Trouble must go back to Reno." He put the dog on the floor, gave it a final pat and moved to the door. "Yes," he repeated firmly. "Trouble must make that journey to Reno. And he must make it – by airplane."

Leaving Mrs O'Ferrell deeply mystified by this cryptic statement, he returned to the big living-room. Most of the guests were there, and in the center of the room stood Don Holt, the sheriff. Beside him was a man who would have been a figure of distinction in any company, tall, erect, with snow-white hair. Chan's heart was touched as he noted the sightless eyes.

"Morning, Mr Chan," cried Don Holt. "Great day, ain't it? I brought my Dad along – want you to know him. Father – Inspector Chan, of Honolulu."

Chan took the groping hand in his. "To meet an old-time sheriff of the mining camps," he said. "An honor I have always longed for, but never dreamed I should encounter."

"Old-time is right, Inspector," replied Sam Holt, with a grim smile. "And the old times – they don't come back. I sure am glad that you're on hand to give my boy a lift."

"I am plenty happy, too," Chan assured him.

"Well, we're all ready for business, I reckon," Don Holt said. "Miss Beaton here has just been telling me that she's got to go to Reno to get her tooth-brush – and – and – I said I guessed we'd better let you decide."

Charlie smiled. "A diplomatic reply. You put all the young lady's disfavor on me."

"Then you don't think—"

"There were, you recall," Chan continued, "five – no, six – people not in view at a certain fatal moment last night. None of the six must cross state line—"

Swan pushed forward. "What about me? I've got a dozen appointments today. And not so much as a clean collar on this side of the line."

"What a pity," Chan shrugged. "Give us a list of what you desire from your residence – and the location of same. Also – if you so desire – the key." Swan hesitated. "We go there in any case," Chan added meaningly.

"Oh, very well," Swan agreed.

"Say – that's an idea," young Holt said. "Miss Beaton – if you'll give me a list—"

"Not quite the same," she smiled.

"Well – ah – er – maybe not, come to think of it," he admitted, suddenly embarrassed.

"We will take Miss Beaton's brother with us," Chan suggested. "He may be given the list."

"That's a fine idea," Holt cried. The girl shrugged and turned away. "Now" – the young sheriff turned to Chan – " before we go, I guess we better have a talk. Upstairs – what do you say?"

Ah Sing suddenly appeared from the dining-room. He stood for a moment, staring at Sam Holt, then hurried over and grasped the old man's hand.

"Hello, Shef," he cried. "Haply see you."

"Hello, Sing," Sam Holt answered. "I'm happy to – er – to see you, too. But I ain't sheriff no more. Things change, boy. We're old men now."

"You go on being shef fo' me," Sing insisted. "Always shef fo' me."

On the handsome face of Sam Holt appeared an expression that was a mixture of regret and resignation. He patted his ancient friend on the back affectionately, then put his arm about the other's shoulder.

"Take me upstairs, boy," he said. "I want to see that there study. Used to know my way about this house so well – I could travel it in – in the dark. But now – I sort of forgit. Lead the way, Sing."

With loving solicitude the servant helped him up the stairs, and his son and Charlie followed. When they all reached the study, Sam Holt turned to Sing.

"More better you run along now, boy," he remarked. "I see you later. Wait a minute. You catch 'um Dudley Ward – tell him Sam Holt's up here."

Sing departed, and the old man began to move slowly, feeling his way about the room. His son stepped forward to assist him. "This is the desk, Dad," he said. "Where we found the loose tobacco – and the boxes with the jumbled cigarettes." He added aside to Chan: "I've been all over the case with him this morning."

"An excellent course," nodded Charlie heartily.

"And here," the boy went on, "these are the windows, Dad."

"There used to be a balcony out there."

"There still is. That was one of the last places Landini was seen alive. By the aviator, you know."

"Oh, yes – by the aviator. But Sing – Sing saw her last?"

"Yes – when she sent him to bring the blanket."

"Needn't go all over it again," his father objected. "My memory's as good as yours, I reckon. Give me a chair, son." He sat down in a velvet-covered chair before the fire. "Poor Ellen Landini. Mighty curious, Mr Chan, that she had to come way back to this house to hand in her chips. Knew her, long ago. Beautiful. Beautiful girl. Somebody's comin' down the hall."

Dudley Ward appeared in the doorway and greeted the old sheriff cordially.

"Jes' wanted to pay my respects, Dudley," Sam Holt said. "Tell you I'm sorry about – all this. Poor Ellen – I was jes' sayin'. Kyards always seemed stacked against her, somehow. You too, boy, you too." He lowered his voice. "Don was tellin' me that story – mebbe a son – a kid somewhere –"

"Maybe," Ward said.

"Who knew about that, Dudley?" the old man continued. "Of course, Mr Chan – and that other three – Swan, Romano, Ryder? And Sing, I reckon. Of course, you'd tell Sing. But who else?"

"Why – nobody, Sam. Just this woman – this Cecile. The woman who told me the story first."

"Nobody else, boy?"

"Not that I know of."

"Well – 'taint important. Don tells me you're all goin' off to Reno – you run along an' git ready. Don't let me keep you."

When Ward had gone, Don Holt got up and shut the door. "Anything happen last night?" he inquired of Charlie.

Quickly Chan reported the assault on Sing. Both men received the account with rising indignation. Charlie ended with the information that Sing was limping this morning.

"Oh, yes – that bench in the next room," Don Holt said. "Still – maybe that's not the tie-up. Might have cracked it when this guy hit him and he fell. No – Sing's got nothing to do with this – we can bank on that. I ain't going to waste any time on Sing."

Sam Holt was idly plucking with his thin old hand at the arm of his chair. "Ain't it about time Cash Shannon showed up, son?" he inquired.

"Ought to be," the boy agreed. "Cash is a cowboy down at the stables," he explained to Charlie, "and a deputy of mine. I'm havin' him up here today to keep an eye on things while we're all away. I'll go down an' see if he's got here yet."

"Shet the door when you go out," Sam Holt suggested. When he heard it close, he said: "Mr Chan, I'm sure glad you're with us on this case. I reckon, from what Don tells me about ye, you an' me would sort of think along the same lines. I ain't never had no use for science – the world was gittin' along a whole lot better before science was discovered."

Charlie smiled. "You mean fingerprints, laboratory tests, blood analysis – all that. I agree, Mr Holt. In my investigations of murder I have thought, always, of the human heart. What passions have been at work – hate, greed, envy, jealousy? I study always – people."

"Always people – you said it, Mr Chan. The human heart."

"Yes – though even there, one meets difficulties. As a philosopher of my race has said: 'The fishes, though deep in the water, may be hooked; the birds, though high in the air, may be shot; but man's heart only is out of our reach.'"

Sam Holt shook his head. "Mighty purty language, that is, but man's heart ain't always out of our reach. If it was, you an' me wouldn't of made no record on our jobs, Mr Chan."

"Your statement has truth," Chan nodded.

For a long time the former sheriff of the mining camps did not speak. His sightless eyes were turned toward the fire, but his hands were busy. He seemed to be gathering some invisible substance from the arm of his chair with his right hand, and depositing it in his left.

"Mr Chan," he said suddenly, "how close kin you git to the heart of Ah Sing?"

"It overwhelms me with sadness to admit it," Charlie answered, "for he is of my own origin, my own race, as you know. But when I look into his eyes I discover that a gulf like the heaving Pacific lies between us. Why? Because he, though among Caucasians many more years than I, still remains Chinese. As Chinese today as in the first moon of his existence. While I – I bear the brand – the label – Americanized."

Holt nodded. "You've stated the case. These old Chinese in this stretch of the state ain't never been anything else. Maybe they didn't admire the ways of the stranger – I dunno. Which I wouldn't of blamed 'em. But they was born Chinese, an' they stayed that way."

Chan bowed his head. "I traveled with the current," he said softly. "I was ambitious. I sought success. For what I have won, I paid the price. Am I an American? No. Am I, then, a Chinese? Not in the eyes of Ah Sing." He paused for a moment, then continued: "But I have chosen my path, and I must follow it. You are sitting there as one about to tell me something."

"I'm sitting here wondering," Sam Holt replied. "Can I make you understand what Ah Sing's been to me – a friend fer fifty years? I used to take the Ward boys an' him camping, up where it's really high. We used to lay out under the stars – why, I'd ruther cut out my tongue – than say a word – but duty's duty – an' this is my boy's first big case —" He stopped, and held something out to Chan. "Mr Chan – what is this I been pulling from the arm of my chair?"

"It is light, airy fuzz," Chan told him. "Sort of fuzz readily yielded by wool blanket in contact with velvet."

"And the color, man – the color?"

"It – it appears to be blue."

"Blue. Landini sent Sing fer a blanket. He came back with it after you found the body. Came back with – a blue blanket. You sent him away with it. Yes, Don was tellin' me. He took it and went out – he never laid it down?"

"That is quite true," said Chan gravely.

"He never laid it down – that time," the old sheriff continued, his voice trembling, "but – God help me – that blanket had been in this room before."

Neither spoke. Chan regarded the old man with silent admiration.

Sam Holt rose, and began to stumble about the room. He found an unobstructed path, and started to pace it.

"It's all clear, Mr Chan. He was sent fer that blanket – he came back with it – Landini was here alone – he threw the blanket over that chair – he shot Landini with her own revolver. Then he snatched up the blanket, tidied up that desk, went through the room next door – open because he'd planned it all – and when the stage was clear, walked calm-like on to the scene with the blanket he'd been sent fer. As simple as that. And do I have to tell you why he killed her, Mr Chan?"

Charlie had listened to this with growing conviction. Now his eyes narrowed. "I was wondering why you asked Dudley Ward whether or not Sing knew about the child. You did it most adroitly."

"The kid," said old Sam Holt. "The kid – there's our answer." He offered Charlie the collection of fuzz. "Put it in an envelope, please. We'll compare it with that blanket later – but it ain't really necessary. Yes, Mr Chan – that lost boy of Dudley Ward's was the first thing I thought of when Don told me the story of the murder." He stumbled back to his chair and dropped into it.

"You see, sir, I knew the way of these old Chinese servants with the boys of the family. They love 'em. Year after year I seen old Sing cookin' an' slavin' fer Dudley Ward an' his brother – takin' care of 'em since they left the cradle – lovin' an' scoldin' 'em an' treatin' 'em always like babies. An' I knew what it must have meant to Sing that they was no little boys in this house, or in the big house down in 'Frisco. Jes' loneliness in the kitchen, no kids beggin' fer rice an' gravy. An' then he hears that there was a kid – only Landini kept it dark – never let its father know – never brought it out here where it belonged. He hears that, Mr Chan, an' what happens? He sees red. He hates. He hates Ellen Landini – an' I kain't say I blame him.

"Even Dudley Ward doesn't suspect what's in the old man's heart. He invites Landini over here. An' Sing gits his chance. Yes, Mr Chan – it was Sing who came into this room last night an' killed Landini – an' I would ruther be hung myself than say it."

"I have somewhat similar feeling," Charlie admitted.

"But you reckon I'm right."

Chan glanced toward the envelope into which he had put the wool from the blue blanket. "I very much fear you are."

The door opened, and Don Holt entered. "Come along," he said. "Cash is here, an' we're off to Reno. Why – what you two looking so solemn about?"

"Shet the door, son," said Sam Holt. He rose and moved toward his boy. "You know what I said to you this morning – about Sing?"

"Oh, but you're all wrong, Dad," the boy assured him.

"Jest a minute. You know how Sing appeared in this room right after the murder, with a blue blanket under his arm?"

"Sure I do."

"Well – if I was to tell you I found blue fuzz from a blanket on the arm of that thar chair over there – what would you say? You'd say the blanket had been in this room before Sing appeared with it, wouldn't you?"

Don Holt considered. "I might," he admitted. "And then again – I might say that it had come back here later – after the murder."

"What do you mean by that?" his father asked.

"Why, when we carried Landini out of the house last night, we wrapped her in blankets. Sing brought them to us here. Blue blankets they were, too. And while I don't exactly recall, we may have laid 'em across that chair before we used 'em."

A delighted smile spread over Sam Holt's face. "Boy," he said, "I ain't never been so proud of you before. Mr Chan, I reckon I've gone and wandered into the wrong pew. What do you think?"

"The wrong pew, perhaps," Charlie replied politely, "but maybe correct church. Who can say?"

VIII

THE STREETS OF RENO

When they came downstairs, Doctor Swan was waiting for them beside the fire. He handed the sheriff an envelope and also a folded sheet of paper.

"A letter to my landlady," he explained. "And a list of things I'll need – you'll find a bag in the closet to put them in. I hope to heaven I'll be able to get home pretty quickly – what do you think?"

"I hope so, too, Doctor," the sheriff replied.

"You – have no clue, I suppose?"

"None at all," responded the young man. "Except that someone, who knew all about how Miss Beaton felt toward Landini, planted that pink scarf and the pin. We're investigatin' that."

The doctor gave him an unpleasant look and turned away.

Romano came up, looking rather forlorn. "Pleasant journey," he remarked.

"Sorry you ain't goin' anywhere," smiled Don Holt.

Romano shrugged. "Me – I have no place to go – and no money to take me there, if I had."

"Does it chance," Chan inquired, "that there exists some errand we could perform for you in Reno?"

"None," Romano answered. "But" – he came closer, and lowered his voice – "would you be kind enough to inquire of Miss Meecher as to whether or not poor Ellen ever signed that new will?"

"Miss Meecher?"

"Yes – an estimable woman – Ellen's secretary. Estimable, but alas – so – what you call – close-mouthed."

Charlie nodded. "Do not fret, I beg of you. That is one of the things we visit Reno to discover."

"Good," cried Romano. "Splendid news. Excellent."

Leslie Beaton and her brother appeared, the latter going at once for his hat and coat. Don Holt had stepped to the door leading to the kitchen, and he now returned with a youth whose costume suggested that a rodeo was impending. Bright blue corduroys were tucked into high-heeled boots, his shirt was yellow silk embroidered with pink roses, around his neck was a crimson scarf, and he carried a two-gallon hat in his hand.

"Folks," said Holt, "this here is Cash Shannon, my deputy. You'll be seein' more of him – if your eyes can stand it."

"Pleased to meet you," remarked Mr Shannon cordially.

"Miss Beaton – I hope you won't mind him – much," Holt went on.

"Not at all," the girl smiled. "He's to keep an eye on me, I presume?"

"Lady," said Cash in a deep emotional voice, "the softest snap of my life. Easy to look at – that's what you are."

Holt laughed. "Don't pay any attention to him. He's such a fast worker he gets all tangled up. A lady's man – jes' born that way."

"Better that than a woman-hater, like you," Cash averred.

"A woman-hater," cried the girl. "You mean Mr Holt?"

"Lady – you said it. These divorcees we git round here has jes' naturally soured him on the sex. Takes a herd of 'em out on a picnic, an' comes back ravin' about their war-paint an' their cigarettes, an' how women ain't what they used to be – an' probably never was."

"Some women," Holt corrected. "I never said all."

"I ain't deaf," Cash returned. "All women, you always said." He squinted his eyes. "Ain't never heard you make no exception – until now."

"Well, let's get going," said Holt hastily.

Dudley Ward appeared, ready for the journey. Miss Beaton went with them to the veranda, pronounced the morning gorgeous and moved on with the little group to the pier. Chan and Don Holt walked with the old sheriff, but he seemed perfectly able to keep a straight course down the path. Cash Shannon came up behind them.

"Say, listen, Don," he remarked in a loud whisper, "you're crazy. If that dame done murder, I'm Al Capone."

"Get the girl off your mind," Holt smiled. "Remember, you're here to watch a lot of people. Sing, and the doctor, and Romano – that little Italian guy. Cecile, too. How do you know they ain't all goin' out the back door right now?"

"I get you," nodded Cash. "Mebbe I better go back."

"Mebbe you had. An' when it comes to this girl, jes' keep one thing in mind. You ain't the sheriff. You're jes' the deputy."

"Yes, sir," responded Cash, and returned reluctantly to the house.

As they were about to step into the sheriff's launch, the front door banged, and Sing ran like a rabbit down the path. He was waving wildly.

"Hey, Boss," he panted when he reached them. "Heah – you catch 'um umbella."

"Umbrella," Ward protested. "The sun's shining."

"Sun him shine now." Sing announced, portentously. "Plitty soon lain him fall. Sing know. You lissen to Sing."

"Oh, all right," Ward grinned. "Give it to me." Sing handed it to him, and retired up the path. "Let's get off quick," Ward continued. "He's forgot to make me put on my arctics. Poor chap – I'm afraid he is getting old, after all."

They guided Sam Holt into the launch, then Ward, Beaton and Chan followed. Don Holt turned to the girl. "Look out for that Cash," he warned. "He's got a Romeo complex. I'll be back on the job myself by sundown."

"Fine," she smiled. "I'll feel much safer then."

The launch put-putted and they swept off over the sunlit lake. As they turned toward Tahoe, they could see the girl waving to them from the pier. A shrill cry from the house caused them to look back. Sing was standing on the steps, waving an arctic in each hand.

They all laughed, and Dudley Ward said, above the noise of the motor, "Great! Two victories over Sing in one morning. I slipped into his room and got his broken glasses." He held up a spectacles case. "Mr Chan – please don't let me forget them while we're in town."

Charlie nodded, but did not reply. The loveliness of the scene, so foreign to anything he had ever encountered before, enchanted him. The vista of snow-clad mountains, of deep blue water, of dark green pines, might indeed have thrilled one far less sensitive to beauty. And the air – he pitied all those who could not breathe such air this morning. Those of the cities, who awoke to the same old scent of gasoline – even those of his own Honolulu, who awoke to an air likely to send them, mentally at least, back to slumber. He was grateful to the fate that had brought him to this spot.

All too soon they reached the Tavern pier. As he walked with Sam Holt along the unsteady planks, solicitous lest the old sheriff's cane become caught in one of the many cracks, he sought to express some of his admiration for the Sierra Nevada country.

"Yes – it's a good place, I reckon," Holt said. "I was born here seventy-eight years ago, and I've stuck close. Read about them

Alps in Switzerland. Used to think I'd like to see 'em. Kain't see my own mountains – no more. Are we alone, Mr Chan?"

"We are," said Charlie. "The others are now far in advance."

"I reckon you an' me – we're goin' to accept Don's explanation about the fuzz on that chair?"

"With the greatest of pleasure," smiled Chan. "On the part of both."

Sam Holt smiled, too. "I reckon so. But that don't mean we don't have to push ahead an' solve this case, Inspector."

"I am keenly aware of the fact," Charlie assured him.

"Nothing else against Sing – except that bench which got kicked over. You kain't prove anything by that. Ain't nothin' else, is they?"

"Not – not much," Chan answered. "Be very careful, please. The next plank is of a faulty nature."

"I remember it," Sam Holt replied. "What was Dudley Ward sayin' about Sing's glasses? They got broke? When was that?"

"A long time ago – so I understand."

"He wasn't wearin' 'em when you come last evenin'?"

"No – his sight was his own."

Holt hesitated. "Mr Chan – the person who mixed them box lids last night wasn't seein' any too well."

"I am forced to agree," Charlie replied.

"Has it jes' happened to occur to you that the story told by that Beaton boy may have been correct? That Ellen Landini may have sent some person for her green scarf?"

"It has occurred to me," Chan admitted.

"And the person came back with a pink one. Mr Chan – that person wasn't seein' any too well, either."

"I understand," Chan replied.

Holt shook his head. "If that boy Sing don't stop poppin' back into this thing like he was the killer, he'll jes' plumb break my heart," he said.

"Cease to worry," Charlie replied sympathetically. "Maybe pretty quick we eliminate him."

"Or else—"

"In any case, Mr Holt," Chan continued, "please be so good as to accept my advice, so humbly offered. Cease to worry."

Don Holt was waiting for them at the pier's end. "Mr Chan – the car's ready for us up in the drive. Dad, what are you going to do today?"

"Never mind, son. I kin take care of myself. I'm havin' lunch with Jim Dinsdale, an' other times I'll jes' loll round an' mebbe do a little thinkin'."

"Well, you be careful," the young sheriff said. "Better keep inside – you don't want any cold – at your age. And whatever you do, watch your step—"

"Run along," cut in Sam Holt. "My God – anybody would think I was a baby in the cradle to hear you. Mr Chan – you got sons, I suppose?"

"Abundantly," Charlie answered.

"They treat you this way?"

Chan took his hand. "Princes have censors," he remarked, "and fathers have sons. A happy day to you – and once again – so proud to meet you."

On the way to the drive in front of the garage, Chan encountered Dudley Ward. "Now we are on our way," the detective said, "to important discoveries, I hope. May I venture the wish that such stirring morning does not find you – as you said last night—"

"Afraid?" Ward finished. "No, Mr Chan. A man is likely to feel a little low at four in the morning. If I have a boy somewhere, it will be happy news for me. I'm starting late, but by heaven, I'll win his respect and affection if it's the last act of my life. It will give me what I've lacked and needed for many years – an incentive – something to live for."

Hugh Beaton joined them from behind. A silent young man, Charlie reflected. He had scarcely spoken all morning; his face was pale and drawn. No doubt the events of the night before were a bit hard on the artistic temperament.

Don Holt herded them into a big closed car, which he said belonged to Dinsdale, and they were off. Down through the scattered village, then on to Truckee, a bit more cheery in the bright morning. There they came on to the main highway, almost clear of snow, and the sheriff stepped on the gas.

They entered Reno through quiet pleasant streets that in no way suggested anything but the average western town. Charlie looked eagerly about him; here was no hint of night clubs, faro games, bars and merry prospective widows. The main street, Virginia, seemed the usual one, save for a preponderance of lawyer's offices and beauty parlors.

"Just a moment, Sheriff," Ward said. "Here's that optician's. I'll drop these glasses now – it will take some time to fix them. If you don't mind."

"Sure, I don't," returned Holt amiably. He waited while a car slipped out of a parking place, and then moved in. Ward left them.

"Well, Mr Chan," Holt remarked, "what do you think of the biggest little city in the world?"

"So far," Charlie told him, "it refuses to sustain its reputation."

"You got to get it gradually," the sheriff explained. "For instance – them black chiffon nightgowns in that window. Not for the western trade, Mr Chan. An' all these beauty parlors – women have gone dippy over war-paint, but the local girls couldn't support so many. And that nurse in the funny dress – with them cute kids – goin' to have a brand-new papa, the poor little devils. Gradually, it soaks in. The best people from the East come here – and raise hell with the West."

But at this end of the street, Chan reflected, the West still ruled. Cowboys whose costumes were a faded imitation of the

Cash Shannon splendor, cattle men and ranchers – and here an Indian woman with a papoose strapped to her back. It was not until Ward returned and they crossed the bridge over the yellow, tumbling Truckee River, that they began to mingle with the best people from the East. Holt parked in front of the new hotel, sliding in beside a long, low, foreign car, over which a glowering chauffeur, also foreign, stood guard. At the left was the dignified white court-house, the heart of the community. They entered the busy lobby of the hotel, and although Charlie never guessed it, he beheld a Patou hat and a Chanel ensemble for the first time in his life.

"I wonder," Hugh Beaton said timidly, "may I go up to my – to our – rooms now?"

He looked so pale and helpless that the sheriff gave him a kindly pat. "You gather up all the stuff you and your sister will need, and—"

"Need – for how long?" Beaton asked.

"How the heck should I know? Jes' gather up some stuff, an' meet us here in this lobby – say, at three o'clock. Run along, kid – an' cheer up." He turned to Charlie. "Why are you lookin' at me like that, Inspector?"

Chan smiled. "Ah – I am just thinking. Is that the method of a good detective? Such a one would enter those rooms simultaneously – he would search – he would investigate correspondence."

Holt shrugged his broad shoulders. "I ain't no detective, good or otherwise. Thank the lord. I'm only a sheriff."

The sleek young man at the desk looked at them suspiciously when Holt asked to be shown to Landini's apartment. "Miss Meecher is up there alone," he said. "She's had a frightful morning. The reporters have been so rude."

"Well, we're not reporters," said Holt. He flashed his badge. "I'm the sheriff from over the line, this is Mr Dudley Ward, of Tahoe and San Francisco, and this is Mr Charlie Chan, of Honolulu."

Don Holt had a carrying voice, and it was not surprising that three young men at once leaped forward from behind nearby potted palms. They represented various press associations and the local paper, it appeared. The passing of Landini was news all over the world. The method of her passing was better still. After a struggle which reached major proportions, the sheriff and his companions got away, and started upstairs, where Miss Meecher awaited them. As the elevator ascended, Chan thought of Henry Lee, the steward, with a wry smile. "I shall watch newspapers," Mr Lee had said.

Miss Meecher greeted them at the door, a repressed, middle-aged woman dressed in black. Very proper-looking, rather grim, but breathing efficiency.

"Come in, gentlemen," she said. She met even Chan without a change of expression – a remarkable woman indeed, he thought. "A terrible thing, this is. No one, evidently, thought to telephone me the news."

"So sorry," Chan remarked, "but up to this morning, no one in authority knew of your existence. The others – Miss Beaton and her brother – were perhaps too overcome."

"Perhaps," she answered. Her voice was as crisp and cool as the mountain air. She added: "I am glad you are here, Mr Ward. Someone will have to attend to – to the services."

Ward bowed his head. "I'd already thought of it. I shall take full charge – it seems to be my duty. No one else appears to be interested – outside, of course, yourself."

She nodded. "Thank you. Then that is settled." Efficient. No time for emotion. Just – what's the next thing to be done? Well – do it – and move on.

"Might I ask?" Ward continued, "how long you have been with Madame Landini?"

"Over seven years," Miss Meecher replied. "I came first as secretary – lately I have more or less combined that post with the one of – maid. Times have not been so good – with any of us."

Dudley Ward leaned suddenly forward. "I'm sorry," he said, and his voice trembled. "I do not wish to seem abrupt. But there is one question I must ask you – and I cannot hold it back – I cannot wait. I have heard it rumored – that my wife had a son – my son – about whom she never told me. You can understand my feeling in this matter, I'm sure. I want to ask you – I want you to tell me – was there any truth in this rumor?"

Miss Meecher stared at him. The same expressionless face. "I cannot tell you," she said. "I do not know. Madame never mentioned the matter to me."

Ward turned away, and sat looking out the window at his right, across an open space toward the white court-house which had figured so largely in the life of Ellen Landini. Finally Chan broke the silence.

"Miss Meecher – the sheriff here will tell you that he authorizes me to speak for him—"

"That's right," Holt nodded.

"Had you heard any word from Madame Landini, Miss Meecher, at any time, that might lead you to believe she considered her life in danger?"

"None at all. Of course, she carried a pistol, but that was from a fear of thugs, robbers. I'm sure she was not afraid of any of her intimates. She had no reason to be."

"There are three or four men, Miss Meecher, about whose relations with Landini I wish to make inquiries." The woman's expression finally changed – a little. "Oh, most pleasant inquiries," Chan assured her. "Nothing of scandalous nature. I would mention John Ryder. Her second husband, you know."

"I know."

"She never heard from him? Had correspondence with him?"

"I don't imagine she thought of him, any more."

"Have you the slightest idea why she separated from him? After many years, it would seem he still bears wound."

"I can give you a notion," Miss Meecher said. "Madame's scrap-books of clippings from all over the world always traveled with us. In an early one, when I first came to her, I once read a certain item. Just a moment." She rose briskly, went into the other room, and reappeared with a worn old-fashioned book. Opening it, she handed it to Chan, and pointed.

Chan read slowly and carefully a newspaper clipping, now yellow with age:

ELLEN LANDINI SNOWED IN

Recently Divorced San Francisco Singer in a Cabin "Up the Ravine."

SAN FRANCISCO, Feb. 9 – Ellen Landini, the singer, formerly the wife of Dudley Ward, of this city, but who was recently married to John Ryder, a mining man, is snowed in for the winter at Calico mine, in Plumas County. After their marriage Mrs Ryder gave up her career and took the trail with her husband over the Sierra Nevada Mountains to the Calico claim, of which he is manager. Heavy snow fell soon after the couple had established themselves in the superintendent's cabin up the ravine.

Some mining men who have come down from that country say snow is twenty-five feet deep on the level, and that it is one of the hardest winters northern California has known in many years. Twenty-five feet of snow means candle-light all day in the cabin and no fresh grub and little if any mail; snow on the ground until June and no chance to get out with comfort before summer.

Chan handed the book to the sheriff, and looked at Miss Meecher. "It has aspect of romantic situation," he remarked, "rather than grounds for divorce."

"That," the woman replied, "is what I remarked to Madame when I read it. I – I was somewhat younger at the time. Madame burst into loud laughter 'Romantic, Mary,' she cried. 'Ah, but life is not like that. Romantic to find yourself shut up in one room for eternity with the most colossal bore since the world began! A sullen egotist, with the conversational powers of a mummy. In a week I loathed him, in another I despised him, in a month I could have killed him. I was the first person out of that camp in the spring, and I thanked God it was only a few miles to Reno.' I am quoting Madame, you understand, Mr Chan."

Charlie smiled. "Ah, yes – that would, I have no doubt, happen. It begins to explain Mr Ryder. If you do not incline to object, I would remove this clipping."

Miss Meecher looked startled at the idea, but then remembered. "Oh, of course," she said. "It won't matter particularly now."

Chan took the book from the sheriff, and carefully cut out the tale of Landini's second marriage. Meanwhile, Dudley Ward sat, still silent, by the window, apparently hearing none of this.

"We proceed," Chan continued. "And in the course of our proceedings we now arrive at Mr Luis Romano."

Miss Meecher so far forgot her stern aloofness as to permit herself a shrug of disgust.

"Romano," she said, "we haven't seen him in months. You don't mean to say that he is in this neighborhood?"

"He was at Mr Ward's home last evening. I gathered his attitude toward Madame Landini. What, if you please, was her attitude toward him?"

"Oh, she tolerated him. He was a harmless little idiot. Why she ever married him I'm sure I don't know – and I'm just as sure that Madame didn't, either. He liked to be petted, pampered, looked after. But there is no real romance in that – and she finally sent him on his way."

"Making a settlement – which she later ignored."

"I'm afraid she did. She couldn't help herself. She owns a great deal of real estate – but ready cash has been very scarce."

"Speaking of real estate – she drew up a will, leaving her property to her new attraction – Mr Hugh Beaton. I am eager to know – was that will ever signed?"

Miss Meecher suddenly put her hand to her cheek. "Good heavens – I never thought of that. It was – it was never signed."

Even Dudley Ward looked up. "Never signed, eh?" cried Don Holt.

"No. It came from her lawyers three weeks ago. There was something in it that wasn't quite right. She was going to have it fixed here – but she kept putting it off. She was always – putting things off."

"Then Luis Romano inherits her estate?" Chan said thoughtfully.

"I'm afraid he does."

"Do you think he knew this?"

"If he didn't, it wasn't his fault. He kept writing, trying to find out whether or not the will had been signed. He wrote to me, privately. But of course I didn't tell him. Perhaps – perhaps he wrote to her lawyers, in New York."

Chan sat for a moment quietly, considering this startling possibility.

"We drop that for the present," he said finally. "I turn now to Michael Ireland, the aviator. Would you talk about him, please?"

"There's nothing to say," Miss Meecher answered. "I believe there was once a sort of love-affair between him and Madame. It was before my time. Since she came here, she's enjoyed riding about in his plane. But the affair was over – on her side, at least. I'm sure of that."

"And on his side?"

"Well – I suppose I must tell everything. I did overhear him making love to her here one evening. But she only laughed at him."

"So – she laughed at him, eh?" Again Chan considered.

"Yes – she told him to stick to his wife. She reminded him that when she first saw him, he had just come home from the war, and was in uniform. 'It was the uniform, Michael,' I heard her say. 'I loved every man who wore one!'"

Chan's eyes narrowed. "So Ireland served in the war? A steady hand. A clear eye. An expert—" He saw Don Holt looking at him with amazement. "What of it?" he added hastily. "Miss Meecher, there is one I have saved to the last. I refer to Doctor Swan."

"Contemptible," spoke Miss Meecher, and her thin lips closed tightly.

"So I have gathered," Charlie replied. "Since you have come to Reno, he has visited Madame?"

"He has."

"Ah, yes – he lied to us about that. But visits were necessary if he was to follow his trade."

"You mean – as doctor?"

"Alas, no. I mean as blackmailer, Miss Meecher."

The woman started. "Who told you that?"

"No matter. We know it. We know that Madame had long paid him two hundred and fifty dollars a month. Why did she pay him this money?"

"I – I don't know," the secretary said.

"Ah – I am so sorry to contradict a lady," Charlie went on sadly. "But you do know, Miss Meecher. You know quite well Landini paid him this money because he had somehow become aware of the birth of her child. She paid it to him because he threatened that, if she did not, he would acquaint Mr Dudley Ward, the child's father, with the facts. Come – Miss Meecher – this is not the time for double dealing. I want the truth."

Dudley Ward was on his feet. Perspiration gleamed on his forehead as he faced the woman. "I – I want it too," he cried.

Miss Meecher looked up at him. "I'm sorry," she said. "When you first came in – I wasn't sure – I wanted a moment to think. I – I have thought. It doesn't really matter now, I suppose. You may as well know. Yes – Madame had a son. A lovely boy. I saw him once. Dudley – she called him. He would have been eighteen next January – if—"

"If – what?" Ward cried hoarsely.

"If he – had lived. He was killed in an automobile accident over three years ago. I'm so – so sorry, Mr Ward."

Ward had put his hands out, feebly, as though to fend off a blow. "And I never saw him," he said brokenly. "I never saw him." He turned, and walking to the window, leaned heavily against it.

IX

TROUBLE TAKES WING

The three other people in Landini's small sitting-room looked at one another, but did not speak. For a time Ward continued to stare out the window. At length he turned; he was pale, but self-controlled and calm. Blood, the young sheriff thought to himself, will tell. The cowards never started on that rush of '49, and the weaklings died on the way, but Dudley Ward was descended from a man who had reached journey's end. His voice was steady as he said. "Thank you so much for telling me."

"I knew, of course, the child was dead," Chan remarked, "when you told us Romano was Landini's only heir. You have, perhaps, Miss Meecher, some documents regarding the boy's death?"

She rose. "Yes. I have the telegram that was our first news of it, and the letter that followed from his foster-mother. Madame always kept them close to her."

She opened a desk drawer, and producing these, handed them to Dudley Ward. They waited while he read them. "That is finished," he said finally, and returned them.

"Madame read that letter over and over," Miss Meecher told him. "I want you to know, Mr Ward, that she adored this boy. Though she rarely saw him, though he regarded himself as the son of – of others – he was always in her thoughts. You must – believe this."

"Yes," Ward said dully, and again turned to the window.

"Then it is true," Charlie said to the woman in a subdued voice, "that Doctor Swan was blackmailing her about this matter?"

"Yes – he was. She did not want Mr Ward to hear about the boy – even after – the accident."

"Recently she stopped the payments, and Doctor Swan – perhaps he threatened her?"

"He was very violent and abusive about it. I don't believe he had a successful practice, and it appeared that this money meant a lot to him. I don't know that he actually threatened her life, however. But he was a man capable of almost anything."

Chan nodded toward the desk. "I note there long strips of paper with printing. Am I correct in calling them proofs of book?"

Miss Meecher nodded. "They are galley proofs of Madame's autobiography, which I have been helping her to write for the past few years. The book is to be published very soon."

"Ah," returned Charlie, a sudden eagerness in his voice, "would you, perhaps, object if I took same with me and perused them? Some little detail, some chance remark—"

"By all means," Miss Meecher replied. "If you'll be kind enough to return them. As a matter of fact – I'd like to have you read them. I'm afraid you've got rather a – well, a mistaken idea of Madame. If you had really known her as I knew her—" She stopped, and a terrible dry sob shook her thin shoulders. It passed in a moment. "She was really the kindest person – the victim of a wrong impression fostered by her many marriages. She was just restless, unhappy, always seeking romance – and never finding it."

"No doubt she has been misjudged," Chan returned politely. "Public opinion is often an envious dog barking at the heels of greatness. Ah, thank you – you needn't wrap the proofs. This large elastic will suffice. You shall have them back at very earliest moment. Now, I think, Mr Ward, if you are willing, we will trouble this lady no longer."

"Of course," Ward answered. He looked at Miss Meecher. "There were – photographs – I suppose?"

"Many. They belong to you now." She started on her efficient way, but he laid a hand on her arm.

"Please," he said, "a little later. I – I couldn't bring myself—If you will be so kind, you might gather them up for me."

"I will," she promised.

"You have been so good, Miss Meecher," Chan remarked, bowing low. "Always I shall remember your frankness. It is of such great help."

"There's just one thing," the secretary returned, "that you might do for me."

"You have only to name it."

"Trouble," said the woman. "Trouble, the dog. He and I had much in common – we both loved Madame. I should like to have him, if I might. I am certain Madame would wish it."

"I will despatch him to you with the greatest speed," Chan promised. "Perhaps – by airplane."

"Thank you so much. He – he will be company for me here." And Charlie saw, as he took his leave, that at last there were tears in the eyes of the aloof Miss Meecher.

The three men rode down in the elevator, Chan and the sheriff both slightly uncomfortable at the feeling that there was something they should say to Ward and neither being able to put it into words.

"There are a number of things I must attend to," Ward remarked, when they reached the lobby. "I fancy I'm not concerned in your further investigation here. I'll meet you again on this spot at three."

"That'll be fine," the sheriff said, and Chan nodded. Ward disappeared, and Holt added: "Dog-gone it, I wanted to say something about the kid, but I jes' plumb couldn't."

"There are times," Charlie told him, "when words, though meant in kindness, are but salt in the wound."

"There sure are. Well, what do you say? I had breakfast at six, and it's nearly one. Let's eat, Inspector."

Into the rather effete dining-room Don Holt brought a breath of the West. Women in smart Paris costumes looked up admiringly as he passed, and registered a startled interest at sight of the broad figure which followed meekly at his heels. Ignoring them all, the sheriff sat down and with difficulty selected a man-size lunch from the French items on the menu. When the waiter had departed – a friendly waiter who treated them like old pals – Charlie ventured a question.

"You propose to visit local police?"

Holt grinned. "No – reckon I'll give them a bitter disappointment by passing them up. Nothing to gain, that I can see. Say, won't they be sore! All this lovely publicity, an' they on the outside, lookin' in. But you're going to be all the help I'll need, Mr Chan. I can see that, right now."

"Sincerely trust you are not too optimistic," Charlie answered. "Can it be you glimpse light of solution ahead?"

"Me?" cried Holt. "I ain't got the slightest idea what's goin' on. But some men – well, you jes' look at 'em, and you get confidence. You're one like that."

Charlie smiled. "I should gaze more often in mirror," he replied. "Myself, I am not so sure. This is hard case. However, Miss Meecher was mine of information."

"Yeah – you got plenty out of her, didn't you?"

"Our success was gratifying. We learn – what? The background of Landini's second marriage – that to John Ryder. Snowed in with him up the ravine – the poor lady has, even at late day like this, my sincere condolences. We learn what may prove vastly important clue – new will was left unsigned, and Romano is happy heir. Did he know this? If he did, then case may end a very simple one. We learn that Swan's blackmail concerned the dead son of Landini, hear of the doctor's anger when payment at last was ended. Also, that Michael Ireland made love, and was repulsed. Is our motive hidden somewhere among these?"

"Also – though I can't see that it means anything – we hear that Ireland was in the war," Holt remarked. "I must say, Mr Chan – you acted mighty mysterious right there. Last night you said some pretty queer things, too – but I want to assure you here an' now – I ain't going to ask any questions."

"Thank you so much," Charlie said. "But as clues pop up in this case, I promise I will draw them to your attention. We work on the matter together."

"Yeah – but with different brains," grinned Holt. "Well, here's one I guessed right. Filet mignon does mean steak – but not much of it."

After lunch they visited Swan's lodgings. The landlady, who appeared to be waging a battle against age with the assistance of various drug-store preparations, was suspicious at first, but soon succumbed to Don Holt's charm. From then on, she was almost too solicitous. However, they managed a search of the rooms, with absolutely no result, and then proceeded to gather up the articles the doctor had listed.

"Well, I reckon we're jes' errand boys, after all," remarked Holt, as he tossed an armful of gaudy shirts into the suitcase. "And I wanted to get something on this bird, the worst way."

"Ah," nodded Chan, "you still hold him responsible for awkward situation regarding Miss Beaton's scarf."

"He put it there, of course. That's plain enough."

"If he did," Chan continued, "then he also persuaded Landini to grasp it before he killed her. I am plenty sure of that."

"Well, maybe he did," said the sheriff.

They returned presently to the hotel. Ward and Beaton were sitting in the lobby, the latter with two large bags at his feet. A little later they were on their way down Virginia Street. Dudley Ward sat silent, and as they passed the optician's, Chan turned to him. "You recalled the spectacles of Sing, Mr Ward?"

Ward came to himself with a start. "No – by George – I forgot all about them—"

"Permit that I go," Charlie suggested. "I need not climb out over luggage, you will perceive."

"That's very kind of you," Ward answered. "Just charge them to me. I have an account there."

Holt parked some distance down the street, and Chan got out. He walked back to the optician's, through a colorful western throng, and going in, made clear his errand. The optician remarked that Sing should have come himself – the frame should have been adjusted on him.

"Sing has but little interest in the affair," Chan remarked. "Which is a great pity, since his eyes are so very bad."

"Who says his eyes are bad?" the man wanted to know.

"Why – I have always understood that he could see very little without these spectacles," Chan returned.

The optician laughed. "He's kidding you," he said. "He can see about as well without them as with them. Except when it comes to reading – and I don't guess Sing does a great deal of that."

"Thank you so much," Charlie responded. "The charge is to be made on Mr Dudley Ward, of Tahoe."

He returned and handed the glasses to Ward. Holt started the car and in a few moments they were again out on the main road west, rolling along between the snowy hills.

Charlie was turning over in his mind this latest news. Sing was really not deprived of much when he broke his glasses. It was amusing how fate was constantly exonerating the old man. It had probably not been Sing who mixed the box lids.

No one seemed inclined to conversation, so Chan settled in his seat to meditate on the puzzle of those lids. They went over a bump. "Excuse me, folks," Don Holt said. The galley proofs of Ellen Landini's autobiography fell from Chan's lap to the floor of the car. He picked them up and carefully dusted them off. If he had been as psychic as he sometimes pretended to be, he would have known that the answer to this particular puzzle was at that moment in his hands.

Something more than an hour later, they drove up before the Tavern garage. As they alighted, all rather stiff from the ride, Don Holt looked up at the sky.

"Clouding a bit," he commented. "Sort of a dampness in the air, too. Perhaps Sing was right, Mr Ward. Shouldn't be surprised if we had rain – or maybe snow."

"Sing's always right," Ward answered. "That's why I took the umbrella. And I felt a little uncomfortable about the arctics, too."

They stopped for a moment in the big lounge of the hotel, where a welcome fire was blazing. Charlie took Sam Holt by the arm, and led him to a far corner of the room.

"How was the fishin' down to Reno?" asked the former sheriff.

"A few minnows," Chan answered. "But as you and I know, Mr Holt, in our business, most innocent-looking minnow may suddenly enlarge to whale."

"True enough," the old man answered.

"Being somewhat pressed for time," Charlie continued, "I will leave to your son the pleasure of detailed account. Suffice to say, once more our good friend Sing is clear of suspicion." He related his conversation with the optician.

Holt slapped his leg with keen delight. "By cricky, I ain't had so much fun bein' wrong since I played roulette on a crooked wheel, an' run the owner out of Angel's Flats. I sure got off on the wrong foot with this case. Which it served me right – fer I didn't have no business suspectin' that boy – the years I've knowed him. Well, that's out. He didn't mix them lids, nor bungle that scarf business. Who did?"

"At present," Chan returned, "only echo is on hand to answer."

"You'll be answerin' fer yourself soon enough," Holt nodded. "I git more confidence in you every time I hear you speak."

"It will remain one of the triumphs of my life," Chan replied, "that I stood in such high favor with honorable family of Holt. Should events not justify your esteem, I leave this lovely country in the night."

Don Holt joined them. "Hello, Dad," he said. "How about the coroner?"

"Jes' got here an hour ago," his father answered. "Slow, as usual. Down at the mortuary now."

"Reckon we'll have to get his report later, Mr Chan," the young man said. "By the way, I was talkin' to Dinsdale this mornin', an' he agreed to take a few of the suspects off Dudley Ward's hands. It'll be a load off your shoulders, too. Cash an' me is both down here, an' between us we can handle 'em, I reckon. I thought maybe Swan, an' Romano, an' Hugh Beaton, an' – er—"

"Hugh Beaton would not come over here without his sister," Charlie smiled.

The sheriff blushed. "Well, we could fix her up, too," he said. "It ain't fair to Ward, all the trouble he's had, to load these strangers on him. And it's so near you could go on investigatin' as usual. Dinsdale's all tied up with painters an' decorators now, an' he tells me there's only one room ready tonight. It ain't a very good one – so I thought I'd bring Swan back with me an' put him in it."

Charlie nodded. "I yield him with great pleasure. It will, as you say, narrow my watching."

"Well, we may as well get goin'," Don Holt remarked. "It's comin' on dusk."

Chan shook hands with Sam Holt. "Until we meet again," he said. "Aloha."

"Same fer you," Holt replied. "An' thanks fer that news about Sing. I'll sleep better tonight."

Ward and Beaton joined them, and they went down to the sheriff's launch. The afterglow was fading on tall distant peaks as they swept over the darkening lake. Presently they tied up at Ward's pier. Dudley Ward and Beaton went on ahead. Charlie waited, and helped with the mooring ropes.

"I'll just leave Swan's bag in the boat," Holt said. "I needn't have brought it, in the first place. Not much of a thinker, I reckon."

They were walking up the path. Suddenly Chan put his hand on the young man's arm. "As resident of semi-tropic country," he remarked, "mostly sprinkled with palms, I have vast interest in these lofty pines. Could you give me name of variety?"

"Why – they're just pines," said Holt. He sought to move on, but Chan still held him.

"We have a tree resembling the pine on our island of Oahu," the detective went on. "It is called the ironwood. At one time I knew the Latin name, but – a busy life – those things escape. It was – it was – no use, I cannot recall."

"Too bad," Holt answered, squirming.

"Fine examples of the ironwood border the road to the Pali," Charlie continued. "The bark is much less sturdy, less thick, than that of your trees. Do not go, please." He ran across the snow to pick up a large segment of bark that lay at the foot of a nearby tree. "You behold how thick the bark of your trees is," he added, and handed the piece to the sheriff. "Shall we continue now to the house?"

At the foot of the steps, Holt suddenly stopped and stared at Chan. "What'll I do with this?" he asked, indicating the bark.

Charlie grinned. "Toss it away," he said. "It does not matter."

Sing admitted them, and they found Leslie Beaton and the resplendent Cash seated before the fire. "Back already?" Cash inquired. "Well, this day sure has gone fast."

"Not for Miss Beaton, I reckon," Holt said.

"Oh, indeed it has," the girl cried. "Mr Shannon has been telling me the most amazing things—"

"Yeah," nodded Holt, "I can imagine. He ought to write for the magazines, old Cash."

"Never do that," said Cash. "I want my audience where I kin see it. I sure had one nice audience today."

"Yeah," agreed Holt. "An' how about the rest of these people? Any of 'em still around the place?"

"Sure – they're all here – far as I know."

"Anything happen?"

"Not a thing. That aviator – Ireland, I guess his name is – dropped in on us a while ago. I reckon he's in the kitchen now."

Holt turned to Sing, who was fumbling about the fire. "Look here – Sing – go catch 'um Doctor Swan. Tell him I want to see him." The old man went out. "Well, Cash – much obliged. I guess I can carry on from this point."

Cash frowned. "Don't you think you ought to leave me right here, Chief?" he inquired. "I'd keep my eyes open—"

"Yeah – I know you would," Holt grinned, "but Mr Chan will do that – an' he'll look in the right direction. Say good night to this kind patient lady that must be nearly dead from the sound of your voice, an' go out to the boat. I'll be with you in a minute."

As Cash reluctantly departed, Doctor Swan came downstairs. "Ah, Sheriff," he said, "back safely, eh? Did you get my bag?"

"I got it. It's waiting for you out in the launch."

"Waiting for me?" Swan looked slightly startled.

"Yes – we're moving a few people down to the Tavern, and you're the first to push off."

"Of course – that's quite all right. I'll just get my hat and coat, and say goodby to my host."

Sing had appeared on the stairs. "Boss – he sleep. Say, keep evahbody out. My tell 'um you say goo'by. Hat an' coat light heah." He removed the latter from a closet. "Goo'by, Doctah."

With a somewhat dazed air, Swan got into his coat. Holt led him outside and, calling to Cash, turned the doctor over to him. When the sheriff returned to the living-room, he found Leslie Beaton alone.

"Why – where's Mr Chan?" he asked.

"He just ran out the back way," the girl explained. "He told me to tell you to be sure to wait. And he asked me – as a favor to him – to keep you company."

"Always thinking of others. Fine fellow," the sheriff said.

Silence fell. "Nice day," said the sheriff.

"Lovely."

"Not so nice tonight."

"No?"

"Looks like rain."

"Really?"

"Sure does."

More silence.

"Wish I could talk like Cash," the sheriff remarked.

"It's a gift," smiled the girl.

"I know. I wasn't there when they passed it."

"Don't you care."

"I – I never did. Before."

"Are you moving the rest of us to the Tavern?"

"Yes. There'll be a nice room for you tomorrow. Do you mind?"

"I think it's a grand idea."

"Yeah. Cash'll be there."

"Where will you be?"

"Oh – I'll be around, too."

"I still think it's a grand idea."

"That's – that's great," said the sheriff.

In the meantime, Charlie Chan had hurried to the kitchen. Cecile was alone there, with Trouble. "Your husband?" Charlie cried.

"He's just gone," Cecile answered. "Did you wish to see him?"

"I wanted him to do an errand for me," Chan explained. "I desired that he convey Trouble back to Miss Meecher, in Reno."

"You can catch him, I think," Cecile answered. She snatched up the startled dog, and thrust it into Chan's arms, "Michael will be glad to do it, I'm sure."

"Thank you so much," Chan cried and rushed out the door. As he approached the field, the hum of a motor rose on the still evening air. At the first sound of the engine Trouble leaped to life. He trembled with excitement, threw back his head, and time after time he barked a short happy bark. He was almost overcome with joyous anticipation.

As Charlie ran on to the field, he saw that the aviator was about to take off. Near the whirring propeller stood Dudley Ward's boatman. Chan shouted as loudly as he could and hastening to the side of the plane, he held up the dog and explained what he wanted.

"Sure, I'll take him," Ireland answered. "We're buddies, ain't we, Trouble? Crazy about flyin', this dog is."

The detective handed over the excited little terrier, and fell back to a safe distance. He stood and watched the machine taxi across the snowy field, then rise against the green splendor of the pines, and finally melt away into the fast-darkening sky. Deep in thought, he turned and walked back to the house.

When Charlie entered the living-room, the sheriff looked up with an expression that was almost one of relief. "Oh, there you are," he cried, rising hastily. "I was waitin' for you."

"The wait, I trust, was not unpleasant," Chan smiled.

"No – but, of course – I got to get back now. Well, Miss Beaton, I'll be seein' you. I hope your brother got all the things you wanted."

"If he got half of them," smiled the girl, "I'll be in luck. Poor Hugh – he's so artistic." She said goodby and ascended the stairs.

"I also will say goodby," remarked Charlie, and walked with the sheriff out the door and across the veranda. When they reached the path, he added: "Also, I desire to tell you that I just turned Trouble over to Michael Ireland. He is taking the little fellow back to Reno by plane."

"A great idea," said Holt heartily. "Saves time."

Chan lowered his voice. "It was not to save time that I did it."

"No?"

"No. I would like to call to your attention the fact that Trouble was wild with joy at sound of the motor. He was not afraid of the plane tonight."

"Does that mean anything?" asked Don Holt.

"It might. I incline to think it does. In fact, I believe that in this case Trouble is what my old friend, Inspector Duff of Scotland Yard, would call the essential clue."

X

ROMANO'S LUCKY BREAK

The young sheriff stood for a moment, staring across the lake at the last flickering of white on Genoa Peak. He removed his two-gallon hat, as though to give his mind a better chance.

"Trouble," he said, "a clue? I ain't gettin' it, Inspector."

Charlie shrugged. "Nevertheless," he replied, "such statement is based on facts equally well known to you."

Don Holt restored his hat. "Ain't any use, I reckon," he remarked. "You jes' go your way, an' I'll go mine, an' when you get to the top of the hill, drop a rope for me. By the way, when the coroner finishes, maybe you'd like to have a talk with him?"

"Very much indeed."

"Can you run a motor-boat?"

"Sometimes I have been permitted to drive the one belonging to my son, Henry – as a generous recognition of the fact that I paid for same."

"Good. I may give you a ring tonight. I'll send Cash up to spell you here." The sheriff paused. "I wish I had a good sensible deputy in this neighborhood," he added sadly. "A married man."

Chan smiled. "I could bring Miss Beaton to the Tavern with me. Pleasant spin over lake would do her vast good."

"A great idea," agreed the sheriff heartily. "Keep it in mind. Well, good luck. I'm sorry I ain't any use to you."

"Nonsense – you must not be discouraged. I remember well the first important case which came to me. Could I make distinguished progress? Can an ant shake a tree?"

"That's about the way I feel – like an ant."

"But you are indispensable. These are, as my cousin Willie Chan, baseball player, would say, your home grounds. I am only stranger, passing through, and it has been well said, the traveling dragon cannot crush the local snake." They walked together toward the pier. "Do not believe, however," Chan continued, "that I consider myself dragon. I lack, I fear, the figure."

"And you don't breathe much fire," Holt laughed. "But I guess you'll get there, jes' the same."

Cash and Doctor Swan were standing near the launch. The latter held out his hand to Charlie.

"Inspector," he remarked, "I fear we must separate for a time. But we shall meet again, no doubt."

"Such is my hope," the detective answered politely.

"I – I don't wish to seem overly curious – but was your visit to Reno successful?"

"In many ways – amazingly so."

"Splendid! I realize it's none of my affair, but Romano has been speculating on the matter all day, so I am moved to ask – does it happen that Landini signed the will – the one leaving her property to Beaton?"

Charlie hesitated but a second. "She did not sign it."

"Ah," nodded Swan. "A lucky break for Romano. Good night, Inspector. I shall see you, no doubt, at the Tavern."

"Good night," Chan answered thoughtfully.

Cash was already in the launch, Swan followed, and Don Holt took his place at the wheel. In a moment they were off.

Charlie stood watching the little boat as it sped along the brief three miles of shore-line that separated Pineview from the Tavern. Swan, he reflected, would not be far away if he wanted him, and Swan was the sort of man who might be wanted at any moment.

Walking slowly up the path, Chan paused at the foot of the steps. There he stood for a moment, staring up into the branches of the lofty pines. His glance moved thoughtfully from the lowest branch of the tree nearest the house to the balcony outside the study. He retreated a few steps to obtain a better view of the study window. Suddenly a light flashed on inside. Sing appeared and drew the curtains.

Deep in meditation, Chan proceeded, not up the steps, but around to the rear of the house. There were various sheds and a good sized garage between him and the hangar. From one of the sheds, a man emerged.

"Good evening," said Chan. "It was you, I believe, who brought us down in the launch last night?"

The man came closer. "Oh – good evenin'. Yes – I'm Mr Ward's boatman."

"You do not live on the place?"

"No, not now. I'm here jes' July an' August. Other times, when Mr Ward wants me, he telephones my home down t' Tahoe."

"Ah, yes. You just now assisted Mr Ireland in the starting of his plane. Did you by any chance do the same here last night?"

"Lord, no, mister. I wasn't here last night. Soon's I landed you all at the pier, I scurried back home. Mr Ward said I wouldn't be needed no more, an' we was havin' the weekly meetin' of the contract bridge club at our house."

Charlie smiled. "Thank you. I will not detain you further."

"Terrible thing, this murder," the boatman ventured. "Ain't had one o' them round here in years."

"Terrible, indeed," Chan nodded.

"Well – I guess I better be hurryin' back to supper. The wife ain't none too pleased with me today, anyhow. Say, mister – you don't happen to know anything about a psychic bid, do you?"

"Psychic?" Chan frowned. "Ah, you refer to bridge. I don't play it."

"Well, maybe you're right," replied the boatman, and hastened round the house, evidently bound for the pier.

The door of the garage was open, and Chan stepped inside. Only a flivver there at present, he noted – perhaps a larger car could not as yet make its way up the road from the Tavern. For a while the detective explored the place as well as he could in that dim light. He had just come upon a long ladder lying at the rear, when one of the doors banged shut, and he had to hurry to make the opening in time. Sing stood just outside, about to adjust a padlock.

"Hullo," cried the old man, startled. "Wha's mallah you? You no b'long this place."

"Merely taking look-see," Chan explained.

"You look-see too much," grumbled Sing. "Some day, some place, you get in, no can get out. Why you no min' own business, hey?"

"So sorry," Chan replied humbly. "I go now and buy a fan to hide my face."

"Allight. Plenty time you do," Sing nodded.

Feeling decidedly embarrassed, Charlie walked toward the house. Always, he reflected, he seemed to be coming off second-best in encounters with Sing. He stamped the snow from his shoes, entered the rear door and heard at once the voice of Mrs O'Ferrell.

"Take that out iv here," she was saying in a loud voice. "I won't have it in me kitchen."

"It will not injure you." It was Cecile who answered.

"That's as may be," replied Mrs O'Ferrell, "but I've cooked f'r thirty year without – ah, Mr Chan – is it you?" she added, as Charlie appeared in the doorway.

"Indubitably," replied Charlie, "and deeply sorry to interrupt."

"Sure, 'tis nothing," Mrs O'Ferrell replied. "I was just tellin' this Frinch girl that I've cooked f'r thirty year without guns in me kitchen, an' I ain't goin' to start now."

Cecile produced a small revolver from the folds of her skirt. "I am so nervous," she explained to Chan. "All the time, since last night, I am so jumpy and nervous. So I ask Michael to bring me this – from Reno."

"An' now we can all be nervous, an' with good reason, too," the cook added.

"There is no cause for alarm," Cecile assured her. "Michael has taught me—" She paused.

"Mr Ireland taught you to use it," Chan finished for her.

"Yes. He – he was in the war, you understand."

"An aviator, it may be."

"Ah – he wished so much to be an aviator. But no – that did not happen. He was sergeant of infantry." Cecile started for the door. "Do not fret, Mrs O'Ferrell. I will take this to my room."

"An' look which way ye point it, even there," admonished Mrs O'Ferrell. "Thim walls on the third floor is none too thick." She turned to Chan, as Cecile went out. "I don't hold with guns," she said. "The way I see it, the fewer guns they is, the fewer people gets killed."

"You are exponent of disarmament," smiled Chan.

"I am that," she replied firmly. "An' it's a lonely thing to be – among the Irish."

"Among any people, I fear," Chan replied gravely. "I have paused here, Mrs O'Ferrell, to offer most humble apologies. It was not possible to retain the little dog at Pineview. It was not even possible, under the circumstances, that you should bid him farewell."

The woman nodded. "I know. Cecile was tellin' me. It's sorry I am to lose him – but if there was thim had a better claim—"

"There was one who had such claim," Chan assured her. "I am so very sorry. I trust I am forgiven."

"Don't mention it," said Mrs O'Ferrell.

Charlie bowed. "He who keeps the friendship of a prince," he said, "wins honors. But he who keeps that of a cook, wins food. My preference runs to the latter – when the cooking is as superlative as yours."

"Ye have a nice way of talking, Mr Chan. Thank ye so much."

As he spoke with Mrs O'Ferrell, Charlie had been conscious of music in the distant living-room. Walking down the passageway and pushing open the door, he saw that Romano was seated at the piano, and that Hugh Beaton stood beside him. Only a few lights were on in the big room, the reflection of firelight was on the paneled walls, the scene was one of peace and harmony. Romano played well, and Beaton's voice was surprisingly good as he sang, not very loudly, words in a language Chan did not recognize. The detective tiptoed toward the fire and dropped into a chair.

Presently the music stopped and Romano, leaping to his feet, began to pace the floor excitedly.

"Excellent," he cried. "You have a really excellent voice."

"Do you think so?" Beaton asked eagerly.

"Ah – you lack confidence – you lack courage. You need the proper push – the proper management. Who has arranged your concerts?"

"Why – the Adolfi Musical Bureau – mostly."

"Paugh! Adolfi – what does he know! A business man – with the heart of a plumber! I – Luis Romano – I could manage you. I could make of you a huge success. Do I know the game? Signor – I invented it. From one end of the country to the other I would make you famous – in Europe, too. For a salary, of course —"

"I have no money," the boy said.

"Ah – but you forget. You have Landini's money – and there is plenty believe me. I know. Plenty – though mostly now in real estate. Times will change – the real estate will sell. A house in Washington Square – an apartment building on Park Avenue – a summer place at Magnolia—"

"I don't want them," Hugh Beaton said.

"But you should leap at the chance. I tell you, you need confidence. A voice like yours – all this money to exploit it – I will assist, gladly."

"I gave a concert in New York," the boy told him. "The reviews weren't very good."

"The reviews! Bah! Critics are sheep – they never lead. They follow. The path must be pointed out to them. I could arrange it. But first – you must believe in yourself. I tell you – you can sing." Suddenly Romano walked over to the chair where Charlie was sealed. "Mr Chan, will you kindly give this foolish boy your opinion of his voice?"

"To me," Charlie answered, "it sounded most beautiful."

"You see!" Romano turned to Beaton, gesturing violently. "What have I told you? A layman – an outsider – one who knows little of music – even he says so. Then will you believe me – Luis Romano – born with music in the very soul? I tell you that with Landini's money—"

"But I won't take Landini's money," the boy repeated stubbornly.

Charlie rose. "Do not worry," he said. "You will not be called upon to take it. It was not left to you."

Romano leaped forward, his dark eyes glowing. "Then the will was never signed?" he almost shouted.

"It was not signed," Chan told him.

Romano turned to Beaton. "I am sorry," he said. "I will not be able to accept the position you have so kindly offered me. I will be otherwise engaged. But I repeat – you have a wonderful organ. You must believe. Confidence, my boy, confidence. Mr Chan, if Landini died intestate, her property is left—"

"To her son, perhaps," Chan answered, keenly regarding the Italian.

Romano paled suddenly. "You mean – she had a son?"

"You yourself said so, last night."

"No, no – I had no real knowledge on that point. I was—"

"Lying?"

"I was desperate – I explained that. Any chance that offered – have you ever been hungry, Mr Chan?"

"You were telling the truth, unconsciously, Mr Romano. Landini had a son – but he died three years ago."

"Ah – poor Landini! That was just before our marriage. I would not know."

"So I fancy her property is yours, Mr Romano."

"Thank heaven for that," remarked Hugh Beaton, and started up the stairs.

Romano sat, staring into the fire. "Ah, Landini," he said softly, "she would never listen to me. Time after time, I tell her – you must cease to procrastinate. You must not for ever put things off. You say, I will do this, I would tell her, and you never do it. Where will it finish? It has finished in fortune for me. She never took to heart what I said – and now that means fortune for me."

For a time Charlie stood gazing down at this temperamental man whose sudden changes from one mood to another presented him with one of the greatest puzzles of his life.

"Yes," he said slowly, "the murder of Landini means fortune for you."

Romano looked up suddenly. "You will think I killed her," he cried. "For the love of God, don't think that! Landini – she was dear to me – I worshiped her – I adored her marvelous voice – do not think I would silence that—"

Chan shrugged. "For the present, I do not think at all," he answered, and turning, went upstairs to his room.

His last words to Romano were not quite accurate. Seated in a chair before his fire, he thought very hard indeed. Could

Romano have known that the will was unsigned? In that case, would he have made the determined effort to become the manager of Hugh Beaton? To acquire some portion of Landini's estate, by way of Beaton's pocket? No – hardly. And yet – ah, yes – his suggestion of the managership had been made with Charlie in the room, listening.

Might that not have been, then, a sly trick – for the man was undoubtedly sly. To make Chan think that he expected nothing, that he had resigned himself to the idea of Landini's money going to Beaton. When all the time, he knew only too well—

Charlie sighed ponderously. A problem, that was. And Cecile? Sending for a pistol – would a guilty person, who had already fired one pistol in that house, openly parade another? Probably not. But – might that not be a gesture of innocence, staged for his especial benefit? Cecile was another sly one – her eyes betrayed her.

Leaning back in his chair, Chan considered the situation. About time, he reflected, that something definite, something a little less hazy and preposterous in the line of a clue, offered itself. Suddenly remembering, he rose and took the galley proofs of Landini's autobiography from the table where he had laid them a moment ago. Adjusting a floor lamp, he read the first three chapters of the woman's story. They were well written, he thought, with a touch of wistful nostalgia for the days of her youth that rather touched him. Especially since the scene of those days was his own beloved Honolulu.

A glance at the wrist-watch which his daughter Rose had given him on his latest birthday told him it was time to prepare for dinner. As he left his room, at a few minutes before seven, he saw Dudley Ward in the study at the front of the house. He went there at once.

"Ah, Mr Ward," he said as he entered. "We are to have your company at dinner. You are brave man."

"Sit down, Mr Chan," Ward answered. "Yes – I'm coming to dinner. I have had many sorrows in my life, but I have never yet tried to share them with my guests."

Chan bowed. "A true definition of hospitality," he replied. "Mr Ward – if I could find proper words – but such, alas, evade me."

"I understand," Ward said gently. "You're very kind."

"And speaking of kindness," Charlie went on, "I am telling myself that I must not impose upon yours. I was brought here for a certain task. That task, I am sorry to say, is now accomplished."

"And you should have your check," said Ward, reaching toward a drawer of his desk.

"Please," cried Chan. "That idea had not occurred to me. What I meant was that I should no longer impose upon you in rôle of guest—"

"*That* idea," Ward interrupted, "had not occurred to me. My dear sir, the sheriff has asked you to stay. I demand that you stay – at least as long as you see a chance of solving this unhappy puzzle."

"I had no doubt of your feeling. But have you thought of this – embarrassment might arise."

Ward shook his head. "How so?"

Charlie got up and closed the door. "At moment of murder," he remarked, "five persons were wandering alone in house. In Swan, Romano, Miss Beaton and Cecile I presume you have no great personal interest. There was one other."

"One other? Pardon me – but I have been so terribly upset."

"The last person to see Landini alive."

"Sing! You can't mean Sing?"

"Who else?"

For a long moment Ward was silent. On his face was an expression that Charlie had seen before. Where? Ah, yes, on the face of Sam Holt whenever the matter of Sing's possible guilt came up. The old Chinese, Chan thought, was a man who was much beloved.

"Surely you haven't found anything—" Ward said at last.

"So far, nothing," Charlie answered. "We have been combing the hair of an iron donkey."

"Just as I thought," Ward nodded. "Mr Chan, I have known Sing since I was a child, and no kinder soul ever lived. I appreciate your speaking to me about the matter – but I'll take a chance on Sing." He rose. "Perhaps we'd better go down to dinner. I don't like to keep Mrs O'Ferrell waiting—" He stopped suddenly. "Five persons, you said, unaccounted for."

"I said five," Charlie admitted.

"Six, Mr Chan. Haven't you forgot Mrs O'Ferrell?"

"Indubitably. But what interest could that lady have had in Landini?"

"None whatever, that I know of," Ward replied. "But accuracy, Mr Chan – accuracy. I should have thought you would be a stickler for that."

"It is true, I always have been," Chan assured him. "We will, in the future, call it six."

He opened the door into the hall. Sing was standing very close to it.

"You hully up, Boss," the old man cried, "or mebbe bimeby you no catch 'um dinnah."

"Coming right along," Ward said. He insisted on Charlie's going first and they stepped into the hall. Sing went limping ahead of them and, still limping, disappeared in the direction of the back stairs.

XI

A BALCONY IN STRESA

The rest of the party awaited them in the living-room: Leslie Beaton, a charming picture in a blue gown by the fire, her silent brother, Romano, looking undeniably cheerful, and Ryder, grim and dour as always.

"Are we all here?" Ward asked. "I don't see Doctor Swan."

Evidently Sing had not kept his promise to pass on Swan's farewell. Chan explained the matter.

"Indeed," Ward answered. "Miss Beaton – may I have the honor? I trust I am not to lose any more of my guests."

As they moved into the dining-room, the girl said something about leaving on the morrow, and Ward murmured his regrets. When they were all seated, their host remarked: "Someone was singing down here this evening. Rather well, too."

"I hope I didn't disturb you," Hugh Beaton said.

"Disturb me? I enjoyed it. You have a remarkably fine voice."

"What did I say to you, Mr Beaton?" Romano cried. "You would not believe me. Yet my opinion is highly regarded in some quarters. Even Mr Chan agreed—"

"Ah, yes," Charlie said. "But I am glad to have the corroboration of Mr Ward and yourself. For I am no expert. The croaking raven thinks the owl can sing. However, in this case, it was no owl I heard."

Beaton smiled at last. "Thanks, Mr Chan," he remarked.

"What is wrong with this brother of yours?" Romano demanded of the girl. "He has a great gift, and does not trust himself."

"The artistic temperament, I'm afraid," Leslie Beaton remarked. "Of late, Hugh has lost faith in himself. One of his reviews in New York was bad, and he can't seem to recover."

"One of them!" Romano shrugged. "Ah, he knows nothing of life. He needs a manager – a man of intelligence and musical taste –"

"Yourself," smiled the girl.

"I would be ideal," Romano admitted.

"You could at least teach him self-confidence."

"That – yes. A bold front – it is vital to success in the modern world. And I could teach him more. At present, I do not believe I am available. But I would be glad to find a substitute."

"That's good of you," the Beaton girl replied.

Her brother stared morosely at his plate. A silence fell.

"I am so sorry you're leaving Pineview," Ward said presently to the girl. "But then, I realize there is little entertainment here."

"It's a charming place," she murmured, and in the silence that again fell upon the company, Charlie realized the strain it must be on the host to keep up the conversation. Modestly, he sought to help.

"There is vast entertainment here," he said. "Particularly for me. At home, I am amateur student of trees. I know the palms – the coconut, the royal, all of them. But I must confess myself shamefully ignorant of the coniferous trees."

"The what?" asked Leslie Beaton.

"The coniferous trees. Those bearing cones, you understand."

She smiled. "I've learned something today."

"That is good," he told her. "Learning which does not daily advance, daily decreases. Myself, I am fond admirer of study.

He who listens to the chatter outside the window, and neglects his books, is but a donkey in clothes."

"That sounds very sensible," she assured him.

"I believe so. For that reason, I shall, if I can find leisure, study the pines, the firs and the cedars. I am slightly familiar – in books – with the Scottish, the Corsican, the umbrella pine. The Austrian, too. Mr Romano, when you fought so bravely on the northern front, you must have come in contact with Austrian pines."

"With many things I came in contact," Romano told him. "Maybe an Austrian pine. Who shall say?"

"No doubt. I am at a loss to classify the local variety. Perhaps, Mr Ryder, you can help me?"

"What should I know about it?" Ryder demanded.

"But you have been mining man in these parts. You have been snowed in among these very trees." Ryder gave him a startled look. "Is it too much to hope that you are interested in this subject?"

"It certainly is," the other told him.

"Ah," Chan shrugged, "then perhaps I must pursue my studies alone. In a certain family of pine, the bark grows much thicker near the ground, and becomes more fragile as one ascends. Are these pines of that family? I must investigate. Alas – I have not much of the figure for tree climbing." He gazed blandly about the table. "I envy you all your delectable slenderness."

Sing appeared at that moment with the main course, and as the conversation again lagged after his departure, Charlie deserted the pines, a subject which did not seem to interest his hearers to any extent, and launched into a little talk on the flora of the Hawaiian islands. Miss Beaton, at least, became an ardent listener. She asked many questions, and the dinner hour slipped by.

"I've always wanted to go to Hawaii," she told him.

"Save it," he advised, "for honeymoon. Any husband seems possible under Waikiki sky. And the kind you will achieve – he will appear Greek god."

The dinner presently ended, and they returned to the living-room, where Sing served coffee, and cordials from Dudley Ward's precious stock. For a time they sat and smoked, but before very long, Charlie arose.

"If you will pardon me," he said, "I go to my room."

"More study?" asked the girl.

"Yes, Miss Beaton." His eyes narrowed. "I am reading very interesting work."

"Would I enjoy it?"

"Not, perhaps, so much as I. Some day, we will allow you to decide." He paused for a moment beside John Ryder's chair. "Excuse, sir, that I intrude my business on this pleasant scene, but I would be greatly obliged if you would grant me an interview above."

Ryder looked out from the cloud of cigar smoke that enveloped him – an unfriendly look. "What about?"

"Need I tell you that?"

"If you wish me to come."

Chan's usually kind face hardened. "He who acts for the emperor, is the emperor," he remarked. "And he who acts for the sheriff – is the sheriff."

"Even if he's a Chinaman?" sneered Ryder, but he rose to go.

As Chan followed him up the stairs, hot anger burned in his heart. Many men had called him a Chinaman, but he had realized they did so from ignorance, and good-naturedly forgave them. With Ryder, however, he knew the case was otherwise, the man was a native of the West coast, he lived in San Francisco, and he understood only too well that this term applied to a Chinese gentleman was an insult. So, no doubt, he had intended it.

It was, therefore, in a mood far less amiable than was his wont, that the plump Chinese followed the long lean figure of Ryder into the latter's room. The door, as he closed it after him, might almost have been said to slam.

Ryder turned on him at once. "So," he remarked, "judging from the conversation at dinner, you have been prying into my private affairs."

"I have been asked by the sheriff of this county to assist in important case," Charlie retorted. "For that reason I must examine the past of Madame Landini. It is with no glow of self-congratulation, my dear sir, that I find you lurking there."

"I lurked there, as you put it, very briefly."

"One winter only?"

"Just about that long."

"In a cabin – up the ravine." Charlie removed a bit of paper from his pocket, and passed it to Ryder. "I found this among Landini's clippings," he explained.

Ryder took it and read it. "Ah, yes – she would save that – among her souvenirs. To her, I suppose, it was a mere passing incident. To me, it was much more." He handed back the clipping and Chan took it, staring silently at the mining man. "What else do you want to know? Everything, I fancy. Good lord – what a profession yours is! You may as well sit down."

Charlie accepted this grudging invitation, and Ryder took a chair on the opposite side of the fire.

"I'd always admired Landini," the latter began, "and when she split with Dudley I followed her, after a decent interval, to New York. I found her in a rather discouraged mood. She said she'd marry me – give up her career – it was a case of whither thou goest – you know. A grand overpowering love. And it lasted – nearly a month.

"You see, I was bound for the mine, and she came along – a great lark, she thought it. Then it started to snow – and she couldn't get out. So she began to think. Night after night, with only the candles burning, she talked of Paris, New York, Berlin – what she'd given up for me. After a time, I talked of what I'd given up for her – my peace of mind, my freedom. And our hatred for each other grew.

"Toward the end of the winter, I fell ill – desperately ill – but she scarcely looked at me. She left me there in my bunk, at the mercy of a stupid old man who worked for us. When the first sled went out in the spring, she was on it, with scarcely a goodby to me. I told her to go – and be damned. She got a divorce in Reno – incompatibility – God knows I couldn't argue that."

He was silent for a moment – staring into the fire. "That's the whole story – a winter of hate – what a winter! There is no hate in the world such as comes to two people who are shut up together in a prison like that. Can you wonder that I have never forgotten – that I never wanted to see her again – that I did not want to see her last night, when Dudley foolishly invited her here? Can you wonder that I loathed the very mention of her name?"

"Mr Ryder," Chan said slowly, "what was in that letter Landini wrote to you just before she died? The letter you tore open, read and then burned in the study fireplace?"

"I have told you," the man replied, "that I did not receive the letter. I couldn't, therefore, have opened it, read it or burned it."

"That is your final statement?" Charlie asked gently.

"My only statement – and the truth. I did not go to the study. I remained in this room from the time you left me until you saw me again on the stairs."

Chan got slowly to his feet, walked to one of the windows and stared out toward the empty flying field. "One more question, only," he continued. "This morning, at breakfast, you remark to Mr Ward that you have noticed Sing's eyes are bad – that he requires glasses. When did you notice that?"

"Last night, just after I came," Ryder answered. "You see, years ago, when I was a kid, I used to spend a lot of time at this house. One summer I taught Sing to read. English, I mean. I asked him, when we came in here last night, if he'd kept it up. I couldn't quite gather whether he had, or hadn't, so I picked up a book from the table and told him to read me the first paragraph. He held it very close to his eyes – couldn't seem to see very well. I made up my mind I'd mention the matter to Dudley."

Chan bowed. "It was most kind of you – to teach him the art of reading. But then – you are very fond of him?"

"Why shouldn't I be? A grand character, Sing. One of the real Chinese."

The implication was not lost on Charlie, but he ignored it. "I, too, have great admiration for Sing," he replied amiably. He moved to the door. "Thank you so much. You have been very helpful."

Slowly he walked back along the hall to his own room, passing as he did so the spot where, only a few hours before, he had found Sing unconscious from a brutal blow in the face. So much had happened since, he had almost forgotten that incident. Among his many puzzles, he reflected, the assault on Sing was one of the most perplexing.

He entered his room, closed the door and took up again the galley proofs of Ellen Landini's story. Seated in the chair beside the floor lamp, he read two more chapters. The spell of the woman's personality, as it crept from these inanimate sheets, began to take hold of his imagination. Warm, glowing, alive, she wrote gaily and with increasing charm. Her earliest marriage, those glorious days in Paris when first she was told that she was one of the gifted, would walk among the great. Her enthusiasm was contagious.

Chapter Six. As he stared at this caption, it came to him to wonder how many chapters there were in all. He turned to the final galley, and worked back from there to the beginning of the final chapter. Twenty-eight, it was. Well, in twenty-eight chapters, perhaps he could find something that would help him.

His eyes fell casually on the beginning of that last chapter. The names of foreign far-off places – always they intrigued and held him. Almost unconsciously he began to read:

"After my marvelously successful season in Berlin, I came for a rest to Stresa, on lovely Lago Maggiore. It is here, on a balcony of the Grand Hotel et des Iles Borromées that I write the concluding chapters of my book. Where could I have found a more beautiful setting? I gaze in turn at the aquamarine waters, the fierce blue sky, the snow-capped Alps. Not far away, I am enraptured by Isola Bella, with its fantastic palace, its green terraces of orange and lemon trees rising a hundred feet above the lake. The thing that has always made life worth while for me—"

Charlie's small black eycs opened wide as he read on. His breath came faster; he uttered a little cry of satisfaction.

Twice he read the opening paragraph from start to finish, then rose and paced the floor, overwhelmed with an excitement he could not suppress. Finally he came back and lifted that particular galley from the company of its fellows. Galley one hundred and ten, he noticed. He folded it carefully, placed it safely in the inner pocket of his coat, and patted affectionately the spot where it reposed.

He must show this to the young sheriff. That was the fair thing to do – no clues should be concealed. And he had now, he thought exultantly, the clue he had been looking for, the clue that would ultimately lead them to success.

XII

SO YOU'RE GOING TO TRUCKEE?

Charlie had sat down again and was plunging with renewed hope into the sixth chapter of Landini's story, when Sing knocked on his door. Cash Shannon, the old Chinese announced, was below, and desired to speak with the detective at once. Recalling his conversation with the sheriff, Chan went immediately downstairs. Ryder and Ward were smoking by the fire, Miss Beaton and her brother had evidently been reading, and Romano sat at the piano, his playing suspended for the moment. The resplendent Cash stood in the center of the room, smiling his confident smile.

"Hello, Mr Chan," he remarked. "Don wants you to run down to the Tavern fer a while. He says to take his boat. I come up in her, an' she's out there now, rarin' to go."

"Thank you so much," Charlie answered. "Miss Beaton, would you perhaps enjoy brief spin on lake?"

She leaped to her feet. "I'd love it."

"Air ain't so good tonight," suggested Cash, his smile vanishing. "Kinda damp. Rain or snow, mebbe."

"I'd love that, too," Leslie Beaton added.

"Things is pretty dull down to the Tavern," Mr Shannon persisted. "Couldn't recommend it as no gay party."

"I'll be ready in a moment," the girl called to Chan from the stairs.

Cash continued to stand, gazing sadly at his hat. "Sit down, Shannon," Dudley Ward suggested. "You're to stay here until they return, I take it."

"Seems to have worked out that way," Cash admitted. He looked at Charlie. "What ideas you do git," he added.

Chan laughed. "Sheriff's orders," he remarked.

"Oh – I begin to see it now," Cash replied. "An' I broke a date with a blonde to come down here."

Leslie Beaton reappeared, her face flushed and eager above the collar of a fur coat. "Hope you won't be long," Cash said to her.

"There's no telling," she smiled. "You mustn't worry, Mr Shannon. I'll be in the best possible company. Are you ready, Mr Chan?" Out on the path, she looked aloft. "What – no moon?" she cried. "And not even a star. But plenty of sky. And such a joy to get a breath of fresh air."

"I fear our friend Cash does not approve our plans," Chan ventured.

She laughed. "Oh, one afternoon of Cash is sufficient unto the day. You know, I think there's a lot to be said for the strong silent men."

She got into the launch, and Chan took his place at her side. "Trust my avoirdupois is not too obnoxious," he remarked.

"Plenty of room," she assured him. He started the motor, and swung in a wide circle out on to the lake. "It *is* a bit damp and chilly, isn't it?" the girl said.

"Some day," he replied, "I should enjoy privilege of escorting you along Honolulu waterfront, accompanied perhaps by lunar rainbow."

"It sounds gorgeous," she sighed. "But I'll never make it. Too poor. Always too poor."

"Poverty has its advantages," Chan smiled. "The rats avoid the rice boiler of the lowly man."

"And so does the rice," nodded the girl. "Don't forget that."

They sped along the shore, great black houses, bleak and uninhabited, at their left. "You have learned, I take it, that your brother is not to inherit the estate of Landini," Charlie said.

"Yes – and it's the best news I've had in years. Money that came that way wouldn't have done Hugh any good. In fact, it would probably have ruined his career."

Chan nodded. "But now – his precious career is safe. You must not be offended, but Landini's death is, I suspect, a great relief to you."

"I try not to think of it as such. It was, of course, a terrible thing. And yet – we're frank in these days, aren't we, Mr Chan? – it has released my brother. Even he, I believe, feels that."

"You have talked with him about it?"

"Oh, no. But I knew, without being told, that he was heartsick over his predicament. He never really intended to become engaged to her. She sort of – well, jollied him into it. She had a way with her, you know."

"I know," Chan agreed.

"Somehow, I couldn't help feeling sorry for her at times, in spite of everything. She was still seeking romance – she needed it, you might say, in her business. And she was thirty-eight years old!"

"Incredible!" cried Chan, with a secret smile at the young girl beside him. "Poor, foolish Landini." The lights of the Tavern popped up ahead. "One question I would like to ask, if I may," he continued. "You said last night you had met Doctor Swan before. Could you tell me the circumstances?"

"Surely. It was over in Reno. Some people had taken me to a gambling place – just for a lark, you know. Doctor Swan was there, playing roulette."

"Did he have aspect of confirmed gambler, please?"

"He seemed pretty excited, if that's what you mean. One of our party knew him, and introduced us. Later, he joined us at supper. He sat beside me, and I talked to him about Landini. I wish now I hadn't."

"You still believe he placed your scarf in Landini's hands?"

"He must have."

Chan nodded. "He may have. I cannot say. But should you meet him tonight, please do me one vast favor. Assume that he did not try to involve you, and be cordial to him."

"Cordial to him? Why, of course – if you ask it."

"That is so good of you. It happens that I have small plan forming in rear of my mind, and I shall require your help. This much alone I need tell you now – I am eager to watch Doctor Swan while he gambles."

"I don't know what it's all about," the girl smiled. "But rely on me."

They were now beside the pier. Chan tied up the launch, and walked with the girl up the steps of the terrace to the Tavern. The lights were blazing in the big lounge; Charlie pushed open the door and followed the girl inside.

Don Holt at once came forward and took charge of Leslie Beaton, with that shy manner of his which was at the same time full of authority. Moving on to the fireplace, Chan encountered Dinsdale, the manager, Doctor Swan, Sam Holt and a small nervous man in a black suit.

"I don't know as this is any picnic for you," the young sheriff was saying to the girl. "Jes' thought maybe you'd like to come for the boat ride."

"That part of it was fine," she assured him.

"But this don't look so gay, does it?" he said, his eager look fading.

"Oh, I don't know. Who's the little man in black?"

"Well – he's the coroner."

"Good. I've never met a coroner. Having new experiences all the time. Up to last night, I'd never met a sheriff. And I got through that all right."

"You sure did, as far as the sheriff's concerned," Don Holt said. "Now – er – Mr Chan an' I got a little business, an' then I guess I'll be free for – the rest of the evening. I'm afraid that's about all that's goin' to happen – jes' the rest of the evening."

"That sounds exciting enough for me," she smiled.

He left her with Dinsdale and Swan before the fire and walked down to the far end of the big room, whither Charlie had already led Sam Holt and the coroner. "Well, Inspector," he said, "I reckon you've already met Doctor Price?"

"I have had that pleasure," Chan returned. "He assures me that Landini was murdered by person or persons unknown. He has, you will observe, caught up with us in our search."

"The usual verdict, of course," the physician remarked. "Unless you gentlemen have some evidence of which I am not aware." He waited for an answer.

Chan shook his head. "It is now less than twenty-four hours since the killing," he remarked, looking at his watch. "Our researches in that time have been amazingly extensive, but lack definite results. It is the same old story. Like pumpkins in a tub of water, we push one suspect down, and another pops up. However, we do not despair. Tell me, Doctor – what of the course of the bullet?"

Doctor Price cleared his throat. "Ah – er – the bullet, which was of thirty-eight caliber and obviously from the revolver of the deceased, entered the person of the deceased four inches below the left shoulder, and after that pursued a downward course—"

"Then it was fired from above?"

"Undoubtedly. The deceased may have been struggling with her assailant, she may have fallen to her knees, and the assailant, standing above her, fired—"

"How close was weapon held?"

"I cannot say. Not very, I believe. At least, there were no powder marks."

"Ah, yes," Chan nodded. "One thing more interests me. Could the dec – I mean, the lady, have taken any step after the wound was received?"

"Which I asked him myself," put in Sam Holt. "He don't know."

"There might be two schools of thought on that problem," the doctor said. "You see, the human heart is a hollow muscular organ, more or less conical in shape, situated in the thorax between the two lungs. It is enclosed in a strong membranous sac, called the pericardium—"

"He jes' runs on like that," Sam Holt explained. "The sum of it all is, he don't know."

Charlie smiled. "At least, you have the bullet?" he inquired of the sheriff.

"Yes – Doc gave it to me. I got it over there in Jim Dinsdale's safe, along with Landini's revolver."

"Excellent," Chan nodded. "And who would have the combination to this safe?"

"Why – nobody but Dinsdale and his bookkeeper."

"Ah, yes. Dinsdale and his bookkeeper. Presently we may give more thought to the safe. Mr Coroner, I thank you so much."

"Don't mention it," returned Doctor Price briskly. "I am staying here with Jim overnight – anything more I can tell you, you have only to ask. Glad to have met you. I'm turning in now – want to get an early start in the morning."

He went down the room, said something to Dinsdale and disappeared toward a distant corridor. Charlie and the two Holts joined the little group by the fire.

"Draw up and sit down, gentlemen," Dinsdale remarked. "I was just telling Miss Beaton how glad we'll be to have her come down here tomorrow. Of course, the Tavern isn't officially open, and things are a bit dull, but we can show her a little excitement, I reckon. There's a few newspaper reporters coming up from San Francisco on the morning train, and they'll stir things up. They usually do."

"Newspaper reporters," cried Don Holt in dismay.

"Yes – and that Reno bunch will be back here tomorrow. They've been prowling round the neighborhood all day. Claimed they wanted to find Mr Chan."

"Well, I hope it's Mr Chan they find," Holt said. "Lord, I wouldn't know what to say to 'em."

"The secret," Charlie told him, "is to talk much, but say nothing. Not your specialty, I fear. Leave them to me – I will act as buffer. I have the figure."

"Tomorrow sounds interesting," Leslie Beaton remarked, "but how about tonight? Where's the night life around here?"

Dinsdale laughed. "Night life? I'm afraid you'll have to come back later in the summer."

"Oh – but I've heard the gambling wasn't all on the other side of the state line," the girl continued, and Charlie gave her a grateful smile. "There must be a few places—"

"There ain't any in my county," Don Holt said firmly.

"Well, let's get out of your old county, then. I feel like going places and doing things. Surely there must be a city, or a town, or at least a village, nearer than Reno."

"Well, there's Truckee," Dinsdale ventured dubiously. "Summers we sometimes run over there in the evening. Not much doing now, I'm afraid. But there's two or three restaurants, and a movie – and you might dig up a game."

"Not if it's in Sheriff Holt's county," the girl said mockingly.

"But it ain't," replied the sheriff. "It's over the county-line, so you can't tell – it might turn out to be the modern Babylon you're longing for. Get your coat, an' we'll have a look at it." His manner was gay enough, but there was a note of disappointment in his voice.

"That'll be grand," the girl cried. She went over to Sam Holt's chair, and bent above him. "You're coming with us, you know," she said.

"Shouldn't do it," he answered. "But say – I like your voice. Sounds lively. Full o' spirit, which young folks' voices is generally too tired nowadays to suit me. Sure, I'm coming. Fresh air never hurt nobody."

Leslie Beaton turned to Swan. "Doctor – you don't mind a little game, as I recall."

"Well, really – I think I'd better stay here," Swan replied. But his eyes had brightened.

"Nonsense – we won't go without you," the girl said, while Don Holt stared at her in amazement.

"Oh – in that case – " Swan stood up at once.

Dinsdale felt he should stay at the Tavern – a guest is a sort of responsibility, he explained, and there was no one about to take his place in the office. He offered his car for the trip, along with certain vague suggestions of the "So you're Going to Truckee" order.

But Truckee, when they had covered fifteen miles of snowy road and rolled on to its startled main thoroughfare, responded with the gloomiest welcome imaginable. Even the spirits of Leslie Beaton drooped at the prospect. Tired old store-fronts listing, it seemed, with the wind, a half-darkened drug store, the lighted windows of a few restaurants dripping with steam. Don Holt drew up to the curb.

"Here you are, folks," he smiled. "Night life in these parts. I don't know what you're looking for, but it ain't here."

"Isn't that a light in the Exchange Club, over the Little Gem Restaurant?" Doctor Swan inquired.

"It might be, at that. I'm afraid you have the gambler's instinct, Doctor. Maybe we are in Babylon, after all. Anyhow, it won't hurt to inquire."

Holt led them into the Little Gem. An odor of fried fish and other delicacies of the lake country nearly bowled them over. The proprietor of the establishment, a swarthy Greek known locally as "Lucky Pete," was shaking dice with a customer.

"Hello, Pete," Holt said. "What's the big excitement in these parts tonight?"

"Dunno," returned Pete, stifling a yawn. "Is there any?"

"Jes' dropped in to find out," Holt said. "A few friends of mine – from Reno."

Pete nodded. "Pleased to meet them. The slot machines are over in the corner."

"Nothing doing upstairs?" Holt asked.

"Not these days – no. Tables all covered – times is bad. A few members of the Club – prominent gentlemen of the city – they play poker."

Chan stepped forward. "Is this a private game – or can anybody enter?"

Pete surveyed him critically. "You can go up an' ask," he suggested.

"Doctor Swan – what do you say? Shall we purchase small supply of chips?" Charlie inquired.

"We'll take a look, first," Swan replied cautiously.

It appeared there was an inner stairway, which identified Lucky Pete as the real steward of the Exchange Club. The five, led by Don Holt, ascended. Charlie and old Sam Holt brought up the rear.

"Watch what you do in this place, Inspector," Holt said. "A Greek! How did a Greek find Truckee – unless they closed all the other towns to him?"

"Greek people," Charlie answered, "appear to be born with geography of the world in one hand."

In the big bare room above, half hidden in darkness, were numerous gambling tables, covered with brown canvas. Under the solitary light, five men played poker with soiled cards.

"Evening, gentlemen," said Don Holt. "Things don't seem to be prospering round here right now."

"Not much doing," one of the players responded. "Unless you'd like to sit in on this game."

Holt looked around the faces at the table and shook his head. "I hardly think so. We've got jes' a few minutes—"

"Small contributions gratefully received," said another player, who had the pale face and artificial-looking hair of a croupier.

"We might take brief turn to try luck," remarked Charlie. "Doctor Swan – what is your reply? Ten dollars spent in chips by each – and leave in one half-hour, win or lose?"

Swan's eyes glittered, his cheeks were flushed. "I'm with you," he replied.

"Good," Charlie replied. "It is now nine-thirty. Gentlemen – we drop out at ten precisely. May we squeeze in?"

Don Holt gave Chan a dazed look. "All right," he agreed. "Miss Beaton and I will wait downstairs. Father—"

"Git me a chair, son," the old man said. "I sure do like to hear the sound of them chips again. What is it, boys – straight, whisky or draw?"

"Draw," answered one of the boys. "How about you, Dad? Oh – excuse me."

"I'll jes' listen in," explained Sam Holt. "That's all I'm doin', nowadays."

"Would you be so good, gentlemen," remarked Chan, "as to explain to me the value of these chips? I am, you understand, a novice."

"Yeah," returned the man with the pale face. "I've met them novices before."

Don Holt and the girl returned to the aggressive odors of the room below.

"Like something to eat?" the sheriff inquired.

"Never wanted anything less in my life," she smiled.

"Well, I guess we better order something, anyhow. It'd look better. You can't go huntin' night life, an' not spend any money. A table, or the counter?"

She walked past several tables, studying the cloths. "The counter, I believe," she told him.

He laughed. "That's pickin' 'em," he nodded. They sat up to the counter. "Now, what would you like? Wait a minute – I meant to say, what will you take?"

"How about a sandwich and a glass of milk?"

"Well – you're fifty per cent right, anyhow. Stick to the sandwich – that was an inspiration. But as for the milk—"

"No?"

He shook his head. "No. It don't do to pioneer in the West any more. Jes' play safe an' make it what's known in these parts as a 'cup cawfee.'"

"I'm in your hands," she told him.

Pete appeared, and Don Holt ordered two ham sandwiches and two cups of coffee. As the man departed, the sheriff glanced toward the stairs. "Well, Inspector Chan is sure revertin' to type tonight," he remarked. "You take a Chinese, you jes' can't keep him away from a gamblin' table."

The girl smiled. "Is that what you think?"

"Why shouldn't I think it? Say, I hope he's good – those boys up there invented the game. At ten o'clock we leave – if I have to draw a gun. Your big fling at night life ends then, so make the most of it while you can."

She gave him a quick look. "You're not so very pleased with me this evening, are you?" she inquired.

"Who – me? Why – why, sure I am. Maybe I'm a little disappointed – you see, I been tellin' myself perhaps you *would* like the county-seat, after all. It's quite a busy little town, but of course—"

"Of course – what."

"I don't mean that you're to blame. It ain't your fault. You're jes' like all the other girls, that's all. Restless, always wantin' excitement. I see it on the parties I take out from the Tavern. What's got into the women nowadays? The men are O.K. They'd like to relax, an' take a look at the mountains. But the girls won't let 'em. Come on, boys, is their slogan. What'll we do now? I want to go places, an' do things."

"Don't you?"

"Don't I what?"

"Want to go places, and do things?"

"Sure – when there's somewhere to go, an' something to do. But when there ain't, I can sit all the way back in my chair, an' not have any nervous breakdown."

"Everything you say is pretty true," the girl replied. "Women are a bit restless – and I'm as bad as any of them, perhaps. But I've got too much spirit to sit here on this very unsteady stool and be unjustly accused. It wasn't my idea – coming out to find a gambling house tonight."

"But – but you suggested it."

"Of course I did. However, it was only to please Mr Chan. He told me he was eager to watch Doctor Swan while the doctor was busily engaged in gambling."

A look of perplexity clouded Don Holt's fine eyes. "He did? Well, then – say, I reckon there's a pretty humble apology due from yours truly."

"Nothing of the sort," the girl protested. Pete appeared with the repast, and she smiled at the thickness of the sandwich that stood before her. "I wonder if I could really open my mouth that wide," she went on. "It's worth trying, don't you think?"

The young sheriff was still puzzling over her news. "So Mr Chan wanted to watch Swan gamble," he mused. "It's too much for me. I wonder what the inspector's got on his mind."

In the room above the inspector appeared to have much on his mind, including a rapid, tense and deadly game of poker. Scarcely once since it started had he taken his eyes from Doctor Swan. Every move of the latter's hands as he made his ante, pushed out his bet, lost or raked in the chips and sorted them, he watched with extreme care. Either because of this absorption or due to inexperience, Chan played badly, and his stack of chips was close to the vanishing point.

"Ah," he murmured, "how true it is that dollars going into a gambling house are like criminals led to execution. Doctor, might I trouble you – would you exchange ten white chips for a blue?"

"Gladly," nodded Swan, "but – pardon me – you are offering me a red chip, Mr Chan."

"Forgive the error," smiled Charlie, correcting it. "Not for worlds would I cheat you, my dear Doctor."

When Don Holt came to get them at ten o'clock, Charlie held up one white chip. "Behold," he said, "my stack has melted like snow under stream of hot water. I use my last chip to ante." He took his five cards, glanced at them, and threw them down. "No cards," he said. "The situation is hopeless. I withdraw."

Swan remained in for the hand, lost it and also stood up. "I'm about even," he remarked. "A lot of hard work for nothing." He counted his stack, and pushed it toward the banker. "Seven dollars and twenty-five cents," he added.

"Better stick a little longer, gentlemen," the banker said in a hard voice.

"No," Charlie said firmly. "We go along now – with the sheriff." The five hard-boiled gamblers looked up with sudden interest. "Ten o'clock – is that not correct, Sheriff?"

"Jes' ten," Don Holt returned. "Time to get goin'."

There was no further protest against their doing so from the gamblers, who appeared to have lost all interest in the noble sport themselves. Presently the little group from Tahoe was out in the car, and the sleeping town receded rapidly behind them.

"I think it was lots of fun," Leslie Beaton cried. "So quaint and unusual."

"But not very profitable," muttered Doctor Swan. "Eh, Mr Chan?"

"Profit and pleasure so seldom found on same street," Charlie answered.

When they reached the Tavern, Swan said good night and retired to his room, down the same corridor as that into which the coroner had disappeared. Dinsdale suggested that Miss Beaton come and look at the suite he was preparing for her. "There's a small sitting-room, with a fireplace—" he was saying, as they moved away.

Chan turned quickly to the Holts. "Humbly suggest you owe me ten dollars," he said. "The amount of money invested in poker game just now. Place it on your expense account for county to pay."

"Hold on a minute," Don Holt replied. "I ain't getting this. I'm glad to pay the ten, of course – but what did we get for it?"

Chan smiled. "We eliminated Doctor Swan from list of our suspects."

"What!"

"I am, perhaps, getting a few paces ahead of myself," Charlie conceded. He took galley one hundred and ten from his pocket, and gently unfolded it. "Tonight, I am perusing the autobiography of Landini, and happy luck smiles upon me. Will you be so good as to read aloud to your honorable father, the first paragraph of Chapter Twenty-Eight?"

The young sheriff cleared his throat. "'After my marvelously successful season in Berlin, I came for a rest to – to Stresa, on lovely Lago' – Lago – say, what language is this, anyhow?"

"It is Italian," Chan told him. "Lago Maggiore – the second largest of the Italian lakes, I believe."

"' – Lago Maggiore,'" continued Holt uncertainly. "'It is here, on a balcony of the Grand Hotel et des – des – more Italian – that I write the concluding chapters of my book. Where could I have found a more beautiful setting? I gaze in turn at the aquamarine waters, the fierce blue sky, the snow-capped Alps. Not far away, I am enraptured by Isola Bella, with its fantastic palace, its green terraces of orange and lemon trees rising a hundred feet above the lake. The thing that has always made life worth while for me is color – plenty of color, in personality, in music, in scenery. I have pitied many people in my time, but none more so than one I knew who was color-blind – '"

"By the Lord Harry!" cried old Sam Holt.

"' – color-blind,'" repeated his son doggedly, "'a poor luckless soul to whom all this gorgeous beauty would seem as a mere monotonous prospect of dull gray; lake, mountains, trees, sky – all the same. What a tragedy!'"

"Color-blind," Don Holt said again, as he laid down the galley.

"Precisely," nodded Chan. "A person, who, sent for a green scarf, comes back with a pink one. A poor luckless soul who, having murdered Landini and desiring to give semblance of order to desk, places on the yellow box the crimson lid, and on the crimson box, the yellow."

"Mr Chan," old Sam Holt said, "you've sure struck the right lead now."

"Who was this person?" Chan went on. "That remains to be discovered. One thing I know – it was not Doctor Swan, who for one half-hour tonight sorted so carefully the chips, blue, red and white. He is eliminated, but we proceed with high heart now, for we may be pretty sure that the person Ellen Landini pitied – the one who would not have enjoyed to sit with her on the balcony of the Grand Hotel et des Iles Borromées – that is the person who murdered her."

"So you think," Don Holt said slowly, "that she was killed near the desk? By someone who was in the room with her at the time?"

"I am certain of it."

"Then why all that talk about pine trees, and pieces of bark lying on the ground?"

Chan shrugged. “Might it not be that I am truly amateur student of trees? But what is the use? Can you make public believe that policeman is something more than dumb brute thinking only of man-hunt? Can you convince it that he may have outside interests of gentler nature? Alas – can you borrow a comb in a Buddhist monastery?”

XIII

FOOTSTEPS IN THE DARK

Dinsdale and the girl returned at that moment, and Charlie hastily restored galley one hundred and ten to his pocket.

"Sorry I can't put you higher up," the hotel man was saying. "The view would be better, of course. But I'm using only the ground floor at present, and just the one wing, at that."

"It's awfully good of you to take us at all," Leslie Beaton assured him. "Now, Mr Chan, hadn't we better be going? I just remembered poor Cash."

"For whom, perhaps, time does not travel so rapidly as it did this afternoon," Chan replied. "You are quite right, we must hasten." Don Holt and the girl went outside, and Dinsdale followed. Charlie turned to the old sheriff. "Good night, sir. We have something to work on now. As I recall – you once enjoyed camping journeys with Sing—"

"Funny," said Sam Holt, "the way you an' me – we always come back to Sing. I was jes' thinkin' of him myself. Yes, I camped with him, but I don't recollect he was color-blind. Leastways, he never showed it ef he was."

"You are quite sure? An unusual number of Chinese are."

"Dog-gone it, Mr Chan," cried the old man, "let's try not to think about Sing. Why should we? Fine character, he's always been. Model of all the virtues."

"Ah, yes," nodded Chan, "the real virtues. But was murder any great vice in era from which Sing dates? I think not – if the motive was good. The motive – that was what counted then. And would count today, with Sing, I think."

"I ain't listenin'," Sam Holt replied grimly.

Charlie smiled. "I cannot find it in my heart to blame you. It will, you may well believe, pain me deeply if I have traveled all this distance to put an ornament of my own race in hangman's noose. But let us not anticipate."

"Good advice, that is," the old man agreed. "But hard to follow, at my age. I said this afternoon I'd sleep better tonight – but – I dunno. Don't seem to need much of it at my age – an' it ain't so easy to sleep when you kain't tell the daylight from the dark. Somethin' tells me this case is goin' to change the world – fer a few of us. My boy—"

"One of finest young men I have had the honor to meet," Chan put in.

"I know. I wouldn't tell him, Mr Chan, but I know. Ain't never paid much attention to girls, Don ain't. But I heared somethin' in his voice tonight when he was talkin' to the Beaton girl—"

Chan laid his hand gently on the old man's shoulder. "A splendid young woman. Most of her life so far has been devoted to her brother. She knows the meaning of loyalty."

Sam Holt sighed with relief. "Then that's all right. Ain't nobody's opinion I'd take before yours, Mr Chan. Yes, that's all right – but that boy Sing! By the lord, Inspector, I'll be a happy man when we git out o' the woods on this case – even ef I kain't see the mountain-tops myself." He held out his hand. "Good night."

There were deep understanding and sympathy in their handclasp. Chan left the old man standing by the fire, his sightless eyes turned toward the open door.

Dinsdale spoke his farewell on the terrace, where flakes of snow were beginning to sift gently down. "More of it," the hotel man grumbled. "Is spring never coming? Seems to me the weather's all haywire these last few years."

Miss Beaton and the sheriff were waiting beside the launch. "Water's churning pretty lively," the latter remarked. "I'll take you back."

"Ah, yes," nodded Chan. "But I am sorry to remind you that, though we walk a thousand miles along the way with a friend, moment of goodby is still inevitable."

"For which remark," Don Holt replied, "you draw the back seat, an' the snow that goes with it. Hop in."

The pier lights faded suddenly behind them as they nosed into impenetrable dark. From out the soft blackness of the night came the drifting snow, thicker now, cool and refreshing. Chan lifted his face, delighting in the touch of the whirling flakes, so different from the liquid sunshine of steamy Honolulu days. Again a feeling of renewed energy swept over him.

Unerringly Don Holt found the lights of Dudley Ward's pier, and they moored the boat. Sing let them in, muttering vaguely on the ways of people who never knew when to come home, and the steadily multiplying labors in this house. Romano and Cash were alone in the living-room, the latter in the midst of a rather conspicuous yawn.

"Here we are – back already," remarked Don Holt.

"Thought you'd all been drowned," said Cash. "Maybe we might as well stay on fer breakfast now."

"Wait till you've been asked," suggested Holt. "All serene, I take it?"

"Sure – everybody in bed hours ago – except me an' the perfessor, here. He's been tellin' me all about music. I reckon I'll be a wow on my ukulele from this on."

"Most exciting to meet you, Mr Shannon," Romano remarked. "Always I have deep interest in Wild West cinemas."

"I don't know what you're calling me, Mister," returned Cash. "Don't sound very complimentary, but I'm too sleepy to care. Well, Don, do we hit the down trail now?"

It appeared that they did, and the two departed. Miss Beaton said good night and hastened upstairs. Chan was hanging his hat and coat in the closet at the rear, when Romano approached him. "If possible, I would enjoy word with you," he said.

"The enjoyment would be mutual," Charlie returned. "Shall we sit here by the fire? No. Sing, I perceive, is annoyed – we will retreat to my room." He led the way upstairs, and politely proffered a chair before the fireplace. "What, my dear Mr Romano, is hovering in your mind?"

"Many things," Romano replied. "Mr Chan, this news I have heard today – this fortune that has dropped into my lap – it works a vast difference in my life."

"A pleasant one, no doubt," Chan replied, also taking a chair.

"Naturally. From a pauper I ascend suddenly to the position of a man of property. What is my first reaction? To get away from this spot, lovely as it may be – to hasten to New York – to realize on my inheritance, and then to move on to the continent, where alone I feel at home. I shall sit in the twilight while the band plays in the Piazza at Venice, and I shall be grateful to Landini. I shall climb the stairs of the Opera in Vienna – but I perhaps move too quickly. What I am asking, Mr Chan, is – how far has this matter of Landini's murder traveled to solution?"

"So far," Charlie told him, "we have been ringing wooden bell."

"Which, if I interpret correctly, means you are nowhere?"

"In that neighborhood," Chan replied.

"Alas, it is unfortunate," Romano sighed. "And we unlucky ones who are unable to give satisfactory account of ourselves – how long must we languish here, waiting?"

"You must languish until guilty person is found."

"Then we may go?" asked Romano, brightening.

"All those of you who are not concerned – yes. All those who will not be required to give evidence at trial."

For a long moment Romano stared into the fire. "But one who had such evidence – one who had, perhaps, assisted in the arrest of the guilty – such a one would be forced to linger here?"

"For a time. And he would undoubtedly be commanded to return for the trial."

"That would be most unfortunate for him," replied Romano suavely. "But long ago I find there is no justice in this American law. Ah, well – I must be patient. Paris will be waiting, Vienna will still be the same, and I shall sit again in the Opera at Milan. Perhaps direct once more – who knows? Yes – I must – what you call it? – bide my time." He leaned forward and whispered. "Did you, also, hear a noise outside that door?"

Chan rose, went softly over and flung it open. No one was there.

"I think you are unduly nervous, Mr Romano," he said.

"And who, I pray, would not be nervous?" Romano replied. "All the time, I feel I am watched. Everywhere I go – every corner I turn – prying eyes are on me."

"And do you know why that should be?" Chan said.

"I know nothing," Romano answered loudly. "I have no part in this affair. When Landini was murdered, I was in my room, the door closed. I have testified to that. It is the truth."

"You had nothing else to say to me?" Chan inquired.

"Nothing whatever," Romano said, rising. He was calm again. "I merely wished to tell you I am very eager to go to New York. It means nothing to you, of course, but I am praying for your sudden success, Mr Chan."

Charlie's eyes narrowed. "Sometimes success comes like that. Suddenly. Who knows? In this case it may happen."

"I hope with all my heart it will," bowed Romano. His eyes were on a table by the fire. "Is it that you have written a book, Inspector?"

Charlie shook his head. "Landini has written book," he replied. "I have been perusing galley proofs of same."

"Ah, yes. I knew of Landini's book. As a matter of fact, I assisted occasionally in the writing."

"Were you, by any chance, present when last chapter was written? Same was composed, I believe, at Stresa, on Lago Maggiore."

"Alas, no," Romano answered. "I was detained in Paris at the time."

"But you know Stresa? I understand it is beautiful spot."

Romano raised his hands. "Beautiful, Signor? Ah, the word is not enough. Oh, bella, bella – Stresa is heavenly, it is divine. Such coloring in the lake, the sky, the hills. Beloved Stresa – I must not forget – it is one of the places to which dear Ellen's money shall take me. I really believe I shall have to make a list. There are so many lovely places." He moved toward the door. "I hope I have not troubled you, Signor," he said. "Good night."

But he had troubled Charlie slightly. What did this interview mean? Was Romano concealing important evidence? Was his door, after all, not quite so tightly closed as he pretended at that moment when Ellen Landini was shot?

Or was he merely seeking to divert suspicion to others? Always he gave the impression of slyness; what could be slyer than for a guilty man to hint that perhaps he could tell something if he chose? And that play-acting about a noise at the door – rather hollow, rather unconvincing.

Charlie stepped quietly into the hall. All was silent below, and cautiously he crept downstairs. No one seemed to be about, so with only the flickering fire to show him the way, he went to the closet and removed his hat, his overcoat, and those strange arctics which had come into his life when he decided to take this simple little trip to Tahoe. Returning to his room, he placed all these articles within easy reach, got out his flashlight and inspected it, and then – settled down to read the autobiography of Ellen Landini.

At one o'clock Charlie stopped reading, put down the galleys and stepped to his window. Pines, lake, sky, all had disappeared; the world seemed to end three feet away in a mixture of white and black. The outlook appeared to give him immense satisfaction; he was smiling as, with some difficulty, he got into the arctics and fastened them. He donned the unaccustomed overcoat, put his black felt hat securely on his head and took up his flashlight with a steady hand. Extinguishing all but one of his lights, he went into the hall and closed the door silently behind him.

It was the back stairs he chose tonight, and all down their length and along the passageway to the back door, he half expected to encounter the ubiquitous figure of the aged Sing. But no Sing loomed in his path. He let himself out on to the snowy back porch, and started toward the garage where only a few hours before he had come upon a ladder. The amateur student of trees was again immersed in thoughts of his favorite line of research.

But fate intervened, and Charlie did not visit the garage that night. For, flashing his light cautiously along the path, he suddenly perceived that there were fresh footprints ahead of him. Someone else had left Pineview by the back way tonight – and not so long ago.

To one who had hitherto known footprints only as something to be found in sand along a sunlit beach, the idea was fascinating. Almost unconsciously he followed the trail, up the flight of outdoor stairs that led to the road, which was some distance above the house. There he paused, and considered.

Who had left this house since eleven o'clock, which was about the time the snow had begun to fall? Had one of his charges escaped from his care? The falling snow was rapidly covering these tracks, but they seemed fresh ones, none the less. The quickest answer appeared to lie ahead.

He began to travel, as rapidly as his girth permitted, down the road that led in the direction of the Tavern. The wind howled through the long fragrant aisles of the pines, the storm wrapped him in a damp embrace. But he made speed, for his energy was great, and the languor of the semi-tropics was far-off and forgotten.

About half a mile down the road he came to the house of Dudley Ward's nearest neighbor. He remembered having seen it from the water – a great rambling barracks built of wood. Its windows were closed and shuttered for the winter, no sign of life was anywhere about it. And yet – the footprints which Charlie followed unmistakably turned off at this point. Turned off, and went unerringly down the path to the rear door.

A bit skeptical now, Charlie did the same. Perhaps, he reflected, he was merely on the trail of a watchman, or some equally harmless person. For a moment he stood on the rear porch. Then he reached out and tried the back door of the deserted house. A little thrill ran down his spine – for it opened at his touch.

At any rate, this was not housebreaking, he thought as he went inside. He found himself in a passageway, similar to the one in Ward's house, and again he stopped, alert for some sound of human habitation. The wind rattled the windows and sighed around the eaves, but nothing moved or seemed to live in these empty rooms. Yet at his feet, Chan's flashlight showed him, was a trail of loose snow leading off into the dark.

He followed this trail, out of the passage into a front hall. Great shadows danced about him on the walls; in distant rooms he saw ghostly chairs and sofas swathed in white. Undaunted, he pushed on, up the carpeted stairs where the fresh snow lay. It led him to a closed door at the rear of the second-floor hall, and there it stopped. He tried the door, quietly, and found it locked.

A brief examination of the sill decided him, and he had raised his hand to knock, when he thought he heard the closing of a distant door. He waited. Undoubtedly stealthy footsteps were crossing the polished floor of the downstairs hall. Charlie was thinking very fast.

He had been in somewhat similar situations before, and had learned that all the advantage lies with the side which attacks suddenly and unexpectedly. Putting his flashlight in his pocket, he moved softly and swiftly to the stairs and began to descend. Half-way down he stopped and so, almost, did his heart. For the person in the hall below had lighted a match.

Charlie crouched close to the wall, the shadows flickered about him, but the life of a match is brief, and evidently he was still safe when the flame expired. Safe – in a way – except for the fact that the unknown intruder was coming rapidly up the stairs.

He had the top position, and there was nothing else for it – Charlie gathered all his strength and leaped, straight into the surprise of his life. For it was obviously a giant upon whom he fell; a giant who kept his footing and took Chan, avoirdupois and all, into his arms. In another second the plump detective from the islands was engaged in a struggle he would long remember. They staggered together down the stairs; their swaying forms hit the newel post, and an old-fashioned lamp that had been established there for thirty years crashed down in a million pieces. Next they were rolling on the floor, Charlie grimly determined to keep in so close an embrace that this terrible stranger would have no chance to square off for a blow. One blow from that source, he felt, would ruin him for ever.

Not in such good condition as he used to be, Chan reflected, as the fight went doggedly on. Getting on in years, easily winded – ah, youth, youth. No use pretending, it left one day, never to return. About this struggle now – he was losing it. Unmistakably. He was on his back, the stranger's hands were at his throat; he sought, vainly, to tear them away. A flash of the little house on Punchbowl Hill, the bougainvillea vine hanging over the veranda – and then the dark, slowly enveloping his senses.

Then the stranger, sitting down violently on Charlie's generous stomach, and the voice of Don Holt, crying "Good lord – is that you, Mr Chan?"

"Alas," said Chan. "At night all cats are black."

Holt was helping him to his feet, deeply solicitous. "Say – I sure am sorry about this, Inspector. Of course – I never suspected. I hope I haven't hurt you much. How do you feel?"

"How does sparrow feel when hit by cannon-ball?" Charlie returned. "A little disturbed. However, I expect to survive. And I am delighted we have met, though I must disparage the details of our meeting. For there is something strange afoot in this house tonight."

"I reckon there is," Holt answered. "I was sound asleep when the coroner came to my room—"

"One moment, please," Chan interrupted. "I will hear that later. Just now I think it important that we investigate a certain door upstairs. Without delay." He got out his flashlight and, to his surprise, found it still working. "Will you be kind enough to follow me?"

Quickly he led the sheriff to the locked door on the second floor. "Track of snow brought me here," he explained. "And behold." He pointed. On the door-sill was more snow, a portion of a heel-print where a foot had recently trod.

"Then somebody's inside," said Holt, in a hushed voice.

"Somebody," nodded Chan. "Or something," he added.

The sheriff raised a great fist, and the sound of his blow against the panel echoed loudly through the house. "Open up here!" he shouted.

In the dead silence that followed there was something sinister and disturbing. Holt rattled the knob, and then moved back a few feet.

"Well," he said, "we already owe for that lamp downstairs. Might as well add a little damage here. Will you turn the light this way, Inspector?"

Charlie illuminated the scene, and the sheriff lunged forward. There came the sound of splintering wood as the lock gave way and the door swung open. Chan's flash swept the room inside. An ordinary bedroom, it seemed to be, as one after another the articles of furniture emerged from the shadows. An ordinary bedroom – and on the floor beside the bed, the motionless figure of a man.

As they stood for a moment in the doorway, Chan thought suddenly of Romano. Romano sitting nervously in that other bedroom, asking what would happen to one who – perhaps – assisted in the arrest of the guilty. Had there been real fear in the Italian's eyes when he whispered: "Did you, also, hear a noise outside that door?"

Kneeling, the sheriff turned the figure on the floor face up. Chan joined him with the lamp – and they were looking into the dead eyes of Doctor Swan.

XIV

THOUGHT IS A LADY

For a moment, while the yellow glare of Chan's flashlight rested idly on the face of the dead doctor, there was no sound save that of the storm roaring about the old house.

"Exit Doctor Swan," said the sheriff grimly. "I wonder what this means?"

"I believe," Chan answered, "it means that blackmailer has met with obvious finish. Was Doctor Swan enclosed safely in room last night when fatal shot was fired at Landini? It never did seem probable. Suppose he hovered about in hall, desiring one final word with his former wife. Suppose he learned who killed her. Would such a man report at once to police? Or would he, instead, see new delightful path for blackmail opening up before his dazzled eyes?"

"Sounds reasonable," Holt agreed.

"I think it happened. Suppose he is summoned down here tonight to receive first instalment of his wickedly earned money. And receives instead the bullet of a desperate person who cannot pay – or, knowing that the demand will be endless, will not pay. Ah, yes, from murderer's standpoint, this would be wiser course. I cannot truthfully say I disagree. But you were about to tell me how you chance to be here?"

"The coroner had the room next to Swan's at the Tavern," Holt replied. "He was waked up about twelve-thirty by the banging of a shutter. The noise seemed to come from Swan's room. The coroner stood it as long as he could, and then he rapped on Swan's door. Well, to cut it short, nobody answered – an' that was how I come into it.

"We saw right away that Swan had left by the window. I followed his footprints to the road, where they turned in this direction. It looked like the doctor was staging a getaway. Say, I didn't stop for anything – I jes' hurried along on his trail. Didn't even have a flashlight – not so strong on preparedness as you are. But I did have a full box of matches – jes' used my last downstairs."

"You walked the two miles or more from the Tavern?"

"Sure – when I wasn't running. When I got to the point behind this house where Swan had turned off, I looked up and got the glimmer of a flashlight back of the hall shutters on the second floor – yours, I reckon. So I pushed open the back door, and came in."

"The back door was still unlocked?" Chan asked thoughtfully.

"Sure."

Charlie considered. "The killer of Doctor Swan must have intended this house as temporary hiding-place for victim," he reflected. "Would he then have departed, leaving door unlocked for any passer-by to enter? I think not. The answer is, of course, he was still in house when we arrived. He may even be here now. Come – we waste valuable time."

Hastily he led Don Holt downstairs and through the passageway to the rear door. He turned the knob. But now the rear door was locked, and there was no key in sight.

"Haie!" Chan cried. "Our friend has made his escape – perhaps while we were tumbling in mortal conflict in the hall. Where was he hiding when we entered?" He made an investigation of the plentiful snow along the passage. "Ah, yes."

Pushing open the door into a butler's pantry, he sadly pointed out to Holt more snow on the linoleum inside. "Let us place order for ample supply of sackcloth and ashes," he remarked gloomily. "You and I, my boy, both walked tonight within three feet of the murderer we so hotly seek. Alas, this winter climate is not so invigorating to the mental processes as I had hoped it would be."

The sheriff returned to the back door and fiercely rattled the knob. "He's got a fine start on us, too," he said.

"Man inclined to exercise would not need to look farther for nice pair of dumb-bells," Chan answered. "Pardon vile slang, which I acquire from my children, now being beautifully educated in American schools. Come, we must seek new footprints leading away from this rear door. They are our only hope."

They ran to the big front door, where somewhat rusted bolts again delayed them. After a struggle, however, they got it open, and hastened around to the back of the house. The snow was very damp now. "Turning to rain," Holt announced, looking up at the sky. "This'll have to be a quick job."

There were, indeed, new footprints in the snow at the back. They led away, not to the road, but around the house, on the opposite side from that which Chan and the sheriff had traveled. Breathlessly the two representatives of the law followed them – straight to the pier. At the edge of the restless water beneath the pier, the footprints stopped abruptly.

"That ends that," sighed Holt. "This guy had a rowboat, I reckon." He stared at the wild waters. "Wouldn't care to be traveling out there tonight," he added.

Charlie was bending eagerly with his flashlight above the last visible prints just before they entered the water. "No use," he said, sighing ponderously. "Fresh snow obscures any identifying marks. Snow, I fear, has been a little too highly spoken of as aid to detectives in hour of need."

They returned to the front veranda of the house. Holt continued to study the lake. "With this rain coming on," he remarked, "I don't believe a rowboat could keep afloat out there."

"If man who killed Swan, and then escaped after we entered house, brought boat," Chan said, "then who was person whose tracks I followed down from Pineview by the road? Did he perhaps carry boat on back?"

"Oh – you followed somebody down here, too?"

"I assuredly did, and I believe he was the man we seek."

"Perhaps he took a boat from this place."

"No – I observed boat-house intact. Might I make another suggestion?"

"By all means. I'm through."

"Might he not have stepped into water and run along shore for some distance? Beach is flat here."

"By golly, that's right," agreed the sheriff. "He could travel by that method for a mile in either direction. Of course, he'd probably leave the water as soon as he thought himself safe. There's an idea – we could follow the shore—"

"In which direction?"

"Why – you take one way, and I'll take the other."

Charlie shook his head. "No use," he said. "Already this gentleman has had twelve minutes' start. As for me, my avoirdupois precludes success – and even your thin legs, I think, would fail."

Holt sighed. "It seemed the only chance," he said.

Charlie smiled. "There will be other chances," he replied. "Do not despair. Our quarry will be caught – but by subtler means than running alongshore in the rain. For I perceive we now have rain."

"Yes, spring has come," Holt answered. "And here I am, too tangled up in murder to enjoy the thought."

"From the black sky, white water falls," smiled Chan, looking aloft. "This may yet prove very pleasant spring for you."

"Oh, yeah?" the sheriff replied. "Well, in the meantime, what next? Here we are, stuck down here, in a deserted house with a dead man – no telephone, and nothing but our feet to get away on. Here's my suggestion. I'll go back to the Tavern and get the coroner, while you go and see what's doing at Pineview."

"So sorry to disagree," Chan said. "Everything would no doubt be quiet at Pineview – everyone in bed and asleep by the time I reached there. No change – save that I might possibly find back door, which I left unfastened, now locked. In such case, I must raise row, or stand in rain until morning. Besides, is it wise to leave this place unguarded? We might return to find our dead man gone. Suppose the killer still lurks among the trees, sees us both depart, and proceeds to follow out hastily the plan I am sure he intended to pursue at leisure – to drop body of Swan far out in lake, to hide it in hills, to dispose of it in some manner. No. Plan for yourself is excellent, but I shall linger here, awaiting return of the honorable sheriff, the coroner and light of another day."

"Well." Holt looked back into the dim empty house. "It's no job I would rise in meeting to ask for, but if you want it, it's yours. But what in Sam Hill will you do with yourself? I'll be gone quite some while."

"There is no need of hurry on your part. First, I shall open front door very wide, seeking to exchange stale air of long-closed house for fresher breath of first spring night. Then, I shall find comfortable chair in parlor, repose in it and think."

"Think?"

"Precisely. Thought is a lady, beautiful as jade, so do not fear I shall be lonely. Events of tonight make me certain I must not neglect the lady's company longer."

"Well, look out for yourself, if you stay here," Holt remarked. "That's not a pretty picture you painted – the killer creeping back. I haven't got my gun with me, or I'd loan it to you."

Charlie shrugged. "I hold with Mrs O'Ferrell – the less guns, the fewer gets killed. However, have no anxiety. The chair I sit in will be like seat for guest of honor at Chinese dinner. It will face the door, so I may note an enemy's approach."

"Then I'll be going—" Holt began.

Charlie laid a hand on his arm. "Already that lady inspires me – I see Doctor Swan, standing on pier tonight, just before you took him to the Tavern in your launch. What was it he desired so eagerly to know?"

"That's right," Holt said. "About Romano and the will. Did Romano get Landini's property?"

"And was he, consequently, a good blackmail prospect?" Chan's eyes narrowed. "It would seem to me, Sheriff, that Swan came here tonight to meet a man of whom, physically, he had no fear. A small man – like Romano."

Don Holt scowled. "But Romano. If he had done either of these killings wouldn't he have been more likely to use a knife?"

"Ah – excellent reasoning," Charlie cried. "I am proud of you. However, you forget – or perhaps you do not know – that Romano, like Ireland, served in the war. An Italian officer – he must have known well the use of the revolver. But no matter – I merely continue to marshal facts for the storehouse of my mind. A pleasant journey to you."

"Yeah – in the rain, on foot," smiled Holt. "Well, goodby – and good luck."

He ran down off the porch and disappeared toward the road in the rear. Chan retired inside, leaving the door open, and moved on into a large living-room. A pleasant place this must be, he thought, on summer nights, with its splendid view of the lake. He removed a sheet from a large chair and placing the latter in what seemed the safest corner, dropped into it. Then he shut off his light, and put it in his pocket.

The rain beat against the house, the wind roared, and Charlie thought back over this wintry case upon which he, detective of the semi-tropics, was now so unexpectedly engaged. First of all he thought of people: of Sing, whose beady little eyes even Chan could not read; of Cecile, jealous and angry last night when she heard the airplane over the lake; of Ireland, clumsy and uneasy when out of his plane, but so expert when in it. He considered Romano, broke and according to his own confession, desperate – but now come into money through Landini's sudden passing. Hugh Beaton, sick of the bargain he had made; his sister, jealous as Cecile, but in a different way – a high-strung, impetuous girl. Dinsdale – since he was including them all – evidently so aloof from all this – but an old friend of the singer, none the less. Ward, who had started it all and encountered two tragedies. Ryder, with the scornful blue eyes above the blond beard, and Swan – dead now in that room above. Had it been, after all, attempted blackmail that led to Swan's death? How young Hugh Beaton had raged at the doctor last night after the murder – and how Michael Ireland and Swan had snarled at each other.

The rain outside seemed to increase in fury, and Charlie decided he had had enough of the open door. He crossed over, closed it and returned to his chair. Once more, he decided, he would take things from the beginning – the sudden shot upstairs, Landini on the floor, the boxes with the mixed lids – ah, he had been over all this a hundred times. But – and he started up suddenly in his chair – there was one thing he had forgotten. Not yet had he carefully considered the events before the murder.

He was back, then, on the train, repeating from memory his talk with Romano; he was riding up from Truckee to the Tavern; again the icy spray of the lake stung his cheeks, he was going ashore at Pineview, the ex-husbands of Landini were drinking before the fire. Then followed dinner – his excellent memory recalled vividly every incident at the table, nearly every word that had been spoken. He heard again the bark of the dog announcing the arrival of the singer – felt again the vibrant, colorful personality of Landini – ah, what a pity her brilliant career was so soon to end.

But beyond the shot that ended it, Chan did not trouble now to explore. He gazed around this strange room, listened for a moment to the spatter of rain at the windows, and then, oblivious to any killer who might return, he curled up comfortably in his chair, drew his overcoat closer and fell into a deep and peaceful sleep. After all, a man must sleep.

He awoke with a start to find the sheriff bending over him. A semblance of dawn seemed to be floating through the house, but the rain still beat against the window-panes.

Beyond Don Holt stood the coroner.

"Sorry to disturb you," Holt said. "We just dropped in."

Charlie yawned, sat up and was about to step to the window for a look at his beloved Honolulu. Then he remembered.

"Anything exciting happen?" Holt wanted to know.

"I – I think not," Chan said. "No – as I recall now – nothing happened. Ah, yes – the coroner. He will want to go upstairs."

He leaped briskly to his feet, and led the way to the room above. The others followed, not so briskly. They could all see, in the semi-darkness, the body of Swan, lying as it had been left by Charlie and the sheriff the night before.

"We need more light here, I think," Chan said. "I will admit some, such as it is." He went to the window, opened it and threw back the blinds. For a moment he stood leaning over the window-sill, then Don Holt was surprised to see him climbing through the window.

"What are you doing?" the sheriff inquired.

"Small polar expedition of my own," Chan replied. He had dropped to a balcony some two feet below the window. It was covered by about twelve inches of snow, now melting rapidly. At one side of the window, close to the house wall, was a spot which had melted more rapidly than the rest, leaving a small hole. Charlie bared one arm to the elbow, and plunged it deep into the crevice. With an expression of triumph on his face, he held up an automatic pistol so those inside the room could see.

"Man who buries his treasure in the snow," he said, "forgets that summer is coming."

XV

ANOTHER MAN'S EARTH

Chan handed the revolver to the sheriff and began a rather cumbersome climb back into the room.

"Guard weapon well," he suggested. "It may prove valuable – who knows? How many cartridges exploded, please?"

"Why, one, of course," the sheriff replied.

"Ah, yes – the bullet from which, now reposing in poor Doctor Swan, the coroner will later obtain for us. You may handle pistol freely, Sheriff. The killer we deal with does not leave fingerprints – even with his footprints he is careful man. In spite of his care, however, his discarded weapons may yet tell us much."

"You think so?" inquired Holt.

"I hope so." For a time Charlie stood studying the revolver as it lay in the sheriff's hand. "This one has somewhat old-fashioned look," he suggested.

"Sure does," Don Holt agreed.

"You are, of course, too young to have fought in the war?"

"Too young by six years – I tried it," smiled the sheriff.

Charlie shrugged. "No matter. All sorts of weapons were issued in the war – on many fronts. We must seek other path."

Doctor Price stood up. "All right," he said, "that's all I can do now. We may as well take this man down to the village."

"What would you deduce?" Chan inquired.

"I believe he was shot at close range, and without a struggle," the coroner replied. "Certainly there was no struggle here – though he may have been killed elsewhere, and carried to this room."

"Very probable," Chan nodded. "For that reason, I make no extended examination of the place."

"I don't believe the poor devil had any inkling of what was about to happen to him," Doctor Price continued. "That's just a guess, of course. The bullet entered his side – it may have been fired by someone who was walking close to him – or slightly behind him. All things that we'll never know, I reckon." There came the honk of a horn behind the house. "That's Gus Elkins. I told him to follow us with his ambulance." He yawned. "Gosh – I expected to be on my way back to the county-seat before this."

While Doctor Price and Mr Elkins attended to the removal of Swan's body, the sheriff and Charlie made a tour of the house, restoring it to order, in so far as they could.

"You an' me – I reckon we'll take my old flivver and get over to Pineview," the sheriff said. "We come up by road – lake looked pretty choppy. But say – wait till you hit the road." He kicked aside some broken glass in the lower hall. "Hope you ain't feelin' any ill effects from our friendly tussle."

"He who goes out on the hills to meet the tiger must pay the price," returned Charlie.

Holt laughed. "Sure was a mix-up. I was wonderin' when I walked back to the Tavern what we ought to do next. Somebody had a key to the back door of that house, I said. So I sent a wire down to the owner in San Francisco an' asked him who that would be."

"Excellent," Charlie returned. "It was what I was about to suggest. But now you are moving a little ahead of me on our rocky path."

"I ain't so sure about that," Holt said. "How did you get on with your home work while I was away? Going to do a lot of heavy thinkin', I believe you told me."

Charlie's eyes narrowed. "Alas," he answered, "I fear that, like my little son Barry, I toppled in sleep on to my books."

"Oh, yeah?" Don Holt answered.

In a few moments the ambulance had gone, and Chan climbed into the flivver beside the sheriff. "Feel at home in such seat," he commented. They started with a jerk. "But not on such road. Not much melting snow on Punchbowl Hill."

Daylight had come, but a sullen counterfeit daylight. The rain beat down on the top of the car, and on Don Holt's two-gallon hat as he leaned far out to follow the road – the windshield wiper, he explained, was not working. The wind had died, the pines were silent and dripping; they plowed on through slush a foot deep.

"Wonder how we'll find all the folks at Pineview," the sheriff said presently. "Including the murderer. I guess there ain't much doubt he'll be there, waiting for us."

"He may be," Charlie agreed.

"Well – let's have a check-up. Who's there now? Romano, Ryder and Ward. Hugh Beaton – and his sister."

"A charming lady, Miss Beaton," Chan suggested.

"Yeah – she's all right. But don't get me off the track – I'm countin'. Let's see – well, that's about all – except Sing and Cecile – I sort of had that French dame on my mind, but after this, she don't look so good. That's the list."

"And Mrs O'Ferrell," Chan added.

"Yeah – I can see her plowin' down through the snow to put a bullet in Swan. Say – I never been able to figure out what you meant – about Trouble bein' a clue."

"So sorry," Chan replied. "But we all have our little mysteries to sting us, as summer flies pester the horse. For example, in own mind I am convinced blow received by Sing in defenseless face on night of murder was vastly important clue. But – I cannot figure it. However, we must be patient. You and I – we will both learn in time."

They left the car on the road above and descended the steps to the back door of Pineview. Sing was shaking a duster on the porch. He gave Charlie a slightly startled look.

"Wha's mallah you?" he demanded. "My think you up-stah in bed, you come home back step, plenty wet."

"I was called away on business," Charlie explained.

"Hello, Sing," the sheriff said. "Don't worry about Mr Chan. I've been taking care of him. Anybody up yet?"

"Nobody only me," Sing replied. "My get up sunlise, woik, woik, woik. Too much woik this house. No can do."

Inside, they found Sing's statements somewhat inaccurate. Mrs O'Ferrell was busy in the kitchen, and gave them a cheery greeting. Proceeding to the living-room, they found Leslie Beaton, reading a book.

"Hello – you're up early," Holt remarked.

"The same for you," she replied, "and as for Mr Chan – I don't believe he ever sleeps. Was that he – or should I say him – I saw in the road behind the house in the night?"

"It may have been," Charlie said quickly. "Again, it may not. Elaborate the statement, if you will be so good."

"I couldn't sleep very well," the girl went on. "Can anyone – in this house? My room is in an ell in the rear, close to the road. I went to the window and looked out. I saw a shadowy figure, hurrying up the steps, and fairly running along the road."

"Sounds pretty active for the inspector," smiled Holt. "Do you know what time this was?"

"Yes – it was precisely ten minutes after twelve. I looked at my watch."

Chan leaned toward her eagerly. "Describe this person," he urged.

"Impossible," she answered. "It was snowing hard. It might have been anybody – even a woman, for that matter. I was somewhat worried. I went into my brother's room – he's right next door – and wakened him. But he told me to go back to bed, and forget it."

Hugh Beaton at that moment appeared on the stairs. His face seemed paler than usual; there were dark circles about his eyes, and his manner was extremely nervous. He saw Charlie and the sheriff.

"What's happened now?" he cried. "For God's sake – what is it now?"

"It is nothing," Charlie replied soothingly. "You arise early."

"Why shouldn't I? My nerves are all shot to pieces, in this God-forsaken place. When are you going to let us out of this prison? What right have you—"

"Please, Hughie," his sister cut in. "Mr Ward might hear you – and he's been so kind to us."

"I don't care if he does hear me," the boy retorted. "He knows I don't want to stay here. When do we go to the Tavern? You promised today—"

"And it will be today," Holt said, looking at him with a trace of contempt. Temperamental artists were not in the sheriff's line. "Brace up."

"Tell me," Chan said. "When your sister came in to wake you last night—"

"When she – oh, yes. I remember now. What was that all about?"

"You remember, Hughie," said the girl, "I told you I'd seen somebody leaving the house."

"Oh, yes. Well, did somebody leave? Is someone missing?"

"Somebody did leave," Charlie explained. "We think he returned, however. But not until, in an empty house down the road, he had shot and killed Doctor Swan."

There was silence for a moment. "Doctor Swan," gasped the girl. Her face was as white as her brother's. "Oh, that's too terrible."

"It's no more terrible than the killing of Ellen," her brother said, and his voice sounded hysterical. "We've got to get out of here, I tell you. Today. This minute." He rose and stared wildly about.

"A little later," Holt remarked calmly.

"But I tell you – my sister – she's in danger here. So are we all – but I have to look after her—"

"A natural feeling," Chan said. "Your sister will be taken care of – and so will you. I presume you heard nothing in the night – save, of course, your sister's entrance. You can throw no light on this?"

"None. None whatever," the boy answered.

"Most unfortunate," Charlie rose. "I go to my room to freshen up drooping appearance. I return soon," he added to the sheriff.

He went up, leaving the three young people in the living-room. Cecile was standing just inside his door.

"Ah, Monsieur," she cried. "Your bed is untouched."

"I know," he replied. "I did not sleep last night. Just a moment, if you will be so kind. Do not go."

"Yes, Monsieur." She regarded him with troubled eyes.

"Your husband, Madame? When did you see him last?"

"When he left here just before dinner. Surely you recall? He took the little dog in his plane."

"He did not return to this neighborhood last night?"

"How could he? Such a night. He could not fly in such weather."

"But is he not an expert chauffeur? He could return in automobile."

"If he returned, I did not know it. I do not understand of what you speak, Monsieur."

"He and Doctor Swan – they were not the best of friends?"

"Michael hates him, as you saw yourself. He despises him, and with many good reasons. But why do you ask?"

"Because" – Charlie keenly watched her face – "because, Madame, Doctor Swan was murdered in this vicinity last night." Still he watched her. "Ah, that is all. You may go now."

She left without a word, and after hastily washing his hands and his as yet unshaven face, Charlie went out and knocked on Romano's door. The conductor let him in; he was partly dressed, his face was covered with lather, and he held a razor in his hand.

"Enter, Inspector," he invited. "You will pardon my condition. The hour – it is an early one."

"Events conspire to give me no rest," Chan told him. "Continue, please, to shave. I will repose here, on edge of bathtub. There is a word or two—"

"What do you wish, Signor?"

"You heard no one about this house last night? You saw no one leave by the rear door?"

"I am a sound sleeper, Inspector."

Quickly Chan told him what had occurred. He wished the Italian had removed more of that lather before hearing the news. But – wasn't the swarthy forehead now somewhat more in harmony with the white lather?

"Swan, eh?" said Romano slowly. "Ah, yes – he knew too much, that one, Inspector. Him, he could not hold his tongue. Only yesterday, when we were having long day together, he spoke indiscreetly to me."

"He said – what?"

"Nothing definite, you understand. I could not give you words. But already I thought his greedy fingers counted fresh bank-notes. That is dangerous business – blackmail."

Chan studied the Italian's face. From the first, this man had baffled him.

"And in my room last night," he said, "you, yourself, hinted at knowing something, too."

An expression of vast surprise crossed Romano's face.

"I, Signor? The day is young – you are still dreaming."

"Nonsense. You spoke of—"

"Ah, my English – it is not so good. You do not understand me when I speak it."

"You asked if anyone who could give information in this case would have to remain here after giving it."

"Did I say that? I must have been thinking of Doctor Swan."

"Unusual, if you were," Chan answered. "I should not say you devoted much thought to others. Of yourself, you think. Then consider this – if you have information which you withhold, it will go hard with you when matter is discovered."

"I have no information," Romano answered suavely. "All I can say is, I trust this new murder will speed your search, for speed is what I most desire. In the meantime, you are permitting Miss Beaton and her brother the privilege of changing their residence to the Tavern today. Can you deny the same to me? You cannot. I will not stay in this house another day."

"Ah – you begin to remember, now," Chan smiled. "You are afraid here. You do know something, after all."

"Signor," cried Romano passionately, "you insult my honor. Ellen Landini was dear to me – her memory is dearer still – would I conceal the name of her assassin? No! A million times, no! Anyhow," he added more calmly, "I do not know the name. Must I tell you again?"

"For the present – no," bowed Chan, and left the room.

Downstairs, he found Hugh Beaton nervously pacing the floor, while his sister and the sheriff sat before the fire. The latter's conversational powers seemed to be ebbing fast, and Charlie was happy to help him out. In a few moments John Ryder came down the stairs, carefully groomed as always, remote and aloof.

"Beastly day, isn't it?" he remarked. He glanced at the sheriff. "Hello, Mr Holt. Anything new?"

"Nothing unusual," Holt said. "Another murder, that's all."

"Another what?" It was Dudley Ward who spoke, from the stairs.

Charlie Chan explained, watching both men alternately as he did so. Ryder's expression never altered; Ward looked only a little older, a little more worn, as he listened.

"A nasty bounder, Swan," Ryder said coldly. "But, of course – murder is a bit extreme."

"None too kind to Ellen," Ward remarked thoughtfully. "But then – I guess none of us were, for that matter."

"Speak for yourself, Dudley," answered Ryder warmly. "Don't begin to idealize the woman, just because she's dead."

"I'm not idealizing her, John," Ward returned. "I'm just trying to keep in mind her virtues – and they were many. And it has occurred to me these last few days, that she was not too lucky in her choice of husbands." His eyes were on Romano, sleek and dapper, who was now coming down the stairs.

"Bleakfast leady now," announced Sing, from the rear.

"Come on, Don," Ward said. "You're eating with us."

"That's – that's mighty good of you," replied the sheriff.

"Nonsense. Sing – set another place!"

Sing muttered something about the amount of work in this house, and retired. But when they reached the dining-room, the old Chinese was there ahead of them, briskly and efficiently making a place for Holt.

The meal was eaten for the most part in silence. When it was ended, and they were back in the living-room, Holt informed Leslie Beaton and her brother that he would send his launch for them at nine-thirty, and that they should be packed and ready for the move to the hotel.

"You bet I'll be ready," young Beaton cried. Seeing his sister's eyes on him, he added: "Of course, Mr Ward, I appreciate your hospitality. And the way Leslie's looking at me, I suppose I ought to add, I had a nice time." His tone was childish and disagreeable.

"Hardly that," Ward replied amiably. "But I shall miss your sister and you very much, and I hope you may some day return for a stay under happier conditions."

"You've been wonderful," Leslie Beaton told him. "I shall never forget you. The perfect host – at the most imperfect moment."

Ward bowed. "I shan't forget you," he said.

Romano popped to the front. "There will be a place in your launch for me?" he asked.

"What do you mean?" inquired Holt.

"I mean I also – with deep regret, Signor Ward – am leaving here today for the Tavern. Inspector Chan has agreed."

Holt glanced at Charlie, who nodded. "All right," the sheriff said. "You can have Swan's room. You've heard what happened to him."

Romano shrugged. "Ah – he wandered too far away. Me – I stick close to the hotel."

"Well, see that you do," Holt replied.

Charlie followed the sheriff into the passage at the rear. "Pardon me," he inquired. "You have revolver we discovered in snow?"

"Sure. You want it?" Holt produced the weapon.

"I will take it brief while. When our friends come down to Tavern, I will be with them. Tell me, is there train to Oakland this morning?"

"Yes – there's one about ten-thirty. Say" – an expression of dismay spread over the sheriff's face – "you ain't leaving, are you?"

"No. Not at this date."

"Who is?"

"We will discuss the matter later."

"So long, then." Holt lowered his voice. "Well, we had a nice breakfast, didn't we? But that's about all we got, eh?"

"Not quite." Chan's eyes narrowed. "We received also, from Miss Beaton, very pretty alibi for her brother at twelve-ten last night."

"My gosh," the sheriff said. "I never thought of that."

"I did not believe you would," smiled Charlie.

He went at once to his room where, for a time, he experimented with lampblack and brush on the automatic pistol. Then, leaving the weapon on his desk, he hurried at last to the refreshing solace of his morning bath. He had just finished shaving when Sing appeared in his room with a supply of wood. Chan came out from the bath to find the old man staring at the pistol.

"Hello, Sing," he remarked, "you see that before, maybe?"

"I no see him."

"You are quite sure?"

"I no see him – tha's no lie, Boss."

Charlie's eyebrows went up at this unexpected tribute of respect. "Mebbe you catch 'um killer – hey, Boss?" the old man added.

Chan shrugged. "I am stupid policeman – my mind is like the Yellow River." He paused. "But – who was it said – even the Yellow River has its clear days?"

"No savvy," responded Sing, and started out.

Charlie laid a hand on the thin old arm.

"Delay one moment, if you will be so good," he said in Cantonese. "You and I, honorable Sing, are of the same race, the same people. Why, then, should a thousand hills rise between us when we talk?"

"They are hills you place there with your white devil ways," Sing suggested.

"I am so sorry. They are imaginary. Let us sweep them away. How many years did you have when you came to this alien land?"

"I had eighteen," the old man replied. "Now I have seventy-eight."

"Then for sixty years you have carried another man's heaven on your head, and your feet have trod upon another man's earth. Do you not long to return to China, ancient one?"

"Some day—" The old man's eyes glittered.

"Some day – yes. But a man takes off his shoes tonight. How does he know he will put them on again in the morning? Death comes, Ah Sing."

"My bones return," Sing told him.

"Yes – that is much. But to see again the village where you were born – to walk again on the soil where your bones are to rest—"

The old man shook his head sadly. "Too much woik this house," he said, lapsing into English. "No can go. No can go."

"Do not despair," Charlie returned, dropping his somewhat rusty Cantonese. "Fate settles all things, and all things arrive at their appointed time." He took a clean white shirt from his bag and proceeded to put it on. "A very dull day, indeed," he added, stepping to the window and gazing out at the dripping pines. "On such an occasion, the attire of man should compensate. You understand what I mean – I should wear gay clothes, happy clothes. My brightest necktie, perhaps."

"Tha's light," nodded Sing.

"I have a very red necktie – my daughter Evelyn gave it to me on Christmas, and she herself put it in my bag when I left. It is, my dear Sing, the reddest necktie the eyes of man have seen. And this, I believe, is the fitting day for it." He went to his closet, removed a tie and drew it around his neck. For a moment he faced the mirror, and while he tied the knot, he watched the expression on the old man's withered countenance. He turned about, to give Sing the full effect.

"There," he beamed, "that will brighten this gloomy day. Eh, Sing?"

"Velly good," agreed Sing, and walked slowly from the room. Charlie stood looking after him, his eyes narrowed, his face very thoughtful.

XVI

THAT BOY AH SING

At half past nine, Cash Shannon appeared with the sheriff's launch. When it came to brightening the day and atoning for the weather, Cash took second place to no man. Indeed, at the mere sight of his colorful costume, the weather seemed to be giving up the struggle; the rain had stopped, and the clouds raced madly through the sky as though seeking to give the sun an opening. There was no doubt that the storm was over, nature would soon be smiling but not, probably, as brightly as Cash at the sight of Leslie Beaton.

He appeared slightly surprised at the number of passengers he was to carry, for Romano added himself and his luggage to the group on the pier, and Charlie made it known that his not inconsiderable person was also to be included. However, once they were started, Cash paid no attention to anyone save the girl.

"Well, I guess you might call this the opening day at the Tavern," he remarked to her. "If I was the management – which I ain't – there'd be tea on the terrace, music in the casino, an' flags hanging all over the place."

"What *are* you talking about?" she inquired.

"Any time a girl like you comes to a hotel, ought to be some sort of celebration. That's the way I figure it. Say – how do you get on with a horse?"

"I ride a little."

"Well, we'll change all that. You'll ride a lot, the next few days. Some of the trails are open now an' say – the plans I got—"

"If you will be so kind," called Chan, from behind him. "Please make utmost speed."

"What for?" inquired Cash.

"I have some plans myself," smiled Charlie.

The instant the launch had landed, he leaped ashore and hurried to the hotel. Old Sam Holt was seated by the fire, and greeted Chan with every evidence of pleasure.

"Been waiting to talk to you," he said. "Sorry I wasn't with you last night up the road."

"We have much to discuss," Charlie answered. "But first there is a matter that requires great haste. Where is your son, please?"

"I reckon he's out to the stables. I'll send one of the boys." The old man made his way to the desk, gave the order and returned. "What's on your mind now, Inspector Chan?"

"You will denounce me bitterly when I tell you," Chan replied.

"'Tain't easy to picture that," the old man said. "You mean—"

"I mean I propose to call into this case someone we both agree is absolutely worthless. A scientist."

Sam Holt laughed. "Wal – gener'ly speakin', Mr Chan. Gener'ly speakin'. O' course, mebbe I'm a leetle unreasonable. An' if you cave in on th' point, I reckon I kin cave with you."

"A gentleman I met in San Francisco a few weeks ago," Charlie explained. "An instructor of physics at the University of California, in Berkeley. I had a serious talk with him, and I thought—" Don Holt approached and Chan leaped to his feet. "Mr Sheriff, tell me – have you bullet from body of the recent Doctor Swan?"

"Sure – I got it," Holt replied, producing it. "Another thirty-eight. The coroner—"

"Haste is required," Chan cut in. "Pardon the abrupt manner. But inform me – can we place someone on the ten-thirty train at Truckee – and if so, whom?"

Cash had just entered with Leslie Beaton and her brother. The deputy was loaded with bags, and eternal adoration of the fair sex gleamed in his eyes. Holt laughed.

"I'll say we've got someone we can put on that train," he chortled. "And good riddance, too. Hey – Cash."

Cash dropped the luggage and came over. "What is it, Chief?"

"Get a bag packed, kid. You got to catch the Oakland train at Truckee, an' you got to step."

"Me?" cried Cash in dismay. "But say, I just made a date with Miss Beaton to exercise a couple horses at three o'clock—"

"Thanks a lot," smiled Holt. "I'll be glad to take care of that for you. Get a move on, boy. I'm tellin' you." Cash hurried out toward the stables. "Now. Mr Chan – that's the best idea you've ever had in your life. Where's he goin', an' why?"

"To begin operations," Charlie said, "kindly bring me from safe of Mr Dinsdale, Landini's revolver, and along with it bullet from same which killed her. Also, please obtain for me one very large and strong Manila envelope." He sat down at a writing-desk, and took the pistol which had slain Swan from his pocket. This he laid on the desk. The bullet he had just received from the sheriff, he put in an envelope and marked it. Then he took a sheet of note-paper and hastily began to write.

He had finished the letter when young Holt returned and placed before him the pearl-handled pistol that had been Landini's property, and the other bullet. The latter was put into a second small envelope and marked, and Charlie then proceeded to insert a marked piece of paper in the barrel of each gun. He took the big envelope Holt handed him, wrote a hasty name and address on the outside, and put into it the two weapons and the two small envelopes. He then sealed the flap, and handed the big envelope to the sheriff.

"It bears, you will note, an address in Berkeley. Tell the good Cash to alight at Oakland and visit this man at once. He is to obtain answer to question in my letter – tonight if possible – and wire same to you instantly. Impress upon him great need of speed."

"Fine," answered Holt, looking at his watch. "I'll let him take my car, and he can just about make it. He can leave the car in a garage near the station in Truckee."

He hurried out. Sam Holt, who had been listening, came up. "And this perfessor at Berkeley, Mr Chan," he said, "what does he claim he kin do?"

"He claims," Charlie replied, "that if he has both pistol and bullet, he can tell how far latter has traveled."

"He's a liar," said Holt promptly.

"Perhaps," smiled Chan. "But the wonders of science – who are we to question them? And I have some curiosity to know how far these bullets traveled – especially that one found in poor unhappy Landini. My friend also claims that many times, from portion of thumbprint found on head of shell, he can reconstruct full print of person who had pushed same into carriage. That would be useful in other instance."

"He's a colossal liar," insisted the old sheriff.

"We shall see," Chan told him. "If you will pardon me for one moment, I have telephone call to make."

He went into a booth, and in a few minutes he was greeting Miss Meecher in her Reno hotel.

"So sorry to disturb you," he said.

"That is quite all right," she answered. "Is there any news?"

"None save that of Doctor Swan's unexpected passing, about which you have no doubt heard."

"Yes – a bellboy just told me. It seems rather terrible."

"Entire case is terrible. Miss Meecher, you are in receipt of Trouble?"

"Oh – you mean the dog? Yes, Mr Ireland brought him in last night. Poor little fellow – he just roams about the apartment, looking for his mistress."

"That is very sad. However, he is in kind hands, I know. There is a question, Miss Meecher, which I must ask you."

"I'll tell you anything I can."

"Naturally. You have told me that you and Madame Landini worked on her biography together. Do you recall beginning of last chapter, written on balcony of hotel at Stresa, where she spoke of knowing color-blind person?"

"Why, yes, I do," Miss Meecher replied.

"Did it chance that she mentioned to you the name of this person?"

"No, she didn't. I remember she wrote that herself, and when I came to type it I was slightly curious. But she wasn't about at the moment, and though I meant to ask her later, it slipped my mind. It didn't seem important, anyhow." There was a brief pause. "Is it important, Mr Chan?"

"Not even slightly," replied Chan heartily. "I was, like you, somewhat curious. But it does not matter. My real intention in calling up – I would ask has anything developed you think I should note?"

"I believe not. There's a wire from Madame's attorneys in New York asking me if it is true she never signed the will. It seems Romano is already in touch with them."

"Ah, he is no wastrel of time, this Romano."

"Shall I wire them the truth?"

"By all means. And kindly give my best regards to the anxious little dog. I have great likeness for him."

"Thank you so much," Miss Meecher replied.

As Charlie emerged from the booth, two young men entered the hotel lounge from the terrace. One of them – tall, lean, a bit graying at the temples – rushed forward eagerly.

"As I live and breathe," he cried. "My old friend, Charlie Chan. You remember me – Bill Rankin, of the *San Francisco Globe*?"

"With a pleasant glow," Chan replied. "You were my very good ally when Sir Frederic Bruce was killed."

"And here I am, all ready to be an ally once again. Oh – this is Gleason of the *Herald*. He thinks he's a newspaper reporter, too. What ideas these youngsters get!"

"Hello, Mr Chan," Gleason said. "We just missed you down at Pineview. But we had a nice ride on the lake."

"Let's get down to cases," said Rankin. "This sheriff up here, Inspector, is a swell guy, but he won't talk. That was never your trouble, as I recall."

"Talk was my weakness," grinned Chan.

"Of course, you never said anything, but it made copy. Now, what's the dope? Who bumped off Landini?"

"Surely you do not think I have solved such a problem already?"

"Why not? You've had over twenty-four hours. Not slowing up on us, are you? Getting old – no, I can tell you're not by looking at you."

"The case," said Chan, "has many angles. We labor hard, but it will not be brought to solution in a day. No tree in the forest bears cooked rice."

"Yeah," smiled Rankin, "I'll remind my managing editor. Might make a head-line. 'Inspector Chan Says No Tree in Forest Bears Cooked Rice.'"

"Look here, Mr Chan," Gleason said solemnly, "surely you have some results to report to our readers. That's what they want. Results."

"Ah, this American passion for results," Charlie sighed. "Yet the apple-blossom is so much more beautiful than the dumpling."

"And can we send back an armful of apple-blossoms?" laughed Rankin. "You met my editor once. He wants a pan of dumplings, warm from the oven."

"So sorry," Chan apologized. "I suggest first of all, you get lay of land."

"We got it," Gleason replied. "Say, what was in that big envelope you just sent the drug-store cowboy flivvering off with? We asked him – but of all the nasty tempers—"

"Ah," nodded Chan, "perhaps it was Landini's will."

"Carried it with her wherever she went, eh?" Rankin grinned.

"Just a suggestion," Chan told him. "Who inherits her property? Merely one of the angles."

"By gad – we never thought of that," Gleason cried. "How about it, Bill?"

"What was the name of her lawyers in Reno?" Rankin inquired. "Thanks, Inspector. There might be a story in that. I think I'll take a run over there for lunch—"

"I'm right with you," Gleason assured him. "We'll see you later, Mr Chan. Thanks for the tip."

"It was nothing," Charlie smiled. As the two went out, he walked over and sat down beside Sam Holt. "Ah, the reporters – they are upon us," he murmured.

"Like the pest of the locust," the old man said. "I could hear what ye told 'em. Gave 'em somethin' to think about, eh?"

"I did," Charlie replied. "While we think of something else. Your son has told you all concerning last night, I presume?"

"He did – in a terrible hurry. You think this Swan knew too much about who killed Landini?"

"I'm certain of it. I also, Mr Holt, think there is one other who knows something concerning the matter."

"Yes, Mr Chan?"

"Romano, the Italian, fourth and final husband of great singer – he hinted to me that his door was not too tightly closed on night of murder. Vast numbers were about on that second floor when Landini died. This morning, Romano's courage fails him. He will say no more. We should get together, sir, and put bolster under that courage."

"He's up at Pineview, ain't he?"

"No – he came down with us, and took Swan's room. Your son is approaching – the three of us will descend on this man. We may conquer by numbers."

Five minutes later the representatives of the law were facing Romano in his small bedroom. The conductor, frightened and nervous, sat on the edge of his bed and protested.

"I tell you I know nothing, gentlemen. Mr Chan, he mistakes what I say. *If* – I told him. *If* a person knew, I said. Observe that if, please."

"Look here," said Don Holt, "you know something – don't deny it. You don't want to tell because you're afraid it will delay you in getting back to the bright lights an' spending Landini's money. Well, it might – I can't promise. If I can fix things so it don't, I will. But one way or the other, Mister, you're tellin'. Or I lock you up. Get that, an' get it quick."

"I am – I am so upset," wailed Romano. "This American law – it is confusing. What I saw – it was nothing, really. But I will tell. You understand, I am in my room, looking upon snow of flying field, I see plane alight, and for a time I watch it. Then – it comes to me – Landini will be going now. Have I accomplished my purpose? No. A few bills, thrown to me like I am a beggar – I, who have every right to demand. Am I not the husband? I go to my door. I will demand from Landini a definite appointment in Reno.

"I open that door, you understand. I am on point of moving into the hall. Opposite is the study door, now closed. Before I can move, it opens, and – a man – he steps into my view. I watch him. With stealthy look around he slips silently into the room beside the study – the one at my left as I stand."

"Landini's old sitting-room," Chan nodded.

"Something in that man's manner – it gives me pause," continued Romano. "Me – I am not easily suppressed, but for the moment I am just that. And then, suddenly – from the study rings out – what? A shot, gentlemen. The shot that means Landini's death."

"All right," said Don Holt. "But who was the man?"

"The man I saw," replied Romano, with drama. "The man who slips so slyly from one room to another. That man was Sing – the Chinaman."

In the silence that followed, Charlie heard Sam Holt sigh wearily.

"Fine," remarked Don Holt. "You keep that to yourself now, an' you'll be all right."

"Me – I will keep it," Romano cried. "And I hope – so much – I will be all right."

Charlie and the old sheriff walked together down the corridor. "It keeps comin' back to Sing," Sam Holt said. "Fer all we kin do, Mr Chan – it keeps comin' back to him."

"Quite true," Chan replied, "but consider. Romano is the man who profits most by Landini's death. A man who may well have killed her. And a sly one, like a thief amid the fire. One of the slyest I have ever encountered. Suppose he sought to turn attention from himself? His eye lights on —"

"Poor old Sing," finished Holt, slapping his thigh. "Which is the first it would light on, I reckon. Sing, that looks helpless, an' not so quick on the come-back." He stopped. "Still – I ain't so sure, Inspector."

"No?" inquired Chan.

"No. If Romano was cookin' up a story about Sing, would he ha' done it so dog-gone well? Wouldn't he say he seen Sing creepin' into the study, an' then heard the shot? Would he say he seen him creepin' out o' the study, an' then the explosion came? No, Inspector – I got a sort o' sick feelin' Romano's story sounds like the facts. Sing brings th' blanket, an' finds Landini alone. He goes out, into her old room, opens the windows fer a way of escape, runs back to the study by way of the balcony, kills her an' then gits out the way he came. If he killed her, that's the way he done it, an' Romano is too close to it fer comfort, the way I feel."

"Romano is sly and clever," repeated Charlie. "He studied situation, maybe."

The old man laid his hand on Charlie's arm. "Don't it beat all," he said, "the way that boy Sing keeps poppin' back, an' the way you an' me, we jest go on makin' excuses fer him? What I want to know is – how long kin we keep it up?"

Don Holt was waiting for them in the lounge. "Well, what do you think of that story?" he inquired. "Something behind it, if you ask me. Why, I've knowed old Sing since I was a baby. Reckon I'd better keep a sharp eye on that Romano, after this."

"There ye are, Inspector," Sam Holt said. "One more vote for Sing."

"Won't you stay here for lunch?" Don Holt invited.

"You are very kind," Charlie replied. "But I fear we leave Pineview too much alone. I believe it wiser to return."

"Maybe you're right," agreed the sheriff. "Tell that boatman on the pier I said to run you up to the house. I—"

A young woman summoned him into Dinsdale's office. Chan said goodby to Sam Holt and hurried toward the pier. He was stepping into a launch when Don Holt ran across the terrace and called to him.

"Just took a wire from San Francisco," the sheriff said as he reached Chan's side. "From the owner of the house where we found Swan. He says there's just one person up here has a key to that rear door. He leaves it here in case of an emergency."

"Ah, yes. And he leaves it with—"

"He leaves it with Sing," Holt answered. "You'd better look into the matter when you get to Pineview."

Charlie sighed. "The man who would avoid suspicion should not adjust his hat under a plum tree. He is always adjusting his hat – that Sing."

XVII

THE NET CLOSES IN

Chan found the living-room at Pineview deserted and walked rapidly through it to the kitchen. There conditions appeared to be somewhat chaotic. Sing and Mrs O'Ferrell seemed to be jointly preparing lunch, and the latter was red of face and evidently quite flustered.

"Sing," said Chan sternly from the doorway, "I must speak with you immediately."

"Wha's mallah you?" Sing replied. "My velly busy. You go 'way, Boss."

"I'll say he's busy," cried Mrs O'Ferrell indignantly. "It was understood whin I come to this house I was to do the cookin', an' no wan else. An' here he's been all mornin', stirrin' up hivin knows what. Sure, an' it's me notice they get afther this—"

"Sing," Charlie repeated, and his voice was firm, "come here!"

The old man inspected a pot at the rear of the stove, dropped the lid hastily and came to the door.

"Wha's mallah, Boss? This velly bad time fo' talk—"

"This plenty good time. Sing – you got key to big house down the road?"

"Sure, my got key. All time got key. Plumber come, light man come – they want key. My got 'um."

"Where you got 'um?"

"Hang on hook, in hall, outside."

"What hook? Show me."

"My velly busy now. All time woik this house. No can do—"

"Show me, and be quick!"

"All light, Boss. Keep collah on. My show you." He came into the passage and pointed to a hook beside the rear door. It was empty. "Key all gone now," he commented, without interest.

"Gone – where?"

"No savvy, Boss."

"When did you see it last?"

"No savvy. Yeste'day, day befo' – mebbe las' week. My got to go now."

"Wait a minute. You mean somebody has stolen the key?"

Sing shrugged. "What you think, Boss?"

"Do you know that Doctor Swan was murdered in that house last night? And the person who did it had your key?"

Mrs O'Ferrell gave a startled cry.

"Too bad, Boss," Sing answered. "Solly – got to get back to kitchen now."

Charlie sighed and let him go. "Does it chance you had noticed that key, Mrs O'Ferrell?" he inquired.

"Sing showed it to me whin I first come," she answered. "There was a tag on it, tellin' what it was for. Sure, I niver give it a thought from that day to this."

"You wouldn't know, then, when it disappeared or who probably took it?"

"I would not, Mr Chan. It's sorry I am I can't help you." There was a clatter from the kitchen. "Excuse me, please, sir. Sure, I don't know whether it's me or th' Chink that's gettin' lunch."

Charlie went to his room to freshen up. When he returned downstairs, Ward and Ryder were in the living-room.

"Our ranks are somewhat depleted," the host said. "It's going to seem a little lonely from now on."

"I'll have to be getting back on the job myself very soon," Ryder told him. "If there's nothing I can do for you, old man. I – I don't believe the sheriff can hold me here. Do you think so, Mr Chan?"

"Seems nothing against you," Chan admitted.

"I hear your business is even more prosperous than usual, John," Ward remarked.

Ryder brushed an imaginary bit of lint from the lapel of his beautifully tailored coat. "I can't complain," he admitted. "If I've got nothing else from life, I've at least got money. More than enough."

At the luncheon table, Sing appeared to be in a state of great excitement. He served Charlie and Ward first with chops and vegetables, meanwhile assuring Ryder that the latter was not forgotten. "You wait. You see," he said repeatedly. Presently he appeared, triumphantly bearing aloft an enormous bowl, which he set before the mining man.

"Rice," cried Ryder. "Sing – you old rascal!"

"Like ol' time," chuckled Sing, patting him on the back. "You wait now. You see."

He fairly ran to the kitchen, reappearing almost at once with another bowl. "Chicken glavy. You smell 'um, hey? Like ol' time – when you lil boy."

"Sing – this is wonderful," Ryder remarked, evidently touched. "I've been dreaming of your rice and gravy for nearly thirty years. Nothing has ever tasted so good since those old days in your kitchen."

"Sing goo' cook, hey?"

"The best in the world. Thank you a million times." Charlie thought Ryder had never seemed so human before.

"Ah – er—" Ward looked slightly embarrassed. "It seems that you and I are rather out of things, Mr Chan. You must forgive Sing's peculiar ideas of hospitality."

"Not at all," Chan replied. "You and I will have plenty lunch. And I believe Sing's ideas of hospitality are excellent. With him, old friends are best friends. Who could place blame on him for that?"

"This is a real bowl of rice," Ryder was saying. "Not one of those little bowls. A real, big bowl. And the gravy – come to think about it, I don't know that I'll ever go home."

After lunch, Chan retired to his room to finish the last few galleys of Landini's story. Nothing more of interest had cropped up, but the personality of the writer had steadily grown upon him, and now, as he finished, he was one of the singer's friends, he felt. More than ever, he was determined to find her slayer – wherever the trail might lead.

He went downstairs again. Pineview was deserted. He put on his arctics, for though the spring sun was now warm in the sky, things were a bit damp underfoot. Going outside, for a time he wandered about among the sheds at the rear, trying various doors. All, save those of the garage, were tightly padlocked. At the latter spot he looked longingly for a moment at the ladder. Evidently the pine trees again intrigued him.

He moved around to the front of the house. Much of the snow on the lawn had melted, leaving only a thin coating of slush. Now and again he stopped, to pick up a cone or a fallen branch; idly, aimlessly, the student of the pines seemed to be gathering data on a favorite subject. Murders, the stern realities of his trade, policemen and sheriffs, appeared to be far from his thoughts.

And at that moment, Charlie was surprisingly far from the thoughts of the sheriff. Don Holt was seated in the saddle on his favorite mount, and beside him along the narrow trail under the pines, rode Leslie Beaton. The magic air of Tahoe had brought into her cheeks a color that was not for sale in the beauty parlors of Reno, and her eyes were shining with a new enthusiasm for life.

"It sure was a grand idea Cash had," the sheriff remarked. "Inviting you to go on this ride."

"Poor Cash! What a pity he was called away."

"He's the kind that's likely to get called away," Holt responded grimly.

"He never even said goodby to me."

"They wasn't time. You see, Cash's goodbys is likely to be long an' lingering – like that guy Romeo's. I reckon you're missin' old Cash."

"Cash is a fluent talker."

"I'll say he is. By this time, he'd have told you all about – how – pretty you look."

"Do you think so?"

"I know he would."

"I mean – do you think I look – all right?"

"Fine. But I ain't got the words, somehow."

"Too bad. Cash's absence begins to look like a great calamity."

"I was afraid you'd feel that way. Always been cooped up in cities, ain't you?"

"Always."

"This air is doin' you a lot of good. It would do you more good – if you stayed."

"Oh, – but I must go back East. I have to work for a living, you see."

The sheriff frowned. "Cash would explain to you – that you needn't go. He's pretty convincin', that boy." They came into a clearing, and turned their horses about. Far below lay the lake, reflecting snow-capped peaks beyond. "Mighty nice view, ain't it?" said the sheriff.

"It sort of takes my breath away," the girl answered.

"Makes you a little dizzy, eh? This is where old Cash would have staged a big emotional scene. About how you was the loveliest girl he'd ever met – how he couldn't live without you—"

"Don't, please," smiled the girl. "I seem to be missing so much."

"Oh, you ain't missing a lot. Cash got engaged to three girls on this very spot last summer."

"You mean he's fickle?"

"Well – you know – these fellows that talk a lot—"

"I know. But the strong silent men ought to strike a happy medium now and then – don't you think?"

"I reckon that's right, too." The sheriff took off his hat, as though to cool a fevered brow. "You – you think you could like this country?"

"The summers must be lovely."

"That's jest it. The winters – I don't know. I wish you could come down an' look at the county-seat – before you go away. It ain't a very big town. I reckon you wouldn't like it."

"No – perhaps not. Can we see Pineview from here?"

"It's over there – in that bunch of trees. Gosh – I'd plumb forgot. Pretty big job we got on our hands, at Pineview."

"Does it mean a lot to you – to succeed?"

"I'll say it does. I got to live up to Dad's reputation. He kind of expects it, I guess. But I don't know. Even with Mr Chan's help – we don't seem to be going very strong."

For a moment the girl did not speak. "I'm afraid I haven't been quite fair with you," she said at last. "I wonder if you'll ever forgive me?"

"I reckon so. But what do you mean?"

"About the night of Landini's murder. I can't imagine why I was so silly – but it seemed quite terrible. Involving someone who might perhaps be innocent – getting involved myself – I – I just couldn't."

"You couldn't what?"

"I wanted to think it over – I've done that – and I see I've been a fool. All the time I really wanted to help you – I do now. You know – I was in the bedroom next door when I heard the shot that killed Landini."

"I know."

"Well, somehow, the shot seemed to be on the balcony. So – I didn't just sit there dumbly. I ran to the balcony window, opened it and looked out. And I saw a man leave the study, run along the balcony and disappear through the window of the room beyond – a man with a blanket under his arm."

"Sing."

"Yes – it was poor Sing. It seemed incredible – I couldn't believe it. But Sing ran out of the study just after that shot was fired. I'm so sorry I didn't tell you before."

"You've told me now," Holt replied gloomily. "Gosh – I'd rather be hung myself. But there's nothing to it – duty is duty, an' I took the oath. I reckon we'd better be goin' back."

They started down the trail along which they had come. Again on that homeward trek Holt was the strong silent man – oppressively silent, now. When they parted before the Tavern stables, the girl laid her hand on his arm. "You forgive me for not telling sooner, don't you?"

He looked at her solemnly in the dusk. "Sure I do," he answered. "I reckon, when I come to think of it, I'd forgive you for almost anything."

As he led the horses into the stable, he saw his father sitting alone in the office, near the door. Presently he went inside and sat down.

"Ain't no more doubt, I reckon," he said. "Sing killed Landini. I got it straight from a reliable party this time." He repeated Leslie Beaton's story. "Mebbe I'd better go up an' get him now," he finished.

"Hold yer horses," Sam Holt replied. "We got to consult Mr Chan. Yes – I guess there ain't much doubt – but it don't do to jump too soon. We want to git all the evidence we kin, first. Wasn't the coroner goin' to hold an inquest on Doctor Swan about this time?"

The young man looked at his watch. "Yes – that's right."

"You go over there, son," Sam Holt said. "Pick up anything you kin. There's plenty o' time fer Sing."

As soon as the sheriff had gone, Sam Holt's groping hands sought for the telephone on the desk. In another moment he was talking to Charlie Chan at Pineview.

"Yes," he was saying, "it's Sing, Inspector. The net is closin' in. Matter o' fact, it's about closed."

"As I expected," Chan replied softly. "What do you suggest?"

"Git down here as quick as ye kin, Mr Chan – an' fetch Sing with ye. Don't say nothin' to nobody – but have him bring his bag. Jest a little bag – about what a man would need – in jail."

"Ah, yes – in jail," Chan repeated thoughtfully.

"Ye'll find me in the office o' the stables," Sam Holt went on. "Them reporters drove me out o' the Tavern."

"I understand," Charlie replied. "There is an old flivver here. We shall arrive most speedily in that."

And they did. Twenty minutes later, Charlie pushed open the door of the over-heated little office.

"Hello, Mr Chan," Sam Holt said. "Somebody with ye, ain't they? Well, tell him to wait in th' stable. You an' me needs a little talk."

There was an air of tense expectancy about Charlie as he came in alone and took a battered old chair beside the roll-top desk at which Holt sat. "New evidence has leaped to view?" he inquired.

"It sure has," Holt answered. "After we heard from Romano, Inspector, I got to thinkin'. Sentiment is sentiment, but duty is duty. So I got that doctor over here – the Tahoe doctor that helped Don bring Landini's body down to town the night o' the murder. I says to him, 'Sing brought you blankets,' I says, 'to wrap about Landini. Blue blankets. Do you remember,' I says, 'was they ever laid on a velvet chair in that room?'" Holt paused.

"And the doctor's answer?" inquired Charlie.

"Seems I was a better detective than I wanted to be, Mr Chan," Holt went on grimly. "That doctor took them blankets from Sing at the door, an' laid 'em on the floor beside the body. They never touched a chair. He was dead certain about that. Yes, sir – that blue blanket was in the room before the murder – they ain't no doubt about it."

"I congratulate you on keen deduction you performed that morning in the study," Charlie said.

"Kick me, Mr Chan, an' I'll be more obliged," Holt replied. "Yes, sir – jest as I thought – Sing fired that shot. We got the blanket evidence, the hurt knee from that dressing-table bench. We got Romano, that seen him slip through that room next door, jest before the shot. An' we got someone else – someone who seen him leave the study jest after it."

"That is news to me," Chan remarked. Sam Holt told him of Leslie Beaton's story. Charlie shook his head. "Too many people on that floor at time," he remarked sadly.

"Too many fer poor ol' Sing," agreed Holt. "Got him comin' an' goin', we have. Don wants to lock him up."

"A natural course," Chan nodded.

"I wonder," said Sam Holt. Charlie looked at him keenly. "I wonder," went on the old sheriff. "I've been thinkin', Mr Chan. A blind man gits a lot o' time to think, an' I been at it this afternoon, at it hard."

"You have been thinking of all the clues in this case, perhaps?" Chan suggested gently.

"I have. What you said to Don about the dog. An' all this interest of yours in the pine trees, Mr Chan."

Charlie smiled. "Mr Holt – the best clue of all, you do not know. I did not recall it myself until last night, while I waited alone in creaking house of death. I propose to make a slight narration. I intend to tell you, from start to finish, every event that occurred, every word that was spoken, at dinner my first night at Pineview. Before the murder, you understand."

He moved close to the old man, and in a low confidential voice, he spoke for some ten minutes. When he had finished, he leaned back in his chair and studied Sam Holt's face.

Holt was silent for a moment, playing with a paper-knife on the desk. At last he spoke. "Mr Chan – I am seventy-eight years old."

"An honorable age," said Charlie.

"A happy one, too, because I am here, among my own people, in the country I've always known. But now – jes' supposin' – I was in some foreign country – what would I want more than anything—"

"You would wish to see again your native village – to walk upon the soil wherein your bones were some day to rest."

"You're a smart man, Mr Chan. You git me right away. Inspector – Don ain't never even made ye a deputy. You ain't got no real authority here."

"I am well aware of the fact," nodded Charlie.

Sam Holt rose and stood there, a distinguished figure, a figure of honor, of integrity. "And I – I am blind," he said.

Chinese do not easily weep, but suddenly Charlie Chan felt a stinging in his eyes. "Thank you," he said. "I speak for entire race when I say it. You will pardon me now, I know. I have little errand to perform."

"Of course ye have," said Holt. "Goodby, Mr Chan. An' if it should so happen that I don't ever meet a certain friend o' mine ag'in – give him my love an' say I'm proud I knowed him."

Chan stepped through the door and closed it after him. In the dim shadows several feet away, he saw the bent figure of old Sing. He went over to him. "Come on, Sing," he remarked. "You and I got journey to make." Suddenly he saw looming in the doorway the powerful figure of Don Holt. He seized the old Chinese and drew him back into the shadows.

Don Holt opened the office door. "Hello, Dad," he said. "You know, I been thinkin' some. I reckon I ought to go down to Pineview now—"

"Step in, son," came the voice of the old sheriff. "Step in, an' we'll talk it over."

The door of the office closed behind the young man, and Charlie hurried Sing out to the car in which they had come down together from Pineview. He motioned to the old man to get in beside him, and they set off along the Tavern drive. When they came to the main entrance, Chan turned toward Truckee.

"Wha's mallah now?" ventured Sing. "Mebbe I catch 'um jail, hey?"

"You're a wicked man," Chan replied sternly. "You have caused us much worry and suffering. Jail is what you richly deserve."

"I catch 'um jail, hey, Boss?"

"On the contrary," Chan replied, "you catch 'um boat for China."

XVIII

RANKIN DROPS A BOMB

A boat for China! Charlie could not see the face of the old man who sat at his side in the car that sped along the road to Truckee, but he heard a tremendous sigh. Of relief?

"All light, Boss," Sing said.

"All right?" repeated Chan with some bitterness. "Is that the extent of your remarks? We are doing you a great favor, a tremendous kindness, and you reply, all right. The courteous man, Ah Sing, would not permit his tongue to stop at that."

"My velly much obliged."

"That is better. It still appears inadequate, but it is slightly better."

They traveled along the wet road in silence. Chan's face was grim and determined. This next hour, he reflected, was not to be the happiest of his career. All those years on the Honolulu force, beset with temptations, but always honest, always irreproachable. And now – to come to the mainland, to do what he was doing – would his conscience ever be clear again? Ah – thank the gods – the lights of Truckee were twinkling just ahead.

Chan drove at once to the station. "Train for San Francisco arrives in twenty minutes," he announced. "I have consulted time table." They entered the waiting-room, Sing carrying his small bag. "You got money, Ah Sing?" Charlie asked.

"My got 'um," the old man answered.

"Then purchase for yourself a ticket," Chan ordered. "I am sorry, but we do not also furnish fare."

As Sing returned from the ticket window, the detective noted that he was limping.

"Your knee still troubles you?" Chan inquired.

"Velly bad knock," Sing admitted. He put his foot on a bench, and rolling up his wide trousers, exhibited a considerable expanse of black and blue.

"Ah, yes," Chan said. "The wound you acquired when you bumped into dressing-table bench in Landini's old sitting-room?"

"Tha's when. Aftah my shoot—"

"Enough!" Charlie cried. He glanced uneasily around at the other people in the room, and spoke in Cantonese. "Do not poke your finger through your own paper lantern. The luck is running high for you tonight, ancient one. Be cautious, lest the heart of the law yet harden against you."

Sing appeared to be properly impressed. They sat down side by side on the narrow bench, and for a time, neither spoke.

"The government has fallen upon evil times," Chan said at last. "You understand, it cannot even afford to squander small piece of rope on man like you. Old man who will die soon, in any case. So it says – return to China—"

"I will go," Sing remarked in his native tongue.

"I envy you. You will walk again the streets of the village where you were born. You will supervise the selection of your own burial place. I myself will see that your trunk is prepared and sent to you while you await the boat. Where shall I send it?"

"To the establishment of my brother, Sing Gow, in Jackson Street. The Fish Shop of the Delicious Odors."

"It shall be done. For you, the past died this afternoon. The future is born tonight. You understand?"

"I understand."

"I am the bearer of an affectionate message for you, ancient one. Mr Sam Holt has sent it. He is proud to have known you."

Sing's face softened. "An honorable man. May the four nails of his coffin be of purest gold."

"To match his heart," Chan agreed. His own heart stirred with relief as he heard the approach of the train. "Come," he said, rising. "Your vehicle draws near."

They stepped on to the platform. In another moment the train thundered up to the station. Charlie held out his hand.

"I am saying goodby," he shouted in Sing's ear. "May your entire journey be on the sunny side of the road."

"Goo'-by," Sing answered. He took a few steps toward the train, but turned and came back. Removing something from his pocket, he handed it to Chan. "You give 'em Boss," he directed. "My fo'get. Tell 'um Boss too much woik that house. Sing go away."

"I will tell him," Charlie agreed. He led Sing back to the steps of a day coach and helped him aboard.

Retiring to the shadows close to the station, Chan stood watching. He saw the old man drop into a seat and remove his hat. In the dim gas-light the wizened face was stolid, emotionless. The train gathered momentum, and Ah Sing was swept quickly from view. Still Chan hesitated, deep in thought. For the first time in his life – but this was the mainland, strange things happened here. And after all, Inspector Chan had no real authority.

When he got back to Tahoe, Chan again turned in at the Tavern gate. The stables were dark and deserted, and leaving the Pineview flivver parked in the drive, Charlie entered the hotel. Dinsdale was alone beside the office desk.

"Good evening, Mr Chan," he said. "Warming up a bit after the rain, isn't it?"

"That may be," Charlie replied. "I fear I had not noticed."

"No – I suppose you're a pretty busy man," Dinsdale returned. "By the way – of course it's none of my business, but – er – are you getting anywhere?"

"So sorry. There is nothing yet able to be announced."

"Well, of course, I didn't mean to butt in."

"Ah, but you are naturally interested. You were old-time friend of poor Madame Landini, I believe?"

"Yes. I knew her even before her first marriage. A beautiful girl – and a fine woman. I hope you haven't been judging her entirely from the view-point of her discarded husbands."

"For a time, I made that error," Chan replied. "Then I read Madame's own life-story, and my opinion changed. I agree with you – a splendid woman."

"Good!" cried Dinsdale with unexpected vehemence. "I'm glad you feel that way. Because if you do, you'll be almost as eager to see her murderer hang as I am. By the way, we'll be having dinner in half an hour. Please stay, as my guest."

"I will be only too happy," Chan bowed. He indicated a youth who had just come in and taken his place behind the desk. "Would you be so kind as to have this young man call Pineview, and inform whoever answers that I will not dine there tonight?"

"With pleasure," Dinsdale answered.

"And now – if you can tell me the number of Mr Sam Holt's room?"

"It's number nineteen – at the end of that corridor over there."

At Charlie's knock, Sam Holt called for him to come in. He entered to find the old sheriff standing in the middle of the room, adjusting his necktie.

"Hello, Mr Chan," he said, as he reached unerringly for his coat, which lay on the bed.

"Ah, you know my step," Charlie remarked. "It indicates, I fear, the heaviness of my person."

"Nothin' o' the sort," Holt replied. "It's the lightest step in the whole shebang, except mebbe that Miss Beaton's."

"But my weight—" Chan protested.

"I don't keer about yer weight. You step like the tiger, Inspector Chan."

"Yes?" sighed Charlie. "But a tiger who lets his prey escape."

"Then I take it ye've gone an' done that errand?"

"I have done it – yes."

"Ye ain't regrettin' it, are ye?"

"Not unless you are, Mr Holt."

"Which I reckon I'm never goin' to do, Mr Chan. Howsomever, I'm glad to see ye first – before ye've talked to Don. I ain't told Don anything yit."

"The wisest course, no doubt," Charlie agreed.

"It sure is. Ye know. Don really is in authority here. 'Taint with him like it was with you an' me. He's took the oath, an' he's honest, the boy is. Reckon he'd feel he'd jest have to go after a certain party, an' bring him back. An' ye kain't depend on juries no more, Inspector."

"I fear you are right."

"In the old days – wa'al,. it would ha' been different. But – they's women on the juries now, Mr Chan. An' women ain't got no sentiment. They're hard, women are – since they took to runnin' the world."

"I have noticed that myself," Charlie nodded.

"Yes, I jes' figured we better give that certain party all the start we could." The door of the room beyond the bath opened, then slammed. "It's Don," Sam Holt whispered.

"I will await you both in the lobby," Chan whispered back. "It happens I am dining here tonight."

He made a guilty sort of exit, aided by old Sam Holt, who was looking rather guilty himself. Reaching the lounge, he selected a chair and sat down by the fire. In a few moments, a door from the terrace opened and Leslie Beaton entered.

"Hello, Mr Chan," she cried. "Glad to see you again. I've been out admiring the view. It's marvelous."

"You like this mountain country?" Chan asked.

"I love it." She urged him back to his chair, and took the one beside it. "You know – sometimes I believe I'll stay here. Would that be a good idea, do you think?"

"Happiness," Charlie told her, "is not a matter of geography."

"I suppose not."

"Wherever we are, life is the same. The sweet, the sour, the pungent and the bitter – we must taste them all. To the contented, even the cabbage roots are fragrant."

"I know," she nodded. "Would I be contented here?"

Chan shrugged. "I seek to win reputation as philosopher, not as fortune-teller," he reminded her. "If I were essaying latter role, I would say it would depend on whether you have a companion or not. You cannot applaud with one hand."

"Oh, well – I'm sorry I brought the matter up," laughed the girl. "Let's change the subject – shall we? Looking around for a new topic my eye lights – inevitably – on your necktie, Mr Chan. I'm not accustomed to making personal remarks, but somehow that's the sort of necktie one just can't ignore."

"Ah – one might call it red," he replied.

"One couldn't very well call it anything else," she admitted.

"It was present from my young daughter, Evelyn, on recent Christmas," he told her. "I had forgot I was so brilliantly adorned. But I remember now – I put it on this morning. For a purpose."

Young Hugh Beaton came up at that moment, in a rather cheerful mood for him. Even one day at the Tavern seemed to have proved good medicine. He greeted Charlie in friendly fashion, and led his sister off to the dining-room. Presently Romano appeared, arrayed in evening clothes as though he were about to conduct an opera.

"Mr Romano – how do you do," Charlie remarked. "You quite confound me by your formal attire. When I – I must disgrace dining-room with necktie such as this."

"What is wrong with the necktie?" Romano responded. "Me, I dress not for others, but for myself. You should do the same. Attired as I am now, I feel I am already back in some metropolitan center, such as New York. The thought – it gives me great happiness. The reality – it will be sublime."

"Patience," Chan counseled. "In time, the mulberry leaf becomes silk."

Romano frowned. "Not so comforting, that. The process sounds complicated. But in the meantime, one may still eat." He moved away.

Don Holt and his father appeared. "Hear you're staying for dinner," the former said. "Fine! You'll sit with us, of course."

"But I am Mr Dinsdale's guest," Charlie protested.

"That's all right – we'll take a table for four," Dinsdale said briskly, coming up just then. He led them into the dining-room. Don Holt looked a bit disappointed, for he knew discussion of the case must now be postponed until later. Chan, however, was deeply relieved. He had no desire for such a discussion with the sheriff of the county at the moment. Indeed, he did not look forward to it at any moment.

Toward the close of the dinner, Dinsdale was called away. Don Holt lost no time.

"I reckon Dad's told you about my talk with Miss Beaton this afternoon," he began. "The way I see it, that puts the murder of Landini right in old Sing's lap. It's like I told you at the first – I've knowed Sing ever since I was a kid. Always been fond of him, too. But when I took the oath of office, there wasn't anything in it about protecting my friends. I got my job to do, and—"

He was interrupted by the arrival of the amiable Bill Rankin, who leaned suddenly above the table. Chan sighed with relief.

"Hello," cried the reporter. "All the forces of the law, breaking bread together. Gosh – think of the poor criminals on a night like this. Well, what's the good word to send down to the yawning presses?"

"You must find your own words," Charlie told him. "Has your day disclosed nothing?"

Rankin dropped into Dinsdale's empty chair. "We had a nice time in Reno. Called on Miss Meecher. I suppose you know this sleek boy named Romano stands in line for all Landini's property?"

"We do," said Don Holt shortly.

"Well, Romano was at Pineview the night of the murder," Rankin went on cheerily. "Sort of puts the lad in the running, doesn't it? He knew the singer – and the money – was slipping away from him in a couple of weeks. He knew Landini had a pistol in her hand-bag. Need I say more?"

"Thank you so much," grinned Chan. "Gentlemen, our case is solved. Odd we did not think of this ourselves."

"Oh, you thought of it all right," Rankin laughed. "But what I'm getting at is – wouldn't you like to think of it all over again, just for tomorrow morning's paper?"

"Has libel law been repealed?" Charlie asked blandly.

"Libel? Innuendo, Mr Chan. A game at which I am probably the most expert player west of the Rockies. Well, if that little point doesn't interest you, maybe you'll answer me a question."

"I must hear it before I can answer it," Charlie replied.

"You'll hear it, all right. Why did you take that old Chinese servant, Sing, over to Truckee this evening in a flivver, and put him on a train for San Francisco?"

Charlie Chan had known a long and active career, but never before had he encountered such an embarrassing moment as this. In the dead silence that followed the innocent dropping of Rankin's bomb, Chan looked across and saw the fine eyes of Don Holt ablaze with sudden anger. Old Sam Holt's hand trembled as he hastily set down his water glass. Charlie did not speak.

"You can't keep that dark," Rankin went on. "Gleason ran over to file a couple of stories with the telegrapher at the station, and he saw you. What was the big idea?"

The reporter looked directly at Chan, and was amazed at the answering look he received from one who had, a few moments ago, appeared so glad to see him.

"I took Sing to Truckee as a favor – from one Chinese to another," Charlie said slowly. He rose to his feet. "Sing desired to make a visit to San Francisco, and as there were several points I wanted investigated down there, I decided to permit that he go. The matter means little, one way or the other, but I prefer that for the present you write nothing about it."

"Why, sure – if you say so," Rankin returned pleasantly. "It just seemed rather queer, that's all."

But Charlie was already walking rapidly away from the table. Don Holt and the old sheriff followed closely at his heels. He moved on, straight through the lobby and into Dinsdale's small private office. As he expected, the others did the same.

Don Holt came in last and slammed the door shut behind him. His face was white, his eyes dangerously narrowed.

"So," he said, through his teeth, "you took him there as a favor – from one Chinese to another? Some favor – if you're asking me!"

"Hold yer horses, Don," his father cried.

"I've been double-crossed," the boy went on. "I've been made a fool of—"

"Wa-al, ef ye have, son – I done it. I told Mr Chan to take Sing to Truckee. I told him to help him git away – to China."

"You!" cried Holt. "To China! An' all the time you knew he was guilty as hell. You knew he went into that room – you knew he fired that shot— "

"I knew all that, son."

"Then how could you let me down like this? Get out o' my way!"

"Where you goin'?"

"Goin'? I'm goin' after him, of course. Am I sheriff of this county, or ain't I? You two sure have took a lot on yourselves— "

Dinsdale opened the door. "Telegram for you, Don," he said. "They're phoning it from Truckee. I've switched it in here." He looked in a puzzled way at the young sheriff's face, then withdrew and closed the door.

Don Holt sat down at the desk and took up the receiver. Chan looked at his watch and smiled.

"Hello! Hello! This is Don Holt. What! What! Say that again. All right. Thanks. Mail it up to me here, if you will."

Slowly the young man swung around in the swivel chair, and his eyes met Charlie's. "What was it you asked that bird down in Berkeley about them pistols?" he inquired.

"It was a simple question concerning the bullets," Chan replied calmly. "What does he say?"

"He – he says both them bullets came from the gun that killed Swan," Don Holt answered perplexedly. "He says neither one of 'em came from Landini's gun."

"Wa-al," drawled Sam Holt, "them scientists kain't always be wrong. Now an' then one of 'em's bound to strike the right lead."

Don Holt stood up, and gradually the puzzled look faded from his face. He smiled suddenly at Charlie.

"By the Lord Harry!" he said. "Now I know why you was always talkin' about pine trees."

XIX

CHAN CLIMBS A LADDER

Don Holt walked up and down the small room excitedly. "It's beginning to straighten out," he continued. "The dog – I'm gettin' that, too."

Charlie nodded. "Good little Trouble. It was he who set me on correct trail that very first night. Already I had experienced my first doubts. Of the five unaccounted for at time of killing, not one offered alibi. You will recall I commented to you on that. Strange, I thought. The guilty, at least, usually has alibi ready and waiting. I wondered. Could it be that the guilty was not among those five? Could it be he was among those standing in my sight when supposedly fatal shot was fired?"

"Then we went out and talked with Mrs O'Ferrell," the young sheriff said.

"Correct. Landini had remarked she would take dog with her in the plane. 'He loves it,' she had said. But according to story of Mrs O'Ferrell, Trouble had wailed and cried most pitifully when plane arrived over house. No happy barks of anticipation such as I reported to you when, on subsequent evening, he heard sound of plane. Instead, every evidence of grief. Why did he grieve? I considered. As all those who know me have learned to their distress, Chinese have proverb to fit every possible situation. There is one – I recalled it as I talked to Mrs O'Ferrell."

"What is it?" Don Holt asked.

"The dog, wherever he is, knows his master's mood," Charlie quoted. "Poor little Trouble – did he know that, at moment plane was over house, Landini was dying? Yes, I cried inwardly, that was it. Why not? In terrific din made by airplane, a dozen shots might have been fired and gone unheard. But by some sixth sense which we cannot explain, the dog was aware. He knew that when the airplane had landed, and we all stood with the aviator in the living-room and Ryder strolled down the stairs, Ellen Landini was already dead. She was dead some time before the firing of that shot which brought us all to her side.

"The shot we heard, then, had been merely to mislead. Who had fired it? Sing, probably. From the first I suspected him – last night I was sure. For I recalled the dinner on the evening of my arrival at Pineview – before I had even seen Ellen Landini. I recalled what Ryder had said: 'Always a friend in need, Sing was.'"

Holt nodded. "So Ryder said that, did he?"

"He did, and his statement was quite correct. A friend in need. All the way from chicken gravy and rice, to the firing of a deceiving bullet from the study window into the pines."

"Do you know what was in that letter Landini wrote to Ryder?" Holt asked.

"Alas, no. There are several things which I must yet accomplish at Pineview. The message from professor at Berkeley is important, but our evidence is not complete. I propose to go now and complete it. But first, I must ask a thousand pardons. When I set Sing on road to China, I was, I fear, law-breaker myself."

"That's all right," Sam Holt remarked. "Don't you apologize, Mr Chan. I ain't goin' to. We saved this young hot-head here from a mighty embarrassin' situation."

"I reckon you did," Don Holt agreed. "I'm sorry for anything I said."

Charlie patted the boy on the arm. "You were remarkably restrained. And you will note, I did not answer back. I recalled our conflict last night in hall of empty house. With most complimentary intention, I add that the man who has once been bitten by a snake, fears every piece of rope in the roadway."

The sheriff laughed. "Well, I'll take it as a compliment, anyhow. And I'm glad you got Sing out of the way. I don't suppose he thought he was doin' anything wrong, but if he was around here now, I'd sure have to arrest him as an accessory. By the time I'm through with this business, I probably won't know where he is."

"You certainly will not," Chan smiled, "if you are depending on your honorable father for help. Or on my humble self. I go now to Pineview to investigate those matters which I mentioned. After brief talk with your father, you will know precisely how to act." He glanced at his watch. "Give me, however, one hour."

Holt nodded. "One hour, exactly," he agreed.

The moon was shining and a warm breeze was blowing through the pines as Charlie traveled the lonely road back to the house where he had been a guest for several days. Now his moment of triumph was drawing close, but he was not in a mood to gloat. As in so many other cases, he found it impossible to view things from the standpoint of a scientific machine. Always he thought of people – of the human heart. For that reason, his own heart was never to know elation in moments such as this.

But by the time he had driven into the Pineview garage, he had put aside his regrets. He was brisk and businesslike. Now at last he lifted that ladder at which he had only this afternoon cast longing eyes, and boosting it to his shoulder, he cautiously carried it around the house to the front lawn. A light streaming from the dining-room windows indicated that Ryder and his host were still lingering over dinner.

Placing the ladder against the tall tree from which, Chan was sure, that piece of bark had fallen, he climbed aloft, his plump figure finally disappearing among the thick branches. There, for a time, his flashlight played like a will-o'-the-wisp. Finally he found what he was seeking – what he had sought in vain that afternoon on the ground – the bullet Sing had fired from the open window of the study, in order to provide an alibi for a friend. This bullet would complete the story told by the two pistols down at Berkeley: he took out his pen-knife and began to dig it from its resting-place.

With the slug securely in his pocket, he lowered himself from among the branches and found the ladder. He had gone half-way down it when he was aware of a tall, able-bodied man waiting for him in the darkness below.

"Oh – is it you, Mr Chan?" said Michael Ireland. "Cecile seen somebody from the window, and she sent me out to get him – whoever he was. Her nerves ain't none too good, you know."

"So sorry I have disturbed her," Charlie replied, stepping on to the ground. "Assure her, please, that there is no cause for alarm. I merely pursue my harmless investigations."

"Sure," remarked Ireland. "Can I give you a hand with that ladder? Kinda heavy, ain't it?" They carried the ladder back to the garage.

"I was not aware that you were with us tonight," Charlie said. "Did you make the journey by plane?"

"Yes. An' I was wantin' to talk to you, Mr Chan."

"I am a great believer in the here and now."

"Well – it's Cecile. Always kinda nervous an' flighty – you know women. Since this Swan business she's all on edge ag'in – an' she telephoned me to come over an' take her home. I says,

I ain't so sure the sheriff will let you leave – but she just set off the fireworks – you know how it is. So I said I'd ask."

"I know how it is," nodded Charlie. "But you are now asking wrong person."

Ireland shook his head. "No, I ain't, Mr Chan. I called up the sheriff a little while ago, an' he said everything down here was in your hands. He said you would tell me when Cecile could go."

Charlie considered. He glanced at his watch. "Ask me again in half an hour – if you will be so kind."

"O.K.," Ireland answered. "In half an hour." He started away, but suddenly stopped. "Say – what's going to happen in half an hour?" he demanded.

Chan shrugged. "Who shall say? If you will pardon me now, I remain in open for few more minutes."

He waited while Ireland went reluctantly up the back steps and reentered the house. Then he removed from his pocket an enormous bunch of keys. With this in his hand, he disappeared among the sheds at the rear of the garage.

Some ten minutes later, Chan went into the house by the rear door. Mrs O'Ferrell, Cecile and Ireland were in the kitchen, and they regarded him with anxious eyes as he passed. He went on up the back stairs, walking as quietly as the tiger to whom Sam Holt had compared him. Reaching the hall above he leaned over the stair-rail and listened; far in the distance, in the dining-room, he heard voices. He went into his room and locked the door behind him.

For a short time he was busy at his desk, and it was obvious that fingerprints concerned him. Then hastily he began to pack his suitcase. When everything was accounted for, he stood the case in the hall, placed with it his overcoat and hat, and again listened. The sound of voices still came from the dining-room. After a brief visit to the study, he returned to the hall, gathered up his things and went downstairs.

The firelight flickered in friendly peaceful fashion on the walls of the great living-room. Chan set down his luggage and stood for a moment, looking musingly about him. He was reliving a scene; the scene in that room at the moment, two nights ago, when Michael Ireland came in for a drink. He pictured Beaton and Dinsdale beside the fire, Ward preparing the highball, Ireland waiting expectantly in that big easy chair, Ryder strolling nonchalantly down the stairs. Five men in all six if you included Chan himself.

The picture faded from his mind. He walked slowly through the passage that led to the dining-room, and stood there in the doorway.

Ward and Ryder were seated at the table, coffee cups before them. Impelled by his innate sense of hospitality, the former leaped to his feet.

"Hello, Mr Chan," he cried. "We missed you at dinner. Won't you have something now? Sing!" He stopped. "Damn it, I keep forgetting. Sing, Mr Chan, has disappeared."

"No matter," Charlie answered. "I have eaten a sufficiency, Mr Ward. But I appreciate your kindness, none the less."

Ryder spoke. "Perhaps Mr Chan can throw some light on the disappearance of Sing?" he suggested.

Charlie drew a chair up to the table. "I can," he nodded. They waited in silence. "I am grieved to tell you, Mr Ward, that all evidence uncovered has pointed with painful certainty to Sing as the person who fired that shot at Landini – the shot that took us up to the study to find her dead body on the floor."

"I don't believe it," Ward cried hotly. "I don't care where the evidence points. Sing never did it—"

"But if Sing himself admits he did—"

Ward stood up. "Where is he? I'll go to him at once."

"That, I fear, is impossible," Charlie replied. "The sheriff was about to arrest him when – he dropped from sight."

"He got away?" Ryder cried.

"For the time being," Chan answered. "He may yet be apprehended." He turned to Ward. "I am so sorry, Mr Ward. This must be a great shock for you, I know. I have paused for brief moment only to inform you that with deep regret, and with warm glow of thanks for your hospitality, I leave this house at once. There is nothing more I can do."

"I suppose not," Ward replied. "But you must not go until one thing is settled. I promised you a thousand dollars to undertake the search for my boy— "

"But the search was so brief," Chan protested.

"No matter. There was nothing about that in our agreement. Wait here just a moment, please. I shall write you a check."

He left the room. Charlie turned to see an unaccustomed smile on the face of John Ryder.

"You find only pleasure in the escape of Sing," the detective remarked.

"Need I conceal that, Mr Chan?"

"Sing was very good friend of yours."

"One of the best I ever had."

"Ah, yes – chicken gravy and rice," nodded Charlie.

Ryder made no answer. In another moment Ward returned, and handed Charlie a check.

"I accept this with crimson cheeks," Chan said, and having placed it in his pocketbook, he looked at his watch. "It is time I am going," he added, and rose to his feet.

"Won't you have a farewell drink?" Dudley Ward suggested. "But you don't drink, do you? It's just as well because, come to think of it, there's nothing to drink. Poor John and I have been sitting here with parched throats all evening – you see, Sing had the keys to the sideboard, and the cellar, too."

"Thank you so much for reminding me," Chan cried. "I was on point of forgetting." He took from his pocket a great key-ring, on which hung more than a score of keys. "This was entrusted to me by your servant – just before his escape."

"That's a bit of luck," Ward answered. He took the keys and stepped to the sideboard. "What will it be, John? A cordial with your coffee?"

"I don't mind," Ryder said.

From the sideboard Ward took four cut-glass decanters, and set them on a tray. He placed the tray before his friend. "Help yourself," he suggested. He secured a larger and heavier decanter, and put it at his own place. "Mr Chan – you won't change your mind?"

"I am great believer in proper ceremony," Charlie answered. "In old days, in China, refusal to drink parting libation would be slur on hospitality of the host. A small taste – if you will be so good."

"Fine," Ward cried. He placed another glass before Ryder. "John – give the inspector – which do you prefer, Mr Chan?"

"A little of the port wine, please." Suddenly Chan's voice grew louder. "One thing more. In China, in the old days, refusal of the host to pour the parting libation himself might well have been regarded as a slur on the guest."

There was a sudden silence in the room. Charlie saw Ryder hesitate, and look inquiringly at Ward. "But I do not press the point," Charlie continued, with an amiable smile. "You understand, I recall my first dinner at this table. I recall how courteous you were, Mr Ward – how you served the cocktails yourself – how nothing was too much trouble – until that tray of decanters was put before you. And then – how you shouted for Sing – how Sing had to return from the kitchen before the cordials could be served. Ah – these little things – they register in the mind of a detective. Many hours later I remembered, and I said to myself – can it be that Mr Ward is color-blind?"

He paused, and another tense silence filled the room.

"It was an interesting question," Charlie continued. "Only tonight I answered it once and for all. There were two varieties of ink on your study desk upstairs, Mr Ward. Black on the right, red on the left. A moment ago I slipped in and took the very great liberty of changing the position of the inkwells. You will forgive me I hope." He tapped the pocket into which he had put his purse. "The check you just gave me was written in red ink, Mr Ward. So you are color-blind, after all."

"And what if I am?" Ward asked.

Charlie leaned back at ease in his chair. "The person who killed Landini was first sent by her for a green scarf. He returned to her bringing a pink one. Later, in vague impulse to straighten the desk and alter the look of affairs, he put a crimson lid on a yellow box, a yellow lid on a crimson one. No, thank you, Mr Ryder." He waved aside the glass Ryder was holding out. "I could not quite bring myself to drink with a man I am about to arrest for murder."

"Murder!" cried Ward. "Are you mad, Inspector?"

"No – it was you who went mad – night before last in the study."

"I was in the living-room when the shot was fired. You saw me there."

"Sing's shot into the pine trees – yes. But alas, Landini was actually killed in noise and confusion of the moment when airplane was roaring over the house."

"At which moment I was turning on the lights of the landing field. You heard what the aviator said— "

"That those lights flashed on while he was above the house. And he was correct – they did. But you, Mr Ward, did not turn them on." Charlie took an envelope from his pocket and held up, very carefully, the wooden handle of an electric light switch. "Short time ago, aided by bunch of keys from Sing, I entered shed at rear of hangar from which light was managed. I removed this article from its place. On it are two sets of fingerprints. Each set is from the fingers of your faithful servant, Ah Sing." He dropped the switch back into its envelope. "Two very good alibis," he added. "Sing's shot into the trees – your claim of having turned on the lights. Both gone. Both useless now."

Looking up, he saw that a terrible change had come over the usually genial Ward. He was trembling with rage, his face was purple, his mouth twitching. "Damn you!" he screamed. He snatched up the heavy decanter from the table, and his muscular arm drew back to strike. Then his eyes strayed to the door at Charlie's back, his purpose faltered, and, as suddenly as it had come, his fury passed.

"Cool off, Dudley," said the voice of old Sam Holt from the doorway. "I told you when you was a kid that temper of yours would finish you some day."

Dudley Ward slumped into his chair, and covered his face with his hands.

"I guess you were right, Sam," he muttered. "I guess you were right, at that."

XX

AFTER THE TYPHOON

The old sheriff stepped into the room, and Don Holt followed. Charlie looked at his watch.

"One hour, to the minute," he remarked to the younger Holt. "Fortunate you are man of your word. I feared I was about to lose a most important piece of evidence."

"Then you got what you came after?" Don Holt inquired.

"I got it." Chan handed an envelope to the sheriff. "Handle of light switch from shed at rear of hangar," he explained. "On it, fingerprints of Sing who turned off lights on landing field when unhappy evening had ended. Also, more fingerprints of Sing, who evidently turned them on in first place."

"So Dudley Ward never went near them lights," nodded Holt.

"Such is the inference we must naturally draw," Chan agreed. "I am handing precious cargo over to you. Also, in this other envelope, bullet from Landini's gun, which I have recently dug from pine tree."

Ryder pushed forward, his expression unpleasant and contemptuous as usual. "And you expect to convict my friend on evidence like that?" he cried.

"It will all help," shrugged Chan. "We will in addition trace the owner of a revolver which now reposes in Berkeley."

"That may not be so easy," sneered Ryder.

"Perhaps not." Charlie turned and looked at Ward. "If difficulties arise, we can still bring back to this scene the accessory to the crime, Ah Sing. Of course, in such case, he also would suffer punishment—"

Ward leaped to his feet.

"Oh, stop it," he cried passionately. "What's the use? Let Sing alone. Let him go. I killed Landini, and I killed Swan, too."

"But look here, Dudley—" Ryder protested.

"What's the use, I say?" Ward went on. "Forget it, John. I've nothing to live for – nothing to fight for. Let's get on with it. Let's get it finished. That's all I want now." He sank back into his chair.

"I am so sorry, Mr Ward," Chan said gently, "that my visit to your home must finish in such manner. Let us, as you say, get on with it. I will detail a few happenings in this house night before last, and perhaps if I am wrong, you will correct me. You and I went with Madame Landini to the study. You accused her of hiding from you knowledge of your son. She denied it, but you were not satisfied. The airplane appeared, you left presumably to turn on lights of landing field. When you left, Landini was wildly seeking to communicate with John Ryder.

"You could not turn on lights until you located Sing, who had keys of everything about this house. You found him on rear porch, on his way to manage lights himself. You sent him along, telling him that later he must bring blanket to study for Landini's dog.

"With more questions for Landini, you returned to study. She, meanwhile, has written letter to Ryder, who has refused to see her. When you enter, she is on balcony waving to aviator. 'Oh, it is you, is it?' she says. 'I'm freezing – get me my scarf. It's on the bed in the next room. The green one.' The great Landini, giving orders as of old. You go into next room, return with pink scarf. She snatches it from you. Did she chide you then? Did she say, I had forgot you were color-blind? No – the questions are only rhetorical. They do not matter. She decides Miss Beaton's scarf will do. And then – your eye lights on the desk – on the letter she has written and addressed to John Ryder."

Charlie paused. "I wonder what was in that letter?" he said slowly.

"You seem to know everything," Ward answered. "What do you think was in it?"

"I believe that news of your son's death was in it," Chan replied.

Ward did not speak for a moment. He sighed wearily. "You *do* know everything," he said at last.

"You were curious about that letter," Charlie continued. "Always a little jealous of Ryder, perhaps. You asked Landini what it meant. Your unhappy temper grew hot. You snatched up the envelope, ripped it open, and read. Landini was asking Ryder, your best friend in the house, to break to you gently the news that your boy had died.

"Died – and you'd never seen him. Your temper was terrible then. Murder was in your heart. From the drawer of your desk you removed a revolver – an automatic – and turned on the woman. She screamed, struggled with you above the desk, the boxes of cigarettes were unset. The aviator was once more just over-head, the din was terrific. You cast Landini from you, she fell, you fired at her from above. And the roar of the plane died away in the distance. Just as the roar of your frightful anger was dying away in your brain.

"You were dazed, weak, unsteady. A neat man, always, you unconsciously sought to straighten things on the disordered desk. It came to you that perhaps it might help to pretend Landini had been shot from the balcony. You dragged her to the window – and from her hand-bag, opened in the struggle, her own revolver fell. You examined it – the same caliber as yours. At that moment, Sing entered the room, beneath his arm, a small blue blanket.

"What happened then? Whatever it was, it happened quickly. Whose idea was it – the alibi of the shot to be fired by Sing? Yours or his – that does not matter. He was your loyal servant. You knew that he would protect you as he had protected you from your childhood. He was your keeper of the keys."

"That says it," old Sam Holt cried. "Keeper of the keys. For sixty years Ah Sing had been slammin' the doors on the Ward family skeletons, an' turnin' the keys on them. I know all about it – don't I, Dudley? An' he'd 'a' done it this time – only Inspector Chan had his foot in the door."

"I'm afraid he did," Ward muttered.

"So you left it all to Sing," Charlie went on, "and hurried down to the landing field to greet a new guest. Ah, your manners, Mr Ward – they were always so perfect. But a golden bed cannot cure the sick, and good manners cannot produce good man. You made the aviator welcome, and we came inside. While up above, Sing kept the faith. As my friend, Inspector Duff of Scotland Yard, would say – he carried on."

Charlie rose. "We need no longer shade the scene with dark pictures of the past. I do not dwell on murder of Swan. It is not for his death that you will be tried."

"I'm sorry I won't," Ward answered grimly. "Because I rather imagine I did the world a service there. A dirty blackmailer – he was at the door of the study when I – when Landini died. When I went to him later on to take him things for the night, he threatened me, demanded money. I told him I would get him some the next day in Reno, and I did. Last night I telephoned to him he could get it if he'd meet Sing at the house down the road. Then I got to thinking – he would suck at me, like a leech for ever. So I didn't send Sing – I went myself. And when Swan came, eager for his first drop of blood – I finished him. Yes – I'm rather proud of what I did to Swan."

"And I am very grateful," Chan said. "We needed that revolver of yours, Mr Ward – as cherry trees need the sun. I wondered at first why you did not toss weapon into lake, but remembering the famous clarity of Tahoe waters near the shore, I applauded your wisdom. You planned to come back later with boat, and carry both Doctor Swan and the pistol far out – but ah, the best-laid plans – how often they explode into disaster." Charlie nodded at Don Holt. "Sheriff – I am turning this man over to you. With only one question in my mind – who, on the night of Landini's murder, struck the loyal and faithful Sing that cruel blow in the face?"

Ward confronted the detective, and a red dangerous light was gleaming in his bloodshot eyes. "What's that got to do with it?" he cried. "My God – don't you know enough now? Are you never satisfied? What's that got to do with it?"

"Nothing, Dudley," old Sam Holt put in soothingly. "Not a thing in the world. Mr Chan, I reckon we won't insist on knowin' the answer to that."

"Of course not," answered Charlie promptly. "My connection with the case is now completely finished. I go to procure my things."

Ten minutes later the two Holts, Chan and the now silent Ward, stepped into the sheriff's launch. Ryder had been left in charge at Pineview, and Don Holt had also persuaded Ireland to remain overnight. The little boat cut its way through the silvery water; on distant peaks gleamed the snow that was still a nine days' wonder in the eyes of the detective from Hawaii.

They walked up the Tavern pier toward the hotel. "I asked the coroner to be ready," Don Holt remarked to Chan. "We're driving down to the county-seat right off, an' takin' Ward with us. By the way, I'd like to stop at the Tavern for just a minute. I wish you and Dad would take Ward around to the drive. That is – if you think I can trust you."

"We have enjoyed brief lapse," Charlie replied. "However, I believe we are now quite safe custodians."

"Yes – I reckon you are. An' that lapse – I'm grateful for it. Sixty years of loyalty an' love – say, jail would have been a fine reward for that."

As young Holt entered the Tavern lounge, the two newspaper men from San Francisco leaped upon him. It appeared that the coroner had been a trifle indiscreet, and a torrent of questions was the result.

"Nothin' to say," the sheriff replied. "Only this. I just arrested Dudley Ward, an' he's confessed. Nothin' more – only – give all the credit to Charlie Chan."

Rankin turned to his companion. "Did you hear what I heard? A mainland policeman giving the credit to Charlie Chan!"

"They grow 'em different up here in these mountains," Gleason answered. "Come on – the phone's in the office. I'll match you for the first call."

As they disappeared, Holt saw that Leslie Beaton was seated near by.

"Fine," he cried, as she rose and approached him. "You're the very person I wanted to see."

"Dudley Ward," she remarked, her eyes wide. "Why – that's incredible."

"I know – but I can't discuss it now. I'm in an awful rush. I want to say – Cash will probably turn up here early in the morning."

"You mean – he'll be company for me while you're away?"

"Yeah – I'm afraid he will. I wired him to take a little vacation in San Francisco, but he's the sort who will see through that. Yes – he'll pull in here at dawn. And the first thing he'll do – he'll want you to take a ride up to that clearing where we was this afternoon."

"Will he really?"

"Sure. An' I wish – as a sort o' favor to me – I wish you wouldn't go."

"But what shall I tell poor Cash?"

"Well, you might tell him you been there already."

"Oh! But Cash isn't the sort to be put off with an excuse like that."

"No, I guess he ain't." The sheriff turned his hat about in his hands, staring at it as though it were something that caused him much embarrassment. "Well, then – you might – just as a favor, too – tell him you're going to – to marry me."

"But would that be the truth?"

"Well – I know you ain't seen the county-seat yet— "

"I haven't – no. But I've seen the sheriff."

He looked at her, his fine eyes glowing. "By golly. Do you mean that?"

"I guess – that is, I reckon I do."

"You'll marry me?" She nodded. "Say," cried Don Holt, "that's great. I'll have to run now. But I'll be seein' you."

He started off. "Just a minute," said the girl. "Let me get this straight. Is it you I'm going to marry – or Cash?"

He came back, smiling. "Yeah – I don't wonder you're sort o' mixed." He took her in his arms and kissed her. "I reckon that might help you to remember," he added, and disappeared.

Charlie and Sam Holt were waiting beside the car, in which the coroner was already at the wheel. A dim figure huddled in the rear seat. "Mr Sheriff," Chan said. "Your prisoner informs me he will plead guilty." He took out his pocketbook and removed a narrow slip of paper. "So I imagine you will not require this check for evidence at the trial."

"What is it?" Holt inquired.

Chan explained.

"No, we won't need it," said Holt, handing it back. "You jes' keep it – an' use it."

But already Charlie was tearing it slowly across and across. He tossed the pieces into the air. Dudley Ward leaned suddenly forward from his place in the rear of the car.

"You shouldn't have done that," he protested.

"So sorry," Chan bowed. "But I could not enjoy spending the money of one whose association with me ended in disaster for him."

Ward slumped back in the car. "And I always thought," he murmured, "that Don Quixote was a Spaniard."

The sheriff had seized Chan's hand. "You're a grand guy, Charlie," he said. "Will you be here when I come back tomorrow?"

"If you come early – yes."

"Don't go till I see you. By that time, maybe I'll be able to think up some words that'll tell you what your help has meant to me."

"Not worth mentioning," Chan replied. "In this world, all sorts of men could help one another – if they would. The boat can ride on the wagon, and the wagon on the boat. Good night – and my best wishes for – for ever."

Charlie and the old sheriff watched the car start, then walked around the Tavern and out upon the pier. Near the end of this stood a sheltered group of benches, and on one of these they sat down together.

"Kinda hard case," remarked old Holt.

"In many ways," Chan agreed. He contemplated the snow-capped mountains, gorgeous in the moonlight. "From the moment I made up my mind that shot we heard was but empty gesture, I was appalled at possibilities. Did Hugh Beaton climb to balcony and kill Landini, and did his sister fire shot to protect him, as she had protected him all her life? I wondered. Or did Michael Ireland shoot Landini from plane, and did Cecile fire again to save her husband? It was intriguing thought, and for a time I played with it. But no – I told myself sadly that jealous wives are not so obliging. Then I recalled the serving of the cordials that first night at dinner – and at last my eyes turned toward the guilty one."

"He never was no good, Dudley wasn't," mused Sam Holt. "I knowed it from the days he was a kid. Terrible temper, an' a born drunkard. Yes – even the giant redwoods – they got rotten branches. The family of Ward had theirs, an' Dudley was the last – an' rottenest. If his name had come up sooner – I could ha' told ye. That time long ago Landini run away from him – he was tryin' to beat her. Sing stepped in – good ol' Sing – locked him in his room – helped Landini git away. I tell you, Mr Chan, when Landini hid the news of that baby from Dudley Ward, she knew what she was doin'. She knew he wasn't fit to care fer it."

"Poor Landini," Charlie remarked. "What unlucky fate she had when matter of husbands comes up. Romano – grasping as he was – I imagine he was the best – and the kindest."

"I reckon he was," nodded Holt.

"I presume it was Ward who struck Sing that night of the murder?"

"Sure it was. I didn't think we needed to humiliate him no more – but sure, he struck Sing. An' why? Because Sing had the keys to the sideboard, an' Ward wanted booze. He wanted to git drunk an' fergit what he done, but Sing had sense enough to know how dangerous that would be. So he refused to give up them keys, an' Ward knocked him down. I used to see him in them tempers as a boy. He's no good, Mr Chan. We don't need waste no sympathy on Dudley Ward."

"Yet Sing would have died for him. Would never have left him, if he hadn't seen Ward's pistol on my desk this morning, and thought his master was in danger. When, as he thought, we blundered and selected him as the murderer, he was delighted to go away. I believe he would have gone to the gallows just as cheerfully."

"Of course he would. But Sing never saw Dudley Ward growed up. He saw him allus as a little boy, beggin' fer rice an' gravy in the kitchen."

They rose and walked back along the pier, the waters lapping peacefully beside them.

"After a typhoon there are pears to gather," Charlie mused. "From this place I take away golden memories of two men. One was loyal and true beyond all understanding. Of my own race – I shall recall him with unseemly pride. The other – yourself, Mr Holt."

"Me? Oh, hell, Mr Chan, I ain't nobody. Never was. Jes' been goin' along fer seventy-eight years, doin' the best I kin."

"The greatest of Chinese emperors, being asked to suggest his own epitaph, replied in much the same vein," smiled Charlie.

In the Tavern lounge, he bade the old man good night. As he turned, he saw Leslie Beaton approaching.

"Ah," Chan remarked, "I perceive my necktie now has serious competition. I refer to your cheeks, Miss Beaton."

"Excitement," she explained. "You see, I'm engaged. At least – I think I am."

"I know you are," Charlie told her. "I also knew you were going to be, from the moment I saw the young sheriff's eye light upon you."

"You really are a great detective, aren't you?" she replied.

Chan bowed. "Three things the wise man does not do. He does not plow the sky. He does not paint pictures on the water. And he does not argue with a woman."